SINS OF OMISSION

FERN MICHAELS

THORNDIKE PRESS

An imprint of Thomson Gale, a part of The Thomson Corporation

THOMSON

™

GALE

Detroit • New York • San Francisco • New Haven, Conn. • Waterville, Maine • London

LIBRARY OF CONGRESS CATALOGING-IN-PUBLICATION DATA

Michaels, Fern.
    Sins of omission / by Fern Michaels.
      p. cm. — (Thorndike Press large print famous authors)
    ISBN-13: 978-0-7862-9185-4 (lg. print : alk. paper)
    ISBN-10: 0-7862-9185-0 (lg. print : alk. paper)
    1. Americans — France — Fiction. 2. World War, 1939–1945 — France —
Fiction. 3. Large type books. 4. France — History — 1945 — Fiction.
5. Hollywood (Los Angeles, Calif.) — Fiction. I. Title.
PS3563.I27S55 2007
813'.54—dc22   2006034999

Published in 2007 by arrangement with The Ballantine Publishing Group,
a division of Random House, Inc.

Printed in the United States of America on permanent paper
10 9 8 7 6 5 4 3 2 1

For my children, Cindy, Suzy, Patty, Mike, and Dave, who over the years have given me their love and their respect and helped me keep things in perspective. For Kelly and Billie, my grandchildren, who share their childlike wisdom and treat me to ice-cream cones as long as I pay. Then there's Fred and Gus, four-legged creatures to be sure, who make me laugh and keep my feet warm. You're mine and I love each and every one of you.

For my children: Cindy, Sue, Patty, Mike, and Greg, who over the years have given me their love and their respect and helped to make so happy in perspective. Particularly to Billie, my grandchildren who share their chuckle wisdom and bless me to the green comes as long as I say. Then there's Fred and Sue, four-legged are most to be sure, who make me laugh and keep my heart warm, you to have and to each and every one I love.

PROLOGUE

The Academy Awards! The night of the year all Hollywood waited for. Even in his wildest dreams, Reuben had never, ever believed the Motion Picture Academy would single him out for an award, but here he was, backstage, waiting for his name to be announced.

He paced, he smoked, he jammed his hands into tightly balled fists, the cigarette smoke swirling upward making his eyes water. Talk about being nervous! What must it be like for the nominees who had to wait for the winners to be read before they knew whether or not it was their lucky night? Reuben had known about his special award for weeks, and still he was as nervous as a hungry cat. Earlier that afternoon he had written a speech, but he hated speeches. He preferred spontaneity. Ah, the hell with the speech, he decided abruptly; he'd wing it.

What would the small statue feel like in his hands? he wondered. Solid, most likely. Would he keep it at home or in the office? An

honor, one the Motion Picture Academy said he deserved for all his contributions to the industry throughout the years. If you counted the blood, sweat, and, yes, the tears he'd shed for the business, then he certainly deserved the award. But without his friends, would he be standing here now, waiting for the precious gold statue to be placed into his hand?

He peeked through the curtain at the cheering audience. There were people out there who thought he had it all — a beautiful wife, handsome children, the presidency of Fairmont Studios, loyal friends who'd die for him. Was that having it all? No, it wasn't. Reuben realized then, in one split second, that, honor or not, he didn't care about the award because the one person in the world he really cared about wasn't there to share in his happiness. No, he didn't have it all.

Exhaling, he tossed his cigarette away, watched it fall to the wood floor with a small spatter of sparks. Absently he crushed it out with his shiny black dress shoe. Any minute now they would call his name and he would walk out onto the stage — Reuben Tarz, president of Fairmont Studios. For one crazy moment he knew he would chuck it all, his mansion in Laurel Canyon, his title, the studio, even his family and friends, to be a winemaker in France. His eyes burned as he strode onto the stage the moment his name was called. For some reason he hadn't pre-

pared himself for the blinding lights. He knew his friends and family were out there in the audience, in the second row just a few yards from the podium where he was standing, but he couldn't see them. Maybe that was good. He'd stare into the blinding light and say whatever came into his head. A minute and a half, ninety seconds of thanks to those sitting in the second row. *She* should be here, but she wasn't. He had to pretend she was.

"And now for a special award for all his many valuable contributions to this industry. For a man whose list of accomplishments is so long and prestigious he made me promise not to bore you by listing them. Suffice it to say we all know what this man has done for all of us in Movieland. . . . Here, then, to accept the honorary Oscar for Special Contributions to the Industry . . . Reuben Tarz, president of Fairmont Studios!"

Alice Simpson, resplendent in a swirling silver dress, floated over to him, statue in hand. She kissed him lightly on both cheeks, then handed him the gold statue. Reuben watched as she undulated off stage in a cloud of winking silver.

Aware then that he was the sole focus of countless pairs of eyes, he cleared his throat and stared out into the audience he couldn't see. The deep huskiness of his voice surprised him, and he had to clear his throat a second time. Ninety seconds. He began with a wry

9

"This is quite an honor for a guy from Brooklyn. . . ." The audience roared and cheered. When they settled down he continued. "I want to thank the members of the Motion Picture Academy for honoring me this evening. So many people . . . one in particular . . . gave me my . . ."

Max was sitting next to Daniel and Rajean; at least that's what Daniel had told him earlier backstage. Jane was there, with one of her gentlemen friends, and then Bebe, Simon, and Dillon.

". . . gave me the encouragement I needed to barge into this business and make it a better place for all of us. If I've succeeded" — he held the statue aloft — "and I think someone's trying to tell me I might have in some way . . . I want to thank those dearest to my heart, for without them I might be a panhandler in Brooklyn instead of standing here tonight." Obviously he couldn't mention Max by name because of his underworld connections, but he had to thank him somehow. Arthur — that was Max's middle name, thank God he'd remembered it. . . . "My friend Arthur and his . . . support gave me the confidence to leap ahead while he watched the road behind me; Daniel Bishop, my lifelong friend, who is more brother than friend, deserves more than just thanks; Jane Perkins, for being there when I needed a friend; and, of course, thanks to my wife,

Bebe, for her support. Sol Rosen also deserves my thanks for giving me a chance to prove myself." *Say it now, Reuben, acknowledge Mickey and what she's done for you. Say the words out loud for the world to hear. Your speech will be printed in all the morning papers, Mickey will see it sooner or later. . . . Say the words.*

He placed the statue down on the podium but held it tightly before he went on. "There is one other person I have to thank. Without her help, her encouragement, and her love, I don't know where I would be. She isn't here tonight, in fact she's half a world away." He raised the golden statue again this time, high and proud. His eyes burned brightly with unshed tears. "This sign of my achievement should bear the engraved name of . . ."

PART ONE

CHAPTER ONE

Soissons, France October, 1918

Sleet pelted the tall windows of the hospital at Soissons, which sat upon a gentle rise of countryside about fifty kilometers from Paris. Reuben Tarz attempted to disguise his limp as he passed between the neat rows of cots, his watery gaze searching out number twenty-seven, his friend, Daniel. Reuben's heart gave a sickening lurch when he saw a strange man in Daniel's assigned bunk. Disoriented and fearful, he spun around, hardly recognizing the savagery of the sound that erupted from his throat. "Daniel!"

"Can't get enough of this place, eh?" Daniel's even, steady voice came from somewhere behind him.

Reuben whirled at the familiar sound, forcing his eyes to focus on the row of hospital beds beneath the gallery windows. "How did you know it was me?" he asked curiously. "Why did they move you over here?" He tried to keep the anxiousness out of his voice.

15

Daniel made a sound deep in his throat, almost as though he were laughing. "Because they're supposed to take the bandages off my eyes tomorrow. The cast comes off my shoulder, too. I knew it was you because I heard you make the same sound when we were gassed. What are you doing here, Reuben? I figured once they'd patched up that leg of yours, you'd be long gone, back to the front, or to the States. I never expected to see you again."

"You aren't exactly seeing me," Reuben said wryly. "And why in hell would you think you'd never see me again? Do you think I saved your blasted life so I could take a powder? We're friends, we've been to hell and back. That means something, doesn't it? Besides, you're just a dumb kid and someone has to look out for you. I have a plan." Reuben dropped to his knees to whisper. "Or should I say Marchioness Michelene Fonsard has a plan?" He waited to see if Daniel's excitement would rise to the level of his own.

"Madame Mickey? The lady who brought me flowers from her own greenhouse?"

"The same. She's come up with a way for both of us to go to her château for some R and R. What that means is that we're out of this fucking war. We're going to get fresh eggs, good red meat, and lots of strong red wine. What d'you think?"

Daniel didn't answer for a long time, and

16

when he did, Reuben had to bend over to hear him. "What if I'm blind, Reuben? We both came to Soissons at the same time, and you were as blind as me from the gas. You've been out for two weeks, but I'm still . . . here. And what is it we have to give to get all this good country living?"

"You, my friend, don't have to give anything. I'll be doing the giving, or the taking, however the case may be." Reuben's grin broadened at Daniel's expression of awe.

"You mean . . . she wants . . . you'll do *that?* Jesus! One of the nurses told me about Madame Mickey. They say she's old, around forty. That's twice as old as you!" Daniel flushed a brilliant scarlet, which only added to Reuben's amusement.

Reuben changed positions to ease his injured leg. "I look at it this way. Madame Mickey has everything any other woman has, plus a heart as big as all outdoors. If she wants to be our benefactor, why not? We certainly have nothing to lose. You don't want to go back to the front, do you? I sure as hell don't. This war can't go on forever, and I intend to outlast it. I want the same for you. Madame Mickey has some influential friends in the War Office. Did you know that Captain Eddie Rickenbacker stayed at her house in Paris when he had leave?" Reuben watched Daniel's face at the mention of Rickenbacker, hoping the name would lend credibility to

17

Madame Mickey's reputation. "And," he added for emphasis, "guess who's a personal friend of hers, one so famous he autographed a picture of himself for her, taken while he was in full uniform? 'My love for you endures,' it says. Signed B. J. Blackjack Pershing himself!"

"That's all very fine, Reuben . . . for you. But where do I fit in?"

"You'll be right beside me. Daniel, you have to learn how to be gracious when someone offers you something. Always accept. I'm accepting this for both of us. We'll mend, get our health back, have a little fun, and then head back to the States. I told you I'd take care of you, and I will. I made a promise to you and to myself. You're going to be 'the finest lawyer in the country,' to use your own words, and I'm going to be . . . I don't know yet, but I do know I'll be wearing silk jackets, walking on thick carpets, serving the best caviar with chilled champagne. I'm going to have a mansion with a whole battalion of servants and money to burn. And if I get in trouble along the way, you'll be the hotshot lawyer who'll get me out of it. We made a deal, Daniel."

"What if I can't see when they take the bandages off? Then what? What if I'm blind? B-l-i-n-d! How will I go to law school then? Are you going to lead me around on a string?"

"Damn you, Daniel, shut up," Reuben

growled. "You aren't going to be blind. I'm not. I couldn't see very well for a few days, but my eyesight is almost restored. I still have to have the treatments, so will you. And just for the record, yes, I would lead you around on a string. I'd find a way for you to get to law school if I had to go with you. You got that?"

The eighteen-year-old soldier sighed. There wasn't a whole lot left to believe in, but he did believe in Reuben. Reuben was the brother he never had, the uncle he'd always wished for, the father he would have died for. Reuben was his friend. Reuben had saved his life and was willing to believe in his dream of finishing his education and becoming a good lawyer. Reuben believed in him. And if it took the rest of his miserable life, he would repay the debt.

Reuben's gray eyes sparkled mischievously. "Madame Mickey tells me her cousin's daughter by marriage is expected shortly after Thanksgiving. Her name is Bebe and her father is a famous movie-maker in California. You'll have a pretty girl to pal around with. We'll never have to smell carbolic and dead sweat. We'll be civilized, Daniel. Do you know what that means? This . . . this hell we've lived through . . . we've earned this!"

Daniel was silent, but his head dipped ever so slightly in agreement. Reuben always managed to make sense out of chaos. "I think I'll

be out of here in another couple of days. I'm with you, pal. Tell Madame Mickey I'd be honored to accept her invitation. Did I tell you she brought me flowers from her greenhouse again yesterday?"

Reuben guffawed. "She calls it her hothouse. I can tell you —"

"Never mind," Daniel said hastily.

Reuben didn't know why he felt the need to stake out the boundaries of his commitment to Daniel. To take care of Daniel, to watch over him, somehow enabled him to make sense of his own life. Daniel was good, he was honest, and he was honorable, and if Reuben had anything to do with it, he would stay that way. He reached down to tousle Daniel's pale blond hair.

"When you're discharged, Madame Mickey will pick us up in her motorcar. She's promised to teach me to drive."

"How old is this Bebe?" Daniel asked. It grated on him at times that he'd never had a girlfriend, while he knew that Reuben had had scores and had been intimate with all of them. After all, Reuben was a virile man. Bebe was probably ten years old. Reuben still thought of Daniel as a boy. Christ, he'd gone through the war the same as Reuben had; that should qualify him as a man. He waited, holding his breath, for Reuben's reply. Think of me as a man, he pleaded silently, so I can think of myself the same way.

"Fifteen going on sixteen. Same way you're seventeen going on eighteen. I understand she's a beauty. If you can't think of anything else to do, you can talk her to death."

Daniel flushed again and changed the subject. "Does this country estate have a library?"

"Don't they all?" Reuben answered blithely. "I haven't been to the château yet, but Madame Mickey's told me a lot about it. When she'd make her rounds at the hospital we talked, sometimes for hours. The château has everything. We're going there to live again." Reuben's heavy voice conveyed the somberness of his memories. "The trenches are something we'll never have to see again. Shrapnel-seeded meadows, the jagged rubble heap of La Boiselle, the frostbite, the chilblains, jaundice — it's all behind us. No more cold nights with just each other for warmth. We won't have to carry a rifle and we won't ever have to kill anyone again. We can bury our savagery here, outside the doors of this hospital, the day you're discharged. We'll be Daniel and Reuben again, starting fresh."

Daniel felt Reuben's embarrassment at his outburst. He couldn't remember Reuben ever showing so much emotion, even when they were first getting to know each other those many months before in boot camp, when he talked of being a boy from Brooklyn, shunted around from one family member to another

21

until he struck out on his own and never looked back.

"Well," Daniel began, clearing his throat, "so she's gonna teach you to drive, hey? I bet that's not all she's going to teach you." He grinned beneath his bandages.

This time, Reuben noticed, Daniel didn't blush at all.

"Hey, boy! Rest. I'll see you tomorrow." With a wave of his hand, he left his friend and found himself smiling as he threaded his way through the aisles of cots and wounded men to the great heavy doors that led to the street.

Daniel lay quietly for a long time after Reuben left. If Reuben said he would be able to see again, then he would see. If Reuben said his shoulder would knit, it would knit. He was alive, and Reuben had both their lives under control. All this misery would become a memory. His thoughts came to life as the moans and groans of the other men in the makeshift ward faded. Thank God for Reuben.

They'd been in boot camp together since day one, from the first he had recognized a kindred spirit in Reuben. Then they'd arrived in France and tasted the first bitter dregs of day-to-day combat. At night, groups of men had huddled together, speaking of their homes, their families, their sweethearts. They

would ramble on and show pictures, and eyes would embarrassingly tear and voices break. Daniel would see Reuben's expression change, become vacant. Hardened. The tall, handsome man would walk from the group determinedly, and Daniel would join him. They would talk about their own childhoods, about their lack of any kind of home that could compare with what the other men had.

Daniel was an orphan, a fact he'd learned early on, scrambling in the orphanage for scraps of bread or fleeting attention. Reuben's mother had died giving birth to him, and then his father had died when he was six. After that he was passed from one relative to another, winding up with an aunt, a destitute woman who had made it clear that with six children of her own to care for, she had no time for Reuben. Wherever they lived, Reuben and Daniel had felt extraneous. They were outsiders. Neither of them could remember a cozy Thanksgiving dinner in the bosom of their family — parents, grandparents, sisters or brothers.

The war had brought them together. In the trenches they became brothers to each other while the bitter realities of war embraced them in a cloak of death and destruction. Although there were times when it seemed life offered little more than a thousand ways to die, they'd survived by sharing rations and fears, past emotional traumas, and then

almost identical physical pain — gassed and blinded in the same overwhelming moment.

Daniel shifted on his cot, where he lay bandaged and broken. The one question he tried to push far away, to the very back of his brain, whirled in his mind. Will I be blind? Forever? A recent night in the trenches flashed through his mind. He could smell it and feel it, and his skin began to crawl. Speechless and trembling as the world crashed around them, they sat ankle deep in the muck, waiting out an unusually fearful blitz. Then he remembered the body of that boy landing on him, bleeding, open and steaming at the same time, and the smell of gunpowder and burning flesh. When Reuben had pulled him out they had stared at each other and voiced the same overpowering fear: that they would die on strange soil with no one but each other to care. They'd shared their youth, their dreams, and their innocence over the next few hours, looking deep into each other's souls. When the sun came up, they shook hands in open acknowledgment of their brotherhood. Reuben had said, "We're in this together, and, by God, we'll get out of it together." He would never forget those words and the unbreakable bond they'd formed that night.

Daniel pushed his head deeper into the pillow on the hard cot. He had to believe in Reuben. Believe in Reuben . . . He dreamed

of fluffy white clouds, soft warm breezes, and the slow, joyful unfolding of Reuben's promises.

Reuben stood beneath the portico of Soissons Hospital, an abandoned ruin of a chalet before French forces had marched into the valley and commandeered the building for medical facilities. Before coming here he and Daniel had been treated behind the battle lines. Dealing with the sick and wounded was more difficult for the Americans than for the French because there were no American hospitals, and only those men who were permanently unfit for further service could be sent home. Reuben didn't know if Daniel realized they would surely see action again. It was this knowledge that made Madame Mickey's invitation so attractive. On their own, Reuben and Daniel were doomed to return to the front. If someone could pull a few strings for them, for whatever purpose, why not?

The cold made Reuben's leg ache and the biting wind burned his eyes. The past weeks he'd forced himself to ignore such pain. He was alive, that was all that mattered. Time would heal his wounds. He leaned against the wall and lit a cigarette, trying to shrug deeper into his khaki tunic. He was colder than a well digger's ass, but he wouldn't move toward the barracks that were his temporary

25

home until Madam Mickey had all the paperwork in order.

Private Reuben Aaron Tarz, Co. D, 16th Infantry Regiment, a doughboy. On June 5, 1917, he'd been one of ten million men registering for the draft, but he wasn't one of the ones who shouted "Kill the Kaiser!" He'd enlisted for two simple reasons: three square meals a day and a roof over his head. For his efforts he'd received his pay, killed the enemy, lain in his own body filth, been sprayed for cooties, been blinded and wounded. More than that, he'd stood at attention when the bugles blew at four a.m., the time when a lot of Americans stateside were just going to bed. He'd slogged through sleet and slush, seen every horror there was. Eventually he'd hardened himself to the sight of maggots feeding on dead flesh, of rats that infested the trenches in search of food, any kind of food, even human corpses and gangrenous flesh. If he lived to be a hundred, he would never forget walking up the line, his eyes alert for the Krauts and for Daniel. The hateful cacophony of bayonets clanking against steel helmets, the mountains of dead bodies, the madness, the absolute terror of it all. The nightly muck sweats, the fear of dying, the fear of surviving. They called it a world war, but to Reuben it was his war, very personal and very much his own. It was his fight to stay alive.

Reuben flicked his cigarette into a mound of slush. His feet were cold, his legs ached, and he had a terrible pounding in his head. Back at the barracks he would apply the drops to his eyes and gradually the headache would lessen. It was a hell of a price to pay for three meals that were more slop than food and for a cold roof of stars. But what choice had he? he reflected bitterly. All the ills of the world, all the wars, pestilence, and famine, were brought about by small men, small of stature and small of mind.

With a muttered oath, he pulled his cap over his curly dark hair and yanked it down over his ears. By the time he'd made it halfway down the road to the barracks, the hard, sluicing sleet had soaked him to the skin. His head was pounding as he limped through the half-frozen sludge. Looking up, he squinted through the rain in the direction of the barracks. Another few minutes and he'd be inside, where it was warm. Things were looking up — the way his luck was going, his dreams might even come true. He could almost touch them, and it scared him; he kept wanting to look over his shoulder. But he had guts, he had chutzpah, and that chutzpah would make all the difference. He was going to succeed in this world. In the trenches, he'd climbed over dead bodies literally — now he'd do it figuratively if need be.

Yes, he was Jewish, but only when it was

convenient to be Jewish. During his year in the trenches he had passed for every nationality under the sun. Jews, he'd found out early, were not the most highly regarded of people. But when it came right down to it, he probably wasn't anything except Reuben Aaron Tarz from Brooklyn, New York.

A young man, angry still at his mother for dying during the first minutes of his life and then making him live through his first six years with his father, who had grieved over his wife's death in granite silence until he, too, had succumbed. Those first six years, he believed, had taught him not to cry. He didn't remember too much after that except arriving and leaving, then his aunt's house in Brooklyn, and the years with her and her swarming brood. Those years, he believed, had taught him how to fight for his own space. Six loved children in a cramped tenement in Brooklyn and one begrudged child made that damned near an impossible feat. He'd been thrown out of that house after his temper had erupted once too often. And he had been on his own ever since. Often, in those early days in Brooklyn, he went hungry for days and had a bath and clean clothes only when he could finagle a deal. Soon trouble became his middle name. And trouble finds trouble. The local gang of street boys was well into a life of crime, running numbers and doing shady errands for local small-time

mobsters, by the time Reuben had decided that getting out meant living longer. He'd seen enough of what happened when the low men on the totem pole got into a disagreement. The ones on the ground got squashed. Life held no guarantees, but of one thing Reuben was certain: He'd never go back to Brooklyn.

The long gray barracks were just ahead, low shadows in an already gray background. Only the yellow lights dimly penetrating the ice-glazed windows gave him direction. He couldn't wait to get out of his wet clothes, clothes that would never dry. In the morning he'd have to put them on again and they'd stick to his body like leeches. Well, he'd worry about that tomorrow. Right now he was going to shed the wet wool, slip under his blankets, and pray for the pounding in his head to let up.

No sooner had he opened the door than a chorus of voices surrounded him. "Here he is!"

"Now we can feast!"

"Come on, Tarz, let's get it together here."

"Yeah! Lady Bountiful was here and left you a basket of goodies. Good, loyal soldiers that we are, we didn't touch a thing. Divvy up!"

"What do you have that the rest of us don't, Tarz? That's what we want to know."

Reuben grinned halfheartedly. His bunk-

mates had been riding him ever since Madame Mickey had made her first appearance at the barracks. At first he'd thought she was just another generous Frenchwoman who wanted to help the Americans. Then his buddy George had explained her mission. "My body!" Reuben had squawked. "She's twice my age!" The first night in the barracks after her visit, the men began to talk.

"What a knockout!" George had exclaimed. "Did you get a load of her legs? Sheathed in the finest silk stockings."

"That perfume of hers is enough to make you want to crawl after her on your hands and knees."

"She's a fool for black hair and gray eyes. I heard her say your eyes were gray. 'The color of the sky before a snowfall!' "

"I'll bet she's got beds with silk sheets and monograms and the same kinds of towels. Real soap that smells nice and a telephone in the bedroom. White carpets . . ."

"You're making all this up." Reuben had laughed with the rest of them.

"No," George said seriously, "Madame Mickey's a living legend around here from what I've gathered. And I've been up and around longer than you have." He pointed and flexed his healed arm. "She comes almost every day in a big sleek Citroën, bringing a mountain of goodies just like you've got right here. She's got a warm word and a dazzling

smile for anyone who needs it. And always, *always*, looks good enough to . . ."

"Eat!"

"Devour whole!"

"Make love to!"

"Get lucky with!"

Each soldier had his own idea about what he would do if offered the honor of her company.

"No problem for you, Tarz, right?" they'd heckled.

He remembered how he'd laughed then, and his stomach churned. After that, her special visits to him became routine. She persisted. And persisted. Now he was still unsure of her intentions, but he was ready and willing to go along with anything she said. Why not?

"Well?" the men chorused as they watched him undress.

"Whooeee, look at those haunches! Check those sinewy thighs! And that big broad chest . . . whooeee!" they heckled.

"Go ahead, eat whatever she brought. Just tell me how it tastes so I won't have to lie." Drops for his eyes. He needed them badly, so badly that his hands shook as he fumbled with the dropper. It was George who noticed his trembling, and with a wave of his hand he cut the heckling short and reached for the cobalt-blue bottle.

"Jesus, you're frozen. Toss me a couple of

31

blankets. Now lie still and I'll put these in your eyes. You should've said something, Tarz. Sometimes you gotta ask for help."

"How's Daniel?" George asked. "Do they know yet if he'll be able to see?"

"They're removing the bandages tomorrow. He gets the cast off at the same time. It could go either way."

"That's pissifying," George grunted. "I hope the kid's okay."

Reuben lay quietly on his bunk, careful not to move his head. Within thirty minutes the pounding was only a dull ache. Maybe he could sleep. The others had moved to the far end of the barracks to allow him the quiet time he needed. They were good guys; he appreciated them and liked them. He knew he could have been tossed in with a bunch of hardnoses.

Before he drifted into sleep, Reuben did something he would do only three times in his life: he prayed. This time it was for Daniel. Then he crossed his fingers for luck the way he'd done so often when he was a boy. Surely Daniel's God would listen to a Jew.

That night saw the end of the three-day sleet storm that had nearly paralyzed the activities at Soissons Hospital. Reuben thought it miraculous that Madame Mickey had ventured out to deliver the basket of treats.

■ ■ ■ ■

Rolling onto his side as the last notes of reveille died away, he was uncertain whether or not to leave his bunk. His buddies had cleared the barracks at the first sounds of the bugle and had filed out into the deep shadowy dawn. Even here the army had its regulations and methods for making a man miserable. He felt sorry for George and the other men; they'd soon be receiving orders to return to their divisions. Odd as it seemed, none of them appeared to resent the fact that their two comrades would escape a return to the front. Reuben supposed that in some vicarious way, Madame Mickey and her resources represented a kind of hope for all of them.

It was warm beneath the blankets, but not as warm as Reuben would have liked. He was tempted to gather blankets from other bunks and wrap himself like an Indian, but he had a scheduled treatment for his eyes this morning, and at noon Daniel's bandages were to come off. And at some point he had to get in touch with Madame Mickey to give her the news of Daniel. Now, that particular assignment deserved a second thought.

George had warned him not to chase after the famous lady. He'd coached him for hours. Do this, don't do that. Don't fetch and carry, and for God's sake, don't appear grateful. Be

33

stubborn. Parcel out your favors. Flatter the lady, but always make her think you might be lying. Then look into her eyes and say something genuine, something soft and sweet. It had been all he could do to stifle his laughter when old George issued instructions on the exact way sweet talk was to be delivered. But because George was older and wiser in the ways of women, Reuben had listened. He stored away all the little nuggets of information and knew he'd probably have a use for them before long. He stretched his leg, feeling the tendons and ligaments pulling in the muscles of his thigh. He'd carry that scar for the rest of his life, one of the doctors had told him, To Reuben it was more than a scar; it was a sign that he'd survived. The long indentation where flesh and muscle should have been would remind him of the trenches, of where he had slept and ate and learned about a boy named Daniel.

Throwing back the wooden shutter, he peered through the dirty glass out to the bleak light where the men were gathered for roll call. Today was a new day, a beginning of sorts. If he'd calculated, manipulated, and organized the coming events, he couldn't have done a better job than fate had done. Madame Mickey was his first step toward where he wanted to end up. The only problem was he didn't know exactly where that certain place was . . . yet. Time. Time was always the

answer.

The young sun struggled over the horizon, only to be blotted out by a cloud. That didn't have to mean anything, he would never believe in omens. He'd had enough of that trap when he'd lived with his aunt. It was a new day, pure and simple, a good day for Daniel and himself.

He washed his face and shaved with the new safety razor that King Gillette had issued to every doughboy heading overseas in one of the greatest promotional advertising schemes ever. As Reuben allowed his thoughts to travel back to Daniel, he grew jumpy and inadvertently nicked his chin. What if Daniel were permanently blind? He dunked the razor in the tin of water and at that moment reaffirmed a commitment he had made: he and Daniel were to be brothers.

If he felt fear beyond the possibility of Daniel's blindness, it was of his obligation to Madame Mickey. Reuben had never slept with a woman. He'd done all the touching and feeling that was allowed, but that was as far as he'd ever gotten. Back in New York he had few opportunities to meet girls, girls who would bother with him, at any rate. Empty pockets and hard times weren't attractive assets as far as women were concerned. And he would never pay for the pleasure, not like some guys who saved their pennies for a roll

between dirty sheets. Not Reuben Tarz. Not when having shoes with decent soles and a new shirt every so often were more lasting pleasures. It was only since joining the army that the opportunity for women had presented itself. Now, as a respectable doughboy, clean shaven and adequately clothed, he'd blended into the ranks with hundreds of thousands of other faceless men. The army, the great equalizer. But so far, every time he'd been presented with an opportunity to be with a woman, he'd either been shipped out prematurely or the old familiar empty-pocket problem had dead-ended him.

This was the reason he'd listened to George, even while pretending his advice was old news to him. And if it was true that Madame Mickey thought of herself as a teacher, then she would just have to show him what she wanted. He was very good at following orders and keeping his mouth shut. The sharp rap of nurses' heels clicking down the corridors echoed off the well-scrubbed bare wooden floors of the hospital. The familiar odor of pine tar cleaner, bloody bandages, and human sweat assaulted Reuben's nostrils. It was a stink he never wanted to experience again once he left this place. Hushed sounds, the low whispers, the rattling of trays and rolling of wheels almost distracted one from the smell. Starched white aprons, sunlight streaming through the tall

windows lining the gallery, the officious steps of the doctors, all were underlined by the insidious presence of suffering. Suffering and pain were the masters here, vying for the weak human flesh that was dragged in from the battlefields. Suffering and pain.

Reuben shook his head to clear his thoughts when the nurse instructed him to lie flat on the gurney while drops were put into his eyes. Today his eyes felt rough and scratchy, and he found himself worrying. But instead of voicing his concerns to the doctor, he kept quiet. He was never one to look for trouble. If it found him, that was a different matter.

"You know the routine, Private. Lie still so you don't disturb the compresses," the American staff doctor reminded him. "One of the nurses will be checking on you every so often."

Stretched out fully on his back, his head slightly lower than his shoulders, Reuben was inundated with sounds and impressions. Quick steps, the movements of a cart in the hallway, voices that were too far away to recognize, and words that were too hushed to decipher.

Even before she entered the doorway to the confined treatment room, he was aware of her perfume. It was a heady, intoxicating scent, completely feminine, and it did strange things to him.

Her voice was low, close to a whisper, filled

with a thrilling warmth. "Ah, *chéri.* The doctors told me you were here." She bent to kiss him lightly on the cheek. Reuben smiled, pleased with her throaty laugh. Remembering George's advice, he attempted a casual tone. Instead, his voice came out as uninterested and bored. "You're early, aren't you?"

"But of course, *chéri,* but only because I am so eager to move you and your friend to my château. I have a wonderful dinner planned for the three of us. Special wine from my vineyard, roast duckling, new potatoes, and fresh vegetables. Dessert will be apple tart with heavy rich cream from my dairy . . . for you. Tell me, what do you prefer?" There was a girlish eagerness to her voice when she sought his approval.

The best Reuben could manage was a weak "That sounds fine." How was it that this woman managed to make him feel as if he were twelve years old and had just caught sight of a girl's bloomers for the first time? He was grateful for the heavy blanket the nurse had thrown over him, even though it barely hid his growing erection. Madame Mickey seemed to fill the small cubicle — not her size, but her presence. Although she was standing beside his gurney, not touching him except for that brief kiss, his every pore was aware of her, all of his senses seemed to be filled with her. It was a sensation he had had before when she had come to visit him,

38

asking after his health in that strangely husky, sensuous voice of hers. Early on he'd discovered how it had the amazing ability to sound maternal and whorish at the same time.

"Poor darling," Madame Mickey said softly, "does it hurt?" Her tone was solicitous and personal, but he wasn't certain she was asking about the compresses on his eyes or the erection, full-fledged beneath the blanket.

"I dressed especially for you and for Daniel," she said lightly. "When your compresses are removed you will see the lovely colors I am wearing." She hesitated a moment, as if she were changing her mind, then whispered close to his ear, "For you, *chéri.*" He felt her fingers stroking his cheek. Reuben thought he would explode.

"What are the colors?" he croaked.

"My cape is a delicious apple red and my dress is one shade lighter. My hat is ermine and so is my muff. Here, darling, feel how nice." She moved her muff over his cheek, his hand. He could imagine her breasts only inches away from his face. If he were to turn, just a bit . . .

The fur was soft and cool against his hand. Reuben's erection began to die. The fur felt as if it might have cost a lot of money. And the food she was promising made him suddenly want to gag. He had friends at the front who would kill for a slice of roast meat and a fresh potato; he himself had been one of those

men just weeks before. He tried for a smile and wondered if it looked as sickly as he felt.

"You are going to love my chatêau," Madame Mickey continued to babble, obviously unaware that anything was amiss. "There you will find everything to make you comfortable. All will be at your disposal, of course. You have only to ask for what you want. *Le monde* is yours, Reuben. Do you know what that means in English?" Reuben shook his head. "It means the world, darling. I can give you the world, and I will. My late husband, dear Jacques, left me a fortune, as you already know. When he knew he was dying it was his last wish that I not want for anything in this life, despite the war, despite everything. I've done my best to live up to his wish."

Reuben was silent, reflective. Madame Mickey seemed to sense his uneasiness. "I must be on my way, *chéri*. I have many more flowers to deliver and baskets of sweet rolls and jam. My cook was busy for two days. I must do my part for the wonderful men who are helping to make France safe once again. *Vive la France!*"

"Long live America!" Reuben blurted.

Madame Mickey chuckled. "I like your spirit, Reuben. Yes, we all do our part, each in his own way. I must be off." Lightly touching his compresses, she added, "Soon you will be under my own special care." Her last words seemed to carry heavy meaning as she

leaned over and kissed Reuben square on the cleft of his chin. Her fingers traced the deep dimple. Reuben shivered and felt the beginnings of another erection. "I will see you and your friend at one o'clock. Au revoir, *chéri.*"

CHAPTER TWO

It was just past noon when Reuben walked stiff-legged down the hall to Daniel's section of the hospital clinic. His hands were in his trouser pockets and his fingers were crossed. He felt both relieved and anxious. Relieved because his eyes felt less gritty and he could see much better; objects were sharper and his eyes were watering less. But he was anxious for Daniel. Ignoring the pain of his leg wound, he hurried through the wards and was brought up short when he saw the doctor and a nurse with a basin in her hand standing beside Daniel.

I'm here, Daniel. The thought was so intense that for a moment he believed he'd spoken aloud. Reuben didn't realize he'd been holding his breath until he noticed Daniel's shoulders jerk and heard the doctor warn his patient not to open his eyes yet. Thick gauze-pad dressings beneath the swath of bandages were being unrolled, layer by layer. Reuben also hadn't realized that his

benefactress was watching from the far end of the corridor. When the heady scent of her perfume wafted toward him, he turned to face her. Even at this distance the apple red of her cape and the pure white of her hat stood out sharply against the gray-green of the clinic's walls. He wanted to see her face, to see her eyes. Would they mirror that soft, solicitous tone of voice? Or would they be calculating and hard, waiting to see if Daniel was blind and judging what that would mean to her plans? Reuben turned again to Daniel, refusing to think about anything but this important moment. Everything depended upon what happened now; the outcome would govern the rest of their lives. He drew in his breath and waited.

Daniel's moment of truth had arrived. The doctor moved so his back was to Reuben, blocking Daniel from his sight. There were no more offered prayers. The one he'd said the night before was of the miracle category. In the dark hours of the night God had either made things right or He hadn't.

Reuben saw the round eyepads drop to the floor. He remembered his own agony at just this moment, and his innards twisted with fear. Daniel's tortured cry of "I can't see!" ripped through to Reuben's soul. He tore across the space that separated them and was at Daniel's side when the doctor issued his cautions not to panic and to give his eyes

time to adjust to the dim light. Reuben placed a firm hand on his friend's shoulder, calming him. "Another minute or so and then again — but slowly — open your eyes," the doctor instructed.

The seconds ticking by were small, separate eternities. Reuben remembered his own tortured unveiling, and his thoughts then that no one was there to comfort him. Madame Mickey, he'd discovered later, had been standing exactly where she was now.

"Now, Daniel, open your eyes slowly. Your vision will be clouded and it will remain that way for some time. You'll be able to see things, but not in detail and certainly not clearly unless you're quite close to them. Open your eyes, Daniel," the doctor urged.

Daniel's head was turned now so that Reuben was directly in his line of vision. His eyes flickered behind reddened lids, then he squinted and blinked gently in his first efforts to make out what was in front of him. Daniel's first thought was that Reuben looked beautiful, although sharp creases of concern tightened the line of his mouth and narrowed his heavy dark brows. He smiled at the blurry shapes before him and closed his eyes again. The sigh he breathed sounded like an explosion in the quiet. "I prayed, you know, for days and sometimes all through the night when I couldn't sleep." He opened his eyes cautiously a second time to confirm his sight.

This time he smiled.

"Mazel tov!" Reuben shouted, squeezing Daniel's shoulder. He looked down at his white knuckles and eased his grip. Wasn't there something more he should do or say? Perhaps not. He'd prayed to Daniel's God, and He had listened. Maybe there was a trick to all that praying after all. Pray for someone else and maybe then you had a chance of having your own prayers answered. His thoughts were interrupted by the doctor's weary voice.

"I've decided you should keep the cast on for at least another week, Daniel. You can leave the hospital if you think you can manage. Madame Mickey is waiting to take you to her château. Most of the paperwork is done, so all you have to do is dress and leave. Good health, son." He patted Daniel on the head and shook Reuben's hand. All the rest of the day, as the doctor walked through the wards, he remembered the grateful look in Reuben's eyes. He'd seen bonds form between men who'd soldiered side by side before. Often it was the most unlikely of pairings, like this one — Tarz, urbane, streetwise, and slick; and Daniel, innocent and trusting.

Daniel rolled back on his bunk, sweat glistening on his face. "I thought for sure . . . I'd hoped . . . prayed . . . but Jesus, I'm glad to see you. Did you pray before they took your bandages off?"

"Me? Pray?" Reuben asked in mock outrage. "It was the luck of the draw, kid. We were either going to be all right or we weren't. The damage was done out in the field weeks ago. Praying would have been kind of silly." He hoped his words of bravado were loud enough for Madame Mickey to hear, but when he turned to look at her, she was gone.

Reuben was annoyed. Why hadn't he been able to tell Daniel that he'd prayed for him last night? The words had stuck in his throat, as if such an admission were impossible for him. Not for the world or all the Madame Mickeys in France would he admit that he'd been too afraid to pray for himself when he lay with his eyes burned by the gas and his head swathed in bandages. Something in Reuben made him feel undeserving of God's intervention.

A smug expression washed over Reuben's handsome face; his silver-gray eyes were made brighter by the drops. "It's time to go, Daniel, so let's put this place behind us and get on with our lives. Madame Mickey is waiting."

Marchioness Michelene Fonsard could barely contain her excitement. She considered herself a lusty good woman who made amends for her sexual liaisons by doing good deeds for the parish curé. The curé prayed for her each Sunday because of her healthy

donations to the church and for her generosity with her husband's renowned Bordeaux wines. A true patriot to the very core of her French heart, she considered it an honor as well as a duty to minister in any way she could to the casualties of the terrible war that had been decimating her country. The soldiers she visited at several hospitals and clinics were the recipients of her generosity in many ways. She spent her days in her Citroën, covering distances along sometimes treacherous roads to deliver her cook's homemade goods and preserves, to read to some of the men and talk with others, always ready to soothe with her gentle woman's touch. Flowers picked fresh from her greenhouse were always welcomed by the convalescents. She brought cheer; she brought hope.

Some called her saintly and beatific, like the parish curé. Others insisted she had the classic features of an aristocrat from a long line of handsome royalty, which always amused her. The soldiers thought of her as a beautiful angel, larger than life, and it was said that a lover or two revealed that her hair reached almost to her ankles and always smelled delightfully of her perfume. She owned fabulous diamonds and emeralds but preferred to wear the least ostentatious. Although refined in her taste, she always kept up with the latest style and fashion; and as sedate and meticulously groomed as she was

through her years with her famous and doting husband, at night, alone, Mickey Fonsard gazed into the mirror and saw the plain face of a peasant, open and honest.

She had been only fifteen when she married Jacques Fonsard, who was three times her age. True to his word, he'd given her wealth beyond her dreams, all from his famous wineries. She, in turn, had given him the best years of his life. In the end she held his naked body against her full breasts the way a mother would hold a suckling babe and watched his erection die for the last time. The smile on his face made her grieving bearable. He'd died exactly as he'd always hoped he would.

Each time Michelene spent a franc, each time she took a new lover or performed a good deed, she knew that Jacques, wherever he was, approved. Marchioness Michelene Fonsard never looked back, nor did she look ahead. And she lived each day fully, as though it could very well be her last. If nothing else, she considered herself a happy woman.

Soon she would be happier. There would be a young, hard body in her bed. She was happy that Daniel could be ministered to in a warm, loving atmosphere. Naturally she'd realized the way to get to Reuben was through his protectiveness for his friend. Such attention would win his gratitude, but humility . . . Ah, that was a different matter entirely.

With her experience, she knew Reuben, young though he was, was not like all the others. This one, she mused, was a cut above the rest.

Madame Mickey had never been in love. She'd cared deeply for Jacques, of that she had no doubt. But so often of late, with death and suffering all around her, she wondered if she would ever truly experience that much talked and written about euphoria of being in love. Sometimes she ached for that warmth when her passions were spent and her lover rolled over to drift off to sleep.

In so many ways Reuben Tarz was a boy. Yet when those boys came out of the war they were men — men in the world of men, but boys in the ways of a woman and the boudoir. Her mission — and she accepted it gladly — was to make a man of Reuben. When they went their separate ways, Reuben would be a man to be reckoned with. She would instill in him a sense of confidence, integrity, loyalty, and motivation. And — equally important — she would teach him that whatever he wanted was within his grasp. All these qualities she admired in men, knowing she possessed each of them herself. As for social polish, Reuben had much to learn, of course, but she knew he would be a quick study. The proper haircut, the right tailor, exposure to correct etiquette, and he would be magnificent.

In the early days of her marriage, while they

waited for the grapes to ripen, Jacques had taught Mickey languages and geography; she had a natural ear for one and a thirst for the other. Now she could converse easily in seven languages, and her favorite, after her own native tongue, was English.

What wonderful plans she had for Reuben! She'd motor to Paris with him and show him her beautiful house, where Jacques liked to play after the first planting of the young vines. Reuben would love Paris, especially when this damn war was over and things returned to normal. General Pershing had confided to her personally that they were only weeks away from an armistice, but she needed no confirmation that the Germans would be suppressed. From the beginning, Michelene had every faith in her countrymen and the Allied forces, and that life would always go on as it had: wonderful, beautiful, and pleasurable.

Her mind, agile as always, devised a series of *divertissements* to please the senses and delight the soul. The Loire River, the only true French river, would be of interest to Reuben. The Mer de Glace would be a must. She'd introduce him to the Matterhorn and Mont Blanc. A two- or three-hour drive with picnic baskets to Rouen to see the quaint, gabled houses and the crooked streets would be another treat. The cave at Peche-Merle on the Sange River — now a chapel — would add to Reuben's French education. And she

must not forget the Cathedral of Notre Dame. Her second favorite spot was the site of Grosse Horloge, the big clock whose single hand had told time for more than four hundred years.

Michelene Fonsard's long, tapered fingers tapped the steering wheel impatiently. Her thighs tingled and tightened when she saw Reuben, accompanied by Daniel, approach the Citroën. Her smile embraced them, warmed them like a cloak as she settled them into the backseat. On the way home she kept up a running commentary on the conditions of the war whenever they asked specifics; otherwise she kept the conversation light and vivacious, telling them funny little tales of the villagers near her château and the eccentric ways of her friend, the curé.

Daniel loved listening to her and complimented her on her exquisite English, but while they both were amused by her little stories, it was news of the war and the German advance that occupied their thoughts. The frequent German raids and intensified activity all along the front in the north of France indicated that a great German offensive was close at hand. The French thought the Allies would be able to hold without difficulty until the Americans could gain position and provisions. Provisions . . . That was the key word in this chaos. With all of America's wealth, manpower, and ability, there was

still the inescapable fact that the great country was totally unprepared for war. American forces were confronted by the mighty German military offense and compelled to stand by almost helpless and see the Allies suffer unspeakable losses. Provisions, the lack of them, the inability to move them across France to where they were needed most, could be their undoing.

"*Mon Dieu!* I am sorry!" Madame Mickey's apology broke into the worried thoughts of her two passengers. "This road is abominable, so rutted and bumpy. It is beyond repair, I am afraid. All the young men are gone from the village; there is no one to repair it. Hold tight to the straps, it gets worse before it gets better." Her voice in melodious apology held a chuckle.

A flock of scrawny winter birds took flight, seeking refuge in the bare branches of the trees as the Citroën chugged along. Overhead the sky was heavy with angry clouds. Daylight was fading, bleeding into night. Reuben sat beside Daniel, bundled in thick lap robes. Mickey had the headlamps on now, their eerie light casting long shadows onto the road. The drive from the clinic was longer than he'd expected. For some reason, he'd thought the château was no more than a few miles away. Already they'd been driving for almost two hours. Now, more than before, he appreciated the woman's generosity and

dedication in visiting the hospital.

"Here we are," Mickey announced as she turned the car and continued driving down a side road that was bumpier than the last. "We're on my property now and the château is still quite a few minutes from here. Tomorrow, in the light, I will show you the boundaries from the top floor. The view is *magnifique* and one can see for miles."

Both Reuben and Daniel craned to get a good look as they caught sight of the impressive estate Mickey was fast approaching. Daniel's thoughts turned inward. Just another short while and he could rest. In the trenches, at the front, he'd been bone tired, but it couldn't compare with the exhaustion he was feeling now. The concern for his eyesight, the pain of his broken shoulder, the grim uncertainty of the future, and the possibility of having to return to the front — all had taken their toll on him. Such exquisite relief he felt, to know he wouldn't be blind; he felt as though he could sleep for a week. Surely his company would not be missed this evening if he asked to retire early. Reuben would entertain Madame Mickey. A small grin tugged at the corner of his mouth. When would Reuben have time for French lessons?

Reuben's thoughts turned inward: What would be expected of him?

"We have arrived, my darlings," Madame Mickey announced gaily as she brought the

Citroën to a stop. "When you are fully recovered, Reuben, we will begin the driving lessons."

Reuben felt a moment of sheer panic, the same immobilizing fear he'd experienced when at eight years old he was caught stealing apples from the neighborhood greengrocer in Brooklyn.

"Come, come, I want to show you my home. Reuben, help Daniel. He appears tired, *pauvre petit.* We must get both of you indoors and into warm, dry clothing." Her eyes were on Reuben the entire time she spoke. "*Chéri,* you are limping. It is the cold," she advised. "A warm bath, warm clothes, dinner, and a nice fire and you will be fixed. No? We will have soft music — Brahms, I think. I will play the pianoforte for you. If you beg, I might even sing."

"I'd like that," Daniel said wearily.

Reuben smiled. "So would I."

"It is settled, then. Come, come, I, too, have the chill."

Reuben wished he could see better in the dim light as they climbed the stone steps to the great carved doors. Well, tomorrow was another day. Perhaps he wouldn't be so busy entertaining Madame Mickey and could go off for a walk to acquaint himself with his surroundings. His eyes widened at the splendor of the château as he looked over his

54

hostess's shoulders. An old woman with a white cap and apron stood holding open one of the two fan-lighted doors. Inside, the entry foyer was warm and well lit. A spectacular chandelier — the likes of which Reuben had glimpsed only in the lobbies of New York's grand hotels — hung from a frescoed ceiling across which paced horses and hounds against a woodland background. A graceful curving stairway led off to the left, while a patterned Persian carpet ran its full length to the upper floor. His sensitive nose picked up the aroma of something delicious baking in the kitchens. Against the side of the staircase nestled a divan the same bottle green as the carpet, its watered-silk fabric inviting to touch. Dark wood tables held vases of flowers from Mickey's famed greenhouses. Reuben wanted to know it all, see it all, but he was being whisked down the corridor that was concealed behind the stairs to a makeshift bathing room. Later he would examine his surroundings. Someday it might be helpful when he made his own selections in furnishings and style.

Two old women and a boy of about twelve stood ready when Reuben and Daniel arrived for their bath. In the middle of the room stood two huge wooden tubs, half-filled with steaming water.

Reuben stripped down to his bare skin, and

his cast-off uniform and boots were immediately removed by the boy. Boldly he stepped in front of the old servants, who eyed his naked body admiringly. The older one pointed at the tubs, urging him to pick one and get in. He settled himself luxuriously as pail after pail of hot water was poured over him. The woman handed him three cakes of soap and gestured. One was for his hair, one for his face, and the other was for — Jesus! She'd grabbed herself in the crotch to make sure he understood. Weakly he smiled his understanding and nodded. She cocked her head to the side, sharp eyes questioning like a crafty New York pigeon.

"I'll do it!" Reuben said loudly. Misunderstanding, the old woman reached for the washcloth. "No!" he cried; and immediately began to lather himself. He knew he'd used the wrong soap on his genitals when she and the others began to laugh. The sound was so genuine and good-natured that Reuben could only join in, sharing the ridiculousness of the moment.

Cackling to herself, the old woman joined her companions to help remove Daniel's clothing. Reuben watched out of the corner of his eye as the trio stripped Daniel down and helped him into the second tub. He grinned, observing as he had so often in close quarters his friend's generous endowments. Madame Mickey had chosen the wrong man.

While he himself was standard issue, Daniel was gigantically hung. Someday he was going to make some lady very happy.

An hour later Reuben emerged from the tub, the skin on his hands and feet puckered but squeaky clean. Someone had laid out clothes for him — soft wool trousers in a gentle shade of tan, slippers that looked like shoes and fit perfectly, soft white underwear, and a crushable sweater the color of the sky on a summer day. None of the items were new, which he supposed accounted for their comfortable softness. After slicking back his dark curly hair and shaving, he examined himself in the mirror. "Reuben Tarz, you are a handsome devil. Daniel, I can truthfully say I feel like a freshwater eel. How are you doing?"

His face scarlet, Daniel mumbled something that sounded obscene. Both women had the third bar of soap and were scrubbing him industriously as the young boy stood ready with the towels. Daniel, his bad arm draped over the tub so as not to wet the cast, was holding on with the other so he wouldn't slide beneath the surface.

Reuben turned his head so Daniel wouldn't see him laughing. "That's enough, ladies," he ordered. "Out! Enough! Help him out!" He waved his hands, making scooping motions. Both old women cackled gleefully.

"You son of a bitch!" Daniel cried. "I saw

you laughing! Do you know what they did to me? Should I tell you?"

"Only if it felt good." Reuben grinned.

"Well, did it?"

"Dammit! Now they're going to dry me. Reuben, get them off me!"

"I can't. They have their orders. You wouldn't want Madame Mickey to be displeased with them, would you? They're old, like grandmothers. Let them have their fun. They're remembering what it was like. How can you deprive them of a little enjoyment?"

"I don't like it," Daniel muttered, his face flaming.

"Yes, you do. Don't ever lie about things like that. It feels good, let it feel good. They aren't taking anything away from you. Come on now, get dressed and let's find our hostess."

Dinner was a wonderful experience visually, and exquisitely gratifying to their taste buds. The dining table had to be at least eighteen feet long according to Reuben's calculations. Six candelabras gleamed in the reflected surface of the polished mahogany. High ceilings, tapestried walls, crystal, china, and a fine silver service complemented the sumptuous meal. Reuben's attention wandered constantly from his meal to the room, then to Madame Mickey. In this soft lighting her features gave off a warm radiance, and her

58

eyelashes appeared to be soft shadows outlining her sparkling eyes. The gown she had chosen to wear was a simple black sheath that swung to the floor, skimming her hips and rising to a deep scoop revealing her generous bosom and the unexpectedly graceful arch of her throat.

Reuben sighed with contentment at the meal's end. Noticing Daniel's discomfort, Madame Mickey took charge. "Come, my darlings, we will have coffee in the drawing room and then it is bed for both of you. Tomorrow, if you like, I will show you around." The slim black ribbon at Mickey's throat held a modest gem. A diamond, Reuben guessed, and probably quite valuable.

There had been pictures in magazines of rooms like this, and once or twice he'd gone to the nickelodeon and seen lavish movie sets on the silver screen. Unlike the heavy Victorian furniture he was used to in the States, Mickey's furniture seemed to Reuben the essence of lightness and space. The richness came not from bulk, but from style and fabric. This room was decorated in faded gold and pale blue, so different from the red and Oriental patterns back home. Flowered chair cushions, long, luxurious curtains in that same faded gold, all conveyed a feeling of age and permanence and comfort. Security. That's what this represented, he decided. Nothing seemed new or was deliberately

ostentatious. These furnishings gave the impression that they'd been collected over hundreds of years. Tomorrow, when he wasn't so tired, he'd come into this room and dig his bare toes into the lush carpeting.

A log snapped in the fireplace, shooting sparks upward. Mickey smiled, reflections of the flames dancing in her eyes. "This, Reuben, is my favorite part of the day. More so now that I have two charming companions with whom to share it."

Reuben's stomach churned. The evening was almost over. The languid, inviting expression in Mickey's eyes was doing strange things to him. Suddenly he realized she'd mentioned bed for both of them, but she hadn't specified where they were to sleep.

"Now isn't this better than the hospital at Soissons? Ah, how forgetful of me. Cigarettes. I have American cigarettes. Lucky Strike, I believe. Please, help yourself. Americans like and expect a cigarette after dinner, isn't that so?"

"Allow me," Reuben said gallantly as he struck a match to the heel of his shoe.

"There is an easier way to do that, *chéri.* See, on this little table beside the cigarette box is a tinderbox. Strike it on the side. Gentlemen do not use their shoes in polite company."

Reuben's neck grew warm, and Daniel sniggered. He had blundered — a gaffe,

Mickey would have called it. "Sorry," he mumbled. He turned to light Daniel's cigarette only to hear Mickey admonish him a second time.

"Never three on a match, *chéri.* What is the warning in the battlefield about lighting a match? Ah, yes . . . it gives just enough time an enemy needs to put you within his sights and shoot. Ah, I see by your faces that you believe women do not know about such things. I frequent the dressing stations and hospitals, remember? As a matter of fact, the very first time I learned about the danger of lighting a match on the battlefield was in a poem written by a young Canadian who was attached to the Red Cross. I became so enamored with his work that I helped him find a New York publisher. I have a copy of his work, if it interests you."

"Canadian, you say?" Daniel asked, his curiosity piqued.

"*Oui, chéri.* You know, they have been here even before you Americans. Would you like me to read something?"

"Please. Don't you want to hear something, Reuben?" Daniel asked hopefully.

"Then it will be my pleasure." Madame Mickey searched the bookshelf beside the fireplace for the thin volume bound in leather and autographed especially for her. She spoke briefly of the author as she scanned the volumes. "His name is Robert Service, a

61

Canadian attached to the Red Cross. Being part of a mobile unit, I met him several times at different dressing stations and hospitals when he brought in the wounded." She rifled through the pages, searching for a topic that would be of interest to them. "Ah, I think here we have it. It is something he wrote and titled 'My Mate.'" When she read, it was in a rather adept Cockney accent.

> I've been sittin' starin' at 'is muddy pair of
>   boots,
> And tryin' to convince meself it's 'im.
> (Look out there, lad! That sniper 'e's a dysey
>   when 'e shoots;
> 'E'll be layin' of you out the same as Jim.)
> Jim as lies there in the dugout wiv 'is
>   blanket round 'is 'ead,
> To keep 'is brains from mixin' wiv the mud;
> And 'is face as white as putty, and 'is
>   overcoat all red,
> Like 'e's spilt a bloomin' paintpot but it's
>   blood.

Daniel and Reuben listened intently, both of them moved by the pathos in the poem. But it was the next stanza that choked them.

> Now wot I wants to know is, why it wasn't
>   me was took?
> I've only got meself, 'e stands for three.
> I'm plainer than a louse, while 'e was 'and-

some as a dook;
'E always was a better man than me.
'E was goin' 'ome next Toosday; 'e was
  'appy as a lark,
And 'e'd just received a letter from 'is kid;
And 'e struck a match to show me, as we
  stood there in the dark,
When . . . that bleedin' bullet got 'im on the
  lid.

Reuben and Daniel were silent, too moved even to look at each other. They understood the kind of friendship Robert Service wrote about. They had seen it, and they had experienced it.

Mickey crushed her half-finished cigarette in a crystal dish. "I must say good night, my darlings. I've had a busy day and I'm tired. I feel the headache coming on. My servants will see to both of you. You have only to ring this little bell. They have all your medications, your night clothes, and will turn down your beds." She glided from her chair to theirs and kissed both of them lightly on both cheeks. "Sleep well, my brave warriors. And sleep as long as you like. I think you'll find my beds quite comfortable."

Reuben was flustered, uncertain of himself. Was he supposed to follow her? Was it possible he'd misinterpreted what he thought was to happen? Would she come to him later when Daniel was asleep? Was he supposed to

go to her? Damn, why hadn't some rules been set down? Did she think he was accustomed to these circumstances and knew what to do? He found it difficult to look at Daniel, who was busy arranging the cigarettes into neat rows in the little enamel box.

Best to pretend indifference, he decided, to behave as though he knew the score. Simply yawn, get up, and stretch, and somehow convey to Daniel that something would transpire later. If nothing else, he wanted to appear worldly, but how? The hell with it, he thought, angered by his own insufficiencies. He'd made a deal to come here and do — what? The exact conditions of his stay had never been explained. It was his bunkmates in the barracks who said he'd be "servicing" the legendary Madame Mickey.

A strange sensation descended upon him, something akin to fear. Perhaps there was something wrong with him. Perhaps he didn't measure up. Screw it, he decided. I'll take the R and R.

"I'm ready to turn in, Daniel. Who's going to ring the bell?"

Daniel grinned. "You're the man around here, you ring it."

"I don't like that smirk on your face," Reuben said coolly.

"Smirk? Sorry, my friend, that's a grimace of pain. My eyes are aching and burning. Aren't yours? And my shoulder itches. All I

want is a bed and sleep. Ring the damn bell and let's hit the sack."

In her room directly above the drawing room, Mickey heard the tinkle of the bell. Footsteps followed, muffled on the carpeting. They'd be undressing now. The beds were already turned down. The hot chocolate would be placed on the little bedside tables in exquisite porcelain cups. Then the eye-drops, the ointment, the little pills with a swallow of water. Minutes ticked by. The chocolate would be finished, the lights would go off, the covers pulled up. Ah, in seconds Daniel would be asleep, and Reuben would . . .

She'd never waited like this with any other lover. Always she'd brought them to her bed upon their arrival. Of course, they'd been experienced lovers, eager to please. Again and again.

In the dark comfort of his bed Reuben refused to admit that he couldn't fall asleep — refused to accept that he was waiting with anticipation for his door to open, waiting for the invitation to go to Mickey's bed.

In his first restless sleep he dreamed he was running around the room in his skivvies. Mickey was laughing, mocking him, calling him a boy, a little boy. The dream passed. A little before dawn he reached out and grasped the deep restful sleep his body desperately

needed.

Reuben woke at noon, crawled from beneath the covers, and noticed that a fire had been started in the fireplace at the foot of his bed, that the room was warm and cozy as well as luxurious. A ewer of hot water had been prepared and left for him to wash and shave. Ready to face the day, he assumed an attitude of nonchalance when he descended the stairs to search for Daniel. Both his friend and Madame Mickey were seated in a small alcove off the dining hall, talking quietly over coffee. A breakfast setting had been put out for him, he noticed, but the others were finished eating.

"Did you sleep well, Reuben?" Mickey asked, concern in her voice.

He smiled. "I think I had the best night's sleep I've had since leaving the States. How did you sleep, Daniel?"

"Very well, and I think I've just put a big dent in Mickey's larder. Wonderful breakfast. Don't look so disapproving. Mickey asked me to call her by her first name. We're not being formal."

"But of course you must also call me Mickey. All my good friends ignore my title. It is of little importance. Only bank accounts are important in France. Now, what will you have for breakfast?"

"Eggs?" Reuben asked hopefully.

"And ham and sweet rolls and fresh juice. Fresh fruit also, if you like. We must have you healthy again," she said, smiling. She rang the bell, speaking rapidly in French when the maid appeared. Minutes later, a platter of golden eggs and pink ham stared up at him, accompanied by sweet rolls dripping with creamery butter. He gulped the refreshing juice and didn't question the miracle of fresh fruit in a war zone.

"I'm pleased, so pleased," Mickey said. "You've both slept well, you've eaten a hearty breakfast, and now you're going to rest. I must leave you darlings for a short while. I'm off to Marseilles. I'm certain you can find ways to amuse yourselves. I'll return before dinner. We'll have time to talk then. Now, if you'll excuse me . . ."

Both men stood. Reuben made a grimace that passed for a smile. Daniel grinned. Mickey called over her shoulder, "If you wish to brave the outdoors, ask Nanette for warm coats. Don't get chilled." Then she was gone, and all that remained of her was the scent of her perfume. Reuben rang the bell for a second cup of coffee. Daniel held his cup aloft for a refill.

"Tell me, how was last night, Reuben? Not details," he said, flushing a rosy red. "Was it good? Did . . . did you make her happy? What was it like with her? Where did you spend the night?"

Reuben was tempted to lie, but he didn't. "I spent the night in my own bed, alone. Nothing happened. I'd tell you if there was anything to tell."

"But I thought . . . nothing?" Daniel exclaimed.

"Nothing," Reuben affirmed. "I'll tell you the truth. In a way I was relieved and in some way I was disappointed. Now, can we drop the subject? I know you're itching to get into the library, so let's do that first. I'll read off the titles, but you aren't to try to do any reading yet, agreed?" Daniel nodded happily. "An entire room filled with books. What could be better?"

Across the foyer from the drawing room they found the library. The tall windows allowed daylight to spill into the room, illuminating every corner. The room was cold, no fire had been laid in the hearth, but it was cozy despite the temperature. Leather chairs and chaises and small tables with reading lamps, a massive desk near the glass-paned doors leading to a small garden outside, and a dark Turkish carpet were all the furnishings necessary. The vaulted atmosphere was created by ceiling-high bookshelves, each holding a burden of leather-bound books, their spines lettered in gold. There were books in several languages, but Reuben was happy to note that an entire section had been devoted to

English.

Daniel came to a dead stop in front of one shelf.

"Reuben," he faltered.

"What is it, Daniel?"

"I . . . even close up, I . . . can't make out the letters. I'm scared. I thought I'd be able to see better today than yesterday." He tried to hide the quavering in his voice, the trembling of his hands. How he hated feeling this way! He was supposed to be a man now and accept things that couldn't be changed.

"It . . . your eyes will be fine," Reuben assured him. "It was exactly the same for me, too. I kept thinking I'd end up selling pencils on a street corner. Don't forget our eyes were burned. It will ease, I'm telling you. Just don't forget to use your eye drops. I just wish there were something I could do to make it easier for you."

"Why? Who was there to make it easier for you? You had to go through it alone. If you could, then so can I," said Daniel.

"That's the right attitude. But you're wrong. I did have someone. Madame Mickey kept me sane, kept me hopeful. She talked to me for hours, she made me believe I would see. The will is half the battle she would say. It wasn't just me she encouraged, either. I'm very grateful to her."

"When did she get smitten with you, Reuben? You never told me."

69

Reuben laughed ruefully. "I don't know that she is smitten with me. She talked to me for hours about her life with her husband. She said I was a good listener. She loves life. I can't pick a time, really. One day she came up to my bunk, we talked of ordinary things, and then she invited me, just like that."

"How did she find out about me?"

Reuben grinned. "From me, of course. I asked her to check on you and let me know how you were doing. Every day she brought me a report on your progress."

"She could have invited anyone, Reuben. Anyone! She picked us. I hope she's right about the war being over soon."

"I hope so, too. I've had enough, we've given enough. I want to put this war behind me and go on. With or without Mickey's help."

Reuben wasn't ready to discuss the Mickey issue further, not even with Daniel. He hadn't figured it out in his own head yet. All he knew was whatever happened, however it had happened, he and Daniel were now a team. With will and motivation, he would succeed one way or another. Daniel would ultimately get to law school, that much was definite. "Why don't I put a record on the phonograph for you," he offered. "You can sit here and rest your eyes. You've been up for a few hours now, so you should have some compresses for at least an hour. What do you say?"

"Fine with me. What will you do meantime?"

Reuben smiled. Daniel's anxiety was something they were both going to have to deal
with. One way or another he had to wipe
away Daniel's fear, but he didn't know how
. . . yet. Maybe as Daniel's eyesight improved,
his confidence would return. "First I'll go
outside and get some air. Walk around this
little country house and see how it looks from
the outside. Then — hey, how much of the
house have you taken in so far? Did Mickey
show you around this morning?"

"Just as much as you, I guess. She was waiting for me when I came downstairs and took
me right in for breakfast. Why?"

"Good! Then I'll reconnoiter while you're
resting and report back with the details of my
mission. Okay?"

When Reuben returned an hour later he
found Daniel stretched out on the leather
sofa with his slippers off and his feet propped
on cushions. His good arm lay across the cast
of the other, and for one crazy moment Reuben thought he was dead. Daniel stirred at
the sound of his footsteps.

"Reuben?"

"Yes."

"How long have you been gone?"

"Only an hour."

"It seems longer."

"Yes. Keep the compresses on a few min-

utes more," he urged when his friend began to rise. "It's not as though you have somewhere to go. They help, so keep them on as long as you can tolerate them." Did his voice sound as paternal to Daniel as it did to himself? He burst out laughing when Daniel spoke.

"Yes, Father. I know you mean well. That's how a father would sound, isn't it, Reuben? Since I never had one, I have to rely on stories I've heard and my books."

"I wasn't trying to sound paternal. Brotherly, perhaps. As little as I can recall, my own father wasn't a man of many words. Months went by and he hardly spoke to me."

"Do you know how often I wished I had parents? I mean, I had them, but I don't know who they are. I kept thinking all the time we were at the front that if I died there wouldn't be anyone to send the telegram to. That thought was terrible. To come over here and fight and die and be buried or left somewhere in the trenches to rot and no one would care."

"Yes, but neither of us has to worry about that now. We're alive and we buried our savagery back there in the trenches. I didn't save your life for you to fret and stew about yesterday. It's behind us, Daniel."

"Did I ever thank you, Reuben? You know what I mean — a real thank-you? Someday I'm going to be able to thank you properly. I

know you think I'm just a dumb green kid, and I guess I am. I'll grow up, though."

Reuben let his shoes scuff the carpet. To cover his embarrassment, he lit a cigarette and put it in Daniel's hand and then took one for himself. "Someday I'll take the thanks out of your hide," he joked gruffly. For some reason the words didn't sound like a joke when he uttered them. To cover his confusion, he asked, "Well, do you want to hear about what I saw or not?" He placed a little crystal ashtray on Daniel's chest.

"First I walked through the house. I counted twelve rooms, and that doesn't include where the servants sleep — that's a separate wing. They have four rooms off the kitchen. There's a lot of color here. Color makes a difference somehow. I never gave it much thought before, but it can make something look big or small. It's amazing, Daniel. The furniture is kind of spindly, as you know, fragile-looking, but I tested out a couple of the chairs and they hold my weight just fine. I saw furniture like this in a moving picture once, it was about the French Revolution and the women wore these high white wigs." Reuben knew that Daniel liked details.

"There's mirrors everywhere. Over the fireplaces, over little tables lining the hallways, like the one over that long piece of furniture in the dining room, I think I heard Mickey call it a buffet last night. And there are paint-

ings, and the walls are all covered in tapestry where they're not painted with hunting scenes like in the foyer, and countrysides and, get this, some kind of goddesses with their breasts exposed and men with all their equipment hanging out in this room that's big enough to hold a ball — band and all!"

Daniel was impressed. "I hadn't realized it was so big. Imagine one person having twelve rooms all to herself."

"Mickey didn't always live alone. She said they entertained a lot, and most of the rooms are bedrooms. Almost every room has a fireplace. There are hundreds of little statues and dishes and bowls full of Mickey's flowers, and draperies. Maybe they're junk, maybe they're treasures. I don't know. There're oil paintings everywhere. Every one is signed."

"Are they beautiful?"

"I guess so. They're just pictures to me. There's a sunrise and one with ladies in a garden and another of two naked ladies lying side by side. They didn't make me want to hurry out and buy a paintbrush, if that's what you mean. Besides, I'd be lucky if I could draw a straight line."

Daniel chuckled. He couldn't wait to go around the house on his own when his eyes were better to see how apt his friend's descriptions were. "What else?"

"Mickey and her husband must have loved

clocks. There's one or two in every room. For as long as we're here we'll know what time it is every second of the day. I walked through the kitchen and my mouth watered. Good smells in there, Daniel. Dinner tonight is going to be tasty again. I checked out the wine cellar and it's stocked to the brim. There's a root cellar and a storehouse as well as a dairy. Madame Mickey could feed a division of men if she wanted. We'll never starve, I can tell you that!"

"How rich do you think she is?"

"I think the lady has more money than you or I can ever dream of having. The Fonsard Wineries are the largest in all of France. At the clinic she used to talk about shipping their wines to the States. Maybe when the war is over she will. We really stepped into it, Daniel."

"Is there a stable? I've always liked horses. Actually, I like all animals. Someday I'm going to get myself a dog. Not one of those squeaky little things, either. I want one that howls and barks and craps where it shouldn't. I want it to beg for food and lick my face and come when I call it. Someday," Daniel mused softly. So many somedays. Would they ever come?

"You got a name for this mutt, too?" Reuben laughed. "Male or female?"

Daniel snorted. "A boy dog, of course. I'll call him Jake, after my best friend at the

orphanage. Well, he was my best friend before someone took him to work in their factory. I really missed him. I think about him a lot and wonder if he signed up when I did."

Something pricked at Reuben, something he couldn't identify at first. And then he had a name for it: jealousy. Daniel never mentioned Jake until now. Here he was going to name his dog after this fellow. Well, he'd go Daniel one better: he'd get the dog for him. It would be his flesh-and-blood gift, more important than a silly name.

When he began to describe the exterior of the château to Daniel, he forced a lightness he didn't feel into his voice. "It looks smaller than it really is from the road because the major part of the house is in the back. Reminds me of a fairy-tale house; you'd almost expect gnomes and elves to come running out. The roof is tiled, real clay tiles, those half-round gray ones. And most of the windows are stained glass, the top of them anyway. That's another thing — when the sun shines through them there's a rainbow in the room. And some of the windows have designs on them. We couldn't see them last night when we drove up, but the entrance leading to the house has huge stone columns that have frescoes on them. See, I know that word because Mickey uses it. They're kind of weathered and the paint is peeling, but they're still elegant-looking. In the spring,

flowers and rosebushes must surround the house. I didn't look in the greenhouses yet. Well, that's it, Daniel. Someday I'm going to have a house like this. I'll call it my summer home, just like the Vanderbilts and Rockefellers I read about in the newspapers back home. I'll pattern the house after this one. I can smell money here, pal. And when you have money, you have power. I think that's what I want more than the money, but they go hand in hand. Power! I even like the sound of the word."

Daniel flinched under his compresses. The reaction rose from a combination of things. First was the intensity in Reuben's voice. Daniel believed that Reuben would indeed be powerful someday. Wealthy and powerful, an awesome combination. But the second reason was personal: his life was in Reuben's hands, and his friend's words served to bring everything he had been thinking about right out into the open.

The truth was, Daniel had never before slept in a room such as the one he had slept in last night. Large, luxurious, and, best of all, private — the fact that it was all his made him want to run back upstairs and look at it and touch it to make sure it was real. He was overwhelmed by the sumptuous environment Reuben had just described. Mickey was a dream come true for both of them, but to Daniel she was truly the angel he had heard

about, more nurturing and generous and bountiful than he could ever have imagined.

It was a miracle being in this house, and when his eyes were closed he was desperate to open them again and feast on his surroundings. With all his heart and soul, he hoped that Reuben knew what he was doing.

The road back to where he came from rose eerily in his mind. It was studded with places like his spare cot in the barrackslike dormitory of the orphanage, the deathly lonesome, seemingly eternal holidays he had endured there, in the place where he had felt utterly lost from God's eyes. From there he'd moved even further, into the black hole of the war. . . . The thoughts began to paralyze him with sadness, especially now that he was finally experiencing the real thing: a home.

CHAPTER THREE

Mickey returned home after the shroud of evening had fallen. She came in like a whirlwind, chattering easily about her day. "Beastly, darlings, the trip was beastly, but I had to do it. Now my time is yours for the next few days. More rest for you today, but tomorrow I will begin your French lessons. We will play chess and bridge, and if you don't know how to play, I am here to teach you. You, in turn, will teach me to play poker and roll the dice. I have always wanted to learn. Now I wish to get out of these heavy clothes and into something more comfortable. I will be back almost before I am gone and we'll have a spicy drink before the fire. You will tell me what you did today and I will tell you what I did." Seconds later she was out of the room, her perfume lingering behind her as always.

For nine days, each evening was the same as the one before. On the tenth, Reuben decided he was annoyed. Not by so much as

a look or touch did Mickey let her intentions be known. Somehow he couldn't shake the feeling that he wasn't measuring up, that somewhere along the way he'd become a disappointment to his benefactress. He wished he knew when and where she had decided that she didn't want him after all so he could go back and try to analyze it. Madame Mickey was a beautiful, sensuous woman, generous of heart and sweet of nature. And he wanted her.

Mickey watched the expression in Reuben's eyes shift from anger to annoyance and knew the time was almost right. She had paid close attention to his every gesture. After all, she was an expert in the art of seduction. But he still wasn't ready. Soon, though. Now the game was really on.

Although the nights proved torturous for Reuben, the days following Mickey's return from Marseilles were comfortable and filled with contentment. Both Reuben and Daniel were on the road to recovery — Mickey saw to that. Because Daniel's eyes were very much improved, she allowed him to read while it was fully daylight. At night, knowing the lamplight would strain his eyes, she forbade him even to think of burying his nose in a book. For his part, Reuben followed all the rules of her ministrations as an example to Daniel. To fill their free time, Mickey

80

provided other forms of entertainment: word games, music, even a lesson in French cooking.

Both Reuben and Daniel found themselves falling into Mickey's routine, yet always upon rising, Reuben would go to the long, mullioned windows of his bedroom and stare out at the countryside, finding it difficult to believe that not very far to the north the Germans were preparing for the great offensive against the American forces. Through his window, even on the dreariest days of late winter, the land was sweetly undisturbed, the air crisp and clear and waiting for the promise of sunshine. At the front, he knew, the land was disemboweled by artillery, the air thick with the smell of gunfire and powder and the stench of the trenches. Though the same sun would shine on the battle zone, it would lack the golden warmth and would hold no promise.

The threesome made it a point to breakfast together, munching their way through crisp toast made from homemade bread fresh from the ovens and heartily spread with luscious jams and jellies put up from fruits grown on the estate, and lightening their coffee with fresh dairy cream. Coffee, almost impossible to get, was brewed with chicory and one of Mickey's secret ingredients. If coffee was unavailable, they would drink chocolate from the generous supply Mickey had set aside for

herself when she knew war in her homeland was imminent.

After breakfast they would carry their cups into the paneled library. There, Reuben and Mickey would take turns reading aloud to Daniel, who soaked up each work like a sponge. "He is insatiable," Mickey grumbled good-naturedly on several occasions. "He will need proper tutoring soon." When the room grew thick with smoke they moved to the parlor for their French lessons.

This was Reuben's favorite room, despite the feminine furnishings and spindly-legged tables. Here Mickey was reflected in each object that had been chosen to grace the mantel or armoires and étagères. Seashells from the French Riviera, a coin collection under glass, her precious Monet and Renoir. And on the far wall, where the winter sun found itself rivaled for brilliance, was a Van Gogh. A field of sunflowers, yellow and orange and deep green shadows for contrast. Little crystal dishes, vast vases of flowers, thick peach-colored carpeting bordered with a pattern of grape leaves and dark purple fruit. The mantelpiece was Italian marble, the hearth wide and deep, holding logs thicker than Reuben's leg and almost as long. Gilt-edged mirrors, venetian blinds slanted to catch the last ray of sunshine, and satin draperies trimmed with golden fringe. And always the colors were soft, muted, each pat-

tern cleverly chosen to blend into the next.

Madame Mickey's wardrobe seemed to be endless. Unlike the sleek, tailored clothing she had always worn on her trips to the clinics and hospitals, here Reuben noticed that she preferred simpler dresses in soft, elegant colors that brought out the tawny freshness of her unadorned skin and the golden lights in her chestnut hair. Chanel was a young designer with whom Mickey was acquainted in Paris. The styles were revolutionary, and Mickey wore them to perfection.

"Her name is Gabrielle, but everyone knows her as Coco," Mickey explained about her friend, "and one day she will be famous, I promise you. She is what the fashion world awaits. This is a world in which women will take their place, Reuben. There will be little room for snug hobbled skirts and painful boned corsets. Ease of dress, that is the secret of Coco's designs. Away with corsets, away with them forever. Long, simple lines; supple, easy fabrics and knits. Trousers that have slim legs and flare at the bottoms, somewhat like the ones sailors wear. Bell bottoms, I believe they're called. Short jackets, jersey knits, and I have seen her wear a coat that she patterned after General Black Jack Pershing's. A trench coat, it is called. Horrible name, wonderful coat. Many elements of her designs are borrowed from a man's haberdashery."

During their French lessons, Reuben and Daniel found Mickey to be a hard taskmaster. Often she would tap their knuckles like an old schoolmarm. "Someday you will thank me for this," she kept saying over and over. Reuben doubted it; Daniel just smiled.

It was obvious from the beginning that Daniel had a greater aptitude for learning a foreign language then Reuben. Daniel worked diligently on the verbs and syntax, and late at night, after Mickey retired, he would quiz Reuben so he, too, could have his lesson prepared for the following morning. Somewhere along the way he'd become attuned to Reuben's feelings, and he knew Reuben hated to be mocked or made to appear foolish. Mickey's gentle gibing was embarrassing to him. Twice he'd blustered that he didn't want to learn a stupid, damn flowery language and stomped out of the room in frustration. Unperturbed, Mickey had kept on with the lesson. She never referred to Reuben's outburst and had smiled warmly, when, after his temper had cooled, he had returned.

After an hour in their respective rooms, where Reuben and Daniel would dose their eyes and apply compresses, lunch would be served, usually a meal of thick, hearty sandwiches and robust soup. If weather allowed, they would then embark on their daily walk, which covered several miles and always ended at the stables, where Mickey would treat her

horses with sugar lumps and green apples stored from the autumn before.

"All gentlemen ride," Mickey declared. "It is an art, and I will teach you when your health returns. One must be fit to control an animal." Then she'd looked at Reuben and said, "One day, when you are rich and powerful, you will have a country estate and invite others who are rich and powerful. They will all know how to ride. It will be expected of you. Do you understand, *chéri?*" Reuben nodded. Then she fixed her gaze on Daniel. "And you, my learned friend, will be one of those rich and powerful people who visit Reuben. You will be the most famous lawyer. I feel this," she said dramatically, crossing her arms over her chest.

Tea and cakes would be waiting in the library when they returned to the château. After that, they spent an hour on the finer points of bridge and chess. When both were over, after they'd discussed their strategies and errors, Mickey handed out paper and pens and gave a test on what they'd learned during the day. Reuben hated the tests, thinking them juvenile, but he complied. Daniel, on the other hand, loved playing school and always received a beaming smile from Mickey.

The ninety minutes before dinner were allotted to bathing and choosing the proper attire. Casual suits and dinner jackets had appeared in each of their rooms one day, along

with shoes, ties, shirts, belts, socks, and underwear. An old man from the village arrived the day after the clothing did, equipped with tape measure and pins to tailor each article of clothing to perfection.

Dinner, which was always bountiful, was for eating but also for learning. Which fork, which knife, which glass for which wine; how to open a napkin and how to fold it when finished. They learned how to seat a lady and to help her from the table. Mickey educated their palates to the use of wines and spirits, a skill at which Reuben showed himself to be adept. Mickey said it was yet another indication that he would be a success. If there was anything Daniel disliked, it was lessons in breeding and etiquette, although at Mickey's rebukes he would merely flush. "I'll make gentlemen out of you if it's the last thing I ever do," she declared with determination.

Coffee and brandy followed dinner, with talk of the war, what was happening in America, and books. Like Daniel, Mickey was a voracious reader. Their conversations were lively and spirited and usually lasted several hours.

Finally Mickey would peck each of them lightly on both cheeks, saying, "Well done," then wave cheerily and retire upstairs to her rooms.

And always Reuben didn't know if he was relieved or angry at her sisterly show of affec-

tion. When he was alone he admitted that he wanted more. On the third day of his stay he'd decided that Mickey was beautiful. Only at night in his dreams did he allow himself to lust after her. When he woke, frustrated and puzzled, he would punch his fists into the pillows and groan angrily. Why was she torturing him like this? If it was a game, didn't she know he would be a willing player? But there couldn't be a game until both players were in agreement and rules set down. Rules . . . Who makes the first move? Certainly not him; he was a guest. Of course, she was a woman, and as a rule women wanted to be asked, or so he remembered old George saying, but then, most of everything George had said had turned out to be just so much manure.

Worst of all, he found himself staring at her all the time now, imagining all kinds of wonderful things: how her lips would feel on his, how silky her skin would be, how she'd look lying naked beside him, how she'd taste. It was almost beyond his imagination all the wonderful things an experienced woman like Mickey could do to him. Once when they were walking he thought his head would blow off in excitement when he pictured himself settling urgently between her legs. George had said it was a feeling that had no equal. Mickey had looked at him, looked at him as though she knew what he was thinking.

Another time, while they were playing chess, he'd let her capture his knight because he was watching as her pink tongue moistened her lips in concentration of the game. She'd looked fully aware of his thoughts then, too.

It was a game, Reuben knew it in his gut. Who would weaken first? By God, he'd wait her out no matter how long it took. With that decision made, he set a precedent that he was to follow for the rest of his life: Never make the first move. Watch your adversary and then go in for the kill, but only after that adversary has made the first move. The only thing that confused Reuben was that Mickey wasn't exactly an adversary. He also decided it didn't really matter how long he'd have to wait — because although she had begun the game, when it ended, he'd be the winner. In all games there was a winner and a loser. He would never, no matter what he'd have to do, be a loser.

After that, Reuben felt better. Having sorted it all out in his mind, he became an active player. When he walked behind Mickey's chair, he'd let his fingers trail along the back of her neck. When sitting beside her at the bridge table, he'd let his knee touch hers ever so slightly, and he wasn't quick to draw away — nor was she. Over the candlelight dinners he'd stare at her bosom and give her the sensuous smile he'd practiced in front of the mirror in his room. He'd watch her draw

in her breath before he turned away. Another time he'd alluded to his sexual prowess, with Daniel egging him on. He'd seen a spark of anger in her eyes and grinned.

Just last evening when she'd come to peck him on the cheek, he'd turned swiftly so her lips met his. Her eyes had widened and she was the first to turn away, but not before Reuben had seen her body shudder. Hold out the bait and then yank it back was one choice piece of advice from George that seemed to be working. Fine for George to say, but his old buddy hadn't given any advice on how to get her to actually bite. Probably because it was assumed by all of them that Mickey herself would initiate everything from the beginning. Jesus, how wrong they'd all been.

"Today I feel we are like the Three Musketeers. Do either of you feel like that?" Mickey asked. They had been out walking for most of the afternoon in the crisp November air.

"When you are truly well," she continued, speaking to both her companions with a broad smile, "we will motor to Gascony. D'Artagnan and his brave musketeers, even Cyrano de Bergerac, came from Gascony. You see, every day we learn something." She looked directly at Reuben when she spoke. Instead of answering her, he gave her his practiced smile. Her eyes closed sleepily, then

she reached for a flower and placed it gently between her breasts.

Daniel was oblivious to the byplay as he windmilled his arms. His cast had recently been taken off; movement was no longer limited. Now he could bathe himself and wet his entire body. The world he was living in felt good.

Mickey stepped between the two of them and linked arms. They literally danced the next few yards. When they stopped, on the crest of a hill above a small village, they could hear shouting and singing.

"*Mon dieu,* what in the world is that racket?" Mickey cried.

"Looks like there's a parade, or else you're having a party," Daniel said, laughing.

The three of them looked at one another in wonder. Could it be? Finally?

"Hurry, darlings, we must see what this is all about."

Daniel and Reuben took Mickey's hands and ran down the hill, watching and listening to the Frenchmen as they waved their arms about, speaking rapidly. Some were singing while others laughed and slapped one another on the back.

It was November 11, 1918, and the Armistice had just been signed.

"We must celebrate!" Mickey exclaimed.

"It's over, Daniel," Reuben said quietly. "Our men made the difference. I feel kind of

proud, don't you?"

"Damn right." He wiped his eyes, and Reuben realized his own were misty. "We were the lucky ones, Reuben."

"Yes," Reuben said, touching his friend's shoulder. Then he grinned. "I agree with Mickey! We need a celebration!"

The threesome spent the next few hours drinking several bottles of the finest champagne Mickey's wine cellar afforded. The celebration lasted through dinner and into the early evening.

Mickey felt like a young girl, sharing secrets of her youth while the young men listened and spoke of theirs. The conversation inevitably brought them through myriad experiences that elicited both laughter and sometimes tears; their glasses were never empty. When she had listened to Daniel, tipsy and rambling, a lopsided grin on his face and hope in his eyes, tell again of his dream of becoming a lawyer, Mickey decided to begin now to help him realize his goal. Mentally she calculated what it would take over the next few months to put this person into action and determined to make arrangements immediately.

When she watched and listened to Reuben, she was aware that no matter how much he drank, or talked, or listened, a part of him was sitting beside her, tasting her, wanting her.

The atmosphere in the room was jubilant and warmly familial as they finished the last bottle of champagne. Mickey was the first to rise. Hugging them, and kissing them both on each cheek, she wished them a good night's sleep, first Daniel, and then Reuben. Daniel's kisses were wet and childlike and made her smile. Reuben's sent a shiver down her spine. It was difficult not to remain face-to-face with him and say, Yes, I want you now — more than ever. I want to taste you until I have my fill and then taste you again. His eyes burned into her even as she ascended the staircase. She knew he had followed deliberately for just that purpose. But when she looked back at him, she couldn't fathom what was behind that smoldering gaze.

It was odd — she'd been having the strangest feelings the past few days. One minute she wanted to drag the young American upstairs to her bed and the next she wanted to curl next to him with her head on his shoulder. It was unbearable when he was out of her sight. And she hadn't been joking when she'd referred to the three of them as the Three Musketeers. *Amour.* Was it possible she was falling in love with the virile, handsome young American? How could she be sure, never having been in love before, not with her husband and certainly not with any of her *amants.*

Perhaps she *was* beginning to fall in love.

In matters of the heart, when one partner loved more than the other, that one, she knew, would eventually hurt to the soul. Did she want that? Did she want to experience that kind of pain?

And what about Reuben? All she had to do was crook her finger and he'd come like a lamb. A niggling voice within urged her to send both young men back to America. *Before it's too late,* the voice warned. "No!" she cried fiercely. *But what if the young man becomes so enamored of you he, too, falls in love? You will grow old before him. Do you wish to tie yourself to a gigolo? That's what he'll become if you keep him here. You'll never know if he truly loves you or merely the easy life your money can provide. Send him home!* "He's young," Mickey whispered, "but old enough to make his own decisions. If he wanted to go home, he'd have said something."

Mickey turned off the lamps. The near darkness felt good. One could hide in the darkness of a room or in the darkness of one's mind. One could hide from the world in any number of ways, and that world would pass by.

Now she was feeling sorry for herself. In the whole of her life she'd never felt this way. *Go after him, take what you want. Give what you want, but never give all of yourself.* One of her many lovers had told her that once: Never

give all of yourself, for when it's time to walk away, there will be no reserve to carry you through. She smiled wickedly. All right, Reuben Tarz, you shall have ninety percent of me. Right now!

Her room was softly lit, the bed turned down, her silky white nightgown folded neatly on her pillow.

Fingers moving feverishly in their haste, she ripped at her clothes. The silky nightgown rustled softly as it fell about her. With lightning-quick motions she removed what little makeup remained, washed her face, and applied a light dusting of powder. She washed her mouth as well as her hands to rid herself of the smell of nicotine and wine. A light spritz of her favorite perfume and she was finished.

The moonlight streamed through the windows, creating silver shadows everywhere. The room looked exquisite, she decided, perfect for making love. Impatiently she waited until all was quiet outside her door. Then, feeling as giddy as a schoolgirl, she stepped down the hall to Reuben's room. Softly she opened the door. His room was also bathed in moonlight; it fell across his bed in a giant beam. It seemed to Mickey that the young American glowed in the near darkness. Fleetingly she wondered if it was a sign of something. In the end she simply didn't care.

Kneeling by his bed, she whispered in his ear, her fingers trailing gently the length of his cheek and down his neck. The coverlet had slipped from his neck. How broad his chest was, how muscular his arms. How very, very young.

"Come, *chéri*," she whispered.

Reuben woke, instantly aware of her presence. He lay quietly, giving himself up to her touch and her scent. He shuddered and felt her smile in the moonlight.

"Come with me now, to my room."

Reuben swung his legs over the side of the bed, his hands clutching the edge of the plump mattress. Mickey dropped her head into his lap, and he shuddered. She was whispering again as her tongue did strange things to him, things he never wanted to stop. He drew in his breath, expelling it in a loud hiss. With all the force he could muster, he grasped her shoulders and pushed her backward. Heedless now, he stood in his nakedness, staring down at her. At last he reached for her and drew her up and close. With one fluid motion he enfolded her into his arms and in seconds they were both in bed.

Eager to be close to him, Mickey knew no shame. Her fingers tore at her gown as she urged him with her hushed whispers and moist kisses to remove it. Oh, to be finally naked against him, to teach him her special secrets!

His mouth sought hers, his arms locked her in a hard embrace. Wave after wave of desire coursed through her as she answered his kisses and inspired his caresses. Her tongue darted into the warm recesses of his mouth; her arms wound around him, making him her prisoner. Soft hands caressed and stroked her back, smoothing along the curve of her waist to the fullness of her hips and bottom, pressing her close to her desire. Her breasts were taut and full beneath his hands. Soft moans escaped her parted lips as he aroused her to the heights of her passion. He devoured her with his eyes, covered her with his lips, igniting her sensuality with teasing touches of his tongue against her fiery skin. His fingertips grazed the sleekness of her inner thighs, and, helpless, she felt her body arch against his hand with a will of its own, to aid in his explorations.

His mouth became part of her own, and she heard her heart beat in wild and rapid rhythms. They strained toward each other, imprisoned by the designs of yearning, caught in an embrace that ascended the obstacles of the flesh and strove to join breath and blood, body and spirit.

Gently, in the darkened room, he laid her back against the pillows, leaning over her, nuzzling her neck, inhaling the heady fragrance that was hers alone. Blazing a trail from her throat, his lips covered her un-

guarded breast, and she shivered with exquisite anticipation. Gradually she became unaware of her surroundings, oblivious to time and place; she knew only that her body was reacting to this man, pleasure radiating outward from some hidden depth within her. She allowed herself to be transported by it, incapable of stopping the forward thrust of his desires, spinning out of time and space into the soft consuming mists of her sensuality.

Her emotions careened and clashed, grew confused and wild, her perceptions thrumming and beating wherever he touched her. And when he moved away from her she felt alone. When he returned she was whole again, wanting and needing, wanting to be needed in return. The feverish heat of his skin seemed to singe her fingers as she traced inquisitive patterns over his arms and back and down over his sleek, muscular thighs.

Reuben had never touched a woman this way, but somehow he knew he could touch a thousand women and none would feel the same to him as this one. None could have the unexpectedly smooth skin that tantalized his fingers and tempted him to seek more secret places.

Suddenly the room grew dark, jealously veiling the sight of him from her eyes. She wanted to see him, to know him, behold the places her fingers yearned to find and her

lips hungered to kiss. "The lamp," she whispered, hardly daring to make a sound, afraid to break the spell. She barely recognized her voice; it sounded husky, throaty, sensuous, even to her own ears. "I want to see you," she whispered brazenly. "I want to know you, like this . . . naked. All of you." It was a plea, a demand, exciting him with its fervor, arousing his desires for her to a fever pitch.

Soft, golden light flooded the room, and he stood there before her, just out of reach. Her gaze covered him, sizzling and searing, lingering at the swell of his manhood and grazing over his flat, hard stomach. Dark patterns of lustrous curling hair molded his form into planes and valleys, covering his chest and narrowing to a thin, elongated arrow that pointed below. Thighs thick with muscle supported him, the scars of his wound breaking her heart. His torso tapered and broadened again for the width of his chest. Her arms stretched out for him, beckoning him to her.

He was filled with an exhilarating power . . . the power that only a woman can give a man when she reveals her desire for him, welcoming him into her embrace, giving as well as taking, trusting him to carry her to the highest star, where passion is food for the gods and satisfaction is its own reward.

In the lamplight he gazed down at her, possessing her, held in the spell of the moment, watching her eyes travel the length of his

body. Her lips parted, full and ripe, revealing the pink tip of her tongue as she moistened them. She was leaning back against the pillows, one knee bent, hiding her most secret place from his sight. Breasts proud, their coral tips erect, invited his hands and his lips. When he reached out to touch her, an answering voluptuous stretch revealed her womanhood where a fine feathering of downy hair caught the light, gilding her body in a soft, shimmering glow. She was beautiful, this lioness with the hungry eyes, beautiful and desirable, setting his pulses pounding anew, unleashing a driving need in him to satiate himself in her charms, to quell this hunger she created in him and to salve an appetite for her that was ravenous, voracious.

He moved into her embrace, felt her arms surround his hips, aware that she rested her cheek sweetly against the flat of his stomach, rubbing against his soft, curling hairs. His hands found the pins in her hair, pulling them impatiently, removing them, eager to see its dark wealth tumble about her shoulders and curl around her breasts. Silky chestnut strands, scented and shining, rippled through his fingers, cascading from his hands down the smooth length of her back and onto the pillows. She lifted her head, looking at him, her eyes heavy with passion. He had been right in likening her to a lion, a wildcat of the jungle. Dark lashes created shadows

on her high cheekbones; upward-winging brows delineated her features. The full, ripe body, tinged with gilt, tempted his hands and invited his lips.

Her teasing touches grazed his buttocks and the backs of his thighs, slipping between them and rising higher and higher. She took in with her eyes all she touched with her fingers, the masculine hardness of him, feeling it pulsate with anticipation of her touch; and when her hand closed over him, a deep rumbling sounded in his chest, issuing from his lips in a barely audible moan.

He lay down beside her, reaching for her, covering her breasts with his hands, seeking them with his lips. But her appetite for him had not been satisfied, and she lifted herself onto her elbow, leaning over him, her hair draping over her shoulder to create a curtain between them. Again she touched him, running the tips of her fingers down his chest, hearing his small gasp of pleasure. The flat of her palm grazed his belly, and her lips followed her hand's downward slope.

The swell of her hips and the rounded fullness of her bottom filled him with a throbbing urgency. Nothing short of having her, of losing himself in her, would satisfy. He was afraid the touch of her lips would drive him over the edge, past the point of no return. Impatiently he drew her upward, pushing her back against the pillows, trapping her with

his weight. He wanted to plunder her, drive himself into her, slake his thirst, knowing his needs could be met only in her.

Her mouth was swollen, passion-bruised, and tasting of himself. Her arms wound around him, holding him close as she pressed against him. His hand caressed her breast, just skimming the rosy tip, and his lips followed hungrily, tasting and teasing until a golden warmth spread through her veins, quickening her already erratic pulse. Her hair became entangled round his neck, and he brushed it aside before resuming his sensual exploration. His lips lingered now in the place where her arm joined her body, then traced a patternless path back to her full, heaving breasts. She clung to the hard, sinewy muscles of his arms, afraid she would fall into a yawning abyss where flames were fed by passion.

His hands spanned her waist, tightening their grip to lift her above him. His mouth tortured her with teasing flicks of his tongue, making her shudder with unreleased passion. She curled her fingers into his night-dark hair, pushing him backward, away, pleading that he end the torment, only to follow his greedy mouth with her body, straining her flesh against his.

A throbbing ache spread through her, demanding to be satisfied, making her seek relief by the involuntary roll of her hips against the length of his thigh. He held her

there, forcing her bottom forward, driving her pelvis against him.

Suddenly he shifted, throwing her backward and settling on top of her, looming over her. For a thousand times, it seemed, his lips and hands traveled her body, starting at the pulse point near her throat and seeming to end at her toes.

He whispered French words of love, words she'd taught him, praising her beauty, celebrating her sensuality. Her body seemed to have a life of its own, and she succumbed to it, turning, opening like the petals of a flower. His searching fingers adored her, his hungry mouth worshiped her. Lower and lower his kisses trailed, covering the tautness of her belly and slipping down to the softness between her thighs.

She felt him move upon her, demanding her response, tantalizing her with his mouth, bringing her ever closer to that which had always eluded her and kept itself nameless for her. Her body flamed beneath his touch, offering itself to him, arching and writhing, reveling in the sensation that was within her grasp, reveling in her own femininity. She felt as though she were separated from herself, that the world was comprised only of her aching need and his lips. Exotically sweet, thunderously compelling, her need urged him on, the same need that lifted her upward, upward, soaring and victorious, defeating her

barriers, conquering her reserves, bringing her beyond the threshold of a delicious rapture never dreamed of or suspected, even in her fantasies.

And when his mouth closed over hers once again, he had proved her a woman and had not cursed her for it. He had allowed her to rise victorious in her passions, leaving her breathless and with the knowledge that there was more, much more. She was satisfied yet discontent; fed and yet famished. She wanted to share the ecstasy he had given her, participate in the sharing, and only with him.

Grasping her hips, he lifted her as though she were weightless. He brought her parted thighs around him, and when he drove downward, she felt as if she were being consumed by a totally different fire — one that burned still but left the sensibilities intact. Yet there was that same driving need deep within her, deeper and more elusive than she had experienced the first time. She struggled to bring herself closer, needing to be part of him this time, needing him to be part of herself. These fires burned deeper, brighter, fueled by his need for her, his hunger to be satisfied.

Tears glistened on her cheeks. She was triumphant, powerful, a woman. In this man's arms she knew she had been born for this moment, that all her life had been leading up to what she was experiencing with this magnificent American. Together they had

found the secrets of the universe.

Reuben lay back among the pillows, Mickey cradled against his chest. He knew that there would never be a moment to equal what he'd just experienced. There would be other women, he was sure of it, perhaps even a wife someday, but they would never do for him what this woman had just done. He closed his eyes and listened to his heart pound.

His last conscious thought before drifting off into a contented sleep was, George, you son of a bitch, you didn't tell me the half of it.

The purple dawn was wrapping its arms around the château when Mickey crept from Reuben's bed and made her way down the hall to her own room.

How cold and forlorn her bed felt. She wanted to be back in Reuben's bed with her head on his shoulder. Tears streamed down her cheeks. She'd known it would be like this . . . and now there was nothing she could do. She'd tasted her fill of the American, and she wanted more. Would always want more.

But how long would she be able to keep him? Six months, a year? At forty-three, she was old enough to be his mother. Hardly the basis for an enduring romance. In the end, would he be the one to ask to leave, or would she send him on his way? Where in the world would she get that kind of strength? Oh, why

hadn't she listened to herself, to that little voice that had warned her?

CHAPTER FOUR

Sitting at the breakfast table the next morning, Daniel knew immediately that something had changed. There was a different look about Reuben, a softer, more mellow expression around the lines of his mouth. There was a glint in his friend's eyes and a ready smile about to break across his face. Mickey positively bloomed. Daniel was quick to notice that she had allowed the natural brightness of her eyes to replace even the smallest traces of makeup. She appeared younger, even more vital than before, and the smile that played about her lips was almost coquettish, like that of a young girl keeping a secret. Even Mickey's usual lively chatter was no distraction from the way her eyes glowed each time she allowed herself a glance at Reuben.

Thus Daniel arrived at the obvious conclusion: Reuben and Mickey had finally tumbled into bed together. The thought provoked a certain ambivalence in him. On the one hand

he was glad for his friend because they both deserved the best life had to offer; but there was a certain sadness in him because he was going to be left at the gate when the three of them became two. He sighed, recognizing that the idyllic perfection of his time at the château might soon be ending. Perhaps not, he thought, remembering Bebe Rosen's visit after Thanksgiving.

"Ah, *chéri,* your thoughts are elsewhere this morning, and they are not pleasant, I think," Mickey said suddenly, breaking into his reverie. Her smile was as bright as a summer day and seemed to envelop him in its warmth. "Did you hear a word I said?"

"I'm sorry, Mickey. I was" — he searched for the right phrase — "woolgathering."

"I said I was going to the village this morning to bring you the tutor. You are ready for this next step in your studies. Monsieur Pierre Faroux is a scholar. *Extraordinaire.* He will read to you and he will teach you whatever you wish, philosophy, language, law, art, music. He is a rare individual. He was a wonderful friend to my husband and myself. He will take you under his wing, *chéri,* and in six months, a year, you will be eligible for any university you choose."

"Mickey, I never even finished high school. I can't afford college, and law school seems a million miles away. Reuben's got all these ideas but . . . I just don't see how —"

"Bah! Your mind is quick as lightning. Begin today solving the future's problems! Be gracious. Let Monsieur Faroux share his knowledge with you. He is an old man now with nothing in his life but his books. And you love the books. You will make him happy."

"I'll try," Daniel conceded. He glanced at Reuben.

"Mickey's going to teach me to drive the motorcar today, Daniel. So while you're having lessons I will be gadding about the countryside." Reuben hesitated, realizing how that sounded. "Do you think that's unfair?" he asked.

Daniel pretended not to hear the anxiety in Reuben's voice. "Of course it's fair. Please don't crash into a tree this first time out, or run over a cow."

"You worry too much, Daniel."

And you don't worry enough, my friend, Daniel thought to himself. Six months, a year, she'd said. Had Reuben picked up on her intimation? And if so, how did he feel about it?

Monsieur Faroux arrived two hours late; he, too, had celebrated the Armistice. He was a little man with a shock of white hair that stood on end, making him appear taller. His mustache was spiky and also white, curling at the ends. He possessed incredible eyes, the color of taffy, crowned by the same white spiky hairs as his mustache. He wore a heavy

wool sweater two sizes too large and baggy trousers that had once been black but were now muddy gray. His hands, though, were of a much younger man, the fingers perfect for playing the piano or violin. But it was the taffy-colored eyes that mesmerized Daniel: he read in them all the things Mickey had said about the old scholar. He worshiped the old tutor on sight and flushed when the Frenchman kissed him soundly on both cheeks.

"So, you are my new *élève!* Come, we go to the library at once so I can choose our lessons for the day. Go, go, you are in my way," he said to Mickey and Reuben, shooing them toward the door.

"Come, *chéri,* we are in the way here. Daniel, do not forget to have your eye treatment and you must rest for a while. Pierre will read to you when you have the compresses on your eyes."

"Yes, yes I will see to everything. Go, so we can begin our work."

Reuben searched Daniel's eyes to see if he was in agreement. What he saw there assured him. Except for the day his bandages came off, Daniel was the happiest he'd ever seen him.

Reuben and Mickey strolled side by side to the barn. He wanted to say something to her,

to tell her how wonderful the night before had been, but her behavior was so casual, so . . . so ordinary, as though nothing had happened between them. He didn't want to be gauche, so he contented himself by returning her warm smiles.

George had said you never let a woman know how important she is to you. Never let her see how much you want to bed her. You're a man, that's taken for granted. Women know their place, and it's next to a man, when that man wants them.

"Now, *chéri,* you wait here and I'll drive the Citroën out."

Reuben watched her run ahead, imagining her bottom jiggling deliciously under her sable coat. He could feel the heat between his legs, feel himself stiffening. Before allowing himself to think twice, he was running after her, overtaking her just as she was about to open the wide barn door.

"I want you here, now!" he said hoarsely.

She continued to open the door as though she hadn't heard him. Reuben's heart fell; feelings of inadequacy welled in him. Why was she so uninterested? Had his inexperience been so obvious the night before? Hadn't he pleased her? He followed her into the shadowy barn.

The combination of sweet-smelling hay and Reuben's manly scent was so heady, her own breathing was as labored as his when she

finally spoke.

"Here? In the barn? Like animals?" She turned to look at him, felt his gaze pierce her, felt the intensity of that gaze tingle her spine and quiver through her thighs. "You want to fuck me? Or do you want to make love to me: Animals or lovers, Reuben? Which?" Her voice was throaty, deep inside her chest, the tone suggestive, provoking. Actually she didn't care how he wanted it, only that he wanted her. Immediately upon awakening she had wanted him, wondering what he thought of her, wondering if he found her woman enough to slake those irrepressible passions he'd unleashed the night before. Was her waist slim enough, her skin smooth enough? Did her breasts please him? Her sex? Would he ever want her again?

"Like an animal," Reuben said. "Against the wall. Standing up. Now," he insisted, pushing her backward.

"Is this how Americans do things? In barns, in awkward positions?" she purred, already anticipating the feel of him between her legs, stirred by the powers of her own femininity that he would want her again and this time would be the aggressor.

"I don't know what Americans do, and I don't care. This is what I want to do." He moved toward her, hands reaching to span her waist, pulling her against him, feeling her flesh yield.

"Then do it!" *Mon Dieu!* It was as though she'd unleashed a sleeping tiger within herself. She let her hands brush open his overcoat and pulled at the buttons on his trousers, reaching through the soft wool to find him. Her breathing came in quick, hard gasps. His hands were raising her skirt, searching for the fullness of her thighs, groping for the hot bare flesh exposed at the top of her stockings. He laughed when he slid his hands around to her buttocks, slipping them beneath the lace edges of her panties. The sound was sly, amused, satisfied at finding her bare skin.

"Do you think you are the only one with strong passions, *chéri?*" she asked, grazing the flesh of his belly with her finger, searching for and capturing that which would be her prize. "I anticipated this, and if you hadn't followed me in here, I would have called you in, saying the Citroën wouldn't start." A smile played across her lips as she continued. "I, too, know what I want, and I want you, Reuben. I want you. Fuck me! Fuck me, now!"

"Then open your eyes," he ordered as he pressed her onto the nearest hay bale. "I want you to see what I'm doing to you."

Mickey leaned back, obeying him. He pulled away her panties, picked up her legs, and wrapped them around his waist, exposing her to his plunder. Gazing upon her open,

waiting sex, he felt himself stretch almost beyond the limits of his control. "Keep watching . . ." His voice was a gravelly whisper now. "Look," he ordered again as he drove into her fully, in one long, quick motion.

"Quickly, *chéri,* for I cannot stand it. Faster! Faster," she moaned, all the while watching their wild, wonderful, unbearable joining. When he withdrew from her a little so she could see him hard and glistening, she pulled him back, urging him onward. One last violent thrust and both cried out at the same time.

"Mon Dieu! Mon Dieu!" Mickey raked her fingers through his crisp dark hair. "We are animals!" she cried in a voice she barely recognized as her own.

"Was it good for you?" Reuben asked. Suddenly he was unsure of himself, worried that it might have been over too quickly, that he'd slaked his thirst for her too greedily.

Mickey smiled as she smoothed down her dress and rearranged her clothes. "*Chéri,* don't ever ask that of a woman, for she may lie to you. There are many who pretend. You must know, here" — she thumped her breast — "if you pleased me or not. Do you think you pleased me?"

"I know I pleased you now," Reuben groused good-naturedly. "I know you liked it because I watched you. I saw your face and it

was beautiful."

"Ah, yes, because you filled me with yourself. Yes, *chéri,* it was wild and wonderful, the exquisite release. I wanted more. I always want more. You will never be able to give me all I want," she warned softly.

Reuben's neck grew warm. "Would Madame care to place a small wager?"

Mickey looked deeply into his eyes. "No," she said simply. "I think you may be the exception, and that frightens me."

Reuben's first driving lesson was exhilarating. He drove the roadster as though it were a windup toy, whipping it around corners, over ruts and gouges in the road, with no mind to the speed he was traveling. He laughed uproariously as Mickey blessed herself over and over. She cursed him, screaming for him to drive in a straight line. "We are not going to hell, *chéri,* at least not today. Slow! This is supposed to be pleasurable, not miserable. You are making my teeth ache!"

Reuben continued to laugh as he put the touring car through its paces. When at last he braked by the side of the rutted road, he pulled her to him. "All you had to do was say: 'Stop! I want to make love with you again,' and I would have stopped." He kissed her soundly, passionately. Her quickened breathing made Reuben smile. When he

released her, she gasped.

"You had my life in your hands, Reuben," she said, trying to sound severe. "If you care to place yourself in danger, that is your decision. Do not take liberties with my life. Start the engine and I will take liberties with you. Start the engine!"

When the Citroën began to move forward, Mickey foraged into the folds of his overcoat and then into his trousers. He was delicious, this one, she thought as she lowered her head onto his lap. Before she took him into her mouth she ordered, "Now drive as you should."

Reuben's foot pressed the accelerator the same moment her mouth closed over him. For what seemed an eternity, he felt himself being hurled forward, racing toward an unreachable destination. He didn't know if he was driving on the road or had left the earth entirely, shooting off into space. All he knew was the pleasure of being in her mouth. When he shuddered again and again, reason overrode passion and he braced himself against the brake pedal, grinding the car to a halt.

"Mon Dieu!" he moaned as Mickey began to laugh.

"Now it is my turn, Reuben, and I will request your full attention."

"My pleasure," Reuben answered. He would do whatever pleased her.

115

"And mine." Turning toward the back of the car, she threw her sable over the seat and scrambled after it. Reuben quickly followed the length of her silky leg and the promise of her favors. After nestling deep into the fur, Mickey ran her fingers through his hair as she searched for and found his mouth with her own. Oh, how she loved the feel of him, the touch of him! The way his lips evoked a cry in her throat and how his fingers had learned and knew her body almost better than her own.

He was tall and slim and hard-muscled. Her greedy fingers could not touch him enough, her hungry mouth ached to taste every morsel of his flesh. And always there were the words: beautiful and loving, praising her beauty, adoring her passion, filling her head and warming her heart, throbbing through her and creating an aching need for him.

Somewhere, deep in the recesses of her mind and logic, she knew she was being wanton, even barbaric. But she didn't care. All she cared about were the slim hips poised above her and the honeyed words falling from his lips.

His mouth sought hers; his strong, sinewy arms locked her in an urgent yet tender embrace. Wave after wave of desire coursed through her as she answered his kisses, her tongue darting into the depths of his mouth.

Her hands caressed and stroked his back, bringing him closer still. Her breasts were taut, their pink crests hard nubs beneath his palms. Soft moans of ecstasy escaped her parted lips as he proved himself to be an artful lover.

His thighs twined with hers, and she was completely aware of his body and the driving desire he held for her. A deep wave of yearning spread through her belly. Drawing up her knees, she yielded herself to him, inviting their union.

Her eyes opened, bathing him with the splendor of her passions. Every turn and curve of her body was a song, a lyric poem. And when she whispered the pleasure she took in him, her voice was deep and husky, reminding him that she was a woman like no other.

Together they found the culmination of their desires. Together they breathed as one, falling, drowning in the sea of their desires. They lay together on the rich Barguzin sable for a long time, touching each other. There were no words; none were necessary, all had been said and experienced.

It was dusk when Mickey heard Reuben's stomach rumble ominously. "*Mon Dieu!* What kind of woman am I? I gave you no lunch," she cried unhappily.

"You fed me in other ways," Reuben said

quietly. "Mickey, I have never —"

Mickey placed a gently finger over Reuben's lips. "Shhh, do not say the words. It is too soon, and I don't know if you should ever say them. This is now, *chéri.* Tomorrow and the day after tomorrow will take care of themselves. Words, my darling, can wound one's soul if they do not come from the heart. Always remember that. During lovemaking it is allowed," she added hastily. "Often one lover will say sweet words to the other because that is what they think they want to hear. It is better to say nothing. Do you understand, *chéri?*"

"Yeah, sure," Reuben said, sounding for all the world like a chastened schoolboy.

"Do not pout, *chéri.* These things must be said now so there is no hurt to either of us later. You must understand the difference between love and lust. There is a very big difference. Someday you will love a woman so much you will want to offer her your soul. Lust is a mingling of two people for the moment. Lust is when a man or a woman walks away and never looks back. Love is when a man or a woman looks back and . . . smiles."

Reuben's mood turned sour. "Have you ever loved like that?" He hated asking the question, but he had to know.

"But of course, *chéri,*" Mickey lied smoothly. "But of course."

Reuben ground his teeth together so hard

118

he thought his jaw would crack. Angrily he climbed back into the driver's seat and threw the roadster in gear. Mickey was jerked forward unexpectedly, forced to hang on for dear life as the car roared down the road. But she hardly noticed how fast Reuben was driving, so intent was she on the blinding tears in her eyes.

CHAPTER FIVE

The days leading up to Thanksgiving passed swiftly. The dinner hour was the end of a busy day that began at dawn. The Three Musketeers met, dined, and talked. Daniel was full of praise for Pierre Faroux and regaled Mickey and Reuben nightly with his accomplishments. Once or twice, so pleased was Pierre with his pupil's progress, he stayed to dinner to assure Mickey that she'd made the right decision about Daniel. He was so quick, so bright! Faroux insisted his pupil had already far surpassed what Americans required for a high school diploma and was now plowing through college-level material.

Reuben beamed like a proud father when he listened to discussions on law and other matters. It was clear that Daniel was holding his own and several times bested the old Frenchman with queries he couldn't respond to. Daniel's thirst for knowledge was being sated at last.

If Daniel was aware of the change in Reu-

ben and Mickey, he gave no sign. He was so caught up in his studies, he was almost oblivious to their private little exchanges. When he noticed the hand touching, the knowing smiles, the intimate glances, he was pleased for his friend.

It was a glorious time for Reuben as well as for Mickey. They were together constantly, taking care of the château, working companionably in the barn with the animals, seeing to the massive wine cellars, and always making love at any time of the day in any given place. Theirs was a robust, spontaneous relationship in which both of them reveled. Often they'd walk for hours, their hands entwined, overseeing this task or that domestic problem.

It wasn't only Daniel who was receiving an education. In subtle ways and often in blunt, forthright words, Mickey was teaching Reuben the ways of the world. The only difference between Daniel and Reuben was that Reuben didn't ask questions. Everything Mickey said, everything she alluded to, every nuance, every warning, was tucked away — but not before it was categorized and filed in his brain. He had the wonderful ability to stop and search his mind for a second, then come up with exactly the right answer whenever Mickey quizzed him. He'd laugh when she showed surprise. "I never forget anything."

"Elephants are like that," Mickey joked.

The night before Thanksgiving, Mickey presented Reuben with a book that had arrived from America. She had things to do, she said, a surprise, and he should read while she finished her preparations.

Reuben accepted her offering — the latest Zane Grey novel — with pleasure and settled himself in the library with Daniel. He showed Daniel the new book. "It's a tale of the joining of East and West by rail."

Daniel looked up long enough to smile, then settled back in his chair, the reading lamp aimed at the book on his lap. Reuben shook his head and smiled at his friend — his learned, literary friend. Then he, too, began to read.

In the kitchens Mickey huddled with the bevy of extra cooks she'd hired from the village. "You understand now, it must be just the way they do it in America. The turkey is to be at least thirty pounds. We have that," she said, ticking off items on her list. "Chestnut and raisin dressing and candied yams, white potatoes that are mashed, turnips that are also mashed, vegetables fresh from the root cellar, peas, beans, and carrots. I have secured some Echiré butter, the best in the world, and you will make light fluffy dinner rolls that melt in the mouth. They must melt in the mouth because that is what Reuben

hungers for. The pies are to have a flaky, delicate crust — pumpkin, mince, pecan, and one berry. Blackberry, I think. We must use canned berries from the storeroom. Do you think he will notice the difference?" she asked the cook fretfully.

"No, madame. It will be perfection."

"*Mon Dieu,* I almost forgot the soup. Noodle, and there is something called a noodle pudding that Reuben likes. I have it written down here somewhere. Nanette made the noodles last night. And we must have a garden salad of some sort. You will have to forage in the cellar. If you can't come up with something that is going to be perfectly fresh, at least make it look pretty. Americans like fresh raw vegetables." She shrugged to show she herself couldn't understand. "Fresh ground coffee, but don't grind the beans until you are ready to boil the water. Tell me, did I overlook anything? Will there be enough time for you to prepare all of this for three o'clock tomorrow?"

"There is no problem, madame. It will be a feast fit for a king!"

"I'll select the wines now. There must be flowers on the table. The best linen cloth and finest dishes and crystal."

In the wine cellar Mickey leaned back against one of the huge barrels that hadn't as yet been tapped. She'd gotten so much pleasure out of arranging this special dinner

for Reuben and Daniel. She'd do anything, anything at all, to bring a smile to Reuben's face and that warm, intimate look to his eyes.

These past days had been so exquisite. She would no longer fool herself.

She was in love with the young American, deeply in love. And expert that she was in the ways of men, she felt he, too, was in love with her — for now. Yet she refused to listen to his pleadings and his vows of eternal love. Of course they were words she wanted to hear, words she would remember and dream about when he was gone. Because one day, all too soon, he would return to his own land, where he belonged. Until then each day, each hour, was to be lived to the fullest.

She wondered if the arrival next week of Bebe Rosen — the daughter of her American cousin Sol Rosen — would affect her relationship with Reuben. Certainly she and Reuben would have to give up most of their private time to entertain the visitor from California. Already Mickey felt jealous. Bebe would be vivacious and pretty. If she was anything like Mickey had been at her age, she would flirt with Reuben, try to play boy-girl games with him. And what would she, Mickey, do? Stand by and eat herself up with jealousy? Perhaps she was being unfair. Bebe might be a bookworm like Daniel, or she might be shy and keep to herself. . . . Not likely, since she was Sol's daughter and — from Sol's own descrip-

tion — spoiled rotten. Sol had said she was a brat, a willful, spoiled young woman who pouted and finagled and manipulated till she got what she wanted. In other words, a handful.

Bebe's skin would be smooth and flawless without the need of rouge and mascara. She'd be lithe and shapely, wearing the latest in American fashion. And she'd be able to talk to Reuben about things in America. They would have so many things in common, mainly their youth.

What would Reuben think when he saw the two women side by side, the fresh-faced girl and the middle-aged woman he was living with? Her heart thudded in her chest. If it was going to happen, let it happen now before Reuben's hold on her became so overpowering she'd do foolish things to keep him. At the beginning of the affair she'd sworn to herself that she'd never do anything to mar her dignity. As Marchioness Michelene Fonsard, she had an image to protect. When Reuben finally left her he'd remember her that way, not as some *midinette* begging him to stay, offering him money, anything so he wouldn't leave. The thought made her cringe.

No, she would not let her fears run away with her . . . or her jealousy. Jealousy could destroy. If there was one thing she didn't want to do, it was destroy what she had right

now. She would treat Bebe kindly and gently, the same way she treated Daniel. Tonight she would pray that the young girl would find Daniel an engrossing companion.

Two weeks wouldn't be an eternity. They would all survive young Bebe's visit, then give her a rousing send-off when she was ready to leave for England for the second leg of her European visit. Mickey laughed. Here she was arranging for Bebe's departure and she hadn't even arrived yet.

Mickey deposited the wine bottles in the kitchen and ordered a pot of hot chocolate and a plate of cake. While she waited she wondered if anyone would ever go to this much trouble again for Reuben. Tears burned her eyes but she willed them away with a fierceness she didn't know she possessed.

Reuben and Daniel put their books aside for Mickey's late night snack.

Something was wrong, Reuben could sense it. Mickey's eyes were too bright, her smile too tight. She'd been acting differently these past few days. Not exactly preoccupied, but she wasn't always totally with him. Several times he'd caught her gazing through him as if he weren't there. Once he questioned her, thinking he'd done something to offend her or that she was tiring of him. She'd wrapped her arms around him and looked deeply into his eyes. "No, *chéri.* If you did something to

displease me, I would tell you. We made a bargain, did we not? Honesty at all times. Sometimes I think honesty between two people is more important than love." He'd let it drop then, but the strange look was still in her eyes.

Maybe it was the young girl who was coming to visit. Mickey had joked about keeping her busy, entertaining her. She'd said something like "you young people will have much in common," implying that she was old; the same old sore subject. He hadn't seen it that way at all and told her so. Although she'd acted amused, her mood had changed and she'd been warm but silent after that.

It was Reuben's first experience with jealousy, and he didn't know how to handle it. If he had more experience . . . if he'd had women, girls even. Old George had said women fought with each other over men, pulling hair and scratching at each other. He'd called them cat fights.

Reuben's eyes were questioning when Mickey pecked him on the cheek. She blew Daniel a kiss. "Good night, *chéris*. No, no, don't get up. I will see both of you in the morning."

Reuben nodded, thinking it must be "that time of the month." He felt better almost immediately. Now he could spend some time with Daniel.

"Are you happy, Daniel?" he asked, leaning

back against the soft cushions of the settee.

"I was thinking about that earlier in the evening. I am, thanks to you. There's so much to learn, and Monsieur is being patient with me. He never seems to tire of my questions. My head just buzzes. What about you, Reuben? We see each other only for breakfast and dinner. Listen, if you think it's time for us to leave or . . ." He floundered for the right words. "Don't stay on my account. Promise me."

"Daniel, look at me. Do I look like I want to leave? I'm having the time of my life. It's not time for us to leave yet. And don't worry, I'll let you know. This is good for both of us."

"You're happy, then?" Daniel's voice was full of concern.

"Very happy. I'm learning, too. We're going to make a good business team someday. Now, tell me what you think of Bebe Rosen's visit. What do we do with the young lady? Mickey wants us to be sure she has a good time. That means you must give up several hours a day, and so must I."

Daniel blinked at the intensity in Reuben's voice. So . . .

"Another thing. Next month it will be Christmas. We have to think about a present for Mickey. I have all our pay intact. We must get her something so special, she can remember us after . . . you know . . . when we leave."

"Maybe Bebe will have some idea," Daniel

said thoughtfully. "Girls always know about things like that. Mickey already has everything. What could we give her that would make up for all this?"

Reuben shook his head. "The cost of the gift isn't important. It's the thought and the effort that goes into the gift. We're going to have to be inventive and original. I did sort of have an idea, though."

"What is it? Daniel asked.

"It might not work. I'm going to go to the village tomorrow and make some inquiries. If I get the right answers, I'll tell you tomorrow."

Daniel shrugged. "That's fine with me. Listen, I hate to bring this up, but have you thought about going back to America?"

"No, not yet. I think we're going to stay for a while." Reuben smiled at Daniel's happy face. "In the meantime, I mentioned trying to get a job in the village, and Mickey convinced me there was plenty of work here. She asked me to come up with things I'd like to get involved in, and I think I've got some ideas. For instance, I'm sure her wines would be great in the States."

"Have you mentioned it to her yet?"

"No, not yet . . . but soon, very soon. I don't like mooching off her like this."

Daniel read Reuben's thoughts and changed the subject. His friend would handle it, and besides, he felt exactly the same way.

There didn't seem to be any way he could pay her back now. Someday, though, he knew he would turn himself inside out to do just that.

"How are your eyes, Daniel?" Reuben asked. "The truth."

"Much better. They hardly tear at all now. By late afternoon, though, I have to have the compresses. It feels good to keep them closed for an hour or so. Can't see things at a distance too well, but I can see. That's enough for me. I'm going to have to wear glasses later on. That doesn't bother me, though."

"Good! And the shoulder?"

"A little stiff in the morning, but otherwise no problems. How's your leg?"

Reuben laughed. "A bit stiff in the morning, but okay. Depends on what I'm doing. The other day I was moving some grape boxes, and it bothered me. We're both going to be fine, considering we came *that* close to being dead."

"I know. Sometimes I wake up in a sweat. I try not to think about it. Each day it gets better. How's your vision?"

"Impaired. I have very little sight in my left eye. The right one isn't quite normal. How do you think I'll look in spectacles?"

"Reuben! You never said a word! Why? Why didn't you tell me?" Daniel cried.

"Because I was afraid you'd think the same

thing was going to happen to you. There's nothing either of us can do about it. And I know you, Daniel, you'd start feeling guilty that you fared better than me. It's over. We're both going to live with it."

"If you'd gone back, if you hadn't come after me . . . you'd have gotten the medic to help you quicker. You should have told me."

"Daniel, listen to me. A life is more important than a set of eyes. I'd hate it if I was blind, but I'm not, and neither are you. If I had it to do over again, I'd do the same thing. You would have done the same for me."

"I don't know about that. I probably would have been too scared. I'd have frozen on the spot."

"That's what you say now. Back then you would have done what had to be done. So let's just drop it for now, okay? I think I'll try to read for another hour and then turn in. Mickey might quiz me tomorrow," Reuben said with a crooked smile. "Have you ever read Zane Grey, Daniel?"

"Yes, but I can't say he's a favorite of mine. It's hard to believe Mickey likes that kind of writing. Sometimes I can't quite figure her out," Daniel muttered, his eyes already on the book in his lap. But he was only pretending to read. Someday . . .

Mickey's surprise Thanksgiving feast stunned Reuben and Daniel.

"Is it a good surprise?" Mickey asked them. "Tell me the truth, is this like it is in America? I could do only what you described to me."

"So that's why you asked all those questions." Reuben grinned. "It's perfect. I've never seen so much food at one time. Who's going to carve this magnificent bird?"

"You are, *chéri*. I will show you how." She felt so wonderful standing next to him as she instructed him how to carve into the bird and then slice down. They loved her surprise. Perhaps, though, it would make them sad thinking about America. But when she looked up at Reuben, there was no sadness in his eyes at all; they held only warmth, dark and gentle, the way they always did when he gazed at her with love. She released her breath with a soft *swooshing* sound.

Their plates filled, Mickey surveyed her guests. "A prayer for this bountiful table is in order. Daniel, will you do it?"

Daniel nodded. "Bless us, oh Lord, for this bountiful dinner." It was a short blessing because he was starving. The Lord would understand.

An hour and a half later, the Three Musketeers retired to the library for their coffee and pie. Thirty minutes after that, they were sound asleep on their respective chairs.

When they woke, tired and sluggish, Mickey suggested a walk and elicited a promise that afterward, Reuben and Daniel would teach

her how to play poker.

"For money?" Reuben queried playfully.

"But of course. It is no fun to play for matchsticks or raisins."

Reuben grinned. "What do you say, Daniel, a little five-card stud?" Already the walk was forgotten.

"Sounds good to me. Shall I explain the rules?"

"I must warn you, I have never been lucky at cards," Mickey said ruefully. Three hours later Daniel and Reuben were down twenty dollars. Mickey had won the last three pots, the first with an inside straight, then a flush, and finally a full house. She laughed gleefully as she recorded her winnings.

"Do you have any idea how hard it is to get an inside straight?" Daniel grumbled. "And a full house. I've never had one of those."

"Beginner's luck," Mickey said charitably. "Tomorrow will you show me how to shoot the dice?"

"*Roll* the dice," Reuben muttered. "I suppose you want to play that for money, too." It wasn't exactly a question.

"If you want to play for raisins, it is all right with me. But money is so much more exciting," Mickey teased, but then her eyes locked with Reuben's. "I'm tired. Winning money is an exhausting business. Good night, *chéris.*" She blew kisses in their general direction, then mounted the stairs to the second floor.

Reuben grinned. No kiss on the cheek meant he was to join her when he was ready. There would be other, more meaningful kisses.

It was near midnight, the witching hour, when Reuben made his way down the hall to Mickey's room.

Mickey stood on the inside of the door, her ears attuned to her lover's footsteps. She sighed. At first she'd thought he wasn't going to come to her, but then she'd heard the water gurgling in the pipes and knew he was taking a bath. Earlier she'd done the same thing, just to be clean and fresh . . . for him. The door opened; she was in his arms and he was loving her.

The French silk robe fell open under his commanding fingers, and when he captured her breast, its pink nipple rose to greet him and bring him delight. Slowly he teased her ear with his tongue, following the pulse points to her neck and throat. He wanted her urgently, but he would take her slowly, deepening the pleasure. His hands traced the contours of her body, following its curves, caressing its hollows. He explored the depths of her mouth and the silkiness of her thighs. This was Mickey, his lover, as familiar to him now as the back of his hand and yet, some-how, always new territory to be charted.

Her emotions were charged, more finely tuned than ever before, and when he closed

her hand over the proof of his desire, she communicated her own demands.

She hurried him with her kisses, excited him with her soft mewlings and murmurs, undulated beneath his caresses. She wanted him now, desperately. She felt she would erupt with a wildness too long contained. There would be time later for luxuriating in his arms, to have his hands soothe this fever, to have his lips take possession of her inch by inch. Now she needed completion.

Her thighs opened, her back arched, and he became a part of her. In the white heat of her passion she entrapped him, feeling him stroke within her, locking her legs behind his, to take him deeply inside her, where the warmth was building.

Her body exploded into thousands of shimmering, shattering jewels as the waves of her passion swept her under, and she rose to the surface crying Reuben's name over and over.

Spent, they lay back in the mound of soft pillows. Their mouths touched, tasting of each other. They lay naked together without benefit of covers, and when they sought each other again it was with tenderness. Their mouths were gentle, and their fingers softly caressed. And when their passions quickened, Reuben calmed her with his touch and crooned soft words of love.

His mouth became a part of hers, and her heart beat in a wild, broken rhythm. They

strained toward each other, caught up in the designs of yearning. Together they mounted the obstacles of the flesh and joined breath and blood, flesh and spirit.

CHAPTER SIX

The day after Thanksgiving the air was cold and crisp. The sun shone in that particular light of early winter that was more silver than gold. Mickey and Reuben labored to polish the Citroën touring car on the pebbled apron outside the barn when the postman arrived. Mickey was on one side of the car and Reuben on the other, their eyes meeting every few seconds, their light laughter a pleasant sound in the afternoon quiet. Reuben's eyes adored Mickey. She had changed since those early days at the hospital. Gone was the sophisticated lady. Her preferred dress was casual, soft clothing that barely skimmed her figure. Her slacks, a revolutionary style she had adopted, were nipped at the waist and fell in long straight lines to her ankles, her round bottom accentuated by the clever fit and tailoring. Even her hair, newly coiffed with a little fringe of bangs and a coronet of braids, gave her an air of simplicity and freshness.

Mickey read the happiness in Reuben's eyes and took full responsibility. He'd told her earlier, when she'd handed him the polishing cloths, that he was happier than he'd ever been in his life thanks to her. "I don't ever want this to change!" he exclaimed, his eyes darkening. "Do you hear me, Mickey? Whatever it takes, whatever you want, I'll do it."

She'd wanted to caution him, to admonish him, to say all those sophisticated and wise things she had been saying all along, but she couldn't. In just a matter of weeks all her resolve had fallen away. Her own gaze was as intense and passionate as Reuben's, but still she had difficulty with the words.

"Smile, Mickey," Reuben said quietly. "At me, not at the postman." And she'd rewarded him with a dazzling smile that warmed his heart.

"Numbers," she murmured as she sifted through the pile of letters.

"Only if you make it an issue," Reuben said forcefully. "You know it doesn't make any difference to me. When are you going to get that through your head? It doesn't matter," he said, enunciating each word carefully.

"For now, no, it doesn't matter. But later?" She shrugged. There was a desperation in her voice, a sadness in her eyes. She wanted to believe him and she did, for now. But later . . . what then?

As if reading her thoughts: "Later, you and

I are going to have a talk, the conversation you always avoid because you are afraid to hear what I have to say. You, Michelene Fonsard, are a coward," Reuben said heatedly when he saw her shaking her head. "Later, I want it settled between us."

"Yes, yes. Later we will talk. It is a *promesse*. Continue with the Citroën while I take the post into the house. There is a letter from America which I must read. Would you like me to bring you an apple when I return?"

"Two," Reuben said. "We'll sit in the hay and eat them together."

Mickey chuckled. "You are a hopeless romantic, my love. But I will bring them."

Reuben continued his labors on the car, his movements fast and furious as his arms reached for the center of the hood. He wanted his position settled, once and for all. If Mickey wouldn't or couldn't come to terms with him, then he and Daniel would have to leave. He wouldn't be jerked about like a puppet on a string.

His arms trembled with the exertion. The thought that kept creeping into his head surfaced again: He wanted to marry Mickey Fonsard. He didn't care about age, all he wanted was to be near her, to be able to love her. To awaken beside her, to find her across the table from him, to reach out and touch her when they sat before the fire. And then the niggling inner voice attacked him: *What*

happens to your dreams of making it on your own? Of becoming successful in your own right? You want power and wealth. Your own power and wealth. Someday you'll want children and Mickey can't give you that.

"There're orphans!" Reuben shouted, the sound of his voice echoing off the side of the barn.

Which do you want more? the voice whispered. *Mickey or the freedom to find your own future?*

"Shut up," Reuben answered through clenched teeth. "It's not that simple. This is now. I have the rest of my life for all that other stuff."

But what about Mickey? Every day she grows older . . . older . . . older.

Reuben shivered despite the heavy wool sweater he wore. His attention wandered from the polishing. Little puffs of vaporized breath escaped his lips into the cold air.

A parade of chickens trekked past him. He wondered inanely if it was a family or just a bunch of chickens taking a walk. He dropped the cloth he was holding and watched the chickens. Where were they going, and why were they in a group?

Numbers . . . Him and Daniel. Him and Mickey and Daniel. A unit, a family. Man didn't do it alone. Somewhere, someplace, there was always a woman. That didn't mean he couldn't do it on his own. It just meant it

would be easier if there was someone to share with. The chickens scattered; wings flapped, and gravel spurted behind them. Disgust showed on Reuben's face. So much for chickens and families.

Mickey settled herself in the kitchen with a cup of tea. First she opened the letter from Sol Rosen. A vague feeling of foreboding washed over her as she unfolded the crackly paper. Bebe was due to arrive within the week.

Mickey straightened the pages on the table. The letter was in Sol's handwriting, tight and cramped.

Dear Mickey,

I hope this letter finds you well. We were all relieved to hear you came through that bloody mess unscathed. Each day as word reached us about the war we thought of you.

I'm sending this letter ahead of Bebe's departure and hope that it reaches you before she arrives in France.

Mickey, for this favor of taking Bebe, even if it is for a short while, longer if you want, I will owe you a favor in return. Know that you will only have to ask and it will be granted. You can call me on it anytime.

As I said to you in my last letter, you are my only hope. Bebe needs a woman

like you in her life. She's become wild and uncontrollable. She's the darling of the newspapers here. They can't wait to print what she does next. Each escapade is worse than the last.

I've tried to be both mother and father to her, but what she doesn't need right now is more indulgence from me. As it is, when I told her I was sending her to you for a vacation she only agreed to make the trip if I bought her a Russian lynx coat. I don't know any other sixteen-year-old girl who has such a coat! Like a fool I got it for her. That's how desperate I am to get her out of here.

The enclosed bank draft should cover all Bebe's needs.

Mickey, listen to this foolish man's confession and don't think me maudlin. I love Bebe so much it hurts me to see her carrying on like some two-bit floozie. Behind my back my friends call her a tramp. This is breaking my heart. I've made some bad business decisions because of the affairs in my house. You will put me forever in your debt if you take care of Bebe and return her to me a proper young lady, like her mother, rest her soul.

Warm affection,
Sol

Mickey read the letter a second and third time. It sounds, she mused, like Bebe needs a keeper. Sol must be in quite a state. To admit he had failed with his daughter and had made some bad business decisions made the matter doubly serious.

For a moment Mickey almost forgot the jealousy she'd felt at having a pretty young lady as her guest. From what Sol was saying, Bebe didn't sound like she'd be much of a companion for serious-minded Daniel. What in the name of God was she to do with her at the château? Paris and the town house would undoubtedly suit Bebe better, but there she'd need a chaperone. Mickey shuddered to think how that would shatter her present blossoming idyll.

Curious now, she turned the bank draft over in her hands. Money enough for two years! *Mon Dieu!* Sol must be desperate.

Her head was beginning to pound, the usual painful indication that she was upset. First Reuben with his need for a commitment, and now this. Perhaps she should settle things with Reuben first and go on from there. Reuben would be happy. She would be . . . happier?

With a sigh, Mickey rose from the table and stuffed the letter, envelope, and all behind a stack of heavy mixing bowls in the cupboard. Reuben would come looking for her soon, and she didn't want him to see her agitation.

She was supposed to take something to him. What was it? . . . Ah, yes, apples. Ripe, juicy apples.

"It's about time!" Reuben called cheerfully as he watched her walking toward him, rubbing the apples on her sides to bring up their shine. "I was about to call out the gendarmes."

"I had to go all the way to the root cellar for these," she teased, holding up her gifts. "Here is your apple, darling." She tossed one of the rosy treasures to Reuben, who caught it deftly. "You look frozen, Reuben. Look how red your hands are. Come, let's go into the barn, where it's warm and we can talk. Bring the lap robe from the backseat."

Reuben's heart thudded. Mickey was finally going to talk to him about their situation. At once he felt giddy and fearful.

Minutes later they were settled comfortably in a mound of sweet-smelling hay, the lap robe over them. Overhead the sun shot through the ceiling-high window, lacing them with streaks of pure gold. Now that her mind was made up to talk to Reuben, Mickey felt relaxed. Her features were softer, her eyes warmer, her touch more gentle as she leaned against him.

Reuben was aware of all these changes and certain now that he was making the right decision. "I want to marry you," he blurted out.

Mickey was silent for a few moments. Idly she let her fingers trail through Reuben's thick dark hair while she composed her answer. "Darling, there's nothing I would like more, but it cannot be. What we have is so precious, I cannot take the chance that we'd ruin this wonderful feeling. Marriage, I'm afraid, would make all the difference in the world. The difference in our ages matters." She hushed him gently with her fingertips to his lips before she continued. "One very special reason is the most important one to face: I can't give you children, and one day, my darling, you will want children. Because I love you, I cannot take that away from you. Yes, you heard me right, I love you. I never thought I would say those words to any man, much less one half my age. I do love you, with all my heart."

"I don't care about children. I can always adopt children. I want *you*. I want us to grow old together." He hadn't meant to say that, hadn't even thought about it, and now, as he read Mickey's face, he wished he could take the words back. Old age for him was so far into the future it didn't even bear thinking about. Mickey's old age was . . . closer at hand.

"Ah, you see, it creeps in in soft, subtle ways. It will always be there, pushed far back into your mind until I do something to anger you or if I displease you and the devil will let

you pull it out. In the beginning it won't matter too much, but later, when it happens more often, you will start to pay attention and wish you had done so much earlier. It's enough for me, Reuben, that I can admit to you openly, to say the words aloud, that I love you as I've loved no other man, and I'm sure I will never, ever, love this way again. Now that I've said the words, you don't appear to like them. You are scowling, *chéri.*"

He was scowling. He felt angry, but he didn't know exactly why. She was telling him what he had wanted to hear these past weeks. In her own way she was allowing him to see her vulnerability, the nakedness of her emotions, something she'd guarded so carefully.

"That pretty much makes me a gigolo, doesn't it," he said in a flat, emotionless tone. "I'm living off you, and so is Daniel. The word *protégé* is far too generous. I really haven't done much now, have I? I've taken you to bed, made love to you, eaten your food, drunk your wine, polished your car, and lazed about. I really haven't contributed much. In fact, I haven't contributed anything."

Mickey untangled herself from the lap robe and leaned up on one elbow. Her eyes were hot and smoky-looking in the sunbeam-laden shadows of the barn. "Never a gigolo, Reuben. My lover, *oui.* I understand why you think like this and how you must feel. I can't

change circumstances. But I can refute what you say about not contributing. Who is with me when I see to the cellars, the account books, speak with my men in the fields? You. Who helps me in a thousand and one other ways in my other administrative chores? You! Anyway, I want to give to you, I must give to you. That's how I show my love." Her eyes clouded momentarily. "I've taken your love, love that should have been saved for that special woman who will be at your side, bearing your children and walking beside you as you climb the ladder to success. I don't know if it was wrong of me or not. Selfish, of course. What are we to do, Reuben? Think logically and help me to understand what we should do."

It was hard for Reuben to get the words past his lips, but he had to say them. "How long am I to stay here? Till you get tired of me? No lies, Mickey. I heard the stories about you before I came here. They said when you tire of your lovers, you send them off with a fistful of francs and a jewel. Is that what you'll do to me? I can't even get Daniel and myself back to America. I need to earn money. I can't just keep taking from you. For Daniel, yes; for myself, no."

Tears burned Mickey's eyes. "I'm not buying you, Reuben. Yes, I did that with one or two others. However, I never told them I loved them, nor did I pretend. It was what it

147

was. The francs and the jewels were so they would have a nest egg. Or perhaps I hoped they would keep the jewel to remember me. I could never send you away. When it is time to leave, it will be you who will make the decision. I love you too much, I am too selfish to send you off. As for your passage to America, if you decide to return, I will lend you the money at an agreed-upon interest rate. I trust you to pay me back. If you stay, your business is helping me with the management of the wineries. I will have my 'right hand,' and you will have a 'position.' I'll pay you a salary. If you can't see yourself doing that, I can send you to Paris to look after several shops I have there. You can stay in my town house. Tell me what you think."

"I think you are trying to push me away . . . manage a Paris shop," he said with contempt. "And when will I see you? At your convenience?"

"I will not dignify that remark with an answer."

"I want you to marry me."

"I think you want too much. One never, ever, gets the whole pie. Only pieces, and some only get slivers. You see, what we have now is best. If there are to be changes, you will be the one to make them. You needn't feel pressured. For myself, I could go on for the rest of my life like this." Thinking about her last statement, Mickey knew it for the

awful lie it was. How very difficult it was to be young.

Reuben felt as though he'd been kicked in the stomach.

Mickey could not bear to see the torment and defeat in his eyes. She pulled him to her and laid his head on her breast. "Life is never easy, *chéri.* I learned in my life that one must take happiness where one finds it. You don't look back nor do you look forward. Enjoy it now because it may . . . Never mind, *chéri.* I love you and you love me. That is all we have to concern ourselves with. Ah, and we must remember our friend, Daniel. He is so happy, and we, you and I, are the cause of it. You and I together are lighting up the world for that young man. If you give him more time here, he will be better prepared to continue his studies and realize his dream. Perhaps what we should both do for now is think of Daniel and what is best for him. That way, neither of us will lose. But we must both agree. And after we agree, we must finish polishing the car." She tickled him under the chin, her eyes sparkling, until he laughed, a deep resonant sound she loved to hear.

The bad moments were over — but not forgotten. On the other side of the car, as Mickey put her final efforts into the motions of her hands on the polishing cloth, her heart fluttered wildly. Just a few more days.

CHAPTER SEVEN

Sixteen-year-old Bebe Rosen, all ninety-three pounds of her, arrived in Le Havre aboard the SS *Americus* days after her father's letter was delivered to Mickey Fonsard.

Bebe Rosen was thought to be a beautiful young lady, a consensus with which Bebe herself wholeheartedly agreed. She was just five feet tall, but gifted with those long, elegant bones that lend gracefulness and the appearance of height; of course, as might be expected in one so young and lively, she added to this illusion with outrageous high-heeled shoes. Most of her fellow passengers on the *Americus* thought her to be at least twenty years old, and because of the color of her hair, which could be compared to the palest sunbeam, they had dubbed her "Golden Girl," a title she loved. Her eyes were electric, green as bottle glass, fringed with a lush double row of dark eyelashes and crowned with fine arched brows. Her high cheekbones, always lightly dusted with pink rouge, gave

definition to her delicate nose. Her jaw was sharply carved and served to enhance the elegance of her incredibly long neck. Lips, full, ripe, and rouged, would part to reveal small, perfectly aligned white teeth.

Bebe wasn't just beautiful, she was elegant and sophisticated, an ethereal, pale vision that suggested vulnerability and fragility that only heightened her charms. She demanded compliments and adoration the way a baby demands its bottle and its mother's arms.

Her crossing had been first class, naturally, and she had let it be known from the instant she'd placed her foot aboard the luxury liner that her father was a famous American film-maker. There was already a certain aura of glamour attached to the West Coast movie business, and this announcement provided Bebe with instant popularity and the best seat in the dining room. She also had a bevy of eligible young men flitting about like bees to a flower. In spite of her youth, Bebe already knew how to use this power to get what she wanted.

She lied about her age whenever it suited her, and on the voyage across the Atlantic it suited her perfectly. Cocktails would be served to a young woman of twenty, milk to a child of sixteen. She lied about other things, too. For example, she said her brother was a famous lawyer who ran the legal department at Fairmont Studios, the family enterprise.

She lied and said she'd been in several movies herself, and these exaggerations made her listeners believe that Fairmont was a first-rate studio instead of the third-rate quickie grinder that it was. She lied about her friendships with famous actresses and actors and hinted that certain male stars had courted her with gifts too valuable to mention.

Even the stodgy captain of the *Americus* had fallen under Bebe's wily charms and asked her to talk her father into making a film aboard his ship; naturally, he'd gladly play the role of captain. She'd humored him. Later, dazzling listeners with a merry smile and mischievous eyes, she had called him a fat old man with bad breath, so ugly he'd break the camera lens.

Bebe Rosen had been the darling of the crossing. It had been a gay crowd to begin with because of the Armistice and the promise of a return to normalcy at last. And if she had left any young man's heart shattered, she could not have cared less. What she did care about were the darting, envious glances of all the other women aboard the liner.

She was already a little tipsy on champagne when she tripped down the gangplank in her high heels, waving a gay *au revoir* to one and all. Her eyes searched for Aunt Mickey's solicitor, who was to escort her to the railway station to book her passage to Marseilles. First class, of course, complete with sleeping

berth, which she would not need during the three-hour trip, and a private sitting room.

It was a beautiful day for late November, crisp and cold with a bright sun warming the passengers still milling about the pier. Bebe smiled, wishing she were going along with the crowd to Paris. The pier was mostly quiet now, with all of the baggage having been sent on to different hotels or stored in automobiles waiting to take the last departing passengers to their destinations. A lone gull dove low, its wings spread, but as it neared land suddenly it swooped upward again. It appeared lonely, Bebe thought, almost as lonely as she felt. Damn, where was that attorney who was to meet her? She felt foolish as she tapped her foot, first in annoyance and then in anger.

As the minutes ticked by she grew more nervous and felt more abandoned. She wasn't afraid of the dark, not really. Back in California she thought nothing of going from one party to the next at midnight. But California was her territory, her place. This was a foreign country filled with people who hardly spoke her own language. What if she missed her train? Mickey would be worried. If Sol knew she'd been left standing on an abandoned pier, he'd have a fit, too. Perhaps she should throw a tantrum, her usual course of action when things didn't go her way. She glanced around again at the almost deserted harbor. A family of five, obviously waiting for some-

one to meet them, stood in a cluster off to the side. She'd seen the plump woman on the ship eyeing her coat and probably comparing it with her own mink. She'd been dressed to the nines with jewels and shimmering dresses that did nothing for her sallow complexion and horsey teeth. The woman's husband had flirted with Bebe every time his wife's back was turned. Bebe snorted in disgust. Men were all alike — tomcats.

Twenty minutes later an old man shuffled toward her. Effusively apologetic, he introduced himself, saying he had experienced car trouble. He was as old as God, Bebe thought. Just like Aunt Mickey to send some old creature to take all the fun out of her travels. Mickey was acting on Sol's orders, of course.

This trip was in fact a punishment for associating with the wrong type of people. Ha! If her father wanted to believe she was romantically involved with gangsters, let him. All she'd done was party and have fun. It was Eli, her brother, who was up to his neck in trouble. Perhaps it was a good thing she'd come over here now. If Eli was going to go to jail, she didn't want to be around when the mud began to fly.

Bebe smiled in the darkness of the Daimler. Not only had she wanted a trip to Europe, but she'd also gotten the Russian lynx coat she'd been eating her heart out for. If a dashing young Frenchman swept her off her feet,

Sol would have no one to blame but himself.

Closing her eyes, she conjured up an image of Mickey. The last time Bebe had seen her aunt she'd been only seven or so, just a little girl. A wealth of dark hair and laughing eyes, gold earrings, and a smile always on her face. Bebe had liked Mickey, that much she remembered. A free spirit, Sol called his cousin. A wealthy free spirit. Often, when Sol was angry, he would compare Bebe with Mickey. Secretly, Bebe accepted it as a compliment.

Squirming down into the seat, Bebe imagined the wonderful time she'd have with Mickey. They'd go to bistros, have parties, and she would be introduced to wealthy and glamorous Frenchmen. She completely ignored the trunk filled with lesson books and the promise of a private tutor. It would be easy to get around Mickey.

Back in California there were people who had unflattering things to say about Bebe. She knew the names they called her behind her back — and it wasn't just the newspaper reporters, but her friends as well. It was her own fault. She had never bothered to defend herself against the image the reporters presented. Deep inside she wasn't anything like the person they portrayed. She was lonely and she was bored. Going to parties and flirting with her beaux was her only fun. Eli was always off doing something or other that would eventually lead to trouble. Sol was

always at the studio, often later than midnight. The housekeeper didn't care what she
did or where she went. Quite simply, no one
cared about Bebe Rosen.

"Poor little rich girl," that's how she
thought of herself when she lay in bed at
night.

Someday she would meet a young man who
would sweep her off her feet and love her for
all of her life. They would have children
whom they would both adore. It wouldn't
matter what he did for a living; he could be a
shoe salesman or sell insurance, anything,
just so long as he loved her and loved her. It
wouldn't matter if they had an ordinary life,
he would be her Prince Charming come to
rescue her from this loneliness. Or perhaps
they would live on the English moors; she
would be Cathy to his Heathcliff. Romantic
notions played in her head. One day she
would be Cinderella and the next Cleopatra,
but always there was some man, handsome
and good, there to save her, to love her.

Eli called her a spoiled brat. She never
bothered to explain to her brother that her
selfish ways and temper tantrums were a
defense against feeling lost and alone. It was
an attitude that crept up on her, and she
didn't know how or when it began. She had
no inclination to change. It was enough for
her to know that inside she wasn't any of
those things people said about her. She was

Bebe Rosen, and she ached. To reveal herself would be agony; to hide behind this facade was safety. She never knew what was expected of her, so she never seemed to fit or belong. Confusion was a way of life for Bebe, never knowing or understanding who or what she was supposed to be.

Even now, jouncing along in the Daimler, she felt she had to decide who she was supposed to be before she met with Mickey. Was she going to be Bebe Rosen who cared only for herself? Or could she chance being herself, the little girl inside, the shy sixteen-year-old who desperately wanted a new beginning?

Party girl, she decided. It was safer. If the time came when she had to tone down her image, she could do it overnight. Her father said Mickey liked fun and excitement. If she allowed her vulnerabilities to show, Mickey might leave her out and attend parties and social functions without her, burdening her with school lessons and a stodgy old tutor. Mickey was expecting a handful, Bebe knew. Why disappoint her? Besides, who in his right mind could fault this beautiful Golden Girl with the laughing eyes and charming smile?

"Monsieur, do you know why I'm to go to Marseilles instead of Paris? I thought my aunt would be living in Paris," Bebe said, leaning over the seat.

"Madame Fonsard felt safer at the small château. She is a loyal Frenchwoman and felt

she could do more for the war effort from there. She seems to prefer the château these days to Paris. She leads a quiet life. The war is a reminder to us all to treasure those things and the way of life that means the most to us. You'll enjoy the village, mademoiselle."

"Doesn't she ever go into Paris?" Bebe questioned, disappointed.

"For the moment, mademoiselle, her attentions are not there. As her *avoué,* I can handle most things for her." His voice was creaky, like a hinge needing oil. If this man was Mickey's attorney, Bebe felt sorry for her aunt. Her father would have put the old man out to pasture a long time ago. But she was in France now and would have to learn new ways and new approaches to doing things. And it really wasn't any of her business what her aunt did. Unless, of course, it affected her own whims and desires in some way.

For the first time Bebe felt a chill of fear. What if her aunt didn't like her? Most adults didn't for some reason. Worse yet, what if she didn't like her aunt? What if her aunt didn't have the maternal qualities that she craved? Make the best of things and cut her visit as short as possible — if her father would allow the visit to be cut short.

A château in the country. That meant no bright lights and no parties. She'd read a book once about a young girl who was sent away to an old aunt in the country, and her

only entertainment was taking long walks and gathering leaves to paste in a book. Bebe shuddered. She just knew she would die of boredom.

In California her life had been wildly exciting even during those times when the school principal suspended her for smoking in the girls' bathroom, kissing boys in the hall, and generally acting like a hoyden. School, discipline, and authority were simply not enjoyable. She was bright and intelligent, more so than most of the youngsters in her class, and it was a simple matter to catch up in her studies after one of her numerous expulsions.

Bebe kicked off her red shoes and curled her legs under her. She wished she had something to hug to her chest, something warm and alive to squeeze her back. Tears pricked her eyes. It was always like this when she started to think too heavily. It was so much easier to laugh and carry on because your heart didn't ache even if you were just pretending to be happy. Please, she prayed silently, let Mickey like me and let me like her in return.

"How much farther is it?" Bebe asked the lawyer.

"Not too much longer, Miss Rosen. We'll be there before you know it."

The old man irritated Bebe. She'd asked him a simple direct question and he'd responded the way her father had when she

was six years old. He probably thought her dim-witted. Wearily, she shook her head. There was no point in trying to carry on a conversation with him, she decided; because of his age he couldn't do two things at once even if one of the things was talking and the other was driving the stupid car. She slumped back onto her seat and thought about the racy friends she'd left behind in California.

CHAPTER EIGHT

Mickey hadn't slept all night. Even now, with dawn just minutes away, she still couldn't sleep.

It was all due, she knew, to Bebe's imminent arrival that afternoon. The three of them would go to the depot to meet the girl. Beyond the initial meeting and a beautifully planned dinner, she'd made no plans.

Since sleep was out of the question, she knew she should get up and go to the kitchen to make an herb poultice for her eyes. With luck she could diminish the dark circles Reuben had noticed the night before. After arguing with herself for a good fifteen minutes, she swung her legs over the side of the bed, then debated a moment over which robe to wear, the ruffled filmy one or the warm flannel. Since it was early she opted for the warm one. As she padded down the carpeted stairs, she scolded herself. She was a mature woman, knowledgeable in the ways of the world. One slip of a girl shouldn't be having this effect

on her. Ah, but when it comes to matters of the heart, there are no rules, she told herself. Emotions, she had discovered, were the single thing upon which one should never rely.

Mickey rattled around in the kitchen, making more noise than she intended. When the old housekeeper appeared at her elbow, she jumped in surprise and almost squealed her fright. The old woman shooed her to a spot at the table and placed a cup in front of her. Coffee would be ready soon, she said, and she herself would make the poultice since Madame either used too much or too little of the dry herbs. Miracles could not undo days of damage to delicate eyes, the old woman grumbled under her breath.

At eight o'clock Mickey was at the breakfast table waiting for Daniel and Reuben. She'd bathed and donned one of her favorite dresses, designed just for her by Coco — a deep burgundy wool jersey with huge pearl buttons down the bodice and on the sleeves. The hemline was shorter than fashion decreed, but Coco had said she had beautiful ankles and should show them off. Her hose matched the dress, as did her shoes. Jewelry, Coco had advised, would ruin her magnificent creation; sheer elegance did not require jewelry, she'd emphasized impatiently, her spritelike body and little hands in constant motion. Power was the ultimate aphrodisiac. Mickey had been in a hurry the day she'd

picked up the dress, and while she'd promised not to wear jewelry, she hadn't understood what Coco had meant about the aphrodisiac . . . until this moment.

The depot was a cacophony of noise when the train from Le Havre pulled into the station. Steam hissed and whistled through the air, blocking visibility for the Three Musketeers. Departing passengers jostled one another, some good-naturedly, others angrily. There were mountains of luggage everywhere. Mickey found herself looking for the most expensive trunks, the most elegant chapeau boxes, and when she sighted them she didn't need to see the name *Barbara Rosen* engraved on the handles to know to whom they belonged. There were seven trunks and nine hatboxes. A wry smile tugged at the corners of Mickey's mouth. There were times when she herself had traveled with just as much for as little as ten days — a trunk of shoes, one for lingerie, another for daytime dresses, and one for evening wear; still another case for purses and evening bags, at least two for furs depending on the season, and the last one for casual wear, those outfits of which one was uncertain.

Mickey sucked in her breath. If Bebe was anything like she was, she would wait for the crowd to disperse, then disembark from the train looking bored and put out, pouting at

the inconvenience of travel. Instead of allowing her coterie of young admiring men to help, Bebe would expect Mickey and her guests to do her bidding. Daniel would be of little help because of his recently mended shoulder; it would be up to Reuben to carry the heavy trunks unless she could prevail upon a porter. And so far all of them appeared to be occupied — the price one paid for making a grand exit.

When at last Bebe stepped onto the platform, Mickey's first thought was that the girl looked ridiculous in her oversize fur coat and teetering high heels. A child playing at sophistication. Her second thought was that the young girl was probably the most beautiful creature she'd ever seen. She didn't know whether to laugh or cry. A swirling cloud of vapor enveloped all of them for a second, giving Mickey the time she needed to orient herself. When she could see clearly she called to Bebe. "*Chérie,* over here!"

Hearing Mickey's voice, Bebe drew in a deep breath, then loosened the heavy fur and shrugged it back the way she'd seen some of the actresses do in her father's films. She felt a little silly as she advanced toward her aunt. Her eyes went immediately to Reuben and Daniel, then back to Reuben. Handymen? Servants of some sort? The tall one with the black hair was handsome as the devil himself. Sol would probably cut off his right arm to

get him into a film. In the blink of an eye she sized up both men. The second time she blinked she decided she wanted the dark-haired one for herself. If her friends in California could see this man, they'd drop in a faint. He was just the type they all said they were going to marry someday. Hmmm, marriage? She concentrated on the tall man, willing him to meet her gaze. He didn't seem the least bit interested in her. Well, she thought, shrugging, time would take care of that.

The younger and shorter of the two was mesmerized by her, she could tell, but the taller one had eyes only for Mickey, and there was something in his gaze she had never seen before. Something strange squeezed at her heart, and in that fleeting moment she wondered if she was making a mistake in choosing the party-girl role. It wasn't too late to play Barbara Rosen. Look at me and smile a greeting, Bebe pleaded silently. He turned then, a smile on his lips — but it wasn't for her, it was over something her aunt had said to him. Their eyes met, his bored and indifferent, hers challenging and determined. Excitement raced through her when he looked away. Bebe prided herself on her knowledge of young men. This one would never, ever want someone like the real Barbara Rosen. At once she made up her mind to have him. Bebe Rosen, party girl, rushed to her aunt, but not before she favored Reu-

ben with a wicked grin. "Think about *that,*" she muttered under her breath.

"You're all grown-up, *chérie,*" Mickey cooed against Bebe's smooth, satiny cheek. Reuben heard the last whispered word "almost," and smiled.

"*Tante* Mickey, how wonderful it is to be here. You're as beautiful as the last time I saw you . . . only older," Bebe countered in response. She glanced at Reuben. "But we're forgetting our manners, *Tante.* Introduce me to these fine-looking gentlemen."

"But of course, *chérie.* You Americans are so . . . impatient. Bebe, this is Reuben Tarz, and the other smiling young man is Daniel Bishop. My house guests. Ah, I finally see a porter. Wait here for me, *chérie,* I'll return in minutes. Entertain this young lady while I'm gone," she said to Reuben and Daniel.

Reuben's eyes narrowed. Had the others picked up the tremor in Mickey's voice, he wondered. Bebe Rosen was responsible for that tremor, and he himself was feeling strange, almost out of his depth. He felt a vague sense of fear. Not the kind he'd felt during the war — this was different, and so unexpected he couldn't define it. His gut told him that some way, somehow, this girl was going to damage his relationship with Mickey. A troublemaker, he was sure of it. Anger at his own inability to be tolerant of the girl and at the sappy expression on Daniel's face

166

made him clench his jaw, afraid he would say something that would in some way hurt Mickey. He made up his mind then: he did not like Bebe Rosen's bright eyes and creamy skin, he didn't like her youthful figure and calculating smile. He did not like Bebe Rosen, period. Commenting snidely to Mickey about aging . . . The girl reminded him of a baby shark, all glittery eyes and sharp teeth. And Mickey had heard her, of that he had no doubt. The little snit should be put in her place, and at once, but the chances of that were almost nil. Mickey would handle things in her own sweet way, which meant Bebe would get away with her obnoxious behavior. And she'd ruin everything, bit by bit . . . day by day. He did his best to stifle the rage building inside.

"From the looks of your luggage you must be planning to stay for some time," he said coolly.

"As long as it takes," Bebe said just as coolly.

"Takes for what?"

"Why, to get to know all of you. How long have you been . . . guests of my aunt? And for God's sake let's all talk English. My French is so rusty, everything I say comes out as 'Pick up the pencil.' " Daniel threw back his head and laughed uproariously. Reuben grimaced.

"Well?" Bebe demanded.

"Well what?" Reuben said gruffly. It was almost impossible for him to believe that this painted doll standing before him — this mannequin in ridiculous shoes — had just turned sixteen. With some small measure of consolation he remembered Bebe wasn't really Mickey's niece, but a cousin. It made a difference. In France, Mickey told him, cousins, especially young ones, used the term "aunt" out of respect.

Returning to the platform with a porter, Mickey caught the flinty look in Reuben's eyes and felt her heart soar. So, he didn't much care for Bebe Rosen. It was difficult for Reuben to hide his emotions; it was suddenly apparent that he also had a temper, something she'd decided they needed to improve upon but not just yet. Daniel was more open, and he seemed to be enjoying a sprightly conversation with Bebe as her bags were loaded into the car.

"Bebe, you and Daniel will sit in the back and Reuben and I will be in the front. Reuben will drive."

"Does he double as chauffeur?" Bebe asked sarcastically.

"Heck, no," Daniel interjected. "Reuben just learned to drive, and he's doing it for the experience. You know, the more you do something, the better you get at it."

"Imagine that," Bebe said quietly.

Sitting directly behind Reuben, cramped

between Daniel and hatboxes, Bebe noticed Reuben's stiff shoulders and how his head didn't move an inch as he guided the big car down the roads. She listened to Mickey and Daniel prattle on about the château and their Christmas plans and all the things they were going to do. Every now and then she nodded or interjected a word; the rest of the time she tried to figure out who Reuben and Daniel were and how they fit into the picture. Guests could mean many things — working guests, guests on a temporary basis, and guests that did . . . other things.

Bebe knew she could have Daniel and maybe even her aunt eating out of her hand in a day's time, but Reuben would probably bite that hand off and toss it back to her. She wondered why. No one had ever taken such an instant dislike to her before. Reuben made her feel that she was infringing. But on what and on whom?

The tall American was her aunt's lover, she was sure now. Just the thought of the good-looking man in her aunt's bed made her angry. She was so . . . so old, almost as old as her father, who was at least fifty. Sixteen-year-old logic questioned her aunt's right to take a young lover.

For the first time since getting into the Citroën, Bebe looked out the window. All she saw was trees and winter desolation. Her stomach churned as the car bounced over

ruts in the road. Where in the name of God did her aunt live? In America she would have called this place the boondocks.

"How much farther is it, Aunt Mickey?"

"Kilometrage? Perhaps . . . *dix,"* Mickey said.

"Please, Aunt Mickey, talk to me in English. I know only a few words of French — and before you offer to teach me, let me tell you that I really don't want to learn. I don't ever see myself using your language in the future." She hadn't meant to sound so surly, but there was no way to retract the words now.

Reuben bit down on his tongue to stop a sharp retort. The girl was after all Mickey's guest, and it wasn't his place to chastise her. Maybe he should simply ignore her comments and say something positive . . . but what? He unclamped his jaw. "You could take a nap if you don't care for the view. You must be tired after your long trip." He could sense Mickey smiling next to him. She was pleased with his response. He felt better immediately.

Bebe blinked and flushed a bright pink. She waited a moment to see if Mickey would endorse Reuben's words. She wished she hadn't noticed the sly smile on her aunt's face. He must be smiling, too. She turned to Daniel and spotted a cigarette case peeking from his pocket. "Give me one of those cigarettes," she said in a choked voice.

Once again Reuben bit down on his lip.

Bebe was too young to smoke, but he knew Daniel, gentleman that he was, would not refuse her. He let out his breath with a quiet sigh when Mickey spoke. "*Chérie,* you are much too young to be smoking. And I'd rather no one smoked in the car . . . it leaves an odor for days. Would you mind, terribly?" she said, turning in her seat. She smiled to take the sting out of the request.

"No, of course not," Bebe said reluctantly.

"Sometimes," Mickey said kindly, "this trip can be very boring, especially if one is driving alone. Today there are four of us, and we should be happy. I'm delighted you are here and hope you will enjoy staying with us. We do have a routine and there are certain rules. I don't think they'll pose a problem, but if they do, we can talk about it."

"What kind of rules?" Bebe asked haughtily. She was being put in her place, an outsider, a visitor. Damn. She risked a glance at the boy sitting next to her, and their eyes met. Daniel smiled and Bebe found herself returning his smile.

"Simple rules. There is the matter of privacy. The use of the bathroom, mealtime. Nothing major, more a show of consideration for others. I don't anticipate a problem, do you, *chérie?*"

"Of course," she said quietly. Not to agree would be ridiculous.

Reuben wanted to turn in his seat and swat

the girl, and he didn't know why. She was going to be a handful as well as an interloper. He stopped the car to allow a farmer leading four cows to cross the road, then pivoted to get a better look at the invader in his life. "Have you ever seen a cow before?" he asked quietly.

Bebe stared into the clearest, grayest eyes she'd ever seen. His jaw, she thought, looked as though it were chiseled from quarry stone. "Wh-what was the question again?"

"I asked you if you'd ever seen a cow. Those four-legged animals are cows the farmer is leading across the road. They give milk." He thought at that moment that she looked like a frightened bird fresh from its nest instead of the hellcat who had stepped into the car. What could she possibly be frightened of, he wondered.

"No . . . I mean yes, in . . . California," Bebe stammered.

Reuben smiled, a winsome, boyish smile that sent chills up Bebe's arms. "Those are California cows . . . these are French cows."

Mickey fidgeted on her seat. This exchange of conversation was unexpected. Eye contact between a male and a female was all-important, and she wasn't imagining the heightened awareness the two had of each other. Something was slipping away from her, something she couldn't grasp. There was friction developing between the two young

people, and if there was one thing she didn't want, it was to be placed in the role of peacemaker. That would only call attention to her age, and she would come out the loser. God, why did this child have to come here now, when things were so perfect? Why couldn't she have waited until later to visit France? Mickey sighed. It was her own fault: she could have said no to Sol. Now there was nothing any of them could do but be hospitable to the girl.

The rest of the trip was made in silence. When the powerful car drove through the village, Bebe gasped. Reuben smiled. "This is our closest town. I don't imagine this quaint village is anything like Hollywood, but it's all we have to offer. You will come to love it as we do." Reuben smirked. The girl's gasp had been one of horror — not pleasure. In a pig's eye she would come to love it. "You'll get to meet the entire village at Christmas. We're looking forward to it. It will be a pleasant break from lessons." A malicious smile tugged at his lips when he heard her mutter, "Bastard!" under her breath.

"Not really." Daniel grinned. "He's my best friend and a hell of a nice guy. You have to get to know Reuben; he doesn't make friends easily."

Bebe glared at him. "You are, of course, entitled to your opinion. I think he's a shmuck."

"What's a shmuck?" Daniel asked.

Reuben's eyesight might have been poor, but there was nothing wrong with his hearing, even if Daniel was keeping his voice down. "A shmuck is someone to be pitied or despised. At least she didn't call me a shlemiel. They're Yiddish words, Daniel. Unflattering, to say the least, but we can mark them up to Miss Rosen's fatigue." Daniel found himself grinning. Miss Rosen's stay was going to be anything but dull.

"We're home, *chérie*. This," Mickey said, waving her hands about, "is my château. Your father fell in love with it when he was here many years ago. He had to drag your mother away; she wanted to stay forever."

It was on the tip of Bebe's tongue to say that wouldn't happen to her. She'd cut out of this place the first chance she got. And go where? she thought sourly. She'd imagined Christmas would be spent in Paris; Sol had told her Mickey always spent Christmas in Paris. Just another lie from the old man so she would do what he wanted.

Reuben held the door for Bebe as she climbed out. He bowed gallantly, a wicked grin on his face, and she suppressed the urge to kick him. "What about my trunks?" she asked sweetly.

"What about them?"

"Who's going to bring them up to my room?"

Reuben leaned against the car. "It's like this, Miss Bebe. Daniel has a bad shoulder. I have a bad leg. Your trunks weigh tons. What I suggest is you unpack in the barn and carry your things upstairs. We can all help."

"My father said you had servants!" Bebe whined to Mickey.

"At one time I did, and then the war came. Now I have only a cook and a housekeeper."

Reuben felt his anger rise in defense of Mickey and struggled to keep his tone civil and even. "We all pitch in here. We hope you'll do the same. What would you like to do first? See your room, freshen up and then take the contents of your trunks upstairs, or vice versa?"

"But it will take at least a hundred trips!" Bebe cried.

"Not that many, *chérie,* if we all help. Come along and I'll show you to your room." Bebe glared at Reuben but followed her aunt meekly.

"Jesus, Reuben, what was that all about?" Daniel demanded when the women were out of earshot.

"Mickey's been upset about Bebe's arrival. Couldn't you tell? That girl is a spoiled brat, Daniel. I don't want her taking advantage of Mickey. Do you?" he demanded.

"Hell no. Look, maybe she's just scared. She's new to France, and I bet she's bone-tired from the crossing and then the train

175

ride. Maybe you should go easy on her, she is just a kid."

"That one tired!" Reuben guffawed. "She's not tired, she's plain old nasty. She's going to be trouble, and I can see now why Mickey was so —" Reuben stopped himself from saying "afraid," even though he believed it to be true. "So worried."

"She's pretty," Daniel said shyly.

"No, Daniel, she's beautiful. When Mickey was her age I bet she looked just like her except her hair is dark. They have the same high cheekbones and the same straight nose. The only thing is, I don't think Mickey was ever like Bebe. And she was already married at that age. I don't like her," Reuben said. "And for some ungodly reason she brings out the worst in me."

"First impressions aren't always sound, you should know that. All I'm saying is to give the girl a chance."

"And all I'm saying to you is keep your hands off her. She's trouble." Reuben could see Daniel bristling. He'd never given orders before. "She'd chew you up and spit you out in two minutes. I hope you listen." He placed a gentle hand on Daniel's shoulder to take the sting out of his words. "Come on, we can at least get started by carrying in some of these hatboxes."

No sooner had the front door closed behind them than they heard Bebe shout from

upstairs. "Only one bathroom? You mean we all have to share it, to take turns?"

They were just in time to see Mickey throw her hands in the air and stalk to her room. "I'm going to change my clothes and I'll be down to help shortly," she called over her shoulder.

"Don't bother, we'll take care of it . . . get some rest," Reuben said. He and Daniel dumped the hatboxes in the middle of Bebe's room. "Come on, we're not doing it all," Reuben told her sourly. "They're your trunks."

Bebe turned to follow Reuben and almost fell. He swung around, grabbed her, and carried her to the bed, where he dumped her in a heap. "It might be a good idea to take off those shoes. You'll kill yourself on the stones and gravel." He waited a moment until the outrage on her face had faded. She had nice legs, that much he noticed, and she smelled rather good, flowery and sweet. When she made no move to take off the bright red heels, he left to ask Mickey for a pair of serviceable shoes Bebe could wear temporarily. He handed them to the girl, who contemplated them with disgust.

"These are at least three sizes too big. Whose are they?" she demanded. "And they're the ugliest things I've ever seen."

"They'll serve the purpose for the moment," Reuben snapped. "You'd do well to pay attention to the way a real lady dresses

177

— and I'm talking about your aunt. If you want to pretend to be grown-up, then behave like a grown-up."

"Just how old are *you?*" Bebe demanded sarcastically.

"I'm four years older than you. I'll be twenty-one in another month. Is there anything else you want to know?"

"Yes," Bebe sneered. "How does it feel to be twenty years old and a gigolo?" The minute the words were out of her mouth she was sorry.

"What did you say?" Reuben said through clenched teeth.

"No-nothing. I'm sorry," Bebe muttered. God, if she'd been home and said the same thing to one of her brother Eli's friends, she'd be missing her front teeth and have two black eyes. "I said I was sorry. Let's just drop it."

"You ever say that to me again, you'll regret it," Reuben said coldly.

Daniel stared at them, his mouth dropping in surprise. Something fluttered in his chest. You didn't *ever* cross Reuben Tarz.

Twelve trips later, Reuben was about to close the barn door when Bebe approached him, hands on hips, lips pulled back angrily. "What about my trunks? You aren't going to leave them here, are you? They'll smell and get all black and moldy."

"As a matter of fact, I am leaving them here. If you want to carry them to the house

and up that narrow stairway, then do it. Nothing will happen to your trunks here." The urge to slap this petulant brat was so strong, Reuben had to clench his fists to keep from doing just that.

"You . . . you . . . you're hateful!" Bebe cried. "How can my aunt stand you? She doesn't look desperate for companionship. My father —"

"Your father has nothing to do with this conversation, so let's leave him out of it. I'd like to close the barn door if you don't mind." What he really wanted to do was put his hands around her neck and strangle her.

Bebe felt tears sting her eyes. She wanted to reach out to the young man with the cold eyes and say she was sorry; they got off to a bad start and . . . it was all her fault. And she would have said those things if Reuben hadn't reached out to take her arm and lead her from the shadowy barn. She completely misread his intention, thinking he was going to strike her.

"Take your hands off me! When I want to be manhandled, it won't be by someone like you." She felt a second prick of fear when Reuben turned to her, back stiff and gray eyes dark with anger. "You should do something about that temper of yours," she blurted out, "before it explodes and hurts the people around you."

Reuben turned and began to walk away.

"You've just met me and already you hate me," Bebe yelled after him. "I've seen you fighting with yourself not to pound away at me. I'm tired, I'm hungry, and I need a bath. I'd like to call a truce."

An alien sound escaped Reuben's lips, but he kept on walking.

Bebe was right behind him. "Did you hear what I said? What's wrong with you? You're still angry, and that's stupid. You're not grown-up at all, because if you were, you'd be able to handle any situation, and that includes this one. You're a boy trying to act like a man and probably fucking my aunt!"

Reuben pulled up short, and Bebe slammed against his back. She tried to back away, but he reached for her. Somewhere in the back of his mind he was aware of her slender shoulders, her sweet scent. But overpowering everything was an anger so intense that he actually felt the beginning of an erection. It stunned him. "You," he said slowly, enunciating each word carefully, "disgust me. And if you were the last woman on earth, I wouldn't fuck you. The man hasn't been born who would want anything to do with you." With that, he gathered every ounce of strength he could muster to drop his hands and stalk back to the house.

Bebe took off the oversize shoes and raced after him. "If you think you're getting the last word, you're mistaken. I find you incredibly

arrogant and obnoxious, and my aunt must be insane to have anything to do with you. You're nasty, you're inconsiderate, and you are so hateful you make me want to puke." She made a gagging sound in her throat. "Furthermore, I wouldn't let you touch me if you got down on your knees and begged me. *You,* Reuben Tarz, disgust *me!*"

She gave Reuben a shove that sent him sprawling in the dirt and then fled to the house, certain he would follow and beat the living daylights out of her. She was sobbing as she gathered her things together for the bathroom, and it wasn't until the door was locked behind her that she felt safe.

Tears streamed down her cheeks. What was wrong with her? Why was she always doing the wrong thing at the wrong time? Maybe she deserved Reuben's words in some way. She knew better, and still she'd gone ahead and baited him. Why couldn't she ever keep her mouth shut? Obviously Reuben had a vicious temper and knew how to be as nasty as she. But she'd also seen a glimmer of something in his eyes, something she'd seen in other young men's eyes, back in California: arousal.

"Lights! Camera! Action! Cut!" she muttered, her tearful face turning thoughtful. She stepped into the hot tub. Later she would think about her next performance, but not until she was sure where she'd gone wrong in

the barn.

A warm bath always made everything right. Bebe hummed the words to a popular song as she lathered herself. When she was soaped from head to toe, she craned her neck to examine herself in the long pier glass across from the tub. If I truly make up my mind to go after you, Reuben Tarz, you aren't going to have a prayer of escaping me. *If* I make up my mind . . .

Reuben stormed his way into the house, slamming the door behind him so hard the handle rattled. What in the hell was happening to him? How could one young girl upset his life like this? He'd reacted to her instead of ignoring her as he'd promised himself he would. He'd been so happy — they'd all been happy. Until today. Perhaps he was too sensitive, too protective of Mickey. But Mickey was just too goddamned important to him, and no little snot from California was going to interfere.

Once in his room, Reuben could feel the tension ease between his shoulder blades. His heart stopped its furious thudding, and the pounding in his head gave way to a dull ache he could live with. He knew if he lay down and closed his eyes for fifteen minutes, he'd be a fit dinner companion who could laugh and smile and carry on a decent conversation.

But willing his mind to blankness was impossible, Reuben decided. His thoughts were on Bebe Rosen, a serpent in his Garden of Eden. Then he remembered his erection. Angrily he beat his fists into the plump pillow. This was only the first day of her visit and already he was like a wild dog trying to catch its tail.

Suddenly the room was too confining, the pillow too soft for rest, his thoughts too wild. His leg was aching like a son of a bitch, the sure sign of a change in weather. Snow, probably. He could hardly wait to get into a hot tub.

He began to strip down, folding his clothes neatly at the foot of the bed. He took dress trousers and a snowy-white shirt from his armoire, then paid careful attention to his tie, finally picking one that Mickey especially liked. In just a little while he'd be sitting next to her at the table. Later on they'd make love.

He was happy and he was contented, a feeling he'd never experienced until he had come to this château. And it wasn't just the physical side of their relationship that contented him. It was being near Mickey, taking her hand at odd moments, her light touch as she walked by him. Their eyes meeting and speaking a language only the two of them understood. The warm smiles, the gentle touches, their total commitment to each other. That's what was making him what he was.

Reuben's stomach rumbled. The clock on the mantel told him he was already late taking his bath; he'd have to hurry if he wanted to make dinner on time.

The bathroom door was locked. Reuben knocked, knowing as his knuckles touched the polished wood that he wasn't going to like what he heard.

"Yes?"

"It's Reuben. How much longer will you be?"

"Hours!" the voice answered gaily.

"That's too long," Reuben called through the door. "Daniel and I both have to bathe, and dinner is in an hour. Please hurry."

"Oh, poo, I can't hurry. You'll just have to wait. I'll call you when I'm finished."

Reuben could feel his shoulders tighten again. If dinner was delayed, the lamb would be dry and tough. Mickey liked things done on time, and so did he. They'd established a routine, and now this intruder was trying to change things.

"I'll give you exactly fifteen minutes. If you aren't out of there by then, I'll take the door from its hinges. I'm counting as of now."

Reuben rolled his eyes at the squeal of outrage that shrilled through the door. He turned to see Daniel approaching with his towel and robe.

"Are we having a problem?"

"We'll know in fifteen minutes," Reuben

184

said flatly. "I guess we're going to have to set up a schedule for using the tub. Everything was so peaceful till she arrived. I detest her."

Daniel's thoughts whirled. So what if the girl took a little longer in the bathroom? As far as he knew, none of them had told her she had a time limit. Reuben did have a point about the schedule; he liked things done on schedule, too, but he was realist enough to know that extenuating circumstances prevailed from time to time. "In a day or so she'll get the hang of the way we do things here. Getting angry isn't going to solve anything. So I'll take my bath later, after dinner. I don't mind in the least." He changed the subject when he noticed Reuben stiffen. "It feels a little like snow, doesn't it?"

Reuben nodded. Daniel always made sense. He couldn't let this child get to him. Obviously she was one of those cats who liked to stir up trouble out of pure spite. "My leg's been aching all day. That's why I was so eager to soak. Is your shoulder bothering you?"

"Aching like your leg. I guess winter is finally here. The windowpanes downstairs are starting to frost over. I don't know if I'm glad or sorry."

"Hell, Daniel, let's not be sorry about anything except maybe that spoiled brat in there." Reuben jerked his thumb toward the bathroom door. "Did you have Christmas at the orphanage?"

"Well, sure, but it wasn't like a family Christmas. We had a tree that we all got to decorate with popcorn and berries and a few ornaments. I always wanted to know what Christmas was like with a family. Jake said it wasn't much. He said they didn't even have a tree unless one of his older brothers stole it, and even then it wasn't any good because they didn't have anything to hang on it. He said it smelled good, though."

Reuben swallowed hard at the mention of Daniel's boyhood friend. He hadn't forgotten the dog Daniel wanted to call Jake. "Well, this year we'll both know what it's like. Let's cross our fingers that Miss Uppity in there doesn't spoil it."

"Reuben, do we have enough money left to get a present for her?"

"Yeah, we have something left. We'll ask Mickey what to get for her. I understand the principle of giving. Don't worry." Reuben checked his watch and banged his fist on the door. "Your time is up!" he called.

"Go away! If you had a time limit, you should have told me. I got here first!" Bebe cried childishly.

"I'm going to count to five, and if you aren't out of there, the door goes down and you'll fix it. One! Two! Three!" The formidable grin on Reuben's face puzzled Daniel.

Bebe hopped from the tub and wrapped herself in a huge towel. She stomped to the

door and threw back the bolt. "You are a god-damn bully, Reuben Tarz." She tried to shoulder past him, but he blocked her way.

"No, no, no. You drain the water, wipe out the tub, and take all your junk out of here. Now!"

"Kiss my ass!" Bebe cried angrily. Again she tried to shoulder her way past Reuben.

"Mickey's cook is too old to clean up after you. I'm certainly not going to do it, and Daniel can't stretch his shoulder that far. Mickey is your hostess, so we all know you'd never expect her to do it. That leaves you! As for kissing your ass . . . forget it." He turned to Daniel and winked. "It must be something they do in California."

Tears streaming down her cheeks, Bebe grasped the towel around her as she tried to drain the water and clean the tub at the same time. The moment the towel started to slip, Reuben and Daniel discreetly withdrew. Reuben shook his head with disapproval as Bebe's curses filtered out to the hallway.

"Where did she learn words like that?" Daniel asked, shocked.

Reuben snorted. "California, land of sunshine and decadence."

When Bebe finished her chore she stormed past them, eyes blazing. Back in her room, she sat down on her bed with a thump. She let the tears flow, not caring that her eyes would be puffy and red. Who was going to

see her but her aunt and those two officious clods?

And where in hell *was* her aunt? Leaving everything up to her lover, that's where she was. Hiding out. Afraid to face her. Ashamed to face her, probably. Bebe blew her nose lustily, then threw the lace-edged handkerchief carelessly into the corner.

The room was a mess, her clothes in heaps on the floor, her shoes scattered all over. It would take days to sort through everything and place it in the armoires. She really doubted the furnishings would hold all her belongings, and she'd die before she'd ask the others for extra drawers or closet space. She'd had enough humiliation today to last the rest of her life.

This was a fend-for-yourself operation. There would be no one to pick up after her, no one for her to order about. If she wanted something, she'd damn well get it herself or learn to do without. Wait till her friends in California found out she was forced to clean the bathtub! Of course the only way they would ever know was if she told them.

She was so hungry she felt like she could eat a horse, hooves and all. She looked wildly for something to wear. Helter-skelter, the clothing flew as she searched out her underwear and stockings. She pulled and tugged until she found a wrinkled yellow dress with a high neckline. It looked demure and virginal

with its little lace collar and cuffs. She searched through the pile of clothing until she found a pair of shoes with a sensible pair of heels. "Clod!" she muttered.

Bebe stared at her damp hair. The curling ringlets would never dry. The best she could do was fluff it out with her fingers and hope it didn't mat, making her head look like a ball with fuzz on it. It would take her hours, maybe even days, to find the makeup case that held her perfume and powder. She'd go to dinner with a shiny, well-scrubbed face. She'd keep quiet and speak only when spoken to. And the first time the chance presented itself, she'd kick Reuben square in the groin. The thought lightened her mood considerably. She tripped into the library, where Mickey was pouring wine into four glasses.

It was a pleasant enough evening, and by ten o'clock Mickey was ready to call a halt to the long day. "Come along, Bebe, we will go upstairs together. I know you must be exhausted from your travels. I can assure you a wonderful night's sleep on my goose-down bed. Tomorrow you will feel refreshed, and possibly, if I am right, you will go for a walk in the snow with me. We have so much to talk about." Bebe followed her obediently.

Mickey put her arm around the young girl's fragile shoulder and was stunned to feel it trembling beneath her touch. With an unex-

pected surge of suppressed motherhood, she led the girl to her room, helped her undress, and then loaned her a nightgown rather than have her paw through the stack of clothing in the center of the floor.

"Would you care for some hot chocolate, *chérie?* It will be no trouble for me to go down and get it."

"No, Aunt Mickey. I'm fine. And I — I'm sorry about the way I behaved. I have no excuse," Bebe blurted out.

"It is of no importance. I was young once, too, believe it or not. Perhaps in a few days you will feel more kindly toward Reuben and apologize to him. But only if you want to."

"He hates me!" Bebe cried, sensing there was sympathy to be earned.

"No, *chérie,* he does not hate you. He does not like the way you behaved. You are one of his countrymen, and he took your behavior personally. You will make amends, I am sure of it."

"You said my mother liked it here at the château and didn't want to leave. What was she like, Aunt Mickey? I never knew her, and Papa doesn't like to talk about her."

"She was very beautiful. Not just on the outside, but on the inside as well. She was a gentle, giving, caring woman, and she made your papa very happy. When she was pregnant with you, she said she knew it would be a girl. She had such wonderful plans for the

two of you. She said she'd never give you up to a nanny but would take care of you herself. Your father was devastated at her death. Your brother should have been brought here to me. I offered to take him, at least for a while. You, too. But your father said he didn't want to rip the family apart. I know he tried his best with you and Eli, and I also know he was far too indulgent because he loves you so much. I understand Eli is constantly in trouble, but that will change when he discovers who he is and what he wants to do with his life. Someday Eli will be a wonderful painter. You, Miss Bebe, leave much to be desired at the moment. I'm here to help you, but only if you want my help."

"Someday I'll be just like you, Aunt Mickey," Bebe said sleepily. "Maybe then someone will love me."

Mickey had to strain to hear the last words. Tears pricked at her eyelids, and her heart went out to the sleeping girl. "Poor lost lamb," she whispered as she brushed wisps of golden hair from the smooth forehead. "I tortured myself for weeks about you. I thought that Reuben would certainly be attracted to you, that he would compare us. My instincts were right, little one. There is something about you that Reuben finds . . . I don't quite know what it is, but it is something I feel. You and I are like night and day to him. One of us is a woman, an older

191

woman, and the other is a young girl on the brink of womanhood. I love this young man more than I have ever loved a man, and I know in my heart that I am going to lose him in some way to you. If you were worthy of him, I could . . . I could accept it and let him go, because true love is wanting the other person's happiness more than your own. And you, little Bebe, want Reuben, I saw it in your eyes. Against my better judgment I have allowed him to consume my life. I cannot share him with you. Whatever I have I will willingly share, but not Reuben. Not now." There was sorrow in her voice when she whispered her final good-night. "If you take him from me, then he's not worth having, but don't expect me to *give* him to you."

At the door she turned for a last look at the girl cuddled in bed. "You couldn't possibly love him as I do. I wish you had never come here," she murmured. Then she closed the door softly behind her, her eyes bright with tears.

Bebe scrunched her face into the downy pillow and laughed gleefully. When sleep finally reached out to her, there was a smile on her face. Playing at falling asleep had been one of the first things in her acting repertoire. Reuben Tarz was as good as hers.

It was hours later, past midnight, when Reuben slipped into Mickey's warm bed. He drew her to him and whispered, "It's snow-

ing outside." Mickey smiled as she returned to sleep, this time in Reuben's arms.

CHAPTER NINE

The comfortable room was oppressive with the roaring fire. Reuben was feeling lethargic and useless; the vineyards were at rest for the season. After some initially trying days, Daniel and Bebe were settled into a routine of lessons, with Faroux just as easily teaching two bright students as one. Mickey spent long hours going over her financial records and keeping wine charts. Reuben read every book in the crowded library that dealt with winemaking. He'd asked thousands of questions and was surprised at Mickey's expertise. While she didn't actively operate the wineries, she knew to the day and hour what went on. It was time now for him to ask her if he could take over some of the responsibility, have a more active role in running the business.

When Mickey lifted her head from the ledgers in front of her, Reuben smiled at her and mouthed the words, "You are so beautiful." Mickey returned his smile with a rogu-

ish wink.

Reuben closed his book. "Mickey, have you given any thought to my suggestions of last evening?"

"Yes, considerable thought. I'm not sure . . . what if . . . I don't think my wines are —"

"No doubts," Reuben said coolly. "You have first-quality wines. It's time to share them with the rest of the world. Once in a while you have to take chances. Remember what you said about the young woman who designs your clothes? Your instincts told you she was going to be famous someday. A feeling, that's all you had to go on, and you went with that feeling. I feel the same way about the wines . . . it's time. You have to strike while the iron is hot, Mickey. If you don't, someone else will get the jump on you. I want us to jump in with both feet. The only thing we can lose is some of our time and a few cases of wine."

"What if the foreigners don't like our wines?" Mickey asked, frowning.

"The Fonsard wineries and their product are the finest in all Europe. When you have the best, there is nothing to dislike. Talk to your bankers in Paris. If they agree that it's a sound move, will you give the go-ahead?"

"Yes. Yes, I will. But . . ." Mickey faced him anxiously. "Reuben, it will be an all-consuming job for you to undertake. When will we have time together?"

"Is that what's bothering you?" Reuben laughed. "Don't you know I need you at my side while I work on this? I am going to need your French expertise! My American ingenuity will do the rest."

Once Mickey made the decision to go ahead, she felt much better. It did make things simpler, and Reuben was right, there was no reason to stagnate. The past several harvests had yielded some of the best wine Fonsard ever produced. Sharing it, becoming known, would be something Jacques would have done, had he lived. She felt sure the bankers, conservative though they were, would see that it was a good, sound investment for Fonsard. Most important of all, it would give Reuben something worthwhile to do. And working side by side would take them both away from Bebe. If there was any one thing that helped her make up her mind to endorse the idea, it was this.

"Partners?" Reuben grinned.

"Partners," Mickey agreed. She knew then she would do whatever she could to make this man happy. Anything.

During the second week of December, Reuben dragged Mickey to the wine cellar, where she kept a small office. Ledgers, receipts, and bills were filed neatly in stacked boxes. Together they pored over the ledgers until Reuben learned Mickey's bookkeeping sys-

tem. They decided to visit Château la Fonsard in Bordeaux, one of the largest wineries in the region. There Mickey would place Reuben in the expert hands of her head vintner, a position Reuben might assume someday. Monsieur Poitier had been grumbling about retiring, but since he lived on the château grounds he could remain available for consultation.

The days were full and demanding for Reuben, and he loved every minute of them. Mickey thought she'd never been so happy. At night she prayed that nothing would ever spoil her happiness.

The days raced toward Christmas and the holiday season. Four days before Christmas Mickey called a halt to lessons and told Reuben they were on a holiday from their office in the wine cellar. It was time to decorate the house, shop, and get things ready for the villagers who would visit the château to share the celebration.

The château took on new life as Mickey's "petite family" did their utmost to please her — trips to the fields for evergreens, trips to the village to shop, mysterious packages arriving by post from Paris, and hours shared in the kitchen helping Nanette prepare the feast and goodies. It was Reuben who swung the ax that toppled a twelve-foot fir tree. Everyone clapped their approval with cold, numb hands. Then they all tugged and pulled

the monstrous tree to the sleigh, laughing and giggling like children. Mounds and mounds of fragrant balsam for the mantel, the staircase banister, and the doorways were added to the sleigh.

Her face rosy with cold, Mickey laughed and said, "I think, little ones, that we must walk back to the château, there is no room in the sleigh. Also, we must gather holly and leave our tribute to the birds by hanging pieces of suet and bread. Once we return to the château we will feast on cake and hot chocolate. Bebe, you are frozen! I told you to dress warmly, that this would take hours. Perhaps we can find a spot for you in the sleigh. What do you think, Reuben? We'll save the poor child's frozen feet."

"I think," Reuben said as he hefted the last pile of balsam onto the sleigh, "that she should walk like everyone else. Before we left I told her to go back and get warmer gloves and boots. It was a suggestion she chose to ignore."

"*Chéri*, she could get frostbite."

"She won't," Reuben said callously. "She has to learn, Mickey. I know she's young, but she thinks we talk just to hear ourselves like she does. She can walk with the rest of us."

Bebe listened to the exchange with mixed emotions. Almost from the moment she had boarded the sleigh she'd been sorry she hadn't run back into the house for warmer

198

gloves and a hat, to say nothing of the boots. Silly, stupid pride made her automatically reject any suggestions from Reuben. Well, she was paying for it now; she'd never been so cold. The pity in Daniel's eyes made her ashamed. The concern in Mickey's face made her want to weep. But it was the anger and contempt she saw in Reuben that made her determined to walk back to the château if it killed her.

She stared directly at Reuben, making a controlled effort to keep her teeth from chattering. "I think we should get started. It will be dark soon."

"Bravo!" Daniel whispered as he reached for her arm. She quickly pulled it away but smiled at him, a crooked little grimace

"I'll get back on my own, Daniel. I can't let him get the best of me, Not yet, anyway."

Daniel trudged alongside her. "Bebe, this isn't a game. It's not you against Reuben. You have to stop thinking there's a contest between the two of you. Don't spoil things with hate and anger."

"I don't hate him, he hates me! I just don't know why. These past weeks I've tried to do everything he said, and I hardly ever sass him back — but I just know he's waiting for me to step out of line. He still isn't satisfied. I didn't ask to ride in the damn sleigh, did I?"

Daniel hated it when he had to defend his friend. He liked Bebe. He liked the way she

could laugh at herself when she made what she called one of her ridiculous mistakes. He liked the way she hunkered down to learn the French verbs. And when she made a mess of the language, her friendly little winks and crooked smiles delighted him. He particularly treasured her small confessions and some of the secrets she shared with him on their walks over the frozen fields. So often he wished that he could confide something in return, but he had no secrets, only hopes and dreams. He told her about the dog, and wanting to call it Jake. She'd smiled and said she understood. She'd confided in return that the nicest, the warmest feeling she'd ever felt in her life was when Mickey cradled her in her arms the first night she'd arrived. She wanted, needed family love, but she had nothing to give in return, so how could she expect anyone to give her something so precious? Be yourself, he'd said, the way you are with me. The rest will fall into place. And always, after every serious talk, she'd look at him with tears in her eyes and ask, "Why does he hate me, Daniel?"

"With Reuben you have to prove yourself," he'd reply reluctantly. "It's either black or white. There are no gray areas with Reuben. You have to understand that." He'd pat her shoulder awkwardly and she'd smile — and immediately he'd feel a sense of disloyalty to Reuben.

"Just concentrate on putting one foot ahead

of the other," he said to her now. "It's only another kilometer or so. I know a shortcut. Do you want to take it?"

"Not on your damn life," she said, teeth chattering.

"I had chilblains, so did Reuben. It's not pleasant. At least take my scarf."

"No. I'm not going to get chilblains. If I did, your friend would say I got them on purpose to ruin Christmas for everyone. I'll be fine, Daniel."

When she slogged into the courtyard of the château, Bebe thought she was one step away from death. All she wanted was to get upstairs and crawl into bed. It would take hours to get warm. Maybe she'd never be warm again. But instead of running ahead she looked Reuben square in the eye and asked, "Do you need me to help carry the greenery inside?"

Reuben was about to say yes until he saw the look on Daniel's face. "No, you did your share. Go inside and get warm. Later you can help string the garlands and decorate the tree."

Mickey felt herself swoon at the look on Bebe's face — unbelieving, then relieved, and finally transformed by a warm, wonderful smile. She was beautiful, all rosy cheeks and windblown hair.

An hour later Bebe was submerged in a tub of hot water. Nothing in her life had ever felt as good as the warmth that caressed every

inch of her flesh.

Daniel sat on his bed, patiently waiting his turn in the bathroom. He toyed with the idea of knocking on Bebe's door and . . . saying what? That Reuben was . . . Again he felt at a loss. What exactly was Reuben? Possessive, protective? Would Bebe understand that? Probably not; he wasn't even sure he understood what he was thinking. He pictured Bebe in her room crying her eyes out. And here he sat, caught in the middle.

Bebe needed some kind of support, but how was it going to look to Reuben if he took sides? Reuben, he knew, would consider it a betrayal on his part if he got too close to the girl. Before Bebe's arrival, the three of them had agreed that she was to be his companion and study along with him while Mickey and Reuben were busy with the wineries. Now, it seemed, that was changing.

Be Bebe's friend but don't get involved? Bullshit! If today was any indication of what things were going to be like, he would have to get involved. Out there in the snow he'd felt like crying for the girl. If he'd had his way, he would have slung her over his shoulder and carried her back.

She was certainly plucky, she'd proved it again today. In some ways she reminded him of Jake. How many times Jake had admonished him, Don't let them see you cry, don't ever let them see you cry — if you do, you're

lost. The words brought back memories — and, as usual, the one that stayed with him was the one he wished to forget. . . .

It was autumn, and all the leaves were like burnished gold, and the pumpkins were ripe in the field behind the orphanage. Jake had taken him by the hand and said they would snitch a little pumpkin for Bennie and Stevie, two five-year-olds who slept next to them in the dormitory. Daniel hated the idea of snitching but knew the little boys would love the pumpkin. They were halfway across the dry field when they saw an injured sparrow. They forgot about the pumpkin then, and it wasn't until later that Daniel ran back and grabbed the first one he saw, a tall, spindly one that was lopsided and without a stem. Stevie and Bennie never noticed.

Jake had big hands, bigger than his own, and they'd been so gentle with the tiny sparrow. "He can't fly. And if he can't fly, he can't be free," Jake said with ten-year-old logic. "That makes him like us. We aren't free either." They tried everything to patch up the little bird, but his wing was so tiny and they didn't have a knife to whittle a splint. They fed him crumbs soaked in milk for two days, and when they returned on the third day, the sparrow was lying on its side, its legs straight in the air. It was the first time he and Jake had seen death. He remembered crying, long and hard. Jake hadn't cried, but his eyes were

wet. "We have to bury him," Jake said, "or some wild animal will eat the body." So they scooped out a hole in the ground with their bare hands and covered the bird with leaves before piling the dirt on top of it. He'd kept right on crying, not caring what Jake said about not letting anyone see. At last Jake had put his arm around him, and they'd walked back to the orphanage together. Jake cared, but Jake was tough.

Bebe was like Jake, Daniel decided, tough on the outside, where it counted, and soft on the inside. He made up his mind to be Bebe's friend the way Jake had been his friend. If his friendship got in the way of his feelings for Reuben, he'd figure something out — but not until he had to.

As he trotted down the hall for his turn in the bathroom, Daniel felt about 110 years old.

When Bebe finally came downstairs hours later, she felt weak as a newborn kitten and wanted only to sleep. But she wouldn't give Reuben Tarz the satisfaction of lacing into her again. She'd force her eyes to stay open, eat dinner, and help with the garlands. One way or another, she'd get through the evening in grand style.

And she did. Dinner that evening was actually one of the more pleasant meals she'd attended since her arrival at the château. Reu-

ben seemed to be particularly polite and hospitable; when he addressed her directly she was so surprised she almost fell off her chair. She could feel herself flush, and she stammered like a little girl trying to please, knowing she was making a bad job of it. Reuben looked amused until he noticed Daniel glowering across the table. Then, for his friend's sake, he did his best to stifle the dislike he felt for Bebe.

"Mickey, why don't we wait till tomorrow to hang the garlands? I think we're all tired this evening. That cold air was brutal. If Daniel's eyes feel anything like mine, we should be resting with compresses."

"I think tomorrow will be fine. Let's schedule our decorating for midafternoon so Bebe and I can shop in the village." Mickey smiled warmly around the table, knowing everyone would be in agreement. The trip to the fields in the biting cold had done her in, too. "Tonight there will be hot chocolate instead of coffee, and then we'll retire. I think we've all earned a good night's rest."

Bebe was so relieved she wouldn't have to struggle through the evening, she almost cried. She looked up to find Reuben staring at her directly. Flustered, she knocked over her wineglass, and in her attempt to mop it up she spilled her water. This time the tears erupted. "It's your fault," she screamed at Reuben. "If you wouldn't stare at me like

205

that, I wouldn't have spilled the wine. You're so damn spooky, you scare me!" She pushed back her chair and ran up the stairs, with Daniel right behind her.

"*Chéri,* were you staring at the child?" Mickey asked softly.

"I guess I was, but I wasn't seeing her, if you know what I mean. I think she's over-tired. Aren't young girls usually nervous and irritable every so often?"

Mickey laughed, a rueful sound that did not go unnoticed by Reuben. "I suppose so, but it's been a long time since I was a young girl. I'm sure tomorrow will be better for all of us. Bebe is excited about our shopping trip. She said she has something special she wants to get Daniel. So special, she said, his eyes will light up with happiness. What do you think it could be?"

A small stab of jealousy flashed through Reuben. Bebe was going to get his friend something that would make his eyes light with happiness. Only a book could do that. He chuckled inwardly. He was getting a pocket watch for Daniel, a real Swiss time-piece with his initials and the date engraved by a friend of Mickey's. What could that spoiled brat give Daniel that would be better than his own gift? It had to be a book. After you read a book, you either memorized it or you forgot it. A timepiece was forever.

Reuben forced his mind back to the present.

206

"I thought you said you were finished with shopping," he teased.

Mickey leaned back in her chair. "One is never done. Please, you must give me a clue to the present you and Daniel got me. I have never seen such secrecy. Just one little hint?"

"Nope. You give me a hint about mine," Reuben countered playfully.

"Absolutely not. It wouldn't be a surprise then. Anyway, you shouldn't be getting a present — you're Jewish," Mickey said, smiling.

"Ah, penalized for being what I am. I'm nothing, Mickey. I don't even know if I believe in God."

"Of course you do. You told me long ago, you prayed to Him for Daniel, so you do believe. Don't ever say that, *chéri,* for He might punish you."

Reuben didn't like the direction the conversation was turning. "What would I have to give, to promise, to get you to rub or even tickle my back?" His eyes were hot and smoldering as he leaned across the table.

"Give? Promise? Such unadulterated nonsense. Simply ask me." Mickey could feel the heat starting to build within her.

"I'm asking."

"It sounds like a demand to me."

Reuben laughed. "Will you please rub and tickle my back?"

"But of course! We'll tickle each other's fan-

cies!" Instantly Mickey became aware of the smoldering fires deep within his eyes, of the sudden tightening of the cords in his neck. The sensation of touching became overpowering. She imagined she could feel his smooth skin and rippling muscles beneath her fingertips. She hungered to run her hands through that thick mane of black hair, to hear him moan his delight. And then, when he would turn over to take her in his arms, her lips would graze the flat of his belly and the hairs that pointed downward. . . .

He knew her little joke even before she uttered the words. It was a cue, a perfect little opening to their lovemaking. He adored her when she writhed and stretched like a cat beneath his touch. Even this moment his fingers ached to touch her, to run the length of her body, to bring her pleasure.

They both forgot the chocolate and climbed the staircase to the bedroom. Neither of them was aware that just a few feet away from them, Bebe lay exhausted on her bed, sobbing her heart out to Daniel.

"I want to go home, Daniel. I hate it here! No, that's not true, I like it here. I like Mickey and I like you. It's Reuben who's making me miserable! Why, Daniel, why? Why does he treat me like he does?" Her golden hair was a tumble, her lower lip pouting to hold back tears, her delicate chin trembling.

Daniel shrugged, his puzzlement evident. "Bebe, why did you scream like that at the table? All you did was spill the wine. It wasn't a catastrophe. If I'd been sitting in Reuben's chair, I'd have been looking at you, too. You shouldn't take offense so easily."

Playing devil's advocate didn't come easily to Daniel, and he was uncomfortable with it. "It's not good for you to keep thinking that Reuben hates you. Don't play games to get your own way, Bebe. It won't work here." Then a bolt of lightning hit him. "You aren't . . . you don't . . . what I mean is, you don't find yourself attracted to Reuben, do you?"

Bebe bolted upright, her golden hair tumbling to below her shoulders. "Where did you get such a stupid idea? I may be young, but I know about the birds and the bees. They're sleeping together, you know it and so do I. I have eyes and ears, and what's going on is . . . is . . . decadent. In America everyone thinks all Frenchwomen are whores, even my father."

"Are you referring to Mickey?" Daniel challenged.

"No . . . yes . . . Oh, I don't know. She's so religious and saintly, giving money to the church and doing all kinds of good things for the poor, and then she takes a man half her age to bed. What does that tell you?" There were shards of ice in Bebe's eyes, a sharp bitterness in her voice.

"You're jealous of Mickey!" Daniel accused.

"I am not!" Bebe retorted angrily.

"Yes, I believe you are," Daniel mused. "I believe you want Reuben for yourself. You like Mickey, you may even love her, but she has something you want. You want Reuben. Admit it. Once you do, you'll feel better. It'll be our secret." Daniel didn't know where this insight was coming from, but even as he spoke, it all began to fall into place. "I'll never tell," he assured Bebe. "And you'll have me to talk to. I think you need a friend, Bebe, a friend you can be honest with."

"Daniel, I don't want to talk —"

Daniel ignored her protest with a wave of his hand. "There's no room for you in their relationship. You have to accept it. You can't continue to cause friction. I can see through you, Bebe. You keep acting up, causing scene after scene, hoping Mickey will come to your defense, and that will drive a wedge between her and Reuben. It won't work, and you'll be the one who's hurt in the end."

"Don't be so smug." Bebe began crying again, huge tears rolling down her cheeks. "So what if it's true, and I'm not saying it is, so what? Who cares?"

Suddenly she threw herself at Daniel, bursting into racking sobs. He'd never been this close to a girl before, and he didn't know what to do with his hands. Bebe was hugging

him tightly, sobbing on his shoulder. Almost of its own volition, one of Daniel's arms surrounded her and the other stroked her golden head. Strange, wonderful feelings washed through him, but a stranger feeling warned him that he shouldn't take advantage of the situation.

It occurred to him that he was mopping up after Reuben. Reuben had created this problem with Bebe, for whatever reason, and here he was trying to make things right. Was this a harbinger of things to come?

It never occurred to him that Bebe Rosen would and could use him to get to Reuben. He totally forgot that she had grown up among actresses; blinded by her soft arms around him, he wasn't focusing on the fact that she was capable of playing a role and giving an excellent performance.

"Daniel, I don't know what I would have done without you these past weeks," Bebe said, sniffling. "You've been so good to me. You're always there when I need someone. I wish I had a friend like you in California. All my other friends are fake and racy. The gossip columns say I'm just like them, but I'm not. I do like to have a good time, but I've been . . . a good girl. Do you know what I mean?" Her voice held a childish, innocent note. "C'mere," she whispered, drawing him close. "I'm still a virgin. Bad girls aren't virgins, are they? Don't blush, Daniel, we're

friends, and friends can talk about anything. Are you a virgin, too? I'll bet you are. You don't have the same look in your eyes that Reuben has."

"Reuben's older. . . ." Daniel wished his neck didn't feel so hot; he knew his face was scarlet. It felt the way it did when he was running a fever.

They sat together far into the night, sharing secrets and confidences while Reuben and Mickey made love again and again.

It was still dark, with hours to go before dawn, when Bebe finally fell asleep, her hand curled sweetly under her cheek. Daniel kissed her brow, lightly breathing in her warm, clean scent. For a moment he felt almost light-headed. When he became aware of a thread of heat flowing through his body, he quickly left the room.

Under the covers in his own bed, in the darkness, he reached out for sleep with both arms, welcoming it like a long-lost friend.

CHAPTER TEN

The following morning at the breakfast table Bebe watched the glances exchanged between Reuben and Mickey. Daniel was acutely aware of Bebe's interest and felt the skin on the back of his neck crawl.

"Dress warmly, *chérie*," Mickey advised Bebe. "It is quite cold out, and even the little village shops are drafty"

Mickey was dressed in a tailored gray wool dress and knee-high black leather boots. Already waiting on the chair in the foyer was her Russian sable coat and elbow-length gloves. Her long dark hair would be pulled beneath the matching head-swathing cloche of the same sable.

A few minutes after the dishes were cleared, Bebe and Mickey left in the Citroën for the village. They went from shop to shop, with gaily wrapped bundles and sly expressions on their faces. They purchased the standard Christmas gifts: warm mufflers, gloves, socks, and sweaters; books, some of them rare, oth-

ers popular fiction from America; hand-engraved book marks for each of the books was a last-minute gift idea.

In the tea shop, Mickey double-checked her list, then sat back with a satisfied sigh. "Now we can have lunch, *chérie*. Hot soup and crusty bread with melted butter. It sounds delicious, no?"

"Yes, I'm starved," Bebe agreed. "Tell me, Aunt Mickey, what did you get for Reuben and Daniel, or is it a secret?"

"Only from Reuben and Daniel. I have a pocket watch for Reuben, which I did not actually purchase. It was my father's, the one thing he left me when he died. I have had the crystal replaced, and the jeweler polished and engraved it for me. It is a beautiful timepiece, and very, very old. Over one hundred years I would suspect. For Daniel, a set of law books. As always, I wonder after the fact if I bought the proper gifts. What do you think?"

Bebe fought with herself not to say something sarcastic. She knew Reuben would love the timepiece simply because it came from Mickey. Who wouldn't be impressed to receive a gift that meant so much to the giver? And of course Daniel would be in heaven with his own set of law books.

Mickey's eyes sparkled when she paid the check. "Now, *chérie,* we will drive down the road to see about your gift for Daniel. I know you've been waiting all morning for just this

moment."

Bebe giggled. "Yes, I have, but we can't take it today. Oh, Aunt Mickey, are you certain it's all right? You don't mind?"

"Of course not. If it will make Daniel happy, then it will be a most welcome addition to the household. I'm so pleased that you want to give Daniel something special; he is a very special person. I know that if I ever needed him, say when I am old and gray and sitting in a rocking chair, he would come and do what he could for me. That is the kind of person he is."

"I know what you mean. But shouldn't you be saying all this of Reuben?" she asked guilelessly.

"Reuben is not Daniel. Yes, Reuben would come if I were in trouble and sitting in that rocking chair by the fire. The difference is I would never ask him. It is something I could not do. You see, *chérie,* I would not want him to see me old and wrinkled. That is a secret between women, a confidence I share with you. You will not share this with anyone else, *chérie.*"

"No," Bebe said honestly. To grow old and wrinkled had to be the most awful thing in the world. Already there were lines around Mickey's eyes and a slight droop to the sides of her mouth in the corners. Her own skin was fresh and supple without a trace of a line or blemish. She had youth and resiliency

while Mickey had middle age and wrinkles. There simply wasn't any comparison.

The ride to Yvette and Henri Simone's farm was made silently, each woman busy with her own thoughts.

It was a beautiful little farm, and Bebe loved it at first sight. She tried to liken it to her home in California and then to the château, but it was completely different in every way. For the first time she realized that she wasn't in the least homesick for California or her friends. Once in a while she thought about Eli, but the only time she missed her father was when she didn't get her own way about something.

"Here he is, your little Jake. He can leave his mother any time you are ready, *chérie,*" Yvette said cheerfully.

Bebe bent down to scoop the round ball of fur into her arms. The puppy nuzzled its head against her, its little pink tongue lapping at her cheek. He felt so warm, so good to hold. "Daniel is going to love you, little Jake. He is going to be beside himself with happiness." She cuddled the puppy closer and sighed happily. "I can hardly wait to see his face when he sees you." She'd never given a present this meaningful, and she loved what she was feeling. She wished there were something just as wonderful to give Reuben and Mickey. But her heart told her this was a one-time offering, something she'd probably

never do again for anyone. Daniel was special to her and Jake was her gift to him, one she was giving from her heart. "You're special, Jake, just as special as Daniel. Please make him happy," Bebe crooned.

Yvette nudged Mickey. "Did you ever see anything more precious?" she whispered. "Already she is in love with our puppy and she has to give him away. She must be very fond of Daniel."

Mickey's heart fluttered. She, too, was stunned at the look on Bebe's face. If Reuben could see her now . . . "What did you say, Yvette?" Mickey asked fretfully.

"Henri will bring . . . Jake on Christmas Eve and leave him in the barn after dark to be sure the surprise isn't given away." Yvette chuckled. "He will travel with a hot water bottle and a little clock to remind him of his mama. For the first few days only."

Mickey smiled. "Why didn't I think of that?"

"Because, Michelene, you have other things on your mind." Yvette winked knowingly, adding a classic Gallic shrug for emphasis. For years she'd been Mickey's closest friend; they'd shared tales of their lovers over wine at the end of a long day. Henri was Yvette's third husband, but only when she was in the mood to have a husband.

"He's so beautiful," Bebe said, turning to Mickey with the puppy in her arms. "I want

217

to keep him for myself. Look how bright his eyes are."

"Did Henri finish the collar?" Mickey asked.

"Just last evening. Here it is." Yvette took a braided leather collar from the shelf. A small piece of brass was fashioned next to the buckle, complete with a spidery inscription that read *Jake, Christmas 1918, from your friend Bebe.*

"Ooooh, it's just perfect!" Bebe squealed.

"I guess we'd better be on our way. This afternoon we are to decorate the château. We'll see you and Henri Christmas Day. Come early, Yvette, so we can talk a little."

The two old friends moved out of earshot. "How does it go with your . . . amour, Mickey?" Yvette asked. "You have a special look in your eyes, you act differently — does this mean you have finally fallen in love?" At Mickey's expression Yvette continued happily, "It's wonderful, is it not?"

Mickey nodded shyly. "More wonderful than I thought possible. I pray each night that nothing happens to spoil it."

"Then you must not be foolish. Marry the *homme* so that nothing goes awry. Do you understand me?" Yvette whispered.

"But of course. If it is meant to be, it will happen."

"*Non.* You must make it happen, Mickey. None of us gets any younger. Why do you

think I snapped up Henri?"

Mickey hugged her friend affectionately, and they went back to where Bebe sat, holding the puppy.

"You must give petit Jake back to his mama for now," Yvette said as she reached for the contented puppy, which had fallen asleep in the girl's arms.

An hour later Mickey ground the Citroën to a halt in front of the château. Like conspirators, she and Bebe trundled their packages inside and spirited them upstairs.

It took a full two hours, with everyone doing his share, to get the huge fir tree into the stand, erect and shown to its best. Bebe clapped enthusiastically when Mickey stood back and exclaimed, *"parfait!"*

Daniel was dispatched to the attic with specific directions for finding the hand-blown glass ornaments that had been in Mickey's husband's family for years. Reuben was on a ladder waiting for the Christmas angel. Bebe was sorting through colored candles to be mounted in the little saucers that would be hooked onto the tree.

"A delicate job," Mickey warned. "We must be careful of fire, so they must be placed only on the tips of the outer branches. . . . I thought you were stringing the popcorn and berries, Reuben."

"That's women's work," Reuben teased.

"Besides, I'm the only one tall enough to reach the tip of this tree."

"I'll do it," Bebe offered, "just as soon as I finish with the candles. I think Reuben should put the candles on the tree. I don't want to make a mistake and have the tree catch fire."

Soon Daniel returned with the box of ornaments. This was a part of the Christmas holiday that Mickey adored. She explained each heirloom glass ball and teardrop ornament to Reuben, Daniel, and Bebe, the way her husband had explained them to her when they were first married.

Bebe listened to Mickey's stories with rapt attention. At home in California a servant stood a tree up and decorated it. It was done mostly for show, and all she'd ever been interested in were the presents underneath, presents bought by someone else in her father's name. Her thoughts drifted back to California, the Christmas dinner for all the stars dressed in their silks and satins and bejeweled from head to toe. Inevitably, the guests would drink too much wine and liquor, and the holiday celebration would end with tears, recriminations, and curses. Bebe had hated it, dreading all but the gifts.

She continued to watch Reuben out of the corner of her eye. She loved comparing him with the men she knew back in California. Reuben always came out on top: he looked clean-cut, he was American, and he was

handsome. If only he'd smile at her. He was so unaware of her it was insulting. She could have been a bump on a log for all he knew or cared. The only time he noticed her was when she did something to call attention to herself, and always in an unflattering way.

Now Reuben teetered precariously on the top of the ladder. "Well, where's the angel?" he demanded.

"Bebe has it in her hand," Mickey said.

"Well, fetch it here! Don't stand there looking at it! And be careful on the ladder," he admonished her.

Bebe walked haltingly to the foot of the ladder, the angel clutched in her hand. One step, two, three, four, five, and he was leaning down to take it from her, their faces inches apart. A feeling of lightheadedness came over her. It had to be the scent of the fir tree, the aroma of the cherry wood and pine cones in the fireplace. Or was it the nearness of Reuben? In that one brief instant, as she stared directly into his eyes, she'd seen something, something she had never seen before: his awareness of her.

Finally.

Mickey was also aware of that brief instant. She tried to cover it by chattering to Daniel, then excused herself, saying she had a blinding headache and had to take some tablets and rest. In a curt voice she left instructions for the rest of the decorating.

Reuben stared at the doorway for a long time until Daniel took him by the arm and led him to the sofa by the fire. "We're taking a break. Hot chocolate and cigarettes. We can decide who's going to do what before Mickey comes back. She's been getting a lot of headaches lately, hasn't she?"

He didn't expect an answer and was surprised when Bebe offered one. "She gets them only when I'm around and Reuben is in the same room."

Reuben glared at her. Daniel held his breath, waiting for the outburst. He tried to cover the bad moment. "I . . . I don't . . . think that's necessarily true, Bebe. She had headaches before you got here," he stammered. "Isn't that true, Reuben?"

"Yes," Reuben grated. Damn this troublemaking child. Mickey's headache was purely a feminine trick she used when she didn't want to deal with something. He was annoyed now, just short of being angry. God, he hated these times when Mickey pouted and went off to her room. They were supposed to be having a fun afternoon after all their weeks of hard work. Well, dammit, he was going to enjoy himself!

"No! No, Daniel, no hot chocolate. Wine. We're going to have a party, just the three of us. And" — he wagged a finger — "you can't have a party with hot chocolate. The best house wine, what do you say?" He enjoyed

the devilish look on Bebe's face and ignored the concern in Daniel's eyes. "At least three bottles. Now that I'm the expert on Mickey's vintage, I'll go to the wine cellar and choose the right Bordeaux. Bebe, come along with me. Daniel, you stoke the fire and get the mistletoe separated so we can hang it. Mickey was adamant about placing it everywhere."

Reuben followed Bebe from the room, then stopped in midstride, telling her to go on ahead. When she was out of earshot, he returned to Daniel. "That's not betrayal you see on my face or think you see in my eyes. It's anger, Daniel, and anger is an honest emotion. I don't ever want to see you look at me like that again." His voice was so chilly, Daniel flinched.

"I'm sorry," he muttered, dropping his gaze to stare at his shoes, refusing to meet Reuben's eyes. By God, he *had* been thinking all those things. How did Reuben read his mind like that?

When at last he looked up, Reuben was gone.

The decorating came to a screeching halt a few minutes before the dinner hour when Bebe, after too much wine, giggled and said, "I feel like one of the Three Musketeers." Reuben laughed, but it was not a pleasant sound.

"That position has been filled, Bebe.

Mickey is the third Musketeer. She named us that after we arrived." He laughed again, pouring more wine all around.

"Aunt Mickey is too old to be a Musketeer," Bebe said, giggling uncontrollably. "Aunts aren't musketeers. We're young, so *we're* the Three Musketeers! So there!"

Reuben held his glass aloft, a smile on his face but not in his eyes. "To the Three Musketeers!" Daniel, drunk and giggly himself, halfheartedly joined in the toast.

Bebe held her glass next to Reuben's and clinked it. "Drink it all and then we have to smash the glasses in the fireplace. That's how they do it in the films."

Mickey got up from her window chair. She'd been so certain Reuben would follow her upstairs — so certain she'd even turned down the bed. Instead, he'd watched her leave with a cold, hard look in his eyes. For a long time she'd stood at the top of the stairs, listening jealously to the merriment below. She'd wanted to cry, but she hadn't. She was behaving just like Bebe, and that young girl was more observant than she'd thought. And now the last straw — Bebe calling the three of them the Musketeers. Her eyes burned with anger, anger at herself.

She could stay here and have a tray in her room, lock the door in case Reuben tried to come in. *Punish him, the way you did the oth-*

ers when they didn't do what you wanted. "That was a long time ago. This is different," she whispered to herself in the lonely darkness of her room. "This is real."

Mickey avoided staring at herself in the mirror because she knew she wouldn't like what she saw. She combed her hair, letting it flow loose behind her back. It didn't make her look younger, just haggard. Quickly she piled it on top of her head and added a jeweled comb. A dab of scent, some powder to her cheeks, a little rouge, and she was ready to join her three tipsy guests.

The heady scent of the evergreens almost drove her backward. She smiled at her guests and clapped her hands. "Well done!" When Reuben glanced at her suspiciously, Mickey turned away. She recognized that look: it meant Reuben would not play her game — or anyone else's, for that matter.

"It's almost time for dinner. I took the liberty of getting the bath ready for whoever is going first."

"Mademoiselle Bebe is going first," Reuben said gallantly. "Fifteen minutes!" he said, holding up ten fingers.

Bebe giggled. "That's ten!"

"Then you have only ten. Daniel goes second, and I go last."

Daniel tripped over his own feet in his haste to follow Bebe and leave Reuben and Mickey alone.

225

"I do believe we are the bad children, Daniel. I don't feel like a bath, do you?" Bebe whispered at the foot of the stairs. Daniel shook his head. "Then let's just change our clothes, and no one will know the difference."

Daniel ran the suggestion over in his mind. All he had to do, really, was change his shirt and put on a tie. He nodded again.

"Fifteen minutes. I'll meet you at the top of the steps. Rub some soap over your hands and brush your teeth. That's how I always fooled my father." Bebe giggled.

"Did it work?" Daniel asked incredulously.

"Every time."

Downstairs on the sofa, Reuben leaned close to Mickey. "How's your headache?"

"I didn't have a headache, Reuben. You know I didn't, so let's not pretend. I acted like Bebe, and I'm sorry. I don't expect you to understand this, but there are times when I look at Bebe and feel —"

"Old?" Reuben asked bluntly.

Mickey shivered. "Yes. Old. When I start to feel like that, I have to go off by myself and get my thoughts together. I'm sorry if I spoiled the afternoon."

Reuben leaned closer, his breath wine-scented. His tone was as serious as Mickey's. "I don't expect you to understand, but it's not important to me . . . the difference in our ages. I love you. I don't love Bebe. I don't even like her. I grant you she's young, she's

pretty, and someday she's probably going to be a beautiful woman — but she'll never be you. If you keep on like this, I'm going to walk out of here. We had an understanding, Mickey. You're going to spoil it if you keep comparing yourself to Bebe. Send her to Paris if you can't bear to have her around."

Tears glistened in Mickey's eyes. "Forgive me, Reuben."

"There's nothing to forgive. When you love someone, there are no rules and no apologies, only understanding."

When Daniel didn't appear at the assigned place fifteen minutes later, Bebe went to his room. At the sight of him, she burst out laughing. He was sitting on the edge of the bed, his eyes glassy, his mouth hanging slack. Apparently he was trying to put a clean sock over his shoe. Bebe knew Reuben would throw a fit if he saw his friend in such a condition. "Come on, Daniel, we'll sneak down the backstairs to the kitchen and get you some coffee. Here, let me run this brush through your hair. I'll do your tie in the kitchen. Hurry, I think I hear Reuben coming."

Like two naughty children they crept down the stairs to the kitchen. Old Nanette took one look at Daniel and hurried to the stove. She poured the coffee generously and laced it with strong brown sugar. Three cups later,

Daniel raced to the sink and vomited until his sides ached. Bebe just shook her head, watching as Daniel gargled and rinsed his mouth. She wasn't amused when he stuffed a wad of parsley in his mouth to kill the sour taste of the wine.

Later that night, after Mickey and Reuben retired, Bebe and Daniel sat in front of the fire. At last Daniel broke the silence. "Thank you, Bebe. I shouldn't have gotten so blotto, but everyone else was drinking. I didn't have as much as you," he said in an accusing tone.

"That will teach you not to do what everyone else seems to be doing just to be part of it. The reason I'm not in the same shape as you is because I dumped half of my wine in the fire. I know how much I can drink before I lose control. Both of us did what Reuben wanted, you for your own reasons, me because he finally talked to me and paid me some attention. I felt absolutely giddy when my aunt went upstairs, because Reuben looked at me. She was jealous of me. I liked the feeling," she whispered. "It doesn't make sense, does it? I like her a lot, and yet I was glad I could get under her skin."

Now that she'd started to confide her true feelings, Bebe couldn't seem to stop talking. "I wonder if he thinks I'm pretty. He was this close to me —" She placed her fingers an inch from Daniel's face. "He was thinking

about me all afternoon. I could tell. When we were in the wine cellar I could have gotten him to kiss me if I'd wanted to. Daniel, are you listening to me?" Bebe stamped her foot to get his attention.

"No. I mean yes. I'm listening, but no, Reuben wouldn't have kissed you. I know what I'm talking about. Bebe, you have to stop thinking about him. It isn't going to work out. Don't torture yourself."

Bebe stamped her foot again. "You don't know everything, Daniel Bishop. You don't know anything about women or girls. All you know is what's in books. You make me mad!"

"I make *you* mad? Do you know what you make me? Crazy, that's what." As Daniel spoke, his hands gripped the sides of his throbbing head. "I went through a war and didn't have half the problems I have now. I never know what to say to Reuben anymore. I keep sticking up for you. That makes him mad, and he thinks I'm being disloyal. If being loyal to you makes me disloyal in Reuben's eyes . . . I can't help it," he said miserably.

Gently Bebe took Daniel's hands away from his head. "Do you know what, Daniel? I bet I can get Reuben to sleep with me. I bet I can. How much do you want to bet?"

Daniel pulled away from her instinctively. "I don't want to bet anything. Because you'd lose. You shouldn't be talking like this. The

only way you could get Reuben into your bed is to tie him there when he's either drunk or sound asleep. Forget it. Get the thought out of your head!" He should get up — get up right now and go to bed. He didn't like this conversation and knew it was going to get worse before it got better.

"You're probably right about getting him in my bed. His, then. I can get him to . . . to . . . you know, do it. Let's make a bet. Ten dollars? Fifty?"

"Stop it, Bebe. I'm telling you, Reuben will never . . . he won't. Forget it!"

Bebe ignored him. "Sure he will. You're upset, Daniel, and I know why. You don't want your idol to have clay feet. He's only human, you know. Come on. A wager — me and Reuben. If I don't succeed, I owe you a favor that can be called in anytime during our lives. If I succeed, you owe me the favor. It's simple." Bebe sat back and shot Daniel a look of distaste. "You're a coward. I can see that now. You want to bet, but you're chicken. You know I'll win. Admit it, you know Reuben will cave in."

"Damn you, okay! How will I —"

Bebe clapped her hands in triumph and finished his sentence. "Know if I'm successful? You'll know. Trust me. Is it a deal, then? If so, we have to shake hands on it. That's more binding than a written contract, did you know that?"

"It's no such thing," Daniel said hotly. "A written contract can't be disputed. You have to go to court. A handshake is just a man's way of sealing a bargain."

"Fine, then let's make up a contract. Let's see what Monsieur Faroux taught you. Legal and binding, a contract that can't be broken by either of us. Still game?"

Daniel knew he was in over his head, boxed into a corner with no way out. I'll kill you, Reuben, if you fail me on this, he vowed silently.

"We have to set a time limit. Sometime during the next month. Maybe we should make it two weeks. I think we're going to Paris after the New Year. What do you think?"

"I don't think anything," Daniel snarled. "You're the one who's doing all this. I'm betting against you, remember?"

"You're very foolish, Daniel," Bebe said sweetly.

They sat together for another hour. With each word Daniel wrote, he felt sicker and sicker. Something deep inside warned him that he was going to lose, that Bebe would win and go about her business and destroy what Reuben held dear.

It was a mess, and what was worse, he still liked Bebe. If he were older, smarter, he'd be able to talk her out of what she was contemplating. Still, there should be something he could say, something to make her stop and at

least think about the consequences. At least he had to try.

"Let's say for the sake of argument that you do seduce Reuben in either a drunken state or by some trickery. Do you want him like that? I think — and this is just my opinion — he'll hate you forever if you do that to him." He could tell by the excited look in Bebe's eyes that his words weren't making a damn bit of difference.

"Oh, poo, men aren't like that," she said airily. "What's one little tumble in the sheets? He might like it so much he'll come back a second time. I am still a virgin. That's supposed to count for a lot. He might even want to make an honest woman of me, ask me to marry him. Is that so impossible?"

"Yes," Daniel replied, a horrified look on his face. "And you're deluding yourself if you think it will happen. I've known Reuben a lot longer than you have. I know how he thinks and feels. You might win now, but in the end you'll lose. Mark my words."

"That doesn't make sense," Bebe said, standing up and stretching languidly, like a cat. "I don't like riddles late at night. Besides, I didn't say I would do it for sure. I . . . we just made a wager. I can exercise it if I want. It isn't carved in stone."

She dropped to the floor next to Daniel and gently nudged his leg until he uncrossed it. Then she cuddled against him. It was a scene

and a feeling that would stay with him for a long time. The fire burning and crackling, the wind howling and whipping through the château like some mad demon bent on revenge. A nice end to a nice day — with the exception of the past few minutes.

"Do you like me, Daniel? You know . . . like?"

"Sure. Do you like me?" He wondered where the conversation was going.

"Of course I like you. My father would like you, too. He wouldn't like Reuben, though. Do you know why he wouldn't like Reuben?"

Daniel shook his head. "Why?"

"Because Reuben is just like him. When you see all the things you don't like about yourself in someone else, you don't like that person. That's how I am, too. I'm like my father. I think he'd do whatever he had to to get to the top." She giggled. "You can't have ideals in Hollywood. Speaking strictly for myself, if I wanted something bad enough, I'd kick and scratch, claw and fight, and lie through my teeth to get it. And, Daniel, I want Reuben Tarz!"

Daniel's stomach churned. "Why, Bebe?"

Why? Why did she want Reuben Tarz? She'd asked herself that same question over and over, at least a hundred times. Did she love him? He made her heart soar, her pulses pound, her blood sing. She felt drawn to him as a moth to a flame. There was something

about him that made her want to be near him, to have him smile at her, to touch her.

What she felt for Reuben wasn't a win-lose game the way Daniel thought it was. If he would toss Mickey aside for her, that had to mean she was worthy, a person to be loved and cherished. Suddenly she wished she were older, more experienced, so she could define what she was feeling. Daniel was probably right about having to trick Reuben into bed. If she did manage to get him into her bed, what would she do afterward? Would he hate her as Daniel said, or would he realize that she was worthy of his love? Would he look at her and smile the way he looked at Mickey? Or would he turn away in disgust? The thought made her shudder. I want him. I want to know what it feels like to make love. I want . . . I want . . . I need . . . I don't care about Mickey or Daniel, I care only about Reuben. Whatever I have to do to get him I'll do. And you're going to owe me, Daniel Bishop.

She scrambled to her feet and held out a hand to pull Daniel from his chair. "Come on, I think it's time we went to bed." Quick as a flash she snatched the penciled contract he had written up. Smiling, she folded it into neat squares and slipped it between her breasts. "If you want it back, you'll have to fight for it," she teased.

"It's yours, I don't want it," Daniel said

sourly. "For all the good it's going to do you."

"You're just an old worrywart," she said, skipping ahead of him. At the door to his room she kissed him lightly on the cheek and whispered, "Sweet dreams," before sauntering to her own room.

Sweet dreams, my ass, Daniel thought, grimacing. Why in hell had he allowed Bebe . . . He'd done it. She hadn't twisted his arm. He was sorry now. Like Reuben, he was beginning to realize Bebe was the cause of all his discontent. Things had been so nice, so peaceful, until she'd appeared on the scene.

His gut told him Bebe Rosen was trouble . . . big-time trouble.

CHAPTER ELEVEN

The new day brought a harmony that prevailed right up to Christmas Eve. Mickey continued to explain her special traditions, particularly those that pertained to feasting on a wealth of old family recipes, French foods in creamy rich sauces. There would be pheasant and a ham and a leg of mutton. The vegetables would be crisply fresh, the bread warm and crunchy with Echiré butter as golden as a summer sun, melting in little rivers down the partially sliced bread. Marrons glacés and spiced rum cake that would flame at the end of the meal, she said happily. Dinner would be served in the formal dining room with the best linen cloths and the finest crystal and china. The silver would shine like the first evening star. There'd be coffee in tiny china cups in the library before the fire. When Nanette had carried the last of the dishes back to the kitchen, they would gather round the tree. The candles would be lighted, and they'd sing "O Holy Night" along with

other carols. At eleven o'clock they'd pile into the Citroën and drive to the village for midnight Mass. When they returned to the château the gifts would be opened, and then it would be Christmas Day. Their first Christmas together.

Bebe took her cue from Mickey and prepared carefully for the evening. She took a long, leisurely bath, then washed and curled her hair. It dried into springy little puffs all about her face. She applied makeup, but frugally, just enough to highlight her best features. The only jewelry she wore were diamond studs in her ears. Her dress was emerald green with a wide lace collar studded with tiny pearls, more elegant and sophisticated than any she'd worn since her arrival. She looked good and felt absolutely wonderful . . . until she saw Mickey pass by her room.

Her dress was a cranberry silk with lines so defined and elegant it could have been made for a princess. Her shoes were lizard, and very expensive. Bebe knew a thing or two about shoes since she owned over sixty pairs, but nothing she had could compare with the ones her aunt was wearing. Tonight Mickey wore jewels — in her ears, around her neck, on her wrists and fingers. Diamonds, hundreds of diamonds that sparkled and glittered in the dim light. She'd shine like a Christmas tree, Bebe thought nastily.

All her lightheartedness, her good cheer,

had vanished. She couldn't compete, and she wouldn't even try.

Downstairs in the library, Reuben was pouring their predinner wine. Bebe drew in her breath in a long hiss. How handsome he looked in his dark suit and gleaming white shirt! His tie was knotted perfectly, his shoes had just the right amount of polish. From where she was standing she could see that his nails were clipped and buffed. She liked the authoritative way he gripped the wine bottle. His hair was slicked back, but already it was drying, with unruly strands falling over his wide forehead. He looked up when she entered the room. Thank God she'd had the good sense to dress . . . conservatively yet properly. Reuben did two rare things at that moment: he smiled and he complimented her.

"Pretty as a picture," he said, his eyes warm as he gazed at her. "Your father should put you in one of his films."

Bebe was stunned by the depth of her reaction to Reuben's smile and his compliment. The strength of it would easily carry her through the evening and into Christmas Day.

She wondered what Reuben had given her for Christmas. Whatever it was, she would never part with it. She'd sleep with it under her pillow, and if it was small enough, she'd place it between her breasts.

She was a lovely child, Mickey thought sadly, watching her. And Reuben was right,

she was as pretty as a picture.

If anyone noticed the worry in Daniel's eyes, they didn't mention it.

At dinner, everyone laughed and talked and told stories. "When I was a child there were no presents, just fruit and nuts," Mickey said. "Once I got a straw doll from an old aunt. It was so ugly I cried, but I came to love that doll as though it were a real baby. I still have it somewhere. Probably in the attic at the Paris house. And what do you remember, *chérie?*" she asked Bebe.

"As you know, my mother wasn't Jewish, so we celebrated both the Christian and Jewish holidays. The nicest, the most wonderful present I can remember was a train set. It was supposed to be for Eli, but I guess Mama got the name tags mixed up and it was in my pile of presents. Eli wanted to snatch it from me, but Daddy wouldn't let him. He said if it had my name on it, it was mine. He said something about possession being the law. I played with it every day and then right after New Year's I went to a birthday party and when I got back Eli had smashed the train to pieces just to be spiteful. I never forgave him for that," she said softly.

Daniel spoke of his friend Jake and how they'd sit huddled together, wondering if Santa would find them at the orphanage. "Jake always said we were too big for presents and only sissies believed in Santa. He just

239

said that to make me feel better because I was younger and smaller than he was. He looked out for me."

Bebe thought it a touching story and told him so. She looked pointedly at Reuben and wasn't surprised to see his jaw harden and his eyes grow steely. Ha! she thought. So now I know your Achilles' heel, Reuben Tarz. It's Daniel Bishop. She stored the knowledge in the back of her mind.

"It's your turn, Reuben," she said.

Reuben threw his hands into the air and gave them all a lopsided grin that Mickey found particularly endearing. "I never celebrated Christmas. This is a first for me. I've never been in a church, either. I'll do my best not to shame you." He gazed at Mickey apologetically. For what, Bebe wondered.

While Reuben's physical body sat in the pew in the village church, he himself felt far removed. He didn't belong here, not that there was anything wrong with it. The parishioners were all good, hardworking people, devout and caring. He felt . . . peripheral. And he didn't know if he liked the feeling or not. Someday, maybe, he would go to church just to sit alone on the shiny hard pew and contemplate his life.

He looked around to see where the joy was, but all he saw were bowed heads, rosaries in every hand. It was peaceful and it was cold.

He couldn't wait to leave.

When at last he pulled the car in front of the house, they all piled out and hurried to the door. "You aren't going to put the car in the barn now, are you?" Bebe demanded.

"That's where I usually put it," Reuben replied.

"Not tonight," Mickey said, linking her arm through his. "Who cares if snow piles on top of it? Tomorrow is soon enough. Come before Daniel and Bebe burst with excitement."

Reuben began to understand that whatever was going on, Mickey had a grip on it. "It's your car," he muttered.

Bebe raced into the house, down the hall, through the library, and out to the kitchen. She waved to the old cook as she careened out the back door. Twice she slipped and fell as she raced to the barn. Inside she found the puppy just where Mickey had told Yvette to leave it. He was cuddled into a ball, his new collar standing out against his taffy-colored fur. He was shivering despite the hot water bottle under his little blanket. Bebe scooped him into her arms, blanket and all, covering him with her coat. He'd warm up in the kitchen if she put him by the hearth. Nanette would watch him until it was time to hand him over to Daniel.

This time she walked slowly, careful of her footing. So far the puppy hadn't made a sound. Bebe crooned to it all the way back to

the kitchen.

Nanette immediately threw a braided carpet on the hearth and took the puppy from Bebe. She, too, crooned to the animal, but in French. Bebe smiled. Who didn't love a warm new puppy? "For you, Daniel, just for you."

"Where were you?" Daniel demanded when she returned. "We've been waiting for you."

"Curiosity killed the cat, Daniel," Bebe snapped. "For your information, I went to the kitchen to see if I could help Nanette. She is old, you know. I was only trying to help. I'm sorry if I —"

"For God's sake, Daniel, what's gotten into you?" Reuben interrupted. "This is Christmas, peace on earth, kindness to one's fellow man, that kind of thing."

"Enough! We're all here." Mickey laughed, waving her hands for attention. "Nanette has just brought our toddies and a delicious tray of sweets. We can eat and drink while we open our presents. I think Reuben should hand out the gifts."

Obediently they dropped to their knees and sat on petit-point cushions. Mickey instructed Nanette to turn on the phonograph and open the drapes. Reuben thought he'd never been so happy in his whole life. Here he was on Christmas Day in a warm, wonderful house with the two people he loved most in the world. He didn't have to wonder if the others were feeling the same way. He could tell they

242

were by the expressions on their faces.

Everyone's special present was left for last. Daniel handed Mickey the gift that was from both himself and Reuben. They watched as she undid the red bow and picked at the paper. She pried and jiggled the wooden lid until it popped open. When she could see what lay in the box before her, her hands flew to her mouth. "How did . . . when . . . I can't believe . . . but how . . . ?"

"Do you like it?" Reuben and Daniel asked in unison.

"Do I like it? I love it! I adore it! Bourdelle did it, didn't he?"

"When we told him it was for you, he dropped all his other commissions and worked night and day on it. So you see, we are the Three Musketeers. Forever."

They all stood back to marvel at the painting. "It's an exact likeness of all of us. Exquisite!" Mickey cried. "It goes over the mantel. Oh, thank you from the bottom of my heart."

Reuben's eyes glistened when he opened his gift from Mickey. He felt his throat close when he read the inscription on the back. He knew his hands were trembling, but he didn't care. He wished it were appropriate for him scoop Mickey into his arms, but he held back. To think she cared enough to give him the only thing she had of her father's. In his opinion, that said it all.

Daniel was so excited with his watch, he leapt over the boxes and clapped Reuben on the back. "You son of a gun! Now we both have one. I never had anything so grand in my life. Nothing," he cried excitedly, "will ever be as good as this watch . . . except this set of law books!" He swooped down on Mickey, kissing her soundly on the cheek. Mickey reached for him and kissed him back.

Bebe unwrapped her present from Mickey, a strand of pearls. They were so beautiful she felt a catch in her throat. From Reuben she received matching earrings. Mickey must have helped him select them, but it didn't matter. From Daniel there was a tiny pearl bracelet. She beamed her thanks at all of them. Her glance at Reuben was shy but warm. When he returned it, her heart soared.

"Ah, but there is one more present." Mickey laughed. "Bebe must fetch it from the kitchen. Everyone get ready now. This is for Daniel, and it is from Bebe."

Bebe was back in seconds, her arms full of warm, soft blankets. She dropped gracefully to her knees and held out her arms to Daniel. "It's for you from me for being such a good friend." She felt as though she were offering a platter of gold and diamonds.

Daniel reached out and peered down at the bundle he was accepting. Carefully he removed the warm blanket to stare at the soft velvety head of the drowsy puppy.

"Jesus, Crikey, it's a dog! A pup! A live one! Oh, my God!" He lifted the dog from its nest of warmth and nuzzled it to his cheek. "Look! Look at his collar. Jake! It says Jake! Oh, my God, it says Jake! So that's what you've been up to! All the time you were picking my brain you were planning this, weren't you?" Bebe nodded shyly.

"Reuben, look! It's a dog. It has a collar and a tag. I can't believe this." When the puppy's small pink tongue licked his face, Daniel laughed delightedly, a look of pure rapture on his face.

Only Bebe seemed to be aware of Reuben's black look, the look he was directing at her. At first she didn't understand what it meant. Of course, Daniel would have talked to Reuben about Jake. At some point in time he probably would have gotten Daniel a dog, but its name wouldn't have been Jake. Her eyes pleaded with him to understand that giving Jake to Daniel was something she did from her heart. She'd be damned if she'd let him stare her into the ground. Defiantly she held his gaze, and Reuben was the first to turn away.

Rage coursed through Reuben. How *dare* she! How dare she throw Jake in his face this way! He wanted to pick her up and throw her against the wall, break every bone in her body. He didn't care how pretty she looked or how good she smelled or how she felt

when he touched her. He was almost sure he would have done it if Mickey hadn't laughed. Daniel was *his* friend. He should have been the one to get him the dog. He simply hadn't thought in terms of a puppy for a present, and here this girl, who was still a baby herself, had outshone him. In his mind he was convinced she had named the dog Jake just to get at him.

No, whispered an inner voice. She couldn't know you were planning to get Daniel a dog someday. This is now. Look at your friend. When was the last time you saw him this happy? Let it go. Don't hold it against the girl. She meant well. Daniel can have two friends who want to see him happy. Let it go.

The moment his rage subsided, Reuben walked over to Bebe. "Your present is probably the best Daniel will get in his whole life. He's never going to forget this Christmas. I've never seen him this happy."

Bebe beamed. "I . . . I thought you might be upset. . . . I wanted to give him something special so he'd remember me when I leave." Impulsively she reached up and kissed Reuben on the cheek. "Merry Christmas, Reuben."

Remember her . . . when she left. . . . How sweet she smelled. He was off stride now, his steps jerky as he made his way over to Daniel and Mickey. He peered down at the small bundle and smiled. "Can I hold him?" he

asked. Daniel held out the puppy, and the moment Reuben brought him to his chest Jake christened his new suit. Daniel howled with laughter and rolled about the floor clutching his sides. Bebe giggled and Mickey smiled sadly.

It was a wonderful Christmas.

CHAPTER TWELVE

The first days of the new year kept the inhabitants of the château snowbound. The aftermath of the holidays was a quiet time, since the heavy snowfall insulated them from the outside world. There was no friction, only goodwill.

They were lazy days, yet fruitful as well. Reuben spent long hours with Mickey at his side in the wine cellars. Daniel studied industriously, taking breaks in the middle of the day with Bebe. Every afternoon they trudged through the heavy snow, Jake at their heels. If anything in the world could cement their friendship, it was Jake.

And it was a friendship that would last all their lives.

When Bebe wasn't studying or trekking through the snow with Daniel, she was reading her way through Mickey's library and cleaning up Jake's puddles and messes. She never complained, and it was hard to say whom the dog was more devoted to, Daniel

or Bebe.

Jake was a curious pup, into everything, even the cold ashes in the grates. His paw prints were found everywhere. But everyone was indulgent, and if a mess needed to be cleaned and Bebe wasn't available, Mickey or Reuben bent to the task. If anything, the dog solidified the little family.

Bebe's supposed two-week stay had proved to be more fiction than fact. Her proposed visit to England did not carry her father's approval, so she was in France until her father decided it was time for her to come home. But the truth of the matter was she was more than content to stay; she was in love with Reuben. Just to be near him was almost enough for her. She ignored the intimate relationship he had with her aunt and concentrated on ways to get him to notice her.

It was the end of the month before weather conditions improved enough for Mickey to announce a trip to Paris the following week. It was decided that Bebe and Daniel would take the train and Reuben and Mickey would take Jake and the baggage in the car.

The first few days of their Paris visit were hectic as well as exhausting. Meetings with bankers, exporters, officials of the White Star Line concerning shipping, all left Reuben exhilarated and Mickey baffled at the way things were done. Reuben simply told her it

was the American way of doing things. You promise me something and I promise you something. In the end she'd shrugged and left it up to Reuben to "wheel and deal," as he called it.

Thanks to a glowing letter of introduction from Pierre Faroux, Daniel was enrolled at the Sorbonne, where he attended classes from early morning to late in the afternoon. He was unbelievably happy.

Mickey hired a middle-aged woman as a chaperone for Bebe. The girl protested loud and long, then capitulated when Reuben's face darkened at her protests. Whatever Reuben wanted she did.

When spring rose from its winter sleep to blanket Paris with intoxicating air and lovers walking hand in hand, the sidewalk cafés came to life and Mickey called a holiday. "Someday," she told them, "someone is going to write a song about Paris in the springtime. It is my favorite place on earth." She laughed and said she hoped she'd still be alive to hear it.

"My darlings, we are taking five whole days to see this beautiful city I love. Perhaps when our holiday is over you will love Paris as much as I do."

They started out briskly enough, stopping twice at sidewalk cafés for cafe au lait before the noon hour.

"Ah, I believe I made the little mistake this

morning," Mickey said ruefully. "My feet are aching me. It has been years since I showed off Paris to my friends from other countries. Tomorrow we will ride bicycles."

"That's the best idea I've heard all day," Reuben muttered. His leg felt the pull and strain of all the walking they'd done. It was nice seeing Paris, but as far as he was concerned, they could go back to the town house now and he'd feel his education was complete. He didn't really care about the fierce-looking gargoyles on Notre Dame, and he wasn't impressed with the architecture, either. They'd viewed it in the early morning light with mist hanging over it, and it had looked like a dim prison. But there had been such a look of rapture on Mickey's face when she stood looking at the huge edifice; he hadn't wanted to spoil the moment, so he'd simply agreed that it was beautiful. All he really wanted was to get back to work.

They were sitting now in a café by the Closérie des Lilas. Monstrous horse chestnut trees were full of blossoms, and every time the branches dipped in the breeze the soft petals floated to their square-topped table. They were lovelier than anything Reuben had ever seen back in Brooklyn. But then, New York was not known for its beauty.

"I've never seen so many shops. And the stalls on the quays make me want to buy one of everything. When can we shop?" Bebe

demanded.

Mickey laughed. "We have plenty of time, *chérie*. On the way home we'll stop by the baker's cart for some fresh baguettes, but that is all the shopping we will do for today."

"I should be French," Daniel grumbled. "Monsieur Faroux told me Frenchmen are known for their sturdy legs. Walking is a way of life, he said."

"He was teasing you, Daniel . . . pulling your leg. His own are weak and knobby." Mickey shook her head in dismay to show what she thought of Pierre and his little story. "Come now, my little pigeons, it is time to explore some more and then we will lunch."

They trotted off, refreshed with hot coffee, determined to walk as briskly and be as enthusiastic as Mickey.

This time their walk took them past a district filled with stalls and all manner of shops.

"Come, come, we must pass this area quickly," Mickey said. "Do not look toward that café, for it is full of drunks and smells like the cesspool it is. It wasn't always like this." Reuben looked up to see the name Café des Amateurs on the rue Mouffetard.

"How do you know so much about this . . . this wicked place?" Bebe queried.

Mickey hesitated, but only for a moment. "When I was young my friend Yvette and I used to sit here and watch all the young men

go by and try to entice them into buying us a drink. We were so poor then, we had no money to buy our own. Is there anything else you want to know about this . . . wicked place, as you call it?" Mickey asked.

"No." Bebe flushed at her aunt's expression.

Within moments Mickey relented, feeling her words might have been too harsh. *"Chérie,"* she said, drawing Bebe aside, "there is something I wish to say to you. When you asked me how I know so much about Café des Amateurs I explained to you. I did not apologize. In your life there will be many times when the choice is up to you whether to explain or apologize. Always choose to explain. Never apologize for what you were or what you did. There are certain times in our lives when we may have done things we wouldn't presently do. Will you remember what I've just told you?"

Bebe lowered her eyes. "Yes. I'm . . . I'm sorry if I offended you."

"No, *chérie,* you are not sorry. You put me — how do you say it? — on the spot, purposefully. I have nothing to be ashamed of. I responded to your question."

"But you could have said something in front of the others instead of taking me aside like this. I'm glad you didn't. . . ." Bebe looked over to Reuben and Daniel.

"One must never embarrass a friend or

guest in front of others. I'm not interested in playing the game you wish to initiate."

"Game? What game?" Bebe blurted out, her eyes widening in pretended wonder.

How innocent and green her eyes were, Mickey thought. Outwardly she was the picture of an angel. Mickey wouldn't have been surprised to see her sprout wings at that very moment. "If you don't know what I'm talking about, then of course I must be wrong. We will not speak of it again."

Bebe's eyes grew even wider. "I can't believe you would think that way of me, Aunt Mickey."

Mickey's voice dropped, and Bebe had to strain to hear her words. "Once I was young like yourself. There is nothing you can say or do that I myself did not say and do. I know all the tricks, all the games young women can play. With time I outgrew such childish behavior. When you are a woman, you will, too. Now come along, we've kept Daniel and Reuben waiting too long."

Bebe fell into step with Mickey. When they joined the others Mickey announced that they should all wait one moment until she could find a driver for the rest of the afternoon. Thus Reuben found himself standing alone with Bebe as Daniel wandered off to the side of the street.

It was as though he were seeing her for the first time. She wore a picture-pretty hat of

yellow straw with a cluster of pastel-colored silk flowers draped daintily from the brim. Dipping low over her forehead, the hat shaded her brilliant green eyes. Her dress was of watered silk, the same colors as the flowers. She looked as bright and fresh as the spring day. Reuben was also aware of the admiring glances she was receiving from passersby. His neck grew warm when he realized he was staring. Bebe smiled, a winsome little pout of obvious pleasure. Daniel scuffed his feet on the cobblestones, trying to make his presence felt. When Reuben continued to stare, he cleared his throat loudly. Bebe giggled and slapped him on the back, but she didn't take her eyes from Reuben's unwavering gaze.

Disconcerted, Reuben averted his eyes, spotting a fat robin digging ferociously in the ground for his lunch. It had been a long time since he'd seen a robin. There was something about seeing the first robin of spring and making a wish . . . What did he have to wish for? That time would stop, and hold him here, and things would never change?

"Oh, look, there's a robin. Let's all make a wish!" Bebe laughed.

"Let's not and say we did," Reuben replied. Why did she always seem to know what he was thinking — and why was she always one step ahead of him? She belonged behind, far behind.

Bebe ignored him. "My father always says you should be careful of what you wish for because you might get it! I hope I do!" She squeezed her eyes shut to make her wish, and Daniel did the same. Reuben stared ahead at the robin, who was still digging industriously. Without stopping to think about it, he stretched out his leg and stomped it on the stones. Frightened, the robin took wing.

"Meanie!" Bebe exploded. "I wasn't finished making my wish."

"Grow up!" Reuben mumbled harshly. "Wishes are for children."

"You keep reminding me that I'm a child. So why don't you let me be one? Sometimes I hate you, Reuben Tarz. I never did a thing to you, and you treat me like dirt. I'm tired of it. Either you start treating me properly or I'll . . . I'll . . ."

"Yes?" Reuben drawled, his face expressionless. People were staring at them, but most didn't understand English. And he couldn't have cared less if they'd understood every word.

Daniel stayed as quiet as he could.

Suddenly the sunny day felt cool; the wind whipped around them, fussing with Bebe's skirt and blowing up Reuben's and Daniel's pant legs. Bebe burst into laughter at the sight of their trousers ballooning out from their ankles. Reuben thought she was laughing at him and reached for her, but she

danced away, the wind driving her skirt high above her knees. Two boys on bicycles whistled approvingly, and she laughed louder, acknowledging the compliment.

"I'm waiting," Reuben said.

Bebe screwed up her face in a spiteful grimace. "You're always waiting . . . like some gangly vulture." She pursed her mouth. "I'll wish something bad for you. It always works. I practice it all the time back home. Sometimes I don't know my own powers. You wouldn't believe the things I've wished on people that actually happened. Do you want me to do it to you, Reuben? Do you want me to make you unhappy? To make Aunt Mickey take a second look at you? To wish your good life comes to an end because you don't deserve it? . . . Well, do you?" This time it was she who drawled the question.

Reuben reminded himself that Bebe was a sixteen-year-old spoiled brat, a snotty little girl who'd obviously never been disciplined. Where in hell was Mickey? Why had she saddled him with this detestable child? An uneasy feeling settled between his shoulder blades.

"Wish for whatever you want," he said, making his voice sound disinterested.

At that moment Mickey appeared as if by magic. Her dark gaze took in the scene immediately, but she chose to ignore it. "The man I spoke of will meet us at two o'clock,"

she said brightly. "We have time now to visit the Eiffel Tower, and then we will lunch. Briskly, my pets, so that we may enjoy our lunch all the more."

Reuben's leg was beginning to ache unbearably. He tried to keep a pleasant look on his face, but it wasn't easy. Instead of going home, he found himself staring up at the Eiffel Tower. He knew he could have been just as happy if he never saw it.

Mickey pointed up at the structure towering above them. "One day this tower, just as your Statue of Liberty, will be world famous. You will remember this day."

Lunch was a long, leisurely affair, and it was after two when they emerged to find Mickey's driver waiting. At the look of relief on Reuben's face, Mickey said quickly, "I think I shall take pity on all of us and have this kind man drive us home. We can sightsee again tomorrow."

The town house looked so appealing to Reuben that he wanted to shout with relief. It sat way back from the road, at the end of a long circular driveway bordered by blooming chestnut trees. New spring shoots of green ivy, the color of brilliant emeralds, nested in between the old growth along the aged brick facade. The building's stained-glass arched windows radiated rainbows of deep-hued colors in the afternoon sun. He thought the town house beautiful and already felt it was

home. Home was wherever Mickey was — here, in the country, or at the château in Bordeaux.

Inside the house, Bebe scampered off to her room, Daniel headed for the library, and Mickey watched as Reuben plopped down on a love seat, his leg stretched out in front of him. It was becoming an effort to mask his pain. "It hurts like a son of a bitch!" he gasped. "If I ruined the day by —"

"Non! I should have taken more notice. You should have said something, *chéri."* It was a gentle reprimand. Reuben grimaced as her hand touched his thigh, then sighed in relief when her fingers gently massaged the aching muscles. "I'll get you a hot water bottle and a book. By dinner you will feel much better."

"I could make love to you right here. Right now! I don't care if Daniel, Bebe, or the servants walk in. I want you."

"Good," she whispered, kissing him. "Keep that thought, and this evening we will make wild, passionate love in a comfortable bed. I will do all sorts of tantalizing things to you and —"

Reuben laughed. "And I will kindly reciprocate. . . ."

"Tell me now . . . whisper them in my ear, *chéri.* . . ."

"You first. Ladies always go first."

Mickey threw back her head and laughed. "I will surprise you, how's that?"

"I can't wait," Reuben said gruffly, pulling her close.

"Nor I . . . but we must." She drew away from him. "Rest now, while I get the hot water bottle. Sleep, Reuben; I intend to keep you up all night."

"Mickey," he said as she stood there before him.

"Yes, *chéri?*"

"When are we going to Montmartre?"

Mickey sighed. "I was hoping you would forget about going there."

"I want to go . . . just the two of us."

"Whenever you want. But why you want to see the artificial side of Paris is beyond me. It must be the same in America. It is not real, Reuben. It is a place where pimps and prostitutes do business. Derelicts and drunks frequent the district night and day."

"I don't care," Reuben said stubbornly, a glint in his eye. "I want us to go there together."

"It will serve no purpose, but if you are determined, will this evening be soon enough?" At Reuben's nod, Mickey bustled from the room, her brow furrowed in frustration.

For a long time after that, Reuben sat with a book open on his lap and the hot water bottle on his thigh. He thought about all the times Mickey had gone to Montmartre with her friends and the times she went alone.

She'd told him they drank and danced and picked up lovers, sometimes for just the one night. He hated hearing the words, but he'd pressured her to tell about the district, and she had complied, saying she had no secrets from him. She'd also said she would make no apologies for her past life. He wanted to see, needed to see the kind of life Mickey had once led, not as a young girl but as a woman. He knew he would be better off not going, but he wanted to know everything, every single little thing there was to know about this woman he loved.

At last Reuben dozed, in that fitful half-dream state invaded by demons and ghosts from the past. He was running as fast as his injured leg would allow, from a pack of men, down the Champs-Élysées. When he risked a glance over his shoulder, he saw Bebe at the head of the pack. They cursed, calling him hateful names as they threw huge bunches of grapes at him. Purple juice splattered all over him, on his face, his arms, and on his snowy-white shirt. Wiping his eyes did no good: he was blinded by the dark, sticky juice, which dripped into his nose and his mouth, staining his teeth and choking him. He tried to struggle up from his nightmare, but every time he reached that place of awakening, Bebe pulled and tugged, taunting him, leading the attackers and calling him names he'd never heard before. When he finally woke he

felt disoriented and was drenched in perspiration.

When Mickey descended the stairs at ten o'clock, Reuben stood waiting for her, and her costume — for that's what it was — left him stunned and speechless. She wore a bright red satin dress with a slit up the thigh and a skinny ruffle at the hem; black mesh stockings and bright red shoes; a black boa made of ostrich feathers that hugged her neck and fell all the way down her back; and thick red rouge and heavy eye makeup. Taken at a glance, she looked like the worst kind of tramp.

"Ah, *chéri,* I see you are not amused," Mickey said coolly. "I didn't think you would be. If you want to see Montmartre, you will see it as it is, as I was when I went there. I'm ready."

"I . . . I changed my mind. I don't . . . Where in the hell did you get that outfit? You look like a . . . No, I don't want to go," Reuben said hoarsely.

"That is too bad, because I'm going, alone if I have to. You started this and I'll finish it. You won't rest until you go there." The satin ruffle rustled as Mickey swished through the door. She was halfway to the corner when Reuben caught up to her.

"This is stupid, Mickey. I'm sorry I ever brought it up. Just because I was stupid doesn't mean you have to act the same way. I

want to go back! Dammit, listen to me!" Reuben shouted. "I don't care what you did before. It's none of my business. I'm truly sorry I've been pressuring you about this. Let's forget it!"

"No, Reuben, it will fester with you forever. We are going to Montmartre together or I go alone. Decide," she said in a high-pitched voice Reuben had never heard before.

Thirty minutes later they were seated at a fly-specked, rickety table. A waiter with greasy hair and a scab on the side of his cheek came up to their table and leaned over to take their order. Reuben stretched his neck and straightened his tie. He couldn't look at Mickey, who was busy gazing around the café, her outrageous gold hoop earrings dancing each time she moved her head.

"We would like a glass of wine. That's all," Reuben barked.

Mickey's eyes zeroed in on a man sitting alone at the far end of the café. "I'm going to show you how we did it in the old days, Reuben. Watch carefully." She was off her chair and halfway across the café before Reuben realized what she was doing. In horror, he watched as she pulled a chair close to her and lifted her leg so that the satin dress hiked up to her crotch. All he could see was the black mesh stockings. She leaned over for the man to light her cigarette, her breasts almost spilling from the dress, her tongue moisten-

ing her crimson lips in obvious invitation. She dragged on the cigarette and blew a perfect smoke ring.

The man was reaching in his shirt pocket for money when Reuben roared across the room like a freight train. He half dragged, half carried her to the street. "Son of a bitch! I don't believe you just did what you did!" he thundered, not caring who heard.

Mickey's reply was just as shrill. "Well, you son of a bitch, I can't believe you wanted to come here, and I can't believe you need to know what I did before I met you. Listen to me, Reuben. It wasn't like this when Yvette and I used to come here. It was clean and fresh. The food was good and the wine was even better. We were all friends in those days. We weren't prostitutes and we didn't know what a pimp was. If we wanted to make love with someone, no money changed hands. Sometimes there were gifts, but they meant nothing. You had no right to invade this part of my life, no right at all. I hope you're satisfied. I'm going home now and I'm going alone. I want you to sit here and think about us, and this place. Good night, Reuben."

Reuben was boiling as he walked back into the café. "Wine!" he bellowed. Instantly the waiter slapped a carafe on the table.

Reuben gulped at the thin, sour wine, his head pounding violently. Then he tossed several francs on the dirty tabletop and strode

out of the café.

He was dangerous now, and he knew it. If he didn't walk this anger off, he would do something he'd regret. But instead of walking he loosened his tie with a yank and started to run. His leg burned with the punishment he was inflicting on it, but he ignored the pain. When he was exhausted, he slumped against an old gnarled chestnut tree, fighting for breath. A long time later he realized the violent pain in his head had abated, leaving him with a dull ache he could deal with. He promised himself never, ever, to allow his temper to get out of control again. He also swore that he would never again question Mickey about her past. He would apologize, on bended knee if he had to, and beg her forgiveness.

It was almost midnight when Reuben let himself into the house. He took a deep breath, then climbed the stairs and rapped softly on Mickey's door. She opened it wide for him to enter, and he drank in the sight of her freshly scrubbed face and soft blue nightgown. This was the woman he loved, the woman he wanted to spend the rest of his life with. "I need to know that you forgive me," he said huskily.

Mickey nodded, tears in her eyes. "Of course, *chéri*. We will never speak of this again."

They slept in each other's arms. Forgive-

ness, Reuben thought as he reached for sleep, was just a word.

Except for Montmartre, the all-too-short holiday was idyllic. By day the sun wrapped Mickey and her guests in its warmth, and at night the star-sprinkled sky wove a magic all its own. They gorged themselves on a number of picnics from the heavily laden baskets packed in Mickey's kitchen. Baked ham, roast chicken, pickled eggs, ripe cheeses, and loaf after loaf of crusty French bread filled them to the brim, making them drowsy enough to fall fast asleep in the waking light of the spring sun.

One day Mickey arranged for Reuben and herself to picnic alone. After sharing a special meal, toasted with a fine chilled champagne, the loving couple strolled hand in hand along the mossy banks of the Seine. Since the water had warmed considerably over the past few weeks, they paddled their feet in the clear water. Twice they retired to a private chestnut-shaded spot, making love as only two impatient, passion-driven lovers could, spontaneously and with joyful abandon. Mickey thought her heart would burst with happiness when the blossoms from the trees fluttered down on them as they lay spent, their arms around each other.

"This will be such a wonderful memory, *chéri.*" Mickey sighed happily. "I will never

be able to look at a chestnut tree in blossom without thinking of this time."

Reuben silenced her with his lips and held her tight, nuzzling his face in her hair. He had been thinking the same thing, but his throat constricted, making it impossible to get the words out.

Mickey could see his love-filled eyes change as he tried but failed to speak. How she wanted to prod him — to help with the unfamiliar words — but then they would be her words, not his. She waited, savoring the moment. If they came it would be wonderful, if they didn't she knew what was in his heart. After all, she could feel it beating next to hers.

"I don't ever want this to end," Reuben whispered huskily. "I know this is a holiday, a special one, for all of us. It's like a dream. When things are this perfect you want them never to end. I wonder if these special times are what happiness is. Little respites, time away from our ordinary lives. What do you think, Mickey?"

She loved it when he asked for her opinion, and she was always careful to be as honest as possible, sometimes painfully so. "I think I agree with you. When we share something, it makes life more meaningful. I have enjoyed this holiday tremendously, but it's time to go back to the château. Unless you want to remain here." She waited, not realizing she was holding her breath.

"I'm ready to go back. We have one more meeting with that prissy banker of yours. I think I have finally convinced him that shipping wine to America is in your best interest."

"You prefer the château to Paris, is that it?"

"Yes, and you?"

"There was a time when I wanted to be here only. I found the château very dull. I was younger then and lived only for each day. I thought I was happy as I rushed from party to party, buying clothes and jewels to dazzle my friends. I wanted —" She paused, searching for the right words. "To find love, real love. I wanted to be madly, wildly, irresponsibly, and wickedly in love, totally and to the exclusion of all else. I searched for it frantically, in many places, but always it eluded me . . . until you came into my life. I wish I knew what I did to become so blessed. You, Reuben, are my gift from heaven. Each of us must get that one special gift at some time in our lives. For me it was you. I want to think it's the same way for you. . . . Is it, Reuben?"

Reuben looked up into the mammoth eye of the sun, then down at Mickey. She was so different from when they'd first met, so open, so confiding, so very real. "Yes," he breathed, holding her close. "You carved a niche in my heart."

An enchanting silence fell about them, broken only by their soft breathing and

Daniel's shout.

Reuben swore savagely. Mickey smiled. "I told them to meet us here. Tell me you don't mind," she teased. They drew apart and righted themselves as Daniel and Bebe approached with Jake cavorting between them.

"Mickey, I think Daniel should stay here and continue at the Sorbonne," Reuben said.

"My thoughts exactly. He can bicycle to his classes. I'd like him to stay through September at least."

Reuben sat up, a blade of grass between his teeth, his arms around his drawn-up knees. He looked so handsome, so virile, thought Mickey. Just watching him, familiar tentacles of warmth spread through her body. However, the sight of Bebe cooled her mood immediately. The girl came running up and dropped to her knees in front of them with a dazzling smile.

"We've been sprinting up and down this riverbank for the past hour, and you two lazybones are just sitting here. You have to get your blood flowing." She said the words to Mickey, but her eyes were on Reuben.

"I have other ways to get my blood flowing," Reuben said lightly. He enjoyed watching Bebe flush; she was even prettier with her cheeks crimson. "How about you, Mickey, how do you get your blood flowing?"

"For shame, Reuben. A lady must have her little secrets. Isn't that right, Bebe?" she said

casually.

The flustered girl turned sullen, poked at Daniel, who had plopped down beside her, and was on her feet again, running down the riverbank with Jake. Daniel sat motionless, and when he spoke it was with a disapproving tone. "You embarrassed her," he said flatly, "and it wasn't necessary." Then he rose and ran down the slope to the river's edge, joining Bebe.

Reuben shrugged at his friend's accusation, but his face turned dark.

Mickey placed a gentle hand on Reuben's arm. "He's young, Reuben. He knows where his loyalty lies, but he's confused. I wouldn't be a bit surprised if Daniel is the recipient of a good many confidences from Bebe. You know, of course, even to you he will not divulge them. Daniel has ethics. An admirable trait. Most men . . . well, some men have it. You don't as yet, but you will one day."

Reuben felt himself flush. A lot of things were going to happen to him "one day," according to Mickey. It made him feel like a clod, aware once again that he was a man, but naked of the traits she most admired. Well, hell, when and where was he to acquire them?

Their peaceful reverie was spoiled now. "Let's go for a walk this way," he said, pointing away from Bebe and Daniel.

He reached down to pull Mickey to her

feet, and she bounded up to within an inch of him. "I love you, Reuben, all of you, every inch," she said meaningfully.

"Even with my imperfections?" He meant it to come out lightly, but instead it sounded cold and brusque.

"Yes, even with your imperfections, for they are only temporary."

"Will you love me when I'm perfect?"

"No. For there is no perfect person on this earth. If you come close to perfection, I won't be around to see it. It will take a lifetime for that to happen. I love you as you are."

When Reuben looked away, obviously unappeased, Mickey sighed. "*Chéri*, you appear to subscribe to a double standard. You want me to accept you as you are, and I do, but you want to know everything there is to know about me from the day I was smacked on my bottom. You have pointed out to me in subtle little ways that you do not approve of my . . . past, and yet you want to know every little detail. I am not now who I was. You are who you are now, but you won't always be the same person. That is the way it works." Her voice was steady and direct. "Don't you see that our lives are the reverse of each other? I think we should drop this subject now before we say things that cannot be taken back. I do not like to see that pugnacious look on your face, Reuben."

Reuben seethed. She was right; she was

always right! Every damn thing she said was true. Why did the truth hurt so much, why did he feel so frustrated? Because, he told himself, he wanted desperately to be all those things for her now, not later, when he was old. You are a boy masquerading as a man; that's what she was telling him. Yes, she loved him, but she'd love him more, maybe would have agreed to marry him if he had all those goddamned traits she so admired in other men.

Find a neutral subject, he ordered himself. Something, anything to get out of this mood. Using all his inner resources, he summoned a light, conversational tone. "If Daniel continues at the Sorbonne, what will we do with Bebe? She'll be lost without him. I'm going to be busy in Bordeaux and so are you."

"I'm waiting for a letter from Bebe's father," Mickey said, and shrugged. "As you know, she's been pestering me to go to England. If Sol gives her permission, I'll send her across the Channel to friends of mine, friends who are strict and won't allow her to get away with any nonsense. She could spend the summer there and come back in late September. While Daniel stays here, we can go back to the château, then attend to business in Bordeaux and return with both Daniel and Bebe under our wing. I feel like a mother hen." She laughed. "Do you feel like a rooster, Reuben?"

Reuben threw back his head and laughed. He felt relieved that Bebe was going to be gone and realized that Mickey had managed to prod him out of his sour mood. "Someday I'm going to tell you about my friend George from the army. Yes, Mickey, I feel very much like a rooster. And may I say you are the most beautiful mother hen I've ever seen."

Mickey giggled. "Spoken like a true gentleman." She reached for his hand, squeezing it slightly. "I want you."

"And I want you," Reuben said with a catch in his throat. "I'll always want you. I'll want to hold you, to sleep next to you, to sit across from you at the dinner table, to make love to you every day of my life. Every day!" His voice was so intense, so passionate, tears welled in Mickey's eyes. He meant it, her heart told her . . . for now.

"And I feel the same. For all the days of my life." That was what he wanted to hear, but not all of what she couldn't help thinking. Her reservations were in her heart.

Reuben caressed her cheek lovingly, his eyes luminous. "It's time to go back. The sun will go down soon. Let's go home, Mickey Fonsard."

"Home. I love the sound of that word. It conjures up so many pleasant things to my mind. Does it to you, Reuben?"

"Yes, but only because it is your home, and you have shown me just what that word could

mean. But I'm a guest, remember? I don't even have a key."

Mickey laughed. "I don't have a key either! You know we never lock our doors. Is it important for you to have a key?"

He thought about it for a moment. "Yes and no. Not having a key makes me feel . . . temporary."

"Then tomorrow you shall have a key, but whatever in the world will you do with it?" Mickey laughed.

"I'll carry it on my watch chain. It's a symbol. Do you understand, Mickey?"

"But of course, *chéri.* There is nothing I do not understand about you."

Sitting down to dinner that evening, Bebe was instantly aware of the smug look on Reuben's face. It meant something was going to happen, something that involved her. Reuben looked smug only when he had the upper hand in something. Whatever the announcement was going to be, she knew she wasn't going to like it. In her apprehension she stirred the food around on her plate, making a mess of the vegetables and potatoes.

His own plate empty now, Reuben eyed Bebe's. She hadn't said much during dinner, but he noticed her hands were trembling. She must sense something is going on, he thought. Suddenly he felt sorry for her and was shocked at the feeling. What was Bebe Rosen

really like underneath all the braggadocio, he wondered. Underneath her pretended shyness, underneath . . . her clothing? The thoughts so startled him that he dropped his fork, blinking in surprise. He could feel Mickey's curious frown from across the table. Could she feel his thoughts? Trying to cover his clumsiness, he addressed Daniel.

"Pierre Faroux sent your reports from the Sorbonne today, Daniel. They are something to be proud of. Mickey and I want you to stay on at the Sorbonne and live here in the house. You can come back to the château in September if you agree. With Faroux's help you'll have a high school diploma — we know you're way beyond that, though. In any case, then we can work on law school. What do you think?"

Daniel looked at Bebe first and read only blankness. His gaze then traveled from Mickey to Reuben. Did they want to be rid of him? It was such a foolish thought, he was sorry it even entered his mind. They wanted only what was best for him. More time at the Sorbonne. God, he'd give his right arm to stay longer, and here they were, offering him the opportunity on a silver platter. He stammered his acceptance, then asked, "What about Jake?" The dog, seated calmly by his side, thumped its tail, knowing intuitively it was being spoken about. "Will he go back to the château with Bebe, or can he stay here?"

"It will be better, *chéri,* if he stays here with you. Bebe will be going to England for the summer to stay with friends of mine. Reuben and I for the most part will be in Bordeaux." At the look on Bebe's face Mickey said quickly, "Bebe, *chérie,* why are you looking like this? You begged me, pleaded with me, to allow you to go to England. I promised you could go if your father agreed. I expect to hear from him any day now. You look devastated. Please do not tell me now that you have changed your mind, after I've made all the arrangements. Say something, *chérie!*"

Bebe's world rocked. Separated from Daniel and Jake, and from Reuben as well! They didn't want her. It always happened like this. No one wanted her. Well, she couldn't let them know she was aware of their intentions. Later in her room she'd cry all she wanted to. But not now.

"How wonderful!" she croaked, her eyes bright with unshed tears. "I must buy some new clothes. I'll write to all my friends and tell them I'm finally going. How long ago did you write my father? He will agree," she lied. "We talked about it before I came here. Does he know your friends?"

"Why, yes, he does. But I wanted to be sure. You are happy, then?"

"Happy? I'm delighted!" She jumped up from her chair. "If you don't mind, I'd like to be excused, I'm too full to eat dessert." She

beamed a smile around the table as she carefully replaced her chair.

Reuben stared at her as though she'd lost her mind. Daniel gawked, wide-eyed. The girl was one fine actress, he thought. Didn't they see what they'd just done to her? Were they blind? He could feel her pain, her rejection. Abruptly he excused himself and whistled for Jake, then realized the dog had followed Bebe to her room. By now her door would be closed and Jake would be inside on her bed licking at her tears. Goddammit!

In the now-deadly-quiet dining room, Mickey's heart fluttered in her chest. "I have this feeling," she said so quietly Reuben had to lean across the table to hear her, "we just made a terrible mistake." Reuben could only nod his agreement.

But it was too late to change things.

Daniel hesitated a moment before tapping softly on Bebe's door. He thought he could hear muffled sobs from within. Once again he tapped, this time louder, and called softly, "Bebe, it's Daniel. Please open the door."

Bebe muttered something he couldn't quite make out. Without waiting further, he opened the door and closed it behind him. Jake didn't run to him, merely burrowed deeper into the pillows next to Bebe, who looked up at him, tears streaming down her cheeks. Daniel thought her eyes looked like moonstones,

clouded with pain.

"He's nasty, he's mean, and he's hateful! It's all his idea." Daniel didn't have to ask who "he" was. "He wants to be rid of me just like he wants to be rid of you. Don't you care, Daniel? Why do you let him push you around like he does? Don't you have a mind of your own?" Bebe gulped as fresh tears rolled down her cheeks. "He's worse than my father on one of his bad days. I hate him! Mickey didn't . . . Mickey doesn't care. Whatever Reuben wants is fine with her. She's glad to be rid of us, too. I don't want to go to England. I want to go home! We're prisoners!"

"No, we're not," Daniel said, outraged. "You're upset because they didn't discuss your trip, just announced it cold like that at dinner."

"There's a big difference between wanting something and having something shoved in your face. Why can't I stay at the château? *They* have other plans. *They* don't want me around, it's that simple. They don't want you around, either. For God's sake, Daniel, can't you see what they're doing? They're running your life. They could mess you up forever. You just sit there like a ninny pretending you like the whole idea."

Daniel took in a long, deep breath before answering her gently. "But I do like the idea. I love the Sorbonne. Not many Americans get to study there. They're doing me a favor.

I'll be living like a king, being waited on and going to classes. I'll have the library at my fingertips. I might even make some friends. It's good for me." Bebe's disdainful expression pushed him further. "Listen to me, Bebe, I can't let you talk this way about Reuben. He cares about me, I know he does. Everything he's ever done for me has been for my own good. Mickey, too. You have to change your thinking."

"You're a damned fool," Bebe said sourly as she pushed away from his comforting hand. "Take your damn dog and get out of here. I don't need you. I'm sending my father a cable tomorrow. I'm going to tell him what's going on here, too!" Her voice was so defiant and spiteful, Daniel shuddered. "This place is just like Hollywood. It's a damn . . . den of iniquity! What do you think of that?!"

"I think you're upset. What would you do at the château by yourself? It's way out in the country. No, England is definitely the best choice," he said firmly.

"I wish you'd leave, Daniel. I have a headache. I'm sorry . . . I'm sorry you . . . what I mean is, I'm glad you came in to talk to me, but I'm not glad . . . never mind. We're friends, and that's all that matters. We'll always be friends, won't we, Daniel? No matter what happens." Her eyes implored Daniel to agree with her. He swallowed hard, then nodded, and Bebe threw her arms around

him. Jake bounded from the bed, barking and wagging his tail excitedly.

"Let's take Jake for a walk, Daniel."

"Bebe, it's late. . . . Oh, all right," he capitulated. "I'll meet you downstairs."

The fat little puppy of Christmas was now sleek, but still full of energy and mischief. Jake romped ahead of them, skidding to a stop, waiting until they caught up to him and then darting off again.

It was a lovely evening, the star-shot sky boasting a bright full moon. "Nights like this make me feel wicked," Bebe confided.

"Then maybe we should go home," Daniel grumbled. "I wish you'd make up your mind what it is you want. I'd like to see you happy."

"Don't you think I'd like to be happy? I don't even know what it's like. Can you define happiness, Daniel?"

He struggled with the question. Whatever he came up with would have to be good to satisfy Bebe. "I think Mickey and Reuben are happy. They made their own happiness. I guess that's what each of us has to do."

Bebe stopped in her tracks, hands on her hips. Her eyes blazed. "I asked you a simple question, a very simple question, important to me, and what do you do? You throw Reuben and Mickey in my face. No matter what I ask you, you always bring them into it." Her mouth twisted in pain, and she turned her

back to him.

Anger sparked and then flared in Daniel's eyes. Firmly he reached for Bebe's arm and made her face him. "Don't ever say something like that and then turn away. Reuben is my friend, and he will always be my friend. I want you for a friend, too, but I'm sick of the way . . . what the hell is it you want that you're not getting? What is it you expect from everyone?"

"Just shut up, Daniel. Just shut up. I'm going home," she cried, wrenching her arm from his grip. Confused, Jake sat between them, his big brown eyes curious.

"Run away, that's your answer to everything," Daniel said. "As soon as something doesn't go your way, you run and hide. You can't have Reuben. You can't always get what you want. Life isn't always generous. Remember that, Bebe."

Daniel's words had held her, an unwilling captive, just a few steps from where he stood. "I didn't ask for your advice," she replied belligerently, "and none of what you said is true."

With an arrogant toss of her head, she flounced ahead of him, Jake nipping at her heels. Daniel followed behind. He'd had enough of Bebe Rosen for one night. Twice she turned to see if he was following her. Once she stuck her tongue out at him, and

the other time she rolled her eyes heavenward.

True to her word, the following morning Bebe sent a cable to her father. The remainder of the day she was perky and full of smiles. "You'll see, Daniel, my father will put Mickey in her place once and for all and allow me to go home, or else he'll forbid me to go to London."

When the response to her cable arrived three days later, Bebe locked herself in her room and wouldn't come out. Predictably, she refused dinner and wouldn't open the door even to Daniel. Reuben's threats of breaking the door down met with silence. Mickey calmed him and suggested they give her some time to herself.

Bebe Rosen was making a statement.

"This is ridiculous," Mickey said two days later. "The child is starving herself. How am I to explain this to her father? What in the world is wrong with her? I never behaved like this when I was her age. She must be sick!" Her voice was anxious, her face full of concern.

"Bebe won't starve; she's just being a stubborn, obnoxious child. Leave her alone. Obviously she wants to be by herself, and this is her way of telling you she doesn't want to go to England. You can either give in to her or else let her sweat in her room. If you want, I'll take the hinges off the door. It's up to

you," Reuben said, his cold voice belying his true feelings.

"Two days! What must be going through that head of hers. *Mon Dieu!*"

The following afternoon, after returning from his classes at the Sorbonne, Daniel climbed the steps to the second floor and rapped softly on Bebe's door. "Bebe, it's Daniel. Please, may I come in?"

To his utter surprise, the door opened and Bebe stood there, frowning at him. "Well, don't stand there. Come in. You wanted in, didn't you?"

It was such a pretty, soothing room. He could see how she'd be able to stay here indefinitely. The window was open, allowing for the slight spring breeze to lift the sheer curtains in a gentle dance. Then he detected the stale cigarette smoke, two empty wine bottles standing on the end of the dresser, and plates of half-eaten food sitting at the edge of her dressing table. She must have foraged late at night.

"Why are you hiding in here? What happened?"

Bebe wrinkled her nose, then rummaged in a drawer. Only when she handed him the pink cable from her father did he notice the trembling in her hands, the tears forming on her thick lashes.

Daniel unfolded the pink paper. The mes-

sage was so short he found himself blinking in surprise as he read it again out loud.

You are to do what Mickey says, when she says it. Do not give her any trouble.
Much love, Papa.

"You thought he would intervene or allow you to sail home." It was a statement rather than a question.

Bebe nodded miserably. "No one cares about me. Even my own father. It's . . . a conspiracy," she cried, wiping at her tears.

"Maybe it's parental caring," Daniel said in a conciliatory tone.

Bebe's eyes blazed. "He doesn't want me home. Someday, Daniel, you are going to agree with me on something, and that will be the day you shock the bloomers right off my behind. Don't blush, only girls and virgins blush," she retorted irritably.

The ring of heat around Daniel's neck subsided. God, he hated it when she tried to shock him. If he was more worldly, he'd be able to give back as good as he got. Instead, he stood shuffling his feet like some ten-year-old caught doing something wrong.

At last, hesitantly, he sat down on the edge of the bed. "You are in such a hurry to get to tomorrow, you're missing today and yesterday."

"Sometimes," Bebe said sadly, "you just get

tired of trying."

"But if you give up . . . what's left?"

"I don't know. Endless days, parties, sweet . . . little lies. I'm not a fortune-teller, how do I know?" she said defensively. "You're the smart one, you figure it out."

"Bebe, you can be whatever you want to be. You don't have to live that fast life. You have a good start here. Change, make something of yourself. You'll be going home soon enough, and I'll bet you no sooner get home than you'll wish you were back here."

"Sure, Daniel." There was no enthusiasm in the girl's voice.

The following morning Mickey and Bebe left the house early to shop for a new wardrobe. "Whatever you want, within reason," Mickey told the girl with an indulgent smile. In reality, she was so relieved that everything was all right, she would have promised the moon.

When they returned, loaded down with boxes of every size and shape, Bebe's face glowed. Reuben had to admit that spending money, regardless of the amount, made her radiant, so spontaneous and happy it was hard not to fall prey to her charm.

Bebe Rosen operated on the give-to-Bebe-and-Bebe-gets system: give her what she wanted, and she would give you what you thought you wanted. Bebe always seemed to win, one way or another.

CHAPTER THIRTEEN

It was a black, silky night, the heavens shot with millions of tiny diamonds. It was late, and the walk Reuben and Mickey were taking was something she had suggested just as they were about to go upstairs. Reuben didn't mind, he thought it rather romantic. A perfect prelude, really, to their lovemaking. For hours he'd thought of nothing but Mickey, and now that he was walking alongside her, holding her hand, he felt closer to her than if they were in bed next to each other. Less is sometimes more, Mickey was fond of saying, and he believed it. Tonight was a perfect example.

"I think Bebe is settled, at least for now. We had a wonderful day today, Reuben. There were times when she even turned down something I wanted to buy for her. She'd say she didn't need it or could make do with what she had. For a little while, when she was being particularly loving, I felt like I had a daughter. It was a very nice feeling. . . . I

can feel you frowning, darling. What is it? Still the animosity with Bebe, eh? Well, I can't say I blame you. I know how difficult it's been for you, poor darling. When Bebe sees you sweat, that's when she moves in. I think sometimes it's a question of power."

"We spend too much damn time worrying about Bebe. If we aren't worrying about her, we're talking about her. She's with us physically or mentally twenty-four hours a day," Reuben groused. "I can't wait till she leaves."

Mickey squeezed his hand. "She's a child, *chéri*. We've gone over this so many times already."

"Even Daniel is fed up with her. So can we please talk about something else?"

"What would you like to talk about?" Mickey asked huskily.

"My favorite topic of conversation is you . . . us . . . but I need to know more about the wine industry if I'm to make your world mine."

Mickey was aghast. "You want to talk about wine on a beautiful night like this! You can't have everything yesterday, Reuben. When my husband died, he still didn't know all there was to know of the grape. Every day it is something new. My people will have to teach you, I will make sure of that." And then when you learn all there is to learn, you will decide to go back to America, she said to herself. "It could take years, *chéri*. Years!" she heard

herself say.

Reuben stopped and drew her to him, staring down into her eyes. "I have all the time in the world, my whole life. I want to spend it here with you." His voice was so intense, so passionate, Mickey drew back in surprise.

"But your country . . . you are an American. In time you will come to miss all you left behind."

"I can always go back to visit. There's nothing there for me. Why do you keep throwing obstacles at me? Do you want me to get angry and leave?"

Mickey's heart fluttered. "No, *chéri,* that is not what I want at all. When a seed of fear creeps into my mind I must mention it, talk about it. I am a woman," she said simply, as if that explained everything.

Reuben shrugged. This was the way it always ended. If he pursued it, the rest of the evening would be ruined. He knew when to let go.

They walked lazily, their hands entwined and swinging between them. They were in no hurry to get to the end of the long, curving road. Later they would make a mad dash for the house and race up the stairs.

Mickey leaned into him, her mouth open and avid under his. She could feel his shudders — or were they her own?

"This night was made for us," Reuben said against her cheek. "But," he said, a chuckle

in his voice, "I prefer the comfort of a bed with you next to me. Let's see how fast our feet can get us back to the house."

They were breathless when they crept up the stairs to Mickey's room. As they embraced just inside her bedroom door, Reuben thought his heart would burst with happiness. Mickey wanted him. She loved him. Nothing in his life up to now, nothing to come, could ever take away or replace this feeling. To be loved by this wonderful, passionate woman was the single most important thing in the world. Money, power, worldly goods, all were simple additions to fulfillment in life. For without Mickey, what did they all matter?

Reuben kissed her, but he knew once would never be enough for him. He wanted to cover her body with his lips, to hear her cry out in pleasure, to hear her beg for more. She pressed against him now, urging his passion, but he pulled free and led her to the bed. They shed their clothing, their eyes never wavering from each other. When they slipped between the satin sheets, their sighs mingled, soft and expectant.

In one graceful motion she turned and shifted closer so that his hands could circle the soft mounds of her breasts. His palms cupped them, fingers teasing until their crests became hard and thrusting.

Desire rode him like a wild stallion as she

moaned. Unbearable, sweet pain was all he could feel. She teased him then, her mouth against his, her tongue darting in and out, seeking the warm, moist recesses, lingering until it was she who cried out. She was on top of him now, warm and insistent as she covered his face with kisses, nuzzling his neck, nibbling his ears. Rumbling sounds of pleasure from deep in his chest drove her on.

"Open your eyes," Reuben said, pulling back from her. "Look at us." She glanced down at their joining and saw him hard and glistening before he drew her close again. She smiled in the near darkness and knew there were tears on her cheeks, and on Reuben's as well. This perfect moment, this perfect joining, waiting for release was so exquisite she thought she couldn't bear it another second.

Her body was feverish as she pressed against him, demanding that he release her from the exquisite, piercing torture. He was murmuring into the silky curve of her throat, words he'd said before and words he'd say again, their secret words, full of love and promise.

Reuben reached to encircle her waist. Tightening his hold, he rolled her over to tower above her, his chiseled face staring down into her passion-blind eyes. She was writhing against him now; soft, sensual whimpers of pleasure escaped from her lips. Her breath came in tiny gasps at each slow

downward thrust. Pearls of sweat dotted his brow, dropped to his lashes and then onto her face. She struggled to see him clearly, but in the end surrendered to the pleasure he was giving her.

They cried out their ecstasy in unison, their hunger for each other appeased . . . for the moment.

Reuben's last conscious thought before falling into a deep sleep was that he could allow nothing to destroy this happiness.

Reuben woke to the quiet sounds of the night. He lay quietly, savoring the feel of Mickey's warm thigh against his. He loved waking up like this, knowing if he wanted to, he could rouse her from sleep and do whatever pleased him. She was always a willing partner, more often than not initiating their lovemaking in the middle of the night or early morning, right before he left for his own bed.

He didn't want to go back to his own room. He wanted to lie there and do nothing but think about everything and nothing.

If Mickey would just give him his way, he knew he could learn the wine business and make hers the best in all of France. Oh, she said she was giving him all the leeway he needed, but he wasn't so sure. She was always there, looking over his shoulder, and in a way he couldn't blame her. The only things he had going for him were his ambition to make

a success of his efforts — and youth. He remembered how Mickey had frowned when he'd asked her to consider the wine catalog he wanted to draw up. "We have to show our wares," he'd insisted. "No one buys a pig in a poke." He'd almost had her convinced when he'd mentioned brandies and cognac. Then her frown had returned, deeper. For the time being, he'd let that alone, but he knew he would get back to it.

Château Fonsard consisted of 62 hectares, or 155 acres, of vineyards. Château Michelene, the second vineyard, had been given to Mickey by her husband on their wedding day. She had explained that it was a long-standing tradition for the owner to join his name to the established title of the property. Although Fonsard was larger, both vineyards were prosperous.

The routine at the vineyards, Reuben found, was always the same. The grapes were picked, destalked, and crushed. Then nature took over, but always under constant watch.

He understood the time-honored technique; the wine was made in oak vats, *cuvier,* and allowed to ferment for ten days before it was run off the skins; then the skins were pressed. If the weather was too hot and the fermentation generated too much heat, it had to be cooled by watering down the *cuves* with cool water or, in an emergency, with blocks of ice.

From the *cuvier* the wine was pumped into another vat made of cement, to sit for two weeks before it was *débourbé* — pumped of its heaviest sediment into another cask; then it spent the winter in this particular cask, going through its secondary, or malolactic, fermentation, which rid it of malic acid, making it taste less harsh. Usually a secondary fermentation did not start until March, when the sap rose in the vines, In February the wine was pumped into hogsheads in the first-year *chai*. It stayed in the first-year *chai* for a full twelve months, where it was constantly topped up and occasionally racked into a fresh vat, in some years fermenting slightly on through summer.

The following year it was moved into the second-year *chai,* where it was bunged tight and left to mature for two years, after which it was ready for bottling.

It all seemed simple enough. Reuben was certain he could master it if he put his mind to it. Maybe he was making a mistake in wanting to take over the operation of the two wineries. If he concentrated just on selling and shipping the finest of both vineyards, that might be enough to keep him busy night and day. Still, how could he do justice to selling and shipping if he didn't understand the entire process? Mickey had shared the basics with him, but she admitted she still didn't know everything, and often she had to rely

on the opinions of those in her employ who were more experienced. *"Chéri,"* she'd said, "I have more than enough money to last me the rest of my life. I can, after all, sleep in only one bed, eat off one table, drive one motor car, and buy just so many clothes. It is not really important for me to make the vineyards more productive than they already are. I enjoy my work, but I refuse to be a slave to a business. But if you are happy doing this, we will make some sort of monetary arrangement that is profitable to both of us." He'd let it drop but hadn't given up. He'd pored over books, watched the workers at Château Fonsard, and studied the vines until he got dizzy.

Reuben could feel his shoulders start to tighten. This always happened when he got deeply engrossed in all he had to learn — so much, in fact, he worried that he might not be up to it. Other times he was so confident he thought he would explode with all he was absorbing.

Mickey woke, instantly aware that Reuben was wide awake. What was he thinking, she wondered. And why hadn't he nuzzled her neck the way he usually did when he woke in the middle of the night? She opened one eyelid to peer at the clock on the little table by her bed. It was five minutes past four.

"Is something wrong, Reuben?" she asked quietly.

"No. I don't know why I woke up. I wasn't dreaming. I was just lying here thinking about your vineyards and how much there is to learn. You looked so peaceful, I didn't want to disturb you."

"I don't mind." She rose on one elbow, her index finger trailing along his cheek. "Would you like to talk about it, *chéri*? Although I think on this subject you have already picked my brain clean."

Reuben laughed, a rueful sound. "I realize I'm not going to be out there pruning the vines and picking the grapes, but I should know . . . I want to know all I can learn about wine." He hunkered down, eager to share his thoughts with her. "For instance, if grapes are picked too early, they give more acid wine, right?" He didn't wait for her answer. "Then they need more time to mature in the cask. There are some people who like the oak flavor and some who don't. It's like you're damned if you do and damned if you don't. Why would someone pick the grapes too early?" Again he hurried on. "Mickey, your château manager told me that the grapes are picked when they get sticky. Surely there must be a better way to judge the ripeness than stickiness."

"That's how Jacques did it. My managers are just doing what he did. If you can come up with a better way, I'm sure they'll be

amenable. The vines and the grapes are their life.

"My husband told me fifty years ago he saw men cry and kill themselves because of the phylloxera insect. It lives in the roots of the vine and kills it. Almost all the European vineyards were destroyed. The vintners had to pull each vine and replace it with a clean new cutting. It was a terrible time and one he said he'd never forget. We all talk about it and worry that it could happen again. We must be careful so the parent plant stays healthy. Tell me, did you like the winemaker's calendar I made up for you?"

Reuben laughed. "Yes, and I know why you did it."

"Oh, and why is that?" Mickey drawled lazily.

"You wanted me to see how time-consuming the business is and how busy I'll be."

"You are always one step ahead of me. Jacques made one up for me after we were first married. Again, you see, I was forever complaining that I was left alone. He made little drawings to show me how complex the work was. Even though I was young I understood. And what do you remember of the calendar?"

Reuben buried his face in her hair and repeated the litany of the wine grower. "January, pruning starts on St. Vincent's Day. Bar-

rels of new wine must be kept full to the top and their bungs wiped every day with solution. If the weather is dry, the wine can be bottled."

Mickey's tongue flicked out, leaving a trail of moistness down Reuben's chest. Her fingers traced patterns around his chest. She smiled in the gray darkness when he groaned.

"February," he continued, to her surprise, "is for pruning and taking the cuttings for grafting. You make grafts onto woodstock and put them in sand indoors. If there is fine weather and a new moon and a north wind, you can start racking the new wine into clean barrels to clear it. You have to assemble the new wine in a vat to equalize the casks."

"I don't care," Mickey said throatily. "Please, Reuben, you are not going to go through the other ten months, are you? I believe you. The winemaker's calendar was just my little joke. If you insist, I will stuff my fingers in my ears. I want to do other things."

Reuben laughed, a secretive little sound in the darkness. "Are you saying I'm boring you?"

"That's exactly what I'm saying!"

"You are a brazen hussy, and I love you very much."

"Show me how much," Mickey whispered in his ear. "And don't ever mention the winemaker's calendar in bed again. Swear to me!"

He did. He wouldn't. He swore.

Reuben did not go back to his own bed that morning. He supposed it was an act of defiance on his part, and he didn't care. He wanted to wake up next to Mickey, wanted to start the day beside her. He took in the newborn sun shooting across the room, bathing the bed in warm radiant lights. It felt fresh and clean. A new day. A bright new day.

"Come here, kiss me good-morning," Mickey demanded. She looked around her. "You didn't go to your own bed! Do you realize this is the first time we woke together to face the new day? Oh, Reuben, I'm so happy. . . . Reuben, I think it is time to go to Bordeaux. I must see that all is well there."

Reuben smiled. "I'm all for it . . . whatever you say," he agreed. "When do you want to leave?

"Such impatience," Mickey said languidly. "Will tomorrow morning be all right with you? Shall we all go in the car?"

"Absolutely. We'll have a jolly trip if Bebe behaves herself." He rolled over until he was on top of Mickey, bracing himself with the palms of his hands. "When," he whispered, "are you going to wear that black . . . what do you call that thing that holds up your stockings?"

Mickey smiled wickedly. "You mean my garter belt?"

"Yes. It drives me . . . crazy."

"Then I will wear it every day. You should have said something. What is your feeling about black stockings?" she purred in his ear.

Reuben growled, then rolled off her when he heard Daniel walk by the room, whistling. Bebe's laughter, as she joined him at the top of the stairs, wafted through the door. Reuben lost his erection immediately.

As he dressed he began to mutter. "May is when the frost danger is at its height. Work the soil a second time and every ten days remove the suckers so the sap can rise. Watch for mildew. . . . Start the second racking off the lees into clean bar—"

"Reuben! That is enough. I don't want to hear anymore!" Mickey cried, exasperated.

Reuben sighed and shook his head. "You give me a present, and when I try to show you how much I appreciate it, you tell me you don't want to hear it. I want to prove that I take your gift seriously."

"Then allow me," Mickey drawled. "June is when the vines flower and we thin the roots and tie the best ones to wires. The casks have to be checked daily for evaporation because warm weather accelerates the evaporation. July —"

"All right, all right." Reuben turned to her questioningly. "Tell me, why isn't Château Michelene as prosperous as Château Fonsard?"

"In the beginning, as I said, it was a plaything. Now it yields quite a bit of wine, some better than Fonsard, as a matter of fact. Remember, it is not as large, there are not as many workers . . . a lot of reasons, Reuben."

"I think I can make it the best in all of France. Would you like that?"

Mickey thought about it. "It isn't important to me. If it stays the way it is, that would be fine. If it will make you happy to expand it, to promote Michelene wines, then I am, as you say, all for it!"

Daniel waved good-bye to the travelers. At the last second, Bebe ran back to throw her arms around him. "I'm going to miss you. I'm glad you're going to keep Jake here. Talk to him about me so he doesn't forget me, okay?"

"I promise. Bebe, please, don't cause any trouble at the château. It's only a month. Be as nice to Mickey and Reuben as you are to me. I want your promise."

Bebe stared at him for a long time. "I can't promise, Daniel. You're my friend, and that makes a difference."

Last farewells and hugs and kisses were given with tear-filled eyes. Everyone waved frantically as the car took off, their voices fading as the space between them and Daniel widened. For a long time he stood in the

driveway, watching until the car was out of
sight.

CHAPTER FOURTEEN

Reuben ground the Citroën to a halt in front of the château. "Home!" he exclaimed. "You timed this just right, Mickey. I've never seen such a kaleidoscope of color." He breathed deeply of the crisp country air.

"We have had the honor of witnessing two springs," Mickey said happily. "Spring comes early to Paris and late to the country. We had the best of both. I'm glad you approve."

"I don't much like flowers," Bebe said as she began to pull bags from the car.

Here we go again, Reuben thought to himself. We're not even home a minute and she's complaining already.

"Oh, and why is that, *chérie?*" Mickey said, joining her. "I thought everyone loved flowers."

"There were so many at my . . . all kinds, all colors, the room was sickening." She plucked at a hatbox, eyes averted. Mickey stared at her, waiting. "My mother's funeral," she blurted out.

Mickey put her arm around the girl's shoulder. "I'm sorry, *chérie,* I didn't realize." She looked over at Reuben and saw his jaw tighten.

He was watching Bebe as she gathered her packages together. He couldn't be sure, but he thought he saw tears glistening in her eyes. Suddenly she caught him staring at her and stopped what she was doing, her vulnerability unmasked. As she stood there, open and helpless, Reuben thought at that instant she was one of the loveliest girls he had ever seen. His hand faltered, the bag slipping from his grasp. In that same instant he knew Bebe had read what was in his eyes, and he cursed loudly to cover his confusion. For once she didn't laugh or grimace, but as she turned he saw a lone tear slide down her cheek. So, Bebe Rosen did have feelings after all, she could hurt like everyone else. "I'll be damned," he muttered.

A butterfly flitted overhead, drawing his attention. For some unexplained reason, he found himself wishing he hadn't seen the vulnerable side of Bebe Rosen, for it made her a person now like Daniel and Mickey. He shoved his newfound knowledge onto a shelf at the back of his mind. One day it might prove useful.

Bebe spent the next few hours alone in her room. She had thought it would be nice back

at the château, but now she wasn't so sure. It was obvious that Mickey didn't want her around. If only Daniel were here to talk to. If he were here, would she tell him how her heart had pounded as Reuben looked at her . . . as a man looked at a woman? She studied herself in the mirror to recapture what he might have seen — wondered how she had stood and what expression was on her face to make him almost drop his bag. Both Mickey and Reuben had fallen for her flower story. She had used it on several occasions, and it always worked. Reuben had responded very well to it. . . . She giggled. That's why Mickey was pushing her out. Would Daniel believe her if she told him about Reuben's look? That for a moment his eyes had beheld someone other than Mickey? She hadn't been able to believe it herself. No, she wouldn't have said anything to Daniel. This was something she could hug to herself, and it was better than any secret. She smiled at her reflection in the mirror.

Mickey felt the next days pass with tremendous discomfort. The three of them were thrown together incessantly. Bebe, playing the forlorn only child without Daniel, accompanied them everywhere. Reuben became more and more sullen and then began snapping at everyone. Mickey tried keeping it all inside, but the situation was becoming impos-

sible. She wouldn't dream of taking school away from Daniel, but without him there to balance out the foursome, everything was tense, like sitting on a powder keg liable to explode at any moment. Something had to give . . . and soon.

Bebe couldn't help noticing that Reuben was watching her every step with more than his usual suspicion, and that Mickey looked and acted as if she were waiting for a bomb to go off. The more he pushed at her, the angrier she got. And when she was angry she plotted ways to get back at him. All she needed was an opportunity. Why disappoint them? She was scheduled to leave for Paris in another few days and then on to England. She'd leave them with something to chew on. . . .

Mickey was saying something, but not to her. Although they had just sat down to breakfast, something was going on between Mickey and Reuben: the air was charged with electricity. Bebe withdrew quietly, but her curiosity was piqued. Shamelessly she stood just outside the dining room door, listening.

"What do you mean, you have to go to Dijon tomorrow?" Reuben asked angrily.

"I don't like it any better than you do, but I must. My bankers have graciously agreed to meet me halfway so I don't have to make the trip all the way to Paris. I'll only be gone overnight," Mickey said in a conciliatory tone.

"If you knew you had to do this, you should have planned to take Bebe. Or," he continued coldly, "you should have said you'd go all the way to Paris, and taken her along. I can't go with you because I have to see to the second racking of the lees into the barrels. You knew we were right in the middle of it. I should already be there, but since you've made these arrangements, what am I to do? You're taking the car, and Bordeaux is not exactly on the way to Dijon."

"*Chéri,* I heard from the lawyers only this morning. Please try to understand."

"I don't want you to make the trip by yourself. I care what happens to you, and you drive like a . . . wild woman!"

"A wild woman, is it?" Mickey said, aghast. "You never complained before. Why now, all of a sudden?"

Reuben admitted to himself that he didn't know the answer to her question, or even if that was the issue. Was he upset because he felt this particular banker was going to try and talk her out of expanding Château Michelene? Would the banker refer to him as a gigolo? Without another word, he turned and stomped out of the house, slamming the door behind him.

At the sound of the door rattling on its hinges, Mickey stormed up the steps, her face a mask of fury. He had no right: he had no goddamn right to act that way! After all, she

was going to Dijon because of him. Reuben Tarz was just as selfish as Bebe Rosen.

Mickey ran into her room, slamming the door behind her. She threw herself on the bed and let the tears flow. How could he behave like this after all she'd done? Selfish, miserable man. They were all alike. Why had she thought him different?

Downstairs, Bebe walked from room to room, a smile on her face.

Dinner that evening was a total disaster. Reuben and Mickey glared at each other across the table, neither of them touching their food. Bebe ate everything and took a second helping of meat and potatoes. After she had finished she excused herself, but neither Mickey nor Reuben so much as acknowledged her existence. She went to her room, propped herself in bed with a book, and kept her eyes on the door she'd left ajar. An hour later Mickey went to her own room and slammed the door. In the quiet Bebe heard the bolt shoot home. Thirty minutes later Reuben's door closed quietly. Bebe strained to listen, and seconds later his bolt shot home. She smiled. They were playing the game no one won. She should know, she played it often enough.

She sat up all night listening for the sound of a footstep. Finally she dozed off a little before dawn but was up instantly when she

heard Mickey's heels clicking on the wooden floor outside her room.

Wearing the same clothes she'd worn the day before, Bebe left her room after a sketchy hair brushing and a quick dab at her face with a damp washcloth. She joined her aunt at breakfast and kept up the same cheerful commentary as the night before. She looked ghastly, Bebe thought, appraising Mickey's appearance. Her eyes were puffy, and the circles under them were like smudges of carbon. Her mouth was set into grim tight lines; little wrinkles fanning out around them gave her a hard, barmaid look.

Mickey tapped her fingers on the table impatiently, getting angrier by the moment. Reuben knew she wanted to leave by eight-thirty; his absence was inexcusable. She seethed inwardly and felt the urge to slap the chattering Bebe. But, she did her best to hold her temper in check. After all, none of this was Bebe's doing — there was no use blaming her. Her lapel watch told her it was now twenty minutes to nine. Eh, *bien* — she wouldn't give Reuben the satisfaction of waiting a moment longer. She swallowed the last of her coffee, grimacing as she tasted the bitter dregs.

"Have a pleasant day, Bebe," she smiled, touching the girl's hair as she passed her chair. "I will see you tomorrow."

Mickey's steps lagged as she walked to the

barn. He still had time to come down and apologize. Five minutes later, when there was still no sign of him, she pressed the gas pedal to the floor and roared out of the barn and down the long driveway to the road. Chickens scattered and birds took sanctuary in the trees. "Go to the devil!" Mickey spat angrily. "And stay there!"

Reuben stood by the window, a sullen look on his face, his pocket watch open on the time. He could go down now . . . he should go down now. He should apologize to Mickey before she left. It was all his fault, and he didn't even know how it had happened. One minute they were talking, he was merely complaining, saying how he felt, something Mickey always encouraged him to do . . . and then . . . then they were like two dogs fighting it out in the center of a ring. There had been no winner. If anything, he felt like a loser. He was a cad. A man would have pocketed his pride and apologized.

The sound of the Citroën hurling out of the barn made him draw back from the window. As the powerful car careened down the drive, he jerked open the window . . . but it was too late. He took the stairway running, but when he pushed through the front doors she was already gone, a cloud of dust in her wake.

Reuben tortured himself, going over and over what he should have done. What if she

didn't come back? What if she told him to leave when she did come back? She could do that, he realized. She could do a lot of things. . . .

He paced like an angry bull, called himself every name in the book and then some: he was a low-down dirty louse, an insensitive clod. Never in all the time he'd been with her had she raised her voice in anger, until last night. That meant she was very, very angry at him.

Something skittered around in his stomach and worked its way to his chest. He gave it a name: fear. He hadn't been afraid when he'd crouched in the trenches or charged up the line. He'd been green and stupid, not believing in death, his or Daniel's. Invincible, he'd decided when he set foot on French soil. But he didn't feel invincible now: he felt vulnerable, the way Bebe had looked the day they'd returned to the château from Paris. He didn't like the feeling, and he didn't like the thought. Worse yet, he didn't like the comparison to Bebe. At that moment he turned and saw her watching him from the window. Her smiling face drove him over the edge.

Every problem that ever rode his broad shoulders, either real or imaginary, became Bebe's fault. At that moment he began to plot ways to abuse her, to make her pay for what he was going through. His fury gained intensity as he found himself racing back up to his

room. Now he was furious with himself, unreasonably so. Slamming the door behind him, he began to storm and stomp about the room. One long arm swept across his dresser; brush, comb, and hand mirror sailed in the air and crashed to the floor. He lashed out with his foot, scattering shards of silvered glass everywhere. Next he made for the bed and ripped at the bedclothes. His fist shot out, slamming into the headboard over his bed. Red-hot streaks of pain coursed through him. Again he kicked out, this time at the dresser — and howled his outrage as pain rushed up his leg into his groin. Until that moment he hadn't been aware he was barefoot.

His head began to pound as he watched himself destroying his aunt's tenement apartment. He would get those little bastards of hers back for going through his meager belongings. He'd had enough of their snooping around in the one drawer he called his. He was sick of the crowded rooms and the stench of cabbage cooking on her stove. He picked up the boiling pot and smashed it against the wall, splattering the smelly mess across the tiny kitchen. He felt great, powerful.

Reuben held his aching head between two clenched fists and broke into a cold sweat. What was he doing? Horrified, he stared at the path of destruction his uncontrolled anger had wrought. His thoughts came together,

and he began to tremble. He saw himself standing outside the tenement where he had lived with his aunt, his belongings at his feet. Thrown out like garbage on the street. His fear was palpable — it touched him with angry hands, it screamed in his ears. . . . He sat down on the floor in what just a few minutes before had been his own private room in his own private paradise and looked around him. What now?

Bebe sat in her room listening to Reuben's rampage. Each sound he made echoed to her through the heavy walls.

Mickey had walked out on him. Reuben Tarz was angry. A lover's quarrel. Now the silly bet she'd made with Daniel was beginning to look like a sure thing. All it would take was a little planning. . . . She danced around the room, a smile on her face. "Reuben Tarz, you are almost mine, and you lose, Daniel. . . ." She chanted the words over and over until she started to believe they were fact. "You, Bebe Rosen," she said, addressing her image in the windowpane, "have a new role to play. This performance will be worthy of Clovis Ames." She giggled with anticipation. "Mine, all mine."

What about her aunt? If she did succeed in her little plan, where would that leave Mickey? "Back in Montmartre, where she belongs," she whispered. "If she isn't woman

enough to hold him, it's not my problem." *That's not fair,* her conscience prodded. "It is so fair; she's had him long enough. It's my turn now. In a week's time she'll find someone else to lavish her affections on. Besides, she's too old for Reuben. She can spend all her time now running her wine business. Maybe she'll pickle herself in one of the vats." Again her conscience prodded her. *You'll break her heart. She loves Reuben, you know that; you've seen what they have together. She could even die from her broken heart.* Bebe's eyes squinted into small hard beads. "Hogwash! What about my heart? Look, if Reuben is truly in love with her, nothing I do can entice him. All the plans, all the bets in the world, won't make a difference. But if he doesn't truly love her, he'll fall into my trap. All is fair in love and war. If you are my conscience, you can shut up now. It's too late for you to interfere, anyway."

Bebe was sitting in the dining room having her second cup of coffee when Reuben entered the room, limping badly, his right hand swathed in a pillowcase. She did her best to look concerned.

"Let me get you some coffee. . . . Do you want anything to eat? You look mean enough to eat a bear. Ooops, sorry. Would you care to tell me what happened, or is it a secret?"

"No, I wouldn't care to tell you anything!"

he yelled. "And I'll get my own coffee." A muscle at the left side of his face was twitching.

Bebe sat back down and cupped both hands around her coffee cup, watching out of the corner of her eye as he tried to pour coffee with his left hand. When the pot started to wobble, he set it down quickly and carried his cup to the table. He laced the coffee with sugar and thick cream, then stirred it and lifted the cup to his lips. When he burned his tongue on the hot liquid, he swore savagely.

Bebe laughed. "I could have told you it was scalding hot, but you wouldn't have believed me. You never listen to me," she said in a wounded tone of voice. "I'm glad you burned your tongue. You deserved it. Too bad it wasn't worse."

She had to be a goddamned mind reader. That's exactly how he felt. He wondered how many bones he'd broken in his hand and in his foot: he deserved every one of them. When he was small his mother used to kiss his little injuries, and they almost always felt better immediately. He looked across the table at Bebe, wondering if her mother had ever kissed her injuries. He didn't mean to voice the thought, but once he started to he couldn't take the words back.

"Sometimes. Usually Eli was the one who got hurt. I'd offer to kiss your hand, but I think it's more serious than you think. I

noticed you were limping. I heard you upstairs, so I know you were kicking and knocking about. If you like, I'll ride you to the village on the big bicycle. You really should see a doctor."

"I didn't ask for your advice. I asked you a question and I'm sorry now that I did. I tripped. I wasn't knocking things about," he lied.

Bebe shrugged. "Suit yourself. If it makes you feel better to lie, then lie, I don't care. What I do know is if your hand starts to swell, you have broken bones. I saw enough of my brother's to know. I think he broke every bone in his body at one time or another."

"Thanks for sharing that with me," Reuben muttered.

Bebe blinked. "You are an absolute, total bastard. What my aunt sees in you is beyond me. You're like something that crawled out from under a rock."

"Didn't you crawl out from the rock next to mine?" Reuben drawled.

Bebe stared at him, unable to come up with a suitable response.

"What's the matter? Cat got your tongue, little girl? If you'll excuse me, I have things to do."

Bebe felt herself rise from her seat as though someone were pulling her on strings. Brazenly she walked to the other side of the table and leaned against it, touching her thigh

to his hand as it rested on the arm of his chair. He pulled it away as if he had been burned.

"Sure you do," Bebe said casually, smiling. "I'm sure you have a list of things you think you should be doing so Aunt Mickey will feel she's getting her money's worth." This time she was careful to avoid using the word gigolo, and she stood her ground when Reuben's eyes darkened. He rose and then sat back down in his chair. The look on his face was unfathomable. She crept out of the dining room and hid behind the door to see what he would do next.

In less than a minute Reuben pounded down the steps to the wine cellar. If nothing else, he could drink enough wine to dull the pain he was feeling and the rage and confusion of his reactions to Bebe.

By noon Bebe was so frustrated and bored she ventured as far down as the landing on the cellar steps to see what Reuben was up to. That was her limit, because a little farther down the cellar became a dark, dim hole filled with wine racks and the smells of sweat, mold, and sour wine. She sat down and wrinkled her nose as she tried to adjust her eyes to the semidarkness. She knew there were rats down there and other things that crawled and slithered. It was quiet, too quiet. Was it possible Reuben had already come up

the stairs? Scratchy noises, thin little sounds with barely audible squeaks, made her shiver. Vermin! She must be out of her mind to sit here like this. Then she heard the sound of a cork popping. Reuben — he must be drinking, she realized. What kind of drunk was he? She'd seen all kinds — happy drunks, mean ones, crazy drunks, and drunks that fell on their faces. For a moment she almost felt sorry for him, but the moment passed quickly. She turned and made her way back up the steps to her room. Reuben Tarz could drink himself into oblivion for all she cared. She hoped he fell asleep and the rats nibbled on his flesh.

Her room was tidy, everything in its place prior to her departure. It was a nice room, comfortable, but not nearly as pretty and filled with frills as the one she'd had in Paris. She should return the books she'd borrowed from the library. She should put away her writing materials; all her letters to friends in California were finished and waiting to be posted. Her bed was made, something Mickey insisted each of them do. The only thing she had to look forward to in the long day was lunch, dinner, and maybe a solitary walk. Lord, how she missed Daniel and Jake! She was truly alone with nothing to do. "I can't read another book!" she cried aloud. "I don't want to read another book!"

A bath! Full of bubbles. Long and luxuri-

ous. Perhaps a glass of wine in the tub like they did in films. Clovis Ames always did that. A beautiful crystal glass full of sparkling champagne. It was Clovis's trademark. The "Champagne Girl," they called her. She wondered if people really believed Clovis was naked in those tubs. Clovis was her father's biggest star, and it had been his idea to name her the Champagne Girl and put her in a bathtub full of bubbles in every film she made. Everyone, said the tabloids, wanted to catch a glimpse of Clovis's huge breasts. The set would always be cleared before she made her exit to keep up the curiosity. Once, enjoying the special privileges of the owner's daughter, she'd been allowed on the set during the filming of a bathtub scene. When Clovis stepped from the tub, bubbles clinging to her flesh-colored body suit, Bebe had gasped. She'd really thought the actress was naked under the bubbles.

Clovis Ames was decadent and wicked, or so everyone thought. Bebe thought her the most glamorous, most beautiful woman in the world. Clovis had shown her how to make the most of her eyes with outrageous blue shadow and how to paint her cheeks so there appeared to be a hollow underneath. Shiny lip salve, she said, was a must. "Dress like you want every man to attack you, and they'll stay away in droves but hunger for you . . . at a distance," Clovis had advised. "For some

reason men always want what they can't have. It's better to have men hunger and lust after you from a distance while you watch. This way you can take your time picking and choosing. It's also better than being pawed and grappled with." Bebe followed her advice right down to the letter. That's why she was still a virgin while most of her friends were sleeping around or having unwanted babies.

It was the middle of the afternoon when she decided to take her walk. A long bubble bath and her glass of champagne would be better appreciated upon her return, when she was tired.

Reuben sat on a smelly, empty wine barrel, his legs stretched out in front of him. Empty wine bottles stood at attention, and he saluted them cockily. He'd consumed a lot of wine, but he didn't think he was drunk. He should be drunk. His thinking seemed clear, and he felt absolutely nothing. Not anger, not love, not concern, not anything. Maybe he was dead and didn't know it. He pinched his thigh. Nope, still living.

He struggled to remember why he was here. Something about the wines and Mickey's trip. He rubbed at his eyes. Maybe it was the calendar. He'd been so impressed with himself when he'd learned it almost word for word — and then she hadn't wanted to hear it. Women! She'd said the damn thing was a

joke. She probably thought he was a joke, too. If Daniel were here, he would care. Daniel would want to know when the grapes turned black, and he'd want to know when it was time to pick them, too. Time? For the life of him he couldn't remember when vintage was, the most important thing on the calendar.

Reuben fumbled for the wine bottle and took a swig. "What you do is you pick the goddamn grapes when they're ripe!" He laughed, rocking back and forth on the barrel. And she thought he needed a calendar!

He flipped out his pocket watch with steady hands. God, he'd been down here for ages! For the first time since entering this dark hole he became aware of the smell. It would be in his clothes, his hair, all over. He needed fresh air, but more than fresh air he needed Mickey. Thoughts of Mickey were so devastating he slid off the barrel. He grabbed two wine bottles and staggered to his feet. He had to get out of this stink hole and breathe some fresh air.

The house was quiet, the kind of quiet that shrouds death. He walked to the kitchen and fixed the housekeeper with a steely-eyed look. "Who died?" he demanded. The old woman muttered something and ran for the pantry. Reuben laughed. Well, at least she was alive.

"Bebe!" he shouted. The wine bottles clanking against one another, he made his way

around the first floor of the château, calling Bebe's name.

A warm spring breeze wafted through the open windows. It felt good, so good he decided to stay. Just before he fell asleep on one of the deep, overstuffed chairs, he ran over the day's events in his mind. He blamed Bebe for Mickey's leaving, and he blamed Bebe for his anger and his present condition.

It was dusk when Bebe walked into the kitchen. She was tired. She'd eat and then take the bubble bath she'd been looking forward to. "Nanette, is Reuben here?" she asked.

The old lady jerked her head in the direction of the library. "He's crazy, that one."

Bebe merely shrugged and sat down at the table. She was starved; the long walk had really given her an appetite.

She topped off her dinner with an enormous piece of cherry pie and then stood up. "Is there any champagne up here?" she asked the old cook.

The woman pointed to the little room off the pantry that housed several wine racks stretched across one wall. Bebe made her selection from the cold box, not knowing if it was a wise one or not. It didn't really matter, she was going to have only one glass, and she was playing a role. She was pickier in choosing just the right wineglass. Something long-stemmed and sparkling. Something to make

her feel elegant and sophisticated.

She tiptoed into the library and almost laughed at the way Reuben was sprawled across the divan. He was snoring. "Too bad your amour can't see how handsome you look now," she whispered. But she couldn't help moving closer to gaze down at him and study the planes of his face, the way his hair curled, how his hands were constructed. Reluctantly, she left the room for her own.

The rest of the evening stretched ahead of her. How long could she sit in a bathtub? And when she was finished, what could she do? Read another goddamn book, she supposed. Or, she could . . . she'd been dying to go through Mickey's things, try on some of her elegant dresses and furs. Her jewelry, her perfume. It would lend credence to the role she was playing. Of course Mickey was bigger than she was, but that was why they'd invented safety pins. No one would see her, so it didn't really matter. Her mood brightened when she realized there was one person who would: Reuben. When he woke up he would find himself alone with a young and very beautiful woman. This was the first time she could remember ever being alone with him for an evening. She almost flew into the bathroom.

First she had to find the bath salts Mickey used, the lavender-scented ones. She'd noticed several spare bottles in the cupboard

outside the bathroom. If she touched the ones in the crystal decanter, it would give her away, and this was her little secret. Once she'd rummaged in the attic back home and played dress-up with her mother's clothes. Her father had almost fainted when she'd pranced downstairs in her mother's sequined pumps and satin gown.

The door safely locked behind her, Bebe poured champagne and slid into the fragrant bath. From that point on she was Clovis Ames II. She batted her eyelashes, pouted prettily, raised and stretched one silky leg out of the bubbles, then quickly drew it back to safety. She primped and flirted for the mirror across the room. She made toasts, to the Eiffel Tower, to the Statue of Liberty, to Jake. She made a double toast to Daniel. "To all my good friends, wherever you may be," she said grandly, holding the glass aloft. She hoped she wasn't getting tipsy on one glass of champagne. Once again she raised her glass. "To Reuben Tarz," she intoned, and winked. "This could be your lucky night."

She debated about crashing the wineglass against the wall the way Clovis did. But then she'd have to clean it up, and Mickey would notice that one of her best crystal pieces was missing. Instead, she set it carefully on the towel stand, making a mental note to return it to the dining room later.

At last she stepped from the tub, patches of

bubbles clinging to her arms and legs. She walked to the mirror and surveyed her naked body. Her breasts were neither large nor small — just right, she decided. Tiny waist and flat stomach. She stretched first one leg and then the other. She'd been shaving them lately so they'd feel silky and smooth. Her underarms, too, but she hadn't told anyone. Mickey, on the other hand, had a regular bush under each arm, and her legs were hairy. Bebe thought it disgusting. She turned and looked over her naked shoulder, striking a pose Clovis was famous for. But I'm stark naked, which means I'm more wicked, she vamped into the mirror, batting her eyelashes. Instantly she imagined a dramatic tableau of herself just as she was, with Reuben on his knees, worshiping her body. The vision made her shiver.

Her dressing gown tied securely, Bebe walked softly to the door. She laid her ear against the oak paneling and listened for signs of Reuben on the top floor. When she was satisfied he was nowhere about, she scooted across the hall and pulled Mickey's door shut behind her.

Her heart thumped wildly as she went through Mickey's bureau drawers one by one. She laid out the things she wanted, a black brassiere, slip, garter belt, stockings. . . . There were no bloomers, no sign of panties in any of the drawers. A pair of silky black stock-

ings, their back seams embellished with tiny roses, made her draw in her breath in appreciation. Clovis would love these, she thought.

From the closet she chose a gold lamé sheath with a low-cut neck and a generous slit up the side. Matching shoes nestled in a soft flannel bag on the hanger next to the dress.

Mickey's jewelry box made her gasp in delight. Every stone known to man rested discreetly in layers of black velvet. She fastened diamond teardrops to her ears, a matching necklace around her neck. She chose not one, but two diamond bracelets, one for each wrist. She added a ring to every finger.

A dress like the gold lamé required some kind of hat, she decided. At least Clovis would wear one. Finally she found it, in a box on the top shelf. It was a cloche, puckered and gathered on one side with a delicate array of matching feathers. As she modeled it, she had to peek from behind the feathers that all but covered one side of her face. A diamond brooch completed the ensemble.

Bebe stepped back to view her reflection. She gasped aloud, then threw back her head and laughed. In her opinion, she looked more ravishing than Mickey or any of her father's stars. But something was missing — rouge, lip salve, and perfume. Mickey's perfume

smelled positively sinful. Bebe withdrew the stopper and dabbed herself everywhere, behind her ears, at the pulse points in her neck and throat, between her breasts, in the bend of her elbows and knees. She sniffed appreciatively. It took only seconds to apply the lip salve and the bright red rouge.

God! She wished Daniel were around. She put her hands on her hips and kicked at her hem. Here she was, all dressed up and no one here to voice approval. Secretly she thought she looked whorish, but she didn't care. Clovis always played the vamp or whore.

A wicked grin crossed her face. Maybe Daniel wasn't the one to see her like this. If Reuben could see her now . . . She pictured being at a nightclub and Reuben asking her to dance, felt herself being whisked away, swirling and drunk with happiness in his arms. . . .

Bebe pranced around the room in the gold high heels, craning her neck for glimpses of herself in the long mirror. She reeked of perfume, but it was a wonderful smell, full of lust and sinful promise, at least that's what the bottle said. She looked at the clock and grimaced. What a pity no one was going to see her after all the trouble she'd gone to. Maybe she should finish the champagne and then find out what Reuben was up to. Maybe he'd be awake by now.

At the top of the kitchen staircase Bebe

heard something. She stood frozen on the stair, her heart thumping. It was Reuben, prowling about. If he saw her in Mickey's clothes, he'd be furious. Especially if he was still drunk. She turned to retrace her steps, deciding it would be wiser to hide until he fell asleep again.

The next sound she heard was Reuben sniffing like a hound dog. Mickey's perfume! Her generous hand with the bottle was going to give her away. Bebe slipped out of the high heels and thought her heart would stop when they toppled down the back stairwell. In the silence they sounded like bombs going off. Reuben was bellowing behind her now. Fear engulfed her. Where to run? To the front of the house? Outside? She didn't stop to think, merely thrust open the kitchen door and ran as if the hounds of hell were on her heels. Twice she tripped and twice she lost time in her struggle to get to her feet. He was so close she thought she could feel his breath on the back of her neck. And he was calling names suitable only to a whore. Damn him! Damn him to hell!

If she could just get to the barn and slam the door, she could slide the huge bolt across and keep him out. It took every ounce of strength she possessed to make her legs pump faster. The long, tight dress was gathered up around the garter belt, but she didn't care. On and on she ran, until the barn was in

sight. She was having trouble breathing now, panting, almost faint, but still she kept going, not daring to look over her shoulder. All her sins were going to catch up to her now. Reuben was the devil, and he would make her pay. She could feel tears of shame sliding down her cheeks. Oh, how she wanted to be Bebe Rosen, the real Bebe Rosen, who was playing at dress-up. If only . . . if only . . .

Another few yards and she'd be safe. The barn door loomed in front of her and she ran through it into the darkness of the barn. Frantically she swung at the heavy door, her breathing ragged. She dropped the long dress and used both hands to push. Finally she had it closed and was ready to shoot the heavy bolt across when Reuben slammed his shoulder against it.

"You're not going to get away from me!" he bellowed. "I'm coming in there, and if you don't get out of the way, you're going to get hurt!"

The door rocked beneath her hands, driving her backward. She ran to the back of the barn and almost made it to the hayloft, unaware that the moonlight shafting through the open door was bathing her in its silvery light. She started to cry then, great racking sobs that brought her tormentor to within an inch of her. She dropped to her knees, burying her head in the crook of both bent arms. Reuben jerked her to her feet and dragged

her across the barn. It was dark and she was scared out of her wits, too frightened to utter a sound. She tried once to free herself, but her attempt was feeble at best. She knew what was going to happen and she was powerless to stop it.

When the gown had been ripped down the front she screamed. "Reuben, Reuben, you don't know what you're doing! Reuben, let me alone! Reuben, don't you hear me? *I'm Bebe!*" If he did hear, he gave no sign. He was holding her down and loosening his trousers with his other hand. Desperately she kicked upward with her knees, knocking him off balance. Then she was up and running for the open doorway, her legs straining with the effort.

He caught her there, in the glistening silver light. "Don't you *ever* walk out on me again," he rasped. He ripped the few remaining shreds of the dress from her and took her violently. She tried to speak again, to repeat her name . . . to tell him he was wrong . . . the woman he was violating was not Mickey, that she was Bebe . . . Bebe Rosen, a girl playing dress-up in her aunt's finery. But he was holding a cruel hard hand over her mouth, pressing the feathers of her borrowed hat against her face.

If Reuben heard Bebe's choking sobs, if he felt her fists pummeling him, he gave no sign as he drove into her. When he was spent, he

rolled over on the barn floor.

Bebe struggled to her feet but felt her knees buckle beneath her. She crawled away then, across the few feet it took to be safe, away from him in the shadows. She looked over to the spread-eagled man and spoke in a hoarse, quavering whisper, even though she knew he was too drunk to hear her. "You didn't have to do that, I would have given myself to you. You raped me, you bastard! You stole my virginity, and now I have nothing left to *give*. It was all I had. I was saving myself, maybe for you, maybe for someone else. How could you? How could you do this to me?"

She curled into a ball on the barn floor and listened to her own harsh breathing. She didn't know how long she'd been lying there when her thoughts began to turn black. Hate seethed within her, blasted from her as she looked around for some kind of weapon. It was her turn now. At the sight of a pitchfork leaning against the side wall, she rose shakily, straightened her shoulders with determination, and walked over to it. In an almost bemused fashion, she picked it up and hefted it a couple of times to get the feel of it. Then she willed her legs to obey and slowly walked back to the snoring man.

Oblivious to her nakedness, she stood over him, the pronged fork balanced above his testicles, and kicked him with her foot. When he didn't respond she moved the fork until it

was an inch from his neck. "Reuben," she shouted, kicking him again. His eyes fluttered open, and she moved the fork down to its original position. "You so much as move a muscle and your life will spurt over both of us. You took me like some wild animal! I hate you for that! I don't care if you were drunk or not. I told you I wasn't Mickey. I screamed my name, but you didn't listen!"

He began to speak, but she brought the pitchfork to within an inch of his skin. She watched his face as the words caught in his throat, and she grew calm again, tasting his fear. "Do you know what I'm going to do to you?" she asked slowly, taunting him. "I'm going to jab this fork right down between your legs. Right between your legs!"

Reuben lay quietly, strangling in his own fear. How had this happened? If he'd wanted to, he couldn't have moved. As the pitchfork hovered above him, he waited, trying to gauge the extent of her hysteria.

She was talking too much. He marveled at her calm and tried not to look at her ravished nakedness through the horrible presence of the weapon she held over him. What would the pain be like? he wondered. Probably he couldn't even count on surviving. When Mickey returned the car to the barn tomorrow, he'd be the first thing she'd see, dead and lying in his own blood. Of course, she'd know immediately what had happened. My

God! She'd know. All his plans and dreams
. . . Damn! Damn this . . . child! Why had he
been cursed with her existence? What did she
want from him? He wished he could turn the
clock back. This wasn't happening . . .
couldn't be happening. He watched her eyes
and then slowly drew his gaze down her body,
caught by the sight of a single droplet of
blood trickling down her leg.

When at last he tried once again to move,
Bebe quickly brought the fork down until all
four prongs rested on the dark crop of hair.
She inched it down slowly, grazing his skin
until one prong rested on his now limp and
flaccid shaft. He groaned.

"Bebe, don't do this," he begged. "I'm
sorry. Jesus, I don't know what happened.
I'm sorry, I know that won't make it right.
Tell me what to do to make it right and I'll
do it, I swear. Bebe, don't!"

Bebe laughed, a nasty, exultant sound that
echoed through the barn. "You beg prettily,
Reuben. Well, begging isn't good enough! All
my life I'll remember what you did, but you
won't, will you? Unless, of course, you can
remember in hell."

"Yes. Yes, I'll remember it all my life. And
you'll remember what you did to me. Two
wrongs won't make it right!" he cried. Bebe
laughed again, bitterly.

She had to make up her mind what to do.
Her arm was getting tired, and her stance

made her legs ache. Her thoughts were jumbled as she envisioned herself playing the role of a ravished shepherdess. . . . No, I'm a vengeful warrior princess, she decided. She brought the fork down then, arrow-straight, one prong sinking into the groin, the other three piercing the fleshy part of Reuben's thigh. "I wouldn't pull it out if I were you," she said over his agonized moaning. "It has manure on it. You'll probably get some kind of infection and die. I'm going into the house to get dressed. I'll take one of the bicycles and fetch the doctor. I suppose I could call him to come out here," she mused as she reached the barn door. "What do you think, Reuben?"

Reuben did not respond but lay completely still — probably unconscious, Bebe decided. She set about meticulously collecting Mickey's dress and bits of her underclothes and the hat that had finally been torn from her hair. She walked back to the house at a normal pace. It was late, the roads were dark and she didn't feel like riding to the village. Idly she looked up the doctor's telephone number in Mickey's book and dialed him. When his sleepy voice came on the line, she said there had been a terrible accident and asked him to come. It was a superb role she felt she was playing now. As she spoke the back of her other hand rested on her forehead in melodramatic repose.

When the doctor arrived, Bebe was fully dressed and waiting by the barn. She pointed to Reuben and leaned against the door. The old man gave a cry of dismay — probably identifying with Reuben's pain, she thought dispassionately. She could smell his fear when he turned to look at her. "A tragic accident," she said, smiling. "My aunt will be most upset. You must use all your expertise to save him."

"He has lost considerable blood," the doctor muttered.

"Infection. You must guard against infection," Bebe said solicitously.

"Yes, yes, we must do that. He should be in the house, in bed."

"After you tend to him you can fetch some men from the village to carry him to his bed. My aunt is away, and she should find him in his bed when she returns. It will look . . . so much better. I can boil some water if you need it."

"That won't be necessary; I have antiseptic with me." He didn't wonder at the girl's calm: she was in shock. But he had more important things to concern him at the moment.

Bebe went back to the house and fixed herself a cup of tea, then went upstairs to put Mickey's things back in their rightful place. She retrieved the gold shoes from the back staircase where they had fallen. There was

nothing she could do about the torn gown, so she stuffed it into the fireplace and watched unperturbed as it was swallowed by the flames. Then she placed the necklace, bracelets, and brooch back into their boxes, the shoes in their flannel bag, and the hat in its box. It looked a little smashed, so she lifted it out and kneaded it back into shape. With any luck, she'd be in England before Mickey discovered the missing dress. She did her best to wash away the sinful perfume.

Over a second cup of tea she thought about what had just happened to her. She was alive. Her fear was gone, replaced by the sight of the fear she'd instilled in Reuben. She felt a little sore where he'd brutalized her. Sex wasn't what everyone made it out to be. There hadn't been one enjoyable second. She vowed not to think about this night ever again. It had been a game, a role she'd played for a little while. Now she'd step out of it the way Clovis did. It was over, and Reuben had been paid back for his behavior.

It was almost dawn when two strapping young men, fearful looks on their faces, carried Reuben on a stretcher up to his bed. When the doctor approached Bebe, she put on a concerned face. "Is there something I can do?" she asked innocently.

The doctor handed her three small packets of pills as he searched her face. She seemed to be less disturbed than when he first saw

her. "I don't know how much good they're going to be, the directions are on there," he said, pointing to the packets. "I think he should be in a hospital. You say Madame Fonsard will return tomorrow. Today, actually," he corrected himself. "Is that right?"

"Yes, today, but I am uncertain of the time. How is he?"

"Not good; I'll stop back around noon." The old man shook his head and with a last worried look at Bebe left the château.

Outside in his car he blessed himself. An accident? Not likely. Reuben Tarz's injury was deliberate. Yet in his one lucid moment the young man had said it was an accident, and the young lady had also said it was an accident. He would call it an accident on his medical report. What else could he do? He couldn't help but wonder what Madame Fonsard would call it.

Meanwhile, Bebe took another bath and went to bed. She slept for nine hours and woke once when the doctor returned before dinner.

"Madame is not back yet?" the old man queried.

"No. Is something wrong, Doctor?"

"The young man is running a dangerously high fever. I've been with him the past hour. My medication is not working. He should be watched all the time. He should be in a hospital," the doctor insisted, shrugging into

his coat.

"Then that's what you should do. You should take him to the hospital," Bebe said. She began to walk with him to his car.

"It is so far. I have other patients, one due to deliver a baby almost any second now."

"Then I guess he has to stay here. I can sit and watch him. What am I to watch for?"

As the doctor began to issue instructions to Bebe, Mickey pulled up the drive in the Citroën. She stopped outside the barn when she saw Bebe and the doctor standing beside his car. The two of them stopped talking when they saw her, and with an ugly sense of foreboding, she jumped out of the Citroën and hurried over. When she heard Reuben's name she dropped her purse. It was then that she saw one diamond teardrop earring lying near the fetid reddish-brown stain on the barn floor.

All life and color drained from Mickey's face when she stared down at Reuben.

He was on his way to the hospital in Avignon. It was Bebe who comforted her and offered to go along with her to the hospital. It was Bebe who handed her handkerchief after handkerchief, just the way Clovis Ames had done in *Good-bye, My Love.*

Reuben Tarz lay in critical condition, hovering between life and death, the day Bebe boarded the ship in Brest that would take her

to England.

Although Mickey had made her promise to tell Daniel the moment she arrived in Paris, it was at the depot, while waiting for the boat train, that Bebe finally told him of Reuben's condition and how it had happened. She drew back in alarm at Daniel's incredulous expression. "You waited till now to tell me Reuben might be dying! For three hours we've laughed and joked, and you never . . . What kind of evil person are you?" he demanded in a hoarse voice.

"Evil? *Evil?*" Bebe shrilled. "What about me? Before you get so damn self-righteous, maybe you should give some thought to what happened to *me.* Look at me, Daniel, take a good, long look. Reuben took the one thing I had to give. To *give,* Daniel. He stripped that away from me. I could have killed him, but I didn't. He's not going to die, his kind never does. And as far as Mickey is concerned, Reuben was careless and fell on a pitchfork. She never needs to know what really happened. He was already in bed and being seen to by the doctor when she got back. She's blaming herself for leaving him because she knew he was angry. I told her it wasn't her fault, I did my best to convince her, but she just kept saying over and over that if she hadn't gone or if she had taken him with her, it wouldn't have happened. I called the doctor. I didn't

have to do that. I could have let him lie there and die, but I'm not the monster you're making me out to be. Reuben himself told the doctor in the first few minutes that it was an accident. You just remember one thing, Daniel, and don't you ever forget it: I protected Reuben. I thought you were different, but you're not. You're like all the rest — you don't give a damn about me!" Bebe cried bitterly.

"Oh, two last things," she said, reaching into her purse to withdraw an envelope and a single piece of paper. "There's money in the envelope for train fare back to the château, and I need you to sign this at the bottom."

Daniel scribbled his name without looking at the paper. "What is it?" he muttered after handing it back to her.

Bebe smiled and secured the paper in her purse. "The contract you drew up. The one where we bet I could get Reuben to sleep with me. You owe me, Daniel. Someday I'm going to want to collect."

With a last wave of her hand she tripped up the steps to board the train. After taking a full minute to compose herself, she waved with one hand while she dabbed at her eyes with a small white handkerchief. A cloud of steamy vapor floated in front of her, momentarily blocking Daniel from view. The train whistle shrilled as she murmured, "Cut! You couldn't have done it any better, Clovis."

She settled herself in her compartment.

They'd all meet again, she'd see to it. "Good-bye, Daniel, good-bye, Mickey, au revoir, Reuben my love," she said. Five minutes later she was engrossed in a trashy magazine.

Daniel seethed with anger, his body shaking from head to toe. He wanted to direct his anger at Bebe, but she'd made a certain amount of sense, if what she said was true. And he couldn't direct it at Reuben if he was dying. When he had himself under control, he rushed back to the Paris house and threw whatever was at hand into his valise. Then he rushed back to the depot and waited four hours for a train that would take him to Avignon. To Reuben.

CHAPTER FIFTEEN

He hated the sight and the silence of the sterile hospital. He had thought he'd never have to enter another one and here he was, once again — as a visitor, true, but it made no difference; he still hated the smell, the whiteness, and the nurses' hushed whispers as they walked about on rubber-soled shoes.

Daniel saw Mickey before she saw him. She was sitting quietly, a rosary in her hand, her lips moving in prayer. She sensed his presence and turned. Her eyes filled immediately at the sight of him, and she floated into his arms and laid her head on his shoulder. Her tears gave way to hard, driving sobs. Daniel could feel his own eyes start to mist. "Shhh, it's going to be all right. Reuben's tough, he came through the war and he'll come through this, too." His hands felt awkward as he tried to pat Mickey on the back and stroke her hair at the same time. When she quieted they sat down together.

"This is all my fault, Daniel," she said,

twisting her hands nervously. "I never should have gone to Dijon. I knew he was angry and I delayed . . . thinking he'd come outside to see me off. But he didn't. I've never understood how deep his anger goes. We all get angry at one time or another, but not the kind of anger Reuben carries. I never thought . . . never expected that anger to be directed at me. I should never have gone. If I'd stayed, this wouldn't have happened. How can I live with this? What if he dies? It will be my fault. How could I have been so stupid? I don't know what to do . . . I need to do something . . . something to make a difference. There's nothing . . . nothing either of us can do. I know that, I'm talking to hear myself. Wait and pray. Pray and wait. If he dies . . ."

"I don't want to hear you say that ever again. Reuben is not going to die. He's too . . . young," Daniel said lamely. He remembered Bebe's words: *His kind never dies.* He wondered if it was true.

"I want to see him," Daniel said firmly. "I want him to know I'm here. Where is he?"

Mickey shook her head. "He's delirious. He didn't recognize me. Don't torture yourself. Why do you think I'm sitting out here? I can't bear to . . . Go, I understand."

Nothing in the world could have prepared Daniel for his first look at Reuben. He was white as death and just as still. His skin looked dry and parched. Daniel reached out

a steady hand and placed it on Reuben's forehead, then brought his hand back to his own cheek, feeling the heat. A high fever.

He pulled a white cane chair to the side of the bed, perched on the edge of it, and reached for Reuben's hand. How hot it was, how dry. He swallowed hard. "I don't know if you can hear me, Reuben, and I guess it doesn't matter. I'm here and so is Mickey. She's praying for you. If you could hear, I think you'd probably laugh. But she needs to do it — to pray, I mean. I think it's nice that someone cares enough to pray to God for your recovery. You're going to get better, pal, I know it. Hell, we went through the war, and something like this just isn't in the cards for you. We have things to do, places to go —"

He broke off, choking back his tears. "Can you hear me, pal? Can you give me some kind of sign? You know, flutter your eyelashes, move your finger, anything so I know that you know I'm here," Daniel pleaded. Reuben stirred, his dark head moving from side to side, his lips twisting. Horror filled Daniel at his friend's condition. He ran to the door and motioned for Mickey to join him. "I think he's trying to say something. I think he heard me talk to him. He knows I'm here, I'm sure of it. Did you try talking to him, Mickey? Did he react to you?" Daniel asked hopefully.

Mickey placed a gentle hand on Daniel's arm. "He's delirious, Daniel. I . . . when I tried to talk, to tell him I was here, he seemed to . . . I think it upsets him more. When I simply watched from the doorway, he remained quiet. I . . . can't bear to see him like this, Daniel. Come, we'll wait outside."

"I don't understand how our presence could upset him. If there's any possibility that he can hear us, know we're here, that should give him comfort. He loves you, Mickey, and he and I are friends. I don't understand." Of course he understood only too well, but he couldn't say anything to Mickey. He wished then that he was as ignorant of Reuben's accident as Mickey was. Bebe hadn't sworn him to secrecy; he could tell Mickey what had happened. But if he did, it would be to unload his conscience, and the knowledge would destroy Mickey. For now he had to keep his own counsel.

Mickey reached down to brush Reuben's dark hair back from his forehead, her face filled with sorrow. Reuben's hand lashed upward, brushing her hand away. He muttered something Daniel couldn't understand. Mickey stepped away, her shoulders shaking with silent sobs.

"Mickey!" The agonized, passionate cry from Reuben's lips drew her backward until she was once again at his bedside. Tears rolled down her cheeks as she reached for the hand

that caressed her so often.

"Help me, Dan'l, help me!" came the second cry as Reuben thrashed about the bed. For one terrifying instant Daniel's heart stopped beating. He'd never heard such agony in a voice before.

"I'm here, Reuben," he said, trying to sound calm. "I'll help you. I'll do whatever I can. It's my turn now, to help you. Hey, pal, we're the Three Musketeers, one for all, you know. I'll help." *Even if it means keeping your awful secret. I know there's more to it than Bebe said. I know you, pal.*

A nurse appeared, her uniform crackling about her ankles. Gently she shooed Mickey and Daniel to the foot of Reuben's bed while she attempted to take her patient's temperature. Daniel watched helplessly as Reuben fought the nurse, his movements frenzied. He was shouting now, the words almost incoherent, but Daniel knew what was coming, he could see it in Reuben's twisted features. "You bitch! I'll kill you for this! . . . Get away . . . no . . . Don't . . . Jesus . . . please . . . No! Oh, God . . . Bebe, no!"

Daniel rushed to Mickey, who was leaning her forehead against the door. His arm about Mickey's shoulders, he led her from the room to the small waiting area.

Daniel Bishop entered manhood in the space of time it took him to lead Mickey to her chair. "As you said, Mickey, he's deliri-

345

ous." How calm his voice was, how matter-of-fact. "Reuben called your name and mine, too. He asked for help and . . . I heard the love in his voice when he called your name. As for Bebe, we've known for a long time how he feels about her. I understand he's confused and doesn't know what he's saying. I think we should go outside and get some fresh air, perhaps take a walk. There's nothing we can do for now."

Mickey looked up into Daniel's eyes. For a moment she felt baffled at the change in him. He'd rushed in like a tormented boy and now he stood so calmly before her, a tall, lean young man with kind, compassionate eyes. She clung to him as they left the hospital to walk around the grounds.

They stopped to rest once on a low stone wall. Daniel stared off into the distance, wondering if Bebe's ship had made port. Why had she told him the sordid little story? For sympathy or out of malice? He thought he knew her, understood her, but this . . . Once again Reuben's words rang in his ears. *No, Bebe, no!* Bebe's calm, matter-of-fact voice telling him Reuben had stripped away her virginity. The bet. The goddamn bet! He'd actually signed the stupid paper, but he'd been in a daze and Bebe had taken advantage of his befuddled state. Bebe was an expert at taking advantage of people. More than ever, Daniel was convinced that somehow, in some

way, she had been responsible for the rape —
if there really had been a rape.

"What was he doing in the barn, Daniel?"
He jerked his thoughts back to the present
when he realized Mickey was speaking.

"There was no hay to be pitched. The
manure hadn't been disturbed. Reuben is not
clumsy. I simply do not understand. What do
you think he was doing with a pitchfork?"

"Probably cleaning up the barn, working
off his energy until you got back. Reuben . . .
when Reuben gets angry he does that so he
doesn't dwell on . . . whatever it is that . . .
that made his anger . . . I don't know, Mickey.
When he's well — and he will get well — he'll
tell us." What was it he was going to owe Bebe
Rosen? How quickly she'd snatched the
ridiculous agreement from his hands. No, it
wasn't ridiculous, it was deadly, and it would
hang over his head until she called in her
favor. Bebe had succeeded in driving a wedge
between the Musketeers because she couldn't
belong. What Bebe couldn't have, she destroyed. Still, he couldn't hate her. If anything, he pitied her. If he could pity her
instead of hating her, it would be easier to
deal with the debt he owed her.

"Perhaps you're right, Daniel. But I have
this feeling . . . this awful emptiness in me. I
feel what we had . . . the three of us . . . is
over. Why do I feel this way? Do you feel it,
too? Are we lost?"

He supposed he could have lied, but he couldn't do that to Mickey. He nodded.

"I have this awful feeling," Mickey said sadly, "that Bebe is somehow responsible. Do you feel that, too?" Again Daniel nodded.

Back in the little hospital anteroom, Mickey and Daniel settled themselves for the long wait ahead.

Day after weary day passed. One week led into the next, and still the Two Musketeers kept their vigil. Both were haggard and drawn, yet neither would leave the hospital except to eat and change clothes for fear Reuben would either rally or slip into a coma. It was during one of their brief absences that Reuben became coherent for the first time. The nurse, a kind-faced older woman, raced to fetch the doctor.

"You're in capable hands, Mr. Tarz," the doctor said quietly. Reuben thrashed about in the bed, his entire body drenched with sweat. As the doctor continued to speak softly, the nurse reached for Reuben's hand and held it tightly in her own. She echoed the doctor's words, her voice gentle and motherly.

"I want you to open your eyes, Mr. Tarz, and look at me. Do it now," the doctor ordered in a firm, quiet voice. He nodded approval when Reuben's eyes fluttered open. "Do you know where you are? Do you remember what happened to you?"

Reuben struggled from the black vaporous pit he'd been sunk in for so long. He tried to speak, but his tongue seemed to fill the whole of his mouth. The nurse wiped a moist cloth over his lips. "No," he said hoarsely.

The doctor's voice turned cheerful. "I didn't think you would, at least not right away. It's all right, take your time. You've been here a month now. You injured yourself in a barn with a pitchfork that had manure on it. We've bombarded your body with everything at our disposal. I'm not making light of your injury, Mr. Tarz. You've been very ill, but I think you will mend. It's going to take time, however. I also think you should know that Madame Fonsard and your friend Daniel have been here since the day you were brought in. They leave only to eat and change clothes. They've been staying at a pension not far from here. You have wonderful, caring friends, Mr. Tarz, whose only wish is for your recovery. Nurse is going to feed you some broth now, and later, if you're up to it, you can visit with your friends. I'll be back to check on you later this afternoon. In the meantime, rest."

Reuben gagged on the first spoonful of broth. The nurse wiped his chin and tried again. From somewhere his mind ordered him to swallow, to eat, so he could regain his strength. He wanted to think, but opening his mouth and swallowing drained all his

energy.

When the nurse returned to her chair in the corner of the room, Reuben lay back exhausted, perspiration beading on his forehead. He tried to wipe the sweat away, but he was too weak, his thoughts cloudy and disoriented. The broth he'd taken was bubbling around in his stomach. He wondered if he would die. He moved restlessly, his body sticking to the damp sheets. He was in Paris standing under a blooming chestnut tree, seeing a girl in a pretty, flowered dress walk by, and then he was paddling his feet in the Seine with someone whose shoes were too big. He felt himself slipping into black, murky water. "No, no. Don't do it!" he cried feverishly, his head spinning, spinning. "No!" He fought then, with the bedsheets and the nurse's firm hands. "She should have killed me. I thought she . . . Help me . . ." The water was pulling at him, the oversize shoes in his hands pulling him under, deeper and deeper.

"Come back, Mr. Tarz, come back and talk to me," ordered the kindly nurse. "Now. You're dreaming, and the dream is over. Talk to me, Mr. Tarz. Tell me about Daniel. I want to hear about your friend. I want to hear now."

From far away, past the murky black water full of overhead bubbles, Reuben heard the authoritative voice and struggled to obey. "Daniel . . . Daniel . . . Daniel . . . Yes, Daniel

350

. . . my friend," he murmured as he broke the surface of the black water.

"Yes, tell me about Daniel." The old nurse sighed.

He was lucid then, and coherent. He spoke of Daniel until his tongue failed him. The nurse relaxed her hold on his hand, but she didn't leave his side. Instead, she spoke quietly, explaining about his accident. He was lucky to be alive, she told him.

Reuben listened, reliving the scene firsthand as the nurse described what she'd been told. He swore he felt the cold hand of death touch his shoulder at that moment. It all came back to him then — his own voice, Bebe's screams, the pain of the pitchfork going into his groin, his drunkenness, the old doctor's disbelieving face. The pain, God, the pain. The same pain he was feeling now. A month, she'd said, this woman in white. Daniel, where was Daniel? And Mickey. He'd betrayed Mickey. Reuben could feel his eyes roll back in his head and he panicked, thrashing about in the bed. The fever was sweeping through him, starting in his loins, fanning out to cover every inch of his body until he would explode into thousands of pieces of burned flesh. He'd seen that once, a body exploding, the flesh plummeting down on Daniel. Who would pick up his pieces?

Ah, that feels good, he thought as the nurse placed a wet cloth on his forehead and one

around his neck. "I need to hear more," she said in that same schoolteacherish voice, the one every child had to obey. "I want to hear about Madame Fonsard, too. You call her Mickey. You must tell me now. Don't go to sleep, Mr. Tarz. You must tell me about Mickey and Daniel. Jake misses you, Daniel told me. Who is Jake, Mr. Tarz?"

"Jake . . . Jake . . . Daniel's dog. Jake misses me?"

"Very much," the nurse said gently. "Tell me about Jake."

"Jake . . . peed on my new suit. Daniel laughed." The cloths were replaced with cooler ones. It was easier to think when he was cool.

"Will I die?" he asked. *If I die, she killed me. Someday I'll kill her for this. I can't die, I have to live so I can . . .* "Will I die?" he repeated.

"Not if I can help it," the nurse said cheerfully. "Things are mixed up in your mind right now because of your fever. Once it breaks, you'll be fine."

Reuben believed the kind, gentle voice. He slept then, a feverish slumber, but he didn't slip back into the black hole of unconsciousness. When he woke later he knew where he was and what had happened to him. Pain seared through him, but he made no sound.

The nurse said he was very ill, but he would live. Another voice had said the same thing — the doctor perhaps, he thought wearily. If

he lived, the first thing he would do when he was well was find Bebe Rosen and . . . and . . . He slipped away again, into a sleep that was more restful, less feverish, the terrible pain staying with him.

In the coming days he fought for his life with a determination that had been buried deeply within him. He had to live, to make Bebe pay for what he was going through. If it took him the rest of his life, she'd pay for what she'd done to him.

As Reuben fought for his life and Mickey and Daniel continued their vigil, Bebe danced and partied in London under the watchful eye of her chaperone Pamela, Mickey Fonsard's friend.

She was alone in her room, staring at the calendar in front of her, her face registering shock and disbelief. If what it told her was true, then her tiredness and irritability had nothing to do with late hours, parties, and dancing.

She was pregnant.

There was no way she could switch roles now. This was a fact that would not go away no matter how much she wanted to sweep it under the rug. Babies are messy, and all they do is cry, she told herself. I'm too young to have a baby. I'll be fat and ugly and get pimples on my face. Men had their way with you, and a baby was the result. "Damn you,

Reuben!"

She'd planned on returning to France in September, but not if she was pregnant. Dammit, nothing was working out the way she wanted it to. Daniel had promised to write, and he hadn't; Mickey hadn't written, either. They didn't want her, were glad to be rid of her, so why had she expected them to write, to care about her stay in England? And after she'd gone to such great lengths to keep the secret! She should have told Mickey. Should have screamed it at the doctor so the whole village would know. Good old Daniel considered her confession a confidence and wouldn't tell anyone, she was sure of it. She'd been so damn noble and gallant thinking they'd praise her and turn on Reuben.

And how is dear old Reuben, she wondered bitterly. Still living off Mickey and taking advantage of Daniel, no doubt. Whom did he get angry at these days? Bastard that he was, he was probably laughing up his sleeve that he'd stolen her virginity. She rolled over on her stomach. Soon it would puff out and she'd look like she'd swallowed a watermelon. Oh, God! "I don't want a baby!" she wailed. "Especially Reuben Tarz's baby."

Bebe's thoughts whirled and danced. An abortion! Surely Mickey would know someone who would do it. With Mickey's help she'd get rid of this child, and someday she'd tell him what she'd done. She could almost

see the shock on his face. . . . On the other hand, maybe he'd feel sorry for her if she told him, and try to make things right. Maybe he'd ask her to marry him. . . . Of course there was always a third alternative: she could have this baby, go through the nine months of misery, give the child away, and *then* tell him. Reuben's flesh and blood. He'd never know where the child was, only that he had one somewhere. He'd search the world over until he found it and brought it back, and then they'd live happily ever after.

If she chose not to tell him, but have the baby, give it up, and get on with her life, the knowledge would be the same as the contract she had with Daniel. Card players called it having an ace in the hole.

Tomorrow she would go to two doctors to have her pregnancy confirmed. If she was truly pregnant, she'd book passage to France immediately.

If you ruined his life and he ruined your life, where does that leave things? her conscience whispered. "We can start over after I decide what to do about this pregnancy. I won't think about it again, and if Reuben doesn't know, he can't think about it." *Do you still want him, after all this?* "Of course I want him. I want what he and Mickey had. I want to be loved that way. I can love him the way Mickey loves him. I want him and I'm going to have

him, sooner or later. I'm good at waiting. Real good."

The following days were torture for Mickey and Daniel as they watched Reuben slip in and out of consciousness. Each time he rallied he was stronger, his lucid episodes more frequent. He recognized them now, and once or twice he tried to smile, but the effort exhausted him.

August was almost at an end when the doctor pronounced him well enough for a lengthy visit with his friends.

"At last!" Mickey cried tearfully. "The Three Musketeers together again. Oh, Reuben, I'm so glad you're getting well."

Daniel did his best to ignore the blank look in Reuben's eyes, hoping Mickey didn't notice. His friend wasn't the same. A part of him was gone, and Daniel knew he would never see it again. He wished there were something he could do for his friend, something he could say that would bring the sparkle back to his eyes. Time, he told himself, time would make things right.

He didn't know if he believed the thought or not, but for now it was all he had to go on.

Reuben leaned back into his pillow, relieved that his visitors were gone. He felt physically whipped, his life's blood gone from his body.

If he needed further proof of how sick he'd been and still was, Mickey and Daniel's visit clinched it. He hadn't said three words, and while he'd tried to smile he knew he hadn't carried it off. "A newborn baby has more stamina than I do," he grunted.

Tired and drained as he was, his brain refused to be still. Two months gone out of his life and all because of Bebe Rosen. He was an invalid, dependent on other people for his comfort, and it would be many more months until he was fully recovered, according to the doctor.

If there was a way to make Bebe Rosen pay for what she did to him, he'd find it. . . . His thoughts trailed off into sleep.

In the days that followed, as Reuben mended and regained his strength, he plotted his retaliation in every way imaginable. He gave very little thought to the violence of his anger that night, and when he did think of it he realized that he'd finally exploded, just the way Bebe had warned him he would the first day of her visit. Maybe now that horrible black side of him was gone forever. His anger was responsible for his recovery, he knew. But it was a healthy anger, not that destructive, all-consuming rage that had attacked him in the past.

Every so often the memory of his unspeakable behavior that night crept into his thoughts, and he knew the day would come

when the blame had to be parceled out justly; but for now, to speed his recovery, it helped to lay all the blame on Bebe's shoulders.

Mid-September found Reuben back at the château in his own bed. In those first days he refused to meet Daniel's questioning gaze, which only convinced his friend that Bebe's story was true. When at last he did stare Daniel down, there was defiance in his eyes.

By the first week in October, Reuben was walking about. His appetite improved and he was sleeping soundly at night. No one questioned him about his "accident," and he volunteered nothing. He was aware that both Mickey and Daniel received letters from Bebe, but he didn't ask about her and they offered no information.

It was a delightful autumn day, the leaves burned to a rich copper and a soft westerly wind blew, when the phone shrilled to life. Mickey picked it up and shooed Daniel and Reuben outdoors. For several long moments she listened, gripping the receiver with white-knuckled fingers. When she finally hung up, she started to tremble. *Why now? Why?* Hadn't she been through enough? She tried to square her shoulders, to stop her trembling, but she failed. How was she to tell Reuben and Daniel she had to go to Paris?

She walked to the double French doors and watched Reuben as he talked with Daniel in the late afternoon sun. He should be wearing

a heavier sweater, she thought. Daniel, too, for that matter. It was her fault; she'd shooed them out so quickly.

Lord, she was tired. First the long weeks at the hospital not knowing if Reuben would live or die, and then his return — a triumph that was proving disastrous. What more could she do? God, how she tried. She ached with her good intentions, and her face was stiff from smiling. All she wanted to do was go to bed and sleep for weeks. "I want yesterday, I want things the way they were before his accident," she whispered.

She'd always prided herself on being a realist, yet here she was convincing herself that things would get better. Well, they wouldn't. What she had with Reuben was gone. *But I need to pretend. If I don't, I will shatter into a thousand pieces.*

She did her best to put on a practiced smile and then called her guests indoors. Quickly she explained that she had to go to Paris in the morning, then excused herself, saying she had papers to go over and a bag to pack. Only Daniel's eyes held unasked questions. Reuben's blank look ripped at her heart. He didn't care that she was leaving him; in fact he looked relieved. Tears welling in her eyes, Mickey fled to her room, where she sank down on her bed, her thoughts in a turmoil.

Bebe was in Paris, at her house. And — God! of all things — she'd called to say that

she was pregnant and would Mickey please come and help her. Help her do what, for heaven's sake? Pamela, how could you let this happen? You promised me that you wouldn't let her out of your sight. Sol. Mother of God, what was she to say to Sol? She felt a hundred years old. As soon as she arrived in Paris she would send off a cable to Pamela and demand an explanation.

If she was right in her assessment of Bebe, the girl would want to go to some back-street butcher and abort the child. *Dieu,* Bebe was still a child herself! What am I to do, she asked herself over and over as she paced her bedroom. She tried to tell herself she couldn't be held responsible for Bebe, but she was. She'd given Sol her word that his daughter would be well taken care of.

Mickey remained in her room all evening, asking for a supper tray that she didn't touch. She paced and she smoked until her room was blanketed in a dark gray cloud. When it grew unbearable she threw open the casement windows and watched the smoke trail outside as she smoked still another cigarette.

The night was endless. At first light she carried her bag downstairs and out to the barn.

"Would you like me to go with you, Mickey?" Daniel asked gruffly.

She whirled around. "Daniel! You startled me. No, *chéri,* this is something I must do alone. Reuben needs you here. At the most I

will be gone several days." Or longer, depending on how quickly Pamela answers my cable, she thought.

Daniel stood outside the barn for a long time after Mickey had backed the huge Citroën out and drove off. Last evening she hadn't come out of her room once. And on his two trips to the bathroom he'd heard her pacing inside. Something was wrong, he knew it. He wondered if the trip had anything to do with Bebe.

At last he whistled for Jake, who came on the run, a stick in his mouth. "Not this morning, Jake. Let's go inside where it's warm and get some breakfast and wait for Reuben." Jake scampered ahead and Daniel picked up his feet and ran after the dog, into the house that was his security.

Paris would never be the same, Mickey thought ruefully. She'd never feel the same about this beautiful city again, and all because of Bebe Rosen. She'd hated the train ride because there was nothing to do but think, and she'd done enough of that the past weeks to last her a lifetime. She spoke to her driver: "Stop by the Bank of Paris, please, I want to send a cable."

Inside the austere bank Mickey wrote out her cable. It was short and to the point.

Dear Pamela,

At Paris town house with Bebe, who informs me she is *enceinte.* Please explain by return cable how you allowed this child to escape your watchful eye.

Mickey

Mickey paid her driver and stood a moment looking at her house. They'd been happy here, all of them, even Bebe, when they'd made the trip earlier in the year. It was all a memory now. When next she left here for the château, she knew she wouldn't want to return for a very long time.

She walked through the rooms calling Bebe's name. The girl was in the sitting room with her feet curled beneath her, a glass of wine in one hand and a cigarette in the other. She looked for all the world like the mistress of the house.

"What am I to do with you, Bebe?" she said, getting right to the point. "How in the name of God could you let this happen? What is your father going to say? You're just a child yourself. You aren't capable of taking care of a baby."

Bebe stared at Mickey. "How could I let this happen? It happened. I'm sure I don't have to tell *you* about the birds and the bees. As for my father, he need never know unless you decide to tell him. I certainly have no

intention of telling him. I came here so you could help me get an abortion. You're right about one thing, I'm not capable of taking care of a baby. I don't want it! You must know people who will do this . . . for the right amount of money."

"You sound like you're discussing the weather. You're talking about a child's life. Your pregnancy is too far along for an abortion. If you were so careless as to allow this to happen, you will have to suffer it through. I will not be a part of something so . . . wicked, so criminal! No!" Mickey cried.

"Then I'll find someone myself!" Bebe said defiantly.

"Who? A butcher? Someone who will destroy your insides? If you do that, then I *will* tell your father. No. You will have this child. We will find a home for it, someone who will love it and care for it. I will not tell your father as long as you agree to having this baby."

"You haven't listened to a word I've said," Bebe whined. "I don't want to have this baby. I don't want to go for months looking like a cow!"

For hours they went back and forth. Mickey hammered away at her charge, reciting stories of women she knew who had had abortions — those who'd lived, she added coldly. "Who is the father?" she demanded suddenly.

Bebe shrugged. "Does it really make a dif-

ference? Let's just say he wasn't the man I thought he was. In fact, he wasn't a nice man at all." In the end, Mickey's gruesome stories about botched abortions convinced Bebe to agree to have the baby.

"The day after tomorrow I'll take you to Yvette and Henri's farm. You'll stay there until the child is born, and then with the help of the curé we'll find it a proper home. Once you have recovered from childbirth you will leave the farm, and I don't ever want to see you again. I feel responsible for you because I entrusted you to Pamela and she failed me. I am now going to impose on my dearest friend to care for you, and that is the last thing I will do for you. I can no longer keep quiet, and this probably is not the time to bring this up, but I no longer care. I did my best to be a friend to you. I cared for you despite what Reuben said. I promised your father to take care of you. You never thanked me, you never showed consideration for any of us. You caused trouble between the three of us that cannot be made right. I will never understand you, and I will not try anymore. The position you've placed me in and what you've done is unforgivable in my eyes." Mickey gazed at her coldly. "Now it's late; I suggest you go to bed."

"It's only six o'clock," Bebe whined. Inside, she was furious at Mickey's attitude. Well,

why not, what did you expect, she asked herself sardonically. Warm, loving arms and a compassionate embrace?

"Let me put it to you another way," Mickey said. "I don't want to spend the evening looking at you. This is my house and you will do as I say. Now!"

It was after nine o'clock the following day when Mickey's banker arrived with an answer to her cable.

The contents were so unbelievable, so devastating that Mickey reeled backward with a rush of blood to her head. She reached out to the nearest chair for support, thinking she was going to faint. Somehow she managed to make her legs work so they would carry her to her chair. Time stood still for her as she read and reread the cable in her shaking hands. Her head fell back against the pretty, flowered cushion on her chair. She felt her soul leave her body, the part of her she'd given to Reuben Tarz, the part she'd never shared with anyone; the core of her very being. The cable slipped to the floor. She thought it obscene-looking on the sky-blue carpet. Her leg shot out, the heel of her shoe dragging the square of pink backward. She ground the ball of her foot into the flimsy paper, scrunching and tearing it to shreds. But it didn't matter, the words were engraved in her heart.

Dearest Mickey,

Rest assured my eyes never strayed, even for a moment. If Mademoiselle Bebe is *enceinte* she arrived in that condition. Look to your own backyard, my friend.

Pamela

Mickey's world as she'd known it for the last two years shattered. Anger such as she'd never known surged through her. At that moment she knew herself capable of murdering Bebe Rosen without a shred of remorse; she could easily strangle the girl with her bare hands and walk away. She sat alone, in the dark, all through the endless night, reliving each moment she'd shared with Reuben. When the room grew light and the night laid itself to rest, she looked at herself in the long mirror standing next to her bureau. What she saw pierced her heart: she was a shell of her former self, ravaged and plundered by Bebe Rosen. She looked . . . dead, her soul trampled by Reuben and Bebe.

Life went on, she told herself as she washed her face and brushed her hair. The hands of time would not go backward, nor would they stand still.

You are a fool, Michelene. You knew. You knew and you ignored the facts. When you found your earring in the barn, you knew. When old and trusted Nanette could not look

you in the eye those first days, you knew. You knew! she accused the reflection in the mirror. A woman in love is always a fool, one way or another. Silently, she grieved.

With leaden feet she walked back into her bedroom. But she had neither the strength nor the desire to pack her bag. The memories of this pretty room were hateful now, and she didn't want to remember them. She fled without a backward glance.

Bebe was in the dining room drinking coffee, a plate with two pastries untouched in front of her. Mickey wondered if she could drink coffee, if she could sit at the same table with this — this unnatural child. Life went on, she reminded herself again. There was no way she could undo what had been done. It wasn't until she'd laced her coffee with cream and three heaping spoonfuls of sugar that she raised her eyes to meet Bebe's defiant gaze.

Bebe's first thought was how awful Mickey looked. Her second was that there was something in her eyes she'd never seen before. Then it struck her like a lightning bolt! *She knows!* Coffee splattered on the snowy tablecloth as the cup dropped to the floor.

Bebe had never really felt true fear before, but now she felt it wash over her in giant waves. She swayed dizzily as she bent down to pick up her cup.

Mickey felt a moment of satisfaction when

she saw the fear in Bebe's eyes. *She knows I know.* Which of us will speak, will acknowledge that . . . Reuben . . . The thought was so unbearable, she rose from the table, her eyes on Bebe. "I heard a car out front. Get your things together," she said calmly. They were the last words she spoke to Bebe until they reached Yvette and Henri's farm.

CHAPTER SIXTEEN

The farmyard was a hive of activity when Mickey stopped the car. Cats and kittens scattered, dogs and puppies trotted after the cats, their tails swishing. Chickens pecked the ground, their feathers fluttering wildly. Yvette herself clucked like a mother hen as she listened to Mickey's explanation. Warmhearted as she was, she wrapped Bebe in her arms and kissed her cheek. "All men are bastards, *chérie.* I will take care of you, it is a promise." Bebe laid her head on the motherly woman's shoulder. It was like coming home after a long absence.

"And you, Michelene Fonsard, you are to go home and not come back until it is time for the birth," Yvette said kindly. "I'm glad that you brought this child to me. She will be in good hands. Henri and I will take care of her."

"I knew I could count on you, Yvette. You're a good friend," Mickey said. Yvette looked up sharply, her eyes questioning.

"You would do the same for me, *chérie,* eh? Of course you would."

Mickey didn't bother to answer. All she wanted to do was get back to the château and lock herself in her room to lick her wounds. Twice, blinded with tears, she almost drove the Citroën off the road. Filled with guilt she couldn't name, her thoughts whirled in endless circles. She had the answers now to all her unasked questions. At last, unable to drive any farther, she pulled the car to the side of the road and cried — hard, throat-wrenching sobs. A long time later, her tears dry on her cheeks, she started the car. There would be no more tears. There would be no recriminations, no pointed fingers. The love she felt for Reuben was locked in her heart. It would never change.

Downstairs in the library, Reuben paced. He was so goddamned tired he couldn't see straight, but he wouldn't give in to his tiredness. The thoughts that had him pacing were the same ones he had been grappling with since he came out of his long illness. Always they circled and zoomed in his head, bringing him to the same conclusion. He had to get back on his feet and get on with his life. But how? What would a real man do? Confess? Beg forgiveness? Or would he put the disaster behind him and go on from there? He didn't know. His brain worked at break-

neck speed from morning till night to no avail. He was sleeping fairly well, and that was a good sign. His appetite was ferocious, as though trying to make up for the months of broth and custard. He was mending, slower than he liked, but the result was what was important.

At times he suffered terrible memory flashes and knew they would be with him forever. Bebe could have killed him; maybe she should have. Over and over he asked himself why she hadn't killed him. Why, at the last second, had she aimed the fork away? Chills rolled up and down his body. That first instant of pain had been so horrendous, he knew he'd blacked out. The rest of the summer was an absolute blur.

Mickey's trip two days earlier had something to do with Bebe, he could sense it. And today on her return, she'd been preoccupied. Why? He felt his hands curl into fists. Was he always going to live like this, afraid Bebe would reappear, preoccupied by Bebe, obsessing about Bebe?

All his grand intentions of helping with the vintage were shot to hell. He didn't have sufficient strength to walk through the fields, much less pick and help crush the grapes. Right now he should be in Bordeaux, keeping an eye on things, but so far Mickey hadn't said a word about it. Tomorrow he would mention it, just to have something to say.

Daniel had told him that Mickey had been at his bedside night and day all during his illness. Mickey, he noticed, seemed to have aged ten years. And he was responsible for that. How in the hell did you give back ten years to a person? She was still beautiful, and he still loved her with all his heart, but he felt unclean, unworthy of her. And all sexual desire was gone from him. There was a word for his condition, but he couldn't think of it. It was too frightening, and he didn't want to know if it was temporary or permanent.

In the beginning his nightmares had centered on the pitchfork, but in those dreams it was Mickey holding the weapon, aiming it at his eyes, his throat, his belly. In those dreams her face was contorted with hatred. Over and over she called him a whoremaster.

Some things could never be made right, he told himself in defeat. Sometimes you had to cut your losses and go on. Maybe it was time to pack up and trundle off, go back to America. Pay his dues. Old George had said, If you play, you pay. Daniel called it taking responsibility for his actions. Until he himself came up with something better, he would call it taking the coward's way out.

He lost track of the times he'd gone to his room to count his money to see if he and Daniel had enough to return home. They did, but just barely. Once they set foot on American soil, they'd have to scramble to earn a

living. In his heart he knew the good life, as he'd known it, was about to end. He had to make the decision to bury it and go on from there.

"You look tired, Reuben, why don't you go to bed," Daniel said softly. He had been watching his friend, hating the haunted look in his eyes.

"I've been thinking, Daniel. Maybe it's time for us to go home. Right after the first of the year. Fares will be a little cheaper. We'll have to do a bit of scrambling when we get home, but we'll manage." Reuben paused and looked directly into Daniel's eyes. "If you want to stay here, it's fine with me."

When Daniel answered it was in the new manly tone he'd acquired during the days at the hospital, waiting to see if his friend would live or die. "Yes, I think it's time to move on. These last two years are something I will never forget. And I've had to scramble before, so it won't be anything new to me. It might be a little harder this time because I'm determined to go to law school. But Mickey had such grand plans for you, taking over the wineries. What are you going to tell her?"

Reuben wasn't sure that he liked this new assertive, speak-your-mind Daniel. Later he would figure out where and when the change had occurred in his friend. Even his eyes were different, as though he knew something secret and important.

"I haven't said anything to Mickey," he replied. "I wanted to talk to you first. I've been running it over and over in my mind since I left the hospital. As for the wineries, that was a dream, a wonderful, insane dream. My . . . my accident showed me what reality is. Château Fonsard and Château Michelene were Mickey's husband's dreams. I wanted to make them mine, but that's impossible. Mickey tried to tell me that in her own way, but I chose not to listen. So she humored me. She humored me because she loved me, and what did I do? She doesn't know it, but I kicked her in the face, and when she was down I kicked her again." Reuben raised his hand to block Daniel's question. "Someday, a long time from now, we'll talk about this, but not now. If I try from now till the day I die, I can never make this right. I don't want to leave here any more than you do, but I have to. I have to make my own dreams." Or nightmares, he thought bitterly.

"I understand," Daniel said. He had to believe Reuben wasn't keeping his accident a secret, he was simply waiting for a better time, when it wasn't so raw and painful, to confide in him. He felt some of his anxiety drain away. Maybe now they could get back on their old footing.

Reuben sat down next to Daniel, his eyes thoughtful. "I'm kind of up a tree, Daniel. I'm not sure if I should tell Mickey now or

wait. If I tell her, she might decide to boot us out, and I'm not fully recovered. I need at least another month. If I take advantage of her generosity now, that means I'll be using her. She knows something is wrong. She's such a fine person and I love her with all my heart. I know I'll never, ever meet anyone I'll care for as much as I care for her. Christ, Daniel, I asked her to marry me, pleaded with her, and she said no. If she'd said yes, I wouldn't be going through all this and we wouldn't be leaving here. God, I love her so much. And to top it all" — he touched his groin and winced — "I can't make love to her. Daniel . . . I can't . . . get it up. I . . . haven't actually tried. She's so . . . distant . . . and polite. We're like strangers suddenly."

Daniel felt drained by Reuben's confession. There was little he could do now except pat him on the back in sympathy. "If I were you, I'd tell Mickey as soon as possible, lay it on the line. If, on the other hand, you plan on using your inability to, as you say, get it up, as an excuse, that's the coward's way out. I'm the first to admit I don't know a lot about these things, but Mickey was married to an older man. It's entirely possible that at one time or another he suffered through the same sort of thing. She might even be able to help you."

"It's no use. Don't you think I'd know if . . . forget it!"

Daniel shrugged. "It's your life, pal. I would like to know where we're going, if you have a game plan, that is."

Reuben grinned, but there was nothing humorous in his expression. "I thought we'd take our chances in California, land of sunshine — or Hollywood, to be more specific." What better way to get back at Bebe Rosen? he thought. Sooner or later he'd run into her again, and then he'd take out his revenge.

Daniel's eyebrows shot upward. California. Hollywood. Bebe Rosen. He felt a sudden twinge of pity for the girl. "A job in a studio will be fine. I'll go to school nights, too. Agreed?"

"Who knows, we might end up being janitors. It's the luck of the draw, Dan'l. Being at the right place at the right time also helps."

Daniel was so long in responding, Reuben felt his heart start to flutter. Was it possible he wanted to go his own way? Again he realized that Daniel had grown up while he was in the hospital. If he didn't watch out, they'd end up on equal footing. "Well?" he prompted irritably.

"I don't like the idea of keeping this between the two of us. . . . You'll have to tell Mickey." His words were so emphatic, Reuben winced.

"I know, and I'll do it, but for now we keep this under wraps. I can't believe you haven't

noticed that Mickey is rarely here, and when she is she's in her room. In other words, she's avoiding us, and telling her right now will serve no purpose. . . . By the way, when is Bebe due back from England?"

"Any time now," Daniel answered, trying to sound nonchalant. "Mickey didn't say anything, so I assume she's still there. Maybe she'll stay longer. I had only two letters from her and they were short. She said she was enjoying herself and 'didn't miss us at all, ha-ha.' She also said she goes to parties two or three times a week and has met some handsome eligible bachelors, but they don't have any money and she doesn't want a gigolo. There was something about having a terrible summer cold and going to the doctor's. That's about it." He made a pretense of tying his shoe so he wouldn't have to look into Reuben's face. "I'll ask Mickey when she's coming back. No sense in writing her a letter if she's on her way back."

"The holidays," Reuben said lamely.

"That's what I was thinking," Daniel said in relief.

"I'm about ready to turn in, how about you, pal? I try to put off climbing those stairs till the last minute."

"I'll help you," Daniel volunteered.

"No, I have to do it myself. The pain is a . . . punishment."

Daniel wanted to cry at the agony in his

friend's voice.

Mickey pulled the coverlet up to her chin. Never before had her bed been this cold. Before she retired, Nanette had placed hot bricks at the foot of the bed, but Mickey hadn't gotten into bed, preferring to stare out the window . . . seeing nothing and hearing nothing. With her gaze fixed on the flames in the fireplace as they danced upward, she was almost in a hypnotic state when she heard Reuben and Daniel as they passed her door. Instantly she came back to the present and drew in her breath, feeling her body grow rigid as she listened for the sound of footsteps. She didn't know which she dreaded more, Reuben coming to her room or Reuben not coming to her room.

They'd had so little contact since she'd dropped Bebe off at the farm, and that had been her doing. It was uncharacteristic, but she was behaving like a coward, and she admitted it. Instead of confronting Reuben, she'd chosen to return to her hospital work, leaving early in the morning and returning late, after dinner. In some ways she knew she was acting like Bebe, but she seemed incapable of stopping herself. Prisoners of silence they were — she, Daniel, and Reuben. Reuben would have to make the first move, and then she would react. That was the only decision she seemed capable of living with.

The clock on her bedside table told her an hour had gone by. Reuben wouldn't be coming to her room tonight or any other night. Ordering herself to relax, she returned to the dancing flames, and eventually she slept.

Thanksgiving and Christmas came and went, ordinary days with no special preparations.

Four days after Christmas, Reuben made up his mind to tell Mickey he had booked passage for America on January fifteenth. If it had been up to him, he would have told her that same night, but Henri Simone arrived at the château in the middle of the afternoon in a state of agitation and demanded Mickey go with him to the farm, seeming not to care that she was in bed nursing a sore throat and heavy cold. Henri spoke so rapidly in French, it was impossible for Reuben to follow his conservation.

Mickey didn't return that night or the next.

"Did something happen, Henri? It is too soon. Did you fetch the doctor?"

"Nothing happened. There was no fall, no exertion. Yvette coddles her like a baby. We know it is too soon, and yes, the doctor is there. Yvette said I was to fetch you." In typical Gallic style, he took his hands off the wheel of the car and threw them in the air. Mickey screamed for him to take the wheel and keep his eyes on the road.

"Henri, you don't think Bebe did . . . she didn't do anything to herself, did she?"

"It was my first thought, but no, the doctor said the child wants to come feet first and the cord is around his neck."

"How is Bebe?"

"She screams before the pain comes. She screams when the pain arrives, and she screams when the pain lets up. Her suffering is real, the doctor says. She will suffer more, for it is going to take a long time."

"What are we to do?" Dear God, what if something happens to her? Sol will never forgive me. I will never forgive myself. "How has she been behaving these past few days?" she asked.

"Well. She is at Yvette's side at all times. She cries when Yvette goes to market and then she comes to me. She is afraid to be alone. My heart breaks for her. Yvette scolds her, but it does no good. The baby is too fat," he said bluntly.

"Fat! What do you mean, fat?" Mickey cried. "How do you know this?"

"Because he won't come out is how I know. I know these things, Mickey. I have the animals and sometimes I have to help them. Fat," he repeated.

"You say he. Is it a boy, can they tell?"

"I say it is a boy," Henri said, taking his hands from the wheel to thump his chest. Then, remembering Mickey's hair-splitting

scream, he grabbed the wheel. "When I left she was screaming that the child is to be . . . buried when . . . when it finally comes. She is . . . crazy with the pain."

"No, she isn't crazy with the pain. She hates this child she carries." Mickey patted his arm. "Do not fear, Henri, it will not be buried. Did Yvette find a nursing mother?"

"No, *chérie,* the little one will have to take a bottle. The doctor knows of no nursing mothers. . . . Ah, we are here."

Mickey was white-faced when she entered Bebe's bedroom. Henri was right: her screaming could be heard in the next province. She looked at the pleading faces of Yvette and the doctor. They had obviously been at this for a while.

"That will be enough!" Mickey shouted above the din. "If you are woman enough to get yourself into this condition, you will behave like a woman and bear the pain. Here," she said, giving Bebe a folded washcloth, "bite down on this. We'll help you, but you must help us, too."

Hatred spewed from Bebe's eyes. "Get this bastard out of me and drown it before it cries. Do you hear me?"

Mickey shoved the wadded cloth into the girl's mouth without responding. You are the one who should be drowned, she thought bitterly.

"You take one hand and I'll take the other,"

she instructed Yvette. "Doctor, you will do what has to be done. Now!"

Bebe groaned through the washcloth. This was a part, a scene in a movie, and they were just making her do it over and over again until she had it right. It was just another role for her. A starring role, her most important performance to date.

"I don't know why the laudanum isn't working," Yvette said nervously.

"Because I can't give her too much," the doctor said. "I don't want her going completely under." In his entire career he'd never had a patient like this one. Birth was a miracle of God. Maybe this girl would change her mind once she saw the infant and held it in her arms. Maybe he was getting too old to deliver babies. Maybe this was the way American girls acted. Most of his patients went through birthing with hardly a sound. They nursed their babies and were back in the kitchen in two days' time. I am too old, he thought. First the young man at the Fonsard château and now this. Any fool could add two and two and get four.

Two hours later Bebe Rosen gave birth to a five-pound baby boy with a bluish tinge to his skin. The doctor worked quickly to unwrap the cord from his neck.

"Please," Mickey whispered, "you must save this child." When at last she heard the feeble cry, she raised exultant eyes to Yvette.

She looked down at Bebe, who was now sound asleep. She hadn't heard her son's first cry.

"Come," Yvette cried to Mickey. "We must clean and polish this little gem until he sparkles. Why do I feel like a mother?" she asked happily.

Tenderly the two women ministered to the child, taking turns, crooning and making silly sounds like new parents. When at last the baby was dressed and diapered, they sat back to view their handiwork. "Now. What are we to do with him?"

Mickey stared at the tiny bundle, mesmerized by his perfect features. Reuben's son! And she had helped to deliver him. How beautiful he was. She bent over the tiny basket and picked up the baby, her face bathed in wonderment. Yvette watched as she touched her cheek to the soft, downy head, then moved him slightly until his tiny chest was against her heart. Her smile was radiant when she turned to look at her friend. "What did you say, Yvette?"

"I said, so, what I suspected all along is true. The father of this child is Reuben. Now, tell me what we are to do."

Mickey smiled ruefully. "You will keep this secret, *chérie*." It was a statement, not a question.

"And whom would I tell?" Yvette grumbled. "I have a teat and some fresh goat's milk."

"Who is to feed him first?" Mickey asked.

"Since you are already holding him and he is warm and toasty, I guess you are," Yvette replied good-naturedly.

"But the teat's too big, he's choking. He's so hungry, this little piglet. What does Henri use for the animals?"

"Teats like this, and this is the smallest. His mouth is too small. A dropper! Wait, I will fetch it."

For two straight weeks, night and day, Mickey, Yvette, and Henri took turns feeding the infant with the dropper. They tried the teat at the end of two weeks and the baby gobbled down his goat's milk as if he'd been doing it from birth. Mickey beamed with pride.

"You act like a proper mother, Michelene," Yvette said. "Ah, you feel like one, too, is that it?"

"I cannot express my feelings, Yvette. Has Bebe asked about him?"

"Not a word. It is as though he does not exist. When are you going to tell me how this happened? I am your friend, and you kept this secret, you suffered alone. For shame!"

"I could not tell you because I do not know. Look in my purse and read the cable from Pamela. That is all I know. And as for the rest — what I have surmised — I do not wish to discuss it."

"I can see that. Tell me one thing. Reuben

is not to know about this child?"

"No. Yvette, I have decided to raise him as my son. We will tell Bebe the curé has taken the child to Paris to a family there. What do you think?"

"I think you are crazy and stupid, Michelene Fonsard. You are too old to raise a baby, and people will talk. Bah, you are a fool! But if you weren't going to take him, I was. We will tell the village that Henri sneaked out of my bed. He will like being famous. For you, my friend, Henri will go along with our story."

"I think," Mickey said, nuzzling the baby against her chest, "Reuben and Daniel are preparing to leave. I . . . I haven't been able to face him, knowing what I do. Several times I wanted to go to him to ask, to demand an answer, but I couldn't bring myself to do it. I couldn't burden him with my knowledge. I think Bebe may suspect that I know, but she has said nothing. With Bebe it is so easy to pretend nothing happened. I don't want to know the sordid details. It happened, and what kind of person am I if I can't forgive? Bebe is a child, a sly, manipulative girl who wants her own way. I'm not saying Reuben is faultless. But Bebe could have . . . the pitchfork speaks for itself, and Reuben's . . . lie that it was an accident to protect her . . . I don't . . . whatever will be will be, eh, my friend?"

"You are a better woman than I, Miche-

lene. I would have scratched his eyes out, jabbed him in the groin with my knee, and chopped at his neck. I would have spanked Bebe's bottom till she was sore and then I would have sent her back to her father with a letter telling him what she did."

"You are bloodthirsty, *chérie.* I love Reuben, nothing will ever change that. I knew he would leave someday. That day is arriving sooner than I expected. We've said enough. Here, it is your turn to hold this precious bundle. Be sure to give him as much love as I do. I'll be back tomorrow. Good night, old friend."

Bebe lay propped against the lace-edged pillows, a book in her hand that she had no intention of reading. She was freshly bathed and combed with just a touch of color on her lips. For days now she'd been up and about, sitting on a chair by the window, but she preferred bed. Tomorrow she would get up, dress in street clothes, and leave. There was one last thing to do before this role could be put in the can: she had to wait for Henri to fall asleep so she could visit her son for the first and last time. The infant had been fed and now Henri would struggle to stay awake in case the little one needed its pants changed. Yvette had gone to sleep hours earlier, exhausted, but with a smile on her face when she'd come in to say good night.

Bebe waited patiently, her eyes on the clock. She didn't know what to expect. In all her life she'd never really been up close to a newborn child. Seeing her own for the first time was going to be traumatic. Her hand kneaded her brow in pretended anguish. The scene had been rehearsed mentally and was ready to be shot: she'd look down at the sleeping infant and say something witty and charming, perhaps meaningful . . . to herself. Would she cry? Probably not. When one was being noble, one suffered in silence; it was so much more meaningful that way. Clovis had said no matter what the part was, she always came out as a sympathetic figure in the end. Her fans demanded it.

Bebe didn't need the hands on the clock to tell her she could visit her son now. Henri's lusty snores could be heard from one end of the farmhouse to the other. She made her way across the kitchen next to the huge fieldstone fireplace where the baby was kept. The pink-cheeked infant in the sturdy cradle wasn't anything like what she'd expected. With his tiny thumb in his mouth, already being sucked at in some unknown dream of needs fulfilled, he looked so peaceful, a cherub, a sweet angel down from heaven. Bebe dropped to her knees. Tentatively she reached out a trembling hand, then quickly withdrew it. She reached out again and this time touched the downy head. A smile found

its way to her lips. New chicks felt the same way. The tiny mouth puckered at the unfamiliar touch, and Bebe's did the same. "Oooh, hush," she cooed, "you musn't wake up." God, she wanted to pick up the little bundle, wanted it more than she'd ever wanted anything in her life. For a full five minutes, she argued with herself, anxiously eyeing Henri, who was sprawled on his chair by the fire. He was still snoring rhythmically. The baby probably thought it was music. Bebe smiled at the thought.

The child was wiggling now, struggling to fit his entire fist into his mouth. Bebe stepped back in alarm. "Please, please," she whispered, "don't cry. Please don't cry. I want to drink my fill of you. You're mine, you're my son."

Once the little fist was being suckled snugly, Bebe bent over and picked up her son. How still he was, how very warm! With a strangled sigh she brought him closer so she could kiss his plump, smooth cheek. He smelled so clean, but different from anything she'd ever smelled. Better than a thousand bottles of French perfume. "Flesh of my flesh," she told him. "You're my special miracle, little one. Daniel says his God gives only one to each of us, so you're mine. You'll always be in my heart, right next to Daniel. I wish you could hear me and understand what I'm saying. You're going to grow up in a strange place

and never know me because that's what's best for you. It doesn't matter about me. I don't deserve something as wonderful and perfect as you, but someday I'm going to come back for you. I'll find you and claim you as my own then," she whispered fiercely. "It won't be for a while, but I will come for you. It's my promise to you and to myself." The baby slept on, content in her arms.

Bebe laid him back into his mound of warm blankets. She'd promised herself she wouldn't cry, but the tears burning her eyes overflowed. Almost angrily she wiped at them with the back of her hand. "I have to give you a name. I can't leave till I give you a name." Her brain whirled frantically. Henri was stirring now, and the baby was starting to fret. Name after name raced through her head. John Paul. She leaned over the cradle for the last time. "I christen you John Paul Rosen Tarz." Again she brushed away the salty tears slipping into her mouth. "Good-bye, John Paul . . . for now."

The real Bebe Rosen crawled into her bed and stifled her sobs until she fell asleep.

The next morning Bebe appeared in the kitchen, suitcase in hand, demanding to see Mickey, then to be taken to the depot. Henri stood uncertainly in the kitchen, not knowing what to do. Finally he called Mickey and handed the phone to Bebe.

"And I want the check my father sent you. If you leave now," she said to Mickey, "you can meet us at the depot." Her voice was cold and haughty as she refused to look Mickey in the eye.

"Bebe . . . you can't just . . ." She could, Mickey decided, do whatever she pleased. "You're making a terrible mistake, Bebe."

"If I'm woman enough to have a baby, then I'm woman enough to go off on my own, to take responsibility for myself," Bebe said.

"Your father. I promised. . . ."

"And you kept your promise. I'll write to him and tell him I'm off on my own. I won't involve you. You are, as they say, off the hook."

The moon rode high in the sky when Mickey returned to the Simone farm. It had been a terrible day. At the depot, Bebe hadn't even looked at her as she'd snatched the envelope from her hands and walked onto the train. There had been no sign of her at any window. Henri had gone off to find her but had come back empty-handed. When she got back to the château, Reuben had come to her, saying he needed to talk. All she'd had to do was take one look at his eyes and she knew what he wanted to talk about. So she'd whisked herself away, calling over her shoulder that they would talk tomorrow at breakfast, a late mid-morning breakfast.

Now she faced Yvette as they sat at her

390

kitchen table.

"The child has no name, and he must be christened," Yvette said.

Mickey sighed. "You and Henri are to be the proud godparents. And you must give a suitable gift. Your love will do nicely." Mickey smiled. "I contacted the curé, and it is to be done this Sunday. Bebe will never believe I would take her child. If someday she comes looking for him, she will come to you first. You will alert me and I will go to Bordeaux . . . anyplace, so she doesn't find him. You must swear to me, both of you, that you will never tell her where the child is." Henri and Yvette nodded solemnly, crossing themselves to seal the promise.

Henri went to bed, and the two old friends talked far into the night.

"You have not given Reuben enough time. . . . Time, Mickey, makes things better. Do not do anything foolish."

"It's not me, Yvette. Reuben is the one who has decided to leave. I can read in on his face. He's different. Since his accident he cannot . . . No, it is me," Mickey cried brokenly.

"No, *chérie,* it is not you. He is young, he thinks he failed you. Now he has to go out and prove himself. He must leave, I see the way he is thinking. He does not want to be a burden to you. Did he not do his best to learn the wine business before the accident? That was for you, Michelene, no one else. He loved

you and wanted to earn his keep. He still loves you. This one will always love you. I see it written all over him. Why can't you forgive him his indiscretion?"

"I'm so frightened. What will I do when he's gone? I love him so much, my heart is sore. I feel like I want to die, and I haven't even heard him say the words yet. He is so proud. God is punishing me for my past. I can forgive him his indiscretion, but he cannot forgive himself, I see it in his eyes."

"That is not true. Do you see me being punished? No! And we were cut from the same bolt! No, *chérie,* God does not punish. He forgives. I do not say it will be easy. You are strong, my friend. We are French through and through. Remember that."

"In my empty bed at night and when I dine alone? I find little comfort in what you say, Yvette. I knew this would happen. I warned myself, but I ignored my own warnings."

"Because you were in love, *chérie.* We do strange things when we are in love. Who knows better than I? You will survive. I will see to it."

The baby stirred behind them. They watched as his little feet kicked for a moment and then became still.

"We must come up with a suitable name for this child."

"The name must be French," Mickey said, "if I am to raise him."

"No," Yvette said firmly. "We must pick a name that can be taken as French or American. His parents are American. Promise me that you will never forget that fact. I say we call him Philip. That is very American sounding. For his birth certificate and his identity papers. A double set. A French set of papers with the name Philippe. How does that sound to your ears?"

Mickey rolled the name off her tongue several times. "I think this is one of your better ideas, Yvette. Philippe it is. I must go now. They wonder at the château why I come here so much. God only knows what Reuben and Daniel think. I am a very poor liar, old friend."

"You will learn," Yvette said philosophically.

Mickey kissed the baby's soft cheek, tears welling in her eyes. "I promise you a wonderful life, little one," she said huskily.

Yvette watched her friend until she was out of sight, her eyes filled with concern. Why couldn't Mickey have happiness? She did so much good, had such a gentle, giving heart. "Be kind to her," she whispered silently, her eyes raised upward. "Please, be kind."

Reuben was dressed in a suit with a shirt and a tie when Mickey entered the morning room for breakfast. Not today, she pleaded silently, it can't be today. She wasn't ready to say good-bye. He'd said he wanted to talk, not

say good-bye. He looked so formal, so cool, aloof. Dear God, what was he going to say? Please, let me be able to survive it, she prayed.

At the table, Reuben's movements were stiff and awkward as he reached across to grasp Mickey's hands in his own. How tired she looked, he thought. He felt personally responsible for her drained, exhausted look. Now he was going to deliver a shattering, devastating blow.

His eyes were sad, full of regret at his own betrayal. But he couldn't stay here and live a lie; he loved Mickey too much to do that to her.

"I've been wanting to talk to you, but I sensed you were avoiding me. I . . . didn't ask why because the last time I demanded answers from you a disaster occurred. We're leaving today, Daniel and I." He held on to her hands, feeling and seeing her pain-filled reaction to his words. "I didn't think today would . . . would creep up so fast. Perhaps it is better this way, it will be over quickly. If you had allowed me . . . if you had taken the time to talk to me, it would have just caused both of us more anguish. A man from the village is coming with a car to take us to the depot. I want to say good-bye here, here in this place where . . . where we lived so happily together. I want . . . I need . . . to say . . ."

"Reuben, please, you don't have to . . . to

explain . . . anything to me." She could barely speak. The pain she was feeling weighed her down until she felt she was suffocating.

Reuben hated the look in her eyes, like a beautiful wild creature caught in a trap. He hated having to cause this much pain. The one thing he'd never wanted to do was hurt this woman he loved. How had this happened to them? The truth struck him intensely every time he was forced to remember.

Mickey held herself in check. Now was not the time to give in to her grief. For some time she'd known this day was coming, and she'd halfway prepared for it. But nothing had prepared her for the look of shame and guilt in Reuben's face. If nothing else, she would make this right for him, even if she had to say the words for him so he could move on and not prolong this agony. She bit her lip to stem the flow of her tears, and tasted her own blood. "I understand, Reuben. It is time for you to get on with your life."

Mickey's brave front tore at his heart. God, he wanted to reach out, to gather her close. Part of him wanted to confess his betrayal, to beg forgiveness, to promise her anything; but that would destroy her. How could he destroy what he loved most, just so he could walk away, forgiven? What he was doing was best . . . for Mickey. It didn't matter about him.

There was so much he wanted to say, to let her know. . . . He needed something to take

away with him. . . . He knew he'd come back, after he'd made things right. Should he say it, or was it better left unsaid? Mickey's tears were unexpected, he didn't know how to react to them, silent tears of . . . grief, as though he were dead. In a way, he was. "Please, Mickey, don't cry," he pleaded.

"I don't mean to. I'm sorry. I don't want you to see me this way. I don't want you to go away carrying my tears with you. Oh, Reuben, you don't have to go. Things will . . . I'm sure it's just temporary. . . . These things happen. It doesn't matter!' she cried.

"I'm . . . so sorry," he cried brokenly. "I swear to you I'll come back, perhaps not right away, but I will come back." At these words Mickey turned away. It was as if he had struck her. "Look at me, Mickey, and tell me you believe me. I promise. I've never made a promise to you I didn't keep."

When her eyes met his they were steady. "Reuben, please, I don't want you to make promises. We will say au revoir, and if we are meant to see each other again, we will. It is that simple, *chéri*." Those words sealed her defeat, the weight of it made her lower her head. She couldn't find the strength to look at him.

"I don't know how I can leave you," Reuben said, his voice wavering. "You mean so much to me. You are my life! But I . . ." He almost confessed then, in that one brief

second. But he didn't. If she hadn't lifted her head at that precise moment, he knew he would have. It was more than he could bear, having to read his own betrayal in her eyes. She thought — and he was allowing her to believe it — that he was leaving because he was impotent. How cruel he was being, how selfish! Was his sin then only one of omission? Someday Mickey would understand.

Mickey swallowed hard. "You haven't said where you are going, what you will do, and how you will live. Do you have money?" she asked in a practical tone.

"We'll get by. We'll work. Neither Daniel nor I want to go back to New York, so we decided to go to California and take our chances in the movie industry. That's where things are happening right now."

"Hollywood!" gasped Mickey. Yes, of course. Hollywood. Bebe. Dear God. "Reuben," she said tearfully, "you must wait here for one minute . . . I will be right back. Promise me that you won't leave until I return." Reuben nodded, a puzzled look on his face.

Mickey raced up the stairs, dabbing at eyes that were blinded with tears. Where was it? Where had she put it? Clothing flew in every direction as she searched for the packet of American dollars she'd secured early in the spring, anticipating this very moment. It was important — no, *crucial* — to know in her

heart that Reuben and Daniel would be all right. After all, it was only money. She rifled through the crisp bills. Two thousand; it would give them a good year until they established themselves. Poor things, they were going to be like sheep to the slaughter.

Taking her stationery from the top drawer of the little cherrywood desk, she quickly scribbled a letter of introduction to Sol Rosen for both Reuben and Daniel. A second short note requested that he give them both jobs in return for the favor she'd done him in taking Bebe.

Reuben flushed scarlet when she returned with her offerings, but he accepted both money and letters. "I'll pay you back, every cent. I won't use the letters unless . . . unless things become difficult." This was his chance, the perfect time to ask about Bebe. My God, an actual letter to Sol Rosen at Fairmont Studios. He could almost taste his revenge. "I'm sorry I won't be here to see Bebe when she returns. Say good-bye to her for me and Daniel. Daniel said he left a letter for her on his bureau."

"Bebe . . . won't be coming back to the château. She decided to stay in England. I'll tell her when I hear from her. It's very possible you will see her before I do, if she decides to return home."

Reuben searched her eyes for any sign of knowledge. There was none. So he was off

the hook after all. He would have to carry his guilt with him until he had found Bebe and evened the score. Why had he thought it was going to be easy? Someday, somewhere, he was going to remember exactly what had happened to him that night to make him go so crazy. Someday.

"I hear the car, Reuben," Mickey said, her voice shaky. "Where is Daniel?"

"He's outside, waiting. Please, Mickey, no tears. If Daniel sees you cry . . . I don't know what he'll do."

Mickey stepped into his arms for the last time. How warm he felt, how very alive! She could hear his heart, actually felt it beating. Too rapidly, too hard . . . or was that her own? Tenderly, with exquisite finality, his hand stroked her hair, her neck, the small of her back. Determined not to weaken at the last moment, she bit down on her lip and forced the tears to remain in check. "Au revoir, *chéri*."

From somewhere deep inside him, the Hebraic farewell rose to his lips. "Shalom, my love."

Mickey watched him walk away from her, to the car. Her heart shattered into countless pieces. Somehow, she'd hoped, at the last minute, that he would change his mind.

Daniel rushed up to her; tears streaming down his cheeks, he took her in his arms and turned her so her back was to Reuben. "How,

tell me how to say good-bye? How can I thank you? I don't have the words."

Mickey swallowed past the lump in her throat. "You say it, *chéri*. Not good-bye, that is too final. Au revoir. We will meet again. I know we will. Promise me two things, Daniel," she implored, looking deeply into his eyes.

"Anything. For you, Mickey, anything." *She knows.*

"Promise me you will take care of Reuben for me. I am entrusting him into your care." *He knows I know. Dear, wonderful Daniel.* Their eyes locked in silent understanding.

"I'll do my best, and if my best isn't good enough, I'll try harder. And the second promise?"

"That you will think of me from time to time."

Daniel could only nod. When he had himself under control he said, "You will take care of Jake for me?" Mickey nodded bleakly. "Au revoir, Mickey."

The men climbed into the car that would take them away. It was the end of the world, Mickey thought, the end of her world. All she had to do now was put one foot in front of the other and go back into the château. How could she do it? How could she walk away from the one man she had ever loved, her one true happiness? *You must do it because*

you have no other choice, an inner voice directed her. But she felt bruised, beaten, and too weary to move. Part of her wanted to scratch and claw, to demand he come back and stop this nonsense. The other part demanded dignity and a noble spirit. One step, two, three, four. She wouldn't turn around, she just would not. Five, six. Like lightning she swiveled. The inner voice whispered, *You turned on purpose because you remember telling Reuben true love is when the lover looks back and smiles. You want to see what he does. . . .* Turn, Reuben, look for me, she pleaded silently. How would she be able to tell if he did or didn't, with tears blinding her? She'd feel it, sense it. But he wasn't going to look back. He would drive away from her, out of her life, and she'd never see him again. "Good-bye, my love," she murmured.

There was lead in his shoes and a thousand pounds on his shoulders. There was something wrong with his eyes, he could feel a painful stinging, something he'd never felt in the hospital or during his recovery. His chest was achingly heavy. He felt ill. Insane. He was insane to walk away from this place and the woman he'd grown to love more than life itself. Things would get better, she'd said; he didn't have to go. But she didn't know . . . she thought . . . This time he was really leaving her, going back to America. The lump in

401

his throat was strangling him now. Look back, he told himself; don't leave like this! Even though they'd said their good-byes, he needed one last look at what he was giving up because of . . . At last he turned, straining his eyes. She was there, but was she facing him or walking away? His eyes ached with the strain. If it's true love, you look back. Mickey had said that. Well, he was looking back. But he couldn't see. Angrily he swiped at his watery eyes. He waved and whispered, "I'll always love you." It didn't matter whether she heard him or not; he needed to hear the words. It was a pity he couldn't see Mickey's smile, the smile that rivaled the sun for brightness.

As the château receded from view, Reuben forced his eyes forward. That part of his life was over.

■ ■ ■ ■

PART TWO

■ ■ ■ ■

Part Two

CHAPTER SEVENTEEN

Hollywood, 1921

Reuben and Daniel endured a grueling ocean crossing and then boarded the train in New York, traveling slowly across the continent. They didn't stop for more than a night on the East Coast; their future lay in Hollywood, California.

They didn't discuss Mickey or Bebe during their travels. They spoke only about the future. That morning, before disembarking from the train, Reuben had shown Daniel the two thousand dollars Mickey had given him and the letter of introduction to Sol Rosen. He wondered why his friend's eyes hadn't wavered as he displayed the money.

Daniel watched as Reuben hired a hack to take them to a decent apartment house and listened to the description he gave the driver concerning his requirements. On the way Reuben hung his head out the window and hooted, "Look at that sunset! Did you ever see such a bright one, Dan'l?"

Daniel didn't understand Reuben's cheerfulness. Why couldn't they grieve for a little while? They had left two and a half years of their lives in France. It wasn't easy for him to turn it off the way it seemed to be for Reuben. He wished he were back in France. He missed Mickey; he missed the château and the Sorbonne. He missed Jake. He sighed wearily; he would have to put up a brave front for Reuben's sake.

Reuben pulled the envelopes out of his pocket again and handed them to Daniel. "Here. You keep the money, pal. I'm appointing you our banker. If we're careful, it can last quite a while. I want to start paying Mickey back as soon as possible. With interest. . . . I have a good feeling about California, Daniel. I think we're going to make it here. You're going to school, and I think I want to run one of those big motion picture studios." Reuben laughed at Daniel's incredulous expression. "We'll work our way up. Why not?"

"Just like that, you want to run one of those big studios? What are you going to do, walk off the street and say, Look, I'm here!"

"Hell no. But Hollywood is a land of dreams. Why can't I have a dream? Why can't I run a studio? Give me one good reason!"

"Because you don't know a goddamned thing about the movie business. There're already people running the studios. What do

you plan to do with them? They aren't going to let you walk in and snatch their jobs."

"Daniel, Daniel, we have to work on your imagination. If you want something bad enough, there's a way to get it. I just have to figure out the best way. I learned a few things back in France, and Hollywood will be the perfect place to test them out."

"Here you are, guys." The sound of the driver's voice brought Daniel back to reality. "Crestwood Apartments. There's the vacancy sign I told you about."

Fifteen minutes later they were settled in a clean one-bedroom apartment that was sparsely furnished. The rent was twenty dollars a month and it was on the bus line, three blocks in from the corner of Hollywood and Vine. It had a bathroom with a pink carpet and a sink full of years of rust stains. The beds looked comfortable enough, and the sheets, while thin, were clean and unwrinkled. It was a far cry from the luxury of the château, but, it would have to do.

"Why don't you settle us in and then read through those," Reuben said, referring to the *Citizen's News* and the *Ledger Gazette* they'd picked up on the way to the apartment house. "Maybe they'll have some information that'll help us out. I think I'll go out and check around the neighborhood. That okay with you?"

Reuben left the third-floor apartment and

walked aimlessly, trying to decide where to go. Spotting blue lights in the early darkness, he headed for the canopied doorway they surrounded. Gilt lettering on the heavy blue doors welcomed patrons to the Mimosa Club. What the hell, thought Reuben, shrugging. A man checked him out through a small glass window before opening the door. Stale sweat, staler perfume, and smoke-laden air rushed against him. It was so rank he almost gagged, but he forced himself to take a deep breath, then made his way across the crowded room to the bar. Loud honky-tonk music and shrill laughter grated on him. How was a man supposed to think in this damned racket? Obviously he wasn't. If a man wanted to think, he went to the library or stayed home. If he wanted a drink and a little fun, he came to a place like the Mimosa Club. Reuben squeezed himself next to the bar and ordered a drink.

The customers didn't surprise him. Well-dressed men and women, pimps and their floozies, the usual number of husbands and fathers having a beer and a quick game of cards before going home. Everyone was talking to someone, he noticed. Couples, groups. He appeared to be the only person alone in the crowded room. A little man with pomade-slicked hair and a trim mustache approached the bar. For a few moments he said nothing, merely leaned back and examined his buffed

408

nails. Then: "You new here?" he asked casually.

Reuben almost laughed. Later, at home, he'd mimic the man when he described him to Daniel. "You could say that," he drawled. He towered over the little man by almost two feet. Two of his upper arms would make up the man's skinny chest. But there was something likable about him.

"This is my club. Max Gould." He introduced himself as if he were announcing the arrival of the President and didn't offer to shake hands. So far, he hadn't looked Reuben in the eye, possibly because he didn't feel like craning his neck.

"Reuben Tarz. Do I detect a hometown Brooklyn accent?"

For the first time, Max Arthur Gould looked up into the handsome stranger's eyes. "Yeah. But how did you know? You don't have one yourself."

"I've been in France for a while," Reuben said. "But I'd know that accent anywhere. I grew up in Brooklyn."

Max Gould took a second look at the stranger. He wasn't a flatfoot, that was for sure. He'd detected a slight limp as he'd watched him cut through the crowd. Must've been the war, he decided. "You a vet?" he asked curiously. Reuben nodded. "What's your game?"

Reuben pretended to take his time. What

did he want? "A little information would help. About this town, you know, what makes it tick. A job, money, action . . . whatever." He swung around and ordered a second beer he didn't want. As he ignored Max and concentrated on the beer, he felt the little man studying him.

"I got a table in the back. Follow me and we can talk. This racket is driving me crazy."

The minute they were settled at the private table, Max got down to business. "You're a pretty beefy guy. You look like you can handle yourself."

Reuben looked over to an open doorway. "You mean like those two muscleheads you got doing double duty?"

"Yeah," Max said softly.

"I've done my share both in the war and in Brooklyn." Reuben looked hard at the little man to make sure he'd made his point.

Max Gould always prided himself on being able to read people correctly. What he thought he had before him was a classy young man who knew a little more than how to put his tie on straight — which as he glanced at the handsome man's neck he realized was done to perfection. A perfect Windsor knot.

"Look, I run a good business here. I make money. The people that work for me make money. Everyone is happy. Money," he said, leaning across the table, "is the name of the game. Money is power, but you know that

already, don't you, Tarz? How old are you?"

"Twenty-six," Reuben lied. "But you didn't bring me over here to ask me my age. What's your angle, and don't tell me you don't have one. Everyone's got an angle."

"Relax." Max laughed at Reuben's brashness. "If you're looking for some part-time work, I can accommodate you."

"What's the setup?" Reuben asked. He liked the turn of the conversation.

"A few pickups. Sometimes a few deliveries. Your share is one percent of whatever you pick up. A bonus at the end of the month. If you have to sit on someone, you sit; you're sure as hell big enough. But maybe you don't want to get your nice clothes dirty." Max grinned.

This was exactly what he needed to get him by during the next few weeks. He wanted time to settle into this place, get to know it and feel comfortable without being desperate for money. The two thousand dollars he and Daniel had looked like a small fortune now, but he didn't want to get caught with his pants down.

"Let's talk turkey," he said.

For thirty minutes they discussed Max's possibilities and Reuben's availability. It came down to maybe three pickups a week. Two, maybe three bucks a night and a ten-buck bonus at the end of the month, providing everything went all right. If he was careful,

he could send Mickey fifty dollars the first of every month. "I'm in" was Reuben's final comment.

"If you don't mind my askin', what kind of . . . daytime work are you in?"

Reuben started to itch. Lie or not lie? If he lied, the little man was apt to find him out. If he told the truth, he might decide he could do without him. A gambler at heart, Reuben stared down at Max. "I just got here straight from France. I have a letter of introduction to the head of one of the studios. I guess you could say I'll be working there, doing what, I don't know: but this much I do know, one of these days I'll be the head of one of these studios. Anything else?"

Max almost laughed until he looked into Reuben's eyes. The bugger had admitted to not having a job, yet he truly believed what he'd just said. He stood up and stared at Reuben. For the life of him he couldn't think of a thing to say. He decided to believe everything Reuben had told him . . . except his age, of course. If his instincts were right, this guy might be someone to keep handy.

A buzzer sounded somewhere nearby, and Max told Reuben to sit quietly. He watched, bug-eyed, as cups were emptied and refilled with steaming coffee. His cup was snatched quicker than he could blink. The transformation from speakeasy to sleazy supper club was the slickest, quickest operation he'd ever

seen. He found himself grinning and mockingly saluted Max, who had risen and was jittering around the entrance.

He continued to watch in admiration as Max put the police officers through their paces. First he offered a table for two in the back of the room, followed by the services of two shapely, friendly waitresses in scanty uniforms, who proceeded to fawn and tickle both men under their chins. Out of the corner of his eye Reuben saw a man part a curtain. Instead of the gun he expected to see, a flash went off, and he laughed. He decided this was as good a time as any to leave.

"Leaving already? I hope you enjoyed your coffee," Max said, waylaying him at the door. "You won't believe this," he whispered, "but those two creeps are on the take and still they put me through this. Every second I'm a supper club I lose money. I been takin' pictures, though. Got them by the balls that way. City Hall might be interested someday."

Reuben laughed. Max couldn't help but ask, "What would you do?"

"Squeeze!"

Max's full-bodied laugh followed him out the door.

"Gangsters! I don't think Mickey would expect you to hang out with gangsters just so she could be repaid," Daniel said anxiously

when he'd heard about Reuben's evening.

"Don't worry. If you could have seen how smooth this operation was, you wouldn't give it a second thought. Look, you know it takes all kinds to make this world spin. I didn't just fall off the tree now, did I? I know what's going on, and I'll be careful. If I keep my mouth shut, not give Max the edge, I think I can work and pay Mickey off. Who knows, later on it might pay even more. This is for now."

A lot of things were for now, Daniel decided. He'd voiced his thoughts; the rest was up to Reuben. "I've read through the papers, and I've got some addresses for schools and studios. And everything's ready for tomorrow — I got the landlady to press our suits."

"We're going to spend the next couple of days getting to know the territory," Reuben said. "I'll take the studios and you take the schools. But tomorrow you'll come with me to test the waters. Fair enough?" Daniel nodded his agreement. "We're on our way, Dan'l! You nervous?"

"Like a cat in the rain."

It was one of Hollywood's better days, with the sun shining down on busloads of hopeful actors and actresses trundling their way to their dreams. Sun was important to those struggling to make it in the sinful city. It was easier to accept rejection when the day was ripe and golden.

All these nameless men and women — "the hopefuls," as Reuben had begun to refer to them — believed the myth. Just keep plugging along in the land of magic; there's fame and fortune at the end of the dusty path.

It was a twenty-minute ride to the studio, and Reuben did his best to breathe through his mouth. He hated the scent of unwashed bodies, stale perfume, and the greasy hair pomade that everyone seemed to favor.

"Thirty seats on this bus, Reuben," Daniel hissed, "and fifty people." Reuben laughed. Daniel always counted. They'd been here only a few weeks and were soaking up the atmosphere on a daily basis. Daniel was being tutored by a college professor who had come to Hollywood to become a star, and Reuben had established a good working rapport with Max Gould, had even been invited home to sample his mother Rachel's noodle pudding, but only with the understanding that he not mention business; she thought Max ran a delicatessen.

Reuben and Daniel had scouted Metro Pictures, Universal Studios, and Fox Film Corporation; the last studio had been Paramount. Today they were on their way to Fairmont, Daniel to gather as much information as he could and Reuben to see the big man Sol Rosen. He patted the letters in his breast pocket: he'd need them.

His thoughts turned to Mickey. What was

she doing right now, this very minute? he wondered. Was she thinking about him? If he was in her mind and in her heart, then everything else was bearable. A man could accomplish anything when he had someone to go home to at the end of the day — or the year, he thought ruefully. Or maybe the decade? As always, when he thought of Mickey, Bebe insinuated herself into his thoughts. Today would tell the story. Getting a job at Fairmont was his way of turning the knife . . . in Bebe. She wouldn't get away with what she had done to him and go on her happy, meddling way. His goal was to be in her face at the first opportunity — and in a position of power. He only hoped she'd stay away long enough for him to get there.

When the bus crunched to a halt outside the studio gates, Reuben hung back, letting the crowd stampede by. Then he and Daniel looked at each other, their glances anxious but exultant. This was the day they'd been working toward.

Fairmont's studio lot was huge but unkempt, debris strewn all over. The guards at the gate were dressed sloppily, unlike the natty snap-to-attention men in uniform at the other studios. The buildings here were in dire need of paint and outside maintenance. The actors and actresses, with the exception of Fairmont's one big star, Clovis Ames, were as

third-rate as the studio itself. The casting directors appeared unprofessional and sloppy. The clods directing the calls looked like recruited farmers to Reuben, although most of them had New York accents and talked out of the side of their mouth. An odd combination of traits, he mused, wondering if they were Sol's relatives.

Reuben mounted the seven steps that would take him to the studio head's office. In his mind he wasn't sure if he should approach Sol Rosen as studio owner or as Bebe's father. He decided to play it by ear. Sometimes rehearsed speeches and introductions came out flat and phony.

A middle-aged receptionist with spectacles hanging off her nose looked up at Reuben's entrance. His unusually virile good looks had the usual effect: her hand shot up automatically to pat her crimped and polished hair, and she smiled coyly. Reuben thought her round circles of rouge clownish. He smiled, the practiced smile, showing just enough strong white teeth.

"Can I help you?" the woman asked.

"Reuben Tarz to see Mr. Rosen," he stated, and handed her the sealed envelope.

"I usually open all the mail, unless it's personal. Is this personal?" the receptionist simpered.

"Yes, it is. It's from Madame Fonsard in France. I'll wait while you give it to Mr.

Rosen." He watched as the woman sashayed her way into what looked like Rosen's inner sanctum.

Reuben immediately began to study the waiting area. It was almost bare. Three straight-back chairs that looked uncomfortable as hell, the receptionist's desk and chair, a wastebasket, and a dusty plant that stood in one corner. A crooked picture of a bowl of fruit on one of the walls. The place resembled a room in a mission house. Where was the glitz and glitter he'd expected? Nevertheless, he felt a quiver of excitement. Potential. The place had potential just waiting to be tapped. It had all the right ingredients and obviously no one at the helm.

Reuben was almost glad his vision was impaired when he entered Rosen's office. Even before he stepped through the door he'd known that this office would be an extension of the waiting room outside. In the blink of an eye he categorized it as early prop room and the man sitting behind the desk as vintage prop room.

Sol Rosen stood and waddled over to Reuben in shoes that were too large for his feet. A fat, smelly cigar was clamped between his teeth. He was stocky, pugnacious-looking, and sported a nose that could be described only as a honker. Spiky gray hair stood on end, looking as though it hadn't been combed or brushed for days. His gray suit was un-

pressed, his shirt wrinkled, and his tie full of stains. Reuben knew the man's neck was dirty without having to look and could bet he'd worn the same shirt three days in a row.

Rosen worked the cigar around to the opposite side of his mouth with his tongue. He didn't bother to remove it when he spoke. "What kind of work you looking for? Times are hard here at the studios."

Reuben blinked in disbelief at the whine in the man's voice. He was about to say something until he looked into Rosen's eyes — the same incredible green as Bebe's and just as calculating. Always start high, something told him. If you start low, you sink.

"Something in the front office. Managerial. A liaison, if you prefer," he said coolly. He doubted the man even knew what the word meant.

Sol Rosen gave a horsey laugh. There was no amusement in the sound. "Do I look like I need a leezon?" he croaked. "I run this business myself. You start hiring people to take over and you end up out in the cold. They snatch the goddamn rug right out from under you. I might — and this is a big might, mind you — be able to give you a couple of days' work as extras. You interested?"

Reuben didn't have to think about his answer. "No. I don't think that was exactly what Madame Fonsard had in mind for us

when she wrote you the letters you're holding."

"You telling me you read these . . . these personal letters?" Rosen blustered.

"That's not what I'm saying at all," Reuben said smoothly, his eyes never wavering. "Madame Fonsard read me the letters before she sealed them in the envelope. She expects you to give my partner and myself suitable employment. She said if you couldn't see your way clear to doing as she asked, I was to cable her immediately." Reuben turned as if to leave.

"Hold on, not so fast. What's so special about you and your buddy? And where the hell is this buddy of yours?"

"He's here at the studio checking things out," Reuben informed him. The men stared at each other. Rosen took a step backward and Reuben smiled gently.

"Why's she putting the squeeze on me like this?" The obscene-looking cigar shifted to the left side of Sol's mouth.

"Your daughter was a real handful, Mr. Rosen. But then, that's why you sent her to France, wasn't it? Madame read me your letter, the one where you implored her to take care of Miss Rosen? She put all her affairs aside to do as you requested — and before you can ask what my position was, I ran the winery in Bordeaux." Reuben's stomach tightened when he thought of what he had

just said. None of it was untruth — especially about how Mickey had put *all* her affairs to one side when Bebe arrived. "Madame Fonsard took me into her confidence because she trusted me. She said you needed someone in your offices that you could trust. That's why I'm here. But if you've got no place for us . . ." His hand reached out to open the door before Sol called him back.

"Hey, you, wait a minute." Reuben turned around, a friendly smile on his face. Sol sighed. "Let me see what I can work out here. Come back tomorrow morning around ten, you and your . . . partner. I'm not promising anything. You content to chew on that for the time being?"

"I'll hold off sending the cable, then, and I'll see you tomorrow morning, Mr. Rosen. I appreciate your taking the time to see me." He held out his hand, but Sol turned his back and shuffled across the room to his desk.

When the door closed behind Reuben, Sol sat down heavily and tried to light his soggy cigar. Finally he gave up and took a new one out of a dusty box in his bottom drawer. He bit off the end and spit it across the room. "What chutzpah!" he muttered. Right this goddamned minute that arrogant shit was walking away thinking him an *alter kocker*. "Bullshit!" he exploded, puffing away at his newly lit cigar.

Sol unfolded Mickey's letter and read it

421

several more times. It was worded cleverly, but he wasn't stupid. He correctly interpreted the implied threat. Either he gave these two jokers jobs — jobs that paid decent money — or she would start to take an active interest in her half of the business. Marchioness Michelene Fonsard owned fifty-one percent of Fairmont Studios. A very willing silent partner who, up until now, had never asked for an accounting, never interfered with how the business was run, and never made demands.

His ass would be in a sling if he didn't comply with her request. He couldn't help but wonder how much Mickey had told the man who had just left his office. If he was her lover, which he probably was, then he knew everything. As he contemplated this assumption, Sol got a jittery feeling in his stomach.

He was grateful to Mickey for saving his hide, but only when it was convenient to be grateful. He'd come to Los Angeles because his wife hated the junk business he'd run on Chicago's South Side. With her incessant complaining, she'd convinced him that their fortunes could be made in the movie business. They'd soon found out that the capital from the sale of their junk business wasn't going to get them anywhere in the new boom town called Hollywood. It had been his wife's idea to go to France and talk to her cousin Mickey. Sol had been able to convince

Mickey that a fortune was there for the making in the up-and-coming motion picture industry, and she'd invested handsomely. Actually, she'd contributed almost three-quarters of the capital needed, but on paper they were almost equal partners. Within two years Sol had repaid her a quarter of the money he owed. And until this letter, she'd never mentioned the business. Oftentimes he'd wondered if she was interested at all. Now he knew she was.

In the beginning, when the studio was operating in the red, he'd sent quarterly reports. But when the numbers switched from red to black, he'd developed a bad memory. When Mickey made no comment about the fact that she no longer seemed to be receiving any reports, he felt safe skimming off the top. If his memory was accurate, he was now about three years behind in his reports to Mickey, even longer with his payments.

An inch of thick gray ash from Sol's cigar dropped to his chest. He sat bolt upright in his swivel chair as a horrible thought hit him between the eyes. Tarz was a spy! Mickey had sent him to spy and report back. Somehow he'd weaseled his way into her bed, a young stud, and like all stupid women she'd spilled her guts, and Tarz'd seen a good thing staring him in the face. It was probably his idea to come here and smell things out. Goddammit!

How smart was Tarz? If he or his friend had any brains at all, the cat would be out of the bag in a few weeks. But not if I can help it, Sol told himself. He'd been caught off guard today, but by tomorrow he'd be in command again. And if there was one thing he knew something about, it was greed. Tarz could be had; it was written all over him. As he deliberated about the best way to deal with Reuben Tarz and his confederate, Sol's gut churned and his ears felt warm, sure signs of an increasing self-confidence.

Hollywood. Sin city. City of back-room deals and front-room deals. Everyone washing one another's hands.

Sol hefted himself from his comfortable swivel chair. Now was as good a time as any to go over his books — to find out exactly how much he owed to Mickey.

Outside in the bright sunshine, Reuben fired a cigarette and waited for Daniel. He didn't have to wait long.

"This place is a dump compared with the other studios," Daniel said as he joined Reuben. "What happened in there?" he asked.

Reuben filled him in. "Tomorrow we report back here and we'll both have jobs. You know, there was something in Rosen's eyes I couldn't figure out. And you're right, this place is a dump, but it makes money. I wish I could put my finger on it, but . . . You know,

424

Daniel, this is going to sound crazy, but that guy looked like he was afraid . . . of me! He got indignant and he blustered and tried to con me, but it was an act. I knew he was going to hire us, I just knew it. He was playing some kind of waiting game. I don't know the rules yet, though. It's just a feeling. . . . You know how you can smell trouble? Well, it was the same kind of feeling. I wish I knew what it meant."

Daniel laughed. "If I know you at all, pal, and I do, you'll figure it out!"

A crowd of people stood before them, waiting in line for the buses that would take them back to the city. Most of them milled about with downcast eyes and slumped shoulders. They didn't even have the promise of a job, but tomorrow was a new day. They'd struck out today, but they'd be back again, revved up and ready, hopeful and energized by other success stories.

A young girl wearing incredibly high-heeled shoes tripped past Reuben and Daniel, singing happily. She turned to call over her shoulder, "I got a job for tomorrow. You guys get lucky?"

Reuben nodded. The girl was ideal for moving pictures, bright-eyed and animated — her bow of a perfect mouth smiled back at them merrily. "What've they got you doing?" he asked.

She turned and walked back over to the

wall where Reuben and Daniel were standing. "Not much, standing in a crowd. I've been coming here every day for almost a year. This is my third call. Maybe this time someone will want to take an option on me. It happens," she said cheerfully. "I've done my share of leaning on this wall. When you leave here, you either lean on it and cry, or you lean on it and light a cigarette!"

"Where's your cigarette?" Reuben teased. Up close, he realized the girl couldn't be more than seventeen, maybe eighteen.

She blushed crimson. "I'm not lighting a cigarette because I don't have a red cent to buy cigarettes." She laughed, the happy sound contagious.

Reuben reached into his pocket and handed her a cigarette. She took it, lighted it, and inhaled deeply, a contented smile on her face.

"The only thing that puts a damper on tomorrow's job is that it's with Fairmont," she confided.

"Why's that?" Daniel asked.

"Because they suck your blood, that's why. Fairmont makes you wait for your money, and their directors think they're God's gift to the universe. It's a cut-rate studio," she said authoritatively.

Reuben and Daniel looked at each other with raised brows.

"What'll you guys — My bus!" She started

to run to the stop, then paused long enough to ask their names.

Reuben Tarz, and this is my friend, Daniel Bishop." In two long strides Reuben was by her side, pulling out his pack of cigarettes and handing them to her. "Take these, and congratulations! Maybe we'll see you around."

The girl fought her way onto the bus and poked her head out the window as it began to pull away. "Jane Perkins!" she shouted, waving the cigarette pack. "And thanks!"

"Pretty, wasn't she?" Daniel remarked. "Kind of reminded me of Bebe with all that fluffy hair and green eyes. How old do you think she is?"

"Seventeen or so. Why?"

"She looked like she was taking a shine to you. Didn't you see her flirting?"

Reuben's mouth dropped open. "Me? Go on, get out of here!"

"No, I'm serious. When you gave her those cigarettes she almost fainted. I have eyes. You should use yours, pal."

"When did you get so smart about women?" Reuben was flustered and Daniel grinned, shook his head. Obviously his friend was unaware of his tall good looks and the effect he had on women. Sometimes he was so dumb, it was pitiful.

"I think this is our bus," Reuben called, pointing. "Let's go home and have lunch. I

have to be at the Mimosa Club a little early
today."

CHAPTER EIGHTEEN

Mickey would approve of this small, tastefully furnished apartment, Reuben decided. For the most part all he and Daniel would be doing was sleeping and eating here, and the rent wouldn't make a sizable dent in his bank account. A respectable address was important, and this one was more respectable than the Crestwood. The apartment was on the first floor of a two-family house, on a tree-lined street that smelled of orange blossoms. Temporary. All things now were temporary.

Deep in his heart he'd known that his time in France with Mickey was temporary, even though he'd wished it permanent. He wanted to be back there so badly he ached with the feeling. Yet whenever he wondered where Bebe was, what she was doing and how long it would be before she appeared, the ache magically left him. Now, however, he needed control, no more thoughts of Mickey and Bebe, except maybe late at night when he lay in darkness. A clear, sharp mind uncluttered

with emotional debts and plans for revenge would serve him well.

Daniel watched Reuben as he paced the living room. He knew he was thinking of Mickey, maybe Bebe, too. Reuben's face always softened when he spoke or thought of Mickey and darkened when he thought of Bebe. As close as they'd always been, he felt the same way as Reuben — half of him wanted to return to France, the other half wanted to stay — to protect Reuben from Bebe when she showed. Reuben would always win if there was a contest, and he knew it; so did Reuben.

Suddenly Reuben's pacing became frenzied, his softened features replaced by a hard, calculating look.

"What's eating you, Reuben?" Daniel asked. "Is it something you want to talk about?"

"No. Yeah. Yes, I do." Reuben sat down on a gray-corduroy-covered chair, hunched his shoulders, and slapped the palms of his hands on his knees. Now he was almost relaxed. "I have so many ideas buzzing in my head. I know you think I'm impulsive at times, but when I get ideas and gut feelings, and if something *feels* right, I want to do something about it. Now. Not later, not tomorrow or next week, but now! Do you understand what I'm saying?"

Daniel nodded and leaned forward, listen-

ing carefully.

"I know I could get Fairmont Studios on its feet in no time at all. It's a gut feeling, Daniel. I'm the first to admit I don't know a goddamn thing about the movie business, but I didn't know anything about the wine business, either, and I learned. For some reason I don't think you have to know a whole hell of a lot to make movies. All those other studio heads started from nothing. One was a junk dealer in New York just like Sol Rosen. Now, you tell me what qualities a junk dealer has to have to make movies?" Daniel shrugged, and Reuben continued, not waiting for a verbal reply. "One studio head was a pool hustler from the Lower East Side, and still another was a glove peddler from the Warsaw ghetto. Ignorant immigrants, Daniel. They all came here to the land of milk and honey. They could barely speak English. Right now, right this very second, I know as much as they knew when they first started. I want you to research all the studios, Daniel, and make me a chart. I want to see the highs, the lows, whatever you can find out. I was thinking . . . let's ask Jane Perkins if she wants to earn a few dollars helping with the research. If she can read, that's all we need. Sometimes women see things men tend to overlook. Mickey taught me that," Reuben said, a catch in his voice. "What do you think?"

"I think it's a great idea," Daniel said

slowly. "It's something I can really sink my teeth into. Do you want this from day one, or just a few years, or what?"

"From day one. I want to see what Sol Rosen did wrong and be able to understand it. In detail. Everyone else is making it big, why isn't he? Why is his studio such a joke?"

Daniel felt elated. It thrilled him when Reuben got intense and passionate about things. But he'd also have to make sure his friend didn't get too carried away too quickly. "I know you can do it, but . . . listen to me, Reuben, you have to crawl before you walk. Slow. No rash moves, no rash decisions. From all you said this afternoon, it sounds to me like Bebe's father doesn't exactly trust you."

Reuben slapped at his knee. "You're right. I wish I could put my finger on what it was with Rosen this afternoon, but I can't. Daniel, sometimes there are things you simply know, and what I know is we're going to get jobs. I can't explain it, I just know."

Daniel's heart thumped. He wouldn't admit it, but he had the same feeling. "Reuben, if we do get the jobs, how can I work on the research project?"

Reuben wagged a finger under Daniel's nose. "You are going to be in the perfect place to do all this: the legal department. They probably have a bigger research facility than the main library here in town, and if they don't, you simply requisition what you want

from the town. They'll be happy to comply with a studio," Reuben said confidently.

If there was one thing Daniel loved, it was dealing with graphs, charts, and numbered columns. The research would be a breeze thanks to his French tutor. "Do I do this on my own time, or on Rosen's time if we manage to get the jobs?"

"Either or. I don't think there's going to be a lot for you to do . . . at first. Use your best judgment. Listen, Daniel, and tell me what you think of this idea. Whatever Rosen offers me in the way of salary, I'll ask him to cut it in half. Half the time I'll work in the office doing whatever he wants me to do. The rest of the time I want to be free to go about the studio to learn what's going on, how they operate, what goes into a studio. Rosen may think it's pushy on my part, but I should be able to convince him that I'm serious about learning the business. I want a favorable report to go back to Mickey. I don't ever want her ashamed of either of us. If necessary, we'll work our asses off to prove ourselves," Reuben said, his voice choked with feeling.

"Do you miss her, Reuben?" Daniel asked softly.

Instead of answering, Reuben chose to make a statement. "The minute our jobs are secure, the minute I know we have money in the bank, I'm going back, but I can't go back until I've proven myself. I want her faith in

us justified. We can't ever lose sight of the fact that we have a debt that has to be honored."

Daniel nodded solemnly.

"I wonder if we'll ever hear from Bebe again. Where do you suppose she is?" he asked.

"Who cares! She'll show up out of the blue as though nothing ever happened. Meanwhile she's no doubt whoring around Europe getting the education she thinks European men can give her."

"I can't believe you said that!" Daniel said.

Reuben snorted. "Don't tell me you didn't think that, too. I just say out loud what you think."

"I think you're wrong. She might be a party girl, what they call a jazz baby around here, but she's no whore. Wherever she is, I hope she's happy. Bebe deserves some happiness," he said.

This was what Reuben liked best about Daniel — his defense of anything and anyone, his loyalty, and his friendship. What would he think if he knew what had gone on in the barn? "Thanks for pulling me up short," Reuben said, "and don't ever be afraid to do it again if I get off track. Let's get back to subject one — what's wrong with Fairmont Studios. They have Clovis Ames, one of the biggest stars in the business. We saw hundreds of people buzzing around, so we know they

have a sizable payroll. The studio has to be making money. Why isn't it up there with the others?"

Daniel shrugged. "There could be a hundred reasons. Maybe Rosen has no desire to compete, or he doesn't know how. My opinion would be the latter."

Reuben's eyes grew thoughtful. "Maybe it's like the wine business. When I asked Mickey why she didn't want to expand Château Michelene, she told me one of the reasons was she would have to devote all her time to it. She said if she hired new people, they would rob her blind. I have to assume she knew what she was talking about. So she strives for quality versus quantity. My guess is Rosen is doing the opposite — except they aren't grinding out all that many films, according to Jane Perkins." He sighed. "I suppose in some crazy way there's a method to all of Rosen's business madness."

Daniel threw his hands up in the air. "I saw pictures and posters in the personnel office of some of the latest movies, and none of them looked top-drawer to me. Everything is shabby and run-down."

"That's cosmetic, Daniel, easy to fix, and it wouldn't be costly, either. Some gardeners, some painters, some decent-looking uniforms for the employees, a little glamour for the front offices, a lot of decent advertising. Better scripts for better films. I had some won-

derful ideas for Mickey's wine business. I could take those same ideas and apply them here. I know they'd work."

"All indications point to Rosen liking things the way they are. Older people resist change, you know. Slow, Reuben. Real slow," Daniel cautioned.

Reuben leaned back in the comfortable chair. "Sol Rosen isn't one to resist change. The man gave up a thriving business in Chicago to come here and make it big. Big, Daniel, means money and power, and not necessarily in that order. Rosen has made money, that's obvious, but he is not a power in the movie business. Maybe he's too short-sighted. On the other hand, he may be content with pocketing his profits and living like a king. Bebe told us that. Remember when she described the house and the pool and the tennis courts and all the help they had in the way of servants? She made it sound like they shook money off a tree." Just the mention of Bebe made his head throb. Where in the hell was she, and when was she going to turn up? He rubbed his forehead wearily, trying to exorcise the demon and concentrate on the task at hand. "Go back to your book, Daniel, I have some more think-ing to do."

While Reuben brooded upon various strate-gies to insinuate himself and Daniel into the mainstream of Fairmont Studios, miles away

in Benedict Canyon, Sol Rosen was busy trying to think of ways to keep them at bay.

The stack of financial ledgers bore out Sol's original thoughts. Tarz was here to spy on him. If his rough calculations were correct, he owed Mickey Fonsard over half a million dollars. Where had it gone? It sure as hell wasn't in the bank. Slumping back in his chair with a frustrated sigh, he looked around him. Of course — the house, the pool, the tennis courts, the cabanas, the nine-hole golf course. That's where it was! The renovations on the house alone had cost him a fortune. Everything was the best, the imported Oriental rugs, the mahogany staircase, the Bavarian crystal chandeliers, the tile, everything from Europe. In addition, he had a cook, a laundress, an upstairs maid, and a downstairs maid. Four gardeners were required to tend the lawns, and others were needed for the pool and tennis courts. A steady crew of five worked five days a week to maintain the golf course no one ever played on. He was paying out a damn fortune to live in Hollywood, and it wasn't doing him a damn bit of good socially. Bebe and Eli had gone to the best private schools, wore the best clothes, drove fancy cars, and ate only the best food. The plain simple truth was, he didn't know how to manage money. And he'd refused to listen to the people in his front office. Everything was kept in his head — his deals, his bank

balances, and the actors' and actresses' salaries. Still, he paid front office help, because if he didn't, the other studio heads would make him out to be a jerk. His pudgy fingers ran down his ledger. Twenty-three relatives, mostly his wife's nieces and nephews, were on the payroll. Deadwood. God knew he couldn't fire them when she was alive, and he sure as hell couldn't fire them now that she was dead. Their salaries came out of Mickey's share of the business. And healthy salaries they were. Tarz would find all this out and report back to Mickey. Jesus! He could just picture Mickey taking the next ship to the States and arriving on his doorstep demanding an accounting. Fifty-one percent of the business was hers. The fifty-fifty split was merely a paper calculation; the real contract was in France with Mickey's bankers. Maybe that was why Fairmont never achieved the status and the glory of the other studios, he reflected sourly. His heart and soul wasn't in the business because he owned only a minority forty-nine percent.

At least three times a week Sol had nightmares about Fairmont. Mickey always showed up in his dreams with the contract in hand, saying she was taking over. In one dream she appointed him janitor. Goddammit to hell, he was over a barrel!

Sol mopped at his face with a dirty, frayed handkerchief he'd honked his nose in all week

and bellowed for the maid. "Fetch me a drink — a double whiskey and a beer." Thanks to Eli and his friends, his liquor cabinet was always full. "If it isn't too goddamn much trouble, I'd like to have my dinner now, too."

"Yes, sir, Mr. Rosen. You told the cook —"

"I don't care what I told the cook, I want my supper. Where the hell is it? What am I paying all of you for, to sit on your asses and paint your fingernails?"

"Cook will get your dinner right away, sir," the maid mumbled as she scurried off to fetch his drink.

An hour later Sol pushed his chair back from the table. After consuming three-quarters of a roast chicken, a small mountain of mashed potatoes, a bowl of peas, and two sliced tomatoes, he was finally ready to come up for air. With a loud, offensive belch, he left the dining room, cleaning his teeth with a toothpick.

He shuffled his way into the living room, calling over and over for his son, Eli. God only knew why, probably just to hear the sound of his own voice. Now he had three things on his mind: Tarz, Mickey, and Eli. Jesus Christ, if it wasn't one thing, it was another.

The open French doors beckoned him. Since he was paying a fortune to his garden-ers, he should take a look at his gardens even if it was by moonlight. He walked two steps

down and up three to a pastel flagstone terrace surrounded by fragrant greenery and potted plants. At the terrace balcony he halted, staring into the dim shadows of the garden. For the first time in years he realized he was a lonely man. As his had been a "marriage of convenience," he'd never really been romantically in love with his wife, but they'd been friends of a sort. These days he missed her; he even missed her big, whining mouth. There were few things in life worse than coming home to an empty house. His eyes misted when he thought of Bebe. God, how he missed his little girl. She was the only person in his life that he loved with his heart. His baby — all grown-up now, a person in her own right. She didn't need him anymore. A feeling of grief rushed through him.

Sol walked back into the house, unaware of the clear evening or the tantalizing scent of flowers in the garden. The huge four-story structure was ablaze with lights, at his insistence. He hated coming home to an empty house but would accept one that was lighted from top to bottom. Thus he'd instructed every servant the day they were hired to turn on every light in the house at the first sign of dusk. Not that lighting was going to make him feel better tonight.

The corridor leading to what he called his home office was on the main floor with ornate sconces positioned three feet apart on

both walls. The office wasn't actually an office but two closets placed back to back. The wall separating the two closets had been knocked out, the clothes poles removed along with the shelves. Several years ago he had brought home a battered roll-top desk from the prop room and two straight-back chairs. A dusty lamp with a low-wattage bulb completed the furnishings.

Sol sat at the desk until midnight going over his books. His meaty shoulders slumped, the flab on his upper arms jiggling with his nervousness. Belching loudly, he reached for a plump raisin-filled cookie on a tray, stuffed the whole of it into his mouth and swallowed it, then wished he'd left it on the tray. It was the story of his life; he always regretted what he did after the fact. He sighed wearily. What should he do about Reuben Tarz? Hire him, of course, he had no other choice. Give him the title of assistant to . . . himself. Stash Tarz's friend in the production room. Yes, he'd cable Mickey and tell her that, too. If he paid them both well enough, neither one would squawk. But how much was enough? He'd always liked the sound of the word *negotiate.* Even though you eventually came to terms, someone won and someone lost. Winners and losers, givers and takers. Bullshit!

Sol was halfway up the mahogany staircase when the front door opened. Eli Rosen stag-

gered into the black-and-white marble-tiled foyer and proceeded to throw up all over his shiny patent-leather shoes. Smearing his mouth on the sleeve of his jacket, he giggled, a nasty, whining sound. As he lurched to the stairs, he saw his father for the first time. "Pop, you're up kind of late, aren't you?" He waved his arm backward toward the foyer and almost lost his balance. "Must have been something I ate."

"You're drunk," Sol said. He turned to his son, hating what he saw. Over the years he had tried to find some redeeming qualities in Eli, but when the boy reached his tenth year and none were forthcoming, he'd simply given up and allowed Eli to do whatever he pleased. The young man sitting on the stairs now was the result of his neglect. At twenty-two he was tall and thin, almost emaciated. His skin was sallow and his eyes a dull gray, mean and hard. He had hardly any eyebrows to speak of, and his hair was thick with pomade, standing straight up now in greasy clumps. His face was full of ripe blemishes that he picked at constantly. If he hadn't been born at home, Sol would have questioned his legitimacy.

As if he could feel his father's disgust, Eli raised his head, a miserable look on his face. Tears burned his eyes and rolled down his cheeks. "Pop, I —"

"Get out of my sight . . . and that mess on

442

the floor better not be there when I come down these steps in the morning. You're nothing but garbage, Eli, and one of these days I'm booting your tail out of here. Bebe isn't here anymore to plead for you and to coddle you. Go to bed. You make me sick."

When his father left him, Eli sat for a long time on the stairs, trying to summon enough energy to stand up. After awhile he fell back against the stairs and was sound asleep in seconds. When Sol came down in the morning, Eli was still there. His father's loose-fitting shoe lashed out, striking him in the ribs. Groaning in pain, he woke, disoriented.

"Jesus, Pop!"

Sol's foot lashed out a second time. "Shut up! I don't want to hear anything you have to say. You're scum, a punk, a hood. I have a goddamn gangster for a son!" His face was purple with rage as he swung about to attack Eli again, but the boy was too fast for him, scrambling up the stairs like a crab. "God-damn fairy!" Sol bellowed over his shoulder as he strode out the front door.

Eli staggered upstairs to the bathroom and turned on the faucets. Maybe he should drown himself, then the old man would feel better. If Bebe were here, he'd at least have a fighting chance of coming out even with his father. Bebe always defended him, took his side, and the old man loved her.

Muttering incomprehensibly, Eli stripped

off his clothes and kicked them into the corner. His skinny fingers picked at the jars on the glass shelf over the sunken tub: Bebe's bath salts in every fragrance made. Lips pursed, he picked out a colorful decanter and poured lavishly, smiling when he saw the bubbles swirl and slide backward in the tub. Just the scent made him think he'd hear Bebe call his name any minute. For the thousandth time he wished that he'd gone with her. When Bebe was around he was accepted and almost respected — on his own he amounted to shit and he knew it.

He loved his father, and when he was a boy he wanted to be just like him. For years he'd tried to get close to him, to win his affection, but it was Bebe with her big eyes and soft curls his father wanted. In those early years he'd tried to forget the disgust and shame on his father's face when he looked at him. Was it his fault he had bad skin and stringy hair? He'd been born skinny and he stayed skinny; was that his fault, too? As he got older he realized he'd inherited the worst features of both parents, while Bebe had inherited the best. Such were the quirks of fate; he didn't hate Bebe for her good fortune; on the contrary, he loved her. She was the only reason his father hadn't locked him up in a loony bin.

His bath over, Eli wrapped himself in a plush terry sheet that smelled like Bebe and

trotted down the hall to her room. It was a pretty room, just like Bebe, all frilly and feminine. It still smelled like her, and she'd been gone for a long time. It was cleaned and aired once a week and the sheets changed even if no one had slept in the bed. There was so much sunshine, the room seemed to have a thousand lights. How often he'd come in here and poured his heart out to Bebe. Murmuring soft words of love, she'd stroke his neck and back and tell him things would get better. And she'd believed they would; she wasn't lying when she'd said the words.

Eli walked to Bebe's closet, swung the mirrored doors to the side. Most of her things were gone, but there was still a row of dresses and coats. He rummaged until he found the old flannel robe Bebe wore when the California weather turned cool. It was pink and gray with a velvet cuff on the sleeves. Bebe loved it because it was big and roomy and she could cuddle into it. Eli found himself slipping his arms into it and then belting it around his waist. He hunched his shoulders into it the way Bebe did, loving the feel of it on his naked skin. Jesus, he was tired — too tired to tromp back down the hall to his room. Better he should sleep here with the warm sun streaming into the room. Yawning, he drew back the flowered eyelet cover and crawled between the silky sheets. In seconds he was asleep, his face cradled against the sleeve of

Bebe's robe.

The California sunshine was warm and golden when Reuben strolled to the bus stop like a man with a purpose. He *was* a man with a purpose, he told himself. Today he was dressed nattily in gray flannel slacks with a matching sweater vest, shirt, and tie, his cap tilted at a cocky angle; a navy-blue jacket with gold buttons completed the outfit. His dark curly hair was brushed back with just a trace of pomade, but already an unruly strand was flopping over his wide forehead. His hands were jammed into his pockets and his stride was loose and nonchalant. The observers, and there were many, couldn't feel the fluttering in his stomach or see the wild ricocheting thoughts in his mind. This particular image was one he'd practiced for hours last night. Daniel had laughed himself silly, but in the end he'd agreed that Reuben looked and acted perfectly. "Never let them see you sweat, Daniel, and never let them see how hungry you are for what they have to offer." So he'd gone to work in front of the mirror, practicing an elegant French shrug that was almost second nature to him now. Sol Rosen would be hard-pressed to find fault with him this morning.

The tree-lined street was beautiful, he decided. The sidewalks were swept clean, the gutters cleaner. Birds chirped overhead in

their nests of greenery. The tangy salt air mixed with the fragrant orange blossoms growing in profusion in the front yards. Reuben liked it here. Soon he would belong; he and Daniel would be true Californians. New York was so far away, France even farther, he thought sadly.

By now he was almost at the bus stop and he could see the knots of people trying valiantly to form a line. For some reason Reuben couldn't fathom, all of them seemed to be ignoring the green-striped waiting bench with its colorful advertising. As he approached the bus stop he noticed a young woman with pale blond hair and a stunningly beautiful face. She was beautiful enough to be in films. Her face was artfully made up, not that she needed cosmetics. Huge gold hoops dangled from her ears and jiggled whenever she moved her head. In the space of ten seconds he had her cast in a film, outfitted in a ridiculous costume of gold lamé. A vamp. Seductive and . . . kind of like Bebe.

Packaging. The outside trappings. Important. He made a mental note to apply this thought to his new job. The showy blonde was staring at him, probably wondering if he was a film star the way he wondered about her. Brazenly he stared back until she lowered her eyes. Other people were looking at him now openly, assessing his wardrobe, wonder-

ing where he was going and what he did for a living. The speculation in their eyes was obvious.

The huge bus was trundling down the road now, sliding gracefully to the curb. The last to board, Reuben walked to the rear of the bus and sat down. The blonde was in front of him, and as he stared at her crimped blond hair, he realized it wasn't clean. Also, her scent was overpowering and made him recoil slightly. A smick-smack girl.

A car, he decided. Pretty soon he was going to get a car so he didn't have to ride these damn buses that belched smoke on the outside and stale sweat on the inside. A Stutz Bearcat. Why the hell not? Go for the best, the top of the line. Don't ever settle. If you can't have the best, do without until you can.

Sol Rosen took a good look around his office. Crummy was the only word he could come up with. Reuben Tarz wouldn't fit in here in his hotsy-totsy clothes. Christ, he should have done something about redecorating a long time ago. When his secretary poked her head in the door to announce Tarz, Sol decided she was as crummy-looking as his office. His wife's cousin.

Sol clamped a dark brown cigar between his teeth and grudgingly walked around his desk. He made his hands busy with lighting his cigar so he wouldn't have to shake hands.

But when Reuben walked in and waited in front of him with his hand outstretched, there was nothing Sol could do but stretch out his own. Reuben's grasp was so overpowering, Sol thought his hand would fall off at the wrist.

Reuben pulled out the pocket watch Mickey had given him to check the time, a reminder that he was on schedule and ready to get down to business.

"Nice watch," Sol grunted. "Lessee."

Dutifully Reuben handed it over. While Sol was examining the watch, Reuben sat down, hiking up his trousers to preserve the crease. In one fluid motion he leaned back, a young man completely at ease, and watched as Sol's face went from purple to pink to white. Of course, he'd read the inscription Mickey had engraved on the watch. The older man's hands trembled when he gave the watch back.

"Keeps perfect time, right to the second," Reuben said quietly as he pocketed the watch.

Sol tried to pull his vest down over his bulging stomach. Reuben noticed two of the buttons were missing. Once he was behind the scarred, cluttered desk, the studio head looked more comfortable, Reuben decided. It was time for him to stand up. Mickey had told him towering over sitting men put them at a disadvantage, one they wouldn't care to admit to. They could hardly stand, once they'd settled themselves, without looking

foolish. Reuben gazed benignly at Sol, the picture of relaxation.

Sol grumbled in his throat, then hawked and spit accurately into the spittoon a yard from his foot. "I decided to hire you, Tarz. It's up to us old birds to give you young ones a chance. I'm using my noodle here by hiring you. I think you might be an asset to my studio." Reuben smiled. Instead of the compliment it was, the word *asset* sounded obscene coming from Sol's puckered mouth. "Salary is seventy simoleons a week. That okay with you?"

"No." Reuben's response was so quick, so cool-sounding, Sol's jaw dropped.

"Ain't it enough for you?" Sol demanded. Here it comes, he thought. He sucked in his belly and waited.

"Actually seventy is more than fair. I thought we could work out a deal. . . ."

Sol flushed. "I don't make deals with —"

"You haven't heard mine," Reuben interrupted, unperturbed by the explosive response. "I propose you pay me forty a week. I'll work for you here in the office doing whatever you want me to do from eight in the morning till one-thirty in the afternoon. From one-thirty to five or six, I want to be free to learn this business on my own. What that means exactly is I want to be free to come and go undisturbed. I want to be able to ask questions and get answers. Inside of

six weeks I think I can have some kind of business plan to present to you. I'd like Daniel Bishop to work in the legal department, since that's where his talents can better serve you. And since he'll be starting law school soon, the hands-on experience will be good for him. Fifty-five a week will be a good starting salary. What do you think?"

Reuben could feel his eyes narrow as he peered at Sol. The room wasn't hot, but the man was sweating profusely. A large vein in his temple throbbed as if it might pop any second. Reuben removed his hands from his pockets and strolled about the cluttered room as he waited for a response.

Sol felt his throat constrict. Free, my arse. Snoop! Goddamn spy is what this bird was. He wanted an inside track to find out what was going on at the studio. Once his pal was in the legal department, he'd know everything that went on.

"Oy gevalt," he sputtered. "You don't want much, do you?"

"Not really," Reuben said quietly. "In the long run I'm saving you money. I'm here to work, not sit on my haunches. Trust me."

Sol shifted the cigar in his mouth. "I learned a long time ago never to trust anyone who says 'Trust me.' Your pal ain't going into my legal department because we ain't got a legal department. This," he said, pounding his head, "is my legal department. Your pal

goes into the prop or transportation department. Take it or leave it!"

Reuben walked back to the desk and leaned over until his face was just inches from Sol's. "I don't understand something here. My friend Daniel doesn't know a thing about props or transportation. Why would you be willing to put him on the payroll with a decent salary to sit on his behind doing God only knows what? If you don't have a legal department, it's time you got one." Reuben stopped just long enough to take a meaningful look around the old man's office. "Your bookkeeping can't be all that efficient."

"Don't go telling me how to run my business. Take it or leave it!"

"Then I guess I have to leave it. We came here for honest work, not charity."

Sol could feel the sweat dripping down his back. The son of a bitch was leaving. Well, let him leave! He waited until Reuben was out the door and halfway down the stairs before he rumbled to the doorway to call him back. "Ain't no call for you to be so hotsy-totsy with me," he said. "I ain't giving you charity. I'm giving you a job. I said it was okay. If I ain't got a legal department, what do you want from me?"

"Start one," Reuben said smoothly. "You need one and you certainly have the room. I'd like business contracts drawn up. Two years. Is that agreeable with you?"

"Two years! Two goddamn years! All right already," Sol grumbled.

"But," Reuben said, wagging a finger in front of him, "my salary goes to seventy-five in six weeks. That's how long it will take me to learn this business. Every six months I want a fifty-dollar-a-week raise. Don't look so sour, Mr. Rosen. I'll be saving you a hundred times that much money, down the road."

"Cocky bastard!" Sol spat. "A *chachem* yet!"

Reuben hid his smile. "Someday maybe," he said. "Now, about Daniel Bishop. What shall I tell him?"

Sol rubbed his chin. "I told you we ain't got a legal department. So I'll open up a broom closet or something. Tomorrow morning at eight o'clock. Both of you. You'll be working here with me. That door opens into another small room. I'll get it cleared out."

"That sounds fine, Mr. Rosen. We'll both be here. For now, though, I'd like a pass to go about the studio lot. Strictly as an observer."

Sol winced. There was nothing he could do but issue the pass and usher the *ganef* out of his office. His stomach rumbled ominously as he closed the door. So now he was going to have an office assistant *and* a legal department. But things could be worse. A lot worse, he consoled himself. How the hell could this

scheming little snotnose save him money, he wondered. And how long would it be until his report went out to Mickey Fonsard? He pushed the thought out of his mind. What he would do now was go home to Benedict Canyon, pack up his ledgers and the studio contracts, and bring them back so Tarz's pal would have something to look at. How much savvy could a green kid like Bishop have? He wasn't even in law school yet. All he had to remember was that this was his company, and he ran it the only way he knew how. Maybe Tarz wasn't a spy after all. "And they get ice water in hell," he muttered as he struggled back into his jacket.

Reuben meandered around the studio lot, stopping along the way to introduce himself. His bone-crushing handshake made more than one department head flinch. And when he announced his name and title, he saw fear in every face. Or was it apprehension? Reuben decided he liked the feeling of power he was arousing. How much was due to his image and how much to his title?

So far he'd been to five departments — prop, carpentry, electrical, camera, and editing. Lunch was being served in the dining hall via a caterer when he arrived and introduced himself. He glanced at the silver serving dishes and fine china, then picked up the menu to see what was being served. Mongole

soup, steak, lyonnaise potatoes, stewed tomatoes, garden salad, and floating island for dessert. The reverse side read simply hamburgers and weiners, obviously for everyone else.

"Who pays for this?" Reuben asked curiously.

John Carlyle, the head director, looked up.
He was a small man, round from his neck to
his ankles. "The . . . the studio," he said. Reuben thought he could see the man's hair
bristling at the question.

"Who eats the hamburgers and weiners?"

Carlyle shrugged. "My helpers, the cast,
anyone who wants them."

"Who pays for them?"

Carlyle lowered his fork onto his plate.
"They do." Suddenly he wasn't hungry
anymore. He smiled uncomfortably, waiting
for the next question.

"Is there a personnel folder on you in the
office, John?" The man nodded numbly. Reuben smiled, a cat with a mouthful of feathers.
"Good. . . . Enjoy your lunch, John. It's all
right to call you John, isn't it?"

"Sure, sure. Is it okay to call you Reuben?"

"No," Reuben said, and sauntered off, his
hands still in his trouser pockets. By nightfall,
he knew, every department head would be
storming Sol's office. He laughed, a deep,
rich sound that made scurrying actors and
actresses turn for a second look.

The casting, art, and costume departments

took up the rest of Reuben's afternoon. When he walked out of the studio at five-thirty, he had a working knowledge of what was going on. He itched to dive in with both hands and feet.

Max Gould's plastered-down eyebrows rose a fraction of an inch when Reuben walked through the door at six ten and straddled a chair next to the bar. "How about a cup of coffee?"

"It's yours," Max said, puzzled. He jerked his head at the bartender, who immediately set out a cup of coffee. Max hooked his thumbs in his suspenders. "You looking for a run tonight?"

"No, I just came for coffee. It's good," he said, surprised.

"We grind it fresh every day. It's good you aren't looking for a run because I don't have one today. Tomorrow I will, okay?" Reuben nodded. "You get a job? You look like one of those guys that strolls around on a golf course on his day off."

Reuben listened for disapproval but heard only genuine interest in Max's voice. "I start tomorrow. I'll be Sol Rosen's assistant at Fairmont Studios."

"That's not too shabby. Are they paying you decent money?"

"Pretty decent."

"So how long you think it'll take you to

start running things or even taking over the place?" Max laughed.

Reuben thought about the question before he answered. "A year, give or take a month or so. You want to lay a bet on the time or what? Good coffee," Reuben said, tossing a dime on the bar.

Again Max laughed, but this time he stopped when he saw Reuben's eyes. "I'm not laughing at you, Tarz, I'm laughing with you. You take over that place and I'll clean up. Sure, I'll make book on it. Why the hell not?"

Reuben smiled. "Why the hell not," he said quietly. "I'll see you tomorrow, Max. Good night."

Max snapped his suspenders, making a loud noise just as Eli Rosen walked through the door. The young man's face was a splotchy red. He was trying to grow a mustache and constantly caressed the nubby hairs with his index finger. "I thought I told you to use the back door," Max growled. "Are you trying to give this place a bad name?"

"You got nothing but a mud hole out back. And garbage," Eli whined. "You want to know how much I paid for these shoes? I ain't ruining them even for you, Max. How about a drink and something to eat."

"Did Daddy give you your allowance today?" Max hated this kid with a passion, but he did bring in business. Compared with

Reuben Tarz, Eli was nothing — a pimple on the ass of life. "I see your old man hired on an assistant. Does this mean he's finally going big time?"

Eli ignored him. Max knew Sol Rosen never confided in his son — the question was just one way of giving him a hard time. "So whatcha got for me tonight, Maxie baby?"

Max wanted to tell Eli he had a king-size package of gift-wrapped horseshit, but he didn't. There were times, like now, when he needed this slimy, greasy little weasel. He motioned in the direction of his table in the back.

Eli calmly slid off the stool and followed Max. News traveled fast. If he was patient, by the end of the night he'd have the scoop on his father's new assistant, whoever he was. If Max weren't waiting for him, and he didn't have what he thought was a tough-guy image to protect, he would have run outside and kicked the building and punched his fist through a window. How many times had he begged to work in the front office of the studios? Christ, he'd actually groveled to his father — but the bastard had only laughed at him. Now he felt like crying as he sauntered back to Max's private table.

Reuben decided to sit on one of the green-striped benches while he waited for the bus. His leg was aching, and he hadn't eaten since

that morning. All things considered, though, he was pleased with the way the day had gone. Later in the evening, after a long, hot bath, he would work on his schedule for tomorrow. His head was buzzing with ideas. Relaxed now, almost sleepy, he closed his eyes against the soft twilight — and a moment later he felt rather than saw a man sit down next to him.

"Beautiful evening," said a distinct voice. "That's one of the things I like about California. Damian Farrell here."

Reuben stirred and turned. "Reuben Tarz," he said, offering his hand. "It is a beautiful night. New York was never like this, even in the summer. I'm getting used to this weather real fast."

"You look familiar," Farrell said.

"I was going to say the same thing about you. Have we met?"

"I work at Fairmont Studios. I'm an actor, maybe you saw one of my films." His voice sounded apologetic.

"I haven't seen many films lately. I've been in France and just got back. Maybe I saw you at the studio today. I start work there tomorrow myself."

Farrell snapped his fingers. "You're right. You're the guy that gave Jack Carlyle heart palpitations. That man is the worst director I've ever worked with."

Reuben nodded slightly. You always learn

more when you listen, Mickey had said. He listened.

"I've worked under a few, some worse, some better. Carlyle is Rosen's wife's nephew — was, actually, she's dead now. Most of the studios have this nepotism thing. If they'd only hire people that know what the hell they're doing, things would pick up. I'm thinking of moving on since my contract will be up in another two months. I want to do something . . . important. I've got some great ideas, but no one in the front office will listen. I can't get past Carlyle. Say, what kind of contract did they offer you?"

Reuben laughed. "I'm not an actor. I'm going to be Rosen's assistant. Tell me more about your ideas."

Neither man paid attention as bus after bus pulled to the curb and then glided away. Lavender faded to charcoal as night fell, and still the men talked, quietly at first, then excitedly. The moon crept behind its cloud cover and sailed across the spangled sky, and still the men made no move to leave. When Reuben finally looked at his pocket watch it was ten-thirty. "I think we missed the last bus," he said, grinning. The two men stood and shook hands, with Reuben promising to put Farrell's ideas into the works. The chance meeting was the beginning of a friendship that was to last all their lives.

The small kitchen in the apartment was fragrant with the smell of fried onions and peppers, Daniel's favorite. One end of the table was set for Reuben while at the other end Daniel pored over one of the law books that had been Mickey's gift.

Reuben entered the kitchen like a whirlwind. Daniel looked up and blinked. His friend exuded excitement, an excitement he obviously couldn't wait to share. Daniel closed his mouth as Reuben sat down, his plate full.

"Wait till you hear this, Dan'l," he said between mouthfuls of food. "I met this guy, Damian Farrell, who's one of Fairmont's biggest actors. He was just sitting there waiting for the bus like me. We got to talking, and he said his contract was up in two months and he's thinking about moving on.

"He has an idea," Reuben continued enthusiastically, "and if Fairmont won't go with it, he's going to take it somewhere else. You aren't going to believe this, I swear, but I told him the studio *would* develop his idea. I actually said that! Picture this now. Farrell as Red Ruby, bungling, bumbling jewel thief, and his foil will be Lester Kramer, who will play the part of Whitey Diamond, the cop who is just as bungling, and just as bumbling. Red Ruby

occasionally pulls off a heist and stashes his loot, but can never fence it because Whitey Diamond is always on his tail. A serial, or a series, Daniel. Jesus, the public will go crazy for something like this! I guarantee the box office will quadruple in six months. He also said he'd want double what he's getting paid now. I told him . . . I gave him my word we'd make it a deal. It felt right, Dan'l. You have a whole book on contracts. I want one for Farrell and Lester Kramer that is absolutely foolproof. A series like this could run for years!"

Daniel winced at the word *contract* as Bebe's face flashed before him. "Jesus Christ, Reuben, you got balls! You haven't started working yet and you're already making deals. Did you shake hands on it?"

"Damn right, and a bone-crushing grip it was. We sealed the deal," Reuben said proudly. "You have to think positively and you have to believe. Believe in me, Daniel! Think of the potential. Think about the money! Think, for God's sake!"

"I am thinking . . . about Sol Rosen, the legalities of something like this, and the fact that tomorrow will be your first day on the job," Daniel grumbled. "I'm no aficionado of films, but it does sound damn interesting. I'd like to know how you're going to pull this off with Sol Rosen."

"I'm not going to 'pull it off,' as you say.

I'm going to present the idea, project revenue, and then scare the hell out of Rosen and tell him Farrell has an offer for twice the amount I'm willing to give him. He'd be a fool to turn it down. If I was in his place, I sure as hell wouldn't. Ideas are what make this business. Something new, untried. I already figured out that a studio is only as good as the people who work there, and by that I mean the actors and actresses. Farrell doesn't like his director, John Carlyle. I met him today. . . ." Reuben went on to tell Daniel about his conversation with Carlyle. "Farrell wants a different director for the Red Ruby flick. I asked him if he had one in mind, and he said there's a guy at Fox he'd like to work with. I said I'd put him on the payroll."

"You *what?*" Daniel exploded.

Reuben roared with laughter at the expression on his friend's face. "Look at it this way: This new director, Mike Avery, is a necessary ingredient in this little stew I'm cooking up. Without him it won't work. Fairmont can buy out his contract and give him a bonus to switch over. The guy likes Farrell, so that's going to help. Look, pal, I'm not going to do this tomorrow first thing."

Daniel sighed. "That's a relief."

"I'll wait a couple of days," Reuben said, laughing.

"You're moving pretty fast, pal," Daniel cautioned.

Reuben turned serious. "I have to, or I'll start to think, and right now memories are the one thing I can't afford. I was hoping you'd go along with me on all of this."

"That's what I'm here for. I think it's a swell idea, and I do believe you have a money-maker here. I'm studying these law books, but that doesn't make me a lawyer. Let me read up on everything and promise me you won't do anything till I research it."

"It's a deal. . . . What's that?" Reuben asked curiously.

"A letter I wrote to Mickey. I didn't seal it yet in case you want to put in one of your own."

Reuben thought about it for a moment. He had so much to tell Mickey, but he couldn't dash off a note in a few minutes. Writing to Mickey would take . . . well, he simply wasn't ready to pour out his heart. "Send her my love and tell her I'll write soon when I have something important to say. And be sure to enclose our payment. You're keeping a record, right?"

"Down to the penny. Is there anything you *don't* want me to mention in my letter? I told her to give Bebe our address if she's in touch with her. I miss Bebe," Daniel said carefully.

"Don't look at me like that. It's all right for you to miss her." Reuben stood up. "I guess I'll clean up since you cooked. Then it's a nice hot bath so I can soak my leg. You go

464

ahead to bed. I'm going to go over some of the things I learned today. I'll make notes and then turn them over to you. By the way, we report at eight tomorrow. Congratulations, Daniel, we're employed."

Daniel wondered why he didn't feel as enthusiastic as Reuben. He imagined he could smell the problems that were going to erupt with this new employment. Still, another part of him couldn't wait to put his feet under a desk filled with graphs and charts, pencils and pens: his need to do something for himself.

CHAPTER NINETEEN

A light snow was falling, dusting the French château in feathery whiteness, creating a soft blanket of silence. Smoke from the chimney spiraled upward in lazy patterns as a southerly wind began to whip through the trees at the back of the château. Inside, it was just as quiet and hushed; the baby known as Philippe Bouchet slept. He had two birth certificates, this sleeping child. One said he was Philippe Bouchet, French citizen, the name Bouchet having been Mickey Fonsard's maiden name. The second read Philip Tarz, American citizen. The sleeping child held dual citizenship.

Mickey Fonsard stood over the baby's cradle, a beatific look on her face. How she loved this small, tenderly wrapped bundle. He slept in her room at the side of the bed where she had once made love with his father. The cradle the infant slept in had once belonged to her husband's family. Yvette had helped her clean and polish it until she

466

proclaimed it fit for her angel. He was a good baby, staying awake only to eat and have his bath. Everything Mickey did for the child she did lovingly. She had much love to lavish on him, and she rocked him for hours, crooning and singing lullabies she made up as she went along, often calling him her "plump little pigeon." Once in a while he smiled, either from gas or pure pleasure, when she made baby sounds or sang her made-up songs.

Each day the little one took on a new characteristic all his own. The likeness to both Bebe and Reuben could not be denied. He had Reuben's dark hair, Bebe's mouth. It was too soon to say whose eyes he had, but Mickey thought they would be Reuben's. Now they were tiny little slashes in his plump, rosy face and didn't stay open long enough for her to decide. His feet were large . . . but then, his father had large feet. "Whose disposition will you have, *chéri?*" Mickey whispered.

Yvette poked her head in the door. "And what is our bundle from heaven doing this afternoon?" She leaned over the cradle. "*Mon dieu,* this child is beautiful! He will grow to be as handsome as his father, is that not so, Mickey?" she cooed in whispers over the crib.

"Yes, as handsome as his father," Mickey echoed.

"You have heard nothing?"

"It is too soon. Perhaps I will never hear

anything. I can accept that, for I have this priceless treasure," Mickey said, a catch in her voice.

"So you have decided . . . you aren't going to . . . It isn't fair, Mickey."

"Never!" Mickey said forcefully.

"Ah, old friend, never is a very long time. What are you afraid of? He has a right to know."

"No, Yvette. It would confuse things, and I am confused enough as it is. I cannot handle more at this time. The circumstances of his birth are no longer important. The day I brought this child here I figured out what had really happened. Bebe instigated, led Reuben on, enticed him. He was angry with me, and he fell into her trap. And it was a trap. Nothing will ever convince me otherwise. When you love someone the way I loved Reuben, you know things like this. Perhaps she meant only to tease and flirt with him, and when things went beyond that, she grew frightened and fought him. A man, a man like Reuben . . . would do just what he did. Bebe must have reacted violently, hence the pitchfork. It took me a while to realize she would have said something, blamed Reuben one hundred percent and played out her part if she'd truly been an innocent . . . victim. She chose to remain silent. And Reuben called it an accident to spare me, of course. I've come to terms with it," Mickey said sadly.

"So, you wait. Bah! What a fool you are!"

"No, I do not wait. I exist. There is a difference. If you wish to think of me as a fool, feel free."

"Someday you will be old," Yvette said sourly.

"Yes, I will be old. Everyone grows old, Yvette. Whatever God has in store for me I will accept. Come, let us have tea or wine. This jewel will sleep for at least another hour."

"I have something to tell you, Mickey," Yvette said over tea.

"Why do I have this feeling I'm not going to like what you have to tell me?" Mickey said tartly.

Yvette smiled. "Bebe called me on the telephone last evening. She said she's going to Paris, and wanted to know if she could come to the farm. She asked about you . . . and Reuben. I lied to her. I said Henri had been ill and I hadn't seen you for a while. I think she plans on calling you because she wants to stay in your Paris house."

"Then she doesn't know Reuben has gone back to America?"

"I do not think so. It was not my place to tell her anything."

"Did she ask . . ." Mickey couldn't bring herself to finish her question. Yvette shook her head.

"How did she sound?"

"She sounded . . . like Bebe. We didn't speak that long. She did ask how you were. There was something in her voice I never heard before, a certain . . . maturity. No, perhaps that is the wrong word. I kept waiting . . . dreading . . . but she never asked. I thought she would, I really did. I can't believe she doesn't care. Mickey, how . . . ?"

Mickey chose her words carefully. "I don't think any of us will ever be able to understand Bebe. She can be warm and gentle and caring one minute and then calculating and manipulative the next. The latter is what worries me."

Yvette threw her hands into the air. "Well, I just don't understand how a woman can give up her own flesh and blood. I'll never understand."

"She wasn't a woman when she gave up the child. She was little more than a baby herself," Mickey said gently.

"You mark my words, someday she's going to come looking for this child. If you think you felt heartsick when Reuben left, think how you'll feel when she rips this child from you."

Mickey stared across at Yvette. Her old friend was only voicing aloud the fears she herself dealt with constantly. "We must make sure that never happens. If you feel strongly that she may come here, then I must make arrangements to leave with the child."

"Where will you go, *chérie?*" Yvette asked unhappily.

"To the chalet in Chamonix. I can be happy there as long as my love is with me. You see, my friend, there is nothing else left to me. Stop looking at me with such pity! If you can't stop, go back to the farm," Mickey said sternly.

"Mickey, please, we've been friends for so long and I care what happens to you and because we are friends I wish to speak my mind. It is a wonderful thing that you took this baby because you have much love to offer. You have money and can give this child every advantage the world offers. But can't you see what you are doing to yourself? If you must, go to Chamonix, but hire a nurse for the child. Start to make a life for yourself. You cannot live through a child, even if he belongs to your lover. What if Reuben comes here searching for you? What if he writes or cables and gets no response, what then, *chérie?* His love for you was like none I've ever seen. If you definitely plan on leaving, then write and tell him so. Bah! You haven't heard a word I've said. You deserve to wallow in your misery. I'm going home because I cannot bear to stare into your sad eyes a minute longer, and because it's snowing harder."

"Will you and Henri come to visit me?"

"But of course, *chérie.* After you have settled in and things are running smoothly. I

471

need a vacation. Perhaps I will leave Henri home, eh?" She'd hoped for a small smile from Mickey, but none was forthcoming.

The moment the door closed behind Yvette, Mickey was off her chair and up the stairs. First she checked the baby to see that he was still sleeping peacefully. Satisfied, she started to pack her trunks. Tomorrow morning, at first light, they would leave. She could stay in Chamonix for a long time — years, if necessary. There was, after all, nothing to keep her here any longer.

Mickey sat propped up in her lonely bed staring across the room to the darkened windows. Moonlight washed the floor in a soft silvery light. The stars shimmered in the heavens like a cluster of twinkling diamonds on a length of black velvet. She wished then . . . for yesterday. Realist that she was, she knew it could never be. Perhaps Yvette was right; perhaps she should write to Reuben. If not Reuben, then Daniel. They might write, if only to pay off the loan she'd advanced them. That thought depressed her even more. Better not to be here to open flat envelopes with only money and an obligatory note. Better to drop an informal note to them both.

Mickey crept from her bed like a thief in the night, quietly so as not to awaken the sleeping child. She tiptoed from the room on slippered feet and settled herself at the desk in the library downstairs. She started not one,

but seven notes to Reuben; all of them found their way to the trash basket. She fared no better with Daniel's note. In the end she gave up. She cried for her loss, for yesterday, and for what might have been.

Mickey Fonsard, carrying her adopted son, opened the door of her chalet just as Bebe Rosen arrived at Yvette and Henri's farm. The young girl tooted the horn of her shiny new Citroën and waved gaily, calling out to Yvette and Henri.

"I had to come to see you," she said, rushing out of the driver's side to hug them both. "You look wonderful, both of you. Look, even the dogs and chickens are happy to see me! Please say I can stay for lunch."

"But of course you can stay for lunch, and dinner, too, if you wish. You did not tell me you were planning on a visit. I thought you wanted to stay in Mickey's Paris house." Yvette hoped she didn't sound as nettled as she felt. There was going to be trouble, she could feel it. "You look wonderful, *chérie.* The latest fashion, I see."

"I wanted to look nice when I got here. I went to that designer Mickey uses in Paris, Coco, and she made this up for me. She's outrageously expensive, but have you ever seen anything so elegant?"

Yvette stared enviously at the scarlet walking suit with the fluted skirt. Mickey would

have worn a white silk blouse with such an outfit, but this young lady preferred to expose her long slender neck. Her shoes, purse, and driving gloves were a deep magenta that somehow complemented the scarlet of the suit. A soft felt cloche, trimmed in matching feathers, rested on the front seat. There was no luggage that Yvette could see. She felt relieved. "What do you think of my new hairdo?" the girl continued to babble. "I had it cut and styled in England just before I left."

"Most becoming," Henri said, beaming. "Men love fluffy hair on a woman so they can run their fingers through it. Isn't that so, Yvette?" He held Bebe's arm out and showed her off to his wife.

Yvette shook her own long mop of hair in agreement. When was the last time you ran your fingers through *my* hair, my dear Henri? she thought to herself. She made a mental note to push Henri out of bed later for the way he was fawning over Bebe. She'd married a lecher. She said, turning to Bebe, "You look wonderful, *chérie.* So fashionable it makes me ache to be your age again."

"It's just as I remember it," Bebe said, looking around her. "I can't tell you how often I've thought about this place and you and Henri. I was hoping the dogs would remember me." She stood back to drink in the sight of the stone farmhouse with its gabled windows and heavy oak door. The wide sills on

the windows were filled with thriving colorful greenery. She peeked excitedly into the open doorway. Inside, she knew, would be hot tea and small homemade cakes with Yvette's thick frosting, their insides gingery and fragrant. "I think this is the nicest, the most welcoming home I've ever been in." She wrapped her arm around Yvette's shoulder as they walked over the threshold.

Henri hopped from one foot to the other, hoping his wife would ask him to join them for tea. When she glared at him he turned and left the little courtyard. Tonight he would pay for his careless tongue. But ah, he knew how to sweet-talk Yvette and put her in a good mood. He shrugged. A man was a man.

In the parlor, Yvette poured tea and set out the remembered cakes, then poked around in a basket full of odds and ends for a cigarette. Bebe joined her, fitting her cigarette into a long onyx holder. "I didn't know you smoked, *chérie*," Yvette said.

"I just recently took it up. Everyone smokes these days. Not a lot. It helps me relax. I feel at home here," she added, settling onto the familiar kitchen chair.

"I'm glad you could stop to visit. Where are you going from here?"

Bebe tossed her hands in the air, the cigarette holder clamped between her teeth. "I suppose I'll drive down to the château and get the key to the Paris house from Mickey. I

called and called, but there was no answer, so I decided to hop in my new car and drive here. It was an outrageous experience," she trilled.

Yvette rummaged in the basket a second time, to withdraw a key and a folded slip of paper. "Mickey left this for you. She's gone . . . business or something about the wine . . ." Her voice sounded false even to her.

Bebe's innocent eyes widened and her brows shot upward. "You mean there's no one at the château? What about the house-keeper?"

"On holiday, or else she went with Mickey. I'm not sure. Mickey just . . . what she did was . . . she was in a hurry and said she would be in touch and to give you this should you happen by. . . . I told her you had called," she added, catching Bebe's puzzled expression.

"How strange. I guess she didn't want to see me. I wonder why. The château is empty, you say?"

"For the moment," Yvette said firmly.

"Then that must mean Danny and Reuben are with her." Yvette thanked God it wasn't a question; Bebe assumed . . . "I really miss . . . Daniel," she continued. "I wonder if I'll ever see them again."

Yvette pretended not to see the tears in Bebe's eyes. "Nothing is impossible, *chérie.* If it is meant to be, it will be," she said gently. "Now tell me about your glamourous life in

England." This should be safe ground, Yvette thought gloomily.

"Glamourous . . . at times," Bebe said loftily. "At other times it was quite boring. I missed the cabarets of Paris." She shrugged, indicating it was of no importance. "The men . . . most of them were overgrown boys with only one thing on their minds. Sex," she said authoritatively, "is a participatory event. I had no wish to participate."

Mon Dieu, Yvette thought, I must remember to spring this on Henri tonight when I kick him out of bed. "I see," she said quietly. Her eyes dropped from Bebe's sad face to her slender polished fingernails which were drumming impatiently on the tabletop as she spoke.

"More tea, *chérie?*"

"I certainly had many propositions," Bebe said, ignoring Yvette's offer. "I didn't make many friends among the women my age. For some reason they didn't seem to want to be around me. Mickey's friend said they were jealous. I suppose that's possible." Her tone indicated she didn't believe it. "I'm an American," she said flatly, as if that explained everything.

"I think you're just shy and tend to wait until the other person makes the first move. . . . Sometimes, *chérie,* the other person is just as shy as you. You learn these things as

477

you get older," Yvette advised in a motherly tone.

"You should have had a dozen children, Yvette. You'd make a wonderful mother," Bebe said sincerely.

Here it comes, Yvette thought, and what do I tell this miserable young woman about her son? She gulped the rest of the tea in her cup, tea she didn't want.

"Well, I think I've taken up enough of your time," Bebe said, rising. "Now I'd like to take a ride past the château. For old times' sake. And then I'll head back to Paris. Thank you for the tea and cake. It was wonderful. I . . . I want to . . . to thank you for welcoming me. I wasn't sure if . . . if you would want me to come here. I decided on impulse, the way I do most things. Say goodbye to Henri for me. I — I'll write if you'd like me to. . . ."

Yvette crossed the short distance to the young girl and wrapped her in her arms. "My darling girl, please do write. I would love to hear from you. I get no mail on this miserable farm, so I will look forward to it, but only if you wish to write. Bebe, have you given any thought to going back to California?"

"I plan to return at the end of summer — late August, maybe the middle of September. I'm not sure. If Mickey should get in touch with you, please thank her for the use of the house. Tell her I'll take care of it. And thank

you, Yvette, for being a wonderful friend to me when I needed a friend." Yvette nodded and watched Bebe's eyes circle the kitchen, coming to rest on the slab of slate near the fireplace where the cradle had rested months before. From the fireplace they strayed to the little bedroom door off the kitchen. Now. Now, she's going to ask. Instead, Bebe hugged her again, kissed her soundly, and bolted out the door. Yvette blessed herself over and over as she watched the powerful car surge down the road.

Bebe drove carelessly, narrowly missing a rabbit on the road. She felt she drove well considering she'd had only three lessons. Any idiot could steer a car. Idiots could do a lot of things other people thought them incapable of.

Forty minutes later she ground the car to a halt at the bend in the road. From here she had a perfect view of the château. How lonely and sad it looked, so deserted with no smoke rising from the chimneys. The windows were covered from the inside with something heavy. The barn was closed and probably locked.

Not caring if she ruined the magenta shoes, Bebe slowly walked the quarter mile to the château. At one point the barn loomed directly ahead. Part of her past was there, she mused . . . but she refused to move toward it. She couldn't bear it. The front door, the back

door, and the side door were all locked. A thought popped into her mind: Mickey must plan to be away for a very long time. Where did she go? Why did she go? The urge to kick the door, to break the lock, was so strong, Bebe had to grind her heels into the soft, loamy earth next to the back steps. A window, I could break a window, crawl through, and stay here for a while. *To what end?* queried a small voice. Just to feel again, to smell the scent of him, to touch the things he touched.

Tears spilled from her eyes, caught for a moment on her thick lashes, then streamed down her cheeks. Everything is gone . . . you can't get it back. Why aren't you here to help me? I need you, Daniel, you're the only friend I have.

She sobbed all the way back to the car. Five minutes later, the engine running, she sat swiping pitifully at her eyes. She wailed then, a high keening sound of pure misery. Ten minutes later she was dry-eyed and smiling, driving the car away from the château. Bebe Rosen from California was going to gay Paree.

CHAPTER TWENTY

At the end of ten days Reuben felt he had more than a working knowledge of Fairmont Studios. With Daniel's invaluable help, he was in the process of drawing up a temporary operational work plan. Presenting it to Sol would be an entirely different matter, however. The studio head had followed him with his eyes for the first few days. It hadn't been a comfortable situation.

He'd spent his evenings watching movies, trying to decide what could be classified as good, bad, and indifferent. His conclusion when he watched the last film was that all of them were indifferent. There was a plethora of beauty and handsomeness, but no talent. In the beginning, audiences had hungered for pie in the face, chases, and pratfalls. It was time for a change. Lester Kramer needed better scripts, better direction. And then there was Damian Farrell. Reuben had sat through *Tillie's Punctured Romance* four times, a 1914 movie directed by Mack Sennett. Jane Per-

kins came to mind immediately, and he made a notation to himself. With women as the main moviegoers, romance films should be at the top of the list. Fairmont had none. Jane would be perfect.

To date, the only thing he could give Sol Rosen credit for was the fact that he had copies of every film produced at other studios. For comparison, probably. But why didn't he upgrade his own productions?

It was two o'clock in the morning when Daniel tossed his papers aside. "That's it, Reuben! That's what the problem is. In the beginning distribution was a simple affair. Producers sold copies of films outright to whoever was showing them. They were sold at so much a foot, or by the reel. Maybe ten cents a foot or seventy to a hundred dollars a reel. Quality wasn't important. Rosen doesn't own any theaters like the other studios. No shekels coming in from that kind of operation. Distribution, Reuben, that's where it all is."

Reuben tapped his pencil against his front teeth. "Sol Rosen doesn't *look* stupid. But is he? Who's actually in control of all the money?"

"From what I can tell, his brother handles all the paperwork. Reuben, it's a mess. See this stack of papers? It's a work sheet for every short, every film, every serial made by

Fairmont. I'm sure you've seen all of them in the projection room. Twenty-five thousand to produce. The take should be around one-hundred-fifty-thousand. Doesn't matter if the film stinks. That's the take."

"Jesus," Reuben breathed.

"There's something else. At some point along the way, audiences got tired of seeing the same old thing over and over. Somebody set up an exchange where an exhibitor could trade in his prints and, for a small fee for the service, receive different prints from other exhibitors. Don't ask me who got the money. At some point competition increased, at least I think it did. The rental instead of the sale became the big thing. Producers then received a share of the actual box office drawing power. There's no record showing Sol got any.

"This is the way I interpret it," he continued. "The product — in this case, the film — is not bought or sold. The patrons merely pay to look at the film. The retailers or exhibitors return a share of that income to the wholesalers or the distributors, who in turn subtract their expenses and profits and then pass the remainder on to the manufacturers or producers, in this case Sol or whoever he designated as head of this operation. Lots of room to skim off the top, if you know what I mean."

"I don't think Rosen knows," Reuben

interjected. "And if he suspects . . . what's he going to do? Every goddamn employee is a relative. Obviously he hasn't kept up with the times. I'm no expert, but even I could tell his films are schlock."

"Schlock?" Daniel queried.

Reuben shrugged. "Garbage. Hit-and-miss is what he's producing. No-formula pictures. Westerns, for example. One week the public gets a western, the next week a comedy, and the week after that a romance. He's grinding out the same old thing, day after day, week after week. He's also not capitalizing on his stars. Take Farrell, for example. Women are crazy over him. They swoon when he comes on the screen. Men whistle when Clovis struts her stuff. Everyone laughs for Lester Kramer. People want to see them again and again." Reuben checked his watch. "It's late, Daniel. We should have been asleep hours ago. Too bad we can't get paid for all this time."

Daniel rubbed his eyes and yawned elaborately. "What would we do with all that money?"

"Repay Mickey," Reuben said.

"Have you written her?" Daniel asked quietly.

"I have half a letter finished. I'm no letter writer. I find it a monumental task. I want to do it, know I should do it, but I have difficulty saying what I want to say."

"Practice makes perfect." Daniel's tone stopped just short of severity when he chided, "It isn't fair of you not to write. I'm sure she goes every day to the post. She loves you, Reuben. You can't be so cold as to forget so easily."

"Forget! That's why I'm having so much difficulty writing. I can't forget. I don't want her thinking I'm some lovesick puppy that can't control his emotions. I'll do it, Daniel. I said I would and I will. You sent the payment, right?"

"Last week. Good night, Reuben."

Reuben changed into his pajamas, brushed his teeth, and washed his face. Then stomped his way back to the tiny living room with his half-finished letter to Mickey. It took him an hour and a half to finish the letter he'd started days earlier. Twice he read it over to make sure it said everything he wanted to say. He signed it, "My love for you endures, Reuben." God, how he missed her.

Reuben fingered the material of his pajamas. He knew they'd cost a pretty penny, probably more than some men's entire wardrobes. The shoes at the front door and the jacket hanging on a hook under the hallway mirror had all been bought and paid for by Mickey. Even the food he'd had tonight for dinner was bought and paid for by Mickey. His debt to the woman he loved gnawed at his soul.

Chapter
Twenty-One

Reuben whistled on his way to the bus stop. It was another golden day full of promise and sunshine. The tree-lined sidewalk gave the appearance of a tunnel with lacy patterns of sunshine, even this early in the morning, hopscotching all over the concrete. Daniel sighed happily. He'd had only four hours sleep, but he felt rested. Reuben hadn't gone to bed till almost dawn, but he'd finished his letter. He looked rested, and that pleased Daniel.

"Do you have your speech to Mr. Rosen down pat?" Daniel queried.

"I don't know if it's a speech, exactly. More like a list of questions. How he answers them will tell me how to proceed. Jesus, I had no idea he had so many relatives on the payroll. He's paying out a chunk of money that would pay off the national debt. If . . . if he was getting a return on the money, it would be a different story, but he isn't. I think he's going to be surprised when I show him what I have. Six months, Daniel, that's all it will take to

put this company up there with the others. I know you don't want to hear this, but I'm going to tell you anyway. I asked Max to look into the distribution end of this thing. If he can move booze, he can move film. He's got the connections. Good cover for Max. Good for the studio, too. Sometimes you have to close your eyes to certain things. The decision will have to be Sol's, though. I'll just be the go-between."

"What good is moving film if you don't have theaters to show them in?" Daniel asked.

Reuben sighed. "I told you, Max has connections. Legitimate connections. One hand washes the other, that kind of thing.

"Believe it or not, Max is all right. Like all of us, he has this passion to be someone important. I don't even think it's for himself, but for his mother. That's one for the books, isn't it?"

"I suppose so," Daniel growled. "What happens if some of this backfires and you end up in the clink?"

"By that time you'll be a full-fledged lawyer and will simply bail me out. Don't think about it, Daniel, until it happens. I hate it when you stew and fret about things. Live for today. Yesterday is gone and tomorrow will take care of itself. Don't worry about something that hasn't happened yet and might never happen. . . . Good, here's the bus."

Daniel was so relieved the conversation was

at an end, he tripped up the steps.

Sol Rosen seethed and fumed. His fingers drummed on his desk. A meeting, yet! A request for a meeting, the memo read. Ten o'clock, to discuss business. The guy had moxie. Christ, if only he knew one way or the other . . . did Mickey send him here to spy or didn't she? The cable he'd sent off a week before must have reached her, but there had been no response. Somehow, in some way, Tarz would ferret out everything. It was only a question of time till the ax fell . . . right over his head.

The guy was a worker, he had to give him that much credit. The guards at the gate said he was usually one of the first to arrive, around six-thirty or so, and one of the last to leave.

This morning he'd made an attempt to dress for what he now referred to as the Occasion. He'd had the maid press his suit and turn the collar and cuffs on his shirt. "Make it white," he'd ordered. He could still smell the bleach in his shirt. He'd even spit on his shoes for a little shine. Now he straightened his tie and shook out the cuffs of his shirt. His vest was buttoned, his tie secure inside. All was as it should be as he walked to the door to let Reuben in. Nodding curtly, he motioned him to a seat. "You said you wanted

a meeting, so let's get down to business," he said.

Reuben withdrew a thick sheaf of papers from a brown folder. Sol could see another, fatter stack with a rubber band around it. Christ, he must have worked around the clock to come up with so much paper, he thought.

"I'd like to ask you a question, Mr. Rosen. You don't have to answer it, but if you do, it will be an indication of how we can proceed." At Sol's nod, Reuben continued. "Do you want to be a major studio in this town and a force to be reckoned with?"

Sol swallowed hard. Christ, yes, he wanted to be a driving force, to have people recognize him, cater to him, be sought after. He couldn't trust himself to speak, so he simply nodded. "That's what I thought. You're no fool, Mr. Rosen, and I never thought of you as one. I think, in six months, I can put you on top."

Sol blanched. Six months! "What's in it for you, Tarz?"

Reuben leaned across the desk so that their eyes were level. "Power."

"If you have the power, where does that leave me?" Sol growled.

"Big . . . and rich. You'll be the power behind the power. You've got to give me the go-ahead, though. Don't decide now. Tomorrow will be soon enough. I'm going to leave

these papers with you so you can go over them tonight at your leisure."

"Show me," Sol said gruffly.

"The first thing we have to discuss is your payroll. You have twenty-seven relatives working for you. I'm not saying there's anything wrong with hiring your relatives. What I am saying is, most of those relatives are not qualified to fill the jobs they hold. Like your director John Carlyle. You're paying out three hundred thousand dollars a year in salaries that are going down the toilet. In order to make money, you must spend money. But you've got to spend it in the right place. Now it's obvious that you are spending it and getting no return. Here's why. . . ."

"My relatives ain't crooks," Sol spat out.

"I don't believe I used that term," Reuben said. "If they aren't, as you say, crooks, then that leaves you. Have you been skimming off the top?"

"I should bounce you out on your arse for saying something like that!" Sol barked.

"Why, for telling the truth? It's all here in black and white. You can't dispute it. They have to go, all of them. We'll find jobs for them, jobs that are more fitting to their talents, if they have any. If they have no talent, then they go. We'll hire professionals, men who know the business. That three hundred thousand dollars will go a long way in getting you the best. I'm personally going

490

to take over the distribution of your films."

"Lots of luck." Sol laughed abruptly. "That's the problem, we can't *get* distribution!"

"No, that's not the problem. The problem is your people didn't go about it in the right way because they don't know how. That's what I've been trying to tell you. The next thing you're going to do is buy up a chain of theaters. If you have to, go to the bank for financing. You need control. You can't be content with your colleagues so far ahead of you. The way I see it, you are about one year away from going down the drain."

"Where'd you learn all this stuff?" Sol muttered. He hated the thought of going belly up. He'd be a goddamn laughingstock.

"People talk. I can read. I listen. You helped. It's simply a question of interpreting the facts. And the facts say you're in a mess. I won't make any decisions without your okay. This is your company. Do you want me to help you or not?"

Sol thought about it for so long, Reuben was about to shove the contents of the folder on the floor and walk out. "If I make a deal with you, who else will know about it?"

"Daniel Bishop."

"Is that the truth?"

"Yes."

"Okay," Sol barked nervously.

Reuben stretched his hand across the desk.

491

Gingerly Sol reached for his hand. "I think I'll take a short vacation," he said. "I don't want to be here when you ax the relatives. I don't have the stomach for that."

"I'll handle it. I want a contract drawn up to this effect. You get a copy and I get a copy. Who you show yours to is your business. Daniel Bishop will be the only person to see mine, since he'll be drawing it up."

Sol's eyes were glued to the door long after Reuben made his way to his own office. He started to shake, unsure if the trembling was due to excitement or fear.

Things were a little clearer now. The reason he'd had no response to his cable was that Mickey had turned everything over to Tarz. She wanted no contact with Sol himself. Now he was certain he'd made the right decision in going along with Mickey's protégé. To do otherwise would be fatal.

Did he want to be one of the big five? Hell, yes, he did. Power was what Tarz wanted. Power and money — a marriage that was difficult to dissolve. For some strange reason, he believed everything Tarz said.

His head whirled with thought. If he believed this good-looking kid and trusted him, where did that leave Mickey? He didn't doubt for one minute that Tarz had the ability to play both ends against the middle. When that happened, Sol knew, there was a winner and a loser, and the guy in the middle came out

on top. Final approval. Tarz had said he wouldn't do anything until it had been okayed. That little tidbit would have to be written into the contract. Final approval would keep him on top. Sol reached for a cigar and was pleased to see that his hands were fairly steady now. The cigar glowed red as thin streams of smoke eddied upward to swirl about the room. He leaned back and propped his feet on an open desk drawer. Four days' vacation, that's what he'd give himself. His gut rumbled when he visualized the scenes that would be played out when Tarz lowered the boom on his money-grabbing relatives.

Sol walked from the studio lot, nodding his head first to one actor and then to another. Some of them he didn't even recognize. His thoughts now were on Mickey. Was she a first-class fool and so in love with Tarz she'd turned over her half of the business to him, or was she a shrewd business woman who, with the help of a smart guy like Tarz, could ace him right out of his forty-nine percent of the business? He started to tremble again. He knew then he would do a lot of trembling in the days to come.

Two days later Reuben did two things: he hired a secretary and bought a load of green plants for his office. Margaret, his secretary, was a no-nonsense woman who supported

herself and her mother. She said she gave a day's work for a day's pay and in the next breath said loyalty was her strongest point after efficiency. Reuben hired her on the spot. "After you water the plants," he told her, "find someplace suitable for a conference room and set up two meetings — one with all personnel, and one with the actors and actresses. Call the personnel office at Paramount and get the address of a Jane Perkins. She's an extra. If they don't have it at Paramount, then call every studio till you find her. You might have to go to her home or else you can send someone, someone reliable. Set up a meeting with her."

"Shouldn't I know why?" Margaret queried in a businesslike voice, her pencil poised over her steno pad.

Reuben stared at her. "Yes, I guess you should. I never had a secretary before, so if I don't do something right, call me on it," he said generously. "I want to give Jane a screen test. It's not necessary that she be told that right away. And Margaret, anytime anyone wants to see me, I'm not too busy. I'm here to put this studio on its feet, and the only way I can do that is with everyone's help. I don't want to be untouchable. The last thing is, no matter what I'm doing, no matter where I am on this lot — and you'll always know — if Daniel Bishop wants me, find me. Daniel *never* has to wait to talk to me."

Reuben took a deep breath. "Order the trade papers, *Billboard, Moving Picture World,* and the *New York Dramatic Mirror.* I want to know what's going on in this business. Find out who we cozy up to for the latest gossip."

"I'll see to it all, Mr. Tarz," Margaret said briskly, pushing her pencil behind her ear as she closed the door behind her.

Reuben took over his tasks with a vengeance. More than anything else, he looked forward to seeing the expression on Jane Perkins's face when she stepped into his office and he offered her a screen test. Hollywood, the land of dreams. If nothing else, he would create a dream for Jane. Daniel was delighted when he was told of Reuben's plans and asked if he could sit in.

"You bet! We discovered that girl together. We just didn't know we were discovering her at the time."

When Jane Perkins arrived promptly at three o'clock, Margaret ushered her into the room. Reuben came around his desk, and Daniel got up to shake her hand. "What are you guys doing here?" she asked, her hand on her hip.

"We work here." Reuben grinned. "Fairmont Studios would be most pleased to offer you a screen test. In, say . . ." Reuben pulled out his watch and made a pretense of looking at it. "Exactly ten minutes.

"Everything is set up for you. Projection

has a film they're going to run for you. I want you to pay close attention to it . . . very close attention. In your test I want you to emote the same way, do you understand what I'm saying?"

"She's fainting!" Daniel shouted as he tried to catch the falling girl. "You do have some impact on women, Reuben!"

Reuben called to Margaret, who immediately shooed them aside. She splashed cologne on a linen handkerchief and waved it under Jane's nose. The girl's eyes fluttered, and then she panicked as she struggled to get to her feet.

"Easy does it, Jane. When was the last time you had something to eat?"

"I'm real sorry, Mr. Tarz. Yesterday, maybe the day before, I guess. I'm a little short this week. Did you s-say screen test? I — I'm an extra," stammered the ashen-faced girl.

"You *were* an extra," Daniel said, beaming. "Look, we know your test is going to be fine. You're going on the payroll, and when you leave here today you'll have a contract in your pocket."

"Gosh! Why me? You guys don't even know me. I'm grateful, so grateful I think I'm going to cry."

"Your faint took five minutes. Come along, Jane, we'll get some doughnuts on the way so you have something in your stomach. I want you to give this test everything you've got.

Did you ever see *Tillie's Punctured Romance?*"

"Only a dozen times." Jane smiled. "I can do it. I'm sure I can do it."

"I know you can, too," Reuben said warmly.

At twenty minutes past seven Jane Perkins signed a contract Daniel drew up with Fairmont Studios. Her salary to start was $175 a week and would escalate with each movie she starred in. Reuben handed her fifty dollars from petty cash as an advance on her first week's salary. He wiped her tears with his handkerchief. "Here," he said, offering her his pack of cigarettes. "Buy yourself some food and go home. Celebrate. Be here tomorrow at seven. Can I count on you?"

"I won't let you down, Mr. Tarz, I swear I won't. Just tell me what you want and I'll do it. I can take direction. How am I ever going to thank you for this break?" she said, wiping at her tears.

"For starters you can go back to calling me Reuben, and Daniel is Daniel. Deal?"

Jane smiled tremulously. "It's a dream," she kept muttering as she left the studio.

Reuben and Daniel watched her from the window. Halfway down the lot she tossed the cigarettes in the air and did a high skipping jump and a little dance step. Reuben burst out laughing. "Good flicks with good actors," he said. "We'll do the big stuff with fanfare. We pay out big bucks for the best. We did our good deed for the day, so let's go home

early tonight."

"I thought you were going to see . . ." The name stuck in Daniel's throat.

"Max? I am, but after dinner. If you're ready, let's go."

"Are you going to tell Sol about Jane?"

"I cleared it with him yesterday. He understands, and he didn't voice any objections. Sol's in line, and I think he's happy with the way things are going. He'll pull me up short if I step over one of his boundaries. That's okay with me. We made a deal and I intend to honor it. He okayed Red Ruby and the director from Fox, too."

There was awe in Daniel's face. "Congratulations!"

"I'm tryin', Dan'l. I'm tryin'. I think Mickey would be pleased with what I've accomplished. I think I'll write her tonight and tell her. She'll understand what we did for Jane. I can see her smiling when she reads it." This letter, Reuben thought, would be a pleasure to write.

The Mimosa Club was jumping with sound when Reuben walked in at nine o'clock. On the small stage next to the bar, two young girls were giving a poor imitation of the cancan. Reuben grinned. He'd seen the real thing, and these two needed quite a few more lessons before they had the dance down pat. He winked lecherously at the prettier of the

two as he walked to the back of the club where Max was waiting for him.

"Tell me that was a smile . . . I'm impressed," Max said loud enough to be heard over the sound of the band.

Reuben bared his teeth in a grimace. "Yes, a smile. Can we go someplace where it's a little quieter so we can talk?"

"What's up your sleeve?" Max said out of the corner of his mouth, imitating gangsters he'd seen in the movies.

Reuben imitated Max. "My arm," he said curtly.

Fifteen minutes later Max leaned back in his ruby-red Morris chair and said, "You want me to do *what?*"

"You heard me the first time. No names here, Max. Straightforward business deal. You want it, you're in. You don't and I'm out of here."

"Tarz, I'm not big time. I make a living at this. My territory is small. I'd give my eye-teeth for a crack at your distribution, but I'll be honest, I don't think I can handle it."

Reuben straddled a chair. "You know, Max, if you'd jumped at this, I'd have walked out of here. I appreciate your honesty. Now, let's put our heads together. I'm real interested in a string of theaters here or in New York. You have contacts in the East. Move my film and you're legit, if you want to be legit. I don't care if you move your hooch at the same

time, but if the feds come down on you, my name stays out of it. Take a couple of days to think about it. By the way, your percentage will please your mother. I'm a fair man, Max."

"Yeah, I'll think about it. Does this mean you're off my run?"

"Until you find someone to replace me, I won't leave you in the lurch. I said I was a fair man. By the way, you need a whole row of girls to do the cancan justice."

"You a connoisseur or something?" Max asked curiously. This guy was one hell of a puzzle.

"I saw the real thing in Paris. You should expand, Max. This place is too small."

"It takes money, you know. But I've been thinking about it."

"You have to spend money to make money. Think about that. I'll be by in a few days. Don't take too long, Max. I want to roll on this as soon as possible."

"Yeah. Yeah, yeah."

After Reuben left, Max sat for a long time stroking his chin. Could he do it? Legit. Jesus, his mother would be so happy. Hell, he'd be happy. But he wasn't about to give up the hooch runs. What the hell was he thinking about? His mother thought he was legit now. His head started to buzz. Name after name rolled off his tongue. He fished a pencil out of his shirt and started to write on the blotter. Maybe . . . just maybe . . . But where did

you pull a string of theaters out of a hat? For the first time in a long time Max pushed what he considered his limitations far out of his mind. His gut told him no matter what it took, he should hitch his wagon to Tarz's. The ride would be anything but smooth . . . in the beginning.

In the weeks to come, Fairmont Studios took on a new look. Paint, landscaping, uniforms, and a general cleaning made everyone step back for a second glance. Personnel changes were quick and dry. Those who cooperated stayed, others packed and left. Other changes were more subtle. The word was out that Fairmont was paying top dollar for directors and producers. Actors and actresses stood in line at the gate in the morning, a number of seasoned professionals hoping for a better break than they were getting at the other studios, and hopefuls by the dozen. Scripts, novels, and plays were delivered to the gate. Reuben himself took over the advertising, and his battle cry could be heard all over the studio. "I'm looking for talent!"

By midsummer Reuben felt he had a good roster of capable actors. His directors and producers were the finest money could buy, and he had on hand three scripts that his gut told him would bring in a fortune. The first was a dramatic extravaganza starring Clovis Ames titled *California Madness.* The script

called for deep cleavage, a lot of silken leg, and the bathtub scene Clovis was famous for. Only the director understood Reuben when he said he wanted a beginning, a middle, and an end — in other words, a story that said something. Clovis groused but followed the director's orders. The second was a star-studded adventure starring Damian Farrell as Red Ruby. Reuben himself sat in on the filming, nodding approval from time to time. Jane Perkins was pulled from her bread-and-butter rolls to play Opal Jade, Red Ruby's first heist victim. The third film, which starred Norbert Nesbit in a clown suit performing garden weddings, was designed for laughs, and laughs it got — so much so that some scenes had to be reshot a few times because the crew was so caught up in the hilarity during filming.

Sol beamed his approval, but not in Reuben's sight. In private he rubbed his hands together as he calculated the revenue Reuben's hard work would bring in. Distribution was scheduled for August first. Three days before that date, Max Gould called asking Reuben to stop by the club. "I got what you want. It's time to talk money."

Max was so excited when he rattled off his spiel, he forgot to act tough. He was like a kid with a room full of new toys and not sure what he should play with first. "I got this guy who's willing to drive a truck to New York

for five hundred smackers. I tried to get the price down, but he wouldn't budge. Your stuff is safe with him, though, I personally guarantee it."

"That's good enough for me, Max." Reuben felt relieved; he'd estimated a two-grand bill.

"This same guy has a cousin that might . . . might be interested in taking your stuff to Chicago. That's if you're interested."

"I'm interested. Five hundred for him, too?"

Max nodded. "Now about the theaters. I got you twenty-four. Rat traps, Tarz. You want them, they're yours. You can either rent or buy outright. I set up appointments for you over the next two days." Max unfolded a map and laid it out on the table. It had so many marks on it, Reuben was hard-pressed to follow the routes Max was mapping out. "It's the whole state of California. This is no schlock deal, Tarz. Took me a long time to put this together. I called in all my favors on this one. These guys, they think I'm nuts. I don't think I'm nuts. My business is going to triple with these runs. The best part is . . . never mind."

Reuben nodded. Whatever Max was going to say would come out later, and if it didn't, it was his business. Without the gangster's help Reuben knew he could never hope to distribute Rosen's films. For the next hour the two men talked money.

He was in business!

That night Reuben went home and wrote a long, loving, three-page letter to Mickey. The only thing he didn't tell her was that Max was a gangster. He signed his letter: "I love you with all my heart, Reuben."

CHAPTER
TWENTY-TWO

The village postmaster stared at the pile of mail addressed to Michelene Fonsard. Twice he'd driven by the château to see if she'd returned. Cables were usually important. Letters and cables, all from America. He did something then he'd never done before. He took it upon himself to bundle Michelene Fonsard's mail into a tight packet. He addressed a letter to the postmaster in Paris telling him to deliver the mail to Madame Fonsard's house in Paris. He was so relieved that the mail was no longer his problem, he poured himself a large glass of wine and downed it in two long gulps. Perhaps on her return Madame would reward him for his diligence.

A special messenger was dispatched to Michelene Fonsard's Paris house the same day the thick bundle of mail arrived. A young girl with fluffy hair accepted the mail, smiled, and gave the messenger two francs. She signed a receipt.

Bebe tossed the packet on the foyer table and immediately forgot about it. Today she had other things on her mind. The young man she'd flirted with for two solid weeks had finally asked her to the theater. Right now her biggest decision was what jewelry to wear and should she or shouldn't she varnish her nails.

For the next two weeks Bebe's days were busy and fun-filled. She didn't give the packet of mail a second thought until the night she had a row with the young man when he tried to put his hand up her dress. She slapped him soundly and told him to get out. He turned a deep, angry scarlet and called her a tease and a flirt before he slammed the stained-glass door.

Furious, Bebe paced the drawing room, wearing a path in the fringed Oriental carpet. It was always like this; be nice to a man, and immediately they took advantage. No great loss, she told herself. She felt at loose ends. Maybe it was time to return to California. She'd been in Paris far too long. Finally she settled herself on a chair and picked up the newspaper. It was a week old, but she didn't care. When she came to the entertainment section, she gasped aloud. Staring up at her was a picture of Clovis Ames under the dark black heading "American Films":

California Madness is a smash hit for Fair-

506

mont Studios & Clovis Ames Reuben Tarz, production assistant to Sol Rosen said he "wasn't in the least surprised that *California Madness* was a hit. We simply gave the public what they clamored for."

Reuben Tarz! Production assistant to her father! Bebe felt so faint she put her head between her legs and took great deep breaths. Reuben was in California and working for her father. How had that happened? Was Mickey there, too? Of course she was, that's why the mail was so piled up. Bebe threw a tantrum then, the equal of the one she'd thrown when she was six years old and destroyed her mother's fine parlor porcelain. She lashed out, kicked, and screamed, tossing Mickey's priceless figurines against the wall, upending furniture, and ripping paintings off the walls. When she was finished she was breathless with exertion. Spent, she lay down in a mound of pillows and was asleep in minutes.

Soft gray light was creeping over the windowsill when she woke and stared about the wreckage she'd created. She recalled telling Yvette to assure Mickey she would take care of the house. Now she sobbed as she tried to gather up the broken crystal and porcelain. None of the delicate objects could be repaired. She'd behaved like a hoodlum. How

was she going to make this right with Mickey? Taking a deep breath, she set about straightening the room as best she could. She rehung pictures, fixed lamp shades, and arranged the pillows on the furniture. The broken porcelain and crystal she swept into a box and set in the kitchen. Then she wrote a note explaining what she'd done and apologizing.

A moment later, when she headed for the stairs to change her clothes, she'd completely forgotten the destruction. Her eye fell on the stack of mail in the foyer. She unwrapped the string and carried the thick bundle back to the parlor. Among other pieces were two cables from her father and one from Reuben. There were also five letters from Reuben, thick letters, and four from Daniel. Obviously Mickey was not in California. Bebe's heart lightened immediately.

She weighed the letters, balancing them in the palm of her hand, trying to decide if she should open them or not. A voice at the back of her mind warned her that what she was about to do was wrong. "So was what I just did to this parlor," she grumbled. Reuben's letters were so thick, what could he possibly have to say that would take so many sheets of paper? How else would she ever find out unless she opened them? She settled herself on the lounge chair in the parlor and read them all — first Daniel's and then Reuben's. When

she'd finished she got up, walked stonily to the fireplace, and tossed in the lot. She struck a match on the hearth and laughed as Reuben's sweet, loving words roared up the chimney.

Bebe felt as though the blood would boil right out of her veins. Reuben didn't love her; the letters confirmed her worst fears. Bitter tears of sorrow coursed down her cheeks. Was she so ugly, so unpleasant, so . . . unlovable? She would have licked his feet, killed for him, if he'd asked it of her. Why? What was there about Reuben Tarz that made her feel this way? Or was it Mickey? She did her best to analyze her situation. Mickey was a sweet, gentle person, full of love and compassion. That's why Reuben was so in love with her. She, on the other hand, was young, Reuben's contemporary, spoiled and selfish. She'd made a mistake on her arrival, thought someone her own age would be interested in gaiety and laughter and having fun. She hadn't realized Reuben was looking for a more mature love, the kind Mickey had offered him. She knew she loved Reuben, had loved him from the moment she'd made the decision to be Bebe the party girl. If she'd only taken a few extra seconds before making that terrible decision, Reuben might have seen her as she really was, the way *he* really was — lost and abandoned. He would have fallen in love with her as she had fallen in

love with him.

So many mistakes. And today she'd just made the worst one of her life by destroying Reuben's and Daniel's letters. She sat staring at the ashes of the burning letters, thinking about the mistakes she had made.

She'd borne Reuben a son, a son she couldn't acknowledge, wouldn't acknowledge. A child born of rape deserves better than me or Reuben, she thought. She could have told him about John Paul and he might have done the right thing and married her, but she didn't want him out of pity. "I want you to love me. Reuben, the way I love you. Every night I pray that Daniel's God will forgive me for abandoning our son, the way we were all abandoned. Daniel, you, and I. We're truly the Three Musketeers. All we want is love. You think you have it with Mickey, and I suppose in a way you do, but it's a passionate mother-son love. Daniel . . . well, Daniel will find love someday, but I think he'll make mistakes before he finds what he's seeking.

"That leaves me. Mickey tried to give me her mother love, a love I needed. It would have been so perfect if you'd loved me, too. Both of us would have had a mother and we would have been free to love each other. Oh, Reuben, you are so stupid! I love you. I love you so much I ache with the feeling. How else could I forgive you for raping me, how

else could I give away our son except out of love? I made so many mistakes, and I made them out of love for you. I could make you so happy. You feel something for me, I know you do. I saw it in your eyes, but out of loyalty to Mickey you won't allow yourself to act on your feelings. Loyalty and love are two very different things."

The real Bebe Rosen curled into a ball, her knees almost to her chin. "I can be whatever you want, Reuben, as long as you love me," she whispered.

The following day Bebe booked her passage home.

CHAPTER
TWENTY-THREE

Sol stared at the intimidating stacks of papers on his desk. Notes, memos, contracts, proposals, all from Reuben. Secretaries were supposed to handle this stuff, he thought nastily, and then he remembered who his secretary was. Relatives! He'd been adamant with Reuben about not firing his gum-chewing, nail-polishing secretary, not because she was worthy or efficient, but just to keep his hand in and not allow Reuben too much power. Now he regretted his cranky decision. If Tarz liked memos, he'd scribble one off to him telling him to relocate his secretary. Possibly to the costume or makeup department.

His nerves were like raw ends pricking him as he waded through the stacks of papers. At first glance he didn't see anything he could call Tarz on. Now that the decision making, at least outwardly, was out of his hands, he could look and think objectively about the progress the studio was making. He had no complaints about Reuben at all. In the begin-

ning he'd worked overtime trying to catch him in a wrong move, but so far the kid was straight as an arrow. Sol envied him his cool head, his logic, and his straightforward way of doing business. With Tarz calling the shots he was sleeping better at night, eating wisely, and his eyes weren't twitching anymore. If things kept going the way they had been over the past few months, he'd be able to replace some of the money he owed Mickey. In a year, give or take a few months, he could pay off his debt entirely and possibly buy another twenty-five percent from her, if she was willing to sell.

He was looking at a proposal now that made him blink. "What in hell is this?" he sputtered. Tarz was asking his approval on some kind of short skit: cancan girls, California cancan girls. Different songs, different skits, to show before each movie. It will bring young men, middle-aged men, and old men to the theaters, read the proposal, and it will keep them coming back. Long-legged beauties, scantily clad, with ruffles on their rear ends. Sol sputtered again. It would work; he could feel the excitement building in him. The others had nothing like this. Zukor would go up in smoke when it hit, and so would Zanuck. Sol scribbled his initials on the memo.

At one o'clock Reuben sent out a casting call for twelve long-legged dancers. He

ordered black mesh stockings and what wardrobe called rompers with ruffles. "I can't come up with a name that will suit this review," Reuben grumbled to his director, Carl Maddox.

"Run a contest with the employees and give a prize of fifty bucks. You'll have names growing out of your ears in a day's time."

By closing time the following day, Reuben had picked a name from the two hundred or so offerings and hired a choreographer named Sam Naylor, who agreed to take on the job for an outrageous sum of money. He looked Reuben in the eye and said calmly, "If you want quality and excellence for the Sugar and Spice Review, them I'm your man." Reuben hired the diminutive, balding man immediately. He wrote a memo to Sol saying the man would earn every penny of his salary.

Reuben's voice was brisk and cold as he issued instructions to the choreographer. "I don't want these young women worked like the cancan girls in Paris. You are to give them plenty of breaks and rest periods. I'm sure you know that most of the Parisienne cancan girls live only a few . . . years after they start dancing, and I don't want that to happen here. Hire extras to take the load off the stars. Don't even think about crossing me on this, because if you do, your ass is out of here."

Naylor's voice was low with a musical

cadence to it. "I was going to suggest the same thing to you. I spent two years in Paris studying music and dance. I am well aware of the problem. I think you should know something about me. When I . . . ah, plant my ass, it stays planted. I hate job hunting. So I think we understand each other, Mr. Tarz." They shook hands. The Sugar and Spice Girls were now Sam Naylor's exclusive responsibility.

Reuben Tarz was the picture of comfort with his body tilted backward in his swivel chair, his long legs propped on an open desk drawer. Hands clasped behind his head, eyes closed, he contemplated his progress to date. Things were running smoothly, with only a few snags here and there. But his pose wasn't one of simple relaxation, it was something he did every day around this time — a break to go over the day's agenda. The truth was he was tense, anxious, but he didn't know why. A sense of foreboding seemed to shackle him to his chair.

Rain whispered against the window. Reuben's feet plopped to the floor, and he swiveled around to stare out at the gray day. He was reminded of the war and the cold, dreary, rain-soaked days he'd spent in the trenches. He hated days like this; they made him think about things he'd rather not deal with. Like Mickey. Bebe. It was always either Mickey or

Bebe and not necessarily in that order. Seven goddamn letters and not one response from Mickey. Not even an acknowledgment concerning the money he and Daniel were paying back. Even Daniel had had no letter. Out of sight, out of mind. Obviously she was finished with them and didn't want to be bothered anymore. For one crazy moment he wanted to chuck everything and head to the nearest shipping office to book passage to France. The *Mauretania* was sailing this week, he'd read about it in the papers. And what the hell would you do when you get there? he asked himself. Cry, beg, plead? For what? Wicked thoughts attacked him like angry ghosts in the night. It was just an adventure for Mickey. You were young, she wasn't so young. She gave, you took, that was the bargain. It was all Bebe's fault; as soon as she'd arrived in France things started going wrong.

He hated it when Bebe entered his thoughts, especially when he was alone. When he was alone he had to deal with his hatred of her, his guilt and his love for Mickey. In his mind it was all mixed up. She'd promised to write — no, that was wrong, she'd promised to answer his letters. By now he should have had at least five responses. Maybe she had found someone to replace him. The thought was so horrible, so sickening, he rushed to the window and opened it violently,

leaning out to take great gulping breaths, mindless of the rain.

In that moment he saw her. Stunned, he blinked and rubbed his eyes to clear his vision. But when he looked again, his mind could no longer deny the evidence — it was Bebe roaring through the lot in a super-powered convertible roadster. Bebe was back! Reuben inched his way to the corner of the wall and cowered there like a shell-shocked doughboy. It took him a full ten minutes to move away and return to his swivel chair. He had to think, and he had to think clearly . . . now. "Margaret?" he bellowed. "Tell Daniel I want to see him. Now!"

Margaret had never heard this strange voice before. She peered nervously around the half-open door to make sure it was Reuben speaking, then hurried down the hall to find Daniel Bishop.

Ten minutes later Daniel strolled into Reuben's office with a sheaf of papers in his hand. "I told you I'd have it by the end of the day, and here it is. Relax, Reuben," he said, eyeing his friend curiously. "The S and S Girls are going to net this studio a handsome return. I did a year's projection. I made two copies, knowing you'd want to give Sol his right away."

"That will be all, Margaret. Close the door when you leave, please." Reuben watched, silently until the secretary had left, then he

swallowed hard — twice. Daniel's eyebrows shot upward. "Daniel, I just saw something I never expected to see . . . at least not yet," he said in a voice he barely recognized as his own.

"Louis B. Mayer kowtowing to Sol Rosen?" Daniel quipped. He'd never seen Reuben in such a state. "What's wrong, Reuben? You look like you've seen a ghost."

"I just saw Bebe drive through the lot in a car with its top down in the rain."

Daniel reached out a sympathetic hand to clap Reuben's shoulder. "And I thought you wanted these projections! Did she see you?"

"No. That's not the point. She's here. Why? What does she want now?"

"I don't know if you realize this or not, but she does live here. She's probably home to see her father. You must have known she'd come back at some point. Bebe's return won't change things," Daniel said in a reassuring voice.

"And we haven't heard a word from Mickey. Don't you think that's rather strange?" He jerked his head toward the window. "She must have had something to do with it. I wouldn't put it past her to fill Mickey's head with a pack of lies," he said viciously.

"Why hasn't she written? Why, Daniel?"

He'd been wondering the same thing himself for weeks now. "I don't know. Maybe

she's traveling. There is that possibility. Mickey would not abandon us."

"Daniel, it's time you grew up. Life is hard, and the world outside these walls is merciless. I'm not some sap that walked in out of the rain, and neither are you. I don't know how I know it, but that girl has something to do with why we haven't heard from Mickey. I'll take it one step further — I'd stake my life on it!" Reuben said bitterly.

"That girl can cost us our jobs, Daniel," he continued, his eyes narrowed in anger. "She is her father's darling. One word from her and our asses are out on the street. If I get the first inkling she's up to something, I'll take matters into my own hands. I'll settle that girl's hash once and for all."

So that was what it was all about. Daniel almost felt relief. "Sol won't do that to us. He likes what you've done. The studio has turned around completely. I think his biggest fear is whether one of the other studios will try to get you to go with them. He won't let Bebe dictate how he should run his business."

Reuben snorted. "I suppose she told you that in one of your calculated confidence-sharing sessions."

Daniel felt himself bristling. Why was he always in the middle? "As a matter of fact, she did. She told me she and her brother used to make suggestions to Sol all the time, and he told them the studio was none of their

business. I think you're wrong on that score, Reuben."

Reuben looked out at the darkening day. Driving rain beat against the window. "I have to stop by the Mimosa Club. Don't wait dinner for me, I'll grab a bite at the club. . . . Don't look so sour, Daniel. This is Memorial Day weekend, and we'll have three whole days to do nothing but lounge around. Let's hit the beach, we haven't done that in a long time." It was an effort to speak lightly, to erase the look of worry on Daniel's face. He felt relief when Daniel grinned at the mention of time off.

"Sounds great, pal. I guess I'll see you later, then."

"Wait up for me, Daniel, I want to talk to you about college this evening. I haven't forgotten, you know. We'll talk tonight."

Reuben worked hard in the next few minutes trying to strike the proper pose as busy assistant to a studio head. He stuck a pencil behind his ear and another one in his pocket. He perched his glasses on his nose and scattered papers all over his desk. He waited, his stomach churning with hatred. Bebe Rosen wasn't the only one who knew how to put on a performance.

Bebe was on her way to her father's office, or else she was right outside his door. Reuben wrinkled his nose, recognizing her scent, *Quelques*. His hand started to tremble. "Keep

a tight rein, Tarz," he muttered. The sound of her trilling voice sent shivers down his arms. Without shame he listened as she greeted her father affectionately. The makeshift wall separating Sol's office from his own allowed for crystal clarity. He made a mental note to tone down his own conversations.

"Ohhhhh, Daddy, it's so *good* to be back! I didn't even go to the house, I came here first. What a beastly day! Where's Eli? I can't wait to see him! Are you glad to see me, Daddy? Everything looks so different. Elegant. Who are all these new people? Oh Daddy, I have so much to tell you!"

"You look beautiful, sweetheart. I'm glad you're home," Sol said, wrapping his arms around his daughter. "Maybe you can talk some sense into your brother. He's driving me crazy. He's going to end up in jail one of these days. I'll let him rot there, too. No man deserves a son like Eli."

"Daddy, you've never been fair to him. You don't take the time to understand him. Now that you have an assistant, you'll have more time . . ."

Reuben wondered if Sol had picked up on the sudden hard edge in Bebe's voice.

"How is Mickey?" Sol asked in a nonchalant voice.

"Why, Daddy, how else would Mickey be but fine? She let me stay in her Paris house. We must send her a check because I broke

one of her ornaments. It was just the silliest thing, I . . . bumped right into it, and crash, there it went."

"What's she doing?" Sol asked.

"Doing? The same thing she always does. She's living her own way."

"I sent her a cable some time ago and she didn't respond," Sol said, sounding worried.

Bebe laughed, a tinkling sound that Reuben recognized as one of her "stall for time" laughs. "Well, Daddy, I certainly can't explain why Mickey does or doesn't answer her mail. She talks about you and the studio all the time. She thinks we're just filthy rich, you know. She always looks in the papers to see what the American films are and which ones are produced by Fairmont. She always clucks her tongue, like this." She made a funny sound that made Reuben grimace. "You aren't laughing, Daddy. That was supposed to be a joke. . . . Daddy, why is Reuben Tarz your assistant? I read about it in the papers. He's so . . . nasty and arrogant. I want you to get rid of him. You'll get rid of him, won't you, Daddy? He's just so arrogant. Why, in France he had us all jumping through hoops doing what he said when he said it. He had Mickey wrapped around his finger. He was in charge of the wineries, in charge of the château, in charge of Daniel and me and Mickey, too, I suppose. I can tell you one thing, she certainly danced to his tune," Bebe

said maliciously. "Why did he come here? I can't believe you hired him! I wouldn't be a bit surprised if he had some kind of hold on Mickey and she booted him out. I think he's a gigolo. Mickey . . . well, she just swooned when he was around. It was sickening, Daddy. I wish you could have seen the way they looked at each other. It was so . . . so disgusting. I still can't believe you sent me there. You shouldn't have exposed me to such . . . shenanigans. Daddy, are you listening to me? It's not too late, you can get rid of him, can't you?"

"You're home now, safe and sound," Sol said through clenched teeth. "Listen, as I've said before, studio business is not for your . . . pretty little head. Reuben Tarz is a very capable young man and he's proving to be invaluable. He's turning the studio around, and we're already making money and paying off debts. So don't start on him, Bebe, or me."

Reuben could hear a wet smacking sound as Bebe gave her father a kiss. "I still think he's all wrong for this studio. You'll be sorry, Daddy, when he sticks an ax in your back."

"He has a contract," Sol said as if that were the beginning and the end of the discussion. Reuben bared his teeth in a snarl.

"You are just the darlingest father," Bebe cooed. "You think everyone is wonderful. You even think Mickey is wonderful, don't you?"

"Of course," Sol said curtly.

"Well, she isn't all *that* wonderful. She thinks you are a bumbling old fool who's incapable of running this studio." Reuben heard the quick intake of breath as Bebe gasped. "I'm sorry, Daddy, I made that up. She didn't say that at all. . . . Look, let's get out of here. I'm taking you to dinner."

Reuben listened as two pairs of footsteps went down the stairs, one heavy and one so light it was almost indistinguishable.

He was angry — angrier than he'd ever been. So angry he picked up a paperweight and pitched it across the room. He blinked at the size of the hole it made in the plaster wall. "Son of a bitch!"

If he wasn't careful, Bebe Rosen was going to continue to muck up his life. Already his mouth tasted foul. Her perfume was still in the air. He had to get out of here and get a breath of fresh air before his temper roared out of control.

The rain was coming down in torrents and a soft gray mist eddied about his feet as Reuben slogged his way to the Mimosa Club. He had to get hold of himself. He couldn't let Bebe Rosen get to him; he wasn't ready for her . . . yet.

He'd given up his thrice weekly run for Max and been replaced with a young woman in a tight blue dress and blond hair. Max said she did as good a job as he had. He'd never met the woman and had no desire to. These

days he rarely came to the club, preferring to keep his working relationship with Max a private thing. Reuben sat down at the bar and ordered a cup of coffee and a hamburger. It was dim and smoky in the club and still too early for a crowd. Later the noise would bounce off the walls, but by then he'd be gone.

"You look like a drowned rat, Tarz," Max growled.

"I feel like one. It's raining like hell out there."

"You ever hear of an umbrella? I might have an extra one around here. You get wet feet you catch cold."

"Ask me if I care, Max."

"You also look like you lost your last friend," Max said boldly. Reuben turned on the bar stool to stare at him. "I have only one friend, and I did not lose him. I have things on my mind, that's all."

"Don't we all. Must be a woman, then," Max persisted. "Pal, if I was you, I'd learn how to play poker. Your face gives it away. Hey, bimbos are a dime a dozen. You want a dame, I'll get you a dame. Never hook yourself up with one in particular. First thing you know you start telling her your secrets, and it's all downhill after that. Dames are murder." For once Reuben was tempted to agree with the gangster.

"Not much business tonight. Guess it's the

weather."

Max nodded. "We have a private party later, but Monday nights are usually a little on the quiet side. See that dame down at the end of the bar. She came in here about an hour ago and already she's sloshed. She's not one of my regulars. Just up and walked in. Now I have to worry about getting her home in one piece. She's no drinker, either. Two cups and she's bawlin' her eyes out. Sooner or later I get 'em all in here."

Reuben bit into his sandwich and realized he wasn't hungry. He didn't want the coffee, either. He pushed his plate and cup away.

"I been reading the trade papers lately," Max continued. "You're making a name for yourself, Tarz. I got this gut feeling you're gonna make it to the top."

"I'm gonna try like hell. But the ball didn't start to roll till you came into the picture, Max. I owe you for that."

Max beamed up at Reuben. "Go home, Tarz, and get out of those wet clothes and shoes. It's on the house," he said, indicating the coffee and hamburger.

Reuben put on a halfhearted smile. "Thanks, Max. See you."

"Anytime."

Reuben walked the length of the bar, his eyes straight ahead, his thoughts everywhere but at the Mimosa Club. When the sound of a stifled sob caught his ear, he half turned to

stare at the girl Max had mentioned. "Jane! What the hell are you doing here? If Sol Rosen knew you came here, your butt would be out on the street."

"I just wandered in here. I was walking in the rain after I got off work. It seemed as good a place as any. What I do on my free time has nothing to do with my work . . . does it?" she asked, suddenly fearful.

"It has a hell of a lot to do with it. You're drunk. Why, Jane?"

"If it's a problem, I'll leave," Jane mumbled. She slid off the stool and would have fallen if Reuben hadn't reached out to grab her arm. "Oooooh, I got a little dizzy there for a minute. I'm fine now. You can let go of my arm, Mr. Tarz."

"If I let go of your arm, you'll do a nose dive. You really have a snootful. Where do you live?" Reuben demanded.

Jane waved her arm vaguely. "Out there."

"Out there where?" Reuben grated.

Jane started to cry. She was like a rubber doll as she tried to maintain her balance. "Max!" Reuben shouted down the length of the bar.

"You know her?" Max asked, surprised, as he hurried over.

"She works at the studio. She's so sloshed, she's ready to pass out. I think we better let her sleep it off. You have some rooms upstairs, right?"

"It's not a hotel, but it's goddamn clean!" Max said defensively.

"Good. Let's get her upstairs and out of these wet clothes. Do you think any of your girls might have something that will fit her?"

"I'll check. Wait here."

"Jane, what the hell are you doing here, and why are you drunk?" Reuben demanded sternly.

"It's Bobby. He said he doesn't want a movie star for a girlfriend. He doesn't like it that I make more money than he does. He dumped me. I told him I'd quit. I would, too, Mr. Tarz, but that was just an excuse, he was already going behind my back and seeing someone else. He lied to me, the no-good bum. He's a bum, a stinking bum. How could I love a bum, Mr. Tarz? My friends told me my best friend Stella has sex with him. That's who he was seeing behind my back. I want to be a virgin when I get married. Bobby never said anything about getting married. He's a bum, isn't he, Mr. Tarz?" She began to bawl again, her head in her arms.

"Yes, he is, Jane," Reuben said softly. He found himself cradling Jane in his arms. Awkwardly he patted her damp curls.

Max watched the little byplay as he instructed one of the girls to check out a room. So Tarz was human after all. A dame would do it every time, he thought smugly as he walked back over to the bar. Later, if he ever

528

found himself getting angry at Reuben, he'd remember he was human like the rest. It was always easier to handle a situation when you knew a man was capable of being vulnerable. At least that's what his mother told him. "Just a few minutes and you can take her up," he told Reuben. "Good thing you were here, I don't know what I would have done with her."

"You wouldn't have let her leave like this, would you? You just have to look at her to know she doesn't belong here. You would have taken her upstairs, wouldn't you, Max?"

Max looked embarrassed. "Yeah, sure. . . ."

Reuben smiled.

They were at the end of the bar, their backs to the door, when it opened. Reuben's arm was around Jane as he helped her off the stool to follow Max up the stairway. He heard Bebe's musical trill of laughter and Sol's bellow. "You didn't tell me Sol Rosen was your private party, Max," he hissed harshly.

Max turned on the step. "He isn't. It's Eli's party. For his sister. She just got back from Europe or somewhere. Tell you the truth, I didn't think the old man would show up."

"I'll take the back way out," Reuben snapped.

"Tarz, it's not my fault. Did I know you were going to stop in this evening? Business is business. You should understand that."

Reuben sighed. "You're right, Max, sorry."

At the top of the steps he turned Jane over to a buxom redhead named Delphine. "Take good care of her and see that she's at the studio for her call at seven. Max" — he turned to the little man and handed him a dollar — "send her in a cab, okay?"

"She'll be there. I don't know what shape she'll be in, but she'll be there," Max promised.

Reuben left the Mimosa Club by the back stairway, feeling like a thief in the night. He stepped into three inches of water and cursed loudly as Max handed him a huge black umbrella. He accepted it and sloshed through kitchen garbage and debris in the alley. Three times he poked his head from under the umbrella to see if anyone was following him.

Bebe Rosen was back.

Bebe's eyes widened at the sight of Reuben; she could feel her heart fluttering. She wished he would turn around and see her, at which point she would wave gaily and smile. Who was the girl, and where were they going? Upstairs, obviously. To do God only knew what. For weeks now, ever since she'd made the decision to return home, she'd thirsted for the sight of him, and now that she'd seen him she felt terrible, out of sorts. She should be the one he had his arms around, not some nameless girl who appeared to be drunk. Maybe she was a prostitute. Reuben Tarz with

a prostitute! Not likely, but then, she really couldn't figure Reuben. Mickey would certainly be surprised — or would she? Mickey was worldly and would probably take it in her stride. Men weren't meant to be monks, she'd say with a little laugh. Women, on the other hand, were meant to be virginal until their wedding night. Damn. She'd dreamed, schemed, and planned, looking forward to a surprise meeting with Reuben. He'd see how she'd grown up, how worldly she'd become, and now it was all spoiled. Later, somehow, in some way, she'd go upstairs and see what was going on. If she didn't, she'd imagine all kinds of terrible things. Catch him, her mind ordered, and tell the girl what he did to you. Let him see she hadn't forgotten. Damn you, Reuben Tarz.

"Bebe, you haven't heard a word I said," Eli said. "Who are you staring at? We brought Pop here to show him a good time and already you're popping out."

Bebe turned to face him, forcing her thoughts away from Reuben. "That's nonsense, Eli. I thought for a minute I saw someone I knew, but I was wrong. Remember now, I just arrived home today and I am a little tired."

"We could have done this some other time, Bebe," Sol fretted. "Getting drunk in some gangster's den of iniquity isn't my idea of a good time either."

531

"Oh, Daddy, where else is there fun to go? Eli went to a lot of trouble to arrange this, so please don't spoil the evening. We've ordered all your favorite food, and there's going to be a show later. Be nice to Eli, Daddy. For me, just this once," Bebe cajoled, batting her eyes at her father.

Sol's gaze was paternal and indulgent when he looked down at his beautiful daughter. "All right already. Tonight we'll call a truce."

Eli's movements were awkward and jittery as he hopped around trying to find the best seat for his father at their reserved table. He would have cheerfully killed to have his father look at him just once the way he looked at Bebe. "Here, Pop, this is the best seat. You'll be able to see the show real good from here. Max has a couple of great acts. You might see someone the studio can use."

Sol bristled. "What do you know about what the studio —"

"Daddeeeee! . . ."

Sol looked at Eli with disgust. "Maybe I'll . . . I'll keep my eyes open."

"Now, that wasn't hard, was it, Daddy?" Bebe said, giving him a kiss. Sol didn't answer.

Bebe did her best to have a pleasant evening, but it was an effort to smile at Clovis and compliment her on her latest movie when she joined them at the table. She laughed at Lester Kramer's roguish antics,

but the laughter never reached her eyes. Every ounce of untapped energy went into parrying compliments with Damian Farrell, who said over and over that she was the most beautiful creature on earth and worthy of being one of his leading ladies. Twice she tried to make her way to the upstairs section of the club, only to be turned away at the curtained entrance to the stairway and informed that the quarters above were private. It was midnight when she finally told Eli she wanted to go home.

Sol heaved a sigh of relief and flushed with pleasure when Clovis linked her arm through his and thanked him for a lovely evening. "Eli arranged it, don't thank me," he said gruffly.

"By the way, Sol, where was Reuben this evening?" Lester Kramer asked. He turned to Bebe and smacked his hands together in delight. "That is one young man who just might turn your head, little girl." Bebe smiled wanly.

"My sister's too smart to fall for a creep like Tarz," Eli spat out. "Aren't you, Bebe?"

"Eli, stop acting like my big brother," Bebe said, artfully avoiding his question. "Daddy, you didn't answer Lester."

"This was Eli's party, I had nothing to do with the guest list," Sol said, heading for the door.

"Tarz is a brilliant fellow," Farrell said. "I rather like the chap. He's done all right by

me, and I have no complaints."

"I agree," Kramer added. "How about you, Clovis, what do you think about Sol's new assistant?"

Clovis rolled her eyes and pretended to swoon. "If I was a little younger, I'd want his shoes under my bed. Wait till you meet him, Bebe, you'll fall for him the way every female on the lot has. Unfortunately, he has eyes for none of the beauties, and that includes me," she said haughtily. "Ask your father what he thinks of him."

Bebe shook her head wearily. She hated the look on Eli's face. Poor, poor Eli. Tomorrow she would ask him why he hadn't invited Reuben.

The good-nights over, the Rosens piled into Eli's car. He ground the gears, knowing full well his father was thinking him inept and bungling. He pretended not to hear his father's muffled curse.

Bebe's first sight of the house in Benedict Canyon brought tears to her eyes. The mansion was ablaze in a soft light that spilled out and over the manicured shrubs, bathing them in a soft golden glow. She was home. Tonight she would sleep in her own bed, in her own room. She knew she would dream because she always dreamed when she was upset or overtired. Tonight she was both. Reuben would be in her dreams, and so would Eli. The two young men in her life — one strong

and arrogant, the other weak and ineffectual. But *was* Reuben in her life? Of course he was, he would always be tied to her in one way or another. After all, he had stolen her most priceless gift, her virginity. She would never allow him to forget what he did to her.

Reuben Tarz belonged to her by right of rape.

Bebe was just about to turn out the light and snuggle into her covers when Eli appeared with two cups of hot cocoa. "Just like old times, eh? I always brought you cocoa, do you remember?"

"Eli, I haven't been gone for thirty years. Of course I remember. You want to talk, is that it?"

Eli set the cups down carefully. "If you aren't too tired. Did you have a good time this evening? I did it for you. I'm so glad you're home, Bebe. God, I missed you."

"I missed you, too," Bebe lied. She wished he would leave; he was stinking up her room with his stale liquor breath, and he reeked of cigarette smoke. But he was her brother and she owed him at least her attention for a few minutes. She sighed wearily. "What's bothering you?"

"Tarz. Wait till you meet him. He'll bother you, too. He's goddamn taken over the studio. He's like horseshit, he's everywhere. Do this, do that . . . make this, don't make that. . . . He tells Pop what to do and Pop

does it. He must have some kind of hold on him. He's a smart aleck, sis. Pop should have given me the chance to work with him. He's always grousing about what I do and don't do. Wouldn't you think he'd take me in and show me the ropes? Oh, no, he hires an outsider! Who the hell is that guy, anyway?"

Bebe pondered the question sleepily. "I guess he's someone who knows how to run a motion picture company. Everyone says he's doing a good job. Don't you think so?"

"What's that got to do with it? How does Pop know I wouldn't do a good job? He's never given me the chance. All the other studio heads hire sons and sons-in-law, why can't Pop? He hates me, that's why."

"Blow your nose, Eli, and stop crying. Grown men don't cry. It . . . it isn't . . . manly."

"You never minded before. You said if crying made me feel better, it was okay. You've changed, Bebe," Eli accused.

"I might have said that *then,* this is now. I'd bet Reuben Tarz never cried, even when he was a child. He has that look, if you know what I mean."

"How do you know what he looks like? You've never seen him, have you?" Eli said, staring at his sister suspiciously.

"Oh, Eli, you are such a little boy," Bebe said, thinking fast. "Everyone was talking about how he looks tonight. I just made up

my own image of the man, and that image wouldn't cry. I'm so tired, sweetie, what say we call it a night. We have all day tomorrow to talk."

"We didn't drink the cocoa. I thought this would be like old times. . . . Oh, all right, I'll go," Eli said peevishly. At the door he turned. "It's you and *him* now, right? Before we were allies, now I'm on the outside looking in. Thanks, Bebe. Thanks for nothing."

Bebe flung herself back into the nest of pillows after Eli had left. Damn. When was he going to grow up? She hadn't responded to the "him" because she didn't know if Eli meant her father or Reuben.

Why hadn't she admitted to knowing Reuben? To spare Eli's injured feelings? She wondered then if her father had mentioned that she knew Reuben. No, of course not, they never spoke to each other unless it was to complain about something. Certainly they never shared confidences or carried on a normal conversation. Poor, poor Eli. One of these days she would speak to Reuben about him. There must be something he could do at the studio. One more family member wouldn't make a difference.

Bebe tried to drift into sleep, but Eli was too much in her thoughts. At last she swung her legs over the side of the bed. Why me, she asked herself as she padded down the hall to Eli's room. She knocked softly and

called his name, then opened the door a crack and called him again. "Go away!" came the muffled reply.

Oh, God, he's crying again, Bebe thought angrily as she pushed into the room. "Eli, I'm sorry if I hurt your feelings. I didn't mean to. It's just that I'm bone tired. I was seasick so many times on the way over that I haven't fully recovered. Please, forgive me." She kissed his splotchy face and winced at the puckered, angry-looking skin. She ran her hands through his hair the way she used to. She didn't remember his hair being so full of pomade, but then, she probably hadn't noticed a lot of things about Eli. She patted his back, trying to wipe the pomade on his pajama top. "It will be all right, Eli. I'll make sure it's all right. Go to sleep now. I'll stay here with you till you're sound asleep."

Bebe stayed with her brother for a long time. When she finally got to her feet she thought fleetingly about the dismal state of her family. How would Eli react to the fact that he was an uncle, she wondered. You'll never know, Eli, that there's a little boy somewhere in France who's your nephew. She bent over to drop a kiss on her brother's cheek. The tears on his lashes revolted her. What was happening to her? She'd always loved Eli. No, she corrected herself, she'd pitied him, felt sorry for him, and tried her best to make things easy for him. Now all she

wanted was to be out of his sight.

Back in her room, she found she still couldn't sleep, so she drank the cool cocoa. It was so sickeningly sweet, she gagged.

She punched at her pillow, trying to smooth out a place for her weary head. No matter what she thought about, no matter how she tried to shift her thoughts to other things, Reuben kept intruding. Eli had said something earlier in the evening about going away for the Memorial Day weekend. A party Dickie Hastings was throwing. She'd said of course she would go and even offered to drive. A whole gang of people, Eli said, starlets and leading men. A bang-up weekend, and he was providing the liquor; of course that's why he'd been included. On his own, Eli couldn't make it out the door. Bebe, Bebe, you are a nasty sister, she scolded herself. She punched at the pillow again and again. This time sleep welcomed her, her dreams full of demons and lovers.

Reuben Tarz sat alone, contemplating the ceiling. Daniel had gone to bed an hour before and as far as he could tell, he hadn't moved so much as a muscle since. He himself felt like he was in a stupor, emotionally paralyzed. He remembered his panic attack at the studio earlier in the day and the lengths he'd gone to to appear busy, certain that Bebe would burst into his office and say . . . what?

Jesus, what was happening to him? What was he so afraid of?

Deep down, he knew, It was his one big fear. He'd refused to think about it, to bring the horrible thing to the surface of his mind, but he had to do it now: If Bebe told her father all, Sol might kick his ass onto the street. Jesus, where would he go then? What would he do? What would happen to all the plans he'd made for Daniel to go to college?

At that moment he made a decision — one he hated himself for, but he made it nonetheless. He would woo Bebe. If he had to, he would get down on his knees and apologize. He would smile, he would beg, he would do . . . anything to keep his job at Fairmont. *And the ultimate end?* a small voice inside him queried. The ultimate end to any relationship between a man and a woman was . . . marriage. The thought so paralyzed him, he started to sweat. His breath came in feeble little gasps as he contemplated marriage to Bebe Rosen. *And Mickey?* the same little voice queried. Mickey was finished with him. He no longer mattered to her, was no part of her life. She hadn't responded to either him or to Daniel. Bitter tears of defeat burned his eyes. He wanted to cry then, not for his loss, because tears would never erase what he felt, but for what he'd hoped to gain and now would never realize.

When his emotions were under control,

Reuben got stiffly to his feet. He cursed Bebe Rosen with every dirty word he knew, and then he cursed himself the same way.

When he slid beneath the covers, Reuben gathered the pillow close to his chest. The softness, the cleanness of the pillow slip reminded him of Mickey. His hands caressed the pillow as he gently lowered his head into the feathery down. A tear slipped from his eye, a single tear of loneliness. Mickey's name fell from his lips as he reached out for sleep.

CHAPTER TWENTY-FOUR

On Thursday afternoon, Reuben met Bebe by accident. He'd rehearsed and schooled himself to act nonchalantly, but nothing prepared him for her breathless greeting and her genuine look of pleasure at seeing him. He forced a smile to his lips that was more of a grimace. "Welcome home, Bebe."

Bebe's eyes were warm and full of excitement as she drank her fill of his lean good looks. "How are you, Reuben? You're the last person I expected to see on this studio lot. My father tells me you're doing a . . . remarkable job for the studio. I think that's wonderful!"

Reuben almost grinned. "This . . . nasty, arrogant man thanks you for the compliment."

"Oh, poo, you heard me." She waved a hand airily to dismiss the words. "I was just in a cranky mood. After all, I'd just arrived and hadn't even been home. Say you forgive me."

"There's nothing to forgive. Sometimes I am arrogant and nasty. Did you enjoy your trip home?"

Bebe laughed, a tinkling sound Reuben remembered and didn't know why. Her perfume was still the same. He wanted to sniff, to smell his fill of her, but he caught himself.

"I was seasick most of the time."

Reuben had sworn to himself that he wouldn't ask, but the words came unbidden to his lips. "How is Mickey? Daniel's been wondering how Jake is."

"Mickey is just wonderful," Bebe lied, watching his eyes. "I never saw a busier person. She allowed me to stay in the Paris house for a few months. I thought that was wonderfully kind of her. And Jake is doing just fine at Yvette and Henri's farm. I stopped to visit them. It was like old times except you and Daniel weren't there. I swear, Reuben, I think I was the only one who missed you two. Listen, I have to run. Tell Daniel I'll look him up in the next day or so. I can't wait to see him." She blew him a kiss and was off before he could blink, her perfume drifting behind her.

Reuben stood staring after her, feeling foolish and a little angry. The worst was over. It didn't appear, at least on the surface, that Bebe was holding any grudges. He tried to analyze what she'd just said as he watched

her wriggle her way to her car. Mickey was busy. No one missed him. Daniel's dog was at the farm. It was depressing dialogue.

He realized if he closed his eyes, he could picture exactly what Bebe had been wearing. A soft blue clinging dress with small pink flowers. It had a lace collar and puffy sleeves with lace around the edges. She wore the pearls they had given her. Her hair was different, lighter and puffy, soft looking. Beautiful. Damian Farrell had told him she should have been an actress; of course it was hard sometimes to tell when Damian was serious.

"You look like a man in love," Diego Diaz quipped as he strolled by, his mustache twitching.

Reuben put up his hands. "Not me, pal. Women are . . ."

"Wonderful!" Diego crooned. "I certainly don't ever want to be without a woman. Didn't anyone ever tell you love makes the world go round . . . and round. Of course, if you haven't been in love, you wouldn't know what I'm talking about. You do have that look, though."

Reuben waited while a parade of full-dress Indians passed, only to be followed by a squad of soldiers leading horses. Patience was never one of his better virtues. Instead of waiting and enjoying the warmth of the sun, he chose to leap over a low wall and go around Studio B. He took the steps two at a

time and bumped into Daniel, who was about to open his office door.

"Reuben," Daniel said, smiling. "What's up?"

"Why do you ask?"

Daniel shrugged. "You look . . . different. Is anything wrong?"

"What the devil could be wrong? You're the second person who said I look different. Maybe it's the way I combed my hair this morning."

Daniel peered at him. "No, it's your eyes. They look . . . sort of excited. Look, I wanted to let you know that Jane showed up on time and did an incredible job today. She's okay."

Reuben nodded. "That's good," he said abstractedly. "Oh, by the way, I ran into Bebe a little while ago and she said to tell you she's going to look you up in a day or so. She's eager to see you. She said Mickey is fine and very busy and Jake is at Yvette and Henri's farm and doing well."

So that was it. Daniel did his best to hide his surprise. "I'll look forward to seeing her. See you later, Reuben."

Reuben marched into the small lavatory that separated his office from Sol's and stared into the mirror. A look of disgust washed over his face. He couldn't see anything different about himself. Now, if Bebe had said he looked different, he would have believed it. Women had a knack for that sort of thing.

It was going to rain again, Reuben decided hours later, watching from his perch on the windowsill. He stared at the threatening cloud mass moving across the sky. If he hurried, he might be able to beat the deluge. On his way down the stairs, he called to Daniel, and the two of them left the studio together.

They barely made it to the apartment before the heavy downpour. Damn, thought Reuben. It would be just his luck to have the entire weekend spoiled with dismal wet skies.

CHAPTER
TWENTY-FIVE

A party! A sparkling, glittering rainbow of a party. Hosted by him, of course. A party that would set tongues to wagging for weeks afterward. The kind of party Hollywood deserved. Formal, of course, which meant the stars would be decked out in their jewels and dressed to the nines.

It was time, Reuben decided, for him to step into the limelight, light he deserved for his hard work. He was an idea man, or so the directors said. Idea men came up with ideas, and he'd just come up with one: a party to end all parties. The idea had come out of nowhere when he'd entered his office earlier in the day. He'd tried it out on Margaret and her mouth had fallen open. "Tell me more, Mr. Tarz!" she'd cried. She'd even offered to help.

But ideas were only ideas until they became functional, and in this case functional meant getting approval from Sol Rosen. Tonight, after dark, he'd go out to the Canyon and

spring it on Sol. Of course all he had to do was cross the hall and spring it on him now, but he wanted to think about it a little more, and besides, Bebe wasn't in his office. Bebe would be home. Oh, shit, he groused. This has nothing to do with Bebe, not a goddamn thing.

Then he laughed, a confident, arrogant sound.

It wasn't one of California's starry nights. All day the weather had been oppressive. The heavy scent of orange blossoms that Reuben usually liked hung upon the air like a wet blanket. He'd suffered through several sneezing attacks already. Even now, sitting outside Sol Rosen's house, the air was still and his nose was tickling. Maybe he should turn around and go back to his apartment, but he'd come here for a reason. *You're an ass, Tarz,* a voice inside him whispered. *You know you could have said what you have to say at the office instead of driving all the way out here. Leave well enough alone and go home.* Reuben hated these little conversations he had with his inner voice. Before he could change his mind he pushed open the car door and loped up the steps to the front door. A maid in a starched white uniform opened the door and ushered him into a sitting room off the wide central foyer.

Sol Rosen shuffled in, his eyes wide with alarm. "What's wrong?" he bellowed. "Don't tell me the goddamn studio burned down. I'm not in the mood for bad news tonight, Tarz."

"It's not bad news," Reuben said. "I have an idea and I wanted you to hear it tonight before I give it to the papers in time for the morning editions. I propose a party, a sizzling, glittering Hollywood party that's going to cost some big dough. One month from this weekend. By then we'll have the box office receipts from the Red Ruby series and Jane's *Devious Dolly Darling* clips. I'd like to run a reel of the Sugar and Spice girls with each picture — you know, two for the price of one, that kind of thing. Distribution is set, we can't go wrong. I need your okay for the party, though. I saw both films late this afternoon and they're spectacular. It's going to take you weeks to count your money. The public is going to eat this up."

"Yeah? How much do I have to spring for this party?"

Somewhere upstairs Reuben could hear a phonograph playing. "Maybe thirty grand. I've never thrown a party like this, so I have no idea. It could go over, it could go under. If you want to be on the front page of every trade paper in the business, this will do it, trust me. We'll invite the whole damn industry. What do you think?"

"I say what the hell, it's only money. And you sure know how to spend it, Tarz. Like you said, you gotta gamble once in a while."

Reuben almost jumped out of his skin when he felt hands cover his eyes. "Guess who?" Bebe said, laughing. "What are you two cooking up?" She went around to her father's chair and plopped into his lap, her dressing gown flying open to reveal a silky expanse of leg. She stared across at Reuben with wide green eyes that looked so innocent he could only stare back at her, transfixed.

"We're planning a party to celebrate Red Ruby and Dolly Darling, new films we're producing. It's Reuben's idea," Sol said generously.

"Who's going to plan it?" Bebe asked.

"My secretary, I guess," Reuben replied. "I really didn't get to that stage yet in my thinking."

"A thirty-grand party, honey. Do you think this town will sit up and take notice?" Sol asked.

"Thirty thousand dollars!" Bebe said, awed. "Would either of you gentlemen consider letting me arrange this party? I know what goes over and what doesn't. It will give me something to do and I know the places to go for the best prices. Things like ice sculptures, engraved invitations, musicians, where to rent different things, like flowers, appropriate crystal . . ." She looked hopefully at Reuben,

then craned her neck to look up at her father.

"If it's okay with Tarz, it's okay with me," Sol said fondly as he tussled his daughter's hair.

"Fine with me. I'd like it one month from this weekend. The entire industry. Black tie."

"I'll do a good job," Bebe said excitedly. "I'll start tomorrow."

"If that's settled, I have to be on my way. I want to make the papers before they put them to bed."

Bebe was off her father's lap in a flash. "I'll walk you to your car. No, no, don't get up, Daddy, you're tired." She trotted after Reuben like an adoring puppy.

"I think it's going to rain, what do you think?" she asked in a shaky voice.

"I wouldn't be surprised," Reuben muttered.

He was behind the wheel, about to turn the key in the ignition, when Bebe poked her head in the window. "Reuben . . . I . . . I appreciate you . . . I know my father would . . . Reuben, I'm glad . . . are we ever going to talk about . . . you know . . ."

"Not if I can help it," Reuben said through clenched teeth.

Bebe drew back. "I'll do a bang-up job with the party . . . Dammit, Reuben, it wasn't *all* my fault. You're certainly none the worse for it. Look at you, my father's assistant, and before you know it you'll have him retiring

and be running the studio yourself. Taking over the way you did in France. Good night, Reuben."

"Good night," Reuben growled as he maneuvered the car around the half circle.

He absolutely would not think about this in any way, he told himself. He would deal with Bebe Rosen when he was ready to deal with her and not before.

Daniel was sitting at the kitchen table poring over his books when Reuben walked in. It was after midnight by the time he'd finished running through his evening for Daniel's benefit. "Do you have any ideas?"

"One. I'd make sure word got around that this affair is by invitation only. Stall on mailing them till . . . maybe ten days before. Everyone will sweat wondering if they're invited. The studio will be swamped — you know, you owe me for this, let's see that I'm invited, all that kind of stuff. Keep feeding the papers little tidbits and this will be one grand party. I bet Bebe will do a terrific job. She knows everyone. Wise choice, Reuben. Do you mind my asking if you two made peace with each other?"

"You must be dreaming, Daniel, or else you're overtired. Bebe hasn't changed at all. She doesn't have all her nuts and bolts and don't sit there and tell me she does. I don't want to hear that poor-little-girl routine, either. You have your opinion of her and I

have mine."

"If that's the way you feel, why are you letting her arrange this party?"

"Somebody has to do it, why not Bebe? At least it will keep her out of trouble for a month. Besides, I didn't ask her, she volunteered," Reuben snapped.

"Why don't you just admit you're using her," Daniel snapped back.

"I'm entitled to . . . forget it. Good night, Daniel."

Daniel grinned to himself as Reuben stomped his way to the bedroom. "You aren't fooling me, pal, not for a minute," he murmured.

During the following weeks Reuben paced and worried like an expectant father as he waited for the financial reports on Red Ruby and Dolly Darling's box office success. When he wasn't stewing and fretting, he was busy fielding phone calls and avoiding outright confrontations concerning invitations to what was now being referred to as the party of the decade. Once again, Daniel had been proven right.

"This would be a hell of a time for you to even up all those slights and any other grudges you're holding in the industry." Reuben told Sol the day the engraved invitations were to go in the mail. At Sol's uncertain look, he continued. "I mean it. A lot of those guys out there stomped on you. You're en-

tirely justified in my eyes if you cross off some of these names."

Sol dickered with the idea, remembering various slights and insults over the years, most of them real, some of them imagined. Reuben could feel the man's indecision and wasn't surprised when minutes later he said, "If I crossed off names, I'd be just like they are. Send them all, don't cross anyone off."

"You're a bigger man than I am, Sol," Reuben said flatly.

Sol smirked. "You know, my sweetheart is working her buns off on this. I think she dreams about it. She goes to bed at two or three and she's up at six. This morning she had all her papers and notes spread out on the dining room table. She told me I'd have to eat in the kitchen. A bang-up job, Tarz. A real bang-up job." Sol frowned. "In fact, she's been spending so much of her time arranging this thing, I don't think she's given any thought to an escort for herself. I'd hate like hell to see my honey being escorted by her brother. In my eyes that would be a pissifying shame." Sol's voice was loaded with meaning.

Reuben grinned. "You're always one jump ahead of me. I was going to ask Bebe to be my escort. Time just got away from me." He turned at the office door. "You look jittery, Sol."

"Don't tell me you aren't," Sol blustered.

"I've been hawking the mail room for the past hour. I want to see what your bright ideas are netting this studio. Today's the day!"

Reuben felt his stomach start to churn. He tried for a patient, confident tone. "We've gone over this at least ten times, but if it will make you feel better, let's have another go at it.

"New York said the Red Ruby film grossed half a million. Instead of running it just Saturdays, they ran it Friday, Saturday, and Sunday. Continuous matinees Saturday and Sunday. Dolly Darling grossed four hundred thousand in Chicago. What we're waiting for is our blockbuster, the double feature and the Sugar and Spice short. All these studio heads are scrambling to do what we did. So we gave a little extra with the Sugar and Spice girls. I keep telling you you have to give to get. The trade papers are saying the lines are a block long. I don't know which is the bigger hit, Red Ruby or Dolly Darling. The Sugar and Spice girls are the clincher. A million in New York and a cool million in Chicago. Two here in our backyard. Fifty bucks says I'm on the money," Reuben said arrogantly. "But I'll be stealing it."

Sol was spared making a decision when Daniel walked through the door, his arms loaded down with mail, graphs, and charts. Like a kid on Christmas morn, he was grinning from ear to ear. Reuben felt light-headed

at the look on his face. He gave an imperceptible nod and Daniel dropped his load of papers on Sol's desk. "You did it, Mr. Rosen. You're on top of the heap! I took the liberty of picking up the trade papers early. I had to grease a few palms, out of petty cash," he said hastily.

As Sol's pudgy fingers riffled through the stack of papers, Daniel drew Reuben aside. "Our projections were too low" he said. "We grossed three-quarters of a mil in Chicago and nine hundred thousand in New York. Our own little town gave us top dollar, a million and a quarter. The *Examiner* said — and this is a direct quote — 'Fairmont is at the top of the pile.' This morning, Reuben. The phones are ringing constantly. They've had to put extra guards on at the gate. The whole damn town is out there begging for an invitation to your affair. You did it, pal! You pulled this place out of the muck, and it's right up there on top. I can't believe you're letting Sol take the credit."

"It's his studio, Daniel. I work for the man and so do you. I did what I was paid to do. But there'll be big bucks in it for us. Look, we know what we did, and so does the industry. Letting Sol take the credit is . . . the wise thing to do. Working behind the scenes is fine for now. When it's time to step out front I won't owe anybody anything. I have to admit it's a great feeling. . . . Listen, do

you have a date for this party?"

"Do I need one?"

"You don't *need* one, but you should have one. This is a big night for both of us. Sol just suckered me into escorting Bebe. To tell you the truth, I think we'd look kind of silly walking in together." Reuben grinned. "Why don't you ask Jane? She's a star now, and you two'd look good making an entrance together."

"What if she says no?" Daniel asked, flushing.

"She's not going to say no. She likes you. Get going, and thanks, Daniel, you did a hell of a job on this. When Sol comes down to earth I know he'll recommend a bonus for you."

Daniel was almost at the door when he called over his shoulder, "You're sure she'll say yes? You didn't call her or anything, did you?"

Reuben shook his head. "You're on your own." He turned to Sol. "Well, what do you think?"

"Think? Jesus Christ, I don't know what to think! People want to laugh and Red Ruby is making them laugh. A jewel thief, yet!" Suddenly he frowned. "Maybe we're giving them too much at once."

"No, we are not giving the public too much. They came back for the triple we ran last week. This is no time to be greedy, Sol. This

was a test and it proved itself. Let's face it, you are not an astute businessman. If you were, this studio would not have been at the bottom of the industry. If you're going to fight me on this, I'm going to walk out of here and I'll take Red Ruby and Dolly Darling with me. And even though Nesbit is still in the developing stages, he goes, too. If you insist on being greedy, it'll be your downfall. We've got something good going here, don't fuck it up! I want to hear your answer now," Reuben said coldly.

"Okay, okay." Why was this son of a bitch always right?

Then Reuben moved in for the kill. "After the party, Sol, we'll discuss my position again. Money, bonuses, a percentage . . ."

"Percentage!" Sol squeaked.

Reuben hooked his thumbs into the waistband of his trousers and rocked back and forth on his heels. "Uh-huh — of the net," he drawled.

Net! Sol sputtered, his face red and splotchy.

"Net," Reuben said coolly. "Now, I've got things to do, and I know you want to read your press again, so I won't take up any more of your time."

Sol cursed under his breath for a full five minutes before he returned to the columns of figures that danced before his eyes. A long while later, when the numbers were engraved

in his mind, he decided he liked being the man of the hour. This goddamn town was finally going to recognize him and pay homage. He didn't mind at all that it wasn't justified homage. The fucking bastard really pulled it off. Moxie, that's all it took. Jesus!

The house in Benedict Canyon seethed with activity. Bebe's helpers were shuffling papers and making notes, calling out to one another as they tried to balance figures, the menu, the decorations, and the entertainment while Bebe checked and double-checked everything. Every five minutes she exploded with "This has to be perfect. This has to be exquisite. There's no room for mistakes here, girls. Now, let's go over this again." One of the maids handed her the telephone as she started her lecture for the third time in the same hour. "Yes, yes, what is it?" she said briskly.

"Bebe, it's Daniel. Listen, I just got Reuben to get your father to up the party money. You have twenty thousand more."

"Daniel, really!" Bebe squealed. "Are you sure? I'm already two thousand over and there's not one place I can cut. Thanks so much! Don't tell me how you did it. I saw the papers this morning. Daddy must be in heaven."

"Everyone is happy. How's it all going?"

"Great. Just great. This town is going to

talk about this party for years. You know, I've been so busy, I haven't had time to buy myself a new dress. I wanted to order a new suit for Daddy and Eli, but I . . . we're a family, and when we walk into the Ambassador ballroom I want us to look grand."

"I thought you were going with Reuben. He said he was taking you."

"What did you say?"

"Sorry, guess I put my foot in it."

"You mean he's going to ask *me!* Daniel, did he say that? When? Oh, God, now I have to . . . Daniel are you sure?"

Daniel thought he'd never heard such happiness. "I've got to go now, Bebe, but yes, that's what he said. Keep it under your hat and act surprised, okay?"

"Sure. Oh, thank you, Daniel," she cried happily. "Can you imagine, me walking into that ballroom on his arm? Oh, God, I think I'm going to faint."

Bebe bordered on delirium when she instructed her helpers to carry on because she had something to do. Her face flushed with happiness, she ran up the steps to her room. Going to the party with her father and Eli called for one kind of dress, the kind she'd have to go out and buy. Going with Reuben called for something else entirely, and she had that something else in a tissue-wrapped box, a French creation she'd been saving for a special occasion. There was nothing more

special than going to this party with Reuben. Her hands shook as she plucked the satiny box from its nest in her bottom drawer. Eyes round with pleasure, she drew in her breath the way she had the first time she'd set eyes on the dress. It was silver satin, with a shell-pink overlay that was seeded with pearls and sparkly sequins. She loved the diamond-shaped hem studded with glittering sequins. The overhead light in the Ambassador ball-room would assure that she sparkled all night long. Her evening bag and headband were the same shell pink seeded with the tiniest pearls she'd ever seen. Even her shoes, heels but not too high, were silver satin, but with a delicate shell-pink pattern. In this outfit she would be a vision of loveliness — maybe she'd even boggle Reuben's mind for the first few minutes. Reuben, Reuben, if you only knew how much I care for you. I can forget the past if you can. You don't need Mickey. You need me, why can't you see it? We are going to look so good together. We'll be the handsomest couple there. All of Hollywood will see us and know you're *mine.* Her touch was almost reverent when she replaced the tissue paper over the sparkling dress.

She made her way back downstairs to the busy dining room, humming softly. Lord, there was so much to do! Instead of a hundred white doves in gilded cages, she could order five hundred now. And she could

upgrade the champagne. Instead of a red satin carpet runner, she could order red velvet. More greenery, too, to show off the lavender orchids to better advantage. She shook her head to clear her thoughts. Maybe she should cancel the white linen tablecloths and ask for lavender eyelet with a white organdy overlay. Yes, that was a better idea, she decided, and picked up the phone. Reuben was going to be so elated and . . . and grateful when he saw the result of her efforts. So very, very grateful.

The studio was working overtime in an effort to get as many Red Ruby and Dolly Darling segments in the can as possible. Reuben's hope was that the public would remain loyal to Red and Dolly, but he knew the film industry was fickle. He also knew that every other studio was making a valiant effort to come up with their own versions of Red and Dolly, which meant he had to stay three jumps ahead of them. It was crucial that he come up with something new just as they were jumping in with both feet. That way every imitation they rushed to offer the public would be passé by the time it came out.

In deference to Sol and his ego, Reuben pretended he hadn't read the paper when he arrived at the office. Thus he exuded just the right amount of enthusiasm when Sol read the columns, word by word, that applied to

Red and Dolly. By the time Sol started to calculate the box office receipts, he already had them figured out in his head.

There was no doubt about it, he was a winner.

Reuben found himself at loose ends this particular morning as he waited for a meeting he'd scheduled with Daniel. The only other thing on his agenda for the day was to call Bebe and invite her to the party. With a glance at his closed door, he quickly lifted the desk blotter and withdrew the winemaker's calendar. It was frayed and wrinkled. He smoothed it out on his blotter and stared at it the way he did almost every day before he left the office. His index finger traced the months, and from long habit he recited his litany of winemaking. When he reached the month of December, he found himself wiping his eyes. And then, as always, he got angry with himself and replaced the calendar under the blotter. Time to call Bebe and get it over with. Still, he argued with himself for a full five minutes before he picked up the phone with a reluctant sigh. He announced himself to the maid, then asked for Bebe. "It's Reuben, Bebe," he said when she came on the phone. "I've been meaning to call you, but studio business got ahead of my good intentions. I'd like to take you to the party if you don't have a date."

"I'd like that very much, Reuben. Thank

you for asking me. I was going to go with Daddy and Eli. There wasn't . . . anyone else I wanted to ask," she said truthfully.

"How are the preparations going?" he asked. "Is the money holding up?"

"I was over budget till you added to it. It seems as the days go on this party is getting more and more important, and I do want it to be just right. You and Daddy will be proud."

Bebe smiled as she hung up the phone, then pushed Reuben from her thoughts and returned to the task at hand, assigning the waiters and waitresses, all studio hopefuls, to different stations. The waitresses, each one prettier than the next and with incredibly long legs, would be wearing a short midthigh ruffled skirt with a stiff white crinoline underneath and ruffled panties like the Sugar and Spice girls. The waiters would be attired in swishing black capes lined in red satin with low-brimmed buccaneer hats like the one Red Ruby wore. All thanks to Wardrobe.

Last night, late, after the studio had closed, she'd gone to Lot 5 and watched the skit Damian and Lester had agreed to put on as part of the evening's entertainment. Jane Perkins had also agreed to do a short skit, both condensed versions of unreleased films. It had taken three full days for the prop department to construct a portable stage complete with a curtain that swooshed across it.

It was going to be a wonderful evening. Simply wonderful.

The day of "The Party," as the newspapers referred to it, the real Bebe Rosen was up at dawn, bathed and dressed and on her way to the Ambassador Hotel. She sailed through the hotel lobby like the Queen Mother on a state visit. Her voice, however, was that of a commanding general as she barked out orders and shouted for coffee, running her pencil down the list of things to be done before ten a.m. Wardrobe had promised the waiters' and waitresses' uniforms for nine o'clock; the would-be hopefuls were to arrive at nine for a quick dress rehearsal and to be given their assigned stations for the evening. Alert to every detail, she cast a critical eye over the hotel staff setting up the buffet tables at the far end of the room. Lavender was a wise choice, soft and delicate, the perfect complement for the orchids that would find their way to designated spots an hour before the start of the party. For now they were in boxes of ice in the hotel kitchen, wrapped in waxy tissue.

Bebe gulped her coffee in between screams of disapproval when she noticed wrinkles in the eyelet table skirts. "Have Housekeeping get those wrinkles out now, and I don't want to see any in the overlay, either. You're making more work for yourselves. Do it right the first time! I don't have all day. I see marks on

the silver. I told you I wanted it polished and I *mean* polished," she shouted to someone else.

"What do you mean, the revolving bandstand is stuck! Unstick it. You were supposed to have that checked yesterday!" she bellowed in the voice of a truck driver. "Do I have to do it myself?"

The white doves in their gilded cages arrived at noon just as Bebe was about to throw a tantrum over a hundred pounds of lobster she said smelled funny. Assurances that all fish smelled funny in large quantities made her roll her eyes. Back in the ballroom she was met with a loud drumming sound she'd never heard before. The workers had all stopped what they were doing, silly expressions on their faces. The doves were billing and cooing, either with pleasure or displeasure, Bebe couldn't determine.

"Okay, okay, maybe this was a mistake," she shouted over the sound of the birds. "Wait, I have an idea. Someone get a phonograph and some records."

Three hours later they finally hit on the right piece — Brahms' "Lullaby" — to soothe the excited birds. Bebe's head was pounding as she informed her crew of workers that they did indeed need her. What would they have done if she hadn't been there? "I'm going home now, you all know what has to be done." Before she left, she issued her final

parting shot, one she'd held over everyone's head for days: "You foul this up and none of you will get your picture in the paper! Keep playing that record, and if it wears out, get another one." She absolutely would not think about what would happen when the first guests arrived and the record had to be turned off. How could she have been so stupid? The man at the aviary hadn't said a word about the noise doves made. Then a second horrible thought struck her. What if bird shit came out of the cages, leaked somehow onto the guests? "Oh, my God," she muttered. Then she laughed, so hard she had to pull the car over to the side of the road as she pictured a bird dropping its poop on one of the men's black tuxedos or down some woman's cleavage. She was still laughing helplessly when she ground the roadster to a screeching halt outside her father's house. Peals of laughter followed her up the stairs as she headed for the bathroom to draw her bath. When it was time for the aviary attendants to release the birds, she hoped she would be in the ladies' room. But she didn't want to miss the flight and the thousand pounds of white rose petals that would drop at the same time. Well, it was out of her hands now. Sighing, she slipped deeper into the steamy bath.

Bebe was powdered, perfumed, coiffed, and dressed an hour before Reuben was due to

pick her up. Nervous and jittery, she tried without success to quiet the fluttering of her heart. Now she knew how the poor birds felt in their cages. Hmm, maybe the bright overhead lights were making them bill and coo so loudly. Without stopping to think, she called the hotel and asked to be put through to the ballroom. "Lower the lights or change the bulbs," she told the workman who answered. "That might quiet the damn doves."

"We already did that," he responded. "They're quiet now and sound asleep." There was a hint of laughter in his voice. Bebe slammed the phone back onto the cradle.

When Eli came up from behind and touched her on the shoulder, she jumped a foot. "Eli! Don't do that!"

"I didn't know you were so jumpy," Eli apologized. "Sis, you look like a knockout. You'll be the prettiest one there. That's some dress!" he said approvingly.

"Thanks," Bebe said distractedly. "You look pretty good, too. You look good in a tux. Where's Daddy?"

"Right here," Sol said, joining them. At the sight of his baby girl he rolled his eyes and slapped at his forehead. "Your brother's right, you're gonna knock 'em dead tonight. I hope Tarz appreciates you."

"I hope so, too. Are you waiting for us or are you going to go on ahead?"

"We're going on ahead. I want to be the

first one to see what you've cooked up over there. I know you did a wonderful job, honey. You certainly worked hard enough. Maybe we should put you on the payroll."

"No thanks, Daddy, this was enough for me," Bebe said, smiling nervously.

"I hear a car. Must be Reuben. You look so beautiful, honey," Sol said, kissing her on the cheek.

"I second that," Eli called over his shoulder.

Bebe herself opened the door for Reuben, then she stepped back to drink in the sight of him. How handsome he looked in his tuxedo and snowy-white shirt! All kinds of feelings rushed through her, some good, some not so good. "I'm ready, Reuben, if you are," she said in a shaky voice.

For a second Reuben lost his composure. This elegant, sophisticated young woman couldn't be the Bebe he knew. Usually she was either overly made up or overdressed. Tonight she looked more beautiful than any of Fairmont's stars. "You look . . . nice," he said gruffly.

Nice. That was it, "nice"? Well, what had she expected? "You'll do, too, Mr. Tarz," she said.

On the way to the Ambassador Reuben took note of her silence. "Is anything wrong, Bebe?" he asked.

"Wrong? What could be wrong? What makes you think something's wrong?"

"You're being too quiet — something's got to be on your mind. Maybe if you tell me, we can solve it before it gets out of hand."

Bebe bit down on her tongue. "Reuben, it's the . . . oh, it's the damn birds! The doves in their cages, hundreds of them. They bill and coo. We couldn't shut them up, so we've been playing a lullaby on the phonograph, and we turned down the lights hoping that would quiet them. I made a mistake. I thought the birds would be that one touch, that little extra something that would make the party a real success. My God, what if they . . ."

Reuben threw back his head and roared with laughter. Twice he had to knuckle his eyes so he could see the road.

"You won't think it's so funny if they christen your tuxedo," Bebe sputtered.

"Well, we wanted this to be a memorable evening," Reuben said, choking with laughter. "I wonder how they'll write this up in the morning papers." He burst into another chorus of laughter, and this time Bebe joined him.

Minutes later Reuben slid the car to the curb and got out. A liveried doorman held the door for Bebe. Reuben held out his arm to her, and they stepped onto her red velvet runner. "Nice touch," he said, indicating the runner. "Smile pretty for the sidewalk gawkers."

Inside the ballroom, Sol, Eli, Daniel, and

Jane were still in the oohing and aahing stage. But it was Reuben's reaction Bebe wanted. This time he didn't disappoint her. "Splendid! Actually it's magnificent!" he said sincerely. His eyes wandered upward as did the others to the gilded cages. From somewhere far back in the ballroom the lullaby was still playing. Bebe wondered who was manning the phonograph.

"Bebe, about these birds . . ." Daniel said, indicating the one nearest him.

"Don't say it, Daniel," Bebe said adamantly. "Don't even think it! Just move away and don't stand underneath. Tomorrow we can discuss this, but tonight I don't want to hear another word. Not another word!"

"I think it's kind of funny myself," Reuben grinned, but Daniel noticed he, too, moved from underneath the cage.

The party was a rousing success. The thousand or so guests mingled, ate, drank, and danced. Reuben found himself on the sidelines with Bebe at his elbow, his eyes glued to Sol and all the handshaking that was going on. When he wasn't watching Sol he found his eyes on the bird cages overhead. He laughed the loudest and clapped his hands the longest during the evening's skits, and he enjoyed the looks of frustration on the faces of all the other studio heads. Red Ruby and Dolly Darling were household words now.

"They're going to let the birds loose now, Reuben," Bebe whispered. "I think we should move way to the back."

The moment the French doors were thrown open, the Rosens, accompanied by Daniel and Jane, moved to the far end of the ballroom. The orchestra struck up a good-night chorus, and the birds, free of their cages, circled the huge room. Squeals and shrieks filled the room. Napkins fluttered, handkerchiefs appeared out of nowhere. Stoles and chiffon scarfs hastily appeared on ladies' elaborate hairdos as men opened their dress jackets, hiking them above their heads. Reuben and Daniel shook with silent laughter. Bebe fell into her father's arms, tears streaking her face. The last guest hurried through the door just as the French doors were closed by the aviary men.

"I don't know about any of you, but I think that was better than any movie this studio ever made. Mark that down, Daniel, maybe we can do something with it," Reuben said, laughing. "Let's retire to the kitchen and get some of this fancy food everyone's been eating all night.

"Bebe, this was one hell of a party!" he continued. "I appreciate all the work you put into it, and I know your father does, too. I think it's safe to say it's a memorable event this town will not likely forget."

An hour later they walked through the

confetti and ribbons lying all over the floor. Reuben plucked a spray of orchids from one of the banquet tables and handed it to Bebe. "You don't mind going home with your father, do you?" He didn't wait for her reply.

As Bebe watched him leave, tears in her eyes, she brought the orchids up to her nose. Tear after tear fell onto the fragile petals.

Daniel said his good-nights and followed behind Reuben.

"You're tired, Bebe. It's time for us to leave, too," Sol said tenderly. "We've all earned a good rest."

The morning papers called the party an extravaganza and went on to describe the tons of food, the wild orchids, the white doves. Bebe read the paper, tossed it aside, and went back to bed.

The party was over.

CHAPTER
TWENTY-SIX

Usually in an upbeat mood, Reuben now felt depressed as he changed from his business clothes to comfortable slacks and sweater. With Daniel engrossed in schoolbooks and settled comfortably for the evening, he felt at loose ends. At least he could have brought coffee with him. If he opened the door and returned to the kitchen, Daniel would raise his eyes and stare at him thoughtfully, making assumptions Reuben didn't want made, even by Daniel.

How was he going to spend the long evening that stretched ahead of him? Before he could think twice about it, he found himself spreading out his writing materials on the arm of the chair. He'd write one last letter to Mickey. If she didn't answer this one, he wouldn't write any more. For a long time he simply stared at the paper uncertain how to begin. Did he tell her how well things were going, or should he start with entreaties as to why she hadn't answered any of his other let-

ters? It was obvious she'd received the money they sent, none of the letters had been returned. On the other hand, he could write a long, letter telling her *exactly* why he and Daniel had left. He'd confess to that sordid afternoon in the barn. His stomach heaved at the thought. How could he explain something he himself didn't fully understand? He felt a surge of anger rush through him and did his best to stifle the feeling.

Reuben flexed fingers that were stiff and cramped, an indication that his anger was still with him, albeit controlled. Mickey could have sent at least one letter — telling him to go to hell, to stop writing, something to let him know she was alive and well. If she'd found someone else to lavish her affections on, she should write and tell him so he wouldn't waste his time. That's probably what it was — she'd found someone else and he was half a world away. The decent thing to do would be to tell him. The thin streak of fairness in Reuben asked why he hadn't done the decent thing and told her the truth about that afternoon in the barn.

Within an hour he'd composed six different letters, all full of recriminations, all sounding belligerent. He tore them all up. "Out of sight, out of mind," he muttered angrily as he ripped at his clothes and put on his pajamas. Going to bed early wouldn't kill him. Two hours later he was still wide awake,

tossing and turning, his frustration still with him. At last he swung his legs over the side of the bed and marched to the chair where he'd left his writing paper. He pulled the chain on the lamp, flooding the room with light. Pen in hand, he started his letter.

My dear Mickey,

So much time has gone by without a letter from you that Daniel and I are both concerned that something is wrong.

Bebe returned to California and told us that you are very busy. Too busy, Mickey, to drop a line to either Daniel or myself?

Things are going well at the studio. Sol has given me some responsibility and I've come up with some films that have proved to be winners. The studio held a party to celebrate the success and invited the entire industry. It was a memorable evening.

Daniel is doing well, but I'm sure you know that from his letters. I'm working on a plan to get him into law school. I'd explain it all to you, but it's a little complicated. I think, though, you would appreciate my creativity in this area.

If you have *other* guests at the château and no longer want ties with Daniel and myself you have only to say so and we won't bother you with our letters. I don't understand your silence. I can understand

if you are angry with me, to a point, but please don't take out that anger on Daniel, he doesn't deserve it. Every day he waits for a letter, as I do.

I love you, Mickey. A day doesn't go by that you aren't in my thoughts. I had hoped you felt the same way. I simply do not understand your silence.

My love for you remains constant,
Reuben

Reuben read the letter over twice and then a third time. Christ, he felt terrible, as though a part of him had died. His anger was gone now, replaced with bitterness. With all his heart he believed that what he and Mickey had was a love for all time, forever and ever. Obviously he had been wrong. He'd been replaced in Mickey's affections, there was no other explanation. To continue writing, begging her to respond, made him out to be worse than a lovesick puppy.

Frowning, he tapped the letter on his knee. Did he really want to send this, or was he simply trying to exorcise his own guilt over the decision he'd made about Bebe? Quickly, before he could change his mind, he stuck the letter in his pocket to be mailed the following day. Then he hopped back in bed again, the darkness total, and ordered his body to sleep.

577

Finally it obeyed him.

The rain continued all night, the sound dreary and mournful. Reuben woke with a raging headache that grew worse with the intensity of the rain. It looked like he'd be spending his weekend indoors watching Daniel bake a cake. Daniel always baked cakes when it rained.

With one umbrella between them, Daniel and Reuben sloshed through the rain, jostling each other as they hurried to the bus, only to miss it by seconds. Disgusted, Reuben flagged a hack and crawled into the backseat, Daniel next to him. Somehow he'd known it was going to be that kind of day. When he reached into his pocket for a cigarette, he found he'd forgotten them. But the letter to Mickey was still there. They'd been in such a hurry to get to the bus, he'd forgotten to mail it.

Margaret took Reuben's rain-soaked jacket and brought one he kept in the closet for emergencies. There was nothing he could do about his wet squeaking shoes. "Hold on, Margaret," he said, and retrieved his letter to Mickey for the outgoing mail.

"Mr. Tarz, you have a meeting in a few minutes with the committee for the Motion Picture Directors Association. A car will pick you up in fifteen minutes. And John Mundy returned your call. He's amenable to a meet-

ing to discuss what you can do for him. He said his contract is up in December. And I have the figures you wanted on Paramount Studios."

"Thank you, Margaret. I should be back by noon," Reuben said, shrugging into the jacket she held out for him.

It was mid-morning when Bebe tripped up the stairs, dressed in a sky-blue raincoat with matching hat and umbrella, in search of Daniel. She tossed her soaking wet hat in the direction of a chair and giggled when it missed.

"Let me look at you, Daniel," she said. "My, my, but you're a handsome devil." She giggled again at Daniel's flushed face. "Tell me, what do you think of my new hairdo?"

"I like it," Daniel said sincerely. "You always look wonderful. Stop fishing for compliments."

Bebe pouted. "You're the only one who ever pays me any, and then I have to fish for them. . . . Tell me, do you have any plans for the Fourth of July? Everyone who has a boat is going to Catalina. We don't have one, so we aren't going, and I'm not sure I'd want to in this weather. Some of my friends are going to Big Sur, but I've been there so many times it's already old hat. The desert is out, and that leaves only San Fran. What are you and Reuben planning?"

"We were going to the beach to lie in the

sun, but it looks like I'll be home baking a cake."

"A cake!" Bebe shrilled with laughter. "Why ever would you bake a cake?"

"Because I like to eat chocolate cake on rainy days, that's why," Daniel said stiffly.

Bebe stifled her laughter. "I'm sorry, Daniel, I didn't mean to hurt your feelings. It just struck my funny bone that you'd bake a cake. Men don't usually . . . cook or bake. Listen, will you bake one for me? I love sweet things. Please?" Daniel grimaced but nodded.

"Dickie Hastings is throwing a big party in San Francisco over the weekend with lots of big stars," Bebe went on. "His parties are always a hoot. Eli said we were invited. Soooo, where's your partner?"

"Who? Reuben?"

She nodded. "Haven't seen much of him since the party. I was going to stop in his office to have a little chat. . . . I've really missed you two. I do hope we can stay friends here in California. I don't see any reason why we can't, do you? Especially me and you."

Daniel smiled. "I thought we agreed we'd always be friends no matter what."

Bebe ran her fingers through her fluffy hair and winked at Daniel. "Just wanted to see if you remembered. Well, I have to be going. I'll stop by Reuben's office on my way out. Have a nice weekend."

"Bebe, wait a minute. I've been meaning to

ask you — how was Mickey? Did you see her at all before you left?"

Bebe averted her eyes. "Well, not exactly. She was at the château and I stayed in her Paris house. She didn't bother coming to see me, so I have to assume she was busy. Once, because I was in the area, I stopped by to see Yvette and Henri and, of course, Jake. They were all wonderful. But you musn't worry about Mickey. Obviously she isn't worrying about you."

Daniel frowned. "How do you know that?"

"Have you heard from her?" At his blank look, Bebe smiled. "I thought not. You know what they say — out of sight, out of mind."

"Mickey isn't like that," Daniel said loyally.

"Then why hasn't she written you?" Bebe snapped. "Grow up Daniel. She had her fun with the two of you, playing the magnanimous benefactress. And now it's over. Why don't you just accept it?"

"I don't believe that for a minute."

"You better believe it or you'll end up with egg on your face. I'll just bet Reuben hasn't heard from her, either," she said carefully. "So I guess she couldn't really have loved him after all. You two were just a pleasant interlude. Don't forget now" — she wagged a finger at him — "you're going to make me that cake. Put coconut in the frosting and I'll be your slave forever. Ta-ta." She blew him a kiss and sailed through the door.

This Bebe, Daniel decided as he went back to work, definitely was not the Bebe he'd known in France. He hoped Reuben would recognize the difference.

"Bebe Rosen to see . . . Mr. Tarz," Bebe said to a startled Margaret.

"Why . . . why, Mr. Tarz isn't here right now, Miss Rosen. Would you care to leave a message?"

"No. I'll wait," Bebe said regally. "No, no, don't get up. I can show myself into his office."

"But, you . . . you can't . . ."

Bebe turned, her eyes cold. "I can and I will."

The stocky secretary capitulated. After all, she *was* Mr. Rosen's daughter. But what could she possibly want with Mr. Tarz?

Bebe walked around the spartan office. How like Reuben. No clutter, no nonsense. A workingman's office. She noticed his wet jacket hanging on a hook, she walked over and laid her cheek against the wet wool. It smelled just like Reuben. And his chair — she loved the feel of it. From the prop room, she decided. Everything was from the prop room.

Against her better judgment she went through his appointment book. Director's meeting . . . so that's where he was. The realization that Reuben would probably be

582

gone for hours so disappointed her that she wanted to cry. She'd been looking forward to a few minutes with him in private. Gradually disappointment gave way to anger as she struggled out from behind the desk. A tantrum was brewing just below the surface — she could feel it. But what would be the point?

Peevishly she slid the mail basket across the desk, then placed it on the other side, glancing down at the pile of papers with the cream-colored envelope on top. *Madame Michelene Fonsard* . . . and in Reuben's unmistakable handwriting. Bebe's eyes narrowed. She glanced at the door, then stuffed the letter into her purse. Her heart was beating madly when she exited the office. "Tell Reuben I got tired of waiting," she called over her shoulder.

Fifteen minutes later the mailman stopped by Margaret's desk. She stepped into the inner office and returned with a pile of mail, which she handed over to him. "See you on Tuesday."

He returned her smile. Everyone's thoughts were on the long weekend ahead.

By noon the weather had the entire studio lot in chaos, as anxious men tried to stem the heavy rain from flowing into the different ground-level studios. Yellow slickers could be seen from one end of Fairmont to the other.

Reuben watched the activity glumly from his window, knowing his plans for the weekend would have to be canceled completely. Someone had to oversee the lot, and it wouldn't be Sol. By three o'clock the driving rain gave way to a mournful drizzle. The air was oppressive, ushering in a low swirling fog that set Reuben's teeth on edge. All day he'd been nervous, and the fog wasn't helping matters at all. On a clear day from his position at the window he could see five of the major studio lots. Today, with the smoky-gray fog rolling in, his visibility was zero.

Reuben sat down at his desk, nodding slightly when he realized the mail had been picked up. Might as well clear his desk and check out the lot.

Reuben and Daniel worked alongside the maintenance crew stacking film on higher ground. By five-thirty the worst of the rain was over and only the fog remained. Satisfied that nothing more could be done, Reuben washed his hands and nodded to Daniel. "Time to go home."

Daniel smiled. "We'll have to feel our way."

"I think our best bet would be to walk. It'll take us a little longer, but at least we'll be able to see where we're going."

The moment they stepped outside, Daniel's glasses steamed.

"What kind of weather is this?" he grumbled.

Reuben laughed. "You really didn't think we'd get sunshine three-hundred-sixty-five days a year, now, did you? It has to rain sometime. I can do without this humidity, though. What the hell . . ."

Behind them, horns honked, tires screeched, shrill laughter and raucous shouts filled the air with yellow arches of light fighting with the swirling fog.

"Is everyone ready?" Eli Rosen shouted drunkenly.

"Ready!" came a chorus of replies.

Daniel and Reuben walked over to the parade of cars. "The studio is closed for the weekend," Reuben shouted. "Get these cars off the lot."

"We're waiting for Clovis," Eli yelled from his position behind the wheel of Bebe's car. Bebe herself was in the passenger seat with her silk-clad legs hanging over the door. "Clovis, where are you?" Eli shouted.

"Clovis . . . Clovis, Clovis," Bebe wailed. "Where are you, Clovis?"

"They're drunk," Daniel said to Reuben.

"I can see that," Reuben snapped. "Clovis left the studio a while ago," he informed Eli.

"No, she didn't. She's gointa Frisco with us. She promised. Dinnnshe promise, Bebe?" Eli slurred. The other revelers were catcalling and hooting.

"Clovis promised, yes she did, Clovis promised to ride in our car with us," Bebe

called out. Reuben winced at the drunken silliness in her voice.

The sound of bottle after bottle shattering on the pavement echoed in his ears. Grimly he walked around to the line of cars. "Get your asses out of those cars and clean up this glass," he ordered. "Now!"

"Don't pay any attention to him," Eli shouted. "He's just a flunky my father hired. You don't have to do what he says. You just listen to me."

"Is that a fact?" Reuben snarled as he lifted Eli bodily from the car. "You clean it up, then, if you don't want your drunken friends to do it. None of you belong here, this studio is closed until Tuesday morning. If you don't have a studio pass, you don't belong. Get these cars off this lot and do it now, or I'll call the police — they'll be happy to escort you off this property and off to jail. I'd say that'd be a great start for a long weekend."

The silence that greeted his words was as thick as the fog. The mad scramble to do his bidding, after his words had registered, was worthy of the Keystone Kops. When Eli lashed out drunkenly, Reuben stiff-armed him and then twirled him about until he was outlined in the car's headlights.

Bebe untangled her legs from the car and slid over to take Eli's seat. "You spoil everything, Reuben. I'll drive us to Frisco. We'll leave your precious studio lot if that's what

you want, but you remember something, Reuben Tarz — you don't own Fairmont, you just work here. Gigolo," she muttered contemptuously.

Reuben ripped open the car door and yanked her out. She flopped about in his arms like a rag doll, which so enraged him that he shook her until he thought he could hear her teeth rattle. "I told you once before never to call me that." His hand was raised over Bebe when Daniel shouted to him.

"Don't do it, Reuben! She's so drunk she doesn't know what she's saying. Let her go!"

Reuben grabbed Bebe's wrists and pulled her around until her face was within inches of his own. "Go home, Bebe. This is not a night to drive to San Francisco. Daniel and I will take you home, or you can come with us and I'll explain to your father in the morning. These people, these friends of yours, are drunk and so are you. What's it going to be?"

"Still telling people what to do, eh, Reuben? Well, you can't tell me what to do. In France it was different, but not here." Bebe's face was contorted as she faced him head on. "I'm going with Eli and his friends. Dickie is expecting us. Let me go," she continued in a harsh whisper, "or you'll be sorry."

Reuben's eyes narrowed. Bebe acted drunk, she looked drunk, but she didn't smell drunk. Obviously she was a better actress than he gave her credit for.

"It's 350 miles to San Francisco, and it will take you all night and half of tomorrow to get there. In your condition, you might not get there at all. The coast highway will be treacherous. I've seen you drive," he added pointedly.

Bebe pulled free of Reuben's grasp, glaring at him. "If, and I say *if,* you're so damned concerned about me, then *you* drive me. That's fair enough!" Reuben thought her beautiful at that moment, with her damp curls wisping about her forehead and ears. A Christmas angel. She wasn't angry, not really. She was issuing a challenge — and he found it compelling. Despite himself he could feel his cold reserve start to thaw.

"Don't fall for it," Daniel growled at his side. "She's trying to manipulate you, Reuben."

"We can't let this pack of fools out on the road in this fog. Did you ever try to reason with a drunk? If you take a good look, you'll see the whiskey and gin on the floor in the back. Eli is making a delivery. They're going to make this trip no matter what."

Bebe hopped back in the car and let her head loll against the seat, the picture of a weary, happy drunk. Only she wasn't drunk at all; in fact, she hadn't had a drink all day. She closed her eyes. What was better: going to Reuben's apartment or having Reuben drive her to San Francisco to party all week-

end? Quick as lightning she turned on the ignition, ground the gears. The car bucked forward and then stalled. The other engines came to life, their fog lights dancing crazily in the eerie mist. Bebe laughed uproariously. Reuben clenched his teeth so hard his jaw started to ache. "Get your brother in this car," he barked. "Daniel, get in the back with Eli."

"Reuben, you're not serious about this. . . ." He sidled closer to his friend. "You don't even have your glasses." His voice trembled with worry.

"You don't have to go if you don't want to," Reuben said quietly. "I just can't let these fools go alone. Someone has to watch over them. Don't you understand, they could cause this studio one hell of a lot of trouble if something goes wrong. Are you coming or not?"

Daniel looked around at the ghostly hulks lined up as though for a parade. The chattering and laughter grated on his nerves. Reuben was right about the studio. He was soaked right down to his underwear, either from perspiration or the high humidity. This was ridiculous. He tried one last appeal, this time directed at Bebe. "Come home with us, Bebe," he begged.

"Daniel, I don't want to make a cake. I want to go to a party. Don't you want to go to a party? Don't be a poop. Reuben's a

poop. Reuben doesn't know how to have a good time. Reuben doesn't even know how to smile, does he, Daniel?" She laughed, a deep throaty chuckle. Her voice dropped several tones. "Reuben wants to run this studio and be the boss. Isn't that right, Reuben?"

But Reuben refused to be baited. Without a word he climbed in the car, pushing Bebe over as he settled his large frame behind the wheel. Eli was last to settle himself in the backseat. Horns honked as the cars and passengers hooted in excitement. The fog parted in ghostly shapes, only to return thicker and heavier. Reuben clenched his teeth again.

Bebe swung her legs over the side of the door, started to sing in a voice loud enough for the last car's riders to hear. "We're going to a party, we're going to a party."

"I'd appreciate it if you'd shut up, Bebe, and let me concentrate on my driving," Reuben snapped. "Go to sleep!" Oh, he was just itching for a fight, and he didn't care with whom. He glanced in the mirror. Eli was asleep, his neck resting on a carton of liquor, and Daniel . . . he didn't even think of picking on him at the moment. It looked like his fight would have to be with Bebe if she didn't go to sleep. Instantly his shoulders and arms stiffened in anticipation of the verbal onslaught. Bebe turned completely on her seat to stare at Reuben. In the swirling gray mist

she looked ethereal. Reuben grunted as he concentrated on steering the powerful machine.

"Very well, Reuben, if you want me to go to sleep, I'll go to sleep. Good night."

Another trick, Reuben thought in disgust. Bebe never did what she was told. He risked a quick glance over his shoulder at Daniel, who simply shrugged, as if to say there was a first time for everything.

Reuben tried to settle himself for the long drive ahead of him. Daniel thought he was crazy, and he agreed. What had possessed him to do this thing? Had he actually agreed to drive to San Francisco? No, he decided, not exactly. But he'd climbed in the car, and that had made it official. Of course he could have driven Bebe and Eli to Benedict Canyon and just dropped them off. Now he wished he'd done just that. He looked into the rearview mirror. The other cars, swathed in the murky fog, were not far behind. This was probably one of the stupidest things he'd ever done in his life. Was he trying to make amends to Bebe? Did he want her to think he was better than that person in the barn?

The miles rumbled beneath him. After a few hours the temperature seemed to drop slightly and a soft wind whistled through the open windows. The cool air felt good on Reuben's face, but his eyes were aching with strain and his leg was starting to twitch, a

sure sign of fatigue. Once again he chastised himself, the litany of grievances raced through his mind. Stupid, stupid, stupid.

A thick swirl of mist came through the open window and seemed to enshroud the girl sleeping at his side. Reuben lashed out with his arm to disperse the cloud. Bebe stirred and then settled back to sleep.

"Jesus, Reuben, that stuff looked like a bunch of fat snakes," Daniel said in a tremulous voice. "Maybe you should close the windows."

"I need the fresh air to keep awake. I think it's getting a little cooler. Maybe the fog will lift. It's not bad in some places and in others you can't see an inch ahead of you. I'll get us there, Daniel, don't worry about it. Haven't I always come through for you?"

"Yes, but this is different. Before you never took reckless chances. I don't understand this. We're fools, both of us. I wish this liquor weren't in the car."

"So do I, but it'll be all right," Reuben said tightly.

Daniel inched himself forward until he was leaning over the seat behind Reuben. "Is there any one particular reason we're on this dismal road to San Francisco, a reason I am not aware of?"

"Neither one of them was in any condition to drive. You saw how determined Bebe was to make the trip. I don't know about you, but

592

I know I wouldn't be able to look Sol in the face if something happened to Bebe or Eli when I could have stopped it."

"Is that the only reason?" Daniel asked quietly.

"I have a few others, but that's the main one. Why don't you try and get some sleep."

"With this guy next to me? I trust him only as far as I can see him. When he wakes up he's going to be one angry young man. You pretty much made a fool of him back at the studio, and now you're horning in on his territory."

The long road loomed ahead of them like a never-ending snake. Reuben settled himself as comfortably as he could for the rest of the drive. The fog was lifting slightly, allowing for better visibility. Every now and then, when the road cleared, he risked a glance at Bebe. Each time, something cringed in him at the sight of her sleeping face. She looked so . . . so angelic. Her brother, on the other hand, looked like the devil incarnate.

Bebe peered at Reuben through her fringe of heavy lashes. She caught each furtive glimpse he took of her as a ray of hope. If there was a way to get Reuben Tarz for her very own, she promised herself, she'd find it. More than anything else in the world, she wanted him. And one way or another she'd always managed to get what she wanted. This time wouldn't be any different. After all, she

held all the cards. The day might come when she wanted or needed to deal him the joker in the deck. She smiled as she slipped into sleep. Reuben Tarz was as good as hers.

The sorry-looking caravan arrived at the Sherwood Hotel at mid-morning. Reuben was red-eyed and irritable when Bebe hopped out of the car, stretching luxuriously. "See, Reuben, you were concerned for no reason. We're here, safe and sound. Now it's time to party. Eli! Eli, wake up. We're here, toots."

Eli struggled to wakefulness. Spittle was caked at the corners of his mouth, and his greasy hair stuck up in stiff peaks. Like horns, Reuben thought. He was wrinkled and stiff from the long trip. Red, festering blotches dotted the side of his face he'd slept on. His beady little eyes stared at Reuben. "Carry that stuff in the back and in the trunk upstairs," he ordered Reuben and Daniel.

"You want that 'stuff' carried upstairs, I suggest you hop to it," Reuben said coldly. He stared at Eli until the young man looked away.

"Bebe," he whined, "how are we going to get this liquor up to the party?"

"I have no idea, but I'd be real careful if I were you, Eli, I'm sure they're counting on it." Bebe danced her way to the entrance.

Reuben strolled over to Eli. His voice was quiet, almost musical when he spoke. "Eli, the only reason Daniel and I are here at all is

because you and your sister were too drunk to drive. I suggest you keep your nose clean while you're here. If you don't, you won't have a nose." The moment he turned his back, Eli spit in his direction. Daniel grinned and wagged his finger at the young man, who kicked the car in rage.

"Flunky," Eli muttered.

Reuben stopped in his tracks and turned, his eyes never leaving Eli's face. Slowly he backed Eli against the car. "What did you call me?"

"You heard me the first time," Eli whined shrilly.

"The first time you were drunk — now you're not."

"You work for Maxie same as I do," Eli said belligerently.

Reuben's fist shot out. Eli went down in the gutter, his legs sprawled straight out. "What were you saying?" Reuben asked icily.

"Okay, okay, so you're not a flunky. What makes you so different from me? We both work for Maxie."

Reuben lifted his foot and placed it on Eli's neck. "Wrong, Eli. Max works for Fairmont, and you *owe* Max. There is a big difference. If you agree to behave yourself, I'll take my foot off your neck. Just nod." Eli nodded. "If I hear one more peep out of you this entire weekend, your ass will go back to L.A. in a basket. Do we understand each other?" Eli

nodded again, and Reuben removed his foot.

"I'm too tired to breathe," he grumbled to Daniel as they entered the hotel. "All I want is a bath and a bed. Since we aren't exactly invited members of this party, I wonder where we can sleep?"

"Reuben, Daniel, over here!" Bebe called from the desk. "My friends have taken over an entire floor, so I'm certain there will be a room where you can catch some sleep. I didn't thank you properly for driving us. I do want to apologize," Bebe said, giving each of them a warm, moist kiss. "Thank you, Reuben. You, too, Daniel." Reuben drew in his breath sharply. "Where's Eli?" Bebe called over her shoulder. "Did he get someone to carry his . . . his baggage?"

"The last time I saw your brother he was leaning against the car, but I wouldn't worry about him if I were you."

Bebe turned, her face full of concern. "But you see, I *do* worry about my brother. That's why I came along on this trip. I would much rather have stayed home, but sometimes Eli needs a keeper."

"What you're insinuating is *you* don't require a keeper," Reuben said, amazed at Bebe's audacity.

"Whoops, I think we're here." Bebe laughed at the blast of sound that greeted them when she thrust open the suite door. "I'm Just Wild About Harry" blared from the gramophone.

"I wonder who Harry is?" Bebe giggled. Daniel stared, his mind busily sifting and collating what was happening around him.

"To the City of Hills!" a man said, holding his glass aloft.

Daniel recognized him immediately. Richard "Dickie" Hastings was the hottest director in Hollywood. He was also notorious for throwing the wildest and most decadent parties of the day. For years he had informed anyone who would listen that he had two goals in life: one, to be the greatest director of all time; the other, to go down in history as the party king of the twenties. He was well on his way to becoming the living legend of his prophesies.

"I'll drink to that," Bebe said, reaching for a glass.

Reuben's eyes narrowed and Daniel's jaw dropped at the sight the open door provided. Hastings was standing, glass raised, smack in the middle of the cocktail table, in his boxer shorts, his fat belly jutting out obscenely. Christ, thought Reuben, the bastard was so hairy he looked prickly. Girls and women in various states of undress simpered around him, offering him grapes and cheese. Reuben's eyes continued to narrow until they were mere slits in his face as he watched a budding starlet pour her drink down Dickie's shorts. "You lick that right up, you hear me, darlin'?" Dickie said, laughing lasciviously.

The starlet obliged by pulling at Dickie's shorts, then craned her neck to do his bidding.

"Jesus," Daniel breathed. All three of them were rooted to the spot.

The moment Dickie exploded into the starlet's mouth, he noticed Reuben. "Hey, Tarz," he bleated, "it's a party. Let your hair down, there's enough here for you, too. Who's your friend?"

"They're with me." Bebe smiled uncertainly. This was the first time in her life that she'd seen public sex. She felt embarrassed and couldn't look at Reuben or Daniel. "And they'd like to take a bath and get some sleep. We drove all night," she added feebly.

"We have the whole floor. Take your pick. Take a girl if you want," he said generously.

Reuben carved a path through the writhing bodies on the floor in his quest to get back to the door and hallway. Daniel could feel his cheeks flame as one buxom starlet ripped her dress from the shoulder, exposing large creamy breasts. Reuben looked back once to see if Bebe was following them and saw her cuddling with a young actor who was prettier than any girl in the room. She waved gaily.

"Son of a bitch!" Reuben seethed. He spotted Eli carrying two heavy cartons while he pushed a third with his foot, his face sheathed in perspiration. It was probably the hardest work he'd ever done in his life. "That supply

should keep the party going for at least a half hour," Reuben snapped sarcastically.

"I'll go back and keep an eye on . . . things," Daniel volunteered.

"That's a good idea. If I don't get some sleep I'm going to drop in my tracks. Wake me in a couple of hours."

Back in Dickie's suite of rooms, Daniel tried to make himself as inconspicuous as possible. His eyes searched out Bebe, his main concern. She was still snuggling with the pretty young actor, who was busy whispering in her ear. He hated the blank look in her eyes and her nervous giggle. Eli, he noticed, was doing his best to put his hands up a woman's dress. The ravages of liquor, dope, and too many wild parties showed on her young-old face. She seemed to suit Eli, he thought uncharitably.

"C'mere, Mavis," Dickie called out to her drunkenly. The woman struggled to her feet and wobbled over to Dickie.

"Whatcha want, honey?" she simpered. Up close Daniel thought she looked even worse. Her face was caked with old as well as new makeup. But Dickie didn't seem to mind — or perhaps he didn't notice, as he drew her into his arms.

"You and me, toots," he said, "we had some good times, didn't we?"

"We sure did, Dickie, but you got real famous and didn't need me anymore."

"You got old, that's why," Dickie said drunkenly. "I'll never deny you were the best lay I ever had."

"You want to try again for old time's sake?" Mavis asked hopefully.

"Maybe later." Dickie chuckled as his eyes slid across the room. He knew he could have any woman in the room except maybe Bebe Rosen. What the hell did he want with a crinkly old broad like Mavis? She smelled, too, he thought in disgust. He failed to see the malevolent look on Eli Rosen's face.

At one point Daniel estimated over a hundred people were in the room, eating Dickie's food and drinking his liquor. The bash had to cost a fortune. They were like a horde of locusts foraging on food, drink, and flesh. Daniel felt dirty just watching.

At one point Dickie returned to the room with a towel wrapped around his middle. He greeted each new arrival by name. "I'm so glad you could come. Come on in and join the party."

Daniel wondered if Dickie realized half the people in the room didn't care a twit about him, but only what he could provide in the way of food, drink, sex, and reefer. His eyes returned to Bebe, who was extricating herself from the pretty actor. She pouted and made her way over to Daniel.

"Where's Reuben?" she asked, her full pink lips pursed on the rim of a glass.

"Your lips are bruised," Daniel said disapprovingly.

Bebe shrugged. "That happens after you kiss a lot. Walk me to my room?"

"One of these rooms, or did you engage one?" Daniel asked.

She pointed upstairs. "On the next floor. A girl needs a room where she can repair her makeup and tinkle without sixty people observing her." She barely suppressed a smile at Daniel's embarrassment. "Daniel, you are just too precious for words. Please, don't ever change."

"Do you get some kind of weird pleasure out of making fun of me?" Daniel snapped.

Bebe's eyes widened. "Oh! Don't ever think that, not for a minute. I love you just the way you are, and I don't want you to change — that's all I meant. Sometimes when I say things they don't come out the way I intend them to. I would never make fun of you," she repeated.

Somewhat mollified, Daniel allowed her to link her arm with his. They made their way out to the hall, the strains of "A Pretty Girl Is Like a Melody" following them. "Do you think I'm as pretty as a melody, Daniel?" asked Bebe.

Daniel flushed. "You bet."

The real Bebe Rosen smiled at him. "I know you mean that. Thank you for the compliment. I think we can both use a

breather away from that party. It was wild, wasn't it? Did you see some of those people Dickie hangs out with? I hear Mavis is always around. She licks his feet and he kicks her, supposedly. I thought he was nicer than that. I hate to be disappointed in people. Eli . . . Eli wants to be invited to things like this. I can't make him understand they just use him. Speaking of which, I haven't seen him for a while, have you?"

"Not for an hour or so."

Bebe crinkled her nose. "Let's not worry about him. When is Reuben going to join us?"

Daniel pulled out his pocket watch. "I have to wake him in half an hour. He's . . . he's a little upset."

"Poor Reuben. He doesn't enjoy much of anything. He doesn't know how to relax and have fun. Was he relaxed with Mickey in France?"

"I thought so," Daniel said carefully. Whatever Bebe was leading up to, it was about to come to a head. While he waited for her to make her point, he looked around the hotel room. It was a duplicate of Dickie's, but smaller. A small sofa, covered in the same material as the drapes and bedspread, sat at the far end of the room next to a small table and two chairs. The carpet was beige and soft. No one lived here. People like Bebe just visited for a day or two and then were gone, leaving behind wet towels and spilled powder.

A temporary place. The room irritated him because he'd had enough of temporary places.

An hour later Bebe yawned elaborately. "Why don't you go wake Reuben and go back to the party. I think I'm going to treat myself to a long hot bath and a nap. Do me a favor, Daniel, keep your eye on Eli. For me. Someday I'll tell you Eli's sad story, and then you won't think so badly of him." She kissed him on the cheek and shooed him out the door.

Daniel stared at the closed door with a puzzled look on his face. What was *that* all about, he wondered.

He decided to let Reuben sleep. Bebe was going to take a nap, and there would be nothing for Reuben to do but worry. Besides, he knew his friend needed the sleep.

Daniel himself tried to sleep, but the sounds of Dickie's party prevented it. At last he decided to go back and see if Eli was around. Bebe had said to keep an eye on him; that much he could do.

If anything, the party was louder now than when he'd left. He noticed that half the liquor Eli had brought was gone. The food on the heavy silver trays was dry and unappetizing. Fresh-squeezed orange juice was everywhere, in jars, bottles, and pitchers.

Finally Daniel spotted Eli in a corner with Mavis Parks and another woman. He searched for a chair that would afford him

somewhat of a clear view and settled himself comfortably. After all, he'd promised Bebe.

It was early evening when Reuben stalked into the party, mad as a wet hornet. "I thought I told you to wake me!"

"I didn't see any point. You needed the rest. Bebe took a room and she's sleeping. I have my eye on Eli. It's all under control, Reuben."

Reuben looked shocked. "Bebe took a room?"

"To fix her makeup and tinkle." He winced at the odd look on Reuben's face. "Women tinkle, men piss. It's sort of like men sweat and women swoon."

"Where do you get that kind of information? I'm real curious." Reuben stopped talking just long enough to point beyond a half-open door. "Your sleeping friend is standing in the next room," he said, pointing to the sitting room off Dickie's bedroom.

"I guess she woke up. It was a while ago."

Reuben took a good look at Daniel's eyes. "And just how many drinks have you had, Daniel?" he asked suspiciously.

"One, two, maybe three. Is it important for you to know exactly?"

"I didn't bring you here to drink."

"What the hell am I supposed to do? Sit here and twiddle my fingers?"

"We have to keep our eye on Bebe. She's not asleep in her room, she's over there, and

she looks like she's getting ready to do something. . . ."

"What?"

"How the hell should I know?"

Daniel looked in the general direction of Reuben's worried stare. "By the way, did you know the bathtub is filled with orange blossoms? Not the flowers." He grinned. "A whole bathtub full of orange blossoms. Drinks. You just scoop it out. That's what I did."

"Everybody, listen! Give me your attention!" Bebe Rosen shouted. She was drunk, Reuben thought disgustedly. If there was one thing in life he detested, it was a drunk woman. He tried to look away, but his eyes kept going back to Bebe, waiting to hear what she had to say.

"How much money will you put up to see me take a bath in the orange blossoms?" Bebe shouted from her perch on the back of the sofa.

"Five hundred!" Eli screamed.

"Two thousand!" Dickie called drunkenly.

"We have two thousand five hundred. Do I hear more?" Bebe yelled. A crowd began to gather around her.

As the bids increased, Reuben could feel his back stiffen. Why should he care what Bebe did? He wasn't her goddamn keeper. Her actions were disgusting him.

"Somebody come up with another five

hundred to make it an even ten thousand and I'll do it!" Bebe screamed over the cheering crowd. She kicked off one shoe and then the other.

"Ten thousand!" Dickie shouted.

"Done!" Bebe rolled down one stocking and then the other, twirling them in the air for a second before she tossed them into the leering crowd. Then she was off the sofa, dancing away from Dickie's lecherous hands. She collided with Reuben, their eyes meeting, hers wicked, his angry and sullen. "You didn't bid," she whispered.

Pandemonium reigned in the next few seconds as Bebe stripped down to the buff and headed for the bathroom. The crowd followed, tossing clothes in every direction. Sounds of splashing and raucous laughter bounced off the tiled bathroom walls.

"I think this is an orgy, Reuben." Daniel's voice cracked. He stopped smiling when he caught the look on Reuben's face.

"Have you got any idea where Eli is?"

Daniel pointed. "He went into that room over there with Dickie and Mavis."

A moment later Reuben spotted Eli standing in the doorway of the room he'd entered, a strange look on his face. Before he turned and disappeared back into the room, Reuben noticed that the front of his suit was covered in vomit. He glanced at Daniel, who grimaced and nodded to show that he, too, had seen

Eli's condition. Reuben was halfway to the door when Daniel caught up to him.

Reuben spoke first. "This is all we need. Did anyone else see him like that?"

Both men looked carefully about the room. No one seemed sober enough to have registered Eli's disheveled appearance.

"I guess we'd better go in and clean up the mess," Daniel said, disgust and irritation written all over his face.

Reuben opened the door. Inside, Dickie was naked and sound asleep on the bed, and Eli stood hunched over by the open window, vomiting again. Reuben shook his head in contempt.

"Stay here and watch the door," he said as he moved toward Eli.

The moment Eli realized he wasn't alone, he did something that seemed strange to Reuben — he stood bolt upright, stretching out his arms, trying to cover the opening of the window.

"What the hell are you trying to hide?" Reuben demanded, striding over to the window to investigate.

He had seen enough death in Europe to know there was nothing he could do for the woman lying at the bottom of the refuse-strewn hotel alley. Her head was crushed, surrounded by a pool of blood, her body twisted in a heap of ancient garbage. "Jesus Christ, what have you done?"

Daniel was at Reuben's side in a second. The sight below made him gag. "It's Mavis!"

Reuben ran to the door Daniel had been guarding. "Get him out of here, Daniel. Drag him, slug him, I don't give a damn, just get him down to the car. When you get to the lobby, make him stand upright. I'll get Bebe."

Reuben plowed through the crowd, trying to keep his face relaxed. "Bebe? Bebe honey, where are you," he called, revolted at having to use the endearing term.

"Here, darling," Bebe called drunkenly.

Reuben's eyes searched the crowd of revelers. Bebe was sitting on the commode, stark naked, orange juice dripping from her breasts, her legs crossed, and a cigarette in her hand. Her eyes seemed fuzzy, out of focus. Reuben reached for a bath towel and threw it at her. She dropped her cigarette and threw the towel back at him. He yanked her from the commode, scooped her up screaming and yelling, and carried her from the room, but not before he threw the towel over her flailing body.

"Shut that mouth of yours before I slap you. Your brother or Dickie . . . pushed . . . or witnessed a woman fall to her death in the alley behind this hotel. She's dead. Do you hear what I'm saying? Dickie is sound asleep and Daniel is taking Eli to the car. My money is on your brother. *Do you understand what I*

just told you?"

Maybe it was Reuben's viselike hold on her, or his words. Bebe closed her mouth and passed out in his arms. Reuben carried her down the back steps of the Sherwood and out to the car, where he dumped her unceremoniously in the backseat beside her brother.

Reuben's thoughts raced. The partiers would continue their revelry and probably not bother with Dickie's room, thinking he was with a woman. The alleyway looked like it hadn't seen a human being for months. It was late now, the liquor was almost gone. If he could get back to L.A. before the police were called, he would have a fairly good alibi, and so would Sol's children. He was certain nothing could have been done for the woman, so calling the police would serve no purpose. Eli, Dickie, and a dead woman. He could add; the problem was in subtracting. Take away Eli and that left Dickie. Take away Dickie and that left Eli. Which one was guilty? Dickie looked too done in. You couldn't just kill someone and then fall asleep like a baby. Or could you? Aiding and abetting . . .

Reuben took a good long look at Eli, who was obviously in shock, huddled in the backseat next to Bebe. As the car roared to life, he turned to Daniel. "He didn't do it, he doesn't have the guts," he said.

Daniel only nodded. He knew Reuben was lying.

It was three-thirty in the morning when Reuben drove the Pierce Arrow up the long, winding road in Benedict Canyon to the Rosen mansion. At the entrance, he braked, leapt over the side of the car, and raced up the steps, mission white in the moonlight. He rang the doorbell insistently. He wanted to bang at the door with his fists, but he kept his head. When the overhead lights went on, he returned to the car. He pulled Bebe from the car and draped the towel over her, then he slung her over his shoulder like a sack of potatoes. Eli was slumped on the other side of the backseat. "You'll have to carry that toad," he said to Daniel.

"What the bloody hell . . . ?" Sol Rosen boomed in the dark night.

Reuben hushed him hurriedly. "Your children, Mr. Rosen," he announced. He handed over his naked charge, while Daniel dumped Eli on the foyer floor. Sol's eyes were wild with fear as he stared first at his children and then at Reuben and Daniel.

"What have you done with them? What's the meaning of this!" he bellowed. "I want some answers, and I want them now!"

"Keep your voice down. . . . After I've told you, you'll be glad you did. The servants . . . Help me get these two in bed first."

Fifteen minutes later, Sol spluttered, "I don't believe this horseshit you're feeding me. How in the hell did these two get to San Francisco?"

"I drove them because they were determined to go and they were too drunk to drive. I didn't think you'd want them killed on the road in all that fog. The papers will bear out my story by morning. I drove like a maniac to get back here. The police will want to talk to everyone who was at that party. If we say we got back here at midnight, I think we'll be safe."

"Did my boy do what you said?" Sol whispered fearfully.

Reuben stared at Sol for a long moment. "I don't know, Mr. Rosen. Dickie was passed out cold. My personal opinion is the only thing I can share with you, and yes, it is my opinion that Eli did it. As I said, I can't say that for certain, and it won't hold up in a court of law. Good night, Mr. Rosen. I'll drive your car to the studio in the morning."

CHAPTER
TWENTY-SEVEN

Bebe woke to bright yellow sunshine. Her temples pounded and her stomach heaved. She lay still, her thoughts jumbled. She really had to do something about her bedroom, it was too girlish, too frilly. She needed something a little more sophisticated, something on the tailored side, something that said she was grown-up now. Her eyes were full of grit and still bore traces of the heavy makeup she'd worn in San Francisco. When she moved outside of the covers, she became aware of the sticky bedclothes. Frowning, she thought she remembered that one minute she was in a bathtub full of freshly squeezed orange juice and gin, and the next thing she was naked except for a towel and being carried to the car by Reuben.

Eli. Eli was with her and already in the car when Reuben carried her down the back steps of the Sherwood. Somebody was dead and Eli was going to be blamed. Not Dickie. Dickie passed out. She remembered Daniel

and Reuben talking. Mavis Parks was lying dead in the courtyard. Eli had been dragged out by Daniel.

She wished she could remember more, but she'd been so drunk, splashing around in the tub full of orange blossoms, splashing and taking great gulps of the sticky drink as she was pushed under time and again. She thought it silly and stupid now. Whatever possessed her to do such an asinine thing? Reuben, of course. She'd wanted to rile him, but she hadn't actually succeeded in doing that. What she'd done was act the fool and disgust him. She felt like crying. She never did anything right, no matter how hard she tried.

Her thoughts raced. Reuben and Daniel's quick thinking had saved her and Eli from . . . what? A police investigation. The word she'd heard bandied about last evening was *orgy*. She'd participated in an orgy, and now her father was going to raise unholy hell. The industry was going to raise unholy hell. The public would raise unholy hell. She groaned. There was no way she was going to sweet-talk her father on this escapade. He would probably kill Eli if he thought he could get away with it. This was one time she was going to have to take it on the chin. No excuses. She'd tell her father the truth and hope for mercy. Bile rose in her throat. She flew off the bed, the top sheet stuck to her rear end and trailing behind her like a wedding train.

An hour later, dressed in her old comfortable robe, with her head wrapped in a towel, Bebe sat down on a slipper chair and stared at Eli, who was sleeping fully clothed on the chaise longue. She must have been in a real stupor not to know Eli had spent the night in her room. He'd done it before, but this time was different. God, he was a disgusting mess.

She should wake Eli and talk to him before her father . . . Her head was pounding so badly she thought it would spring off her neck. She leaned back and closed her eyes, hoping to ease the sick feeling. And to think Eli was in this condition several times a week. God!

She tried to peer at the little bedside clock without moving her head. It was ten minutes of nine. Her father would be here soon. She couldn't even begin to comprehend what his mood would be.

One bare foot stretched out to poke at Eli. "Eli, wake up. You have to get up." He was a slug, a dead weight on her chaise. The foot poked again, this time with more force. "Eli, Daddy is going to be here in a few minutes." He didn't move. Bebe leaned over and put all the force she could muster into pushing her bare foot into Eli's groin. He toppled over in an ungainly heap. "Someone's dead, Eli. *Dead.* Now wake *up!*"

Eli shook his head, moaned, and began to crawl over to Bebe. "I didn't do it, Bebe. I

swear to God I didn't do it!"

"Don't worry about God right now, worry about what you're going to tell Daddy. You better worry about what Reuben told him, too. This is one time we're going to pay for our fun. Only it wasn't fun at all. I made a fool of myself, and all because you wanted to go to that stupid party. If it wasn't for Reuben and Daniel, we'd probably be dead on the coast road. Instead, we're involved in a murder."

"You make it sound like I killed someone," Eli whined.

"Reubin thinks you did."

"Bastard!" Eli spat out.

"No he isn't. He saved our necks. I don't want to hear another bad word about him. Do you hear me?" Bebe said wearily.

"You're soft on him. I could see it all night. He must be soft on you, too, to drive us all the way to Frisco. He hates me!"

"Oh, shut up. Your voice makes my head worse. And God, do you stink!" She tried to move away from him.

"Oh, I get it," Eli snapped. "You're going to play the good little girl who was with her big bad brother and I made you take off your clothes to make a spectacle of yourself."

Bebe reared up. "You bid five hundred dollars to see me take off my clothes. That's sick, Eli. My very own brother! Daddy's right, you are a horse's ass." She flopped back against

the chair, her temples throbbing to the beat of her anger.

"Bebe, we have to stick together. Pop will beat the hell out of me. Please, don't let him get at me. Bebeeee."

Even though he was pleading in a whisper, Bebe still had to cover her ears. "You aren't listening to me, little brother. We deserve whatever Daddy decides to do with us. I'm telling the truth. I don't give a damn what you do. Get that through your head."

Eli cowered against Bebe's legs, his arms holding on to the sides of the chair as the sound of heavy footsteps drew nearer, ever nearer.

"Do you," Sol said, bursting into the room and enunciating each word carefully, "have any idea what you two did? I don't want to hear any of your lying excuses. It was your idea, Eli, to go to San Francisco. Bebe, you did not have to go along. Your reputation is shot now. My daughter a tramp! Your poor mother must be turning over in her grave. Your antics can bring the studio tumbling down around our ears. If it wasn't for Tarz, your ass would be roasting in jail, Eli. It still might end up there if we can't cover this up. You had the goddamn nerve to drive bootleg liquor all the way to Frisco. That's going to come out somewhere down the line if Tarz can't cover it up. Murder! A goddamn murder. Someone is dead! *Do you hear me?* I'm

meeting with Tarz later this morning to come up with . . . we'll get a story together. Both of you will remain in this house until I tell you you can leave. Do you understand me?" Sol thundered. "Eli, if you so much as step foot out the door, you will be in the gutter and I will be the one who kicks you there. I do not want my family in the headlines. Do you understand?" he thundered. When no one answered, he went on.

"For the past few months there's been talk a watchdog is going to be appointed by the film industry to oversee Hollywood's morals, and that doesn't mean just the actors, it means all of us. If I can't control my own family, how can I control my studio? . . . Now you can talk, if you have something to say. *No lies,*" he roared.

"Whatever Reuben told you is true, Daddy. I'm sorry. I thought it was going to be fun, but it wasn't. I won't do it ever again. Whatever you decide to do . . . what I mean is . . . I'm sorry," Bebe said sincerely.

"I didn't kill anyone, Pop. Dickie did it. He was so drunk. I . . . couldn't kill anyone. When I saw the body down there, I got sick. Ask Tarz, he saw me throwing up. I wouldn't put it past that bastard to have cooked this all up so he could come in like a white knight and save the day."

Sol's hand shot out, striking Eli full in the face. Eli reeled backward, his head landing in

Bebe's lap and his legs crumpled under him. He started to cry.

"Tarz didn't arrange anything. He saved your skin, is what he did. I don't like it, but the truth is the truth. He has me over a barrel now, thanks to you. I'm going to pay and I'm going to pay big for what you two did last night. Chew on that for a while. I'm leaving for the studio now, and you damn well better think about what I've said. If the newspapers come around, let the servants handle them."

"Daddy?" Sol turned at the sound of his daughter's voice. "Daddy, if I have to stay in the house, can I redecorate my bedroom?" He didn't bother to answer, just slammed the door so hard on the way out that Eli cringed. Bebe shuddered.

"How . . . how long do you think it will be before he lets us out?" Eli asked in a trembling voice.

"A very long time. Until Reuben Tarz tells Daddy it's safe to let us out," Bebe said tearfully. "Oh, how did I ever let you talk me into going to that stupid party. How?" She prodded him forcefully with her foot. "Dammit, Eli, answer me."

Eli got to his feet. "We used to be friends as well as brother and sister, but all that changed when you came back. You aren't even nice to me. I always looked up to you, Bebe. I'm sorry about last night. I wish it

never happened. It's Tarz, isn't it? There's something between the two of you, I can feel it. I'm not blind. I saw the way he looked at you and the way you looked at him. Just how well did you know him in France?" Bebe's sharp intake of breath seemed to float through the room.

"You thought I didn't know about that. I'm not a complete fool, Bebe. I think it's just . . . real shitty the way you've been treating me." He looked down at his sister with tears burning his eyes.

"Not now, Eli. I feel too terrible to discuss something that's so important to you right now. We're going to have plenty of time to talk in the coming days. I'm angry with you, yes, but I'm angrier with myself."

How blank and cold his sister's face was. There was little he could do but leave the pretty bedroom with the warm sun streaming through the gabled windows.

Bebe let her breath out in a long sigh. Now she could redecorate her bedroom in her mind. A bedspread with pleats around the bottom instead of flowered ruffles. Drapes instead of frilly curtains. A soft rose rug, thick and ankle-hugging. Get rid of the knick-knacks and add a few plants. At least one original painting on the wall. Soft and warm, neither feminine nor masculine. Like the guest bedrooms in Mickey's house.

■ ■ ■ ■

Sol's brain churned as he drove to the studio. Thank God for Tarz. A stupid stunt like last night could wipe him out. Bebe was becoming more of a handful than ever, and Eli was a lost cause. When the Hastings thing blew over, if it ever did, he'd boot his keister out and forget he ever had a weasel for a son. Bebe would not toe the line for long, so he was going to have to do something about her. Maybe what Eli said was true; maybe she was smitten with Tarz. If she was, he should be thankful; she could have picked one of Eli's sleazy friends. Tarz . . . He was going to want something, and who could blame him? In his position, he'd have made demands last night. The price was going to be high, that much he did know, and he would pay it with good face.

Maybe, just maybe, the idea he had last night would pay off if he went about it in the right way. He'd throw Bebe into the pot. It would take somebody a lot stronger and tougher than Reuben Tarz to turn down such a beauty. Tarz was young, with healthy animal appetites. He'd taken Mickey on, and she was twice his age. Obviously he'd satisfied her, or why else would she have turned her business over to him to manage? Maybe she'd yank it all away from him if she found out he was

seriously thinking of marrying Bebe. Yes sir, sometimes good things came out of bad.

Sol's steps were lighter, but he still shuffled forward when he walked up the steps to his office. Tarz was his answer.

Reuben sat at his desk with his hands behind his head, every inch the studio executive. Sometimes Lady Luck lets you step in it. San Francisco was behind them now. If he could convince Sol to let him handle the interviews when the police came around, things might be okay. He had a few bad moments when he thought about Dickie, but he consoled himself with the thought that he hadn't seen the crime, only the aftermath. No one, least of all the police, was interested in opinions, his or anyone else's. The police dealt in facts. The only thing that worried him was Eli and his loose lip. There had to be a way to insure his silence. Obviously Sol had long ago given up on his son — he certainly had no control over the young man. On the other hand, Max had a hold on Eli, but how far would Max go for him? A deal. You wash my hands — I'll wash yours. A bigger cut on the distribution? He'd have to think about it a while longer.

That left Bebe. A handful. Sol was definitely going to have to do something about his children before . . . before they . . . What? They were in serious trouble already, at least

Eli was. Nothing was more serious than murder.

Right now, though, he had better concentrate. He had something else to contend with, and that was Daniel. He didn't want Daniel involved in any way with what was going on, so he was going to have to put his plans into action regarding his friend. He should have taken care of it a week before, the way he'd originally planned.

Sol would be late this morning, which would give him time to go down to the prop department and get things under way. If he was lucky, the police wouldn't find their way to the studio until later in the day or early tomorrow morning.

The head of the prop department was a wizened man with curly white hair and crinkly blue eyes, and an iron trap of a memory for every stick, every last item in the department. His jaw dropped as he listened to Reuben, and he hooted with admiration when Reuben spread out his notes on a long worktable. He was still chuckling and slapping at his thighs when Reuben asked, "Well, can you do it?"

"Son, I've had requests for just about everything and anything. So far no one has been able to stump me — and let me tell you, some of these set men are out of their noodle, but I always come up with what they want.

Yes, Mr. Tarz, I can do it. It'll be a challenge, believe me."

"Can we keep it between the two of us?" Reuben asked uneasily.

"As long as you ain't planning on getting fired we can. You get yourself canned and it'll come out the way dirty laundry does. Get my drift?'

"I'm here for the long haul, Mr. Sugar. As a matter of fact, if you know how to keep a secret for your own future good," Reuben said, "I expect to be promoted any day now to vice president in charge of production."

"That means you'll call the shots around here, then," the little man said in awe. Reuben nodded. "Then I guess I better start to work. It's gonna take me about a week, how's that?"

"Too long. The deadline for registration is in a week, and he has to drive east. Two days. Can you do it?"

"Consider it done. It won't hurt me to go without sleep for a night or two."

"It has to be perfect," Reuben warned.

"It'll be so perfect the dean of Harvard Law School will believe he wrote Mr. Bishop's acceptance letter himself and forgot to file it." As the two shook hands, one thought circled in the old man's head: That's got to be one powerful friendship.

Reuben's next stop was Daniel's office. "Close up shop for now, Dan'l. Go over to

the prop department and get a chit from Mr. Sugar for a studio car. There will be someone there to teach you how to drive. All day, till you have it down pat." Reuben raised his hands to brush away Daniel's startled look. "Don't even begin to ask questions, pal, just do it."

Margaret was every inch the professional secretary when she ushered Sol Rosen into Reuben's office. A minute later she reappeared with coffee and danish on a silver tray. Sol sipped his coffee, set the cup down, and spoke.

"In your opinion, what's the best way to handle this?"

Reuben didn't quite know what he had expected, but this — having Sol Rosen ask his opinion — definitely wasn't it. "I think you should let me answer the questions because I was there. They might ask you something and you'll trip up. It could be some minuscule little detail. But only if you agree. I'll say we left around seven and got here about one A.M. I think it's safe to say I was the only one not drinking. As much as I hate to admit it, Daniel had a snootful. He's not used to drinking, so one or two would put him under the table. But he could still function. He's the one who got Eli down to the car. As for Bebe, we can't deny she was taking the orange blossom bath, but then, so

was everyone else. Paramount is going to take the heat in this. So to sum it up, we were there, the three of them had a few drinks, Bebe did her bathtub number, and we left to return here. It wasn't our cup of tea, that sort of party. The police are going to want to know where the liquor came from. I suppose you know by now that Eli had a carload. However, there was liquor at the party when we arrived. I don't know where it came from. Eli got it from Max, who will deny it. We don't want to jeopardize Max and his distribution, so Eli will have to deny the charge if anyone brings it up. Bebe and I will back him up. Do you see anything wrong with any part of what I've just said?"

Sol rubbed his chin. "Sounds pretty good to me. I only hope we can carry it off. This town is already buzzing about the lack of morals and accusations of decadence. This is all we need."

"I want you at my side when I make my statement," Reuben said.

"I'll be there." Why hadn't Reuben said Daniel would be with him and Bebe, to back up Eli's story? Bishop was the kind of guy cops loved, clean-cut and studious-looking. Still, he wasn't about to ask. Now he had to find out what this was going to cost him. "What do you —"

"A vice presidency — in charge of production," Reuben said coolly. "Five thousand a

625

month to start."

He'd known it would be something of this magnitude; there was no point in arguing. He nodded. "I'll send out a memo, and my secretary will release it to the papers."

A goddamn vice president! He wished Mickey were there so he could tell her, but . . . Mickey wouldn't approve of the way the promotion had come about. He'd be able to pay her back now, in one lump sum instead of payments over a period of time. That was the first thing he'd do. Money would have to be set aside for an allowance for Daniel. Pretty soon he'd be rolling in the greenery.

Two days later Reuben ushered Daniel down to the prop room.

It was ten-thirty in the morning when Al Sugar handed over a packet of documents to Reuben, who in turn handed them to Daniel. Both men were silent while Daniel read first one paper, and then the other, until he was finished. His face was white, his mouth hanging open.

"This . . . this says . . . what it says is . . . I'm going to Harvard Law School! Jesus, Harvard Law School!" Daniel cried excitedly. "I . . . Reuben, you have to write Mickey and tell her! When . . . when am I going?"

"In about ten minutes, or as soon as your car arrives. We sent a chit around to the motor pool. You're going in style, Dan'l," Reuben said fondly. "A Daimler. We're signing it

out for an indefinite period of time. Now that I'm vice president, I'll answer to myself. Over there is your wardrobe, two trunks and two valises. You, my friend, will be wearing Diego Diaz's underwear. Mr. Sugar has taken care of everything."

Daniel's shoulders slumped. "Reuben, how can I go to Harvard Law School? I didn't even finish college!"

Reuben and Al laughed. "Sure you did, Daniel, you must have overlooked your diploma," Reuben said, pointing to the packet in Daniel's hand. "It's inside that envelope. So is your acceptance letter from the dean himself."

"Jesus!"

Reuben threw his hands in the air. "This is Hollywood, Dan'l, land of magic, and we just created some for you. All you have to do is make us proud. Straight A's. Leave the girls alone and study till you drop. Is it a deal?"

"Reuben, I . . . Mr. Sugar . . ."

"No sniveling, kid, or the ink on that acceptance letter will run; it isn't dry yet."

This couldn't be happening to him, yet it was. A car horn tooted, and panic suddenly ribboned through Daniel. It was true, he was leaving; he was going to Harvard!

"Here's a map. This envelope has enough money for the trip and your allowance for the first month. As soon as you get settled, write me so I know where to send it every

month." The two men looked at each other. "Good luck, Daniel," Reuben said softly.

"Go ahead, tell me to stop blubbering, I don't care. I'll miss you, Reuben, I really will, and I won't let you down, I promise!"

"I know." Reuben laughed reassuringly. "Make sure you stop when you get tired. There's enough money there for hotels and food."

"Reuben . . . can I talk to you a second, in private?"

Reuben motioned for Al to step back. He leaned over the car. "Reuben, I know that your personal life is none of my business. I was going to talk to you about this later tonight, but . . . this all came up so suddenly. I don't want you to . . . please don't . . . don't marry Bebe," Daniel blurted out.

Reuben threw back his head and laughed. To Daniel it sounded ominous. "Now, where in the hell did that come from?" Reuben's gaze was penetrating as he contemplated Daniel's worried face.

"It's the only thing left, Reuben. I won't ask you to promise me because I . . . I can't ask that of you. Just think before you leap, okay? Now, stand out of my way. I'm driving this car all the way to Harvard. . . . Gas! does it have gas? Where does the gas go?"

Reuben pointed to the cap on the side of the car. "You better get going. You've got a

lot to do in Cambridge before the term begins."

An unfamiliar mist covered Reuben's eyes as he watched the Daimler until it was beyond the studio gates.

"That's a fine thing you're doing for your friend," Al Sugar said quietly. "Illegal, but still a fine thing."

Reuben grinned. "Two bits says they never catch on."

"I made the credentials, so I ain't about to bet against you. I want a copy of his diploma when he graduates." The old man grinned.

"I do, too, and he'll be at the top of his class, you can take my word on that."

Al Sugar removed his greasy cap. "Mr. Tarz, if you say so, that's good enough for me. Pleasure doing business with you. I'll be taking the rest of the day off to catch up on my sleep."

"You earned it, Al. Take tomorrow off, too, if you want. With pay."

There was a quiet to the office building when Reuben walked in. His eyes searched out the lobby and then the stairs. At the top, staring down at him, was a man in a dark blue uniform. So they'd finally gotten around to Fairmont. He took a deep breath and scaled the steps two at a time. He shouldered his way past the man at the top and headed for Sol's office. He passed Margaret, who was sitting at her desk with a petrified look on

her face. Sol looked normal enough, he thought.

"Reuben Tarz, vice president in charge of production. Is there anything I can help you with?"

"The police are here about the Mavis Parks accident," Sol said in an amazingly normal voice.

"Murder, Mr. Rosen," the police officer said coolly.

"I know only what I read in the papers, Officer," Sol replied.

"I understand you were at the party, Mr. Tarz. Would you care to elaborate a little for us?"

Reuben shrugged. "Yes, I was at the party. I drove Mr. Rosen's son and daughter to the Sherwood. It was a bad night. I guess you could say I chaperoned them."

"What time did you leave the party, and who left with you?"

Reuben pretended to think. "Around seven or so. It wasn't our kind of party, if you know what I mean." He half grinned at the officer, but the man remained stone-faced.

"Did you carry liquor to the party?"

Reuben looked outraged. "Of course not! But I won't deny there was liquor when we arrived."

"That party's been described as an orgy. Would you care to confirm that?"

"That's pretty much my opinion, too, Of-

ficer. As I said, it wasn't our kind of party, so we left."

The officer addressed his next question to Sol. "Your daughter took a room at the hotel. Why?"

"I was there," Reuben cut in smoothly. "Miss Rosen wanted to take a bath and freshen up. We were on the road for almost twelve hours because of the fog. At one point, I believe she took a nap. Her brother was with her all the time, if that's important."

"It is," the officer said curtly. "I'd like to talk to both your son and daughter, Mr. Rosen."

"Sol," Reuben interjected smoothly, "why don't you call your house and have the housekeeper prepare lunch, and we'll all go out to the canyon. Call from here."

"Good idea, Tarz. I'm tired of eating this lunch wagon slop. While I'm doing that, bring a car around."

"We aren't finished with you yet, Mr. Tarz," the officer called after Reuben.

"I didn't think you were. You can talk to me all you want. My time is yours. Mr. Rosen told me to cooperate fully."

On his way out Reuben stopped by Margaret's desk. "Call Mr. Rosen's house and ask to speak to Bebe. Tell her we're on our way with the police and to warn Eli. Don't talk about this to anyone, Margaret."

Margaret looked offended. "Mr. Tarz, what

goes on in this office stays in this office. I'll take care of it."

Reuben did a double take when Bebe and Eli walked into the library. Eli's hair was washed and combed without the aid of pomade. He wore a loose-fitting white shirt speckled with paint. In his hand he carried a paintbrush and rag that he hastily shoved into his trouser pocket. Eli painted! Bebe looked demure and no more than fourteen years old. Her face was scrubbed clean and devoid of makeup. Even the varnish she liked to wear was missing from her nails. Her dress was cornflower blue with a ruffle that started at the shoulder and ran to her waist. He wondered where she'd dug it up, but it served the purpose of making her look young and vulnerable.

"I made lunch, Daddy. Sandwiches and salad, is that all right? There wasn't much time to prepare," she said breathlessly. A performance worthy of Clovis Ames, Reuben marveled.

They all heaved a sigh of relief when the police left thirty minutes later.

"How'd we do, Tarz?" Sol asked.

"For now we did all right. They'll be back as other people start to talk and remember."

"That's a relief," Bebe drawled. "Lunch is on the terrace. We are going to have lunch, aren't we? I really did make it myself!"

Reuben raised his eyebrows in disbelief.

"I can make sandwiches and salad," Bebe said defensively. "Eli darling, you'll have to move your easel since there will be four of us out there."

Reuben followed them out onto the terrace. It was beautiful, with wicker furniture and masses of flowering plants. The lawn beyond was perfectly manicured. Someday . . . someday *soon* I'll own something just like this . . . maybe even better, he said to himself. He could almost taste it.

"I didn't know you were a painter, Eli," he said, more to make conversation than anything else.

"I'm not very good," Eli mumbled.

Reuben walked around to look at Eli's work, and his eyes widened in shock. Eli's painting was a seascape full of huge, angry, overbearing waves lashing out at a slim coastline. Angry dark clouds seemed to meet with the swirling sea at the top of the painting. It was beautiful. "I think you might be wrong on that score, Eli," he said. "I'm the first to admit that I don't know much about painting, but if you ever want to sell this, I'd like to buy it."

Eli stared at him suspiciously to see if he was making fun. Then, satisfied that he wasn't, he mumbled something about painting only for his own enjoyment.

Sol grumbled something that sounded like "free-loader" and bit into his sandwich.

"You should have brought Daniel, Reuben," Bebe said. "I really want to see more of him."

Reuben smiled. "That will be a little difficult. Daniel left this morning for Harvard Law School. Three years," he added proudly.

"Harvard don't let Jews in," Sol said with his mouth full.

"Of course they do. And Daniel isn't Jewish," Reuben said quietly.

"He didn't even say good-bye," Bebe said, pouting.

"I'm sure he'll write."

Reuben had finished only half his sandwich and was just starting on his salad when Sol announced that it was time to get back to the studio.

"Bebe, I've been invited to the opening of Café Arevire on Saturday. Would you like to accompany me?" Reuben asked, surprising himself with the unexpectedness of the invitation. Jesus, why had he asked her? He hadn't meant to. Daniel's last warning flashed through his mind.

Bebe's eyes lit up. Everyone was talking about the elegant new bistro. Then she looked at her father uncertainly. "Daddy said I can't leave the house. Can I go, Daddy?"

"How did *you* get invited?" Sol asked suspiciously.

Reuben shrugged. "I have no idea. I don't even know the owner." He didn't explain that he was doing Max a favor by checking out

the competition. "Look, I understand about Bebe, so there's no problem. I wouldn't have asked if I'd known you —"

"No, she can go. It won't hurt to be seen at that kind of affair. It's a hell of a lot better than that orgy."

"Good. I'll pick you up at seven, then, Bebe. Dinner is at eight." Then, with a hint of the old Reuben Bebe remembered from France, he added, "And if you aren't ready when I get here, I'll leave without you."

"I know you will." Bebe grinned. "I'll be ready. I'll even greet you at the end of the driveway, so you don't have to come all the way up here and turn around."

Reuben laughed. "That won't be necessary. The invitation said black tie, so . . ."

"I know what it means." Bebe smiled playfully. "Do you?"

"Good-bye, Bebe."

The police visited the studio three more times, asking for other pertinent details. To Reuben's relief, Daniel was never mentioned. He congratulated himself on managing Daniel's "appointment" to Harvard, which got him out of town quickly. Daniel had to stay clean and above reproach, to lead an unsullied life. Three years from now, when he graduated with honors, his roundabout entrance to the prestigious law school would prove justified.

"I think the police are satisfied with my story," Reuben confided to Sol after the authorities' third visit. "No one seems to be contradicting anything I've said. I don't mind telling you, Sol, that I'm having a hard time with all of this. Even if he is a slimy character, Dickie deserves better than the roasting he's getting."

"What you're saying without saying it, is Dickie didn't kill the woman and Eli did," Sol growled.

"Dickie's done for, Sol. You might as well say his life is over, at least in this town. Your son, on the other hand, is a free man."

"It's not necessary to remind me of your part in all of this. I understand all too well." Sol's eyes grew hard. "If . . . any additional evidence comes out, you'll be as guilty as the man who killed that woman. You withheld evidence. Conspiracy. Aiding and abetting for the betterment of your career."

Reuben's jaw tightened. "And what does that make you? In my book, you're just as guilty as me. I think we should lay it all to rest . . . for now. I know I can ignore my conscience and hope you can do the same."

"You seem to have more experience in matters like this than I do. You better hope some wise guy doesn't recheck the figures somewhere down the line and come up with the right answer."

"That sounds like a threat," Reuben said

coldly. "Why don't you just spell it out for me, Sol."

Sol could feel his blood start to boil. Tarz was a cocky son of a bitch, and he'd like nothing more than to bring him down a peg or two — but not at his own expense. Still, he couldn't let the man bulldoze him all the time. "You got moxie, Tarz. You walk in here with a letter of introduction a couple of months ago, and today you've vice president in charge of production. Someday someone is going to wonder how you got that little promotion."

Reuben smiled grimly. "And of course you'll tell them it was given to me on merit, won't you? After all," he said smoothly, "there is Dolly Darling's success, and Red Ruby is making so much money we can't count it fast enough. The Sugar and Spice reels are grossing astronomical receipts. I snared two of the finest directors in Hollywood for this studio. Jack Evers is considering switching over to Fairmont. If we play our cards right, we can team him with Lester Kramer. And let's not forget the real joker here, Max and his distribution. Without him we'd be down the toilet, and you know it. I took this studio out of the gutter, and in another year you'll be one of the big five. What more do you want?" Reuben slammed his fist on the desk. "I don't owe you or this studio a damn thing, Sol. In fact . . . you owe me."

"No call to get snotty," Sol said, backing down. "We're just having a friendly little discussion. It happens all the time in this business."

"Really! Then mark this down in your appointment book: this is the last discussion of this type that you and I will ever have."

Sol was determined to have the last word. "Don't step out of line and there won't be any more discussions." Before Reuben could reply, he turned on his heel and shuffled back to his office. Behind his desk, on his comfortable chair, he took huge, gulping breaths. He hated confrontations with Tarz because he never came out on top. The son of a bitch would never step out of line. On the line maybe, but he wouldn't cross over. Even though he had had the last word, it was an empty, meaningless victory. He knew it and so did Tarz.

Sol reached for one of his foul-smelling cigars. One of these days he was going to upgrade his tobacco to real Havana. He puffed contentedly. Every business had a bottom line, and Fairmont's now showed black instead of red. Only a fool would quibble with that.

At three in the afternoon Bebe started to prepare for her second date with Reuben. First, she soaked in a scented bath for over an hour, luxuriating in the warmth. If she

was very careful, and if she didn't make any mistakes, maybe Reuben would ask her out again. She'd spent the entire morning writing little notes to herself: Do this, don't do that, remember to do this, forget about doing that, smile, show teeth, smile like a madonna, smile, always smile. Be winsome when the evening called for winsomeness. Don't drink, don't even think about taking a drink. Nibble, do not chew noisily, do not, do not, do not. There were more do-nots than dos. She read the newspaper from front to back, skimming over the lurid details of Dickie Hastings's party in San Francisco.

By four-thirty, her hair was washed, dried, and crimped to perfection. She spent another hour applying makeup that wouldn't look like makeup. When it came time to choose her dress for the evening, she remembered Mickey's advice. Less is more, *chérie*. Simple but well cut. She'd follow Mickey's advice. She had one dress designed by Cristóbal Balenciaga that she kept going back to as she searched through her closet. The soft scarlet material felt sinful, but then, so did she. A narrow satin headband with a cluster of tiny feathers clipped to a small diamond pin was to be worn around the middle of her forehead. She put it on carefully so as not to disturb her crimped hair, then stood back to admire her reflection. "You are gorgeous,

Bebe Rosen," she crooned. "Now for the dress."

On the scented hanger it appeared sacklike, but once she had it on, it clung to her body. She had a bad moment when she couldn't make up her mind if she should wear jewelry or silver shoes. Again Mickey's words echoed in her ears. Jewels must be worn carefully. If in doubt, go without. In the end she settled on a pair of silver shoes that were mere straps. She practiced walking up and down the room, her eyes riveted to her full-length mirror.

The feathery soft fringe that caressed her knees as she walked up and down sent her into excited peals of laughter. "This time, Reuben Tarz, you are just going to eat your heart out, you really are. And when your heart is half gone, I will eat the other half and you will be mine. All mine!"

"Dressed to the nines, I see," Eli said grouchily from the doorway.

"Do I look beautiful, Eli? Do I smell scandalous? Will I knock them dead? . . . Say something!"

"Except for Frisco, I've never seen you look better. And yes, as usual, you will wow them all, but I think all of this is wasted on Tarz." He grinned at her crestfallen expression. "Have a good time, Bebe. When you get home, come and tell me about the opening, okay?"

Bebe was as good as her word. She was sitting on a velvet-covered settee in the foyer when Reuben arrived. "See, I'm ready," she said coyly.

"I see," Reuben commented. "We should be on our way, then."

Bebe's spirits sagged. Not one word about how she looked. Panic surged through her. Maybe the dress was all wrong. Maybe the shoes were too sinful or the headband too theatrical. . . .

"My God!" Sol exclaimed, lumbering into the foyer. "Darling girl, you look like royalty!"

Bebe beamed. "Oh, Daddy, thank you for saying that. Do I really look all right?"

"You'll stop them in their tracks, sweetheart. She's a real knockout, isn't she, Tarz?"

"A real knockout," Reuben agreed. Truth to tell, he hadn't been prepared for just how much of a knockout she would be. His throat felt paralyzed, and all he could do was mutter a few words at a time.

"You look very dashing, Reuben. Handsome and dashing," she said sincerely.

"Wardrobe," Reuben muttered. Bebe leaned against him, brushing her hands along his sleeve.

"Tarz . . . it wouldn't hurt if you did a little business at this opening. It's done all the time. If you get the chance," Sol added hastily. Reuben nodded, his hand on the doorknob.

Outside in the cool evening, he drew a needed breath of fresh air. He should be talking to Bebe, saying something, something gentlemanly, something girls wanted to hear. But what, he wondered desperately. "You're going to kill yourself in those shoes," he blurted out.

Bebe burst out laughing, a sound that almost warmed him. "I practiced all afternoon. If I fall, you'll catch me, won't you?"

"Knowing you, you'll probably drag me down with you." Stupid! he thought wildly. Stupid conversation . . . "Sorry, Bebe. I didn't mean to say that. I'm a little tense about this opening," he lied.

"Good manners are all that count. I read the paper today, so I think I can carry on a conversation about world events."

Reuben looked down to see if she was serious or making fun of him. When he realized she was serious, he laughed out loud. "Somehow I don't think either one of us will be called on to discuss the latest international crises." He laughed again as he held the door for her, and tried not to look at her silken legs and thighs as the scarlet dress slid up over her knees.

"I'm trying, Reuben, I really am. I don't want you to be ashamed of me or sorry you asked me. We always seem to get off on the wrong foot, from the first time we met in France. I'm willing to put . . . *all* of that

behind us and start over. I never . . . I would never . . . if you're worried that I might reveal . . . It's past, Reuben. What happened that night shouldn't have happened. You did what you did; I did what I did. We're both sorry, at least I am. Can we just be friends and start over?"

"I've wanted to talk to you about . . . about that night. I really would like to . . . to make amends, if that's at all possible."

"You have, by asking me to be by your side for this party. The past is over and I want to forget it." Impulsively, she held out her hand. Reuben clasped it for a moment, then — his eyes holding hers — brought it to his lips.

"Friends," he whispered.

"Friends," Bebe agreed. Joy spread through her at that moment, blinding her to the cold calculation brewing behind Reuben's smiling eyes.

The inhabitants of Hollywood consisted of those who had reached the top and those who had not. At no time could this be seen more clearly than on an opening night.

Reuben and Bebe glittered down the runway of the new bistro, which was flanked by barriers and hordes of excited observers lining up to catch a glimpse of anyone walking down the brightly lit runway.

"Now, this is what I call an opening," Bebe said as liveried footmen bearing torches

walked up and down the long runway, guiding the guests into the club. The interior shimmered with candlelight and the happy faces of the specially invited guests. More men in livery escorted each couple to their assigned table.

Reuben and Bebe were seated at a table for two in full view of the dance floor, and two waiters introduced themselves as their servants for the evening. Bebe looked at Reuben, delight radiating from her face. She had been dreaming of this moment for so long. He was so handsome she felt she would scream her happiness or burst with pride. And tonight she had him all to herself. She ordered herself not to gush over him and decided to keep the evening light.

"I'm so glad you invited me, Reuben. I've always dreamed of attending one of these openings and this man Assaro's wonderful, if you believe what's written in the papers. He already has a successful club in New York City and they say he has two in Europe. One in Spain and one on the Italian Riviera. Smile, Reuben, our host is waving at us. I recognize his face from the *Gazette*." Bebe smiled at the suave and pampered-looking man walking sinuously toward them.

"Darlings, how nice of you to join me this evening," Ramone Assaro said grandly. His face was as shiny and red as an autumn apple. His teeth gleamed at them in a liquid smile.

"Mr. Tarz, I've heard a lot about you of late. Perhaps one day we can do business together . . . if the price is right."

"I'm sure that can be arranged. . . ." Reuben smiled and shook the man's hand. "This place has to be seen to be believed. Congratulations!"

Assaro raised his eyebrows. "They were right, you are gallant." He smiled devilishly. "I'll remember what you said. Lunch next week? Thursday at say . . . noonish? I'll call you."

Thunderstruck, all Reuben could do was smile knowingly and nod. The man's eyebrows were painted on, and there was a hint of color on his lips. Wait until he told Max about the competition. When Bebe jerked at his arm, he suddenly remembered his manners and introduced her.

"How . . . sweet you look," Assaro purred. "Where are your pigtails, darling?"

"Home in my drawer." Bebe smiled innocently.

Assaro's face rearranged itself. "Meow. You'll do, darling."

"He's a cat," Bebe snorted the moment they were out of earshot.

Reuben tried not to smile. "Now, now, we're his guests, so let's be nice. You are going to behave, aren't you?"

"Of course I am. I won't embarrass you, if that's what you mean." She huffed. "Lunch

. . . noonish . . . I'll call you . . . And what does he mean, 'do business with you'? . . . I think I *know* what he means, but —"

"That's none of your business, and it's not what you think," Reuben said gently. "Let's just enjoy the evening, shall we?"

"Well, for heaven's sake, Reuben, you must admit his lip color is pretty vibrant . . . everyone knows he's a flaming —"

"For God's sake, lower your voice. Where did you hear that?"

"From my father, who got it from some of the men he — I can't believe you'd have anything to do with those big eyes and rouged cheeks. Sweet, my foot," Bebe snarled.

Reuben tried changing the subject. "There must be at least two hundred people here," he said, his eyes scouring the room.

For the next two hours Bebe and Reuben were approached by directors and producers, actors and actresses, from all the major studios and from Fairmont. Not a moment passed without someone either waving in their direction or stopping at the cozy table. At one point champagne was brought over, compliments of Paramount.

"Sometimes it's embarrassing to wave or greet someone you don't really know," Reuben blurted out after their waiter had placed pheasant under glass for two in front of them. "I recognize their faces, but I really don't know too many of these people personally."

"That's all right," Bebe reassured him. "It's obvious they know you. You wouldn't have been invited otherwise. They're all watching you, or me in this red dress. Our party started the ball rolling, and now . . . just smile, like you're enjoying things. Don't you understand, it's all a game. You're becoming well known in this town. My father used to be invited to occasions like this all the time; then the invitations stopped, he refused to conform, it's that simple. I guess it's your turn. Just don't give them what they think they want."

"What's that?" Reuben asked, puzzled.

"Any indication that you're going to get the jump on them. It's too early yet to do that. I told you, it's a game," Bebe said quietly. "One by one they'll all come around to you. You were invited here for a reason, Reuben. Just relax and enjoy the limelight."

Reuben looked at her long and hard, studying her as she smiled and waved to people and spoke to them with a smooth social ease. She was born and bred for this, he mused.

"Eyes are boring into your back," Bebe whispered.

"I know." Reuben chuckled; he was beginning to enjoy himself.

Zukor and De Mille were next, asking him and Bebe to join them for dinner. "We'd love to, but we have another engagement."

"You're leaving!" Zukor said in surprise.

"What could be more important than this

opening?" De Mille asked, abashed.

Reuben just smiled and raised his champagne glass to them. He was still smiling when Bebe kicked him.

"What do you mean, we're leaving? We just got here and we've just been served . . . I'm hungry. When you take a girl out you're supposed to feed her."

"All right, we'll stay just a few more minutes, until dinner is over. But remember — always leave them wanting more. After we're gone they'll have something to talk about. Not that you need to know, but I'll tell you anyway: I won't be lunching with Assaro, at least not this week. Feel better?"

"He'll eat you alive. Look, there's the guy he's been known to hang around with. Eli knows him. In fact, I think Eli gets most of . . . of his merchandise from him. Russell Stark. He's a married man," Bebe concluded virtuously.

Reuben grinned and shook his head. "Let's say good night to our host. Do you see him?"

"Who could fail to miss those teeth? Real teeth can't ever be that white," she said.

All in all, Reuben thought, it was an interesting evening. He'd even enjoyed Bebe's company and her sour comments on the host. He'd gotten some insight from her, too. Maybe the boss's daughter could be helpful to him in more ways than he thought. She was just as radiant and socially adept as she'd

been at Fairmont's party. Only tonight she didn't have all those birds to contend with. He laughed to himself at the memory as Ramone Assaro rushed up to them.

"But darlings, you *can't* leave! You'll miss my grand entertainment. Duke Ellington" — Assaro smiled — "has promised to give us an evening we won't forget. You can't leave," he said coolly. "No one ever leaves my clubs before the wee hours of the morning."

Reuben smiled his most charming smile. "Being first at something carries its own rewards. Thank you for inviting us. I'll look forward to lunch."

"Good night," Bebe said sweetly, so sweetly Reuben wanted to laugh.

They left then, ushered out by the same liveried footmen in their red and white outfits. They didn't see Assaro's jaw drop or his worried glances as he searched out the other men of prominence in the room. The last thing he needed was to have a gorgeous man start a new trend by leaving early.

It wasn't quite midnight when Reuben swung the studio car alongside the Rosen front entrance. It looked pretty at night, with the moonlight bathing everything in a silvery glow. He knew there would be dew on the grass because the crickets were chirping and chattering, the sound coming from the gardens in back of the house. The mansion was

ablaze with light, and he couldn't help wondering which rooms Eli and Sol were in, or if they were still awake. He felt it a blatant waste of money to burn so many lights.

"Oh, look, Reuben, a shooting star!" Bebe whispered. Reuben looked upward to the star-filled sky and smiled. He'd seen it, too.

"Now we have to make a wish, each one of us," Bebe said in a hushed voice. "Shooting-star wishes always come true. My mother told me that when I was a little girl. Close your eyes tight and wish." Bebe closed her own eyes and wished . . . for Reuben to love her as much as she loved him. She risked a glance at him from under her thick lashes. His eyes were closed and he wore a fierce look.

Mickey . . . please respond to my letters and reassure me of your love. Reuben felt silly but hopeful . . . and if she didn't . . . Bebe would assure him a new place in paradise.

"I'll tell you my wish if you tell me yours," Bebe urged.

"If I tell you my wish, it won't come true," Reuben said.

"Are you going to kiss me good night?" she asked plaintively.

"I hadn't thought much about it," Reuben said. It was a lie: he'd been thinking of nothing else on the ride home. Thinking about how soft her lips were, how her arms would feel around his neck, how sweet she smelled. How she was the boss's daughter, and what-

ever Sol owned would eventually belong to Bebe.

"You better make up your mind pretty quick, Reuben, because I'm going into the house. There really aren't any rules, you know . . . about kissing, I mean. Girls kind of expect it, men want to but aren't sure if they'll get slapped. I expect it and won't slap you." She looked up at him, wide-eyed and expectant. "Well?"

Reuben got out of the car and opened the door for her. "When I want to kiss you, or anyone else for that matter, it will be because I want to, not because it's expected."

"Oh, poo. Stop being so starchy and stiff. You don't have to kiss me. I'll continue to live if you don't, so don't go thinking it's an earth-shattering decision. I had a very nice time this evening. I think I did, anyway. I still don't understand why we had to leave just when the evening was starting to warm up. I think it was —"

"Don't think, Bebe. I know what I'm doing. Ah . . . it was nice of you to go with me. Maybe next time we'll stay longer."

Bebe's sagging spirits lifted. He'd said next time. That had to mean he was going to ask her out again. She was going to have to learn patience.

"Good night, Reuben. Sleep well."

Before he could turn, she reached up and brushed her lips softly against his. Before he

could draw back, she was gone.

In the car driving back to his apartment, all kinds of doubts skittered through Reuben's head. She was so young, so beautiful . . . charming, actually. He'd enjoyed her company and knew he would have kissed her if she hadn't asked him so bluntly. She'd wanted him to kiss her. And then that silly business with the wish. What had she wished for? He'd give up a good deal to know. What would she have done if he'd told her what he wished for? She would have clawed his eyes out. The thought amused him, and he smiled. The smile was still with him when he let himself into the quiet apartment.

In the darkness of his room, with only the moon sifting through the curtains, he finally relaxed. He was moving now, upward. If he could keep up his momentum, he would make it to the top. In the stillness of his room, he analyzed his assets. Youth and his own brand of maturity, his ability to keep a poker face in business dealings, his moxie, as Sol called it. His ability to be ruthless would be his strongest point. If he wanted to survive in this business, he would have to nurture that particular trait. Then and there, he made up his mind that he would be ruthless up front and try to be fair behind the scenes. He couldn't ask more of himself.

Sleep reached out to Reuben then, soft and warm, welcoming him to that peaceful place

where all worries and doubts seemed to fall away. In time he dreamed, images following one after the other. Mickey walking hand in hand with him, dropping his hand, running from him. Mickey offering him a glass of wine and then taking it back, running from him. Mickey holding out her arms to him and then turning to run away. Always he stood rooted to the ground, a disbelieving look on his face. His feet wouldn't move. He was stuck in something . . . his own inadequacy. "Mickey, Mickey," he muttered in his sleep. "Don't you care? Can't you see that you've broken my heart? Mickey, please, come back."

In the morning he wouldn't remember the dream. It was too painful.

"It's not that late, Bebe," Eli coaxed. "As soon as I heard the car I went downstairs and fixed us some cocoa."

Bebe let herself be drawn into Eli's austere bedroom. At night, with the lamps lit, it didn't seem so cold and unfriendly.

"I had a good time," she offered, kicking off her shoes. She curled up on Eli's pillows like a cat snuggling for warmth by the fire.

"Who was there? What did they have to eat? I know I can read about it tomorrow, but hearing it from you will be better."

"It looked like a movie set, that's how perfect it was. There were hundreds of roses, all over the place, in vases, in baskets, deco-

rating the tables in clumps. They were kind of nestled in some kind of waxy, green leaves. The tables were covered in snow-white satin to complement the roses. All the dishes were crystal and silver. It was almost blinding. We didn't eat much, though."

Eli squirmed, inching closer to Bebe. "Why?"

"They started to serve us, and we were leaving. Reuben wanted to leave, so I had to leave, too, but the food we sampled was scrumptious. It must have cost a fortune and taken days to prepare. Lobster, caviar, duckling, pheasant under glass, and lots of French wine. And before you can ask me, yes, there was liquor, and no, I don't know where it came from. One of your . . . business associates was there, Russell Stark.

"Who else was there?"

"Everyone, Eli, just everyone. Over two hundred people. All the bigshots, little shots, too." She giggled. "But if you mean who was there from Fairmont, I can tell you we were well represented. Clovis Ames and a lot of the newer stars that signed on while I was abroad. All the bigwigs were there — Goldwyn, Selznick, Mayer, De Mille, Zanuck, just everybody. Clovis was with Lester and Damian. Reuben spoke to some of the bigwigs, they sort of introduced themselves. You should have seen him, Eli. He looked so . . . professional, so . . . important and powerful

. . . it sort of oozes out of him. Ramone couldn't take his eyes off him, and some of the women there were positively smoldering when they looked at him. I felt very flattered to be with him. Then we left," she finished flatly.

They were curled up together on the bed, brother and sister, their arms entwined at the elbow.

"But why? It sounds like it was just starting to liven up. Doesn't make sense," Eli grumbled. He didn't want the night to be over, he wanted to keep Bebe to himself, to savor the closeness they'd lost.

"Ramone did his best to coax him to stay. This young black man named Duke Ellington was scheduled to entertain. It was . . . heavenly. I just relaxed and enjoyed being with Reuben. It wasn't anything like that disgusting party in Frisco."

"What time did you leave? It's only a little after midnight now."

"Around eleven-fifteen."

"Did he kiss you good night?" Eli asked sourly.

"No, he did not. He put me in my place, but I took it with good grace. I think he'll ask me to go out again. I had such a wonderful time." Bebe snuggled deeper into the crook of her brother's arm. "We saw a shooting star and made a wish. Reuben wouldn't tell me what he wished. If mine comes true, I'll tell

you, but only if it comes true."

Heads together, one dark, one fair, they slept.

CHAPTER
TWENTY-EIGHT

Outside Château Fonsard a steady rhythmic rain was falling, a much-needed rain that made no sound. Rabbits scuttled to their warrens, squirrels to the leafy trees, and birds to their nests, where they tucked their heads under their wings to stave off the wetness.

Inside Château Fonsard, in the newly decorated nursery, the only sound was the raspy breathing of Reuben Tarz's son, who was fighting for his tiny life with every tortured breath. Silent prayers were being offered up by Mickey Fonsard, who sat on a rocking chair next to the sick infant.

Standing in the doorway was the village doctor and Yvette, Philippe's godmother.

"I am exhausted with this vigil, and you, Yvette, look like the walking dead," said the doctor. "How does Madame Fonsard do it? She hasn't eaten or slept in over a week. I have seen patients on their deathbeds who look better. If the child does not —"

"Do not even think such thoughts, Doc-

tor," Yvette whispered. "He will recover, he must, otherwise Michelene will lie down and die. You're sure you've done everything? You've overlooked nothing? Some small method that perhaps escaped you?"

"There is nothing. Do you think I like seeing this little one fighting for his life? If I had a magic potion, I would have used it long ago. The child is in God's hands at the moment. Go home, Yvette, I will stay awhile longer. Eat and try and get some rest. You'll be no good to Madame if you get sick."

"I know what you say is true, but how can I leave my friend when things are so . . . It's been a week, Doctor, and there's been no change. His fever should have broken by now. Why is God doing this to them? Mickey is the kindest, the most gentle, generous person to walk the earth, and this little innocent, what has he done to deserve this terrible thing? I simply do not understand," Yvette said fretfully.

"I have no answers for you. Please, go home to your husband, he needs you, too."

Yvette wiped at her eyes. "And little Jake, what of him? Should I take him home, too?" At the sound of his name, the dog looked up, his tail thumping slightly on the floor. For the past week he'd stood sentinel at the door of Philippe's room. From time to time he'd get up, stretch his thick body, and meander from room to room seeking out those scents

of Daniel that still remained; but always he returned to his position at the door.

"No, leave him. I think Madame gets a measure of comfort from him."

Yvette nodded and left. The doctor settled himself on a straightback chair he'd carried to the room from the kitchen. It wouldn't do for him to get comfortable, for he might fall asleep. Again he marveled at Madame Fonsard's stamina.

An hour later two things happened simultaneously. Jake left his position in the doorway to settle himself next to Madame's chair, and there was a soft knock on the kitchen door. Neither Mickey nor Jake stirred. The old doctor forced his weary body up from his chair and lumbered down the narrow staircase, knowing the person at the door was going to tell him he was needed elsewhere.

The doctor had one arm into his rain slicker when he opened the door. A small boy of ten or so, soaked to the skin, looked up at the doctor with fearful eyes. "My papa has had an accident, you must come."

"Yes, yes, hop into my car." He didn't look back. There was nothing more he could do here.

In the nursery above, Mickey's lips continued to move in silent prayer. At some point she'd noticed Jake lying by her side. One tired corner of her mind registered the fact that the dog had not entered the room since

659

Yvette had brought him. Her left hand dropped down to fondle the dog's ears. As soon as she'd finished her rosary, she started mechanically on another. Hail Mary full of grace . . . he's so little, so innocent . . . the Lord is . . . he shouldn't be paying for other people's sins . . . I wanted to send a cable to . . . With thee, blessed art thou . . . He could die . . . can die . . . and there is nothing . . . Among women and blessed . . . It is I who is being punished. . . . Why, why, what did I do that was so terrible? . . . Is the fruit of . . . Please, God, don't let him die. . . . Hail Mary full of grace . . .

Jake's ears shot up as he rose on his haunches. He looked around before he padded all about the room. When he was satisfied Mickey was asleep and that he was in charge, he moved closer to the baby's crib. His head dropped to his paws, but he didn't close his eyes. Something drove him to stay alert to the strange sounds coming from the sleeping child, sounds he'd heard all week now. His velvety ears shot up a second time when the rosary dropped from Mickey's hands, and he was on his feet in an instant, padding around the room again, his eyes alert, his ears straight up. When he returned to take his position near the crib, he waited a moment, listening to the harsh sounds coming from the crib. His tail swished once and then was still.

All through the night he watched the sleeping child, listening to the raspy breathing.

Dawn was creeping close when Jake rose to walk the perimeters of the room. His ears shot upward and he stopped, his head cocked in the direction of a sound so faint he had to strain to hear it. His tail grew still, his body turning rigid when he heard the unfamiliar sound. He was at the crib now, his paws on the wooden bar running across the slats. The baby was choking, strangling on the thick mucus in his throat. Jake turned and began to paw at Mickey, trying to wake her. He barked then, a deep rough growl, a plea for the sleeping woman to get up and tend to the strange noise. Mickey's head rolled to the side, and she muttered, "Hail Mary full of —" Jake barked again, this time louder, a desperate sound in the sickroom. He leapt onto Mickey's lap, he licked her face, and barked in her ear as he pawed and dug at her.

Mickey struggled to wakefulness as she felt the weight of the dog on her body. Shaking off the remnants of sleep, she pushed at him, her ears now as sharp as Jake's. Her sluggish movements turned feverish as she reached for Philippe and upended him, holding him by the ankles. "Spit it out," she ordered as she smacked the child's back again and again. The deadly mucus in the baby's lungs gushed out. Mickey cried out, and Jake whooped and

woofed, his tail swishing back and forth as he circled the now-screaming baby. Surely now he would be let out to pee, and perhaps a sugar treat was in the offing. Again he barked as Mickey cradled the wailing baby to her chest.

Her body trembling with fright, Mickey sank to her knees beside the crib. Wearily she watched as Jake lifted his leg uncertainly against the rung of the rocking chair. "Yes, yes, I know, it's time to go out, little Jake, but I do not have the energy to walk down those stairs to open the door. There will be no punishment. A hero deserves no punishment. Later, there will be treats when this angel sleeps. I think his fever is breaking now that the mucus has loosened. Whatever would I have done without you, my four-legged friend?"

When Yvette arrived after breakfast, she took in the scene at a glance. Immediately she ran to Mickey and brushed her face against the baby's forehead. Her eyes glowed with happiness but turned stern when she looked at the puddle.

"No, no, do not scold Jake," Mickey cried. "I fell asleep at my post, and he woke me when this angel started to choke. You must let him out for a run, and he deserves a treat. Perhaps two." She smiled happily. "And will you fetch a sugar bottle for Philippe with perhaps one little drop of brandy in it?"

Yvette was a whirlwind, shooing Jake out, but not before she gave him a treat. Bucket and mop in hand, she swabbed at Jake's error, a smile on her face. In seconds she had the crib stripped and placed fresh linen on the mattress. The moment the weary baby finished his sugar bottle, Mickey laid him on his stomach. How she loved this child of Reuben's! She'd come so close to losing him. "My life is yours, little one," she whispered.

"Enough already. It is time for your own bath, Michelene. You smell," Yvette said tartly. "I have turned down your bed, your bath is ready, and I will sit here. It is my turn now. You are so selfish with my godchild, I cannot bear it sometimes. Go, before I take a broom to you."

"Yes, my friend, I have no fight left in me," Mickey said meekly. "Thank you for everything."

"You are very welcome. My eyes will never leave this cherub."

An hour later, fresh from her bath and on her way to her room, Mickey peeked into the nursery. She smiled. Yvette had Philippe in her arms, rocking him steadily and crooning a soft lullaby. "How loved you are, Philippe," she whispered.

CHAPTER
TWENTY-NINE

In the months that followed, Reuben was inundated with invitations to every major as well as minor party Hollywood had to offer. As these affairs were generally more business than pleasure, he made it a point to appear at every function, even if it was only for five minutes, Bebe shining at his side.

Every minute of his day was taken up with meetings, negotiations, talks with bankers, and overseeing the tedious business of the studio lots. With each month the box office draw increased over 200 percent. He was meeting his bank loans ahead of schedule while he charmed and enticed actors and actresses away from other studios — to the outrage of the Hollywood "moguls," as the newspapers referred to the studio heads. Sol happily fielded each phone call of complaint, grinned at the stormy, expletive-riddled diatribes they subjected him to, and laughed aloud at the black line on each monthly financial ledger.

Fairmont was moving into the big time with what Reuben called "blockbuster" movies and "hot property" actors and actresses. His instinct was to allow Farrell and Kramer full rein with Red Ruby which was topping all box office receipts while the public clamored for more. If those two successes weren't enough to push him to the top, the promotion package he worked on for Diego Diaz did. Women clamored for the Latin lover, storming the gates of Fairmont so that extra security guards had to be employed. He watched from his office windows when the first mob of fans threatened to break down the gates. "We just want to see him in the flesh, to touch him, to breathe the same air!" they screamed.

The entire front page of the *Los Angeles Examiner* was dedicated to Diego the day after the threatened break-in. Pictures of hysterical, screaming fans demanding to see the star covered pages one, two, and three. The headline read LATIN LOVER TAKES AMERICAN WOMEN BY STORM. WE WANT MORE! THEY SCREAMED. Reuben and Sol laughed all the way to the bank.

By the new year, the media was calling Reuben Tarz the Golden Boy, the Wonder Boy of Hollywood. Reuben started to look for a house in Laurel Canyon at the end of January when his picture appeared on the front pages of *The Saturday Evening Post, Knicker-*

bocker Magazine, Harper's New Monthly and *Harper's,* and *Scribner's Magazine.* Not to be outdone, *Reader's Digest* ran an article on him with quotes from Sol and the directors at Fairmont. Reuben was pleased with the flattery and the genuine kind things that were said about him. Like a miser surrounded by gold, he hugged his success to his breast, and only late at night in his room did he lament the sad truth: he had no one with whom to share any of the good things that were happening to him. Bebe . . . Bebe was still a meddling child to him, decorative . . . and useful.

On the first day of February a second murder occurred, this one in Hollywood. The front-page headlines announced the death of director William Desmond Taylor. It was a double blow to Paramount studios, which still had its hands full with the Hastings scandal. The *Los Angeles Examiner,* which had been kind to Reuben and Fairmont, attacked Paramount with a vengeance. Reuben followed the account of how Mabel Normand had rushed to the apartment on Alvarado Street to retrieve a bundle of her correspondence. Charles Taylor rushed to the same apartment to get rid of all the illegal liquor, while Adolph Zukor sneaked in to clean up any traces of sexual hanky-panky. Reuben read on about how the police uncovered a cache of pornographic photographs hidden in Desmond's bottom drawer, which meant

Zukor and Taylor were unable to finish their housecleaning. Mary Pickford was questioned and reported that she knew nothing and would pray for Taylor's soul, and would the police please return her photograph. Reuben laughed outright when he read that a letter was found between the pages of *White Stains*, a book of erotica by Aleister Crowley. The scented page was monogrammed with the initials *M.M.M.* — Mary Miles Minter, Paramount's answer to Mary Pickford.

Reuben was keeping score. One down and four to go; Paramount was sure to crumble under this latest blow. Stars were falling by the wayside. Obviously another discussion with Sol was called for, along with another trip to the bank. With Paramount controlling five hundred of the choicest theaters across the country, it would behoove him to be ready to pick up what he could when the time was right. With Daniel gone, Margaret had worked days to compile the list for him. So now his hunch was going to pay off. But was it a hunch, or was it a death wish for the studio that was so large and powerful? Even now he could see the headline: WONDER BOY STRIKES AGAIN. Anyone else would have felt like a ghoul getting ready to pick at the flesh of the dead studio, but not Reuben — he simply petitioned Sol to send money anonymously to the Dickie Hastings Defense Fund.

It took all of three days to tarnish Mary Miles Minter's virginal image and destroy her promising career. The *Examiner* slashed words like *dope angle,* queer meeting places reputed to be dens where effeminate men and peculiarly masculine-looking women dressed in kimonos and lounged around using marijuana, opium, and morphine, all served from elegant tea carts.

The public, incensed at this betrayal by one of their idols, sought to topple another. Howling for vengeance, they now pointed an accusing finger at Mabel Normand, the darling of the Keystone Kops, when it was revealed that some of her appealing effervescence could be attributed to the use of cocaine.

One article stated that her "cokey" habit was singing to the tune of two thousand dollars a month. This, combined with a romantic connection with the murdered William Desmond Taylor, was enough for a bloodthirsty moviegoing public. Mabel soon retired from the screen. Reuben smiled; the irony of it, he realized, was that their misfortune was his good fortune.

Each day he scanned the papers, pointing out to Sol uncomplimentary press notices and denunciations ringing out from the pulpit. The Hollywood magnates didn't fear divine wrath but retaliation at the box office. Reuben kept Sol on course as they prepared to be first in line to pick up what they could

of the Paramount theater chain.

"It won't be long now. The professional puritans out there aren't going to let this alone," he told Sol.

Late in the day he received a call announcing a meeting at Universal to discuss moral rectitude. He and Sol left straight from the office, deep in conversation.

Louis B. Mayer called the chaotic meeting to order and in a breathless, fearful voice announced, "We need a watchdog for this business before we all get flushed down the toilet. I'd like to appoint Will H. Hays to the position. He's a member of President Harding's cabinet and chairman of the Republican National Committee. His salary, which some of you may think outrageous, is going to be earned, every penny of it. One hundred thousand a year." The members in the smoky room drew back in horror to stare at Mayer as if he'd suddenly sprouted a second head.

"For Christ's sake, Louie, Hays is postmaster general. Do you think overseeing the smut mail is enough to appoint him to this kind of job?" Sol bellowed. Reuben blinked at Sol's belligerence.

"Hell yes, Sol," Mayer shouted back. "I've checked this guy's background. He's a Presbyterian elder, a member of the Masons, the Knights of Pythias, Kiwanians, Rotarians, the Moose and Elks. This is the man who can give the Purity Leagues a run for their money.

We can send him to 'neutral' territory; I suggest New York. That's all I got to say. Let's all think about this and meet again tomorrow to take a vote."

A week later, news reporter Elinor Glyn stated that the founding fathers of filmdom had unanimously agreed to hire Will Hays as referee of Hollywood morals.

Within the month, Hays issued his first dictate: Films were to be purified, all screen immorality would be scissored. No more hungry kisses, no more carnality, no more improprieties of any kind, and God help anyone caught off screen doing something he wasn't supposed to be doing, because it would mean instant release from his studio — in other words, the ax.

Reuben had no illusions that the morals clause would get the industry to mend its ways. When word filtered down to him that a "doom book" was being compiled by a host of private detectives unleashed by Hays, he started to sweat. In the end, one hundred seventeen names appeared on the list — two of them starlets from Fairmont. Paramount's top box office draw headed the list, a superb actor named Wallace Reid. Zukor shouted long and hard that he would lose two million a year if he sacked Reid. "It's suicide!"

Reuben moved swiftly by applying to the banks holding the mortgages on two hundred and fifty choice theaters. However, he did

refuse to be a party to smearing Zukor. The next day, the *Graphic's* banner headline read HOLLYWOOD HOPHEADS! . . . and the article said Reid had been spirited away to a secluded private sanitarium.

"Where's the son of a bitch!" Adolph Zukor shouted the moment he hit the front door of Fairmont's executive offices.

"Which son of a bitch are you referring to?" Margaret asked smoothly, her eyebrows raised in questioning arches.

"That Tarz crud and that fat Jew Rosen. where the fuck are they?" Zukor screamed.

Reuben stood at his door. "I'm right here, and I believe Mr. Rosen is in the men's room. If you want to talk, we can talk. If you want to swear and curse and shout, you'll have to go somewhere else."

"You're a goddamn vulture, is what you are," Zukor hissed.

"I've been called worse. Sit down, Mr. Zukor."

"You pipsqueak. Just how the hell old are you, anyhow?"

"Old enough. What does age have to do with business?"

"Plenty. You're robbing me blind. I got troubles coming out my ass, and a pipsqueak's robbing me blind. What the fuck happened to decency?"

"Ask Will Hays. You can hardly blame Mr.

671

Rosen or myself for the . . . indiscretions of your staff."

"You were right there, weren't you? You couldn't wait. My fucking ashes aren't even cold yet."

Reuben leaned across his desk. "My . . . ah, sources tell me that the line to snap up your theaters is five deep. I just happened to get there first. Where did you ever get the idea there was loyalty in this business? One way or another we all feed off one another. If I didn't buy up your theaters, someone else would have, maybe one of your good friends, Mr. Zukor. I don't consider myself a good friend of yours. A business associate, yes; but that's all."

"Was this your idea, Sol?" Zukor pounced on the big man as he took a seat across from Reuben. "Kick a man when he's down, by Christ, that's the lowest thing going. Who is this crud to us?" He jerked his head in Reuben's direction. "Jesus, he ain't even dry behind the ears."

"He's dry enough to put the skids to you," Sol said. "If you can't control your studio, don't come crying to me. It wasn't my idea to hire Hays. I went along with the rest of you because something needed to be done, but Hays is so far out of line, it isn't funny. You guys hired him, so now you're stuck with him. If you want some advice, Adolph, look into *his* background. He was a politician and

672

he hangs out with politicians. Some dirt must have rubbed off on him."

Zukor snorted. "It's a little late for that, don't you think?"

"It's the best advice I can offer at the moment. Good luck, Adolph."

"Shove that luck up your fat ass, Sol," Zukor snarled. "And as for you, Tarz, I hope I'm around the day you get yours. And you will, you know. You get what you dish out." He slammed the door so hard on the way out, the paperweight slid across Reuben's desk.

Reuben turned to Sol with a boyish grin. "Mission accomplished, I'd say. And with this one out of the way, I think it's time to renegotiate my contract, Sol. With a handsome raise. Twenty-five thousand."

Sol frowned. "Are you nuts? You're making sixty grand now." Suddenly his jaw dropped. "You mean twenty-five thousand — a *month?*" Reuben smiled and nodded.

On April 10, fifteen months to the day of his arrival in Los Angeles, Reuben sent the balance of the money he owed to Michelene Fonsard. He put the money neatly in a folded blank piece of paper and slipped it into an envelope. No note, no tender words of love or gratitude this time. There was a bitter look in his eyes and an angry set to his jaw when he mailed the letter from the post office. He was going to give her exactly one month to

cable her response. If she didn't, he'd carve her out of his heart once and for all.

In May, one month later, Reuben asked Bebe Rosen to marry him. She accepted. The wedding ceremony was small and private, held at his new house in Laurel Canyon. His only guest was his secretary, Margaret. Bebe invited her father and brother. It was a late afternoon affair with candles of every size and shape lighted on the terrace where they took their vows. Love, honor, and obey. Till death do us part. Bebe had every intention of honoring it all.

Sol and Eli left at ten-thirty, offering congratulations for the dozenth time. Bebe smiled prettily and winked at Reuben. "I'll go upstairs and get ready." Reuben swallowed hard, hating the happy look on his new wife's face. The overpowering sickness in his stomach at the thought of sleeping with her astonished him.

No matter how hard he tried to get his thoughts in order about what should be considered a normal course of events, he failed miserably. One question kept insinuating itself into his mind: How could you make such a horrendous mistake — now, with all your plans and dreams at your fingertips. . . . Mickey! Mickey . . .

Perfumed and powdered, wearing a nightdress made especially for her, short notice

and all, by Balenciaga, Bebe paced the room nervously. This was what she'd wanted. This was what she'd wanted ever since she'd laid eyes on Reuben. He was hers now, all hers. Forever and ever.

At twelve o'clock her nervousness gave way to irritability. At two, irritability progressed to hostility, and by three-thirty hostility had intensified to a venomous anger. A marriage in name only. A way to lock the studio to him. Tears spilled from her eyes, hot and scalding.

At four o'clock she ripped off the virginal white lacy gown and tossed it in the hamper. Breasts heaving with frustrated rage, she threw on her old flannel robe and ran down the stairs. Her eyes spilled over a second time when she saw her husband sprawled out on the sofa, an empty whiskey bottle on the table. Her mind flashed to an image of him that was almost a duplicate of what her eyes were registering now. Reuben . . . the library at the château. She felt her skin begin to crawl.

"You bastard! You dirty rotten bastard! You'd rather sit down here and drink that rotgut than make love to me. This time it's our wedding night, Reuben! Do you hear me, our wedding night! I ought to kill you! I should have killed you that night in the barn. Damn you to hell!"

"Wha—" Reuben elbowed his way to a sitting position. He looked at Bebe in her ratty

robe, trying to comprehend what she was doing in his house, and then he remembered.

"You don't love me. You never loved me. Why did you marry me? Answer me, goddamn you! I want to know."

"I never said I loved you. I . . . asked you to marry me because . . . because . . . it seemed like the thing to do at the time. The tenth of April was my deadline. . . . I shouldn't have married you, Bebe. I'm sorry."

"You're *sorry!*" Bebe screeched. "I love you. You've known I've loved you since I first met you. What does the tenth of April have to do with anything! What deadline? You're a bastard, Reuben, a real fucking bastard!" Wildly she looked around for something to throw at him. Nothing was heavy enough . . . nothing sharp enough.

At the old familiar look on her face, Reuben became fully awake. "But you love this fucking bastard," he drawled, triumphant and guilty at the same time. With an immediate gut reaction, he realized that it was a nauseating combination.

Bebe's anger seemed to drain from her. "Yes, I do." She wept now, tears running freely down her grieving face.

"Don't, Bebe. Just don't love me." He turned his back to her and pretended he was asleep again. There was nothing more he could say.

Bebe climbed the stairs to the newly deco-

676

rated master bedroom she had dreamed of sharing with her husband. With a muffled sob she threw herself onto the bed and buried her head in the creamy satin-covered pillows. Her tears were bitter and savage. "Bastard!"

When the lacy soft lavender dawn crept up and out of the canyon, she was on the terrace, still dressed in her ratty robe. A stack of writing paper and a steaming cup of coffee awaited her on the table. On this, her first day as Mrs. Reuben Tarz, she was going to write to Mickey. Did Reuben think her a fool? Of course he did. With Mickey out of the way she could make Reuben love her. She always got what she wanted, sometimes it just took a while. Certainly she could wait this time; she had her whole life ahead of her.

The letter was short, sweet, and to the point.

Dearest Mickey,
I just had to write to you to tell you how very happy I am. Daddy wanted to send you a cable, but I told him I wanted to write you instead.

Reuben and I are married! Isn't that just the most wonderful news! We are so happy. Reuben just absolutely dotes on me. He can't seem to do enough for me. Everyone calls us the two love birds. He bills and I coo.

Reuben bought me this wonderful,

magnificent house here in Laurel Canyon and told me to turn it into a comfortable haven he can come home to. He said to decorate it as tastefully as your house. That's a compliment for you, dear Mickey.

My darling is doing so well at the studio. Daddy made him vice president in charge of production. He pretty much runs the studio — the tabloids call him the Wonder Boy of Hollywood! How often he says his success is because of you.

I hope this letter finds you in good health. Please give my regards to Yvette and Henri. Tell them of my marriage and how happy I am. Later, when things aren't so hectic I will write to them.

Much affection,
Bebe Tarz

When she'd finished she signed her name with all the appropriate flourishes and then read the letter over, smiling grimly as she fingered the shiny new plain gold wedding band on her ring finger.

CHAPTER THIRTY

The profusion of living color at the château was like a rainbow gone wild after Paree. Every spring flower was in full bloom, some of the heavier blooms bowing their heads as if in welcome. Mickey watched indulgently as fragrant cherry blossom petals settled around the toddling baby. He reached for them with plump fingers. "Watch," Mickey whispered to Yvette. "Watch what he does." The little boy sniffed a petal, looked at it, and then stuffed it into his mouth. Mickey rushed to remove it. "He is a handful. Yvette, isn't he the most gorgeous child you have ever seen?"

"So gorgeous I am envious that you have this beauty with you twenty-four hours a day. He is a sturdy little boy, his legs so straight. A long torso for one so small."

"Like his father," Mickey said quietly. "These past months he has grown more and more to look like his father. What do you think?"

"A miniature of him, Mickey. It must break

your heart."

Mickey ignored her friend's words. "One day he got up on his feet and the next thing he was walking, exploring, touching. He is the inquisitive one. I love him so."

"I see that," Yvette said. "Come, I had the house opened and aired. Everything is ready for you and this angel. I fetched your mail several days ago. There isn't much, but there are letters from America."

Mickey's heart pounded at Yvette's words. Her voice, though, was calm when she spoke. "I'll look at them later, when my sweetheart sleeps."

"I brought a present for the child," Yvette said shyly. "Henri made the blocks and I painted them. Is he too young, do you think?"

"Not at all," Mickey assured her friend. "He loves to play with anything that is brightly colored. His curiosity is amazing." Both women watched the little boy with the basket of blocks. "See, he will stack them, look at me for approval, and then topple them. He will do it over and over until he tires, an event that usually doesn't happen for a long time. The energy he has, *mon Dieu!*"

"Now that the angel is settled, tell me, have you written to Reuben?"

Mickey shook her head. "It is pointless. Why can't you see that? He is in America and I am here. He is young and I am getting old. You must understand, it is not meant to

be. I have accepted it; you must, too. If you can't, then you must share Henri with me."

"He's yours!" Yvette cried dramatically. "You say these words, but your eyes say something else, old friend."

"I try, Yvette. I will always love Reuben. I don't deny it to you, but, alas, my love wasn't strong enough for that spirited young man."

"Michelene," Yvette admonished her friend softly. "You should have written. Who can blame the young man? You are a worldly woman and wise in the ways of love. He is still a puppy. Your sad eyes break my heart."

"Then you must not look at me, or I will have to hide my eyes."

"That's not what I want." Yvette's frustration was growing by the second. Always when she had these conversations with Mickey, at the end her head would ache as her heart did. "I want you to write to Reuben. Now, tonight. I will come by tomorrow and post the letter for you. I want your promise, Michelene!"

"Pretty words on a page . . . phrases . . . Bah!"

"Your promise, Michelene," Yvette said mercilessly.

"Very well. Tonight when the baby sleeps I will write a letter. You have my promise."

"Very good. I am satisfied." Yvette smiled. "I always miss you when you to go Paris, Mickey. I will bring Henri by tomorrow to

see this gorgeous child. He will be delighted. Already he plans a red wagon. Who knows, by tomorrow it may be finished. . . . Mickey?"

"Yes?"

"Just say what is in your heart."

"That would take many pages. I will say the necessary things."

It was late, the moon riding high in the heavens, when Mickey finally settled Reuben's son in his bed. Of course he didn't understand a word she said, but she read him stories anyway, first in French and then in English. Eyes wide with curiosity and wonder, he sucked his thumb contentedly as he listened to her crooning voice. Usually he was asleep in ten minutes, but tonight it was less, probably because of the trip from Paris and his new surroundings.

Mickey sighed as she glanced about her. She needed a housekeeper, and she needed her soon. One day home and already she had a pile of laundry.

A cup of coffee in hand, Mickey settled herself on the rocking chair before the empty fireplace and sorted through the mail. There were four letters from America — two from Daniel, one from Reuben, and one from Bebe. Carefully she arranged them by the dates and opened Daniel's first, smiling as she refolded the pages and slipped them and the crisp American bills into their envelopes.

"I miss you, Daniel," she murmured.

Should she open Reuben's next or the letter from Bebe? Bebe's, of course. Reuben's she would save till last. Maybe she would be able to sleep tonight after all.

She was dry-eyed when she finished Bebe's lilting letter. A long time later she got out of the rocking chair awkwardly and leaned over the yawning fireplace. Her hands trembled as she laid the letters on the grate. They flamed instantly, sparks shooting upward, the green edges of the American money turning orange and then black.

She'd made a promise to Yvette, and her friend would never forgive her if there wasn't a letter for her to post. What would Yvette say when she noticed whom the letter was addressed to?

A note, that was all that was required. To both of them, of course.

My dear Bebe and Reuben,

Your wonderful news reached me just today. I have been traveling for some months now and just returned home.

I wish you both health and happiness in your new life. I will always remember our times together with affection and warmth.

My love to you both,
Michelene Fonsard

She rocked then, her feet planted firmly on

the floor, the chair going backward and then forward. This was what it was like when you were dead, she decided. A tear spilled from her eye. "Goodbye, my darling," she whispered.

When Yvette and Henri arrived the following morning with the red wagon in tow, Mickey was still in the rocking chair. Yvette took one look at her friend and then at the cold grate. Without a word she picked up the letter in Mickey's lap and saw that it was addressed to Mr. and Mrs. Reuben Tarz. *"Mon Dieu!"* she exploded. "I will not mail this . . . this thing!" Anger laced her strained voice. "Who is Mrs. Tarz?" she demanded.

"Mrs. Tarz," Mickey said, getting to her feet, "is Bebe. I must go to the child, he is crying for me."

"Do they want . . . the little one?" Yvette asked quietly.

Mickey took a deep breath. "They have said nothing about the child . . . thank God . . . nothing."

Yvette watched her old friend leave to tend her precious baby. The sound of the child's whimpering caught her ear. "And I will cry for you, too. It is a gift from the devil to have so much pride. What kind of people are we dealing with here?" she asked, her eyes directed toward the heavens. "Come, Henri, leave the damn wagon, we'll come back another day. We must mail this . . . this . . .

letter to Mr. and Mrs. Tarz. Maybe . . . maybe we won't mail it — I must think on the matter."

Little did Yvette know the old postmaster would bang his dated stamp on the envelope and near-sightedly throw it into the wrong mail sack where it stayed for almost a year, at which point he blessed himself and forwarded the letter to America.

Daniel Bishop's new home beckoned him invitingly. It was a comfortable double room with two desks, beds, and dressers. The two straggly green plants he'd added to the windowsills were thriving now with his care, bright green and healthy-looking — as healthy as he was these days, thanks to Reuben's generosity. With a critical eye, he inspected his side of the room, the neatly made bed, shoes lined up underneath, the dresser bare except for necessities, traveling kit, and his personal grooming supplies. His desk was full of neatly stacked books and pads of paper. Pencils were sharpened, their points sticking out of a cup. His closet held neatly pressed trousers and jackets, all stylish and fashionable, again thanks to Reuben.

The other side of the room, however, was a disaster. Daniel itched to take a broom to it, but he didn't. Gerald, better known as Rocky Rockefeller, had issued a statement the day he moved into the room: "I don't plan to

clean this room till the day I move out." Dust balls skittered to Daniel's side of the room. Clothes hung over the end of the bed, and sitting on Rocky's chair was a month's worth of dirty laundry.

"What we need is a maid," Rocky said boisterously, slamming the door behind him. "Or," he had said another time with a conspiratorial wink, "we could sneak a girl in here and have her do it. It'd be a real pleasure to put on an ironed shirt."

Daniel had had an answer to that statement. "Do it yourself, it builds character," he'd said.

"I picked up your mail, Daniel. It's on your desk. Must be allowance time," Rocky said good-naturedly. "I guess that means we can party this weekend."

Daniel laughed. "That means you party on my money and I stay here and study. How could you have spent all your allowance so quickly?"

Rocky tried to draw himself up to Daniel's full height but failed. "Women," he announced, leering, "are expensive. Listen, Daniel, I've been meaning to speak to you about something. Do you have any money stashed away — you know, a bundle of some kind? Don't look so panicky, I don't want to borrow it. When my father came to see me on Sunday he was talking about a commodities stock that's going to take off. You could

make a fortune, really rack up. My father is never wrong." Rocky's round face beamed.

"What does 'rack up' mean, exactly?" Daniel queried, liking the sound of Rocky's words.

"Hundreds, thousands, millions. Depends on what you go with."

"Jesus!"

"Yeah, but keep a lid on it. My old man sort of let it slip, if you know what I mean. I'm off to the library, but I need to change my socks. You got any clean ones? How about some underwear, mine's kind of gamey."

Daniel grinned and jerked his head in the direction of his dresser drawer, where stacks of underwear and socks, all formerly belonging to Rudolph Valentino, were folded neatly.

"I wish you'd get bigger underwear," Rocky grumbled as he struggled into a pair of shorts. "A guy could die of strangulation wearing these. See you later, and remember, zip up about what I told you."

When Rocky left, Daniel sighed with relief and reached for the top letter on his mail stack. It was from Reuben — he'd seen that much while Rocky was changing — and for once he could enjoy a visit from his friend in private. He ripped open the letter and scanned it for length. Reuben never said three words when one would do.

Suddenly his face filled with dismay. Frowning, he read the short letter a second and then a third time. When he returned it to the

envelope, he muttered, "Reuben, this is the biggest mistake of your life."

The pad of notepaper stared up at him. What should he say? What did Reuben expect him to say? Congratulations and good luck! Well, he was going to need some luck, of that Daniel was certain. When it came right down to it, there really wasn't much else to say when someone got married. With a sigh of resignation, he dipped his pen in the ink.

Dear Reuben,

I received your good news today. I have to admit it was a real surprise. I'm happy for you, and wish you the best of everything.

Everything is going great here. I'm keeping an A average and am pretty proud of myself. I have two invitations for Easter. Rocky asked me to go home with him, and Teddy Vanderbilt asked me, too. I don't want to hurt either one's feelings, so I think I'll stay here. Yes, I'm hanging out with what you call the big-money guys.

Speaking of big money, Rocky told me just minutes ago about a tip his father gave him on Sunday. If you invest heavily enough, you can make hundreds of thousands, even millions. Gather up all the cash you can get your hands on, and if you can talk Sol into mortgaging the

studio, do it. In one fell swoop you can clean up, pay off the bank for the theaters and have a fortune left over. That's the way these guys do it all the time. Surges in commodities don't last long, so keep your eye peeled. Will keep you advised on further developments. Details on separate paper.

Again, congratulations! Tell Bebe I'll write to her as soon as I can. Right now, I have to bone for an exam.

Thanks again for everything, Reuben.

Respectfully,
Daniel

The moment Reuben received Daniel's letter at the studio, he read it and then headed for Sol's office. Silently he showed him the letter and waited for him to digest the contents.

"Do you have the guts, Sol?" he said when the older man was through. "We can head for the bank right now if you do."

Dollar signs danced before Sol's eyes. "We're already in over our heads. What bank would be fool enough to loan us more?"

"I've learned something extremely valuable, and that is the more money you owe a bank, the more they'll lend you. Let's test the waters and see what we come up with."

It was fifteen minutes before noon when they walked into the bank. At four-thirty the

bank's president called Sol and approved the mortgage on the studio, promising to advance one million dollars at nine o'clock the following morning. Sol's face drained of color and he rushed to Reuben's office. "We got it, kid," he said. "One million at noon tomorrow. How . . . how much . . . what if . . ." The thought was so horrible, he couldn't finish.

Reuben smiled grimly.

"There are no what-if's. We stand to clear around seven, possibly eight and a half million. It goes without saying that I get half. Before you squawk, I'll take my half from the net, after we pay back the bank — which'll leave you maybe a million ahead of me. We can sign an agreement right now."

Sol reached for his pen; he'd hitched his wagon to Tarz, and it looked like the ride was just beginning.

"Bebe is going to love this. I'm glad she's your responsibility now, kid. That girl can spend money faster than you can make it. You better have your friend cut you in on a few more deals. You know I won't sleep a minute until this . . . until we have the money in our hands. For a young guy you have nerves of steel," Sol grumbled. "When I was your age I didn't have nerves, but I was a gambler. If we go belly-up, we lose it all, you know."

"We won't. No guarantees in this life, Sol, none at all. You either take a chance when

opportunity knocks or you slam the door. I can feel the money in my pocket." Reuben smiled. He was still smiling when he left the office, earlier than usual.

He didn't go home, even though he knew Bebe would have dinner waiting. Instead, he stopped at the Mimosa Club. "I have something to talk to you about, Max," he said quietly.

"In my office," Max said.

With the door closed behind him, Reuben told the little man about Daniel's tip. ". . . as much money as you can lay your hands on, Max. And when it's time to get out, you squirrel it all away."

"How come you're telling me all this? I thought you didn't . . . How come?" Max blustered.

"You gave me a job when I needed it, even if it was for just a little while. You're not a back stabber; you know how to keep your lip zipped, and you did me a favor that time with Jane. If you want the real reason, it's because I like your mother's noodle pudding. Besides, this squares us."

Max looked puzzled. "I thought we were square when you gave me the film distribution."

"No. We're square now. All the money you can get your hands on," Reuben repeated. "Be at the broker's first thing in the morning. Don't drag your feet on this one."

"Jesus, I'll wear skates if it'll make you happy. By the way, I heard about your marriage. This ain't none of my business, but you don't look like the marrying kind."

"We all have our weak moments," Reuben said sourly.

"Jesus, there's lots of free pussy out there, Tarz. Weak moments can cost you in the end. Sorry, sorry," Max apologized at the look on Reuben's face, "this is none of my business. You want something to eat or drink? I can have it brought here to the office."

"No, I think I'm going to take a walk, a long walk."

Max watched Reuben from the window. He knew a lot of people, but none as unhappy as Reuben Tarz. If only there were something he could do, something to make the kid happy so he smiled when he got out of bed in the morning. With a sigh, he reached for a pencil. With what his mother kept in the pillowcase under her bed and in the toes of her bedroom slippers and what he had stashed, he should be able to come up with close to $800,000. Jesus, he should have asked Tarz what this kind of investment would earn. If he was lucky, he'd probably come out with $75,000 profit. Not bad for a hot tip.

One month and two days after getting into the commodities market Reuben received a telegram from Daniel. It contained two words: Sell immediately. Reuben called Mort

Stiner and told him to sell. He called Max, but the gangster was out for the day, so he called the broker back and told him sell for Max.

"I can't do that, Mr. Tarz," the broker protested.

"I'm his partner, and I'm telling you to sell. If you don't, you won't have any arms or legs left. Sell, goddammit!" Reuben snarled. "You want the studio's business in the future, you do what I tell you."

At noon Reuben left the office. At five he returned with three checks: one for Sol in the amount of $5,500,000; one for Max in the amount of $2,000,000; and one for himself for $3,000,000. He was elated. Three million dollars. Jesus! Wait till he told Daniel. "I love you, Daniel!" he cried happily.

On his way to Sol's office he stopped at his secretary's desk and peeled three hundred dollars out of his billfold. "Here, Margaret, buy yourself a new dress, get your mother one, and take her out to dinner to the fanciest restaurant in town. Now!"

"But I . . . I still have work . . . This is too much. . . . Oh, thank you, Mr. Tarz, thank you so much." All the way home on the bus she kept saying over and over, "He's the nicest man in Hollywood."

Sol looked at the check as though it were a snake. One plump finger counted the zeros,

ticking them off one by one. "Jesus, you pulled this off! You really pulled it off! Put them together here on the desk so I can see what $8,500,000 looks like at one time. My God! This must be all the money in the world, and it's right here. We have to put these checks in the safe till tomorrow morning. The goddamn banks are closed now. Shit, I'm going to sit here all night holding it for safekeeping." When Reuben left, Sol was staring into space, a truly happy man.

At six o'clock he called Bebe to tell her he wouldn't be home for dinner. In fact, he said, "I'll be rather late, so don't wait up for me." He winced at the sound of tears in his wife's voice. You are a bastard, Tarz, he berated himself.

It was almost nine when Reuben cleared his desk. He headed straight for the Mimosa Club. The joint was jumping when he pushed his way inside. Max was leaning on the bar, his eyes glued to the door. The minute he saw Reuben he headed straight over.

"I hear you been calling me all day. I took my mother to the zoo, and then stayed for dinner. She's my mother, what can I tell you?"

"That it's nice to care about your mother. Don't apologize for that, Max."

"Tarz" — Max stopped in his tracks — "I wasn't apologizing. I was explaining. Let's go in the office."

"When I couldn't reach you," Reuben said, sitting opposite Max in his office, "I took the liberty of selling for you. I picked up your check this afternoon. A little unorthodox, but they came across. Here it is."

Max looked at the check and then at Reuben. "Not bad. I thought I'd make around seventy-five grand, so I made a little more. Thanks for the tip."

Reuben frowned. "Max, maybe you better put your glasses on. Take another look at that check, and this time count the zeros."

Max stared at the piece of paper in his hands. "Holy Jesus Christ! This is millions. Is it a mistake? How much of this is your cut?"

"When are you going to learn, Max? This is yours. I do not get a cut. I do not want a cut. You better put it someplace safe till the banks open in the morning. How about something to eat?"

"Eat! You want to eat at a time like this? We should be celebrating."

"Wrong. I want to eat. By the way, keep this to yourself. I'm serious. Sometimes — and this is one of those times — it's best to keep things like this . . . private."

"Yeah, I guess you're right. I don't really have too many people to share this with, anyway. It takes away part of the thrill, if you know what I mean."

"I know exactly what you mean. About that food . . ."

"Yeah, yeah, yeah. Listen, I'll get it for you myself."

It was after one in the morning when Reuben let himself into the house in Laurel Canyon. Bebe rushed from the living room and threw her arms around him, kissing his nose, his cheeks, his mouth. "I'm so glad you're home, Reuben. I waited up. I didn't think you'd want to come into a dark, quiet house. Do you want some dinner? I told the cook to keep it warm."

Reuben shook his head. "I ate, Bebe. I told you not to wait up. You should go to sleep now. I want to write to Daniel and I have some papers to go over."

Bebe stood there, her hands on her hips. "Why are you avoiding me? We're married. What am I supposed to do — pretend we're brother and sister? Tell me what it is you expect from me. I won't force myself on you. Do you want me to move back to my father's house, or what?"

"I just need some more time, and no, I don't want you to go back to your father's house. We have our whole lives ahead of us."

"Good night, Reuben." The words fell like stones from her mouth. Suddenly she swung around and said, "The day is going to come when you really do need me, and I won't be there. Think about that!"

"What's that supposed to mean?" Reuben demanded.

"I said good night. I'm sleeping down the hall. You can have that big wonderful bridal bed all to yourself." With that, she stormed up the steps, the train of her dressing gown swirling behind her.

His little bride was angry.

CHAPTER THIRTY-TWO

In the months that followed, Bebe Tarz led the life of a hermit. Each night she had the cook prepare an elaborate dinner, complete with three and sometimes four kinds of wine. Rarely, if ever, did Reuben return in time to eat it. To while away her time she read trashy magazines and drank bootleg whiskey that Eli brought to the Laurel Canyon house three times a week. In the beginning she was content to spend money by the barrel, courting famous designers and buying extravagantly. Eli egged her on during the afternoons they spent together at the side of the pool. One late September afternoon he introduced her to marijuana, a ritual that fast became a habit.

"I am absolutely bored out of my head," she told Eli in mid-October. "Did I tell you that our marriage has never been consummated? Reuben seems to detest me. He's never here. I don't believe he's seeing anyone else, but I do believe he still loves Mickey."

She told Eli then, because she was high on marijuana, about the time she spent in France, even the part about Reuben raping her. Eli soaked up his sister's confession like a sponge. When he left to return home he felt as though he had something on his nemesis, something he could use later on if things ever got messy. In the circles Eli traveled in, it was called blackmail.

One morning, a few weeks from the couple's first-year anniversary, Bebe curled her lip at Eli and announced, "I am going to throw the biggest, wildest party this town has ever seen. And when it's over, I will either seduce my husband or . . . I will know once and for all if he can still . . . get it up." She giggled at the sight of Eli's acute discomfort. "Did you bring it?" she asked greedily.

Eli was about to say no, until he saw the pleading in his sister's eyes. He was sorry now that he'd introduced her to the addictive weed. When he'd come by for breakfast that morning she was already smoking out on the terrace. If his father ever found out, he'd kill him. Reuben would probably decapitate him. With a heavy sigh, he handed his sister a small paper bag and warned, "This has to last you for two weeks, Bebe." He knew she didn't hear a word he said; she was too busy snatching the bag and rifling through it.

"We'll need some other . . . stuff for my party, Eli," she said distractedly.

"Bebe, your husband will be here. I don't want to go any rounds with him. The answer is no."

She glanced at him a moment, then shrugged. "Then I'll get someone else to bring it."

"Damn you, Bebe! I'm sorry I ever gave you the stuff, and I'm not about to provide you with cocaine. You won't get it from me."

His voice was so forceful, so adamant, Bebe did a double take. "Meanie," she whined.

Reuben chose that particular moment to walk into the house, forcing Bebe to shove the paper bag into her pocket. Eli mumbled good-bye and left by way of the terrace walkway.

"You're home early," Bebe said. It sounded almost like an accusation.

"What does it take to make you happy, Bebe?" Reuben asked quietly. "You complain if I'm late and you complain if I'm early. I could move out — would that make you happy?"

Sullenly she poured herself a tumbler full of gin and swilled it in two gulps. "You want to know what would make me happy?" she said, turning to him. "Well, I'll tell you. A husband. You are not a husband. We're married almost a year, and we have not slept together once in all that time. My question is, what do *you* want? It's Mickey, isn't it? You still want her after all this time. You are a

fool, Reuben. She's old, a has-been. She used you, and like a fool, you let her. Has she written to you even once?" she asked tipsily. "No. I can see by your face that she hasn't. You're carrying a torch for someone who doesn't care a twit about you. You're a real fool!"

"At least she isn't a drunk," Reuben said, eyes flashing. "And she doesn't need reefers to keep her flying high, either."

"You made me this way," she said. "Why don't you get a damn divorce if I make you so unhappy? It's your fault. I want to know something, my dear husband. Men your age are supposed to be virile, with only one thought in mind — to bed a woman. You don't seem to be interested in sex at all. Are you getting it somewhere else, or do you prefer men? What would Sin City say if it knew we'd been married a year and you haven't touched me?"

"I wouldn't brag about it, Bebe. They're liable to think there's something wrong with you. . . . I think this discussion is over. Maybe you should sleep it off," Reuben said, and turned to leave.

Bebe's eyes were glassy now as she let loose with her own brand of drunken harangue. "Reuben can't get it up; Reuben can't get it up; Reuben can't get it up," she sang as she danced around the terrace table. "Hollywood's Golden Boy can't . . . get it . . . *up!*" She backed up fearfully when she saw Reu-

ben stop and come back to her.

"Do you want to see me get it up? Now? Here on the terrace with the servants in the house?" His voice was ominously quiet, and a tiny muscle in his jaw worked convulsively. Bebe was terrified.

"No! Yes . . . no, oh, go away," she faltered. Goddammit, why couldn't this exchange have happened when she was sober and free of marijuana? Oh, God, it was going to happen again, just like the last time. She hacked away, tears spilling from her eyes. "I'm sorry, Reuben, I had too much to drink, I didn't mean what I said. You have your reasons for feeling like you do . . . please, not here, not like this."

"Why not here?" Eyes glinting with suppressed rage, he ripped at his clothes, his jacket, his shirt, his tie. He kicked at his shoes, not caring that they landed in a flower bed. His head was buzzing now with uncontrollable fury as he stared at his wife. One long arm reached out to pull her to him. Although he was aware of her tears, of her trembling, of her fear, the ache in his chest and throat drove him on. Heedless of Bebe's protests, he ripped the smooth pink fabric of her dress down the front, exposing her breasts. A sound rushed from his throat, alien and almost savage.

He was pushing her backward now, onto a narrow chaise, his breath hot and fiery on her throat. Caught in the prison of his arms,

she was making sounds, mewing little sounds like a kitten caught in the rain. He paid them no mind, the pain in his loins driving him to loosen his trousers and at the same time remove her panties. Now the sounds coming from his throat were bitter . . . strangely familiar to Bebe's ears as she struggled to get away from him. It was a futile attempt, however — he only held her tighter; that feeling, too, was remembered. At last she gave up her struggles and lay still. When it was over she stared at him with tear-filled eyes.

There was no remorse in Reuben's face when he stared down at his wife. Her eyes full of shame, Bebe struggled to her feet, shoulders trembling uncontrollably. Stifling her sobs, she stumbled from the terrace.

It was dark when Reuben got up stiffly from his bed. His leg ached and his neck felt as if it were in a vise. Perhaps a bath might ease some of his tension, he thought. He was aware then of the deadly silence in the house. What was Bebe doing? If he went to her and apologized, he knew she would hold out her arms to him and forgive him. He knew it, but he wouldn't go to her. The hard truth was, he was emotionally afraid of Bebe and the hold she would exercise over him if he let his emotions have free rein. Afraid of his wife. It had to be the sickest thing he'd ever heard of.

In the bathroom he turned the tap and water rushed into the huge galvanized tub built to hold two people comfortably. He watched the spurting stream of water swirl and rush down the drain, then fixed the stopper. Hopefully, the hot bath would wash away some of his growing self-hatred. When the tub was full he lowered himself into the steaming water and with a towel folded behind his head stretched out to his full length. He closed his eyes and allowed his memory to travel back to France. It was where he belonged, where he wanted to be. . . .

Later, dressed in his underwear and a robe, Reuben walked outdoors to the bedroom terrace. It was a beautiful night, the kind to be shared. Stars twinkled overhead, the moon aiding them in casting a silvery shadow over the blooming terrace. Everything smelled faintly of flowers, a pleasant scent that teased his nostrils. In the right mood a man could get lost in such beauty.

Reuben leaned on the railing, the outward picture of a happy, contented man. His thoughts soared again, something that always happened when he could get business or Bebe out of his mind. He had enough money to go back to France now. His pockets full, he wouldn't be beholden to Mickey in any way. He'd paid his debt; he'd proved honorable. He'd even added extra money to pay

for all the things Mickey had bought for he and Daniel, plus a bit of interest. Not that he'd gone overboard — just paid enough to cover what he thought of as his tab. If he wanted to, he could travel first class to France and buy a car, drive to the château, and sweep Mickey off her feet. In these musings he always rushed her to the nearest justice of the peace and married her. Abruptly, his thoughts crashed around him. He couldn't do that now, he was married to someone else, someone he didn't want to be married to. Mickey would send him packing within seconds; she wouldn't want to hear excuses or explanations. The time for that was long gone.

All that was left to him now were memories of France and a flesh-and-blood wife. He clamped his teeth together so hard his jaw ached.

It was well past midnight when Reuben made his way to the kitchen for a sandwich. He hadn't eaten since early morning and wasn't sure now if he wanted something to eat or was really going downstairs to see if Bebe was still there.

The French doors in the living room yawned in the silvery night. Frowning, he walked over to close them and saw his wife stretched out on one of the chaise longues. One hand held a drink; the other, a reefer. The sickly-sweet odor of marijuana wafted to

706

his nostrils. At the sound of his approach Bebe raised her head a little to stare at her husband with blank, lifeless eyes. She said nothing.

"It's late, Bebe, you should be in bed," Reuben said quietly.

"It doesn't matter when I go to bed," Bebe said flatly. "I don't have anywhere to go in the morning. I don't have anything to do but play cards and drink. . . . I want a divorce, Reuben."

The word rattled around in his head. Divorce meant he'd failed. Christ, he hadn't even given the marriage a fair trial. Divorce would free them both, but then, what about the invisible bond between them, the intangible thing that ate at him night and day? "We'll talk about it another time, when we're calm and reasonable. Tonight is not the time."

"There will never be a right time, Reuben. You've shackled me to you for whatever your reasons are. But it's not enough. Divorce is our only solution. You will always love Mickey. I thought I could change that. I thought you could come to love me, but you can't. It's not your fault. I've heard about men, and sometimes women, who are capable of loving only one person in their whole lives. I'm sorry that I'm not that person, because I love you with all my heart."

Bebe stood up and set her glass on the table, the reefer hanging out of the corner of

her mouth. Staggering slightly, she made her way across the flagstone terrace. "I will not allow you to destroy me. If destruction is to be my end, I will do it myself. I've taken nothing from you, Reuben. I owe you nothing. So whatever happens to me will be my own doing. Do you understand what I'm saying?" She peered at him in the silvery light with her blank eyes, eyes that once sparkled and made demands.

"Bebe . . . I . . ."

"Bebe, I what?" Bebe mocked. "The damage has been done. Tomorrow we start with a clean slate. I do what I please and you do what you please. You do not tell me what to do and I won't tell you what to do. We'll live in the same house, but that's all we'll have in common. Unless, for appearance' sake, you want me to accompany you to whatever social events you think I should attend. That's it. Good night, Reuben."

Go after her, he told himself, try to make her understand. In silence he watched her weave her way to the staircase, half expecting her to look back, to beckon him, to give some sign that she could be forgiving. But she didn't. Her hand gripping the banister, Bebe climbed the stairs wearily, like an old woman, planting both feet on each step before taking another.

Reuben's eyes were bleak as he made his way through the dark gardens — the one

place on his so-called palatial estate that reminded him of France, where he had found happiness and peace in his love's arms. Wearily he sat down on an iron bench at the foot of the flagstone walkway, where the scent of the ever-present orange blossoms mingled with the fragrant gardenias dotting the path. His shoulders hunched, and he made no effort to stem the tears that burned his eyes and slipped down his cheeks.

He sat there all night, and when dawn crept over the garden he got up slowly. At that moment he felt more weary, more fatigued, than at any time on the front line during the war. Without a backward glance at his beloved garden, he trudged into the house; after soul-searching the whole night through he had only one thought on his mind — to be a better husband to his wife.

But it was not to be. Bebe made her own plans that night, and they did not include Reuben. She was rarely home now, and when she was, the house was full of noisy revelers who drank and smoked reefers and sniffed cocaine till the wee hours of the morning. With reckless abandon, she drank to excess and, immediately upon awakening, reached for her cache of marijuana. Eventually she took less pains with her dress and her makeup; her face became haggard and bloated. Three months later, when she an-

nounced her pregnancy, Reuben's jaw dropped in shock. His first thought was that now he'd never be able to leave her. Then devastation gave way to elation. He was going to be a father! Suddenly the reality of Bebe's physical condition struck home. How could a baby inside her womb survive what she was doing to her body with alcohol and drugs?

On a drizzly, dreary Wednesday morning Reuben forcefully carried Bebe to the car. She was going to the doctor whether she liked it or not.

The doctor was a kindly old man with penetrating blue eyes. His voice was stern when he spoke to Reuben and Bebe in his office after the examination.

"Together you have created this child, and you, Mrs. Tarz, have no right to abuse your body and endanger its life. If you don't give up alcohol and drugs, this child will die. And Mrs. Tarz, that is murder in my eyes." He addressed himself to Reuben. "I know of a place where you can take your wife to regain her health. At first the solitude may bother you, but you will adjust. It is a bit of a rural resort. You'll find good food, sunshine, and a healthful atmosphere. Palm Springs," he said flatly. "I can personally make arrangements for you today if you wish."

Reuben nodded, his mouth a grim, tight line.

"You must be out of your minds, both of you," Bebe shrilled. "I'm not a drunk, nor am I a dope fiend. I can stop whenever I want. I like to have fun — go to parties — and my husband doesn't. This pregnancy isn't —" She was about to say she'd been pregnant once before, but caught herself in time. "— wasn't exactly planned, Doctor. I appreciate your concern, but I can manage nicely. Tonight I'll stay home and knit a pair of baby booties. Will that make you happy?"

"I'm concerned only with the health of the child and yourself, of course, as I'm sure your husband is. I don't see that you really have a choice, Mrs. Tarz," the doctor said sternly.

"Make the arrangements, Doctor," Reuben said.

"I'm not going!" Bebe shouted.

Reuben ignored her. "Make the arrangements. We'll leave in the morning." He turned to Bebe. "This is my child, too, and I will not allow you to harm it in any way. We're going to Palm Springs!"

That night he locked Bebe in her room and then called Sol and asked him to come over to the house. Determined to enlist his father-in-law's support, he explained Bebe's condition and told Sol what the doctor had suggested. "I don't know what else to do," he said when he'd finished, half expecting Sol to

fight him, to yank his daughter out of the house and take her away.

"What do you want me to do, Reuben?" Sol asked quietly.

"Go upstairs and talk to her, tell her you agree with me that this is best for . . . your grandchild. I had to lock her in her room. She . . . I . . . thought she might go off somewhere, try to go to one of those back-street butchers. When she's drinking and smoking she's apt to do anything that pops into her head."

Sol nodded numbly and trudged upstairs. When he returned he looked beaten. "She spoke to me like I was scum," he said in a choked voice. "She said you and I were birds of a feather. I know it's not my daughter talk-ing, but a stranger full of drugs and booze. You don't need my permission to take Bebe away, but I'm giving it to you anyway. I want a healthy, robust grandchild." His shoulders slumped in misery, he walked out of the house in Laurel Canyon.

It was a beautiful morning, with the night's dew sparkling like tiny diamonds on the newly mowed lawn. Reuben looked up at the sound of chittering birds. Their farewell, he thought sadly. They'd fly to some other refuge when he carried his wife kicking and scream-ing to the car. That's what he was doing — seeking refuge, a sanctuary for Bebe and his

unborn child.

He savored the morning, unwilling to go upstairs and start the temporary life he didn't feel qualified for. Everything was on hold now. For the next six months he would devote every minute of the day to Bebe and the child she carried. And it would all work out — it had to. He'd come this far in his life, suffered through Mickey's rejection, made Fairmont a major contender in the studio wars, waded his way through scandal and was still alive to talk about it. He would make it through this, too. Palm Springs wasn't the end of the world. There were telephones, there was the mail. He might be out of reach, but he wouldn't be out of touch. Daniel would say he was attending to his priorities.

When he opened the door to Bebe's room, Reuben was shocked at her appearance. She hadn't bothered to bathe or change her clothes, and her makeup was garish in the early morning light. Her fluffy hair was limp and flat against her head, her usually pretty face was bloated, and her eyes were puffy. But she wasn't in the throes of a tantrum; in fact, she seemed resigned to whatever Reuben would do. "It's time to go, Bebe," he said quietly.

"I know. I've been thinking, Reuben. I don't want anything to happen to this baby. Yesterday I said a lot of wild, hateful things. I guess at the time I meant them, but I don't . . .

what I'm saying is, I'll try." She looked at herself in the mirror. "I know how I look, and I'm so ashamed . . . so ashamed," she cried. "I wouldn't blame you one bit if you were embarrassed to be seen with me. What's-his-name, that guardian of Hollywood's morals, will have a wonderful time at your expense if . . . if anyone finds out . . how bad I am. Look, let's go before I change my mind."

"Bebe, I would never be embarrassed to be seen with you, no matter what your condition. And anyone who says one word about you will have to tangle with me." He realized he meant what he said. "If you're serious about starting over . . . I want you to know I will do everything I can to help you with this pregnancy. All I ask is that you meet me halfway. Can you do that?"

"I'll try, Reuben. I'll try my best," Bebe promised.

"Good girl," Reuben said heartily. "Let's be on our way, then."

"I never noticed how the lawn sparkles in the morning. I don't think I ever heard the birds, either," Bebe said in a surprised voice. "I'm glad the sun is shining." She drew in a deep breath. "The air smells good enough to eat. I wonder if a person can get drunk on flower-scented air. What do you think?"

"I wouldn't be surprised at all. We're leaving now . . . Mrs. Tarz."

At Bebe's startled look, he smiled, a warm,

wonderful smile that warmed her heart.

Overnight Reuben turned into a considerate, caring, devoted husband who catered to his wife's every need. He spent every waking moment with her, enticing her to eat good, nourishing food, sunning with her under a striped umbrella, frolicking in the hot springs that were felt to be therapeutic. They walked, sometimes miles at a time, holding hands and talking animatedly about everything and anything. When Bebe fell to yearning for a drink or wishing she could smoke a reefer, Reuben held her close, crooning confident words of encouragement. And from each setback she emerged stronger and stronger. In a month's time, most of her vitality returned. Eventually she slept less, ate more, was able to keep pace with her husband. To the other guests at the resort, they appeared to be the perfect couple, loving each other tenderly and completely.

Bebe made no sexual demands on her husband, content to be at his side, adoring him as she always had.

By the end of their second month at the resort they were friends, if nothing else. Reuben talked openly of his success at Fairmont and told Bebe about some of his more important deals. A captive, eager audience, she clapped her hands in delight as each new episode was revealed.

By the end of the third month Bebe was brown as a nut, her hair cropped short by her own hands. Reuben told her she looked like a lovable street urchin. Her waistline disappeared and her breasts became fuller. They were together, sitting on the side of their favorite spring, when the baby kicked for the first time. Bebe smiled and reached for Reuben's hand. "Feel your son," she said.

With a fearful look on his face, Reuben felt his child move. His eyes were so soft, so full of awe that tears sprang to Bebe's eyes. How was it possible that something unknown and unseen could affect her husband so? She knew then that he would love their child, be it a boy or a girl, and felt a deep sorrow that neither of them knew John Paul, their first-born.

"How do you know it will be a boy?" Reuben asked in a choked voice.

"Oh, women know these things," Bebe said airily. Crossing her fingers, she wished for a son for her husband, knowing he already had one — one he might never know.

"What if it's a girl?" Reuben asked.

"Then you will have a daughter instead of a son. Would a daughter displease you?" Bebe asked.

Reuben thought about it. "No. I think I would like one of each. Not right away, of course," he added hastily.

"I think I would like a little girl at first. Not

that it matters really," Bebe said gently. "Girls have such pretty little dresses and bonnets. She'd be like a Dresden doll. I think Daddy would like a girl, but maybe he's just saying that. I guess all men want a son."

"It doesn't make any difference, Bebe, as long as the child is healthy," Reuben said sincerely.

"Oh, Reuben, I am so happy. I'm glad you made me come here. And I'm so glad you're staying with me. After the baby is born we can start our lives again. You pulled me back from the brink and I'll never forget it. I did all of this," she said, waving her arms expansively, "for you. I'd do anything for you, Reuben. Anything."

What was there for him to say? He squeezed her hand and Bebe smiled contentedly.

It seemed to Reuben that his wife grew more beautiful with each passing day. Motherhood, he decided, became her. When he received word from Sol that he was needed back at the studio, he left with regret, promising to return within the week.

"You really will come back, won't you, Reuben?" Bebe asked anxiously.

"Of course I will." He cupped her face in his hands. "Give me your word that you'll rest and eat and continue to exercise and take care of yourself. Promise."

"I'll do whatever you want," Bebe reassured him.

It wasn't until the next day, as Bebe reclined under a shady umbrella, that she thought about Reuben's parting words. His priorities were obvious: he wanted to be sure she delivered a healthy child, his child. Yes, he was attentive; yes, he smiled at her; yes, he held her hand; and, yes, he tucked her into bed at night — a bed he didn't share with her. All along he'd acted more like a father and brother than husband and lover. Most devastating of all, he hadn't responded when she'd said they would start over after the birth of the baby. To her, starting over meant living as man and wife. Tears gathered in her eyes. It was the baby — he cared only about the baby. His concern, which she'd chosen to believe as loving and caring, was all for the child. Certainly she couldn't fault him for lying. He'd been truthful; it was her own fault that she had misunderstood. Bitter tears of remorse stung her eyes. Mickey had told her once that you couldn't make someone love you. The bitter truth of the statement hit her now like a physical blow.

Still, she'd given her promise to Reuben to do all the things he requested, and she honored the promise. She ate, not really tasting the nourishing food. She walked aimlessly, her thoughts on Reuben and what he was doing, where he was doing it, wondering when he would return. In her mind she questioned her love and Reuben's indiffer-

ence on an hourly basis. Someday, she promised herself, her husband would love her. Someday.

The studio lot was cast in the pale shadows of early evening when Reuben drove his car through the gate. He didn't like this time of day, when the sun was newly down and the world was in shadows. He preferred sunlight or total darkness. As he mounted the steps to the executive offices, he wondered what was so important that Sol had called him back to the studio.

At the landing he turned and went directly to Sol's office. The older man stood staring out the window but turned at Reuben's entrance. "How's my little girl doing?" he said as soon as he recognized Reuben.

"Fine. You wouldn't recognize her, Sol; she's eating and sleeping without the aid of her 'old friends.' She's stronger and calmer and nicely tanned." Reuben smiled. "The baby is going to be fine. I think we got her in time."

"She's a handful. I'm afraid I spoiled her," Sol said in an apologetic tone.

"Well, I'm sure you didn't get me back here for this little conversation. What was so important?"

"What's your feeling on biblical stories?"

Reuben shrugged. "I can take them or leave them. Is that why you called me back?"

"It's one of the reasons. The grapevine has it that Jim Crocker wants financing for *Moses on the Mount*. How will something like that go over at the box office? Talk is he doesn't want to put his eggs in Paramount's basket because of the recent scandals. Paramount is going down fast. He'll go with the highest bidder. And Rupert Julian has been trying to reach you for weeks now. He says he won't talk to anyone but you." Sol's voice took on a peevish note. "He left his business card."

Reuben frowned. "You could have put all that in a letter. There's something else. What is it?"

"It's that sanctimonious, pussy-licking Will Hays," Sol muttered belligerently.

Reuben tensed. "What about him?" he asked quietly.

"He's sniffing around, him and some of his doom boys. I got a couple of calls, one from your friend Max. He thinks he's on to something with . . . with Bebe. He's looking for headlines, is what he's up to. He blew into Hollywood about two weeks ago. You know in this town everyone knows everyone else's business before you know it yourself. As much as I hate to admit it, neither of my children has loyal friends. All of them will spill their guts with the promise they won't be prosecuted. When your ass is in a sling, you spill your guts."

"Is that all?" Reuben demanded.

"Christ! Isn't that enough?"

"Yes. Yes, it is. The tabloids must be giving Hays all kinds of coverage. Where's he staying?"

"The Ambassador Hotel. If you're planning something, Reuben, I think I should know what it is."

"When and if I do plan something, I'll let you know. I've had a long day driving, so I think I'll head home for a hot bath. How's Eli doing?" he asked, more to be polite than anything else.

"God only knows," Sol replied bitterly. "He's hardly ever home these days. For all I know he could be sleeping in a gutter somewhere."

"Funny Hays hasn't picked up on him, wouldn't you say?"

"He'll get around to him. Eli isn't what you call real smart."

Reuben nodded and left Sol's office to stop off briefly at his own. There, on top of a stack of mail on his desk, were four telegrams from Daniel. Cursing, he scooped up the bundle and left the office.

The night was quiet, with only the faint sound of chirping crickets. Reuben wondered how many people in the world knew the sound crickets made came from rubbing their legs together. Mickey had told him that once at a picnic. He smiled.

■ ■ ■ ■

The house in Laurel Canyon was as dark as a shroud. The help had been temporarily dismissed, and the furniture was covered with sheets and blankets, awaiting his return. To Reuben, it looked like the prop room at Fairmont. He headed straight for the desk in his bedroom, fitted the key he carried on his watch chain into the desk lock, and withdrew a letter from Daniel. After countless perusals, he knew what it said, but he read it again.

Dear Reuben,
    I don't know if this will be important to you or not, but what I'm about to tell you is as close to gospel as it can be.
    My roommate's father told him that Will Hays was a member of President Harding's cabinet and, as chairman of the Republican National Committee, tilted the nomination to Harding. The payola was in the amount of $75,000. He also accepted a loan, the kind that doesn't have to be repaid, from millionaire Harry Sinclair, out of gratitude for pushing Harding into the White House. That's it, pal — hope the information can help you if you need it.
    Have to hit the books now, so I'll sign off and write you a proper letter later.

Take it easy, Reuben, and try to write more often. I miss you, pal.

Your friend,
Daniel

Satisfied that he'd memorized the important information, Reuben locked the letter back in his desk. Tomorrow he would make it his business to stop by the Ambassador Hotel to speak with Will Hays. Jesus, what would he do without Daniel?

He placed two more phone calls, one to Crocker, the other to the faceless name on the business card in his hand. Neither party was in, so he left his name both times, asking simply that they return his call. Now he could turn his attention to his mail and Daniel's telegrams. First the telegrams. His eyes widened as he read. Tips for the market again. It was all Greek to him, but tomorrow he would head for Mort Stiner's office. This time he would keep the tips from Sol, simply tell him they were too risky. But he'd give Max one of them. Oh, yes, he was feeling better by the moment. Power and money, money and power — aphrodisiacs that had no equal.

The first letter he picked up was postmarked France. He stared at it so long, his eyes started to water. Mickey! After all this time. The various postal stamps, which traced the letter's journey back to its source, showed that it had been mailed on June 1, 1922. A

year ago! One month after his marriage to Bebe. His chest tightened and his throat felt constricted. For the first time he noticed the names on the envelope: Mr. and Mrs. Reuben Tarz. The letter fell from his hands and fluttered to the floor. Mr. and Mrs. Reuben Tarz . . . Sol must have had the house mail sent to the studio, he thought irrelevantly. The envelope bore the Laurel Canyon address.

His head throbbed when he ripped open the letter. His eyes burned just as angrily as he read the short congratulations.

It was Bebe! he realized. Bebe hadn't been able to wait to write and tell her. "Goddamn you to hell, Bebe," he said hoarsely. Suddenly it occurred to him that he was damning the wrong woman. Bebe had every right to tell Mickey they were married. Mickey, on the other hand, couldn't be bothered to write, to acknowledge his payments, but she could take the time to send a note of congratulations, and only because Bebe had obviously written her. And where had the letter been all this time? Misplaced? Lost? How ironic that it should appear now. A whole year had gone by, more than a year, and this letter had been lying somewhere. At least it was a communication of sorts. Mickey was alive and well. He would have to be content with that.

CHAPTER
THIRTY-THREE

Halfway around the world in a daisy-filled meadow, a sturdy little boy pulled a bright red wagon filled with flowers. At his side was Jake, whose assignment was to sniff out the flowers for the little boy to pick. Every so often the boy and the dog scampered back to Mickey, who held her hand out for the flowers that were pulled off at the base of the bloom.

"I need a stem, my darling. Jake, a long stem." Mickey laughed delightedly as Jake raced away, his silky ears fanning out behind him. Philippe followed him, tumbling over his own feet twice. Protector that he was, Jake raced back to lick the little boy's face and tug at his shirt. It was no fun when one ran and the other lay on the ground. He growled playfully.

Even though her eyes were glued to Philippe and Jake, Mickey's thoughts were far across the Atlantic. Bebe's latest letter had arrived days before. It was long and rambling,

the contents forgotten save for news of the girl's pregnancy. That had been a devastating blow, and Mickey had felt physically ill for several days.

A baby. Reuben and Bebe's . . . second child. She wondered then, and not for the first time, if Bebe had ever told Reuben about her first baby. She'd visited and written Yvette three letters, but not once had she asked about the child. Nor had she asked after Mickey. Yvette had been apologetic about this; she'd only touched upon Bebe's blatant indifference, preferring instead to share the newsy, chatty aspects of the girl's letters. And now, of course, there would be another letter for Yvette soon, different from the one she herself had received a few days earlier. Yvette's would be full of Bebe's famous husband and how busy they were with all the Hollywood parties and how women, especially the female stars, were so crazy about her good-looking husband, but he had eyes only for her.

The child was back now, holding out a crushed cowbell.

"I would very much like a piece of sugar bread and some" — the little face puckered in thought — "some juice!" he said triumphantly. "Sugar bread for Jake, too, just one little piece." He pushed his thumb and index finger together. Jake's ears shot up at the sound of his name. Mickey watched him as

726

he cocked his head toward the sun, somehow calculating that it was treat time. She thought she loved Jake almost as much as she loved Philippe.

"You would, eh?" Mickey laughed. "Sugar bread and juice and a cookie for Jake. And if I give out these luscious treats, what do I get in return?"

"Two kisses and a hug this big," the little boy said, stretching his arms wide.

Mickey pretended to think. "I can't pass up an offer like that." She leaned over for Philippe, who planted two wet smacking kisses on her cheek. Jake woofed and licked her hand.

"Climb into the wagon and I'll pull you back to the château."

"No, I wish to walk with Jake," the little boy said stubbornly.

Mickey smiled. "If you get tired from the long walk, you'll have to take a nap."

"Will you tell me a story if I take a nap?"

"I have a better idea, you tell me a story." The little boy's eyes sparkled, and he nodded gleefully.

"I think I will sit in the wagon and think of my story. It will be about my papa." He motioned for Jake to hop into the wagon.

"Aha, a double load. That means you must tell me two stories," Mickey teased.

Later, his face and hands clean, Jake settled at the foot of his bed, Philippe sat up impor-

tantly. "My first story will be about my papa. He loves me more than sugar bread. He loves Jake, too. He does love us, doesn't he, *Maman?*" the boy asked wistfully.

"Very much, Philippe," Mickey said softly.

"He can't come to visit me because he is busy fighting pirates and riding a horse. He captures all the bad men and ties them up. If he had Jake with him, he would warn him about the bad people. My papa is . . . a musketeer," he said proudly. "That's my story."

"Not so fast, young man. You promised me two stories," Mickey said, smiling.

"My papa lives in a big castle. He is the king. When he comes to take us with him you will be the queen and I will be . . . What will I be, *Maman?*"

"The prince."

"I will be the prince. He will be wearing his crown and he . . . he will have one for you, *Maman.* My room in the castle will be full of toys. Jake will have his own little house and . . . do dogs wear crowns, *Ma—* ?"

Mickey brushed at the tears on her cheeks. Poor lost lamb, how badly he wanted a father. How selfish she was being! But if Reuben knew, he would take him away. And Reuben was married now with a child of his own on the way. You're all I have, Philippe, and I won't let anyone take you from me. No, you're mine . . . until such time as I . . . until

I decide to give you to your father, and I hope that day never comes! You are my life, little one.

Jake's ears wobbled over his head, and he looked at Mickey expectantly. "No, little one, you stay here and watch my love. I leave him in your capable . . . paws." She leaned over to fondle the dog's silky ears. "I think, little Jake, that you, Philippe, and myself are the true Three Musketeers. Nothing and no one can shake the love we have for one another. In our lives there is no Bebe Rosen. And for dinner you shall have a whole chop because you deserve it. And ice cream for Philippe."

Downstairs in the library, Mickey walked over to the mantel and looked up at the portrait. "This was only temporary, a short span of time that had meaning but no resolution." She gave a halfhearted salute to the portrait. "To all the yesterdays," she said tearfully, "for tomorrow never comes."

She wept then, bittersweet tears of sorrow. Reuben and tomorrow would never come.

CHAPTER
THIRTY-FOUR

Reuben sat at his office desk, his fingers drumming impatiently on the glossy surface that was devoid of all papers. It was early, just a little after six, and his emotions were as impatient as his fingers. Part of him wanted to be here at the studio; another part wanted to be in Palm Springs supervising his wife's activities. The rest of him wanted to be in France. He wondered if he looked as haggard as he felt. He hadn't slept at all in the dust-covered bed but had sat up on a chair covered with a yellow blanket. His fingers picked up momentum, the sound startling to him in the quiet of the office.

It was hard to believe that in less than an hour the studio would be a beehive of sound and activity, but for now this was the only place he could think objectively. He leaned back, his hands clasped behind his head. He'd follow the Jewish creed of doing business: business first, family affairs later.

At two minutes after seven he was on the

phone with Jim Crocker. "I'm going to have to admit my ignorance on this, Jim. In terms of box office I have no idea what a biblical film will do. Convince me, sell me on it, and we can talk dollars. Better yet, come round to the office this morning and we can talk. Do you have any figures on paper? . . . Good, bring everything with you."

At seven-thirty he was talking to the faceless Rupert Julian. He, too, had a property he was interested in peddling if the price was right. "If you're interested in lunch from the wagon, come around noon to my offices and we can talk."

After he'd rung off, Reuben stared at the phone, his drumming fingers silent. *Moses on the Mount* and *Witches and Ghosts.* Jesus. Moses would probably do well with Hays in power. Or would the public ignore horror and something with religious overtones out of spite? "Go with your gut feelings, Tarz," he muttered to himself.

At seven-forty he placed a call to Max and shared with him the second of Daniel's four "hot" tips. "Let's do it," Max said, chortling. Both men were waiting at Mort Stiner's door at exactly eight o'clock.

"This is insane, Mr. Tarz. Where in the hell are you coming up with these . . . Very well, it's your money." The bespectacled man grimaced.

"Exactly. Win or lose, you still get your

commissions."

"Mr. Rosen isn't . . . participating?" Stiner queried.

Reuben grinned. "He thinks it's too risky."

"A very wise man." The broker wiped at his chin with his rumpled handkerchief.

On the way out of the office, Max looked up at Reuben in awe. "What the fuck am I going to do with all this money?"

"Get married and settle down. Your wife will show you what to do with it." Reuben laughed derisively. "Now, tell me who Rupert Julian is and why you sent him to me."

Max looked embarrassed. "Look, Tarz, it's one of those things, my mother knows his mother . . . Well, these two old ladies decided it was time for a really, really good spook film. They swear people like to be scared silly. My mother belongs to all these clubs and organizations, and Sadie, that's Julian's mother, is beating the bushes for her son and this picture he wants to make. Hell, according to the *Examiner,* most of the box office is made up of women, anyway. If you aren't interested, tell him to take a walk. What I was trying to do was . . . repay the stock tip. I'm the first to admit I don't know anything about making movies. . . ." His voice trailed off.

"It won't cost a thing to listen, Max. I told Julian to come to the office around noon, and we'd have some lunch and talk about it. Fair?"

"Yeah, fair. See you around, Reuben."

"What's your hurry?"

Max stopped in his tracks. "You set the rules early on, remember? I haven't stepped over the line. I don't think it would do your reputation any good for you to be seen with me." The little man's eyes were embarrassed and hopeful as he looked up at Reuben.

"Max, how would you like to have some breakfast? I'm buying. And" — he waved his hand under Max's nose — "I only invite people whose company I enjoy to eat with me. Now, you coming or not?"

"Hell, yes, I'm coming — especially if you're buying." Max beamed, his face lighting up like a hundred candles.

It was a quick breakfast of ham and eggs and three cups of coffee each. They talked about the orange crop, baseball, and the possibility of rain for the weekend. It was one of the most pleasant breakfasts Reuben ever had.

At the desk of the Ambassador Hotel Reuben was informed by the clerk that Mr. Hays and his entourage had a suite of rooms on the fifth floor. "No, no," Reuben said, smiling broadly, "don't announce me. I want to surprise Will." He winked slyly at the desk clerk. "You know, you're handsome enough to be in films. Come around to the studio and ask for me."

The startled clerk stared at the card Reuben handed him. "Oh . . . I always . . . yes, sir . . . go right up . . ." He removed his hand from the phone to hold the card closer to his eyes. "I have a day off tomorrow, will that be . . . convenient?"

"Not a minute too soon, in my opinion." Reuben smiled. "Remember now, don't call Will and tell him I'm on my way up."

The desk clerk smiled broadly. "No, sir, I sure wouldn't want to spoil your surprise."

"Good. Oh, by the way," Reuben called over his shoulder, "are you married or spoken for?"

"No . . . no, sir. Is . . . is that a requirement?"

"Hell, no," Reuben called back. "Just curious, that's all."

Upstairs, Reuben rapped sharply on Will Hays's door. Hays himself opened it, and when he saw who his visitor was he smiled widely. He loved it when what he called the high muckety-mucks came to crawl at his feet. Depending on his mood at the time, he either kicked them or made them lick his boots. This guy, he decided at first sight, would do both.

"Where's the doom squad?" Reuben asked as he handed Hays his studio card.

"Around town casting doom and gloom," Hays replied flippantly, chuckling at his own joke.

"I think we can get down to business, then. I understand you *think* you have some . . . unsavory little tidbits about my family that wouldn't look good in print."

"Mr. Tarz, I don't think, I *know.* Quite a dossier, I might add."

"Dossier?" Reuben said nonchalantly.

"Yes, a list of indiscretions, and quite a lengthy one. Worthy of the front page." Hays's huge bat ears twitched. Tarz was big and lean and the look on his face was starting to bother him. "If you think you can come here and intimidate me . . . threaten me . . . you've come to the wrong place. I have a job to uphold. I am," he said, puffing out his cheeks, "the moral conscience of this town."

"What you really are, Mr. Hays, is a fucking sanctimonious son of a bitch! If you print one word about my wife or anyone at Fairmont, I will come down on you like Father Doom himself. Do *I* make myself clear?"

"You can't scare me," Hays bristled. "Just who the hell do you think you are coming in here trying to muscle me? You aren't much of a man if you can't control your own wife."

"My wife is none of your business," Reuben said coldly.

"You aren't very clean, either, Mr. Tarz. I've heard about your . . . underworld connections."

Reuben laughed, a deep mocking sound that made Hays's ears twitch again.

"You aren't a man, you're a muckraker who makes his living by destroying people's lives. I despise men like you."

"If that's what you came here to tell me, consider it done. Now you can leave."

Hays's left eye was twitching now. Reuben smiled. If he wanted to, he could have this guy conduct a whole symphony with his twitching and squirming. This time he chuckled aloud at the thought. "As a matter of fact, Mr. Hays, I came here personally to deliver something to you." He withdrew a folded sheet of paper from his inside breast pocket.

Hays reached for it, then withdrew his hand. "What is it?" he demanded.

Reuben's even white teeth gleamed. "Mr. Hays, this is *your* dossier."

Hays unfolded the paper, his eyes bulging as he read Reuben's written words.

"Now we each have a dossier. Time is money, Mr. Hays, but then I don't have to tell you that, do I? It's been nice talking to you."

Reuben closed the hotel door softly behind him. He could hear Hays snarl "This is a goddamn pack of lies!" but there was no conviction in the man's voice. Maybe the crusader would lay low for a while and not bother the other studios and their stars. If the man had a brain in his head, he'd start worrying. Reuben smiled to himself. Let him sweat.

It was midafternoon when he and Sol

inally came to terms with Jim Crocker and Rupert Julian. Fairmont would take on both directors for both films. The men shook hands with the promise of finalized contracts the following day.

"Send out press releases, Margaret," Reuben ordered.

A good day's business. He'd cut two deals, one on his own instincts and the other according to Max's mother's instincts. And then he had taken care of Will Hays. His stomach wasn't churning — in fact, he felt quite satisfied. Little did he suspect that both films would be the top money-makers of all time. Now he had to find something to occupy his time and his thoughts or he would start to think about Mickey and the letter.

He began to stroll around the studio lot, feeling emotionally bruised and battered. It was the time of day he always checked into each lot to see the progress being made. The time he'd spent away shouldn't matter. Inside a half hour he realized no one had time to talk to him.

"See what happens when you have an efficient, well-oiled machine? You did such a good job, there's no time for play," Damian Farrell said as Reuben walked back onto his set. Reuben snorted agreement.

"Mr. Tarz? Reuben, wait up," Jane Perkins called. Reuben turned to see her pedaling a bicycle in his direction. "I missed you," she

said cheerily.

"Did you really?" Reuben felt please[d]. "How's it going?"

"So wonderful I still can't believe it. We wrapped up at noon today. I've sort of been hanging around, for no good reason. I guess I just don't relish going home to an empty apartment. I think I'll get a cat," she said, hopping off the bicycle. "Do you think that's a good idea?"

"I'm a dog person myself, but cats can take care of themselves. Listen, if you don't have any plans, would you like to catch a bite to eat?"

"I have a better idea. If you don't have anything to do, why don't you come home with me and I'll cook dinner. I was going to make some stuffed peppers. I'm a pretty good cook." The happy smile left her face. "Unless you don't think it's a good idea? I mean, with me being just an actress and you running this place and all . . ."

"I'd love to come to dinner. I can use some good company. If you're finished, we can leave now."

"I just have to take this bicycle back to the prop room and I can leave."

"Hold on!" Reuben said, grabbing the bike from her hands. "Let's do this . . . you sit on the handlebars and I'll pedal us over there."

Jane hopped on the bike, laughing, her skirts riding up above her rolled stockings.

With her legs sticking out in front of her awkwardly, Reuben pedaled the bicycle, wobbling in wide half circles. He burst out laughing when he narrowly missed a tree. Neither Jane nor Reuben noticed Sol Rosen's face at the window of his office.

Jane kept up a running dialogue all the way to her apartment, alternately telling him how grateful she was for what she called her lucky break and for Reuben's saving her from a fate worse than death at the Mimosa Club.

Inside the tiny, neat apartment, Reuben immediately kicked off his shoes and sat down on a white wicker chair with cherry-red cushions. He leaned back and propped his feet on a wicker table full of newspapers and magazines stacked on each side. In the middle of the table a white ceramic unicorn pawed the air with his two front legs — a throwback to the child in Jane, he decided.

"I can make us some coffee now and you can drink it and read today's paper while I make dinner. Is that okay with you? . . . You know, I still can't believe how good you've been to me without wanting anything in return. I was beginning to think there weren't any more good people in the world. I'm glad you proved me wrong."

"Make the coffee," Reuben said gruffly. He liked hearing her say nice things about him. Jane was probably one of the few sincere people he'd ever dealt with.

Reuben was engrossed in Will Hays's interview in the *Examiner* when Jane set a cup of coffee next to the prancing unicorn. "I know you drink it black. If you want cream or sugar, I have it."

"How do you know that? How do you know I drink my coffee black?"

Jane flushed. "That night at the club. I wasn't that out of it. I won't be long. Are you sure you like stuffed peppers? I could make something else. It's not fancy. I'm about as plain in my food tastes as I look."

"Jane, I'm not fussy when it comes to what I eat. I am, however, very fussy about who I eat with."

Jane smiled all through dinner as Reuben ate three helpings of her stuffed peppers. He was no slouch about scooping the mashed potatoes onto his plate, and he proclaimed her sour cream cucumbers the best he'd ever eaten. He shook his head over her offer of a slice of jelly roll but did accept a cup of coffee laced with cinnamon.

"Jane, that was one good dinner," he announced with a satisfied sigh. "I hope we can do it again sometime. I thought by now you would have moved into a house or at least some big fancy apartment. You should think about buying a house. Paying rent is money down the drain. Aren't we paying you enough at the studio?"

"Good Lord, yes. But I haven't had the

time to look for something. I don't know . . . this little apartment makes me remember who I am. I don't want to get like those . . . I'm not one of those people Will Hays writes about. I pretty much bank all my money except what I send home to my parents. I like it here," she said defensively.

"I like it, too." Reuben grinned. "You must have noticed I kicked off my shoes as soon as I got here. That's a sign that a man is comfortable. You have a nice touch, Jane."

"Thanks, Reuben."

She was pretty when she smiled — not beautiful, but she was pretty. "Daniel asks about you all the time," he told her. "After the party he talked for days about the good time you had."

"How is he doing?" she asked. "I bet he's getting straight A's. I never met anyone as smart as Daniel."

"Yes, he is smart, that's why he's at Harvard. Jane," Reuben said impulsively, "do you have much money in the bank? What I mean is, are you interested in the stock market? Daniel gives me tips from time to time; I acted on one of them today, as a matter of fact. There's every chance you could make a nice nest egg for yourself."

Jane's face puckered in thought. "Is it risky?" she asked.

"Everything's risky. Before I leave I'll give you a note to take to my broker. Go down-

town on your lunch hour tomorrow and talk to him. Now, look," Reuben said, holding up his hand. "Don't feel this is something you have to do just because I mentioned it. It's your money, and yes, it's risky. I guess what I'm trying to say is, if you decide to go ahead and invest, use only what you feel you can afford to lose if things don't work out right. . . . Tell me, how're things with the boyfriend?" he asked to change the subject.

Jane made a comical face. "What boyfriend? That's over. I'm footloose and fancy free. And I'm not looking for another boyfriend. I still hurt a little. Pride, Reuben, is such a deadly sin. I don't ever want to hang my head in shame. Do you know what I'm talking about?"

Of course he knew; he lived with it every day. He didn't trust himself to speak, so he simply nodded.

"I was so delighted when I heard you got married," Jane continued. "I hope you're happy." It occurred to her to wonder why he was here, why he'd almost invited himself. She'd heard the rumors, and then his absence from the studio for so long set tongues to wagging. She found it hard to believe this handsome man's beautiful wife was a drunk and dope fiend. How had he gotten involved with someone like that? She wished she could ask him.

"I really enjoyed my dinner." Reuben

looked around. "This place is you, Jane, but if you buy any more plants, you'll have to move. I'll come back again if you don't mind."

"I don't mind at all. I was glad for the company this evening, and I will go down to your broker tomorrow. I appreciate the tip."

"I'll be sending a young man over to your studio lot tomorrow — someone I came across today. I think maybe you two might hit it off, or at least be friends. He's a handsome fella working as a desk clerk at the Ambassador. We'll give him a screen test and see if he can't fit into some of your films. Treat him nice, okay?"

"Of course. . . . Good night, Reuben." Jane stood on tiptoe to kiss Reuben lightly on the cheek. She smelled faintly of cinnamon. "That's for being a nice guy. Now, drive carefully."

Even though it was late, Reuben decided to stop at the Mimosa Club for a drink in Max's back office. There was nothing to go home to but empty, dust-covered rooms.

Max stifled his surprise at Reuben's second visit of the day. He jerked his head in the direction of his office. "You want to drink alone or do you want to talk?"

"Depends on what you want to talk about, Max. Get the drink and then I'll decide."

When Max returned a few minutes later, Reuben was sound asleep on the chair. Max

scratched his head in bewilderment. He poked his head out the door and motioned to two of his bouncers.

"Carry him over to the couch. You wake him up and your ass is grass. Pretend you're carrying your mother to church," he hissed.

When the door closed behind the two bouncers, Max opened the closet and pulled out an afghan his mother had crocheted for just such an occasion. It was purple and red with splotches of yellow throughout. It was loud and bright enough to wake the dead. Reuben didn't stir when Max covered him.

CHAPTER
THIRTY-FIVE

Sol Rosen paced his bedroom like a wounded bull. He felt like bellowing, but there was no one to listen.

For hours he'd been ringing Reuben's phone in Laurel Canyon and getting no answer. It was two-thirty now and there was still no answer. Sol always prided himself on putting two and two together and coming up with the right answer. And he'd done that the moment he saw Reuben and the girl on the bicycle. Jesus Christ, this was all he needed — Reuben out whoring around with one of his own stars while his wife was drying out in Palm Springs. No wonder his little girl had gone off the deep end.

Women! By God, they were always at the root of a problem. Just like Mickey was at the root of his problem. Temporarily diverted from thoughts of Reuben, Sol brooded over the fact that Mickey hadn't responded to his long-overdue payment months before. He'd formally requested an additional twenty-five

percent of the studio, and when she hadn't answered him, he'd sent a letter to her bankers in Paris as well; but they hadn't responded, either. The fact that he'd received neither a yes nor a no could only mean Mickey was content to let things be as they were, with Reuben calling all the shots and reporting back to her. If he could just get that other twenty-five percent, he wouldn't give a shit what Reuben did. Maybe he should write another letter and let her know Reuben was into some hanky-panky with someone other than his wife. How would Michelene like to hear that?

Sol continued to pace, scowling with every step he took. At ten minutes after four he called the house in Laurel Canyon again. He let the phone ring twenty-four times before he replaced the receiver in the cradle. "You son of a bitch!" he snarled. When he dialed the number again at twenty-five minutes after five he laid the receiver on the table. The goddamn phone would ring until someone picked it up and the connection was broken.

At eight o'clock the phone was still ringing. Sol wondered about the durability of the telephone system. At last he broke the connection and called his daughter in Palm Springs. He half expected Bebe to cry, but she didn't. All she said was she would wait and talk to Reuben when he returned.

On his way to the studio, Sol decided he

was as big a bastard as Tarz. What kind of father would tell his daughter what he'd just told Bebe? He began to rationalize his action, telling himself it was his only way of getting back at Reuben, something he'd been wanting to do since the day the bastard had first walked into his office. Reuben deserved whatever happened to him. If he could just sack him, boot his ass out into the street, he'd be the happiest man alive.

Sol barely looked at Reuben when he stomped his way to his office. The newspaper was laid out on his desk with his morning cup of coffee. He glanced at the headlines with disbelieving eyes. WILL HAYS TO RETURN TO NEW YORK . . . after issuing a statement saying all was well in the city of sex, sin, and scandal. Sol's breath exploded in a long sigh until he read on: "Reuben Tarz, vice president of Fairmont, was seen entering Will Hays's suite at midday for a meeting with the fearless crusader. This paper wonders what the meeting was about. Will Hays would only say it was informative. As we go to press, Reuben Tarz was unavailable for comment."

Sol stumbled his way to Reuben's office, ignoring Margaret's shout about being formally announced.

"What in the goddamn hell is this all about?" he snarled, brandishing the newspaper. "I want an answer right now!'

Reuben shrugged. "I cut him off at the pass.

What more do you need to know?"

"How?" Sol bellowed.

"That's my business. I solved our problem, that's the end of it."

"Like hell it's the end of it. You can't trust that mealy-mouthed bastard. How do you know he won't —"

"Inform the public about Eli and Bebe? Take my word for it, he won't."

"It's your fault Bebe's like she is. She never drank or took dope till she married you. I must have been out of my mind to give her permission to marry you. I saw you last night, Tarz, with that girl on the handlebars of the bicycle. You went home with her, and don't goddamn deny it. I tried calling your house till eight o'clock this morning and you weren't there. Just where the hell were you?"

"That's none of your business," Reuben retorted coldly. "My personal life has nothing to do with this studio, and don't ever make the mistake again of asking me where I spend my time. I've been cleaning and scraping your family's slime for too long. From now on you can scrape it yourself."

"Bebe's your wife," Sol blustered. "She's carrying your child. . . . Well, goddammit, say something!"

"There's very little you know about your daughter, Sol. I did not force her to drink, nor did I force her to smoke marijuana or sniff cocaine. Eli introduced her to all three

748

amusements. You lay the blame where it belongs." Reuben got up from his desk and walked around to confront Sol. "Butt out of my personal business, Sol."

"This is my . . . Fairmont is . . ."

Reuben's eyes narrowed. "Your studio, is that what you were going to say? Of course it is. The next time you feel it necessary to remind me of that will be the day I walk out of here leaving you holding the bag. You got that?"

"You're a bastard!" Sol bellowed.

"At least we're in agreement about something," Reuben replied.

"What about Bebe?"

"What about her?"

"Well . . . what . . . I already . . ."

"What you did was put your big foot in your mouth, and now I'll have to pull it out. I'll take care of my wife. Is there anything else you want to discuss? If there isn't, let me get back to work."

"When are you going back to Palm Springs?" Sol demanded.

"When I'm goddamn good and ready, that's when."

Sol was a bull elephant charging out of the office, slamming the door so hard Reuben thought it would fall off the hinges.

Eli whispered into the phone, his ferret eyes sweeping the room to see if anyone was

listening. "Bebe, I can't. Pop will kill me if he finds out. Of course I love you. Bebe, wait till after you have the baby. . . . Bebe, listen to me — don't cry, Bebe. . . . Oh, all right, I'll leave in a little while. Just a little bit . . . No, I can't. . . . That's too much, Bebe. Of course I don't want to keep driving back and forth. If Pop catches on, or Reuben, what will you tell them? . . . Yes, yes, I'll come. You're going to owe me big-time for this, Bebe. If Pop gets after me for anything, it doesn't matter what it is, you better promise me . . . In half an hour. Good-bye, Bebe."

Shit! Now he was going to have to scurry around like a rat to get what Bebe wanted. He was like a wet noodle in her hands.

When Reuben returned to Palm Springs four days later, his wife was in the same shape as when he'd first brought her to the resort. It took him an hour to find all the places she'd stashed what she called her goodies. He was angry now and disgusted. "There was no reason for any of this, Bebe. Why couldn't you wait to hear my side of things? I did not do what Sol accused me of. I ate dinner at Jane's apartment and later stopped in at the Mimosa Club and slept in Max's office all night. Right now I don't give a damn if you believe me or not. This time you will weather this alone. I'll have guards watch you. You brought this on yourself, Bebe."

Reuben stayed in Palm Springs until two of

Max's henchmen arrived to serve as "body" guards. "Meals in her room," Reuben instructed them. "Make her walk three times a day. Let her sit in the sun, but don't ever take your eyes off her. When she goes into labor, call me." To Bebe he said in a cold, deadly voice, "You fuck up this time and I will divorce you. You do anything to harm the child you're carrying and I'll personally retaliate." His voice softened a degree. "I am so disappointed in you, Bebe. You gave me your word. I trusted you to deliver a healthy child for us." With that he turned on his heel and left.

"Reuben, wait," Bebe called after him frantically. "Reuben, does this mean we won't start over when . . . Reuben, please come back. . . . I'm sorry, I won't — Reuben!"

Ten weeks later Reuben was back at the private clinic in Palm Springs. It was a little past midnight and he was pacing the floor like any expectant father. Each time he heard Bebe scream, it was like a knife slicing through him.

The doctor's weary eyes sought Reuben out. "You have a son, Mr. Tarz. I usually like to tell the fathers they have healthy, bouncing baby boys, but I'm afraid I can't in your case. Your son is premature at five pounds, and he's not robust. I can't understand the hard labor we went through since your wife has had a previous child. For some reason she

seemed to be holding back, not cooperating when I instructed her to bear down. I guess I'm just tired; it's been a very long night. You can see your son shortly. My nurse is cleaning him up."

Reuben reeled in shock. Bebe had had another child? But then, why should it come as such a surprise to him? She'd pranced and danced her way all over Europe. God only knew whom she'd slept with. He walked outside, taking deep gulps of fresh air. Christ, he was tired. He decided then, for his own emotional survival, that whatever had transpired in Bebe's life before he'd married her was her business. He would not let his wife know that the doctor had told him.

When the nurse held up his son, Reuben peered through the glass and blinked in shock. He wanted to shout, Take it back, that isn't my son! He'd been expecting a pink-cheeked, plump infant with a sweet, downy head — a miniature of either himself or Bebe. This scrawny, red, puckered bundle looked exactly like Eli. He turned away so the nurse wouldn't see the disgust he felt.

"Did they show him to you, Reuben?" Bebe asked wanly when he came to visit. "Is he beautiful? He will be later. Sometimes new babies look like dried-up prunes, but after a week or so they start to fill out, and . . . What's wrong?"

"He looks like . . . Eli."

"Like Eli?" Bebe shrilled, horrified. "Like *Eli?*"

Reuben nodded. "Maybe they showed you the wrong baby," she squealed. "Reuben, tell them I want to see him. Now! If you don't, I'll scream my head off. *Now!*"

Bebe's wails of outrage rang in Reuben's ears for hours after he left the clinic. He'd wanted this baby, wanted it desperately. He wanted something to love, something of his very own, something he'd created. Instead he'd walked away, in his own fashion denouncing the child because it had the misfortune to look like Eli. Blame something, Tarz, he told himself. Blame . . . blame . . . blame . . .

He had a son.

On leaden feet Reuben returned to the clinic nursery. "I'd like to . . . to hold my son," he told the nurse on duty.

She nodded sympathetically. "We don't usually allow the fathers to hold preemies, but this time I'm going to allow it. Here, put this gown on. He's frail, but he's not going to break."

The minute the nurse was out of sight, Reuben examined every inch of his new son. Satisfied that he had all his parts, he leaned back to savor the feel of the life he'd created. The bundle was warm and snug, the little face screwed into a grimace. How defenseless, how dependent he was! Reuben made a

vow to the warm being in his arms to give him everything life had to offer. "We're calling you Simon," he whispered. "It's a strong name for such a little man, but you'll live up to it. I know you don't understand a word I'm saying, but I want to apologize for my earlier feelings. Maybe someday we'll talk about this day, and maybe we won't. If we do, I won't lie to you. I'll never lie to you, Simon, because I am your father and fathers don't lie to their sons."

The nurse was back, her arms outstretched to take the child. "It's time for him to eat."

"Eat?" Reuben said stupidly.

The nurse smiled. "Yes, eat."

Reuben followed her to Bebe's room and watched as she fit the baby to his wife's breast.

"I hate this," Bebe said through clenched teeth.

Until Bebe opened her mouth, Reuben had thought it a beautiful sight. For the second time that day, he turned on his heel and left the clinic.

The next morning, he left for Los Angeles. Bebe and the baby, along with the two bodyguards, returned six weeks later to the house in Laurel Canyon. Bebe handed Simon to the nurse and immediately went to the phone to call Eli.

Reuben found his life changing; he was now

a parent with a parent's responsibilities — responsibilities that he took so seriously, he became the butt of good-natured jocularity at Fairmont. He woke early in the mornings to accommodate Simon's schedule. He watched while the little fellow took his bottle, had his bath, and was introduced to mashed food. He would hold his clean, sweet-smelling baby for twenty minutes, or until he fell asleep. He returned at noon, or as close to noon as he could, when Simon had his lunch. On more than one occasion when business was heavy he had the nurse bring the baby to the studio.

Several times Reuben found himself featured on the second page of the *Examiner* with a tidbit about how he'd held his son during a business meeting, chuckling and burping him at the same time. A devoted father. Nothing was ever said about Simon's absentee mother. At six o'clock he dropped whatever he was doing, no matter how important, to head home for Simon's dinner and bedtime. In the beginning it was a chore, but as time went on Reuben grew to like his routine and actually looked forward to the time he spent with his son.

He recognized the fact that Simon would never be a strong, robust child; doctors told him, clucking their tongues in sympathy, that Bebe's dependence on alcohol and drugs during the early stages of her pregnancy had

dictated his condition. While Reuben accepted the doctor's words with equanimity, inside he damned Bebe for her recklessness. Each time he looked at her, his eyes accused her . . . until the day he told her he couldn't bear the sight of her another minute. And always, not far back in his mind was the knowledge that she'd borne another son or daughter that he knew nothing about. Where was the child and who was the father? As much and as many times as he told himself he didn't care, he did care. It ate at him daily, no matter how hard he tried to shelve it far back in his mind.

Bebe was absent for long periods of time now — weeks, sometimes months. She called from time to time to inquire about her son's health and the well-being of her husband. In time, Reuben came to welcome her absences and hated it when she was home, upsetting the routine he tried to establish. She took great pleasure in swooping into the nursery at dawn, just home from a party, dressed in glittery sequins and gleaming jewels, her face thick with makeup, high on liquor and marijuana. At such times Reuben could see the confusion in Simon's face. Once, as he was leaving the room, he heard her croon, "Ah, John Paul, you thought I forgot about you. Mama never forgets." When she saw Reuben stop in midstride she stiffened momentarily, then hugged the child and told him the words

were actually lyrics for a new song she'd heard recently. Her eyes were sad but defiant when she kissed the boy and fumbled her way out of the room.

Thus life stumbled on for Reuben and his little family. As his wealth and power soared, his marriage crumbled. There were times when he didn't know where his wife was until he read about her in the social pages of the paper. But he no longer cared; it was that simple.

Spring came early to Massachusetts and Reuben thanked God for the brisk, warm day. If he'd wished for trees in full leaf, flowers in bloom, and a light breeze, not to mention the golden sunshine, he couldn't have done a better job of it than Mother Nature. It was the kind of day to remember.

Daniel's graduation from Harvard Law School and his being here, along with Max and Jane, was a surprise. The moment he read the letter from the dean informing him Daniel was graduating summa cum laude, he'd wangled and finagled for front-row seats. Now they were in the coffee shop having breakfast, a hearty meal that Reuben only pushed around on his plate. "I swear," Jane said through mouthfuls of food, "you are going to bust at the seams, Reuben."

Reuben beamed. "I'm just so damn proud of him. He told me from the beginning he'd

be a straight-A student and that he'd make me proud of him. There has to be a better word than proud, but I don't know what it is. Jesus Christ, summa cum laude! Where else could that happen but here in America? And Hollywood," he muttered under his breath. Jane was right, he felt as though he were going to burst any second.

"The kid is going to be real surprised to see you, Reuben," Max said, dabbing at his mouth. "But I don't know how he's going to feel about seeing me here. I know he thinks I'm a bad influence on you. You keep saying it's all right, and I hope it is. I don't want to embarrass him on a day like this."

"He's past all that, Max. Daniel's all grown up now. I want you here and that'll be good enough for Daniel. Trust me."

"What's he going to do — I mean, where is he going to practice?" Jane asked.

"I hope in Hollywood, but that's up to him. I just want him to be happy and successful. Jesus, I can't believe this!" Reuben said for the umpteenth time.

Max grinned. "The kid must have been real disappointed when you told him you couldn't make it. You just wanted to surprise him, right?"

"Yeah, he was, but he said he understood. I would be here even if he wasn't summa cum laude and if I had to crawl all the way on my hands and knees. I love that guy!" Reuben

exclaimed happily.

"I can't wait to see his face when he sees us sitting in the front row." Jane smiled. "Just like a real family. I guess we are Daniel's family, sort of. I can be his sister, Max can be his uncle, and you, Reuben, you are Daniel's everything — brother, father, above all, his friend."

Forty minutes later they were in their seats, dead center with the stage where Daniel would give his speech. Reuben wondered what Daniel would say if he knew he'd sent a cable to Mickey. Whatever there was between Mickey and himself had nothing to do with Daniel, and she deserved to know about this wonderful day. By now he knew the words to the cable by heart because he'd ripped up twenty-three of them before he'd finally settled on just the right words and the right tone.

Dear Mickey, Daniel graduates Harvard Law School summa cum laude, May 20. Will congratulate him for both of us. Warm regards, Reuben Tarz

How had she reacted to the cable, he wondered wistfully. Proud, certainly — unless, of course, she'd forgotten about him, which he didn't think likely. *Mickey, Mickey, where are you? Are you well? Have you really forsaken us?* With a sigh, he forced his mind

back to the present. This was Daniel's day, and nothing was going to spoil it.

Within moments they called Daniel's name, and there he was, making his way to the podium. No papers, his speech would be in his head. The crazy urge to stand up and shout was so strong, Reuben felt light-headed. Daniel looked nervous. Poor bastard, it must be tough standing up there facing all these people. Look at me, Daniel! I'm here! Daniel, look down. Do it, Daniel, before I bust a gut.

"Ladies and gentlemen, members of —" And then he saw him, sitting in the middle of the row with all the proud parents . . . and he did something then, something so out of character for him that the audience smiled. "Reuben, you came! . . . And faculty," he continued, grinning from ear to ear. Reuben smiled past the lump in his throat. His eyes burned and he didn't care if the whole world saw the tears trickling down his cheeks. He made a circle with his thumb and index finger — Right on, buddy.

The moment the ceremony ended, Reuben was off his chair. Once again Daniel lost his composure and leapt off the stage, his diploma clutched in his hand. "Son of a gun! God, I can't believe you're here! Talk about a surprise! Jane, Max! Jesus, it's good to see you. This guy dragged you all the way here. Some friend, huh?"

"I'm so very proud of you, Daniel," Jane said, hugging him.

"I'm kind of proud of me, too. It was a hell of a three years, I can tell you that, but I had to make this guy proud of me." He poked Reuben affectionately on the arm. "I still can't believe you're all here."

"Mr. Bishop," interjected a strange voice. Startled, Daniel turned and nodded at a tall man wearing a dark three-piece suit. "I've been instructed to give you this," he said, holding out a white envelope. "May I offer my congratulations, Mr. Bishop? Marcus Welstar, Morgan Guaranty Bank." He held out his hand, and Daniel gripped it in surprise.

"Thank you," Daniel said, puzzled.

"What is it?" Reuben demanded as the man walked back into the crowd.

"Never heard of him. Maybe they want to hire me. Wouldn't that be something!" he said, ripping at the white envelope. A moment later, as his eyes scanned the paper he was holding, he gasped. "It's from Mickey. Listen to this:

My dear Daniel,

I have no words to tell you how very proud I am of you on this very special day. My heart is so full for having known you. I hope we can call each other friends for all of our lives.

I took the liberty of writing to your dean

and asked him where he thought you belonged in the legal field. He responded by saying the nation's capital would be your forte. Thus I took liberty once again and had Mr. Welstar outfit an office for you on K Street in Washington. All you have to do is hang up your shingle, as they say in America.

I feel blessed, Daniel, for having known you.

Much love and affection,
Mickey

"It's a deed to a building," Daniel said in awe. "I don't believe this! Reuben, do you see what she's done!"

Reuben nodded. "I . . . I cabled her, Daniel. I thought she had a right to know."

"I take it that means you haven't really been in touch or . . . I wish I knew why . . . Never mind, that's water under the bridge." But of course it wasn't. Obviously Reuben still loved Mickey, and in his heart Daniel knew Mickey loved Reuben. "I thought I was going to set up practice in California so I could be near you. I thought that was one of the reasons I went to law school. . . . Hey! I want to hear all about Simon. Daddy Reuben. Now, that does have a ring to it, pal."

Reuben smiled. "Well, he likes presents." No need to tell Daniel the boy preferred rag dolls and picture books to the exclusion of

other toys. "And listen, Daniel, Hollywood is no place for you to practice law. They call it Sin City these days. Hays is leaving us alone and working behind the scenes, thanks to you."

Daniel laughed. "I thought he had cleaned it all up."

"Only in print. You would not believe what goes on behind the scenes. You're clean, pal, and you're going to stay that way. Things at the studio . . . Hollywood . . . sometimes we cut here and there, skirt the edges . . . that kind of thing. It's best for you in Washington. I want to hear you tell me you understand."

"Of course I understand," Daniel said. "If Washington is where you think I should be, then that's where I'll be. But first I have to pass the bar exams."

Reuben grinned. "I don't think that'll be too much of a problem for you. . . . Now then," he said, linking arms with Daniel on one side and Jane on the other, Max following behind, "what do you say to a little luncheon celebration. I think you've earned it — and besides, I'm starved!"

Sol Rosen's spit-and-polish office, where very little business was conducted these days, irritated the portly man. His head felt as empty as his desk looked. In his hand he held what he referred to as his downfall, a letter from Mickey Fonsard's Paris attorneys. For two

goddamn years he'd been writing both Mickey and the lawyers, offering to buy an additional twenty-five percent of Fairmont, and only now was there a response. He wanted to howl his outrage, and found himself mimicking the prissy-sounding words on the crackly paper. "Madame Fonsard thanks you for your up-do-date payments. Unfortunately at this time she cannot offer any further percentage in the company. Madame Fonsard wishes you to be informed that her fifty-one percent of Fairmont Studios is now being held by Philippe Bouchet."

Sol frowned. Just who the hell was Philippe Bouchet? The date on the legal transfer was 1921, the year Reuben Tarz had come to the studio. That meant he must have known about this guy Bouchet when he'd arrived with Mickey's letter requesting a job. He'd probably been instructed by them to inch his way in and then take over, bit by bit, which was exactly what he had done. It was all a plan, a rotten game, and only Reuben knew the rules. What had they offered Reuben in the way of a reward, he wondered. The presidency of Fairmont, probably, along with power and glory. Bastard!

Sol scooped up all the legal papers and left for his personal attorney's office. Forty-nine percent still gave him a loud voice, and Bouchet was on the other side of the world.

CHAPTER THIRTY-SIX

The Paris garden was alive with noise, birds chirping and the gleeful shouts of Philippe Bouchet as he raced after a fat puppy named Dolly, a frisky kitten named Molly fast on their heels. Jake was already at the finish line, his pink tongue ready to lick at Philippe the minute he sat down. All of them were after a red ball that eluded plump fingers and frisky paws.

Watching them, Mickey laughed. The exquisitely groomed garden would be a shambles before long, not that she cared. "I do believe you are the Three Musketeers," she said fondly to the boy.

"Yes," the boy said, grinning mischievously. "Not Molly. Only dogs and me. One, two, three." He pointed to Jake and Dolly and himself with his pudgy finger. "Like the picture of my papa and Uncle Daniel and you, *Maman*."

Mickey smiled. The legend lived on. Philippe loved the stories of the happy three-

some represented in the portrait that hung in a position of honor over the mantel at Château Fonsard. This year when they started out for Paris for the preschool term, Philippe had insisted they bring the painting with them. He'd also insisted they bring Jake, Molly, and Dolly. Mickey had grumbled a bit but happily stuffed the car like a sausage.

"When are we going back to the château?" the little boy asked.

"When school is finished. You must learn, Philippe, that it is important to have a proper education."

"So my papa will be proud of me. I speak three languages and I'm six. Will that make my papa proud?"

"Very proud. I am very proud of you, too," Mickey said softly.

"When will I meet him, *Maman?*"

Mickey hated the question and always responded in the same way. "When it is time." So far the child hadn't pinned her down to any specific time; he was still content with her response. That would not always be the case, she knew, but she would deal with it at the proper time.

"What came in the post, *Maman?* More business letters?"

"Of course. It is always the business letters." Mickey laughed.

"Open it and tell me about it," Philippe said in the grown-up voice he affected when he

wanted to sound serious.

"You remind me of a precocious squirrel, *chéri,*" Mickey said as she obediently opened the packet from America and quickly scanned the contents. "Now, what is it you wish to know?" she asked, smiling.

Philippe's head went up as he stuffed his hands into his pockets and rocked back on his heels. The little boy looked so much like Reuben with his mannerisms that Mickey's heart fluttered. "Everything."

"Very well." Mickey made a pretense of reading the papers again. "This paper says your brother Simon's grandfather is perturbed about . . . certain matters."

"Why do you just call him Simon's grandfather? If he is my brother's grandfather, then he is mine, too. I should have a grandfather if Simon has one," the boy grumbled.

Mickey's voice grew stern. "We have gone over this several times, Philippe, and I have no wish to do it yet another time. It is unfortunate that you do not have a grandfather. There is nothing I can do about it." She hated herself for the lie, but she had no other recourse. Perhaps at some point in the future she could tell him the truth. "It will do you no good to glare at me, Philippe. If you persist, I will not tell you what else is in these letters."

The boy dropped to the grass and hugged his knees, the dogs and cat at his side. "I will

listen . . . respectfully." He smiled, and Mickey's heart melted.

"Now, listen to me very carefully, *chéri*. This paper," she said, holding up the stiff, folded document, "says you, Philippe Bouchet own . . . Are you ready to hear what you own?" Mickey teased.

"Yes, yes, yes. . . . What do I own, *Maman?*" the little boy squealed. Surely it was a pony cart or a sailboat — something grand, at least. His heart pounded in anticipation.

"You own fifty-one percent of Fairmont Studios in America. Isn't that wonderful?"

Tears gathered in the little boy's eyes. "But I cannot play with a studio, *Maman.*"

"Big boys do not cry when they are disappointed, *chéri*. . . . Now, do you wish me to continue?"

"Yes, *Maman.*"

"All right, now, listen to me. When you own fifty-one percent of something, that makes you the major stockholder. In other words, you are the boss. Your papa works at Fairmont Studios. He is a very important man. More important than Simon's grandfather. Are you following me, Philippe?" The little boy nodded, his head buzzing with questions. "Someday, when you are old enough, you will go to America and take over your studio. You will be your papa's boss."

"How can that be, Maman? Papas are grown-up people. I am only six years old.

That will not be for a very long time." He sounded so dejected and forlorn. Mickey took him into her arms.

"Right now it seems like a very long time, but time moves very swiftly, sometimes too swiftly. You will be president and chairman of the board. It will be a tremendous responsibility, Philippe, and that is why you must study hard so you will be able to operate the studio."

Philippe wiggled in Mickey's arms. He was getting too big to sit on his mother's lap, but he didn't want to hurt her feelings by jumping off. "Will I share the studio with my papa and Simon?"

Mickey's throat constricted. "Only if you wish to do so," she said quietly.

"Yes, I will do that. I will share. Is my father *ever* going to come and see me? Will Simon ever come and see me?" the boy asked wistfully.

"No, Philippe. We've gone over this many times. When you are of age you will go to America. Now, shoo, into the house with you." The little boy raced off, Jake three laps ahead of him, Dolly and Molly doing their best to keep up. Mickey knew where he was going, where she would find him when she entered the house.

"Now everyone has to be quiet while I look at my papa," Philippe said, wagging his finger

at the animals squatting by his heels. "Shhhhh."

How he loved this picture of his papa and his uncle Daniel! They looked like the heroes in his picture books. Surely they did all kinds of wonderful things. "If you were here, you'd build me a tree house, wouldn't you, Papa?" he asked sadly. "I wish you'd come just once. I would be good and you would like me. I would be a very good boy. Jake and Dolly will behave. Dolly is Jake's . . ." He struggled for the proper word. "Maybe baby . . . a girl," he said, laughing. "When I say my god-blesses at night, I do one for you and one for Uncle Daniel. *Maman* says that is right." Tears began to trickle down his cheeks. Jake whined at his feet and Dolly tried to snag his socks with her puppy teeth. Philippe dropped down and cuddled the dogs to his chest. "If he liked me just a little bit, he'd come to see me. Just a little bit . . ."

Bebe Tarz woke one morning in the summer of 1929 with a fierce headache. She lay still, trying to remember what she'd done the previous evening to warrant such vicious throbbing. But the harder she struggled to remember, the worse her head pounded. It frightened her, this inability to remember details that were only hours old. Then her fear turned to panic when she thought she might be losing her mind. Alcohol and drugs

ate at your brain, Reuben had told her once.

The timid knock on her door sounded like a thunderclap to her ears. The maid entered with a silver tray containing her coffee and the morning paper. Thank God, maybe the coffee would help her headache. Impatiently she waved the maid away when she started to open the curtains. What she really needed was a drink. Maybe if she could get through the morning without tapping a bottle, she could think a little better. With an ease born of practice, she tumbled eight aspirin into her hand and swallowed them down with a deep gulp of coffee. But this time her tried-and-true home remedy failed; five minutes later she was in the bathroom throwing up, and when she returned to her bed it was all she could do to climb in. If Reuben could see her now, he'd be nasty and contemptuous toward her, and she wouldn't blame him.

My God, why couldn't she remember where she'd been and what she'd done last evening? Again, she tried to think. Yes, she recalled dressing to meet Adam James, Fox's answer to Miguel Paola, the Latin lover. Adam was a wonderful lover, always telling her how beautiful she was, how glamourous she looked, and how thrilled he was that she wanted him, not her handsome husband, the head of Fairmont Studios.

Bebe massaged her throbbing temples. They'd driven up the coast highway and had

dinner, after which they'd gone to a hotel and made love. Then they'd smoked a reefer each, snorted a line of cocaine, and had a few drinks from Adam's flask. It was around midnight when they'd left. . . . Adam had dropped her off where she'd left her car. And that was it, all she could remember. How and when had she gotten home? God, why couldn't she remember? Maybe if she put it out of her mind for a little while and read the paper, the evening's events would come back to her.

The coffee cup slid unnoticed from her hand when she opened the newspaper to the front page. The headline glared at her: STAR'S WIFE COMMITS SUICIDE OVER OTHER WOMAN. Bebe ran for the bathroom a second time as the finale to her evening surfaced at last. The wrath of God was going to come tumbling down on her head now.

It was all rushing back so fast, her head was spinning. Adam had brought his car to a stop beside hers. They'd both gotten out of his car, and he'd kissed her, a long, lingering kiss. Stupidly she'd professed her love for him in a clear voice, a voice that had carried to the figure crouching alongside her car. Adam had said something equally stupid about loving her, about getting a divorce and marrying her, but she'd been too drunk to do more than laugh at his words.

Suddenly he'd shouted, "Melissa! My God,

what are you doing hiding in the bushes? Spying!"

Melissa was a timid little soul, or so Adam had said previously, so timid she believed anything he said. But the Melissa she'd seen last night was anything but timid. She'd pulled a gun out of her pocket and aimed it first at Bebe and then at Adam, calling them every name she could think of. Too shocked to do anything but stare at the gun, Bebe had listened to Melissa's tearful tirade. Then, when she'd tired of her verbal attack on Adam, she'd switched her attention to Bebe, the gun wavering in her fist.

"Tramp! Slut! Home wrecker!"

"Please, Mrs. James, it isn't what you think," Bebe shouted, not knowing whether she was more afraid of the woman holding the gun or her father and Reuben.

"I'll see both of you smeared all over the papers! Slut! We just had a new baby," Melissa shrieked. "Did he tell you *that?* You don't deserve to live, either of you!" Her voice was shaky, the hand holding the gun shakier.

"Please, I have a son," Bebe pleaded, backing away. "Take your husband home and I swear I'll never see him again. I swear it!"

The handsome actor advanced on his wife. He smiled, hoping she would calm down and give him the gun. Instead, she backed up, the gun still shaking in her hand.

"Do something, Adam, she's crazed," Bebe

screamed. "We could die here!"

Adam lunged at his wife and they struggled. When the gun went off, Bebe buried her face in her hands.

"Please don't kill me, please don't," she sobbed, too drunk and panicked to think clearly. "Please, please, please."

"Shut up, Bebe!" Adam barked. "Melissa is dead; the gun went off when we were struggling. We have to get out of here. Oh, God, I don't even know how she got here. Listen, you and I didn't see each other tonight. No — wait a minute — the restaurant where we had dinner, someone will remember. Maybe we should say we met accidentally and had dinner. That won't prove Melissa knew or didn't know. Look, go home. I'll go home, too, and tomorrow I'll call the police and say she didn't come home this evening. . . . God, where in the hell did she get the gun?"

"I don't know and I don't care," Bebe cried. "She was deranged and could have killed me. You're no hero, Adam, and I don't know what I ever saw in you. You killed your own wife!" She marched around to the driver's side of her car and got in. "Don't bring me into this. She's *your* wife! Well, she *was* your wife." With that she drove off in a cloud of dust, leaving Adam and his dead wife in the bushes at the side of the road. Another performance worthy of Clovis Ames.

"Oh, God, oh, God," Bebe bleated now as

she hopped out of bed. Wild with fear, she started throwing clothes into suitcases. Where would she go, what would she do? Adam would incriminate her. If the situation were reversed, she'd sing so loud they'd hear her in Canada.

Reuben. She had to tell Reuben. He would know what to do. If this scandal were to explode in his face, he'd hate her. But anything was better than going to prison, she thought wildly . . . wasn't it?

She dressed as quickly as she could, throwing on pieces of clothing in a careless frenzy that left her looking no better than she had when Reuben had carted her off to Palm Springs. Oh, God, she'd been safe there, protected. Yes, Reuben could take her back to Palm Springs. Things could be all right again. Christ, right now she'd kill for a drink! "I didn't mean that," she cried. "I'd never kill anyone."

Barefoot, Bebe tottered into the dressing room, picked up the phone, and dialed Reuben's office number. "I want to speak to my husband, Margaret, right now. Right this minute. I don't care what he's doing, get him on this phone!" she cried hysterically. The second she heard Reuben's voice she relaxed. "You have to come home, Reuben! Now!"

"Did something happen to Simon?" he asked anxiously.

"Simon? No, of course not. Why would

something happen to Simon? I want you to come home, Reuben. Immediately!"

"I can't leave right now. If Simon is all right, why should I come home?" His voice was so cold, Bebe started to tremble.

"If you don't come right now, I'll take Simon and leave this goddamn house. I mean it!" she shrilled. "I'll give you thirty minutes and that's it!" She slammed the phone down so hard, she winced at the noise.

The minute she heard the sound of squealing tires in the driveway, she ran down the steps. When Reuben rushed through the door, she burst into tears. Between blowing her nose, wringing her hands, and pacing up and down, she told her husband about her affair with Adam James. "It's your fault, Reuben! If you were a real husband to me, I wouldn't have to go somewhere else to find what I need. You're as much to blame as I am. Get me out of here and keep my name out of the papers. Take me back to Palm Springs and stay with me. We were so happy there, remember? I won't drink, I'll give up the drugs. Make me well again, Reuben, please. You know I love only you. That . . . that woman . . . she was so crazy, she was going to kill me . . . she was going to kill me! Adam will tell, I know he will. Daddy will blame you. He'll fire you. Our names will be all over the papers, and that hateful man — what's his name? — will sling all kinds of dirt

at us. And it's all your fault! Damn you to hell!"

At that moment, Reuben realized how much he hated his wife. Even looking at her sickened him. For all her sobbing and carrying on, he noticed her eyes were dry — dry and calculating. When he had his emotions under control, he sat down on the step beside her.

"You have too much faith in my abilities, Bebe," he said softly. "I will try to do something, but because I'm willing to try does not mean I can accomplish anything."

"Maybe . . . maybe they didn't find her yet. Adam was going to call the police this morning . . . and . . . and tell them she didn't come home last night."

"Was he worth all this?" Reuben asked coldly.

Bebe raised her head. "When you don't have anything . . . yes, for the time, he was worth it." Her dry eyes were defiant.

Three hours later Bebe was bound for Palm Springs with the same bodyguards she'd had on her last visit. Reuben sat in Simon's room, staring at his son. "I don't want to do what I'm about to do, son, but I don't want you to have a mother in prison," he whispered.

It was a full three months before Adam James was officially arrested for the murder of his wife. During that time there was no mention of Bebe Tarz, just speculation about

numerous women involved with the handsome actor.

Bebe was on the mend, suffering only occasional bouts of withdrawal, but living through it. Her memory lapses weren't frequent. She was beginning to feel more like herself with each passing day. Each morning she read the papers, searching for some word, some phrase that would incriminate her. Eventually she began to feel safe — until the morning she read that Adam had been arrested. Reuben would take care of things, she told herself, but she wasn't certain. There'd been no word from him since her arrival in Palm Springs, not even news of Simon. Her father hadn't called, and neither had Eli. She was a pariah now.

Adam James never made it to court. The county prosecutor had no choice but to let him go. "Without a murder weapon and witnesses, I can't put the taxpayers to the expense of a faulty trial. The industry Adam James works for will mete out whatever justice they think he deserves."

Will Hays, paragon of virtue, snuffed out James's career with one breath. Months later he took pleasure in announcing that the actor was working in a filling station and living in a trailer.

Bebe Rosen returned to Los Angeles a changed person. She was tanned and fit, with only faint lines around her eyes to indicate

778

she was anything but a respectable matron married to a studio executive. With genuine enthusiasm she plunged into her new life by redecorating the house in Laurel Canyon. Like a dutiful wife she moved back into the master bedroom, and only she and Reuben knew that she slept on one side of the bed and he on the other. As part of the game she ordered fashionable clothes and gave small intimate dinners that Reuben attended; she played with her son and joined every civic group Los Angeles had to offer. She was a model of decorum.

The hatred Reuben felt for his wife dwindled, replaced with pity. During the long dark nights he hungered for what he couldn't have, his only sin that of omission. He knew he could never love his wife. Once he'd made the declaration to himself, he eased into a new mode of living. Friends now, he and Bebe were able to chat amiably together about business, the other studios, and her civic work. He made a point of calling home at least once a day to check on both his wife and Simon.

Life wasn't blissful, but it was tolerable. Reuben had his work, his friends, and his son.

In early January a cold spell rocketed through California, causing crop damage and leaving frost on the ground for over a week. Bebe and Reuben reveled in the crisp cold air. At night they lighted the fireplace and

made popcorn for Simon. They were speaking civilly to each other, often laughing and making jokes. By the middle of the week Bebe had the sniffles. Reuben ordered her to bed, fearful that the frail Simon would come down with her cold.

"How do you feel, Bebe? Can I get you anything before I turn off the light?" he asked, concerned.

"Do you have a way to keep me warm?" Bebe asked, her teeth chattering. "I already have three blankets on my side of the bed."

Reuben slid under the covers and turned out the light, aware of the distance between them. He lay quietly, trying to pretend he couldn't feel Bebe's shivering. At last he inched over until he was next to his wife, then drew her close, hoping his own body would warm her. "Don't you have anything but this silky thing to keep you warm?" he asked gruffly.

Startled by his actions, Bebe could only shake her head. "You're so toasty," she sighed as she cuddled closer to her husband.

Reuben shifted a little so she would be more comfortable. Even though she was shivering, her body felt incredibly warm. "I think you have a fever, Bebe, possibly a high one," he said in a strangled voice.

"No, I don't. I took my temperature a little while ago. If I feel warm, it's because I'm here with you like this. Reuben, I'd like it if

you'd make love to me. I can feel you. It . . . it doesn't have to mean anything if you don't want it to," she said shyly. "The other two . . . what I mean is we never . . . This would be nice, the circumstances are right, if you know what I mean. Neither one of us is angry with the other." Bebe held her breath as she waited for Reuben's reply. It was so long in coming, she thought she would burst.

Reuben tipped her face up to his with a gentle touch. When his lips met hers, his kiss was tender, moving across her mouth slowly, meltingly. Then he pulled away, looking deeply into her eyes. "Are you sure?" he whispered.

Her answer was to move back into his arms, holding him tightly, offering her mouth again to the tenderness of his. More than anything else, she had needed this, had wanted it for so long. Her heart ripped open then, and great wrenching sobs escaped her parted lips. It had been so long since she'd been held this way, and never by the man who was holding her now.

"What's wrong?" Reuben asked softly, searching her eyes for the answer in the dimness from the night-light near Bebe's side of the bed.

"Nothing. It's just that I need you, Reuben," she said honestly. "So very much. I need you to love me, for now. I need you to want me, for now."

Their nightclothes fell from their bodies like the petals of summer's first rose. His body felt strange and unfamiliar against her own; the stubble of beard on his chin was soft, the way she'd imagined it would be. His touch was searching, tender, as though he were charting her body.

She sighed deeply, urging him on with his search. His lips traced lazy patterns along the sweep of her shoulders and down to her breasts. His effect on her was hypnotic, sensuous, and Bebe willed herself to surrender to the moment and the man. She accepted his nearness, his touch, his kiss on the most intimate parts of herself. She accepted these things the way she would have taken food or warmth or air to breathe, because she desperately needed them to reaffirm herself as a woman.

Bebe lay quietly in Reuben's arms, listening to the furious beat of his heart. There were no beautiful words saying she was desirable and loving and warm. And she felt she had no right to expect them. He'd brought her body to life with his hands and lips. But it was her soul that needed to be reached, and he could not touch it.

Her body was satisfied, her ego fed, yet misery lived in the core of her being. There was no future with Reuben, and she knew it; he'd told her often enough, and this evening's lovemaking reaffirmed any doubts she may

have had. What was she to do now — forget this had ever happened? Forget that she could feel alive only when she was with him like this? Choking back a sob, she leaned into her husband's arms, waiting for him to tighten his hold on her shoulders. Instead, he sighed deeply and rolled over to his side of the bed. Their brief moment was over.

Reuben lay quietly, his mind and body filled with wonderment. He'd finally sustained an erection under normal conditions. He didn't give a second's thought to Bebe; she was someone he'd used to regain his masculinity, the virility he'd thought was gone forever. And it was true: he could function now, like other men. The dreaded pitchfork nightmare was gone. The urge to hop out of bed and dance a jig was so strong, he buried his face in the pillow and dug his knees into the soft mattress.

He was a man again.

Dillon Tarz was born nine months to the day from the night Reuben made love to his wife for the first time. Seven and a half pounds of solid pink flesh with rosy cheeks and a crown of soft golden fuzz on his head . . . and so beautiful that Reuben could feel the sting of tears in his eyes.

His creation.

■ ■ ■ ■

Two weeks after Dillon's birth Reuben picked up the phone to hear Daniel's hushed voice. In silence, his guts churning in protest, he listened to what his friend was saying. "I don't understand, Daniel, how can that happen? All right . . . yes . . . I'll start right now. Don't forget, you're going to be Dillon's godfather. Of course you have to bring a present. Look, we'll talk later, Daniel," he said in his haste to get off the phone.

Forty minutes later Mort Stiner stared with openmouthed astonishment at his client. "Let me understand something, you want me to sell everything, the whole kit and kaboodle? Reuben, that's suicide! Some of your stocks are way down. I suppose your other, ah . . . friends want to sell, too?" The thought came to him that this wonder boy of Hollywood had always been on the money even when he himself hadn't agreed with his buy orders. The second or third time around, though, he himself had acted on some of Reuben's orders. So something was definitely up. The market had been crazy for a while now.

"That's a fair assumption," Reuben replied matter-of-factly. "I'm speaking for Max Gould and Jane Perkins."

Stiner's thin eyebrows shot up, and his glasses slid down the bridge of his nose. Sol

Rosen, the head honcho at Fairmont, wasn't selling, but Reuben Tarz was. His gut rumbled. Rosen had borrowed heavily when his blocks of stock were inflated, but they were down now. It would be just like this wonder boy to cash in and snap up the whole ball of wax. "You're sure this is what you want?" Stiner asked again.

"Where do I sign?"

The broker handed over a sheaf of papers. "Bottom line on all of them. When will your friends be in?"

"Sometime today. I'll want cash on this, no checks. The green stuff, and I'll take it in thousand-dollar bills."

When Reuben pulled his car to the curb outside the Mimosa Club, Max was walking through the door. "Hit the bricks, Max," he said tightly as soon as he finished explaining the situation. "The sell orders are all drawn up. Take cash. The order's in. You got transportation?"

"I'll take a hack, you look like you got better things to do than ferry me back and forth. Is it going to work?" he asked anxiously.

Reuben shrugged. "No reason to believe it won't. But there's no guarantees on anything, so bear that in mind."

Max grinned. "On behalf of my mother's old age and my own, thanks."

Reuben drove like a bat out of hell all the way back to the studio. The powerful car

roared through the gates, the guard racing after his snappy-looking blue and black hat. "What the hell! . . ." he cursed.

Reuben ground the car to a halt outside the doors of Lot 6 and raced inside. "That's it for today. Close up shop! Jane!" he bellowed. "Come with me. . . ."

"Daniel told me the market's going to crash," he told her as she hurried after him. "You have to get out now. If you don't, you could be wiped out. I got you into the market, and I don't want you going to the poorhouse."

Jane laughed. "Slow down, Reuben. Listen, I got out a couple of months ago. I started to get nervous. I was making money, so much that I got scared thinking how I would feel if something went wrong. I'm not the smartest person in the world when it comes to stocks and bonds. It was a gut feeling. I bought real estate and I have a good healthy chunk in the bank."

Reuben stopped dead in his tracks. He stared at Jane and then burst out laughing. "You really got out, you aren't pulling my leg?"

"Honest. I got scared. Should I take my money out of the bank?"

Reuben frowned. "Are you still in that apartment?"

"No. I moved to a house, nothing grand, but it has a pool and some other things. I

paid cash for it. Did I do the right thing? Reuben, can I lose . . . What's going to happen?"

"I think you should go to the bank — now. Tell them you want your money in cash tomorrow. They'll need time to get it together. In the meantime I'll give you the name of a man who will install a safe for you. Other than that I don't know what else to tell you. This thing has me to the wall. Daniel . . . when Daniel was at Harvard he made friends with some incredibly wealthy young men. They warned him and he warned me. All the other tips I passed on came from these same young men. We weren't bamboozled, even once, so there's no reason to doubt those guys now."

"I see. . . . Okay, look — I'll head over to the bank now. Give me the name of the man for the safe and I'll go over to his shop as soon as I finish. Reuben, I don't know how to . . . First you get me a job at the studio doing something I love doing, then you help me with the market, and now this. I know you get all flustered when someone tries to thank you. You aren't really as tough as you appear. Thank you for being my friend." She leaned over, her eyes moist, and kissed him lightly on the cheek. "Maybe someday I'll be able to help you." She laughed. "That's probably the biggest joke of all time, me helping you."

Reuben felt drained to the bone. The hell with the studio, he was going home to his family. Shaken and still unnerved by Daniel's bombshell, he forced himself to drive slowly, so slowly that other cars honked their horns at him. At last he pulled to the side, not caring if the blaring horns sounded or not. Should he have warned Sol? If the crash was as imminent as Daniel said, Sol would be wiped out. If Sol was wiped out, he could step in, cover his losses, and take control of the studio. . . .

Reuben hadn't been home during the day in over a year. The Laurel Canyon estate was beautiful, even majestic, and bought and paid for with his own money. Daniel had advised him to pay off the mortgage as soon as he could, and he'd done just that. He'd also socked away enough maintenance money for at least three years so the house couldn't be yanked away for taxes. The money was in a safe in his dressing room behind his shoe rack. Even Bebe didn't know it was there. In that particular safe he had envelopes with notes written in his own hand — one for insurance, one for the house, one for Simon's and Dillon's education, one for walking-around money, and one for investments. He had no idea what the grand total was, but it was substantial. In another safe in the basement he had other money, money enough to see him through five lean years. That had

been Daniel's idea, too. Also in that safe were three bulging envelopes bearing Daniel's name. Now it looked like he would have to install a third safe. And it was time at last to hand over Daniel's share of the investments.

He and Daniel had come a long way since meeting in France, he reflected. He was thirty years old and rising in the film industry. Where in the hell had he gotten the moxie . . . to move in the way he'd done. Guts? Stupidity? Probably a little of both.

The day would come, he knew, when he'd be in total control of Fairmont. To date he hadn't made a wrong decision. He'd come close with his doubts concerning *Moses on the Mount* and *Witches and Ghosts,* but they were proving two of the biggest money-makers of the decade. He was aceing out Warner with sound, something he was still uneasy about, but his gut told him it would work once the fine details were worked out. Sol had vetoed the idea from the beginning, but when he'd consulted his friend Tom Edison in the East, he'd gradually come around to Reuben's way of thinking. Reuben knew that by the close of the year, synchronous sound film would be the universal form of the future. He'd have 116 recording machines, 20 more than Warner had. Half of all his theaters were being wired for sound production. He'd convinced his sound technicians that the system using optical patterns

along the edge of the film, rather than the discs Warner Vitaphone used, would provide more reliable synchronization. It was a race now between him and Warner Bros., and he knew he'd win — he had to win, to prove to Sol and the other studio executives that he knew his business. The patents were in his name, and that was all he cared about. One day they would make him a multimillionaire.

And now, all he'd done, all he hoped to do, was in jeopardy if the market crashed as Daniel's friends predicted.

Reuben walked into the house with shoulders slumped and a heavy step. Bebe stood silently behind the dining room door, surprised and unnerved at the look on her husband's face. Simon clung to her skirts. "Shhhh," she said. "Something's bothering Daddy. Let's get Dillon and go outside in the sunshine. Remember what I told you, Simon, sunshine washes away gloom. Go along now and wait for me on the terrace."

Bebe tiptoed into Dillon's nursery and picked up the sleeping baby. "It's all right, Mrs. Peabody," she told the nurse. "My husband is home and we're taking Dillon outside for some fresh air. His buggy is on the terrace. You look like you could use a nap. I'll keep him till dinner."

Bebe was halfway down the steps when Reuben caught up to her. He'd changed from his business suit to casual slacks and a bright

blue pullover sweater. Bebe was amazed at how she could still react to his handsome good looks. "Why are you tiptoeing around, and where are you going with the baby?"

"Why, I . . . You looked so . . . fresh air . . . I didn't want him to cry and . . . Why are you home at this time of day?"

"Here, give him to me. Why don't you get us some lemonade and we'll have it on the terrace with the children."

Bebe's face brightened. "Like a real family. That'll be nice, Reuben. Simon is on the terrace waiting."

Simon looked up from the puzzle he was putting together on the wrought-iron table. "Hello, Daddy," he said in a reed-thin voice.

The child was as thin as his voice, Reuben thought. He was a fussy, picky eater, preferring water and soda pop to milk. He gagged on vegetables and refused to chew meat. Most of the time Bebe cajoled, bribed, and spoon-fed him. If the boy had any endearing qualities, Reuben had yet to find them. Simon went back to his puzzle, his thin fingers picking through the mound of pieces that represented a blue sky. Reuben hugged Dillon to his chest. This bundle in his arms was normal in every way.

These days he was giving Bebe an A for effort but wondering how long she'd stay on her good behavior. Knowing his wife, he took it one day at a time.

"I added some cookies," Bebe said gaily, but Reuben detected a nervousness in her voice. Obviously, he'd upset the daily routine by coming home early.

It was a pleasant interlude, he thought later, sitting with his family in the late afternoon sunshine, the scent of the garden all about him. Simon had giggled once when his mother tried to draw him out. Reuben thought it a strange, alien sound. Dillon continued to sleep in the crook of his arm.

Bebe struggled to keep the rare time alive by talking of inane things, household matters and Dillon's *bris.* Reuben responded in kind, smiling and gazing down at the sleeping infant. His wife pretended not to see the worry in his eyes. "We're having turkey for dinner even though it isn't Thanksgiving," she blurted out. "I know how much you like turkey . . . cranberry sauce, too. You'll like that, Simon, it's sweet. And for you, Dillon, a nice warm bottle."

Reuben shook his head. "I'm sorry, Bebe, I won't be here for dinner. I've some urgent business to attend to. I'll catch a bite somewhere along the way."

Bebe's heart fluttered in her chest. If only she could steal this moment, preserve it somehow. Suddenly she felt bereft when she looked at her husband, who was saying words that meant nothing. She wanted to cry out, to reach for him and hold him close; but she

couldn't. It was the same feeling she'd had so many times before when she'd wanted to reach out to her firstborn, John Paul. So much of her life had simply passed her by, and what was left was slipping away from her even as they sat together as a family.

The sun was starting to set when Reuben handed Dillon over to Bebe. "Well, I've got to shower and change. Don't wait up for me, Bebe." He bent over to plant a kiss on top of his wife's head. He patted Dillon's blanket and smiled at Simon, who ignored him.

Bebe continued to sit on the terrace until the cook called her to dinner. Somehow she knew that this was the last of what she called her family moments.

Bebe Rosen started to grieve then, the way she'd grieved when she'd made the decision to give up John Paul.

Three weeks later, the stock market crashed; it was the blackest day Americans had ever seen. Believing, yet disbelieving, Reuben tried to go about his normal business at the studio, but it was impossible. Instead of feeling smug that he'd gotten out in time, he felt depressed with what he was reading in the papers and seeing all about him. And even though he'd acted quickly on Daniel's advice, he'd still lost twenty-five cents on every investment dollar. Fortunately, Jane's small fortune was intact, and Max . . . Max accepted his fortune without a whimper.

Inside a week, Sol Rosen turned into a haggard, white-faced caricature of himself. His eyes were bitter, his mouth a grim line as he worked the columns of figures that spelled disaster for the studio. He'd borrowed heavily when the price of his stocks was inflated, and he'd paid off Mickey. Now Philippe Bouchet could come in and wipe him out completely. If not Philippe, then that devil Tarz. The very real possibility that he would be out in the street with Fairmont falling into other hands was a fact he couldn't dispute.

Things couldn't be bleaker; friends, acquaintances, and even relatives were jumping out of windows left and right as their livelihood slipped away from them. Every day it seemed he was attending a funeral, the mourners' faces as dead as that of the person being lowered into the ground.

A month after the market crash Sol trudged into Reuben's office and slapped a sheaf of papers onto his desk. "I can't meet these payments. The banks are going to call in my stock. I'm wiped out."

Reuben thumbed through the papers, and his eyebrows shot up at the amount Sol owed. "I know this is none of my business, but what do you do with your money? You made a fortune in the commodities market. Who the hell is Philippe Bouchet, and what's this . . . what does the Morgan Guaranty Bank have to do with Fairmont?"

Sol's eyes turned mean and calculating. "As if you didn't know. . . . I'll say this much: when Bouchet comes to take over this place, you ain't going to be here. That's my personal guarantee. I've been waiting a long time to see you fall on your face."

"I don't know what the hell you're talking about, Sol." Reuben's pen flew down the pages, ticking off amounts of money as though they were items on a grocery list. "I can bail you out," he said when he was through.

"Bail me out! Just like that!" Sol said. "And what do you get in return? The chance to suck my blood, dance on my grave?"

"Your stock, what else? You can stay on here doing exactly what you've been doing. No one needs to know but you and me. I can have Daniel Bishop do the legal work. Fairmont will belong to me . . . on paper."

Sol laughed bitterly. "You goddamn son of a bitch! You got out in time! You're heeled now. You are a fucking ghoul, Tarz. I'm your goddamn father-in-law! It would have been the decent thing to do to give me a little warning before the crash. I've been real good to you, and you turn around and stab me in the back. Well, your back is out in the open now, and I hope to God Philippe Bouchet stabs you. You'll own forty-nine percent of Fairmont, not the whole ball of wax. What do you think of that!"

Reuben's face turned white then red. "What the hell are you talking about? I asked you before about Philippe Bouchet. Now, who the hell is he and what's with this forty-nine percent?"

Sol rocked back on his heels. "You poor slob, you really don't know, do you? Well, Bouchet is the bird that owns fifty-one percent of this studio. Here's the ownership certificate; actually it's a copy. You can call Morgan Guaranty in New York, but they won't tell you any more than they told me. Keep busting your ass, Tarz, for Mr. Philippe Bouchet," Sol snarled. It never once occurred to him to mention Mickey or the fact that she had transferred her ownership of the studio. He assumed Reuben knew all about it.

Stunned by Sol's bitter outburst, Reuben reacted predictably. "I don't owe you a thing! I've given this studio everything that's in me to give. I cleaned up your slime, saved your daughter from death and disgrace. I gave you two grandsons, what the hell more do you want from me? And don't think for one god-damn minute that I won't call this damn bank. Another thing, I turned you on to the commodities market and I know you made a fortune. I did that because you gave me a job and I returned the favor. Now, I said I'll have Daniel draw up a contract giving you a lifetime position with the studio in return for

your shares of stock. I'll deal with this Bouchet when it's time to deal with him. I want that stock you own turned over to me in three weeks' time. I'll pay off your debts and pay you five-hundred dollars a week for the rest of your life. Take it or leave it!"

"I'll take it because I have no other choice. But I hope you rot in hell!" Sol stormed out of the office, slamming the door behind him.

Immediately Reuben called Daniel and barked out what he wanted done. "And call that goddamn bank and find out what's going on," he added.

After he'd hung up the phone, he sat for a long time staring at the wall. Sol would honor his agreement; of that he had no doubt.

Daniel Bishop stared long and hard at his law degree hanging on the wall across from where he sat. Something was bothering him, something he couldn't quite nail down. An hour later he was still staring at the diploma.

At nine o'clock that evening he called Reuben in his office. "This is the way I see it, Reuben. Sol's stock certificates are to be turned over to you as soon as the bank gives permission for depositors to clean out their safety deposit boxes. I spoke to the bank president and learned that Sol told me the truth when I spoke to him earlier today. . . . He was not in a good mood, Reuben."

"I didn't think he would be," Reuben said tightly.

"Philippe Bouchet does own fifty-one percent of the stock in Fairmont Studios. He's owned it since 1921. But that's all they would tell me. I'm not going up against that crowd, so we go with what information we have. In short, you'll own Sol's shares, which amounts to forty-nine percent. Morgan more or less indicated that Bouchet is content to let things go on as before. Why not? He collects his percentage regardless. I tell you, this is one of the nicest, slickest pieces of legal work I've ever seen, and that's why I don't want to tangle with it."

Reuben cursed. "Daniel, why do I have this feeling that Sol is laughing up his sleeve even though he's wiped out?"

"Funny you should say that. I had the same feeling myself. He loses and so do you. You thought you were getting the controlling interest, and you end up with forty-nine percent. It was nice of you to give him back his house in Benedict Canyon."

"Do I detect a note of sarcasm, or is it disapproval I hear in your voice, Daniel?"

"Possibly a little of both. I hate to see a man go down for the count. The end doesn't always justify the means, you know."

"On that cheery note I guess I'll hang up," Reuben said coolly. "Oh, are you still planning on coming for Dillon's *bris?* It's late, I

know, but Bebe couldn't make up . . . her mind about what she calls mutilation."

"Wouldn't miss it for the world. Take care, Reuben. I'll get back to you if any problems crop up."

"I'll be here," Reuben muttered.

Dillon Tarz's *bris* was scheduled for noon on a Friday. It was a small affair, with only Daniel, Sol, and Eli in attendance. When Dillon was carried off by his nurse, Sol handed Bebe an envelope. The smile on his face made Reuben look sharply at Daniel.

Bebe ripped open the envelope. "Oh, Daddy, how wonderful! You are the most generous father! The children won't appreciate this now, but they will as they get older. Look, Reuben! Daddy has given Dillon shares to equal twenty-four percent of Fairmont Studios and Simon twenty-five. Did you ever hear of such a generous thing? What a wonderful grandfather you are!"

Sol beamed. Daniel turned his head to hide his smile. Reuben glowered. "Bebe, why don't you see about lunch?" he said tightly.

"You bastard! Daniel!" he shouted the moment Bebe was out of the room.

"He transferred the stock," Daniel said, still trying to hide his smile. "He did it before he signed the agreement. If you want to prosecute your father-in-law, I suppose you can. I know the contracts I drew up are airtight. He

simply outmaneuvered both of us. There isn't much trust in the legal department, Reuben."

Eli sat with his head bobbing like a tennis ball as he tried to follow the conversation. What all of this meant, he surmised, was that Bebe now held the boys' shares of stock, which effectively put her in control of Reuben and the studio. The old man wasn't so stupid after all.

On the way over to the railroad station to see Daniel off, Reuben seethed and fumed. "From now on, we don't trust anybody!"

"Bebe is going to be a hard nut to crack, Reuben. This is the first time she's had the upper hand. I don't even think she knows she has it yet, but Eli will tell her soon enough, probably even as we speak."

Reuben flinched. Suddenly it was all falling apart — everything he'd busted his ass for, sacrificed for, just to arrive at this point in time . . . and now it was being snatched out from under him. There was a certain ludicrous irony to it.

"Well, at least it's in the family," he said at last, sighing. "Have we heard any more from Morgan?"

"Not directly. I asked a few of my friends to look into it. This isn't gospel, but the feedback is Bouchet is not interested in selling. He'll remain a silent partner. Evidently he's satisfied with the way you've been doing things. I expect a letter to that effect shortly.

Your hands are tied, Reuben. My best advice is to roll with the punches. Time has a way of taking care of things. Look, nothing's changed really. You're still in control at Fairmont. Bouchet obviously doesn't give a hoot about what pictures you're making or how you make them. You work, he collects. It could be worse, so appreciate what you have and don't for God's sake look for trouble."

Reuben turned to his friend. "You really have to leave, huh? It's been so good having you here, pal. And I know you're right about everything. It was just such a goddamn shock. I never had a double whammy hit me before and I wasn't ready."

Daniel pumped Reuben's hand vigorously. "I like it here, but I have a life back east. You know, I love the change of seasons. Life can't be perpetual sunshine. Once in a while there has to be some gloom. Otherwise, how can you appreciate the sun?" He grinned. "On that note, pal, I'll say good-bye. Take care, and remember it's your turn now to come east. For my wedding, I hope."

"Daniel, you mean . . . have you . . . Who is it?" Reuben exclaimed.

Daniel flushed. "I'm still thinking about it. So don't pester me. When there's something to tell, you'll be the first to know. Now, god-damn it, good-bye. I'm going to miss my train if I don't leave."

"Go, go already." Reuben laughed. "Write! Call!"

"I will," Daniel called over his shoulder. "I will."

■ ■ ■ ■

PART THREE

■ ■ ■ ■

CHAPTER
THIRTY-SEVEN

Hollywood, 1938

America hunkered down during the thirties — the bad years, as most people referred to them — and fought to survive the terrible market crash. General consensus was, the forties would set the world right-side up.

Europe was hunkering down, too, but for a different reason. War had come to its shores, and people were fighting to survive just as America had.

On every street corner, in every tavern, wherever a cluster of men could gather, the talk was the same. Would America get involved in England's war? F.D.R. said no, but heads nodded sagely. When men were dying, other men had to step in. It was coming, they said mournfully.

Reuben Tarz and his friends had survived the crash, their fortunes remaining intact. Even his marriage had somehow survived, more out of stubbornness and endurance than love. As far as Hollywood and the film

industry were concerned, Reuben Tarz was married with a family, and if he slept alone in his room and his wife slept down the hall in hers, who were they to pass judgment? Who were they to know?

Reuben was forty years old — wealthy, powerful, respected, and feared . . . yet he ached with loneliness. No longer was he Hollywood's wonder boy. These days he was being touted by the media as Hollywood's Superman with a Midas touch.

It had been nine long years since that horrible black Monday of 1929, and he'd survived. Sheer guts alone, Reuben felt, was the reason Fairmont was still one of the top three studios, producing the best films in the industry. He'd worked his ass off during those lean years, often staying at the studio until the wee hours of the morning and surviving on two or three hours of sleep a night.

There were days when he wished he could have devoted as many hours to his marriage. He didn't love Bebe, and Bebe knew it, so there was no point in working at something that would net a zero emotional balance. Work was Reuben Tarz's life these days.

Simon was fourteen, enrolled in a private school where, according to his teachers, his artistic ability was being nurtured. Secretly, Reuben felt the boy drew crazy, morbid, ghoulish paintings that defied acknowledgment. Simon was so much like his uncle Eli

it was uncanny.

Eli had, with the help of homosexual friends, straightened out his life. He lived in Carmel now and had had three private shows, selling all his paintings. Who would have believed the world was eager to buy Eli Rosen's angry, hateful seascapes? Certainly not Reuben Tarz. In the beginning it worried Reuben that Simon adored his uncle Eli, but Bebe had explained that Simon needed a male figure in his life since Reuben was never there for the boy. Still, Reuben feared that his eldest son possessed homosexual tendencies; he dreaded the boy's weekend visits and always found some excuse to be away from home when Simon walked through the door. Years ago he'd simply given him over to Bebe, who smothered the boy and encouraged him to do nothing but breathe and paint.

Dillon was a different matter, however. Reuben had fought for his youngest son and sent him to a private school in Oregon to get him away from Bebe's influence. Dillon was a robust boy with a shock of blond hair and bright blue eyes. He was continually in one scrape after another, owning up to each and every escapade and taking his punishment without a whimper. Once he'd had the audacity to wink roguishly at his father, as if to say, It was great fun and worth the punishment. They weren't exactly pals, but they did have

respect for each other. Dillon, Reuben knew, would prove worthy at some point in his life. When he found time to analyze his feelings toward his family, Reuben realized he was most likely incapable of love, of feeling it, showing it, or admitting it.

The feeling he had for Daniel was so overwhelming, so different from anything he'd ever felt for anyone else, Reuben was incapable of analyzing it. A part of his heart would always belong to Daniel, and that was all there was to it. Lately though, since Daniel's marriage to Rajean Simmons, a wealthy socialite older by fifteen years with a teenage daughter, he saw little of his old friend. Reuben sensed trouble in the marriage, but Daniel refused to talk about it, saying simply that he would handle it.

All of them had come so far, accomplished so much, and all because of Mickey Fonsard. Even Sol was living in the lap of luxury, married now to Clovis Ames. When sound came to filmland, Clovis had been one of the first to be put out to pasture, as Reuben referred to the star's retirement. Then he'd pushed, prodded, and instigated until both Sol and Clovis gave in to him and married in a quiet ceremony. Neither one would admit it, but Reuben knew they were happier than two fleas romancing a dog.

Of the original cast, only he and Mickey remained unresolved. No, he thought ir-

ritably, two other members were successful now, too, thanks to him. Max, good old Max, was now the owner of the hottest nightspot in all of Hollywood — the Lily Garden, so-named by his late mother, was a showpiece. Reservations had to be made weeks in advance, and Max himself decided who entered his portals and who didn't. Reuben had a table assigned to him that no one else ever sat at. If a patron had the audacity to ask why he or she couldn't sit at that particular table, they were shown the door.

And then there was Jane. Another casualty of sound in films, she'd shown an early penchant for producing, and now her knack for recognizing a hot property was equal only to Reuben's. For some time she'd been his top producer, a position she richly deserved.

His world, his friends, his family.

The most important person of all was still unaccounted for, of course, and that was Mickey, his dearest love. How often he thought of her, dreamed of her, wanted her. So many times he'd made plans to go to France, only to cancel at the last minute when he remembered the pain, the anguish of her rejection. No, he couldn't put himself through that again. Instead, he fed off his memories and tortured himself with would-haves, could-haves, and should-haves.

The soft knock on his office door startled Reuben, and he looked up to see his secretary

standing in the doorway. Margaret might knock and open the door at the same time, but she never stepped over the threshold unless Reuben invited her in. Most times, like now, he said, "Yes, Margaret?"

"Mr. Tarz, I'd like to introduce you to my temporary replacement, Rosemary Connors. I think she's going to do just fine," Margaret said quietly.

Reuben rose and walked around his desk. His weary eyes locked with those of Rosemary Connors, and in that tiny fraction of time he fell in love. Confused by the alien feeling, he could only nod slightly, his tongue suddenly thick and awkward in his mouth.

"Miss Connors understands that the job is temporary until I get back," Margaret went on. "I explained about the pay schedule, and I've written out your routine, your likes and dislikes. Is there anything you'd like me to do before I leave?"

Reuben found his voice and offered his hand to Rosemary. How soft, like petals on a flower, he thought. Warm, but not moist. "I'm sure you have everything under control, Margaret, and I don't want you returning until you feel up to it." He found himself explaining about Margaret's mother's death, something his secretary had most likely explained in the outer office. Rosemary held his eyes as he spoke, a warm smile on her lips, showing small, pearl-white teeth. Reu-

ben thought it the loveliest smile he'd ever seen.

She was beautiful, this tall, quiet-appearing woman with a pile of golden hair pulled back into a knot. What would it feel like to run his hands through it? he wondered. Spun gold. Rumpelstiltskin. Enormous blue eyes and a light dusting of golden freckles dancing across the bridge of her nose. So endearing. Dimples . . . he liked that. A strong jaw and a mouth that looked like it was made for . . . kissing. She was trim and tall, and her heels made her taller still. She'd come eye level with him if they were . . . kissing each other. His neck felt warm, his cheeks and ears warmer. Christ, he hadn't felt this way since France . . . since Mickey. In the blink of an eye, he summed her up: a warm, gentle, beautiful woman.

When she spoke her voice was as soft and gentle as she looked. "If there's anything you need or want, I am familiar with office procedure. I've worked as a secretary before."

Reuben's neck grew warmer. She was in her early thirties, he decided. Unaccountably, he grew nervous, shifting from one foot to the other, clearing his throat and apologizing for no reason. And when Rosemary smiled, his heart almost burst out of his chest. What was she thinking? He wondered if he would get to know her well enough to ask.

In the outer office with the door closed

behind them, Margaret frowned. "I don't know what Mr. Tarz . . . he never acts like that. He must have something on his mind, something important. He's a wonderful man, a wonderful boss. I think everyone on this studio lot loves him. He's actually paying me my full salary while I'm on leave. He came to my mother's funeral. I was stunned and so grateful. He sent baskets of flowers. Now, you tell me what kind of boss does that? Best of all, he treats me like a person and not hired help. Now," she cautioned Rosemary, "if you're unsure of anything, you can reach me at home. I've left my number in the folder on the desk. Is there anything you want to ask me before I leave?"

"Is Mr. Tarz married? I didn't see a picture of his wife in his office. Executives always seem to have family pictures on their desks. Wives call all the time. How should I handle that?" Rosemary asked quietly.

Margaret frowned again. This one was beautiful, she thought, gorgeous enough to be in the movies. Maybe that's why Mr. Tarz was so befuddled. "Mr. Tarz is married and he has two sons. As to why there is no picture, I don't know. Mrs. Tarz is the daughter of Mr. Rosen, who owns this studio. Mrs. Tarz is a beautiful woman." Margaret's voice grew stern. "If, and I say if, you have any ideas of becoming . . . more than a secretary, I wouldn't give it another thought. Mr. Tarz

is an upstanding, honorable, ethical man."

"I can see that, Margaret. I feel a good secretary needs to know certain . . . intimate facts. I'm sure you know many things you wouldn't divulge to me out of loyalty to Mr. Tarz, and that's the way it should be," Rosemary said gently.

Margaret drew in a deep breath. "Yes," she said through tight lips. "I guess I'll be leaving now. I expect you to do a good job, and please don't embarrass me with Mr. Tarz. After all, I'm the one who hired you and I'm the one who will have to work here after you leave."

"I know I can never be as good as you, Margaret, but I will try." Rosemary smiled. It was the perfect response, and Margaret left with a lighter heart.

Rosemary turned out to be so efficient and professional that Reuben felt at a loss around her in the first few days of her employment. A week into her job he found himself dictating letters that didn't need to be written just to have her sit in his office. He loved looking at her legs, which were crossed so demurely. Sometimes he'd leave the office just so he could walk past her desk. Then he'd feign forgetfulness so he could walk back in and out again. By the third week he was an accident waiting to happen and wanted desperately to talk to someone about his feelings. Daniel, his first and logical choice, was

caught up in his own problems at the moment. Besides, Daniel did not believe in affairs outside the bounds of marriage.

Reuben zeroed in on Max, knowing beforehand what his friend would say: Go ahead, life is short, take whatever happiness you can get. So Jane Perkins was his next choice, last on the list only because she took his troubles to heart and worried about him like a sister.

Jane hadn't married, although she had what she called several "gentlemen" friends whom she allowed to call on her when she was in the mood for dinner or a night on the town. They were nice men, who had no idea Reuben had dossiers on all of them. Jane lived in a large house with a small pool, two dogs, and three cats. She did all her own gardening and had the most beautiful roses in southern California. Occasionally she sent bouquets to Reuben's office with funny little notes, much to his delight.

So, having decided to confide in Jane, Reuben buzzed Rosemary, his heart thumping. He felt like a damn schoolboy. "Rosemary, ring Jane Perkins for me. If she isn't in, leave a message."

"What's the message, Mr. Tarz?"

"The message? Oh, yes, the message. Tell her I'd like to have dinner with her and to get back to me. Tonight, dinner is for tonight."

"I have it, Mr. Tarz."

Was that disapproval he was hearing in her voice? Of course it was — she probably thought he was happily married. Margaret would have described his marriage as a match made in heaven. Christ, he didn't even know where the other half of his marriage was at the moment, off on another one of her toots. This time she'd been gone for over a month. Daniel said she was in Europe. She'd probably make it her business to see Mickey. The thought sent a flurry of worms skittering around his stomach. Mickey, his first love, his only love. Then what was this he was feeling for Rosemary? Lust? Passion?

Reuben flipped the switch. "Well, is she there or isn't she?" he asked irritably.

"Her . . . her office doesn't answer," Rosemary said in her gentle voice.

"For God's sake," Reuben blustered. This time when he charged through Rosemary's office, he forgot to look at her.

Rosemary blinked at the whirlwind, wondering if she'd be fired because the producer didn't answer her phone. God, she hoped not. She enjoyed working for the studio — and especially for the handsome Reuben Tarz. His smile warmed her heart, and the way he *looked* at her . . . ! But of course that had nothing to do with her in particular; he probably didn't even know she was alive, except when he had a letter to dictate or a call he wanted to place.

Unfortunately she hadn't realized that there would be so much work. Margaret had indicated that there were days when she had little to do but straighten files. Rosemary sighed. So many letters . . . often she had to stay after closing to get them all typed and on Mr. Tarz's desk for his signature. They were always gone in the morning. Probably he dropped them at the post office himself on the way home because he wanted them in the early morning mail.

As it happened, Reuben did drop the letters at the post office, but not in the mail slot. First he ripped them up and then he tossed them into a dumpster that sat next to the mail slot. It wasn't until her fourth week on the job that Rosemary began to wonder why there'd been no responses to the letters. Surely Mr. Tarz's business associates couldn't ignore such important letters. Perhaps the recipients followed up with phone calls to his home. She sighed again. It wasn't any of her business. Once Margaret returned she'd be out of a job, anyway.

The following morning, Reuben stopped at Rosemary's desk, jamming his hands in his pockets to steady them. "Rosemary, would you have dinner with me this evening?"

"Dinner? Just . . . you and me . . . dinner? Ah, yes, of course. I'd . . . like that very much."

"Fine. I'll pick you up at seven-thirty. Leave

your address on my desk. Cancel my appointments for this afternoon, and tell anyone who calls that I'll get back to them tomorrow. I'll see you later this evening."

"Mr. Tarz, if you aren't coming back to the office, how will you know where to pick me up? You did say to leave my address on your desk." Rosemary smiled.

Reuben laughed. "That's a good point. Better write it down now." On his way out, he wondered if she'd leave early to do whatever it was women needed so much time to do before a date. And it was a date.

Following Jane's advice, he'd decided to take the bull by the horns and ask Rosemary outright to have dinner. Well, he'd done that, and she'd accepted. Jane had advised him to "go home, sit in the sun, and think about the evening and the consequences if you allow the dinner date to go beyond just that. Wear a new shirt and your best suit. Women like snappy white shirts and crisp-looking ties," she'd said. "Wear a good after-shave and wash your hair. That's my advice," she'd laughed, "and, Reuben, I've seen Rosemary Connors, and so has every other man on this studio lot. And I'll bet she's just as nice as she is lovely." Her voice had turned serious when she'd said, "Reuben, think about this very carefully. The one thing in this world a person can't count on are emotions." Her eyes turned wicked. "And I want to hear the

outcome. Promise."

"I'm not the type to kiss and tell." Reuben grinned.

Jane threw her hands in the air. "Go on home, Reuben, I have an early call tomorrow."

"Wait a minute, where do you think I should take her?"

"Why not take her to Max's new restaurant. People are killing one another to get a reservation and you have a ringside table. She'll love the Lily Garden. Trust me."

He did.

Rosemary made her way home in a daze. Dinner with Reuben Tarz! The thought of it made her so nervous she could barely open the door to the tiny house she lived in with her two cats, Bismarck and Napoleon, acquired along with the house when she'd divorced her husband of five years.

Normally when she returned home after a long working day she quickly changed into comfortable clothes and played with the cats for a while, fed them, and then made herself something to eat; but today she was in such a dither of anticipation she didn't even hold out her arms to Napoleon and practically tripped over Bismarck, who meowed his displeasure and with a swoosh of his tail marched into the small bedroom, leaping onto the mound of pillows on the bed.

Napoleon waited uncertainly for his mistress's usual kind words. When he found himself alone in the living room, he padded after his companion. Both cats stared at Rosemary, their tails thumping as she pulled things from drawers and hangers in between running back and forth to the bathroom to prepare her bath.

Suddenly she stopped in her tracks. This was a date of sorts, her first in over two years and certainly her first since the divorce. She'd loved her husband with all her heart, until one day he had confessed in a gentle tone that monogamy was not something he could live with any longer. When she had been incredulous, he had patted her and explained that he needed the excitement and challenge of youth and beauty and a certain amount of scrappiness and go-to-hell attitude from a woman.

"You, Rosemary," he'd said, "are too placid, too even-tempered, and you never do anything that surprises me. You are so predictable I know what you're going to say before sounds issue forth from your lips. I detest the fact that we have spaghetti every Tuesday and fish every Friday. And . . . you smile, but you don't laugh."

At the time, she had been too mortified to ask him to explain what he meant by that. Then he'd made his final argument, an insult to which there really had been no rational

response: "You don't excite me, dear, you bore me to tears."

It hadn't been a messy divorce. John had labeled it boring, with no squabbling or backbiting, which only hammered home the point he was trying to make. "The house is yours as long as you make the mortgage payments. You can have the damn cats. They were always sneaking and skulking at my feet, hissing and arching their backs . . . and the furniture, after all, you picked it out," as if anything she would have liked he held in the utmost contempt. It didn't matter that she'd offered to find homes for the cats. John wanted out of the marriage, and that's all there was to it. The man she'd lived with and loved with all her heart had suddenly become a stranger. It was a terrifying experience, one she had quietly swallowed and digested with difficulty. Now she was glad she hadn't given the cats away; they were warm bodies, always there waiting to greet her when she came home.

Well, that was all behind her. A date! Dinner tonight was a date, kind of. She wished she had bath salts to scent her bath. Reuben Tarz was married, she reminded herself, so this wasn't a romantic date, and she'd better clear her head of any such notions. The man probably wanted to discuss business or, for that matter, fire her over dinner to let her down easy. Still, her heart fluttered at the

thought of sitting across the table from her handsome, powerful employer.

Her quick bath over, Rosemary rummaged through her lingerie drawer and was appalled at the state of her underthings. Serviceable, not a scrap of lace anywhere. Cheap, too, but that was all right, one conserved where one could. Everything was clean and ironed, smelling of lily of the valley. Boring, matronly, school-marmish. James was right, she thought despairingly, she was boring. Well, there was nothing she could do about the state of her underwear now, no one was going to see it anyway. What to wear over it was the question.

Finally she selected a mint-green dotted swiss with full layered elbow-length sleeves and big shoulder pads. After she'd slipped it on, she stood back to stare at her reflection. The white piqué collar was definitely demure, more demure than she felt at the moment. But she did like the way the dress fell away from her hips in soft swirls and wished she had silk stockings to accent her legs; unfortunately they just weren't in her budget. Jewelry was no big decision since she owned very little of any real worth. At last she decided on a single strand of small pearls with matching earrings that she'd gotten in the five-&-ten several years earlier. If she slid them under her collar so that only an inch and a half of the fake beads showed, no one would know

the difference.

The young woman in the mirror was no goddess by any means. Neat, yes . . . respectable, certainly . . . but not the least bit sultry or dazzling. In fact, a little . . . boring. Sighing, Rosemary reached for her brush.

Her hair, a rich blond with its own natural wave, came alive under her strokes, easing through the bristles and crackling with electricity. A sign of good health, her mother used to say. Tonight she quickly finger-waved the sides and let the bottom fall softly and naturally to her shoulders. Her crowning glory. John had liked to bury his face in her hair, saying it always smelled sweet and clean. However, he'd done that only during the first year of their marriage.

There was no need for more than a trace of powder, for she had a delicate pink complexion that attested to rest, good food, and a calm existence, but in honor of her evening's engagement she added a light dusting of powder to her nose and a sweep of color to her mouth. Unfortunately, she didn't like the waxy taste and wiped the lipstick off, biting down on her lips instead for color.

Perfume. She looked down at the sparse array of bottles on her dressing table. Lily of the Valley and a bottle of Heaven Sent. Why wasn't there something intoxicating and daring? She dabbed the Lily of the Valley behind her ears. She liked the scent, felt it was

indicative of who she was. At last she was ready for Reuben Tarz. Her heart thumped crazily in her chest when she thought about sitting next to him in his car and then at dinner. Dinner! How would she ever be able to eat? Lord, what if she choked or spilled something and disgraced herself?

A nervous giggle rose in Rosemary's throat when she saw the two cats eyeing her suspiciously. "Out of character, eh? Sometimes things change. Come along, gentlemen, and I will fix your dinner. Warm milk and some shredded fish, how does that sound?" Silly, she told herself, but it hadn't sounded silly before when she'd held long conversations with her cats. One of these days, she felt sure one of them was going to answer her.

The two cats snaked between her legs, rubbing against them importunately. She smiled as their whiskers tickled her ankles. "Here we go, only a few minutes late. Enjoy your dinner."

The snow-white Persian fell to his dish with a vengeance, while Napoleon, the calico, looked at his, backed up a step, and then did his usual dance around it as if to view it from all angles. When he decided it was all he was going to get, he lapped it up in seconds and licked his whiskers as he walked away.

Rosemary looked at her watch. Twenty minutes to go until Reuben Tarz's arrival. Her stomach was growling from hunger, and

she felt as tense as a coiled spring. She bolted for the icebox and broke off a piece of cheese from a large slab wrapped in wax paper. As she chewed slowly and thoughtfully, she glanced around her. What would Reuben think of her little house here in the San Fernando Valley? It certainly wasn't palatial. Perhaps it couldn't even be considered homey. All she knew was she was comfortable with the natural woods and chintz-covered furniture and the nylon curtains. It was her home, and John — through guilt, she realized much later — had given it all to her, preferring to walk away unencumbered, as he called it. She wondered what Reuben Tarz's house looked like, then quickly pushed the thought away. John, Reuben Tarz . . . it was so silly the way she thought of one and the other's name popped into her head. It was silly — she was only having dinner with the president of Fairmont Studios, and that's all there was to it. Anything else was pure fantasy on her part.

Putting it into a business perspective made it easy for Rosemary to think that if her mother were alive, she'd be pleased to see her daughter having dinner with the head of the studio. She missed her mother, who had been her friend as well. Unfortunately she did not take after her mother, who had been outgoing and gregarious. Her father had lived back East for some years now. They kept in

touch on holidays, and recently he'd written that he was planning on remarrying. Rosemary wished him well, although she rarely thought of him and didn't miss him at all. But she did miss her mother and the pleasant times they had shared together. She'd missed her most during the divorce, when she'd had no one to talk to. Being married to James had left her no time for personal relationships, and any friends she'd had from school days had long since scattered. Besides, her mother had been her best friend. There were times, like now, when she wished she'd had more than a normal childhood and home life so she would have something to talk about with other people. There had been no radical ups and downs, no problems, no real long-range goals to shoot for, just placid everyday living. "That's why I'm so darned boring," she muttered.

The doorbell interrupted her reverie.

"Come in, Mr. Tarz. Would you like a drink before we leave?"

"No, thank you, and please, call me Reuben. Would you mind if I call you Rosemary?"

Rosemary smiled, and Reuben felt his heart melt. How lovely she was, how serene and gentle she seemed. She had the warmest eyes and the loveliest smile he'd ever seen. Suddenly he was aware of movement at his feet, and he looked down, confused. Rosemary laughed.

"This is Bismarck, and the calico is Napoleon. I'm afraid their manners aren't what they should be. I don't have many guests, and they don't quite know how to react. It's possible to make friends with them if you tickle their ears . . . if you like cats, that is." She reached for her purse. "Well, I'm ready if you are," she said briskly. To the cats she said, "Behave yourselves until I return."

Reuben chuckled. "Will they?"

Rosemary smiled again, a warm, sweet smile that made Reuben puff out his chest. "It's hard to tell. They're pretty good during the day. Cats are very self-sufficient, you know, and I have a kitty door so they can pretty much come and go as they please. My yard is walled in and they stay around the property. However, I don't go out much in the evenings, so I don't know what they'll do. In some respects they're like children, they crave attention."

Outside, Rosemary barely managed to conceal her excitement at the sight of Reuben's gleaming roadster. She forced herself to continue speaking in an even tone. "Once they pulled all the clothing out of my dresser drawer and made a bed for themselves, and another time they took all my shoes out of the closet and literally stacked them by the front door. I think they were trying to tell me something, but I still don't know what it was." Reuben chuckled as he helped her into

the handsome car, then walked around to the driver's side and got in. Instantly he was aware of her scent — like the sweet peas in his garden. Drawing in a deep breath, he complimented her on her choice of perfume. Rosemary glowed, her eyes bright.

Grinning to himself, Reuben started the car. Just wait till Max saw him when he walked into the Lily Garden with Rosemary on his arm! The old gangster would approve of her. So, for that matter, would Daniel. He himself approved, one hundred percent.

Max was every inch the suave host as he personally escorted the couple to Reuben's reserved table. He allowed himself a slight but serious wink in Reuben's direction, then sidled away. But Reuben knew: Max approved.

Twenty minutes after they'd been seated Rosemary decided Reuben Tarz didn't smile often enough. He was so handsome when his eyes grew warm and his features softened. Something deep inside told her she was responsible for his present comfortable and happy disposition. In the office his voice was never this deep and husky, caring and warm. She liked it. And she was liking him more with each passing moment.

"Do you like the wine? Max and I have been discussing importing wine from Bordeaux. What do you think of the Lily Garden?" Reuben asked anxiously.

Rosemary picked up the anxiousness in his voice. "I don't know too much about wine, but I know what I like, and I like this. Wine goes right to my head if I have even one glass on an empty stomach," she confided. Reuben thought of his wife's incredible ability to consume wine. "And I think this is one of the loveliest restaurants I've ever seen. It's so . . . glamourous, and the lily murals are breathtaking. The sound of the water from the fountains is so soothing. It's . . . pleasant and comfortable for a night spot. I wouldn't think movie stars would frequent such a . . . What I mean is, usually they're said to frequent bistros that are loud and crazy. I'm glad you brought me here." Shut up! she told herself.

Reuben leaned across the table. "A lot of Hollywood stars have been given a bad image by the press. In more ways than you know, they are simply ordinary people. They like to come here to unwind, and you're right, this is one of the most comfortable, the most fashionable places to dine in all of Hollywood. Max is very select with his reservation list. Do you see that balcony over there? A little beyond it are private rooms for private parties for up to thirty people. And the stage show is a knockout."

"Where is the stage?" Rosemary asked, looking around them. They were seated on the first tier of tables, and below them on the main floor were other tables grouped around

a highly polished dance floor. At the edge of the dance floor and directly opposite them, a twenty-piece orchestra grouped on a semicircular platform played soft dinner music. Behind them was a white satin silver-edged drape that carried the Lily Garden insignia, three water lilies in moss green with pale pink blossoms.

Reuben grinned. "This is Hollywood! When the show starts the curtain opens and that platform," he said, pointing in the orchestra's direction, "moves out over the dance floor and revolves, exposing the rest of the stage. Hot stuff, eh?" He chuckled at the look in her wide eyes. "And wait till you taste the food!"

They spent the next few minutes going over the elegant French menu, and when Rosemary couldn't recognize anything but snails and sweetbreads, she suggested that Reuben order for her. She watched, astonished, as he ordered in perfect French: Potage aux concombres, artichauts vinaigrette, lobster thermidor, and for dessert, crepes suzette.

The meal was magnificent, the service superb, and every once in a while Max put in an appearance to make sure they were being treated properly. Reuben and Rosemary chatted as if they were old friends all through dinner, and although they had second thoughts about dessert, the crepes suzette were made to order with a flourish by Ar-

mand, the maître d', and set flaming in front of them.

By now Rosemary felt comfortable enough to ask Reuben the one thing that had been bothering her for days. "Mr. . . . Reuben? I've been wondering . . . All those letters I've typed for you . . . there've been no responses, and I was . . . Is it possible I did something wrong? They all sounded so important. I'd feel just terrible if I somehow —"

"No, no, no, everything is just fine," Reuben said, chuckling. "I followed most of them up with a phone call. There were so many because Margaret was preoccupied and I didn't feel it necessary to heap them on her. I'm sorry I did it to you, though." He took a deep breath and dug into the plate in front of him to hide his face.

Rosemary smiled. "That makes me feel better. These crepes are heavenly, but I'm afraid I can't take another bite!" She jogged her brain for interesting conversational tidbits. Obviously Reuben didn't want to discuss her work or he'd have done so by now. Perhaps this was just a social dinner between a boss and a temporary secretary.

Reuben, too, was searching for something to say, something light and amusing, something he wouldn't be afraid to remember later. This pretty woman seated so near him — he wanted to know all about her. *Ask,* urged a voice inside him. *She seems forthright.*

It's the only way you'll find out. An employment application contained little personal information. He knew she could type and take shorthand, and answer the phone in a professional manner. He knew her age and where she lived and that she had two cats. But he wanted to know *everything* about her. And he loved how she flushed with pleasure when she spoke with him directly, then demurely cast her eyes away to hide it.

"Have you lived in the valley long?" he asked.

"All my life. I'm very comfortable there. Somehow I can't picture living anywhere else. My house must seem tiny compared with your mansion. I've seen photos of it in the pictorial section of the Sunday papers." She flushed again. Was she being too forward?

"What did you think of it?" Suddenly it was important to know what she thought. He didn't realize he was holding his breath until she spoke.

"Pictures are sometimes . . . deceiving," she said gently. She appeared flustered. "It looked . . . grand, very grand, but . . ."

"But?" Reuben smiled through his curiosity. "Don't be shy, tell me what you think."

"I think it might be hard to take such a big house and make it into a . . . a home. By that . . . what I mean is . . . it looked like no one really lived in it." She let out her breath in a

whoosh. "Are you happy there, Mr. . . . Reuben?"

Reuben's expression changed, drew inward, but he spoke without hesitation. "No, I'm not. I think of it as shelter and an investment. I have this friend, Daniel, who once gave his opinion of what a home should be like, and I agree with him. It should be filled with wonderful smells — and not just cooking. I mean people smells, something to indicate real people live inside. Daniel even wanted a pet that crapped on the carpet." He laughed then, a deep, warm sound that wrapped itself around Rosemary like a breath of fresh air. "I could do without that, but if it happened, it wouldn't bother me. Lived-in rooms, furniture and carpets that show life, pictures that are important to the people who live there, memories and big beds with soft sheets and fluffy blankets. Sunshine in every room and all sorts of flowers in every shade of the rainbow . . . What do you think of that?" he said, returning his gaze to her.

Rosemary blinked at the look of sadness in Reuben's eyes. She felt confused. What he wanted was just the opposite of what he had. It didn't make sense. "I think it sounds wonderful. I think my own ideas are the same, and your friend Daniel must be a wonderful person. It all comes down to comfort and a sort of peace that's within ourselves. But if that's what you want, why

don't you have it?" she asked without thinking.

Reuben debated only a moment before answering her. This quiet, serenely beautiful woman would understand, he just knew it. So he told her then about his life with Bebe, everything but his time in France with Mickey. By the time he'd brought his story to a close, the waiters were clearing the table. "I don't want you to feel sorry for me, that's not why I told you about my . . . home life. You're very easy to talk to, Rosemary."

"Thank you, Reuben, I consider that a compliment. I wish there were something I could do to make . . . to help you . . . what I mean is, if there's anything I can . . ."

"There is something you can do. You can see me again. I find myself very . . . I want to see you again," he said firmly. His heart fluttered; she looked so devastated, so wary, and, yes, frightened at his words. He smiled and reached across the table for her hand. She was trembling, and he was almost sorry he'd spoken. Almost.

Rosemary cleared her throat. "I would like that, but you don't . . . perhaps it's this beautiful place . . . you don't know anything about me. People might talk . . . they will talk." Reluctantly she drew her hand away from his. "I can't . . . I'm not the type of woman who can . . . I wouldn't be able to sneak around . . . You're a married man," she

said finally. "What you do and where you go is always news. Even tonight." She thought of the number of people who had waved at them; some had even sent over drinks during dinner. "Seeing me, being friends, might cause problems for you."

Reuben leaned back in his chair, eyes twinkling behind his shell-rimmed glasses. Jesus, she was beautiful! He wished then that there were a beach nearby so he could walk with her, holding her hand. The thought made his smile wider. "I was never one to worry about what other people said or didn't say about me, but I wouldn't be very good at sneaking around, either — nor would I ask that of you. I wouldn't do anything to hurt or embarrass you, Rosemary."

Rosemary's heart raced. All he'd really said was that he wanted to see her again; he hadn't said anything about sex. If she wanted to, she could find thirty-seven reasons not to start up a friendship with this delightful man. If she wanted to. A smile tugged at the corners of her mouth, and she looked down at her wine goblet.

Suddenly the emcee picked up the microphone and began calling everyone's attention to the evening's entertainment.

"Ladies and gentlemen, good evening. . . . Tonight we have a special . . ." Just as Reuben had described, the elegant huge curtain began to rise and the stage before them

slowly began to turn. Although everyone grew quiet with anticipation, Reuben and Rosemary felt that they had been intruded upon. Their intimate dinner had become public fare.

"Look," Reuben said impulsively, "why don't we leave here and go for a walk and then back to your house to have some coffee and check on the boys."

Rosemary laughed. "That sounds wonderful."

"Let's go," Reuben said, getting up to hold her chair. Max was at his elbow immediately.

"Is something wrong, Mr. Tarz?" he asked.

"Not a thing, Max. It was a wonderful dinner. Wasn't it a wonderful dinner?" Reuben said boyishly. "We're just going for a walk."

Max had never seen his longtime friend with such a sappy grin on his face. Obviously this one was a lady. Wait until he called Jane. At last, after all these years, Reuben looked happy. It occurred to him that he'd seen something this evening he'd never seen before: he'd seen Reuben Tarz actually smile with his eyes as well as with his mouth. He sighed happily. And to think it had happened in the Lily Garden. . . .

Rosemary and Reuben walked for hours, up one street and down another. They talked, laughed, whispered to each other like conspirators, their hands and shoulders touching. Reuben couldn't remember the last time

he'd been this happy, and he told Rosemary so and was rewarded with her gentle smile. How could any man in his right mind divorce this lovely woman?

They were strolling aimlessly now, their arms swinging between them. "We should be starting back, tomorrow is a workday," Rosemary said.

"Hey, I'm the boss," Reuben teased.

"So you are, but I can't and won't take advantage. After you drive me home you still have to turn around and come all the way back here." But she didn't want the evening to end, and obviously Reuben didn't, either.

They both laughed. "Okay, Uncle, I'll get you home," Reuben conceded.

On the way back to Rosemary's they remained silent, just enjoying each other's company. Reuben grinned from ear to ear as he tried to imagine what Daniel would say if he saw him now. Sappy, ridiculous. He'd even had an urge to pull her over to sit close by his side but hadn't had the courage to do it.

When they pulled up in front of her house he was thrilled when she turned to him and said, "Coffee? Still in the mood?"

They were mock-arguing about whether or not Rosemary would let Reuben help prepare it when they opened the door. Rosemary was the first one to see what lay just beyond. "Oh, no!"

Reuben looked over her shoulder and was

aware instantly of three things: Rosemary's dismay, the two cats huddled together under a corner table, and a sea of white toilet paper festooned over what looked like the entire house.

"I can't believe this! I am so embarrassed. I don't know what's gotten into them. How can you get angry at a cat?" she asked helplessly.

Reuben sat down on a rocking chair, his eyes on the nervous cats. He laughed then, a deep rumble coming from his stomach and echoing through the house. Rosemary dropped to her knees beside him and laughed until the tears rolled down her cheeks. "Would you just look at them, they know they did something wrong. See, Bismarck is sitting on his tail and Napoleon's got his back up. He's angry. At me, I guess. Or maybe at you. You're a stranger and they aren't used to you." She threw her hands in the air. "They're really good cats," she said, giggling. "I'm sorry, Reuben."

"Rosemary, you have nothing to apologize for. I had a wonderful evening. I can't remember when I've had such a good time. This," he said, letting his arms embrace the room, "is sort of the icing on the cake, if you know what I mean. Believe me when I tell you I had a grand evening."

Rosemary felt her heart begin to pound. What if he kissed her, now, this very moment?

But of course, he wouldn't. Still, she knew exactly what the kiss would be like, exactly how it would feel, exactly how she would feel at that exquisite moment and afterward. She sighed happily, her eyes tender and giving.

It was the perfect moment to kiss her, Reuben thought, but something in him drew back, some warning that he had to go slowly with this wonderful, lovely woman. Tenderly he touched her cheek, his index finger trailing down her face to her throat. "I'll help you clean up this mess and then I'll be on my way."

"That isn't necessary. Oh, Lord, look at those two mischief-makers."

Reuben chortled. Both cats had settled down and were fast asleep. "I don't think they'll get into any more mischief tonight. . . . Can I come back tomorrow evening?" he asked suddenly.

There was nothing coy in Rosemary's response, nor did she pretend to hesitate before answering. "If you like."

He was a whirlwind then, rushing through the house pulling the paper from lamp shades, table legs, and doorknobs. "I didn't know there was so much paper in a roll. Isn't it amazing the things you take for granted and never realize? I plan to store this important information, don't you?"

Rosemary grinned. "Absolutely." No doubt about it, it was good to see a man about the

house. She held out her arms and Reuben stuffed them with the tissue.

"Good night, Rosemary, sleep well."

"Good night, Reuben, pleasant dreams. Thank you for a lovely evening."

Reuben just couldn't push himself out the door. He hung in the doorway, like a lost puppy, happy to have found a warm spot to rest. "My pleasure. I'll see you in the office, then?"

"I'll be there," she reassured him, her voice trembling. "Good night."

"Good night, then." Sighing, he pushed himself from the doorway, then stopped to wave back at her halfway to his car. He waved again as he drove away.

Rosemary didn't move until she saw the car's headlights as a dim flicker in the night. Then she carried the wads of tissue paper to the kitchen, reluctant to dispose of them simply because Reuben had given them to her. The scent of his after-shave lingered wherever he'd held them against his body.

Humming softly to herself, she stuffed the tissue into the trash outside her kitchen door. It had been a delightful evening, and tomorrow was going to be just as delightful, she was sure of it. Her little house seemed to spring to life around her as she set about turning out the lights and locking up. The chintz-covered furniture seemed brighter, more vivid, the waxed floors richer, gleaming

now in the lamplight, the snoozing cats more endearing somehow. Life, she decided, was wonderful.

There was a smile on Rosemary's face as she got ready for bed, taking more time than usual to turn down her bed and wondering if Reuben would ever lie in it. Her cheeks felt hot at the thought. Although she liked sex and had initiated it often with John, he'd been far from a satisfactory lover, content with his own gratification rather than hers. Reuben, she thought, would be a tender yet fierce lover, one who would teach and be open to learning at the same time. Someday . . . She was tingling from head to toe as she squeezed the toothpaste onto her brush; she was still tingling when she lathered cold cream on her face and then wiped at it with a towel because the toilet paper holder was empty. Suddenly she laughed, uproariously, and the tingly feeling left her. For the next ten minutes she went through her closet, trying to find just the right dress to wear to work the following day. At last she chose a peach-colored silk dress that she'd worn several times already. All it needed was a change of collar and perhaps that wide lace dickey she loved — the one trimmed with tiny seed pearls. It was rich and feminine-looking.

Rosemary dropped to her knees and said her nightly prayers as she had done ever since childhood. John had laughed at her, ridicul-

ing her until the embarrassment had driven her into the bathroom each night, where she could say her prayers in private. She wondered if Reuben would understand. Did Jewish people pray on their knees? Maybe she could ask him that, too.

In bed with the light coverlet pulled up to her chin, Rosemary wondered how she compared with Bebe Tarz in Reuben's eyes. There was probably no comparison, she thought dismally. According to the newspapers, Bebe was beautiful, dressed always in famous designer clothes and jewels that cost a fortune. She was the darling of the press. But Reuben hadn't said anything about loving her. In fact, the things he had told her over dinner made her feel that he didn't — couldn't, even. If she was constantly off, sometimes for months, and without a word, what kind of a home life could they share? He hadn't said anything about loving his children, either. Yet she could tell by his voice that he loved his friends Max, Daniel, and Jane.

A feeling she couldn't define rushed over her suddenly. It took her several minutes to identify it as the desire to protect Reuben and minister to his wounds — the mother feelings all women had in them. If Reuben were with her right now, she would wrap her arms around him and croon to him, "I'll make it right, I'll not let anyone hurt you."

He'd take her hand in his and she would bring it to her lips and kiss it and place it on her cheek and whisper soft words.

Rosemary sighed and shook her head. One dinner and she was already taking charge of his life! She snapped out the light and slid down between the cool sheets. "Go to sleep," she ordered herself.

As Rosemary struggled for sleep, Reuben was wandering around his house in Laurel Canyon, seeing it through her eyes. She might be awed by it, might even say it was beautiful, but she wouldn't want to live here. He tried to imagine her precocious cats romping through the luxurious, sterile rooms. Everything looked so new and unused. Surely Dillon and Simon had trampled through some of these rooms — or had Bebe redecorated using the same basic color scheme? For the life of him he couldn't remember. The hell with it, he thought disgustedly. It was a damn house, a place for him to sleep, a fancy address befitting his position at the studio.

Melancholy now, he walked back through each of the still rooms, feeling his aloneness more than ever before. When he was halfway up the wide, elegant staircase, he turned and looked around. A monument to his success. A sound caught in his throat, half laughter, half sob. Little did anyone know he was a casualty of that success.

In his room he stripped down, brushed his teeth, threw water on his face. His bed had been turned down earlier by one of the maids, and on the night table was a flask of warm cocoa. Although he rarely drank it, it was something he'd gotten used to in France and had insisted on having here in his own home. It was a tangible tie with his past, a comforting remembrance of happier days. This night he poured the creamy liquid into a china cup but still didn't drink it. He just wanted to look at it — to know it was there.

"I won't think about Mickey tonight," he muttered as he scrunched his head into the soft down pillow. Instead, he dreamed of her, a sweet, almost unbearable dream full of sorrow and love.

Every night after work for the next few weeks Reuben drove home, bathed and changed his clothes, and headed immediately for Rosemary's house in the valley. Within seconds of walking through her door, stepping over the cats, and smiling at her, he would feel at home and at peace with himself, even after having spent the business day with her in a professional and businesslike way. Being with this delightful, serene, contented woman was better than a walk through a daisy-filled meadow, better than a hand-in-hand stroll in a warm spring rain. Not only did he tell

himself she was what he wanted, he believed it.

The hours from six to midnight were theirs and theirs alone. Sometimes they sat together on Rosemary's soft cushiony sofa, each with a book, but always aware of each other. Often they didn't speak for hours, content with eye contact and warm smiles. Rosemary cooked, plain meals mostly, but always with a rich dessert for Reuben's sweet tooth. They picnicked in the park on weekends, and once they took a basket lunch and shared a late supper under the stars because Reuben had been caught up in a late afternoon meeting that had run longer than he'd anticipated. His weekends were devoted solely to Rosemary and hers to him.

During one particular week in late November, it rained steadily for five days and into the weekend. When Reuben arrived at eight in the morning, Rosemary had a fire blazing in her grate and a huge breakfast waiting. Reuben thought his chest would burst with happiness. The cats watched greedily and Reuben sneaked them bits of bacon and buttered toast while Rosemary pretended not to notice. Regardless of what he did, she could forgive him even to the detriment of her beloved cats.

This lovely woman was his life now. He'd tried to explain how he felt to Daniel, to Jane, and even to Max; when she cautioned him to

drive safely, when she asked how he was feeling, it stirred him deeply. Mickey had never cautioned him during those heady days in France, and Bebe wouldn't even think of it. It was a new feeling for him, this caring, this solicitude, blanketing him with a satisfied contentment. He looked forward to arriving at her house and teasing her with, "See, I made it safe and sound."

He thought he was in love, and he knew in his heart that Rosemary felt something more for him than just friendship. When he was with her he had sexual feelings, even definite arousals, which came upon him without warning and passed just as quickly. Although he was alarmed when his erections left him almost as suddenly as they arrived, he was thrilled that, as he would refer to it in his innermost thoughts, he was "not dead yet." It had been so long since he'd been able to physically manifest his sexuality that he was enormously relieved — but he wouldn't allow the thought of acting on his arousal to enter his mind.

They'd kissed, gentle touches that held just a trace of mutual passion. Each of them seemed to be proceeding cautiously, unsure whether this fragile thing between them would fade or grow. Rosemary considered it a nurturing time, and Reuben seemed to bask in that nurturing.

Having done admirable justice to the break-

fast Rosemary had prepared for him, Reuben pushed his plate away. "You're trying to fatten me up," he teased. "It's been years since I had pancakes and eggs at the same time. And you always make the bacon just the way I like it." He patted his stomach in satisfaction. "I really enjoyed it, Ro."

Rosemary smiled. "Well, you know I love to cook. And it's especially nice when someone is here to enjoy the results. I thought we'd make cookies today. Big fat sugar cookies, crisp on the outside and cakelike on the inside with a trace of orange. You can grate the orange. My mother used to make them for me when I was little. I always had a sugar cookie when I got home from school."

"I get the feeling I'm joining you in the kitchen today," he said in a mock rueful voice. "Will the house smell good?"

"Wait and see," she answered, her eyes dancing. "Are you sure you can handle being in the kitchen?"

"What do you mean? I can wear an apron with the best of them. I've never grated an orange, but there's a first time for everything. Lead the way, my dear," he said, rising. "And while the cookies are baking, I thought we might look at some pictures. I brought along those photo albums you've been asking to see — one of the boys and one of me and Daniel in earlier days. They're in the car. I hope it wasn't presumptuous of me?"

Rosemary felt light-headed. He was going to share his past with her. "Reuben, that's so nice. I'm so happy you've brought them. I want to hear all about your boys, especially the little stories that go with each child."

Little stories, Christ, he'd have to manufacture them, he thought. Well, he was certainly in the right business to do that.

It was a wonderful day full of delicious fragrances filling the little house, snuggly comfort, and a sharing of lives. The insistent sound of the rain, drumming rhythmically against the windows, accompanied their every action. Reuben felt more at peace with himself than he had in a long time. It made him think about what he'd been missing all these years. He turned to gaze at Rosemary sitting beside him, and a fierce feeling of protectiveness consumed him. Nothing was going to destroy this. At that moment he knew he was capable of killing to keep what he had. It was time now, though, for the ultimate test. Was he capable of making love to her? He felt the desire, wanted to consummate his feelings with her, but he was afraid. What if . . . what if . . . Rather than subject himself to humiliation, he'd backed off each time his feelings turned passionate, to the point of . . . What would she think? Certainly she would never ridicule him, that wasn't the Rosemary he knew. No, she would be gentle and kind, and tell him it didn't matter and

that things would get better, but he knew her words would be a lie to save his feelings. It would matter to both of them. His feelings for her were so overwhelming he often felt lost, adrift, and unsure of himself. How could she think of him as a man, a complete man? Jesus, she might even be thinking there was something wrong with her, that she didn't excite him enough to want to make love.

Pit . . . pit . . . pat . . . plop . . . pit . . . pit . . . pit. . . .

"What's that sound?" Rosemary asked, looking around.

Pit . . . pat . . . plop . . .

Reuben stirred himself from his position on the couch. Rosemary squirmed around until she was on her knees, straining to hear where the strange sound was coming from. "I think you have a leak somewhere, honey," he said. "It's splattering on your table." He pointed, grimacing. "I'd better move the lamp and check the attic. Get a pot or something."

Rosemary ran into the kitchen. "It's leaking out here, too. My roof is leaking!"

"Show me the way to the attic, Rosemary, and then set out pots and buckets."

The attic was as neat and tidy as the rest of her house. Dark, spooky corners linked by cobwebs made him smile. Boxes tied with string and labeled were stacked in the middle of the floor. But as Reuben looked at the boxes he saw that they were soaking wet; the

848

rain was nearly pouring through the timbers. There seemed to be no way to stop it.

"How bad is it, Reuben?" Rosemary called up anxiously.

He walked back down the stairs. "Bad. The entire attic is soaked, and so are all the boxes. I don't know too much about roofs, but I think you need a new one."

"Oh, no! I can't afford a new roof. I barely make ends meet on my salary, and I have only a few dollars in my savings account." When she realized what she'd said, Rosemary covered her mouth in embarrassment. "Do you think it can be patched?" she said hurriedly.

In an instant Reuben realized her predicament. The fact that he had probably added to the strain on her budget in many ways over the past several weeks made him want to kick himself. But he wouldn't say anything; he wouldn't dream of embarrassing her more than she already was. "Maybe, but I'd have to go up on the roof to know for sure. That's impossible at the moment, but I can tell you that before this rain stops, the ceilings are going to get ruined and could even cave in. I think we have a serious problem."

"We" have a serious problem. Rosemary couldn't think of anything to say, her thoughts were whirling so quickly.

"I think we should move you out right now, to a hotel or a furnished apartment some-

where. What do you think?"

Rosemary shrugged helplessly. Ruined ceilings, a new roof, the beds, all her treasured furniture would be ruined. It would take her years to recover financially. She had exactly $196 in the bank. She'd planned on buying some lacy lingerie, but now . . . "Damn," she muttered.

Reuben couldn't control his laughter. "I didn't know you knew that word. Come on, Ro, it's not the end of the world. I'll have it all taken care of as soon as the rain stops. Smile now, this is just a temporary thing, and it's going to be only as difficult as you make it. I can't promise it'll be exactly as you left it, but . . . I'll take care of it."

Rosemary's brain raced. Why not? Wasn't she past the point of formality with Reuben? Certainly he was her friend; in time he would be her lover, too — she was sure of it. Swiftly she calculated the hours she'd spent with him; day-to-day love was costly. He was just trying to reciprocate the only way he knew how. She felt her eyes fill with tears. "That's more than kind of you, Reuben. How will I ever repay you?" she asked.

"I'll think of something," Reuben teased. "Come on, let's start getting you packed up. I know a good hotel that will allow you to have the cats, and it has suites with a sitting room, too. You'll have to have your meals out, but I can take care of that. The Lily Garden

isn't far from there, and Max will be happy to accommodate." Reuben took her chin in his hands and stared down at her. "Will you let me do this for you?"

The rain was beginning to seep over everything as they stood there, even overflowing the meager supply of pots Rosemary had hurriedly placed everywhere. As if on cue, a solitary tear rolled down her cheek, and she melted into Reuben's arms.

"I'll take care of everything, I don't want you to worry about a thing," he crooned into her hair.

Reuben happily settled Rosemary into the Centurion Hotel. He bustled about, checking the bathroom, the softness of the bed and the sofa in the sitting room. When he was satisfied the suite met with his approval, he kissed her good night and headed back to his own house, filled with a sense of goodwill.

It was a pleasant suite, Rosemary thought, the colors soft and muted. It was comfortable. She would miss her kitchen, but Reuben insisted Max would provide dinner and she was to order from room service anything else she might need. Reuben Tarz was a generous man to those he cared for, and Rosemary was convinced he cared for her. It occurred to her then that he hadn't shown her his photo albums. Although she'd been looking forward to sharing his past, under

the circumstances she could understand his forgetfulness.

She twirled around the spacious suite like Cinderella at the ball. Suddenly she laughed, a delightful sound that brought the cats, who had been busy exploring their new territory, on the run. "If we were bees, gentlemen, we'd be in clover," she told them.

On Monday morning Reuben rose early. After calling Rosemary to see if all was well, he informed her he wouldn't be in until after lunch. By noon he'd hired two contractors, one to replace the roof and the other to rip out the waterlogged ceilings and whatever walls had to be replaced. New wiring would be installed. On the spur of the moment he ordered a completely new kitchen and bathroom and used the colors she had mentioned were her favorites. During the last two weeks of construction he hired an interior decorator, giving the man carte blanche.

It was during this span of time that Reuben's secretary returned. Reuben got Rosemary a job at Fox, making sure her salary was top dollar. The same week they parted professional company, Rosemary's house was finished. Reuben felt like a proud father as he walked through the house; it was perfect. He was profuse in his thanks to the contractors and beamed with pleasure as he handed over checks in the amount of $19,000. When the last piece of furniture was placed in its

planned position, he drew a sigh of expectation. Even the new refrigerator and cupboards had been stocked with all their favorite foods. He couldn't wait to see how Rosemary would react to everything. It had taken some convincing, but he'd made her promise not to visit the house, but to wait until it was completely done.

Reuben wished there were some way he could tie the house in a big red bow for Rosemary. The thought so energized him that he leapt into his car and headed for the studio. For Christ's sake, this was Hollywood and he had a full-fledged prop department! If he wished to wrap the house in a red ribbon, he'd damn well wrap the house in a red ribbon. If his prop men couldn't do it, no one could.

Four hours later the house at 5334 Poplar Avenue was wrapped in two hundred yards of ten-inch-wide red satin ribbon. The bow resting on the side of the chimney jutting from the slate-gray shingled roof was the largest Reuben had seen. A confection. Rosemary was going to swoon with pleasure. The best cameraman at the studio had been told to snap his picture and enlarge it, frame it, and deliver it gift-wrapped as soon as it could be hand-carried.

"Well done, Tarz!" Reuben congratulated himself. He tried to anticipate Rosemary's reaction as she stepped across her new

threshold. Would her response carry him to that place in his mind where he needed to be, where he wanted to be? So many years to be unfulfilled. So many aches and desires. Rosemary was going to make the difference, he was sure of it . . . because old feelings, remembered surges, were starting to rise to the surface.

Reuben stepped back onto the road for a last look at his handiwork before climbing into the car to pick her up. Her voice had been shaky with anticipation when he'd called her at her office to tell her what time he would meet her at the hotel. By now Rosemary's neighbors had gathered around the house and were gawking in astonishment. Reuben grinned as he settled himself into the driver's seat. The construction and the huge red bow would probably be talked about for weeks. He waved airily to a group of them, and they waved back as he swung his car into the road from the driveway. The men in the group were nodding slyly to themselves, questioning whether the man behind the wheel had ever heard the saying "taken to the cleaners." The women were envying Rosemary and wishing the red bow were for them. Reuben was oblivious to them all, about to explode with pure happiness.

Rosemary carried the last of her valises to the door. She wouldn't be sorry to leave the

hotel — not that it hadn't been pleasant, but she was beyond eager to get back into her own home. When he'd first come to visit her, Reuben had been amazed at her insistence upon staying in the suite at dinnertime and ordering from room service, but she'd soon been able to make him realize it was the most sensible thing. There was something that bordered on the illicit about his visits, or maybe it was the fact that he'd paid the bill for her entire stay at the hotel. In any event, she had felt temporary and cheap, and that had made her very uncomfortable. They still hadn't made love, although their kisses had begun to intensify and their conversation now held many sexual innuendos, something she tried to encourage every chance she could. She would advance just so far, but then inevitably Reuben backed off.

For this special night, Reuben said he had made reservations at the Lily Garden for dinner to celebrate both the completion of the house and also an event at the studio she couldn't even remember. What she did remember was that the entertainment for the evening was a man called Frank Sinatra from Hoboken, New Jersey. An "Eye-tal-ian," according to Max. She had to find a way to nip that in the bud; she had no intention of going to the Lily Garden the first night she could be spending in her new house. Besides, she had other things on her mind.

Rosemary kneaded her hands nervously, her thoughts racing back over her relationship with Reuben. His problems at home and even now had to stem from impotence. Certainly she was no authority on sex, but she did know that a man's erection stayed erect until he was satisfied. Pressed against Reuben at night, as they kissed at her door and lingered, proved to her that any hardness he experienced was so short-lived as to be almost nonexistent. There was no doubt that he cared for her given his actions; and she was sure that it had nothing to do anymore with gentling the relationship along. Not too many women with healthy sexual appetites would . . . No wonder Bebe Tarz strayed. Now that she'd put two and two together, she felt pity for Reuben's wife. Her stomach fluttered nervously. Maybe the same thing was going to happen to her. So far this thing, this sharing she and Reuben had, was little more than a brother/sister relationship with a few kisses thrown in. She wanted more, needed more, and tonight was the night.

In anticipation, she had purchased a sheer black nightie and a set of red satin sheets trimmed in decadent black lace. They were so sinful looking she'd almost taken them back. Her breathing quickened at the thought of them naked together on those satin sheets. Now, as Reuben bent down to pick up her bags, she found it extremely difficult to act

naturally. With his dark hair falling over his forehead he looked devilishly debonair, his eyes sparkling in anticipation of the surprise that awaited her. "One house coming up," he said, and winked. "I'll come back for the other bags and you can gather the boys."

"That's what I like, a man who makes spontaneous decisions," Rosemary said gaily. The tremor in her voice surprised her.

There was a small knot of people near Rosemary's house when they drove up and stray passersby stopped to stare in amazement at the huge red bow perched atop the house. Reuben pulled the car into the driveway and Rosemary leapt out, her face stunned, a cat in each arm. She had to back up and crane her neck in order to stare at the red bow. "Reuben! Did you do this? I . . . the bow is . . . Reuben, you wonderful man . . . I love this! Oh, Reuben," she cried, running into his open arms. "This is amazing! I know, I know, this is Hollywood, land of magic! I will remember this as long as I live. I love you for this, Reuben, I really do!"

"You ready for the tour, Miss Connors?" Reuben asked gallantly. Jesus, he felt good. Wait until she saw the inside. "Close your eyes." Obediently Rosemary closed her eyes. "Reuben, why am I closing my eyes?" she asked coyly. "Is the new ceiling going to blind me? . . ."

Reuben held her arm and gently guided her

through the door. When it was closed to the neighbors and all outside sounds, he took the cats from her and said, "Now open your eyes!"

Rosemary gasped in pure delight at the room before her. For hours she'd been practicing her emotional response to this moment, so that she could do justice to Reuben's efforts to please her — but nothing could have prepared her for the quiet, comfortable elegance of her new home. More than anything, she was aware of Reuben's trembling arm and the excitement in his voice as he took her on a guided tour.

"Oh, Reuben," she cried in a tremulous voice, "you've transformed my house into a palace. It will take me all my life to repay you for this miracle. Oh! Oh!" They went from room to room, Rosemary exclaiming at every turn and laughing at the cats as they delicately examined each nook and cranny with curious heads. "You are such a darling for doing this. I've never experienced anything so grand. I love it, Reuben, I just love what you've done. All this and the red ribbons." She stopped dead in her tracks. "I want to save it! I want the bow, but not now. I can leave it on the house for a few days, can't I?"

"Honey, you can have whatever you want. The bow is yours. When you're ready to have it taken off I'll send some of the men from the studio. Do you really like it, Ro?" Sud-

denly he wished that he'd spent more money, bought more elegant furnishings, but that wasn't Rosemary's style. Less is more, he'd told himself whenever his generosity threatened to get the better of him. And now he was part of something, part of Rosemary and this warm, inviting house. He felt connected, committed. This, then, in his mind, was the stable home he'd never had as a boy. Tears burned his eyes. His emotional cup was running over, and all it had taken to bring him to this moment was a comfortable love and a meager amount of money.

"Rosemary," he said softly, "I don't ever want to hear you say another word about repaying me for this." He fished in his breast pocket for a thick envelope and handed it to her shyly.

Rosemary ripped it open with shaking hands. Then, as she scanned the paper contained within, her eyes fluttered and her knees almost buckled beneath her. "You . . . you paid off my mortgage. Oh, Reuben, I can't allow you to . . . It isn't right. I can't . . . How can I accept all of this? You are so good and generous. How can I ever thank you?"

"You just did. Your happiness is all I want. If doing this makes you happy, I'm glad I was able to do it." She'd said she loved him for what he'd done. This was a new Rosemary, one who had temporarily lost control of her

emotions. The thought made him feel power-ful and protective at the same time.

She was cradled in his arms now, snuggled safely against his chest. And he felt so good, so wonderful . . . but she couldn't let anything happen yet. First she wanted to put the satin sheets on the bed and wear the new black nightie, open the bottle of champagne she'd spotted in the back of the car. If tonight was going to be the culmination of their relation-ship, she wanted it to be perfect . . . so that their togetherness was sealed.

"Reuben, tell me honestly, did you choose all of this or did you have help? Everything is so perfectly coordinated, right down to the alabaster ashtrays. And wherever did you get salmon-colored roses?" she asked breath-lessly, referring to an impressive bouquet in a cut-crystal vase on a polished cherrywood table.

Reuben glowed with pride as he gently stroked Rosemary's sweet-smelling hair. "I remembered your telling me which were your favorite colors . . . and . . . I stressed comfort and relaxed elegance to the decorator."

There was no need for Rosemary to know the decorator had at first turned up his nose in disdain at the small house; the offer of a bonus had miraculously restored the man's interest in taking on such a "challenge." "I hope everything reflects you, Rosemary. If there's anything you want changed, it's all

right with me."

"Nothing. It's perfect, Reuben! I couldn't imagine wanting to change one thing. Thank-you seems so inadequate," Rosemary said fervently, "but it's all I can say. Let's stay home and savor all of this. Max won't mind if we don't go to the Lily Garden, will he?"

Reuben smiled. "I'll call him. I was hoping you'd say we should stay home. I can't tell you how glad I am, Ro, that you feel the same way."

"You sit right here," Rosemary said. She headed for the radio and searched until she found a station playing soft, restful music. When she returned to him, she dropped to her knees and untied his shoes. "I want you to put your feet up on this nice new table. Someone should look at this copy of *Life* magazine." She planted a tender kiss on Reuben's cheek.

He smiled up at her and brought her hand to his lips. "It feels so good to be here, so right."

"For me, too," she said gently. "I'll see about dinner, but first I want to change my clothes. Read, take a nap. I'll wake you when it's time to eat."

Reuben idly leafed through the magazine. He did feel good — very good, as a matter of fact. Tonight . . .

Frustrated with his new surroundings and a mistress who was ignoring him, Bismarck

leapt onto Reuben's lap. Seconds later Napoleon settled himself at Reuben's side. Both cats purred contentedly. Reuben was familiar; Reuben was very good at tickling ears.

Rosemary tiptoed down the stairs and stood for a moment observing Reuben and her cats. She smiled happily. Her life was on an even keel, and tonight would mark the beginning of a new phase in her relationship with Reuben. The sheets had gone on in the blink of an eye. At the last second before pulling up the chenille bedspread, she'd dropped a few beads of perfume on the pillowcases. Her nightie lay in readiness. Tonight, Reuben, she thought, I am going to seduce you, first with food and then with my body.

"Dinner," Reuben said, "was delightful." He'd had too much champagne, and so had Rosemary. The delicate omelets stuffed with wild mushrooms and onions and topped with a whipped cheese sauce had been a light, satisfying repast, the scalloped potatoes that accompanied them so savory he'd had three helpings. Reuben's eyes had popped at the fragrant surprise of a dish of honey-baked apples when Rosemary had reappeared from the kitchen.

Now they were in the tiny garden with their coffee, staring up at the twinkling stars. "Do you think the stars look the same all over the world?" Rosemary asked curiously.

Reuben's contented mood seemed to shatter. How often, when out walking after dinner at the château, had he wondered the same thing? He nodded, not trusting himself to speak.

Rosemary immediately picked up on his change of mood. "Let's each make a wish, Reuben. I know it isn't the first star of the night, but we can do it anyway. And . . . I'll tell you mine if you tell me yours." She smiled. "Wishes are for the child in all of us, don't you think?"

Reuben's jaw hardened. Bebe had done the same thing to him years before, and he'd wished . . . He gave himself a mental shake. No one — not Mickey or Bebe — must be allowed to spoil this evening for him. He deserved this; he wanted it more than anything. This was his time. "All right, who goes first?" he said, smiling at her in the darkness.

"I will. I wish that our lives will always be this good, this gratifying. I wish . . . I hope I'm never a disappointment to you," Rosemary said shyly.

"That's two wishes. You could never disappoint me, so let's concentrate on your first wish. I think we have an excellent chance at it, since I wished exactly the same thing."

"Reuben? . . ."

"Yes?"

Rosemary rose from her chair and pulled Reuben to his feet, her eyes twinkling mis-

chievously. "Let's go upstairs . . . to bed. I want you to make love to me."

He wanted to, more than anything in the world, and by God he would or he'd die trying! Desire surged through him like a river gone wild. He scooped Rosemary into his arms, kicked at the screen door with his foot, and shouldered it open. She was light as a feather in his arms, and he swore he could hear her heart beating next to his own. In the kitchen light he was shocked at the smoldering look in her eyes. Gazing at her, he drew in a deep ragged breath, his own eyes taking on a light of their own.

Beyond her bedroom door Reuben set Rosemary on her feet and drew the length of her body close to his. The silence between them seemed more eloquent than words. Rosemary drew in her breath and felt Reuben tense at the sound. He, too, seemed to have trouble with his breathing. She was conscious of his height, of his nearness, of his maleness. His arms cupped her to him, making her tingle with a pleasurable yearning. In the soft glow of the lamp Rosemary offered her lips to his. His mouth became a part of hers, and her heart beat in a wild, untamed broken rhythm.

Reuben kissed her eyes, her mouth, her cheeks, the hollow of her throat, and she felt a raging fire engulf her as she burrowed her head against his chest. It made no difference

that he belonged to another woman; she wanted him, needed him. She moaned softly as his mouth again crashed down on hers in a savage, unrestrained kiss of passion. The banked fires began to smolder and burst into flame as she felt his searching hands explore her body through her clothing. His touch was scorching, searing, as her own hands ceased to tremble and she caressed his face and ran her fingers through his hair. Moan after moan escaped her as she strained against him, her mouth mingling with his, her tongue searching, darting, to conquer his.

Within moments their clothing lay in a heap on the downy carpet. In the soft shadows of the night Reuben drew in his breath in a ragged gasp as his eyes beheld Rosemary's glistening body. His face was inscrutable in the faint glimmer, but his gaze was almost tangible; she felt it reach her, touch her, and was aware of the all-consuming fire that raged through her.

Her response was unwavering as she stared deep into his dark eyes, hypnotized by them as she felt his mouth melt into hers. Her body took on a will of its own as Reuben caressed and explored every inch of her. Instinctively she moved to the rhythm he initiated and felt him respond to her in a way she had never dreamed possible. Searing flames licked at her body as she sought to quench the blazing inferno that engulfed her. He kissed her ear-

lobes, her eyes, her moistened mouth, murmuring tender words of love as his hands traveled down the length of her, arousing, teasing her, until her breath came in short gasps and her body writhed beneath his touch.

Her flesh grew warm and taut beneath him as he pressed her down onto the softness of the bed. His hungry mouth worshiped her, tracing moist patterns on her creamy skin. His dark head moved lower, to graze the firmness of her belly, then lower still to the silky smoothness between her legs. He parted her legs with his knees and felt her respond to him, arching her back to receive him. Her parted lips were a flame that met his raging, tumultuous mouth. She welcomed him, accepted him, his hardness, his leanness, his very maleness, as he drove into her, straining against his hard, muscular chest, responding to his passion with an urgency that demanded release. The unquenchable heat that was soaring through her beat in her veins, threatening to crescendo into a raging inferno.

He lay upon her, commanding her response as she offered it, rocking beneath him, exulting in her own femininity as she caressed his broad back. The sound of her own heart thundered in her ears — or was it Reuben's that beat and roared about them?

Gasping, she opened herself to him, and the searing, scorching aching erupted within

her, consuming her in an explosion that matched his own.

Reuben opened one eye lazily and gazed at Rosemary; her long-lashed lids remained closed, her breathing slow and regular. Sensing his gaze, she opened her eyes and smiled at him. Words were unnecessary. Reuben slept then, his dark head cradled against her breast. Rosemary lay quiet, body and mind at peace. How vulnerable he looks in sleep, she thought. Defenseless, almost like a child. A truly compassionate man. She was so glad she was seeing this side of the famous man, her man now. Content, she raised her eyes and looked at the bright shaft of moonlight. It was all so perfect. She stirred slightly, and the sweet smell of perfume teased her nostrils. The slight stirring of her body caused Reuben to tighten his hold on her, and he sighed contentedly in his sleep.

Later, when Rosemary's breathing was again deep and regular, Reuben opened his eyes and stared overhead at the moonlight filtering through the high bedroom windows. Yes, he remembered the feel of her lips on his eyelids . . . She'd thought him asleep when she'd done that, and when she'd traced the line of his mouth and nose with gentle fingers. No one had ever moved him in quite this way. It confused him; he hadn't bedded enough women to understand what he was

feeling now. *Liar!* his mind screamed. *Mickey moved you, moved you to heartbreaking tears.* Rosemary had been tender, the way a mother would caress her infant.

Goddammit, he didn't want a mother in his bed! He needed a woman. Christ, Reuben, what have you done!

Theirs was an easy, comfortable relationship. In its own way it was sexual as well as satisfying, but Reuben knew there was something missing, that elusive feeling, that wonderful intoxicating breathlessness he had experienced with Mickey. But for now this would have to sustain him.

It was almost a year into his relationship with Rosemary when Reuben began to wonder why his affair with her never made the gossip columns. While none of his peers were privy to his private life, the industry had in some way decided to protect their own. All of Hollywood was aware of Bebe Tarz's long absences and her life-style, just as they were aware of Reuben's sedate, consistent workaholic regimen. General consensus decreed that if he had found happiness, he deserved to enjoy it. Besides, Reuben never flaunted it in anyone's face. It was easy to give a seal of approval because he was less demanding now; he smiled and was more generous in his dealings with business associates. If there was even a whisper of scandal, the studio's publicity heavyweights squelched it immediately.

And when they closed their ranks, nothing could filter through. In no way did Reuben lose the high regard and admiration of those he worked with. He had consistently come up with cinematic winners, and this affair seemed only to accelerate his successes. After all, he was Reuben Tarz, powerful, respected, professionally infallible, the Wonder Boy, the Golden Boy of Hollywood. For years now he had made a lot of people a lot of money.

In early April of the third year of Reuben and Rosemary's affair, two things happened that turned Reuben's world upside down. Rosemary announced she was two months pregnant, and Bebe returned from a trip to Europe in the same condition.

Reuben sat in his office; the air seemed stale and stagnant. Stiffly he rose from his aged leather chair and walked to his window throwing it open to breathe deeply of the fresh night air. It didn't help. As if sleepwalking, he returned to his chair and replayed the scenario of the last twenty-four hours over and over in his mind.

Why hadn't he shown more happiness, some delight at Rosemary's news? Instead, he'd let shock register on his face. Rosemary had backed down immediately, stammering something about the unexpectedness of it all. Then she'd apologized and cried while he'd sat there like a bump on a log, unsure of what to say. In the end he said all the right things,

that he'd file for divorce and marry her. He'd thought that was what she wanted to hear, but instead she'd gotten angry. "If you'd wanted to marry me, you'd have done it sooner!" she cried. Now she didn't want him to marry her at all — she'd have the baby herself, she said. No begrudged piece of paper would change anything. Besides, it was too late to make the child legitimate anyway. She'd asked him to leave then, something she'd never done before.

He'd gone home in a daze to find Bebe sitting on the terrace, a drink in one hand and reefer in the other. What was it she had said? "I'm home, darling, this time to stay. You'll have to dump that little slut you're keeping. You see, I'm pregnant, and my baby is going to need your name."

Stupefied, he'd turned on his heel and gone to the office.

"My God," he blurted out, "now what am I going to do?"

CHAPTER THIRTY-EIGHT

Reuben stood under the blanket of stars, staring at the empty studio lot. It was ghostly at this late hour, all the make-believe and fantasy locked up behind stout steel doors. During the day so much went on here that someone could get lost for hours on end. But once playtime was over, the make-believe characters went home, as did the employees in the front offices. Aside from four night guards, Reuben knew he was the only person on the entire lot.

Part of him wanted to return to Rosemary and part of him wanted to stay where he was to try to fathom what was happening to him. The one place he wanted to avoid, and knew he couldn't, was his house in Laurel Canyon. How could so much happen in so short a time? Rosemary pregnant with his child. Lovely, sweet Rosemary carrying his son or daughter. He'd never seen her angry or upset. She'd wanted his . . . what? His blessing? Or did she want his face to light up the way it

worked in the movies when a blushing bride of three months announced her pregnancy to the delight of her new husband? A baby was simply not part of his plans. Rosemary knew that; they'd spoken of it often enough. He'd trusted her when she'd said the Catholic method of birth control was safe. It suddenly occurred to him to wonder if this child was meant to trap him into marriage. His disillusionment was so total and all-consuming, he wanted to strike out at something, anything, just to vent his frustration.

Marriage to Rosemary had never been his intention. Obviously Rosemary hadn't accepted that, although he thought he'd made it clear. He liked her, even loved her, but he wasn't *in* love with her, and that made all the difference and explained what he was feeling now.

Choices. Did he have choices? Did he *want* choices? No, he decided, he didn't. But the honorable thing to do would be to divorce Bebe and marry Rosemary and be a father to her child. Their child. But what of Bebe?

Bebe was pregnant with another man's child, yet she expected him to accept that fact and carry on as though it were his own. "Goddammit, Bebe," he cried aloud, "you expect too fucking much of me! How long are you going to make me pay?"

Reuben's shoulders slumped. How was it possible that two women, as different as night

and day, could bring him to his knees like this? His life had been so peaceful, so simple, when he'd lived with Mickey in France.

Christ, he was tired. He had to go home and try to get some sleep; he was going to need his wits about him in the morning when he talked to Bebe. Yet he made no move to leave his position atop a buckboard outside Lot 6. Instead, he pulled out his pocket watch and stared down at the numbers. Three o'clock. Daniel, always an early riser would be up — it was only a three-hour time difference. Daniel always talked common sense and was never judgmental where he was concerned. He might not have the answers, but he would sort through things with his analytical mind. The thought made Reuben feel much better; he hopped down from the buckboard and headed for his car.

The house at the end of the long, curving driveway was ablaze with light. Evidently Bebe was still awake. Waiting for him, probably. His stomach churned. Maybe it was better to get it over with now.

Bebe was on the terrace, waiting for Reuben with a half-eaten tuna fish sandwich and a glass of lemonade at her elbow. She wanted a drink so badly, her hands trembled, but she'd made up her mind to wait for her husband and she didn't want him to see her drunk.

Her life was such a shambles, and she

seemed incapable of doing anything about it. This pregnancy was so unexpected, and the man . . . if he knew, which he didn't, would want to do the honorable thing and marry her. Charles Lefuer was a nice man — a stable, solid banker living in Geneva. Best of all, he'd made wonderful, exciting love to her, and for a little while she'd been able to lose herself in his arms. But when she woke in the morning her thoughts always returned to Reuben . . . her first love, her only love.

Aside from the initial shock of discovering her pregnancy, she'd felt a certain amount of relief that she could at last return to California and Reuben. He wasn't going to like her news, but it would necessitate a certain amount of communication, something she hungered for. He might even be compassionate.

She gagged on the lemonade she was trying to swallow, remembering how she'd felt when, minutes after her return from Europe, Eli had whisked her to his car and told her in a gentle voice about "Reuben's woman." Which had stunned her more, she wondered — her brother's unexpected tone of voice or his actual words? According to Eli, *everyone* knew about Rosemary; Reuben practically lived with her. He'd gone on to tell her the story of the red ribbon on Rosemary's house, and she'd wept then, her soul full of sorrow. She would have died for a gift-wrapped

present from Reuben.

Now she struggled with herself to be angry with Reuben, but it wasn't working. For God's sake, why was she hanging on to a man who didn't want her? "Because," she whispered, "he's the only man I have ever loved or will love. This little bit that I have is better than nothing." She wept as she always did when thoughts of Reuben carried her this far in her soul searching. Inevitably, then, she thought of John Paul, fantasizing about telling Reuben, about traveling to France with her husband in search of their son, about how they'd welcome him with open arms and declare their love for each other. Eli said it was a pipe dream and told her to stop torturing herself, because Reuben would not be forgiving and, if possible, would hate her even more. She always felt sick to her stomach after she talked to Eli because he spoke the truth.

Reuben didn't love Rosemary, that much she knew. He might be enamored and infatuated, but his heart belonged to someone else. Reuben loved Mickey and would always love Mickey. The woman hadn't been born who could make his eyes light with that special look, and his warm smile would never be directed at anyone but Mickey. She'd stopped fooling herself years before. The part of Reuben she wanted and needed was buried back

in France, lost to her as John Paul was lost to her.

Bebe jerked her head upright at the sound of Reuben's car. He was opening the front door, striding through the foyer to the kitchen and out to the terrace. Her back was to him, and she didn't need to hear his footsteps to know he was almost upon her. "Good evening, Reuben," she said quietly.

Reuben stared at his wife coldly, as though she were an intruder — which, to him, was just what she was. "I assume you've waited up to talk with me, although I can't imagine that there's anything more to be said."

Bebe smiled. "I'm sure you must be having some difficulty with what I told you last night. First of all, you should know that the father — Charles — is a fine man, a banker in Geneva. He was someone . . . I need . . . Well, it doesn't matter what I need, you were interested in my needs only if they fulfilled yours," she said without rancor. "I consulted two doctors before I came home and both confirmed my pregnancy. I didn't tell Charles because I don't love him, and I could see no reason to upset his life. I plan on staying here now, in . . . our house. The way I see it, you have two choices. You can divorce me and marry Rosemary — Oh, yes, I know all about her. Eli told me when he picked me up. Or you can send Rosemary packing and return home. Of course, it will be the same kind of

marriage we had before, but you will be home with me during this pregnancy. If you had been a proper husband, I wouldn't have had to go looking somewhere else for what I need, just as you went somewhere else." How tortured he looked, how woebegone. Bebe's heart thumped in her chest.

"Of course you realize that if you leave me, you're out of the studio. You'll have to look for a job somewhere else. Now, I plan on sleeping late in the morning, so why don't we have lunch together on the terrace tomorrow and discuss this further?"

"Bebe, it's not as cut and dried as you think. Rosemary . . . Rosemary is pregnant."

Bebe thought her heart stopped for a second as she attempted to digest Reuben's words. "All that and a house wrapped in a big red bow," she muttered. She laughed, a harsh, bitter sound, then rose and walked upstairs to her room. Only then, with the door closed, did she let the tears flow. Reuben, Reuben, what fools we are! she cried silently.

The following day Bebe dressed carefully in a rainbow-colored dress with a wide sash belt. She wanted to have something to play with to calm her trembling hands. It wouldn't do for Reuben to see her in anything but a position of control. When she walked onto the terrace, Reuben was already at the glass-topped table. She took her seat opposite her

husband, fixed him with a steady gaze, and waited.

For the first time in his life Reuben felt like a trapped animal, unsure of which way he should move to escape the snare. Clearly Bebe was waiting for him to say something, to make a suggestion. He was just as sure that she already had his decision mapped out for him; he would stay with her because of the studio.

His stomach churning, he shoved his lunch plate away from him. "I need more time to come . . . to decide what I want to do. You can't flounce back here and expect me to bail you out again. I've made a life for myself, Bebe. In a million years I never would have believed that both of us . . ." He shook his head as if to clear his thoughts. "You're pregnant, and I'm in the same . . . It's a problem. Are there any other conditions you haven't mentioned?" he asked dryly.

"Only one," Bebe said just as dryly.

Reuben clenched his teeth. "What is it?"

"As of tomorrow Rosemary is just a memory in your life. I expect you'll want to use the remainder of the day to . . . to make provisions for the child. For Rosemary, too. A woman can't work and raise a child at the same time. I want you to be generous. I also want your word the affair is over and that you'll make no attempt to see Rosemary after today. I'll know if you do. Now, you had all

night and all morning to think about this. I want you to know that I was serious about the divorce. If you want one, I won't contest it, but you're out of the studio."

Reuben stood up, his eyes narrowed, his jaw jutting forward. "Very well, you win."

"Sit down, Reuben," Bebe commanded in a steely voice. "I'm not winning anything. In case you haven't noticed, we are both losers. Your days of heaping guilt on my shoulders are over. We both made a mistake. I can and will live with mine, and you will have to live with yours. No dirty games, Reuben. If you so much as blink in that woman's direction, you will be history as far as the studio goes. Just think, you'll be able to say you gave up the love of a fine woman for power and wealth. Mickey would be so proud of you!"

Reuben's hand lashed out before he could stop to think. The welt on his wife's cheek stunned him. He hadn't held back, either.

"Is this going to be a repeat of our rape scenes?" Bebe said coldly. "If so, tell me now and I'll take off my clothes to make it easy for you."

"You never know when to leave well enough alone, do you? I said I agreed, and I'm a man of my word. I'm sorry I slapped you. There's no excuse in the world for a man to strike a woman."

"Go to hell, Reuben!" Bebe snarled as she

marched from the terrace. "Go straight to hell!"

Reuben was in a frenzy as he waited for Daniel to come to the phone. He'd been trying to reach his friend all morning. His foot tapped, his fingers drummed, and his head buzzed with Bebe's demands. Daniel would know what to do.

"Reuben! It's good to hear from you! How are things in California?"

How wonderful Daniel sounded. Reuben calmed immediately. "I need to talk, Daniel, do you have the time?"

"I'll make the time. What's wrong?" Daniel asked worriedly. He listened, his mouth dropping as Reuben's story progressed.

"I'm not in a very good position, Daniel. I gave Bebe my word. I care for Rosemary. I didn't know until yesterday that she . . . She probably always expected marriage. I can't get it out of my head that she trapped me somehow. I have to make . . . Daniel . . ."

"I can't tell you what to do, Reuben. Sounds to me like you made up your own mind and that you made it up before Bebe made her demands. You feel like you've been taken, is that it?"

"Pretty much so. Jesus, Bebe waltzes back into the house pregnant and not a remorseful bone in her body, and tells me what to do. I'm doing it, too!" Reuben cried angrily.

"Hey, pal, don't take it out on me. The first

thing you have to do is be honest with yourself. You're doing this for the studio. You don't want to lose it. Bebe will make good on her threat, that much I know. It's not the end of the world, buddy. You had something few of us get; you had your cake and you got to eat it, too. When it's time to pay you have to pay, no one else is going to pick up the tab. I may be wrong, and it's only because we've been friends for so long that I'm going to say this. I don't think you were in love with Rosemary. I think you were in love with the idea of love. You were searching and have been searching for that same feeling you had for Mickey. But you get that only once. Now, tell me what you want me to do."

"A check once a month. An adequate amount. A letter explaining that I will fund the child's education, all medical bills, and a certain amount, whatever you think is right, into a fund for his future. Don't stint, Daniel. I'll tell her all of this myself, but I also want her to have something legal. I paid off the mortgage on her house, so she's all set in that respect. She should have a car once the baby comes. Make a provision for that. And anything else you can think of."

"I'll take care of it. Should I send the papers on to you or to . . . Rosemary?"

"To me and then I'll mail them to her. Don't forget the doctor and midwife. I want her well taken care of."

"Are you all right, Reuben?" Daniel asked. "Do you want me to come out there?"

"I can hold my own hand, but thanks for the offer. I feel like a fool."

"At least you don't feel like a fool in love. There's a big difference, pal. Look, if you need me, give a call. I'll take care of this tonight and get it in the mail tomorrow first thing."

"How's the family, Daniel?"

"Fine. Rajean is just fine, and of course my daughter is just wonderful. I don't know how I managed to get along before."

Reuben grunted something unintelligible. There was a strain in Daniel's voice he'd never heard before. Living with someone like Rajean would not be easy. Poor Daniel. Tomorrow, after he got his affairs straightened out, he'd give his friend another call. Right now he had to talk to Rosemary.

On the ride down the winding canyon road Reuben had time to muster his chaotic thoughts. If he truly loved Rosemary, he'd be devastated by Bebe's demands. If he truly loved Rosemary, he'd give up the studio and walk away from everything: his wife, his children, and the ostentatious house in the canyon. When had his feelings changed? When she'd made her announcement about the baby? Before?

Obviously the picket-fenced cottage, home-cooked-meal life had been strangling him for

some months now. Looking back, he realized that it had been five months since he'd stopped going to the house seven days a week, pleading business or whatever excuse he could come up with. Rosemary hadn't seemed to mind his absences. Until four months ago he would have sworn that she didn't have a devious, manipulative bone in her body. Now, with the birth announcement, he wasn't so sure. He allowed his mind to wander over the past four months, to other times when Rosemary wanted something or alluded to wanting something. Christ, he'd jumped through hoops to get her something even bigger and better than whatever thing she'd mentioned.

Not that he minded — he loved giving her gifts. He loved her smile and the way she threw her arms about him; and then later in bed she was the madonna wanton. As generous as he'd been, Rosemary had been just as generous with her body, sharing her home and her two gentlemen live-ins. Maybe he wasn't being fair to her. Her shocking news now made everything suspect. Was he overreacting, or was he a first-class chump? After today, it wasn't going to matter. Rosemary had given him back his life when he'd needed it most. She'd been kind and gentle, that he would always remember. And now he was going to walk away and pay for his fling.

When he turned off the engine of his car,

he wondered if Rosemary was watching behind the curtained windows. At his insistence she'd given up her job at Fox and Reuben now supplemented her on a weekly basis. Before her "retirement" she'd been edgy and cranky sometimes, and he resented her tiredness. He wanted her fresh and alert, full of smiles whenever he arrived.

She smiled now when she opened the door. It was the same wonderful warm, gentle smile she always favored him with. How could she smile at him like this when she'd been so angry with him? "Come in, Reuben," she said quietly. "Would you like some tea or coffee?"

"No. Rosemary, I need to talk to you. Please, let's sit in the kitchen, or the garden if you prefer."

"Actually, I prefer sitting in here so I can put my feet up. I hope you don't mind." She turned and walked over to the chair he always favored.

"No, I don't mind." His brow furrowed. Was he mistaken, or was there an edge to her voice?

"Reuben . . ."

Reuben held up his hand. "No, Rosemary, I have something to say and I'd like to go first, if you don't mind. Look, I'm sorry about yesterday. You were bursting with your news, and I acted like a callous adolescent. I have to be honest with you. At this stage of my life a baby is simply not a good idea. I thought

you understood how I felt about that and were seeing to it that you were . . . protected. At least that's what you led me to believe. Now, I'm not trying to blame you, but it was your responsibility since you didn't want me to use a . . . condom. That was the reason for my shock." He paused to clear his throat, then continued. "I'm more than willing to provide for you and the child. I've spoken to Daniel and he's arranging everything. You'll never have to worry about a thing. If there's anything you want or need, you have only to ask. I don't like having to tell you this, but Bebe is home and she's pregnant with another man's child. That, too, was a shock to me. She's given me an ultimatum, and if I don't do what she wants, I could lose the studio. I want you to know I will always cherish our time together, and I will never forget it. But you understand why we can't continue to see each other, don't you?"

Rosemary held his gaze steadily for a moment, then nodded. "Yes, I understand, Reuben. You belong to your wife and that mansion. If I made you happy for a little while, I'm glad. I'm grateful that you will provide for us. It won't do for either of us to talk this to death. I think we knew the relationship was waning. At least I did. You stopped coming as often, you developed excuses, and our lovemaking was almost routine. I'm very fond of you, you know. It's better that we part now

as friends than later on as . . . as bitter strangers. You never really belonged to me, anyway. You were another woman's husband with a different kind of life-style. As you say, this was an interlude." She smiled, got up from the chair, and held out her hand. "Friends, Reuben."

Reuben was so stunned, he was speechless. He nodded dumbly.

"It was nice of you to stop by, to tell me about the plans you made for me," she continued, still smiling in that oddly carefree manner. So much for undying love and total acceptance, Reuben thought dimly. He was out of her life, and she didn't seem to give a damn.

At the door she smiled again, then waved airily as he walked down the flagstone steps. Angry and hurt — had he been taken for a sap, a prize chump? — Reuben strode to his car, got in, and drove off without a backward glance.

Chump? Sap? Neither. He'd taken all Rosemary had to offer and he'd given what he could. They were even.

Givers and Takers.

He could live with it.

Rosemary slid the bolt on the front door. "I'm glad *that's* out of the way. Come along, gentlemen, we're going to have an afternoon snack. Milk for you, fruit for me. Later I'll

886

tell you all about the new addition we can expect soon. There will be four of us then, won't that be wonderful! I might even buy some caviar for you."

As she peeled an orange Rosemary kept up a running dialogue with the cats. "I should start my housecleaning tomorrow and pack up Reuben's things and give them to Goodwill. He won't be coming back here. Then I'll shop for the baby, fix up a nursery, and have my jewelry appraised. I don't think I'll miss Reuben too much. Strange as it may sound I found him to be incredibly boring." She laughed, a delightful sound of pure mirth. "The reason Reuben won't be back is he really thought I wanted marriage. Such a silly man." She laughed again with gusto. The startled cats leaped for cover as Rosemary headed for her bedroom. She stripped the bed and turned the mattress. Such a boring, silly man.

CHAPTER
THIRTY-NINE

The Paris garden was a kaleidoscope of brilliant color, created by conscientious gardeners whose only aim was to please Madame Fonsard. Fragile roses the color of a maiden's blush crept up over trellises beside delicate purple morning glories, their petals as soft as the richest velvet. Scarlet cockscomb, sky-colored bluebells, and brilliant yellow buttercups nestled alongside whitewashed rocks as bees buzzed and flirted with dancing butterflies as colorful as any rainbow after a spring shower.

Mickey Fonsard's eyes took in the garden at a glance, but it was on the dark-headed young boy that her eyes lingered. How handsome he was, how content to be here studying in the garden! He was tall for nineteen — but then, his father was tall. And still growing, she would chuckle fondly when she noticed his trousers creep above his ankles. Perhaps, she thought, he would be taller than Reuben. This boy she called her son reminded

her of a delicate engraving. Everything about him was perfect, and he was so like his father in his mannerisms. There were days when he would do or say something that reminded her so much of Reuben, she wanted to cry.

It was late afternoon, and for some reason she always thought of Reuben at this particular time of day, possibly because it *was* the end of the day and the long night loomed ahead, that time when she would close the door to her room and be alone to remember still more.

The boy was her life. In the beginning, after Reuben left, she'd needed to be consumed with Philippe, but now that he was older he needed her less and less. These days he had his studies, his activities, and his friends. Girls by the dozen stopped at the house to chat and smile winsomely at the young man, who blushed and stammered, unwilling to invite them in. Later he would say that he had no time for giggling girls, he had his studies, because when he was ready to go to America he had to know all there was to know about the film industry. Mickey wondered what monstrous tome he was studying now and craned her head for a better look. He wasn't studying at all, but reading the newspaper. For some reason she felt annoyed and then frightened. She didn't know why.

Philippe watched his mother out of the corner of his eye. He wished he'd covered up

the newspaper, but he'd been so engrossed in the war news, he hadn't seen her until it was too late.

"What are you reading, Philippe?" Mickey asked anxiously.

"The paper . . . The American president says he has no wish to intervene in Europe. They will, though," he said knowledgeably. "At the Sorbonne, everywhere there is talk of the Germans and what they are doing. There will be a war, *Maman,* mark my words. They talk of nothing else at school." To Mickey's ears his voice was shrill and ominous-sounding.

"I don't want to hear you talking like this, Philippe. You are too young to be following war and reading and talking . . ." Her voice trailed away.

"You told me my father went to war when he was eighteen. Why am I so different? Don't you consider me a man, *Maman?*"

They'd had this discussion several times in the past week, and each time Mickey felt more drained, more angry, and more unsure of what could happen. Her voice was sharp, sharper than it had ever been with Philippe. "I want to hear no more of this talk, not now, not later, and not tomorrow. Please, do not force me to forbid you to read the paper."

"I don't understand," Philippe grumbled, staring at his mother. "I am not a little boy any longer. I can read the papers at school if

you don't want me to read them here. Our country isn't strong, *Maman.* Lebrun is . . . Very well, *Maman,* I will put the paper away. You cannot hide from this, isn't that what you've always taught me? Face things, you said, meet them head on. There are no bogey-men. Now I must say the same thing to you."

"You don't understand," Mickey said, wringing her hands. "You simply do not un-derstand."

Philippe threw his hands in the air. "Then tell me what it is I don't understand," he said, exasperated.

"Not today, Philippe, I have a throbbing head."

Philippe was instantly contrite. "I'm sorry, *Maman.*" But all the same Mickey noticed that he secured the newspaper in his book bag.

Indoors, the house seemed dim and gloomy after the sunshine in the garden. No, that wasn't it; Philippe was her sunshine, and he'd galloped up the stairs to his room, taking the sunshine with him. Whatever would she do without him? The thought was so horrendous, Mickey felt faint.

Tea. Tea always made her feel better. Tea laced with brandy would make her feel even better. She was pouring thick cream into the cup when she heard a commotion by the back door. Yvette and Henri. "Thank you, Lord," she murmured, "you always send them to me

when I'm at my lowest ebb." She quickly set out two cups and fixed tea for her friends.

Yvette swept into the kitchen, Henri in her wake. "I had this . . . feeling," she said, thumping her ample bosom, "that something was wrong. So I made Henri drop everything. We left early this morning and we return tomorrow because of the animals. So . . . tell me what is wrong. You see, Henri, you need only to look at this face to know all is not right. Ah, the tea — bah, fill my glass with brandy, tea is for children. Sit, sit, Henri, you are with two beautiful women, enjoy our beauty while you drink and be quiet until I find out what is wrong with my dearest friend. So, Michelene, I am waiting. You see, Henri is waiting, too . . . patiently."

Mickey smiled. How Yvette managed to say everything in one breath was something she would never understand.

"I think it is the newspapers, eh, *chérie?*" Yvette continued. "At the farm we get the paper and we can read. I want to see a smile on your face, Michelene. Now!"

"Philippe devours the papers," Mickey explained tremulously. "All he thinks of is war and fighting. At first when he spoke of . . . these things, I thought it had to do with his classes. Young people are so political, you know. But it's more, Yvette. He's thinking of his father. In his mind he thinks of this as romantic. He's so passionate, so full of life, I

892

think, my friends, I did too good a job when I spoke to him of his father. And when necessary, to make the story more interesting for his young ears, I took the liberty of . . . of embroidering . . . in certain areas.

"Tell me the truth, Henri, what do you think? Are we headed for war like everyone says?"

"I think so," Henri said miserably.

"I think we should all go to Switzerland," Yvette broke in happily. "We will be one happy family. I will cook and you will sit around and dote on Philippe while Henri tends to things. Philippe will . . . Philippe will . . . hate it. He wouldn't go with us, would he?"

Mickey shook her head. "I don't think he even wants to go to America anymore. He never mentions his father these days. I think now that he is a young man, he . . . what I mean is, he now has thoughts and opinions that are his own. Not too long ago, when he was angry about something, he said his father abandoned us and everything I told him was make-believe, like the films his father makes. He broke my heart, Yvette."

"Listen to me, Michelene, we spoke of this many times. You said you knew it would happen and you could handle it. I don't like reminding you that you said the same thing when Reuben left. Emotions, *chérie,* cannot be counted on. The devil is working on you!"

Henri finished his brandy and poured another glass, this one full to the brim. "Perhaps, Mickey, it is time for you to think about writing Reuben or . . . to think about sending Philippe to America. I know this is the last thing you want to hear right now, but you must think along these lines."

An angry retort rose to Mickey's lips, but when she saw the sorrow in Henri's eyes she bit down on her lower lip. "I know, but not yet, Henri, not yet. I'm not ready . . . for . . . I'm not ready."

Yvette reached across the table and took Mickey's trembling hands in her own. "Mickey, you will never be ready. The longer you delay, the worse it will be. I remember the other war as you do, my friend. If, and I say if, there is another one and our country is involved, you . . . Philippe thinks of himself as French, he will want to fight for his country like all loyal Frenchmen. Today, Michelene, the paper said that Germany has aligned itself with Italy. The paper calls them the Axis. Nothing good can come of this — mark my word," Yvette said grumpily. Henri nodded, in complete agreement with his wife.

"Time. I need time. Do you think it's easy to . . . to rip my heart out of my chest?" Mickey cried in a tormented voice. "Stick a knife in me, it would be simpler."

Yvette leaned across the table, her voice the only sound in the quiet kitchen. "You can

pack your bags and take Philippe to America. You can go directly to Reuben, who will sweep you into his arms. At least the boy will be safe, and you will get to see Reuben again after all these years. It is also time for you to tell him . . . all that you know. Time, Michelene, this is the kind of time we should be discussing."

"Bebe," Mickey said brokenly.

Yvette threw her hands in the air. "It is time for you to fight for what you want. Bebe walked away from her baby and never looked back. You owe that woman nothing. She has not changed; her kind never does. The last time I saw her I knew that she was just as selfish, just as nasty, and just as uncaring as she always was. In years she has not once asked about Philippe. That should tell you all you need to know."

Henri came around to Mickey's side of the table and dropped to his haunches. "You have the power, Mickey, to rip the world out from under Reuben and Bebe. You own the controlling interest in the film studio. Exercise that interest. Fight! Fight for what you want. Weak kittens do not survive in this world. I am a simple man, as you know, and I do not know much about business, but this is my advice, from here," he said, thumping his chest.

"Pride will be your downfall," Yvette said gently. "The past is past. It is rare, my friend,

to get a second chance in this world. When it does happen, only a fool would turn away. Now!" she said, smacking her hands together. "I think you should feed us. We have come a long way and our stomachs are empty!"

Mickey wiped at the tears in her eyes. "Yes, it is time for nourishment." For my soul, she said silently.

In his room above the kitchen, Philippe puzzled over the snatches of conversation that carried upward through the fireplace chimney. It was nothing new, these hushed conversations between his mother and her friends. He loved Yvette and Henri and called them uncle and aunt out of respect, but there was a secret they shared with his mother, he was sure of it. He'd asked them, dozens of times, but they said it was his imagination. The only thing he was sure of, whatever it was involved his mother and his father.

Philippe's eyes narrowed and he could feel his shoulders grow tense. He knew if he didn't shake off the feeling, he would develop a blinding headache and be unable to finish the newspaper. He also knew when he took his bath and came back to his room the paper would be gone.

His thoughts carried him to the man who was his father, the man he'd never seen. Until he was twelve he'd believed the wonderful stories his mother told him about Reuben

Tarz. When he repeated the stories to his friends, they'd laughed and called him a fool for believing in fairy tales. "If this famous man is your father," they'd said, "why doesn't he write to you or visit or at least send presents?" He didn't know the answer and when he questioned his mother she'd said his friends were jealous. She was his mother, she said, and mothers didn't lie to their sons. After that he'd stopped asking questions, and if his mother brought up his father's name, he closed his ears to her.

After far too many conversations of that sort, he'd started to doubt that there even was a man named Reuben Tarz. After school he'd spent his time going from theater to theater and to every movie house in Paris to ask if they knew anything about a Hollywood film studio called Fairmont. He'd even gone to his mother's Paris lawyers to ask details of his ownership of the studio. The managers of the movie houses told him yes, there was such a person as Reuben Tarz and he made million-dollar movies in Hollywood, California. The Paris bankers were appalled at his audacity and threatened to tell his mother he'd come to the bank with his questions. The sour-faced banker told him to forget such nonsense until he was old enough to take charge of his affairs. After the interview he'd slunk out of the bank like a whipped dog, anxious and fearful. To this day he didn't

know if the man had ever told his mother or not. It could all be a lie. Just because there was a man named Reuben Tarz who produced films in California didn't have to mean he was his father. The picture of the Three Musketeers over the mantel at the château gave a lie to his thoughts. He realized then that he hated it — he couldn't remember the last time he'd actually *looked* at it.

Philippe could feel the tension in his shoulders start to work its way up to his neck. The headache was inevitable. His eyes fell to the newspaper again. His mother's refusal to think or discuss the news wasn't going to make it go away. If the papers in France were full of war rumblings, they must be the same in America. The American president kept issuing statements every day, as did the British prime minister. If his father cared about his mother or him, he would have gotten in touch, offered to take them to America or even take time out of his busy schedule to see them.

The headache was upon him in a blinding flash. He held his throbbing head in his hands as he made his way to the bed to lie down. Later, he knew, his mother would give him three white tablets to ease the pounding, but for now he had to suffer. His dark eyes were full of sadness as he lowered himself to the soft downy pillows. "I hate you, Reuben Tarz, for abandoning me." But there was no convic-

tion in his muttered declaration.

Philippe slept then, the whispered words from downstairs comforting to the lonely boy simply because there was nothing else for him to cling to.

It was three-thirty in the morning when Philippe woke. He lay quietly, unsure if something had wakened him or if he'd simply slept enough to rest his body. His stomach growled ominously.

How silent the house was. He wished Dolly were here, but she was at the farm with Yvette and Henri now because she was old and feeble. Lord, how he had loved his dogs, first Jake and then Dolly. How often he'd poured out his heart to them. And always he'd felt better afterward because they licked his face and his tears. He'd been devastated when Jake had died and had actually written a letter to his uncle Daniel — a letter he'd never mailed. It was probably still around somewhere since he never threw anything away. He *knew* he still had the thousand or so letters he'd written to his father. But, of course, he didn't write them anymore, there was no point. Reuben Tarz didn't care about him in the least.

Philippe's stomach rumbled again. He knew if he went downstairs, there would be a plate warming on the back of the stove.

Thank God the damned headache was gone. He always tried to keep his anger under

control and for the most part he succeeded, but when something really got to him, his head would start to pound without any warning.

When he looked out the mullioned window over the landing on the stairway, he saw that it was a beautiful evening. He particularly liked a full moon, and he always made a silly wish. But not anymore. Wishes never came true, and prayers sometimes weren't answered, either. They were alike, he thought, although his mother said they weren't.

Philippe's steps lagged as they always did when he walked past the library, past the picture of the Three Musketeers. He hated it now, with a passion. The smiling man looked evil to him, and Daniel's honest-looking face didn't seem the same, either. Only his mother was unchanged. Twice he'd taken the painting down and faced it toward the wall. His mother always rehung it and never said anything. When he was thirteen he'd thrown a tantrum and refused to go in the car if they were taking it to Paris. Gritting his teeth, he'd told his mother the picture was ugly and he was grown-up and grown-up boys didn't salivate over unknown fathers. She'd smacked him, something she'd never done before in the whole of his life, but the picture remained at the château from that day on.

He hadn't meant to enter the library, but here he was, staring at the familiar faces from

900

childhood. He knew every brush line, every hair on his father's head, and he hated ever inch of the picture. The smiling face was false as far as he was concerned. At one time it had been so real, as real as the stories his mother told him.

The urge to lash out, to rip the painting from the wall, was stronger than it had ever been. He clenched his hands, then jammed his fists into his pockets. "Damn your soul to hell, Reub . . . Father!"

His quest for food forgotten, Philippe stomped back to his room.

CHAPTER FORTY

Bebe walked through the neatly tended gardens, marveling at the beauty of the plants and flowers — tended she knew, by a very capable gardener. The roses, however, had been fertilized and pruned by her husband. She stared at some of the delicate blooms in their little nests and knew they survived the California sun because they were fed, watered, and nurtured. They were really no different from people, she thought sadly. If the gardener forgot to water the plants or prune the leaves, they would wither and die. So much like humans. For years now she'd abused her body and her mind because there was no one to care, to nurture her.

She was Bebe Tarz. Period. Not Bebe Tarz, movie actress, not Bebe Tarz, Reuben Tarz's wife, not Bebe Tarz, mother. She was, but she wasn't. In order to be those things she would have had to participate, and she hadn't, not really. All those years she'd wasted in a nightmare world of liquor and drugs — and

all because of Reuben. If only she could go back in time and erase some of her mistakes . . . but that wasn't possible. It was time to accept the fact that she was an alcoholic and a drug addict and that she was pregnant with another man's child, a man whose face she couldn't even remember.

Tears streamed down her cheeks. There were no more chances now, she'd had her quota. Reuben was not about to forgive this latest escapade of hers. The truth was, she couldn't forgive herself. "Oh, God, what do I do?" she cried.

Huge with child now, and waddling like a duck, she made her way to a bench under a shady tree. Wearily she closed her eyes as she tried to sort out her life. She'd loved Reuben, obsessively so. She'd given birth to three sons, one lost to her and the other two just . . . children. Only once had she felt true mother love, the day she'd held John Paul. Where was he, what was he doing? she wondered. Whom did he look like, her or Reuben? God, she wished she knew, wished she had a photograph. Maybe that was where her life went wrong. Her throat felt thick and swollen when she thought of that time in France.

"If only you had been kind to me, Reuben," she murmured. "I know we could have had a decent life if you'd been kind and considerate. I knew you didn't love me, but I thought

I had enough for both of us. I really thought you would come to love me. I did everything I could think of to make you love me, but it wasn't enough. You love Mickey, you'll always love her and she will always love you. I understand now. I understand that you can't love me . . . but you could be kind. I can live with kindness. I know I can."

She wept silently as all her past sins rushed through her like a raging river. It was too late, too late for her and Reuben. Too late for so many things. She yanked at the deep pocket of her maternity dress, drew out a small silver flask, and gulped its contents, wiping at her mouth with the back of her hand.

Drinking was forbidden by the doctor, but she didn't care. There was something wrong with this pregnancy, with the baby she carried. By now she should have felt life, some small movement, but she hadn't. She knew without anyone having to tell her that she was going to give birth to a stillborn child. And it was just as well; Reuben didn't want another man's child. He didn't want her, either.

When she heard her husband's car in the drive, she uncapped the flask and drained it, then angrily tossed it in the bushes. Later she'd send the maid to fetch it, but right now she didn't give a damn about anything.

Reuben knew he had walked into his own

corner of hell when he saw Bebe in the garden. She looked so sad and miserable, he wanted to go to her, to comfort her, but he held back. That was another man's baby she was carrying and she expected *him* to give the child his name. And he would, because he had no other choice. Sweet Jesus, how much was a man supposed to bear? Unable to face his wife, or even enter his own home, Reuben retraced his steps and got back into his car. Where to go, what to do?

An hour later Reuben found himself outside the steamship offices. He'd been there so many times, had tentatively booked passage more often than he could remember, only to cancel at the last minute. He could sit there all night and wait for them to open in the morning. He never had to go home again unless he wanted to. He never had to do another thing he didn't want to. Then his conscience needled him. *It's not that simple. You aren't blameless. The reason Bebe is the way she is is because of you. Make it right, it's not too late.*

"Mickey?" he said brokenly. *Mickey is the past and the past is dead. How long are you going to torture yourself?* "Forever, probably. I can't let go. If I let go, I have nothing. Nothing!" *You have a wife. Go home and make peace with her,* his conscience ordered. *Maybe you can't have what you had with Mickey, but maybe you can have something better.*

"It's too late," Reuben muttered. *How will you know unless you try?* Go home, put the past behind you, pick up the pieces, *and get on with your life.*

"All right, goddammit!" Reuben cried. "One more shot, but that's it. One more time, and if she fucks up, that's it! I go to France. I don't look back, either, and forget that crap about sickness and health, till death do us part. One more time!"

When Reuben drove away from the steamship offices, he felt lighter by about a hundred pounds. Guilt and remorse were awesomely heavy burdens to carry around for all these years. How would he say his last good-bye to Mickey? he wondered. Silently, in his heart? In a letter he would never mail? By trying to save Bebe and his marriage?

Driving back to the house, Reuben forced himself to examine the motivations, the subconscious influences that had urged him in this direction. Was it conscience that spurred him on — or had he just made a pact with the devil?

Bebe entered the ninth month of her pregnancy the following day. It seemed sacrilegious to her to be carrying around a dead child, but there was little she wanted to do about it. Listless and wan, she sat at the shallow end of the pool, her feet dangling in the

cool water. She hadn't had a drink yet today because she felt sick to her stomach. Her ankles were so swollen she couldn't wear her shoes. Perhaps the cool water would reduce the swelling.

Bebe Tarz felt ugly, unloved, and unwanted. Woodenly she glanced down at her hands bracing herself on the concrete ledge. They hadn't been this puffy earlier this morning. She leaned over, trying to see her reflection in the clear water. Suddenly she panicked, afraid that she'd leaned out too far, that her ungainliness might tip her over into the water. She was trying desperately to struggle upright when a long arm reached out to her.

"Let me help you." It was Reuben — Reuben lifting her gently to her feet, talking to her in a soothing, caring tone of voice. "The housekeeper called me at the office and suggested I come home. She said you looked ill. Atta girl, come along, I'm taking you to the doctor. Why didn't you say something this morning? Is it time?"

Her husband's gentle concern was more than she could bear. She burst out crying. "The baby is dead, I know it is! It's never moved once all these months. I think you better take me to the hospital. I'm sorry. I . . . I didn't mean to cause you a problem, Reuben."

"It's not a problem. Can you walk?"

"If you go slowly. In case you haven't

noticed, I'm about as big as an elephant," Bebe said sourly.

Reuben stopped in mid-stride and looked carefully at his wife. He chuckled. "I think you're right. C'mere," he said, scooping her into his arms. "You might look like an elephant, but thank God you don't weigh as much."

Settled in the front seat of the car, Bebe turned to her husband, eyes imploring. "Please, Reuben, don't pity me. I couldn't bear . . . Please hurry, Reuben, but don't drive too fast. Something's wrong, I can feel it."

"You know, you could have fallen into the pool, Bebe," Reuben chastised her.

Bebe nodded. "I thought about it. Deliberately falling in, I mean. I've been thinking a lot about dying these last few days. When it comes right down to it, I didn't think anyone would care."

For a second Reuben almost lost control of the car. "You *what?*" he thundered, risking a glance in her direction in time to see her eyes roll back in her head. "Bebe! *Bebe!* We're almost there. Listen to me, Bebe, hang on, okay? Talk to me, tell me about the last time you heard from Simon. I want to hear what he's doing in that fancy school that's robbing us blind." Reuben felt the first seeds of fear and struggled to remain calm.

"I . . ." She was burning up, she could feel

herself lose consciousness. She tried to respond to Reuben. He hardly ever talked to her, and it must be important if he needed an answer. "I . . ." What had he asked her? He was yelling at her now, calling her name over and over. She heard her voice coming from far away and sounding so odd that she shivered. Maybe she was dying. She struggled to give voice to the thought.

"We're here, Bebe. Don't move, I'll carry you in."

In the blink of an eye Bebe was whisked away on a gurney. Reuben stood in the center of the corridor, certain he'd seen Death follow behind.

He lost all track of time in the hospital waiting room. Evening and darkness came and went several times, dawn worked its way slowly to the noon hour and then to mid-afternoon. He felt bilious with all the coffee he'd consumed, but worse than that, he felt heartsick and angry. At last his patience reached the breaking point; frustrated and angry, he strode to the nurse's station and demanded an audience with the doctor.

"I want to see my wife. Now!" he thundered. "And don't give me any of that busy crap. My studio has endowed this hospital handsomely, and that will cease in exactly five minutes. You tell that to the doctor!"

Exactly four and a half minutes later Bebe's doctor entered the waiting room, a frown of

disapproval on his face. "I just got here, Mr. Tarz, and your wife's condition is unchanged. She has toxemic poisoning."

"You just got here! You mean you went home?" Reuben raged. "You went home and left my wife!"

The doctor backed up a step and then another. For a moment he had a vision of his future at the hospital when the administrators learned that he had provoked Reuben Tarz into withdrawing Fairmont's endowment. It was not a reassuring image.

"Only to change my clothes," he blustered. "Your wife is in excellent hands. We're doing everything we can. I simply don't have the time to sit there and hold her hand. If you want to, I suppose I can see my way clear to allowing that." His tone clearly indicated he thought the suggestion unlikely.

"You're damn right I do. Why didn't you tell me I could stay with her before? If anything happens to my wife, I am going to hold you personally responsible, Doctor," Reuben shot over his shoulder as he stomped to his wife's private room.

All the anger was jolted out of him the moment he crossed the threshold. Nothing in the world could have prepared him for his first sight of Bebe. She was so still, so ashen-looking under the sterile sheets. For the first time, he became aware of his wife's mortality. Death hovered overhead, ready to snatch her

away at any given moment. He wanted to do something, needed to do something. She was so alone, so defenseless.

Reuben realized then, to his own amazement, that he didn't want his wife to die. In the car she'd sounded as if she didn't care whether she lived or died. And who could blame her? Reuben wondered. Jesus, he hadn't called Sol or Eli! He'd spare them what he was going through as long as possible.

He dragged a chair over to the side of the bed and sat down. How dry and hot her hand was. On impulse he began to talk to his wife, the words halting at first because he rarely used them; eventually they quickened, tumbling out of his mouth like a runaway car. He talked of his childhood, of Daniel and the war, and of Mickey, of the time in the barn, his goals and dreams, of Rosemary and his foolishness. He spoke of the studio and the progress he'd made. When he found himself tiring, his words winding down, he gave himself a shake and continued. He talked about Jake and how wonderful it was of her to get the dog for Daniel. By the time a kindly nurse tapped him on the shoulder, his voice had turned to a hoarse croak.

"It's time for Mrs. Tarz's medication now, and I want to sponge her off. Go home, Mr. Tarz, and get some sleep. We'll call you if there's a change. You're no good to your wife

in your present condition. If you were my son and it was my daughter-in-law lying in this bed, I'd tell him the same thing."

Reuben nodded. He was halfway out of the room when he turned back and waved the nurse away so that he could bend over his wife. "I know you didn't hear a thing I said and you probably can't hear me now, either, but, Bebe . . . I . . . Please don't die, Bebe. I want us to start over as soon as you're well. I'll make everything up to you, I swear I will. We'll go away, just you and me. We'll have a honeymoon, a real one. I . . . I . . . *think* I love you, Bebe."

At last Reuben allowed himself to be led out of the room and down the corridor to the main entrance. "Your wife is in good hands," said the nurse. "Please, let us do our job. Come back when you're rested."

It was dark when Reuben walked onto his terrace, unsure of how many days had passed. He looked upward at the meadow of stars. He'd never felt so alone in his life.

Three days later Bebe Tarz regained consciousness, and on the fifth day the doctor performed a cesarean section. The child, a boy, was stillborn. On the afternoon of the sixth day the tiny body was lowered into the ground. Sol cursed Reuben as each shovelful of dirt thumped onto the small casket. Reuben clamped his jaws tightly together.

At his car Eli walked over to him. "Reuben,

wait a moment. Look, I know you don't think very much of me and that's okay, it doesn't bother me anymore. I just want you to know that I know the baby wasn't yours. Bebe told me the day she arrived home. If I were in your boots, I don't know if I could have taken the verbal abuse you just did from Pop. I think you did a fine thing, and if you still want that seascape I painted years ago, it's yours."

"Eli, the ten minutes I spent listening to your father made me want to kill. How you lived through what you did with that man is something I will never understand. You've got guts and I admire that in a man. You've made mistakes and so have I. You rectified yours and I'm going to try like hell to fix mine. As for the picture, I'd be honored to accept it." Reuben stretched out his hand, and Eli, tears welling in his eyes, grasped it with both of his.

"Scum! Slime of the earth!" Sol bellowed. Reuben watched Eli's step falter, but he continued walking, head high, back to his car.

Reuben was out of his car in a flash and running to where Sol stood outside his car. He reached down and grabbed the fat man's shirt. "You ever talk that way to Eli again and I'll kill you! And," he said threateningly, "I'll cut you off where it hurts, at the bank! Now get your ass in that car, and if I ever see you

again, it will be too soon for me!"

His face a mask of anger, he stormed his way back to his car. Even from this distance he could see the tears in Eli's eyes. Smiling, he made a circle with his thumb and index finger. "We're square, Eli," he said, mouthing the words. Eli nodded.

Talk about getting religion, Reuben thought on the way back to the hospital. If he kept this up, he'd be taking on the world. Almost overnight he'd turned into someone he barely recognized. He knew one thing, though: he wanted to get to know this new person better.

Bebe sat propped up on a chair by her hospital window, where she had a clear view of the front entrance and could see Reuben the minute he turned the corner. But although her view to the outdoors was excellent, it was her reflection in the windowpane that held her attention. She was bathed and combed, powdered and shiny. The nurse had tried to get her to apply makeup, but she'd refused. What she really wanted was a drink and a cigarette, both forbidden to her. The doctor had wagged his finger under her nose the evening of the day of her operation and said, "Mrs. Tarz, this would be a good time for you to give up your addictions. You have some time under your belt, the worst is over, so to speak, and if you're determined, you can stay clean and get a head start on regain-

ing your health." She knew he was right, and she wanted to follow his advice.

Reuben had been an attentive husband, so much so she'd kept looking at him suspiciously, waiting and wondering what his motives were. Her husband was never nice unless he wanted something. Eli had said Reuben was at the hospital day and night. He'd also told her about their confrontation at the cemetery. Eli, it seemed, was ready to accept Reuben at face value now and had gone so far as to personally deliver one of his earliest paintings to the house. Her brother was not one of her favorite people these days, she decided. Maybe she was envious of Eli because he seemed happy at last. With the help of his friends, he was making a new life for himself and didn't seem to need her anymore. No one needed her. Oh, Reuben said he did. Reuben had said a lot of things these past days; some she remembered, others she chose to blot out. Why now, after all these years, would he say he wanted to start over, to be a *real* husband to her in every sense of the word? Not that he'd exactly come out and said he loved her, but he had alluded to his new feelings, feelings he said he'd suppressed. . . . She couldn't remember why he'd suppressed them.

Reuben felt sorry for her, was willing to forgive her for carrying another man's child. At the time, he'd mumbled something about

her forgiving him for fathering Rosemary's unborn baby. Maybe someday she could.

They were supposed to go away, possibly to Palm Springs, when she was well enough to travel. Just the two of them, he'd said. A *real* honeymoon, the one they'd never had. She'd asked him then, in a stone-cold voice, what he wanted in return for this affection he was bestowing on her.

"You" was his response. Then he'd stared at her, waiting for her to answer. But, preferring to wait out her options, she'd remained silent. Did he really think she was going to believe him after all this time? The days of wanting, of needing, were gone. She felt dead inside. She had nothing left to give. The stillborn child and her close brush with death made her realize she wanted to live, to have a normal life, to be free from drugs and alcohol. Yes, she wanted to be free. Reuben said he understood all that, and together they would be free — free to start their marriage again, free to love each other, free to make a new life. Just like that, without a word of apology for all the lost years. And he hadn't said he didn't love Mickey anymore, either. He hadn't actually said, "I love you, Bebe," and if he had, she wouldn't have believed him.

"You're too late, Reuben. Years too late." she murmured sadly.

Everyone had their lives on an even keel. Even her father was happy; Clovis catered to

his every wish. Eli was a new man and happier than he'd ever been. Simon was content at his new school, so content he didn't want to come home anymore: when he had a holiday he preferred to visit his uncle Eli in Carmel. Dillon liked it in Oregon, said he was going to become a forest ranger and live in the wilderness with animals. Reuben, of course, was a new man — or so he said — ready to make a new life. Only she was drifting, odd man out. She had no niche, no nest to call her own, no place of sanctuary. The doctor said she was depressed and not to worry because it was normal after what she'd been through. She'd been tempted right then to burden the doctor with the story of her life, but she hadn't. Why should he care, she'd asked herself; he was too busy saving lives and going home to rest.

For a time she'd tried to think with compassion about her stillborn baby, yet she'd felt nothing but relief — relief that it was dead and buried. Daniel always spoke of a person's soul. Did tiny newborn babies have souls? She would have to ask Daniel . . . someday.

The real Barbara Rosen Tarz cried, deep, heart-wrenching sobs of failure.

A long time later, Bebe felt herself being lifted from the chair by strong arms. A handkerchief was pressed into her hand. "Don't cry, Bebe. We'll make it right, but I can't do it alone, you have to help me," Reu-

ben said softly. He felt light-headed when his wife burrowed into his arms. She sobbed, hard, racking sounds that tore at his heart. He knew she was grieving for the past, for all the lost, wasted years. And, as a father would hold his newborn for the first time, he held her gently, crooning soft words of reassurance.

Reuben Tarz made a commitment to his wife then, the commitment he'd made years before but never honored. "I'll help you get dressed, Bebe, and then I'm taking you home. I brought your clothes, that flowered dress I like so much. The first time I saw you in a flowered dress, I thought you were the prettiest girl in Paris."

Bebe snuggled deeper into her husband's arms. She felt as if she'd just been born and was safe in her mother's arms.

But Bebe Rosen Tarz didn't believe a word her husband said.

CHAPTER
FORTY-ONE

There was no sense of "coming home" when Reuben and Bebe arrived in Palm Springs. Reuben was so cheerful, Bebe found herself grinding her teeth in annoyance. It was time to rise to the occasion and start . . . acting her part. Reuben was so patient with her she wanted to scream. *Don't you understand, it's too late! You should have treated me this way years ago. You're too late, my dear husband!*

Why was she here? Why had she even agreed to Reuben's suggestion they try this particular resort? Because it was easier, and all the fight had left her long before. She knew she wasn't fully recovered yet. "Time," Reuben said cheerfully. It was the one thing they had plenty of.

There was no attempt at lovemaking, on doctor's orders. Reuben didn't seem to mind, though. Bebe thought he was secretly as relieved as she was. However, he was solicitous and tender. He cared, he kept saying over and over. Bebe thought the words

sounded phony while in fact they were the sincerest Reuben had ever uttered to her.

There were no calls or mail from the studio. Even Daniel was leaving them alone. They were strangers here to the other guests, and no one bothered them. Three weeks into their stay, Bebe's depression began to lift. Her strength was returning, and for that she was grateful. Of course she still craved alcohol and drugs, but that, too, was getting better. For once she was determined to put her life in order — by herself. Being alive was so important now that she gave herself daily pep talks, emerging stronger with each one.

She knew she was carrying off her role by the look on her husband's face. He, on the other hand, was going to have to do a lot more than mouth a bunch of rehearsed words. Later, when she felt fully recovered, she'd administer the ultimate test: she'd tell him about Mickey and how she'd burned his letters. But she still wasn't sure whether or not she'd tell him about John Paul. In the meantime she would play the game — Reuben's reward for bringing her here. After all, he deserved something for all the energy he was putting into his efforts.

Six weeks later, Bebe was up with the new sun. How strange, she thought, looking down at her sleeping husband, to wake first and observe him like this. She felt faint, familiar

stirrings she had thought submerged. How boyish he looked, how vulnerable. With the exception of a few gray hairs at his temples, he could still pass for that handsome young man she'd fallen in love with in France. She inched her way over to Reuben's side of the bed and sat down on the floor, cross-legged. Her thoughts raced as she stared at her husband intently. You said all the right things, Reuben, things you needed to say, things you thought I wanted to hear, but you still haven't looked at me the way you used to look at Mickey. Rosemary wasn't important enough to think about; this had nothing to do with her, really, nothing at all. But Mickey . . . I'd give up my soul, the one Daniel is always talking about, if you'd look at me just once the way you looked at Mickey. Just once, Reuben. She inched closer to the bed.

Some sound, possibly his wife's heavy breathing, woke Reuben. His eyes flew open and the first thing he saw was Bebe sitting on the floor like a crab staring at him. Fear struck at his heart. He'd seen that intense look once before — in the barn in France. He remained perfectly still. "You're up early, Bebe. Are you feeling all right?" he asked quietly.

"I've been up for quite a while. I've been sitting here looking at you, wondering . . . about a lot of things." She trailed off lamely.

"What things?"

"Just things, nothing important." She rose to her feet and stretched. "I think I'm ready to go home. Let's go today. I can be packed in ten minutes."

Reuben propped himself on his elbow. He kept his voice even and quiet. "If that's what you want, I can be packed in five minutes. Loser carries the bags to the car!" he said, hopping out of bed.

Seven minutes later, Reuben announced a tie. Bebe laughed as she struggled with her heavy valise, but he noticed the smile never reached her eyes.

"Breakfast here or in the dining room?" he asked. "What do you think?"

Bebe pretended to think. "Here on the balcony. I'll have pancakes with lots of soft butter and warm syrup. Bacon, too. Maybe some melon. A pot of jam and lots and lots of coffee. How about you?"

"Mmm, some toast, I think, and maybe some melon." He tapped his waistline and grinned as he pointed to hers. Bebe shrugged; her waistline, or lack of it, was the least of her worries.

She was on her third cup of coffee, Reuben on his second, when the phone shrilled, a sound they hadn't heard since their arrival. They glanced at each other. Daniel, Reuben thought. My father, thought Bebe. Reuben stretched his arm behind him, grappled with the receiver a moment, then brought it to his

ear. "Yes? . . . Daniel, hi!"

Bebe watched her husband, saw the relief on his face, and then the concern. Obviously it had nothing to do with her father, she realized, and continued to drink her coffee. "As a matter of fact," she heard Reuben say, "we're leaving as soon as we finish breakfast. I know there was nothing you could do. Who . . . who's taking care of things on the California end? Wise choice, Daniel. All right, I'll call you when we get to L.A. And thanks. Bebe is fine, we really enjoyed our time here. She's fit as a fiddle and looks better than she has in years. Good, clean living."

"Give him my love," said Bebe.

"Bebe sends her love . . . Yes, I'll tell her. Thanks again, Daniel."

Bebe waited, knowing her husband was going to share his phone conversation with her. She also knew she wasn't going to like what he had to say.

"Bebe . . . I . . . that was Daniel. Max called him because he didn't want to . . . intrude on our time here. It seems . . . what I mean to say is . . ."

"For God's sake, Reuben, spit it out," Bebe said irritably.

"Rosemary's dead. She died last night after giving birth to a little girl. She . . . ah, she has no relatives except an elderly father in the East who is in his late seventies. No one seems . . . The child . . . is mine. Max hired a

nurse to care for the baby until . . . until we can make a decision. The . . . the baby's name is Lily." He sighed. "We have to talk about this, Bebe. I thought . . . Rosemary was so healthy. She looked like she was born to have a dozen children. A decision has to be made, and I have to make it," Reuben said firmly.

"What kind of decision?" Rosemary . . . dead? Rosemary wasn't supposed to die.

"Jane knows a young couple that would be glad to take the child if I . . . I agree to give it up for adoption. I need to know what you think, Bebe."

"You mean you would give up your own flesh and blood?" she found herself asking. How curious her voice sounded, how normal, as though she were discussing the weather.

"If there was no other alternative, yes, I would. I want you to agree so that later this doesn't stand between us. Now, tell me what you think."

"I think . . . we should take your baby back to our house and raise it as ours. We're start-ing fresh. Perhaps this child will help us over the rough spots. I could never ask nor can I expect you to give away your child as though it were a bag of trash. She's yours, Reuben, and I know in time I will grow to love her because she's yours. It won't be easy, but I will try. We could go there now and get her and take her home with us." She smiled at

her husband. "I'll love your daughter, Reuben."

Reuben was in such a state of shock, Bebe had to drive back to L.A. All the way there she kept up a running conversation with her husband about his new child and what she would do for it. She was still smiling hours later when, following Reuben's directions, she finally pulled the car to the curb of Rosemary's house. This is it, she told herself. This is the famous house your husband had wrapped up in a red ribbon to present to his mistress. She was surprised at how little the knowledge seemed to upset her.

Inside the house, Reuben felt like an intruder. When he called out, a motherly-looking woman hurried in from the kitchen, wiping her hands on a flour-streaked apron. Life did go on, Reuben thought inanely.

"Mr. Tarz," she said briskly, "follow me and I'll take you to the infant. She's a beautiful little thing, perfect in every way. You can tell the mother took good care of herself during her pregnancy. Lily weighs seven pounds, nine ounces. She's nineteen inches long and has a gorgeous crop of sunny blond hair. I never saw so much hair on a newborn! The child is just beautiful," the woman kept repeating over and over.

The moment Reuben set his eyes on the sleeping baby, he understood why the woman had gone on and on. Baby Lily wasn't just a

baby, she was a creation. His.

Bebe bent over the crib, reaching out tentatively to touch the downy head. A feeling she hadn't experienced since the birth of John Paul rushed over her. This child that wasn't even hers seemed to cry out to her. "May I?" she asked hesitantly, her hands itching to hold the infant.

"Of course, she's not fragile," the nurse said briskly.

Reuben didn't know what he felt — awe, dread, sorrow, happiness, all four. He sat down on the bed . . . Rosemary's bed. Where was her body, he wondered dimly. He would have to go to the services. Obviously he needed to talk to Max.

"Look, Reuben, she's trying to suck her fist. Hold her for a moment while I gather up her things." Bebe turned to the nurse. "Does the baby have —"

"Lord, yes, she has everything a new baby needs and then some. I took the liberty of packing it all up. Mr. Gould also asked me to pack up a few things I thought Lily might want to have of her mother's when she gets older."

"Yes, all right, but only a few items. I am Lily's mother now. Give the rest to charity or keep them yourself. Is that all right, Reuben?" Bebe asked quietly.

Reuben looked up. "Yes." Lord, what had he just agreed to? "Bebe, are you sure?"

"Good heavens, Reuben, do you want me to stand on my head to say yes? You can't abandon this child. What would that make you? She isn't garbage, you know." She'd said this once before or . . . that's what she'd done, sacked John Paul, had him tossed out like so much garbage. She'd abandoned him, a tiny human being who couldn't fend for himself. And now her husband was going to do the same thing if she didn't stop him. "This is a little person, Reuben. Your flesh and blood. Now let me hold her!"

Reuben watched as his wife cooed and crooned to his new daughter. His first thought was, How wonderful. His second thought was that he'd never seen such a possessive look on his wife's face. A feeling of unease settled over him. Then he tried to flick his thoughts away with a toss of his head. He was luckier than he had a right to be. What woman would take her husband's child by another woman and love it on sight?

"Carry Miss Lily's things to the car, Reuben, and let's go home," Bebe said happily.

It was dusk when Reuben ground the car to a halt in front of the house in Laurel Canyon. He looked across at his wife and his sleeping daughter. "Wait here! Don't move till I get back! Promise?" Bebe nodded, still crooning to the sleeping baby in her arms.

Reuben loped up the front steps to the front door, he threw it open, and rushed back to

the car. Then he scooped up his wife and daughter, carrying them up the steps and over the threshold. "We're home, Mrs. Tarz," he said, beaming at them. Gentleness, compassion, love, and humility flooded through him as he stared at the pink bundle in his wife's arms.

Bebe looked up at her husband, expecting to see a silly grin on his face. Instead, she saw what she'd been waiting for, the look she'd lived for all her life and had almost killed for.

Her sin of omission need never be mentioned now.

"Welcome home, darling," Bebe said, and smiled. I did it, I finally did it. I finally made you love me. You're dead, Mickey. Reuben just buried you and I helped him. Good-bye, dear, sweet, wonderful Mickey. Good-bye, good-bye, good-bye.

CHAPTER
FORTY-TWO

Château Fonsard sat nestled among the trees in their rich autumn coats, the sun gilding them to a burnished copper. Mickey sucked in her breath. It was so beautiful here, she always hated to leave, but leave they must. It was time for Philippe to return for the autumn semester. She wanted to keep him here, but her heart told her Paris and the boy's education were more important than her selfish wishes. Leaving this time was particularly bitter for both of them.

Just last evening Philippe had stormed into the library and ripped the Three Musketeers off the wall. He'd turned it to the wall and then stared at her defiantly. "It's time we had a talk, Mother."

"No," she'd cried, "not now, not when we're leaving tomorrow. I'm asking you, Philippe, to please hang the picture back where it belongs." He'd done it, but his eyes were bitter, his mouth grim.

She'd lain awake all night long wondering

and worrying. How was she to tell him about Reuben? How much should she say? How much did she want to say? Over and over she heard his words: "I am not a little boy, *Maman*. You can't keep telling me stories and expect me to believe them. If you won't tell me what I want to know, I'll find a way to learn for myself." Over and over the words ran through her head until she thought she would go mad. He was angry with her and she with him. It had to be made right before things got out of hand. Now; she would talk to him now when he came down to the car. They'd sit on the steps with the beautiful leaves swirling about.

She saw him then, standing by the car she'd moved out of the barn earlier. He must have gone around the back. Tears rushed to her eyes and streamed down her cheeks. "Reuben," she whispered, "please look back. If you look back, it is love. . . . Oh, Reuben, what am I to tell this son of yours?"

"I'm ready if you are," Philippe shouted. He could see his mother was crying and tried to harden his heart, but he couldn't. He rushed up the path and took her in his arms. "I'm so sorry, *Maman*. Please don't cry. It's just that sometimes I get so frustrated. All I ask, and I don't think it's too much, is that you treat me like the adult I am. If you don't want to tell me about my father, for whatever reasons, I will have to accept it. You are not

930

being fair to either of us, *Maman*. Only where my father is concerned are we at odds. Now, that's all I have to say. Did you forget anything? You always do, you know. Shall I take a last look around?" he asked briskly.

Mickey shook her head. "Sit down, Philippe. You're right — it is time for me to speak of your father. Yes, you are grown-up, and you look so much like him. All the little stories I told you when you were a child were true. Occasionally I added a detail or two to make you smile, but that's as it should be for a little one.

"Your father was much younger than I. I worried about it constantly, but he said age was a number and he didn't care. We were wildly, passionately in love. I think in those days I would have died for him the way I would die for you, because I love you so much. In my heart I believe he felt the same way.

"A short while before you were born, your father had a terrible accident in the barn. Somehow . . . he fell on a pitchfork that had manure on it. He was sick for a very long time. He almost died. I prayed night and day, and your uncle Daniel did the same. Eventually he recovered. But when he did, he was not the same. He was unable to make love, and I believe he thought he'd failed me because of this. He decided to return to America because he thought his . . . affliction

would . . . that he would always have it. I tried to tell him otherwise, but I didn't want him to think I was begging him to stay with me.

"When you love someone deeply with all your heart, you want that person's happiness more than your own. My heart shattered when I watched him drive off for the last time, knowing I would never see him again. Oh, he said he would come back, but I knew he wouldn't. I was able to survive our parting only because of you.

"Philippe, Reuben Tarz, your father . . . he doesn't know about you. I never told him. If he had come back as he said he would, he would have seen you for himself. But he will never come, not for me and not for you. Can you accept this? Can we go on as before? Or will you want to go to America and see your father? I will understand if you do, and I will arrange it when you are finished with school. The decision must be yours. I do not have . . . my emotions are still . . . it must be your decision. There is more to tell you, but this is not the time. For now this will have to do."

Mickey searched her son's eyes for some sign that he wouldn't press that matter. How in the name of God was she to tell him, ever, that she wasn't his real mother? Where would she get the strength to say the words?

More. There was more, but this wasn't the time. Philippe felt a seed of anger sprout, but

the look of torment in his mother's eyes made him gather her in his arms. His voice was low, husky, filled with emotion. "I think I knew, *Maman*. I believe knowing is better than suspecting all sorts of things. I thought for a while that my father abandoned us, that he didn't love either of us. Ah, the stories I used to make up, the things I'd rehearse to say to him. I guess I knew then, but the playacting made me happy for a while. He's never been in touch with you since he left?"

Mickey shook her head. "His wife sent me a little note after they were married. And he sent a cable when Daniel graduated from law school. A formal little message, nothing more."

Philippe got to his feet and reached down to pull his mother to him. "So," he said dramatically, "who needs an American father who earns his living making silly pictures! As for you, *Maman*, there is this professor at the Sorbonne who is dashing and debonair and just your age. A rogue unless I miss my guess. I will introduce you when we arrive in Paris. Now, you have given me enough of your life. It is time for wine, men, and song. Come!" he shouted. "I'm driving!"

"You've had only three lessons," Mickey said helplessly.

"I know, but you've been driving for years and we always end up in a ditch because you won't wear your spectacles. We start fresh

now, no ghosts behind us, eh, *Maman?*"

Only one little one, Mickey thought sadly. Then she smiled radiantly. "No ghosts, Philippe. You say this instructor is handsome and dashing?" Her son laughed, a sound full of happiness.

Forgive me, Lord, for my sin of omission, Mickey prayed silently as she settled herself in the car next to her son.

"I love you, *Maman,*" Philippe said quietly.

"And I love you, Philippe," Mickey replied just as quietly.

"For now we are the Two Musketeers. When I marry we will be three, unless, of course, you become attached to Monsieur Claude Molenaux." Philippe laughed uproariously.

"Who knows, we may be four," Mickey shouted gaily. "To Paree!"

EPILOGUE

". . . the gallant Frenchwoman whose name is important only to me."

Reuben reached into his pocket for his glasses so that he could see something of the audience. He let his eyes travel the length of the second row. Daniel's wife, Rajean, and his stepdaughter weren't sitting next to him; somehow this didn't come as a surprise to him. Max was leaning forward in his seat, a silly smile on his face. And there was Sol, dressed to the nines, with Clovis at his side. Daniel — brother, friend, and confidant — sat next to her, a proud look on his face. Sterling — Daniel was sterling from top to bottom. Bebe, beautiful and glittering, was next to Daniel, Simon on the other side of her, and Dillon next to him. Jane blew him a kiss, and he smiled for the first time.

It was over now, his moment in the limelight. Time to go back to his world in Laurel Canyon. Time to get on with his life. If his memories haunted him now and then, if he

hungered for something other than what he had, no one but himself need ever know. Somewhere along the way, Bebe's ability to role-play through life had rubbed off on him.

"Thank you, ladies and gentlemen."

Backstage with swarms of people congratulating him, Reuben smiled and joked, showing off his award with pride. When at last the crowd thinned, he made his way to a dressing room.

She should have been here. He'd never felt so alone in his life. MickeyMickeyMickeyMickey

The hand on his shoulder was soft. He couldn't see her, but her scent wafted about him. His eyes closed wearily. So much, yet so little.

"Let's go home, darling," Bebe said quietly. "Reuben, I think what you said was just beautiful. I'm sorry Mickey wasn't here to see you this evening. She would have been so proud, as proud as I am. I just wanted you to know I thought it kind and generous of you."

But how could you thank a dead person? Bebe mused. She had personally buried Mickey in her thoughts . . . right outside her front door. Otherwise how could she walk through the door with Reuben and Lily? "Damn you, you're dead," she snarled.

Reuben turned to her.

"Did you say something, Bebe?"

Bebe smiled tenderly. "As a matter of fact,

I did. I talked to Simon and Dillon about this, and they agreed." She reached into her purse and drew out an envelope. "They want you to have this."

Of course it wasn't true; they hadn't agreed at all. She'd had to issue all sorts of ridiculous threats to coerce Simon and Dillon into turning over their Fairmont stock. But if she was going to fight a dead woman, she had to use every weapon at her disposal.

Reuben's eyes grew misty as he stared at the contents of the envelope. This was too much. First the award and now the shares of stock. Fairmont was his . . . almost. One of these days he was going to get in touch with Philippe Bouchet and offer to buy out his shares of the studio. But not tonight. Tonight was for celebrating.

"I know she was here in spirit, my darling. I think you know that, too. I want you to smile now for the children. They need you. I need you, too, Reuben. Can I hold your statue, darling?" How wonderful it felt, how solid and comforting. It should have been hers. Tonight's performance alone deserved an award.

Reuben searched his wife's eyes. Her expression was guileless, her smile warm and trusting. This was the real Bebe standing next to him. He put his arm around her shoulder. "Let's forget the parties and go home and

make some popcorn. What do you say, Mrs. Tarz?"

"I think, Mr. Tarz, the offer is so grand, only a fool would turn it down."

Arm in arm, Reuben and Bebe walked through the crowds, their sons alongside them. They were a family, and they were going home.

Together.